CALLED BY THE DRAGON

MANA SOL

1

It was hot. Blistering hot. The sun had set halfway and Anzi was still sweltering under her clothes. If the stiff wind rising from the direction of the horizon didn't carry off the heat, the desert rabbits and foxes would hide in their burrows in dark underground shade, knowing it was better to go hungry and try again tomorrow. And that would mean nothing for Anzi to hunt.

Unacceptable. This was the final meal. Tomorrow, she would be on her way to the Imperial City, and there would be no more hunts. Tonight had to be perfect, for both Baba and for Oza who had been crying since morning and hadn't stopped once. He was afraid. Not just because he had to leave with her, but because Mama had been inconsolable and raging for hours now.

"Why are you taking them from me?" a woman moaned from within the thatched-roof mud hut. "*O muk-hua*, they're taking my children."

"Enough. They're mine, too. If you're going to be like this, I'll take you to the elders and have them put you back in the quiet house. You'll never see Anzi or Oza again."

After that, the woman fell silent, and Anzi prepared to dart away over the dirt and sand into the darkness, farther out into the desert fringes. She barely knew her mother. The woman was only allowed out of the quiet house on the other side of the village if her husband and the elders allowed it, and for the past ten years, Anzi had only been with her one day out of every month. She never knew what to say to the crazy-eyed woman who stared at things that weren't there and babbled nonsense things.

"Elder Bahren. Welcome to our home. I'm sorry for the noise." Before she could leave, Baba's voice slithered out of the hut like a snake. He had always been good at talking. The elders loved him because of that, which was why they forgave him for his insanity-riddled abomination of a wife. "My daughter just left to hunt. We can sit down for a farewell meal together in an hour."

"Your Anzi is even more a skilled hunter than I know if she can find anything in this heat. But she's always been blessed. Only ten winters and so much promise. Her quick eyes and hands will be missed."

"For the Empire, I can give over even my flesh and blood."

"As we should. And your son?"

"They'll be coming to take them both together."

"A surprise, him being Selected for service. So young." The elder clicked his tongue loud enough for Anzi to hear through the thin wall. "You shouldn't have taken him to Anzi's Selection trials. They only noticed him because he was in your arms when you came out to meet her afterward. I think it would have been better if they had waited until he was older."

"They say he has a gift. Better to give him over while he's still malleable. We live to serve."

"Yes. But a shame you have no one else to carry on your name once they're gone. Still, an honorable legacy."

Honorable legacy. That was what awaited her in the Imperial City. She had known all her life she was different from the other children. Faster. Stronger. More vicious and driven. Most of the villagers thought she had an elder spirit in her. Some just thought she was frightening. She didn't know what to believe. All she knew was that that was the reason she was leaving in the morning with Imperial Army escorts, because she ran faster, jumped higher, hit harder than all the others at the annual Selection a month ago. She was meant for something greater, the proctors had said. Take her home, say your goodbyes. She is ours now.

She wouldn't have been so apprehensive if they had left Oza alone. How could they do that? He was so young, just three years old. What could they have seen in him to take him away before he had even learned his letters? He was small and scrawny and sickly, and he lost his breath whenever he walked too fast. He had already nearly died half a dozen times since birth because of the choking sickness there was no cure for, and he would carry it all his life. He was mute, too, something the other children used to bully him for. Used to. Before Anzi returned the favor in vicious kind and broke bones, drew blood, bit vulnerable flesh.

She had gone unpunished by the adults who never quite knew what to do with her. They still didn't. Most were glad she was leaving even though offered only encouraging condolences to Baba. She didn't care. After that incident a year ago, no one had bothered Oza again and that was all she cared about.

Like her, he was different, but in a different way. He needed to be protected. He needed to be safe—but surely the Empire would care for him better than she ever could. Her heart clenched, and she listened a little longer to his crying from within the hut. So little time…Only three. How special must he be that they wanted him already?

When Elder Bahren and Baba talked about boring things next, she slipped away. She had heard enough, and dinner would be late if she delayed any longer. Baba had already bragged that she could hunt even in this heat, and she couldn't humiliate him. His dark desert eyes always bore into her when he was unhappy in the worst of ways. She ran silently over the mixed dirt and sand, heading for the nearest favorable hunting spot. If she was lucky, she would come back with enough to stay his disappointment.

Like it always did on the fringes of the Adaraat Desert, night fell unnaturally fast and draped the land in darkness. Within minutes, nearly all light is gone, and only by the moon's glow did Anzi hope for prey. Her dark eyes flicked from side to side, waiting for signs of even the smallest scurrying life from where she perched in the fork of a desert acacia tree. Her feet were off the ground so the underground dwellers wouldn't detect movement and flee from the surface, and she drew her hooded brown desert garb tight against her body to keep it from billowing.

There. A twitch in the darkness, the first tantalizing promise of prey. But when she leaped eight feet off the tree and darted over the sandy dirt to stab down on whatever had popped its head out of the scrubby growth, she froze with the short javelin poised over her head. She didn't run or back away, but she held still as the shadowy thing pulled itself across the ground and moved closer to her with halting, jerking wiggles. There were little frills on the head folded back flat against the serpentine neck, and a slender, pointed tongue darted out twice before disappearing again.

Ye gods. She had never seen a wyrm from up close before. Even the tiny ones captured for sale back in the Imperial City market were stowed in cages with iron bars so thick one could only see the tip of a snout poking out between them. This one was different. Too different. It was enormous, and she wished it didn't blend in so well with the nighttime with its pitch black hide. The only comfort was that wyrms had weak, nearly vestigial limbs or none at all, and they only moved as fast as a snake. Anzi was faster than any snake out here in the sands and dry grass. Nothing to worry about.

Except this thing had to be at least three meters long and as wide around as a grown man. Maybe more. How did it make it all the way out here? To be this size, it had to have come from deep desert where only the wyrmskin traders dared to go. She could scarcely believe it hadn't run into anyone with sharp flaying knives on its way here.

It twitched again and sighed with a tired chuff. It was no more than half a meter away now, but it had stopped moving. Was it dying? No good for food since wyrmflesh was toxic, but if she harvested its hide, the money would be good. Maybe she could just…

It snorted, lifted its head—and opened its eyes. She sucked in a knife-sharp gasp, staring into the brilliant gold hue of the irises surrounding vertical slit pupils. Glowing. They were glowing so brightly. So beautiful. So—perfect.

It would be unforgivable to let such a perfect, beautiful thing die.

The thought was so foreign and jarring that she had to blink hard to wake herself from the reverie, but something wrapped tight around her heart and convinced her to stay, to linger. She didn't know what it was exactly that made her kneel then, but in the next moment, her legs were folded up underneath her and she was holding up the creature's head. Small, slender fingers stroked along pitch-black scales, smooth and cool.

There was such human intelligence in the unblinking eyes that the thought of doing them any harm cowed her. Nothing had ever cowed her before.

"I'll feed you," she said. "But you need to go back after. You have to hide."

And she did. Feed the thing, that is. She hunted well, better than she ever had, and she caught not only two foxes but two rabbits in no time at all. But she still needed to take something home, and she explained that to the wyrm as if he could understand her.

He? *It*, she meant. Dragons shouldn't be *he* and *she*. They were beasts, dangerous beasts she should never get attached to. When he was done eating—*it,* that is—she was stunned when it wriggled off the ground and stretched out short, spindly limbs. Small, but not vestigial. They could bear the body's whole weight. Not a wyrm—a dragon? But that was impossible. Dragons couldn't survive in the wild all alone. They needed a rider, a human companion to take care of them. Everyone knew this. Impossible.

But she said nothing as the creature struggled back onto its claws, and when it stared up at her, she jerked her chin in the direction of the darkened desert.

"You need to go. If someone catches you, they'll skin you. You're dead."

It didn't move. It continued to stare up at her and captured her with that spellbinding golden gaze, until at last she gathered her nerve to kick the dirt and scowl at it.

"Go!" she exclaimed. "What are you waiting for."

But she didn't want to let it go. There was something insane and confusing and unspeakable happening inside her, and she didn't like it. Confusing was bad. Confusing was dangerous. And dragons in the wild— that was the most confusing thing she had ever heard of. And yet for some reason she wanted so badly to let it go and keep it a secret, even if that means it was doomed. Even if that meant she was committing a crime—because something told her that it had to happen this way.

It was a hypnotic urge that made her reach forward to stroke the creature's dark frill again, fingers running along the webbing between the flexible spines. She thought she felt it purring, but that couldn't be right. She ripped her hand away, suddenly frightened.

"I'll—be in trouble if I don't go home," she stammered. It was the first time in her life she had felt so flustered, and she scrambled back onto her feet so she could back away. Those eyes must be magic. She could feel them burning inside her like molten metal. "Go—go away. Don't come back."

She fled and didn't look back.

2

Before the jagged mouth of a deep canyon, twelve children in beige desert garb scurried to line up in two rows of six. Towering and narrow, the passage that snaked ahead was far darker than it should have been in the rising light of the dawn, but not a single child betrayed even the slightest shade of fear. They looked straight ahead with wide, alert eyes, some even eager.

A bald man in hardened leather armor paced before them, staring hard at each small head he passed. "Let's get this out of the way. If you die, we send notice to your family with your remains for a burial. That's all. You might have been hand-picked to come here, but you're nothing special yet. Not until you pass through the Gauntlet. And no one feels sorry for you just because you're still knee-high and knock-kneed. Is that understood!"

Twelve childish voices chimed in uniform assent. The man grimaced. These kids got smaller every year. "None of you are going to make it through the Gauntlet on the first try, so don't get any stupid ideas if you want to live to try again tomorrow. Only been done once before, and none of you have the right look in your eyes. You won't get far. But that's why you're here, so you can harden and grow and stop being useless little brats. You're only on the brink, nothing but fodder until you prove your-self. Understand?"

"Yes, sir!"

The man moved off to the side with one final stride, heavy boot falling on the packed sand and dirt with a thump. "Then go!"

The children took off with a scramble toward the gorge's entrance, the rustle of their clothes accompanying their frantic footsteps as they entered the darkened passage. They left behind the commanding officer, who stared after them with a stern expression.

"Bit cruel, isn't it? I think a few would make it here and there if you didn't batter their confidence like that before they even start."

He didn't even turn to look at his adjutant, a slender young man with blond hair, blue eyes, and dashingly high cheekbones. "Be quiet."

"All right, sir. You've got it, sir, no lip from me. Then…want to join the pool we've set up? I've put money on the girl with the long black hair. She's got feral eyes, maybe more used to desert terrain than most of the recruits. She might get decently far."

"Shut up."

"But Captain Sanson…"

"I will put you out in your smallclothes if you don't stop badgering me, you dolled-up palace reject."

Louten pouted. "I knew I shouldn't have taken this post. This place is nothing but dust and rude words."

"Maybe stop chasing the wrong skirts, then. Being banished out to the desert garrison will teach you to slide in under the wrong covers, won't it?" Captain Sanson shook his head. Burdened with an unhardened pretty boy out here in the desert fringes…Louten wouldn't last long, not with the growing rumors of rebel uprisings every year and the sharp, dry sands encroaching on fertile territory more with each season like an unstoppable disease. Not to mention all the dangerous beasts starting to slither out of the desert on top of everything else, too. Louten could barely hold his clothes together without an attendant to help him pull back his perfectly groomed hair; what was he going to do if they were ever raided? Couldn't even stay out of Sanson's way today while he handled the first day of Gauntlet training. Pest.

He peered down the gorge and waited for the first shouts to ring through the eerily dark canyon. He had little hope for this year's batch of the most promising the Imperial City had to offer, because those children weren't the only ones being tested today. If anything, they were only the bait. Playthings.

Someone was coming. They would find out who.

~

BOOTS STOMPED along the sands as the children rushed along the bottom of the gorge. The craggy rock walls on either side towered higher and higher, and the meager light at the top of the divide failed to illuminate the shadowed passage. Tall, stalagmite-shaped stacks of weathered rock stood guard at irregular intervals along the way, some skinny and barely an imposition while others were nearly three meters wide at the base, forcing the runners to clamber around the gigantic monoliths.

Soon, the natural corridor narrowed further. Two meters wide, and then just one, until the children were sliding forward one by one down the descending slope like droplets of water funneling downward. And the deeper they went, the darker it became, until finally the jagged tops of the gorge converged and blocked nearly all the light, leaving only scant, scattered reflections of daylight to glimmer against the rocks and sands.

The children slowed. They glanced between themselves and counted their numbers, only to find they had all made it so far. This couldn't be it, their eyes said. The terrain had been hellish, but they had come almost a full kilometer and there was nothing but dirt and dust. They had expected at least one dangerous beast by now, something that would truly put them in danger so they could prove their mettle.

And then they felt it. The rumble of loose earth under their feet, faint at first but growing stronger. Two of them, a girl with dark hair pulled back in a ponytail and pitch-black eyes as well as a boy with much the same looks, wasted no time in scrambling to climb onto the closest ledges they could find, fingers digging into the crumbling walls and digging for handholds. The other children learned quickly. As soon as they saw the two desert natives leap for safety, they followed suit with all promptness —except for the last pair, too slow by a hair's breadth.

Something burst out of the ground, spraying gritty sand in all directions, and the first screams rang out as the serpent-like creature bashed into the wall and knocked down the two stragglers who had only made it several meters up. They lost their holds and tumbled to the ground in a heap, one curling into the fetal position immediately with a rattling groan. The other was luckier and managed to land on their rear, but he was in no position revel in any relief. With a fearful gasp, he scrambled onto his hands and knees and tried to run for the wall again, but the gigantic wyrm reared up, up, up—and roared as it struggled to throw off something that leaped from behind onto its frilled head and neck. Dark green scales glittered and clinked together as the wyrm writhed, even hurling itself into the wall with ferocious strength and injuring itself. A spatter of silvery blood flew from the creature's gaping, fanged maw and landed on several other children who had yet to make it high enough to reach safety. The serpent was easily seven meters long and as thick around as three trees, and when it reared up, its shadow swallowed them all. They wouldn't make it. They wouldn't make it-

A shout went up when one of them finally identified the shape attached to the wyrm's head. A person! Someone in dark leather armor and white attire underneath, someone who had just lodged their spear straight across the rear of the creature's maw behind its fangs. The beast wailed again and attempted to close its jaw as it thrashed and screamed, but the wooden shaft of the weapon held strong. Whoever it was wrangling the wyrm was strong enough to cling to the head and neck with just their clamped knees. Who was that? The armor was generic foot soldier issue, and they had their head concealed in a white cloth wrap that barely revealed even the eyes. Who? And moreover, what had this person been doing in the canyon ahead of them?

But no time for questions or gratitude. Their rescuer's timely appearance would have to go unthanked. They scrambled back down to the ground and fled, running past the writhing creature—

—and leaped back when the wyrm crashed across their path, barring the way forward.

"Grab rocks to throw with!" someone barked, and the recruits' heads all whipped around to look at the young girl who had just shouted. She was already picking up the sharpest piece of rubble she could find that had fallen from the bashed wall, and she wound back her arm to hurl it toward the wyrm writhing in the sand. Her pitch-black eyes were hard and fierce, and the stray strands of dark hair that had freed itself from her ponytail were pasted to her forehead with sweat. "Don't be idiots! That guy's not on our side. He's using the wyrm to get to us, too!"

They realized in an instant that it was true. With the spear still lodged horizontally across the open jaw, preventing it from closing, the wyrm was hardly a threat as long as they stayed away from its thrashing tail. But the person who had subdued the wyrm, the one who was now effectively *riding* it, even—he was staring at them as he jerked back on both ends of his weapon shaft, making the creature's head rear back as well under his controlling grip. The wyrm hadn't fallen in front of them. That soldier had steered it there. Dark eyes stared out at them through the slit in the white head cloth, and the girl shouted once more.

"A desert native! Don't let down your guard. He can't catch all of us!"

That was true, but what everyone else also knew was that not everyone would make it. Most might, if they were lucky enough to not be the bait. The others, the ones who went first...

"Oh, "Oh, look at that! I knew you were up to something when you didn't meet us at the river choke point, you dirty cheater!"

Another voice rang out, a strong, masculine one that echoed around them. The wrangled wyrm renewed its struggles once more at the sudden appearance of an armored man strolling in from behind it, but the rider gave it another punishing jerk of its spear and forced it to settle.

The newcomer was a young man with a strong, cut jaw and a cleft chin. Sandy blond hair and dark blue eyes glimmered even in the murky half-darkness of the gorge, and the mixed metal and leather armor snugly framed a tall, muscular stature. He approached with slow steps, moving expertly around the wyrm's twitching tail as he twirled a sword in one hand. The air of a trained, confident soldier, but the smile curving his mouth was playful rather than dangerous. He stared up at the creature's bleeding head and grinned, ignoring the gaggle of staring children entirely. "The others shouldn't be far behind, so sadly, you won't be snatching your win this easily. But, hey. Nostalgia. I remember when I was a kid making my first Gauntlet Run here, like those kids. How's it feel to be on the other side now after all these years? Being the chaser instead of the chased?"

He received no answer.

"Oh, come on. No need to be so serious." He twirled his sword in his grip once more before positioning it in front of him with both hands on the haft. "Rookies don't get to clear the Gauntlet on the first try, whether you're here for the First Run like these kids or for the Second, like us. Save yourself some time and just come down. If we're quick enough, I'll split half the kids with you, and we can take the win together this time before the others get here."

Still no answer. Some of the children surreptitiously began edging toward the wall, confused by whatever was happening but still desperate to escape. If those two adults were going to remain distracted, then perhaps this was their chance to—

"Ah, don't move, you little runts." The man hadn't turned toward them, but it was clear who he was speaking to. They all froze, eyes glued to the glinting tip of his sword, and were reminded very clearly they had no weapons of their own. "All of you stay exactly where you are. Uncle Pierro will take good care of all of you—as soon as he gets this lady here to agree. What do you say? Are we going to team up, or are we going to settle this the hard—"

He leaped out of the way just in time to avoid being crushed by the wyrm's diving head, which bashed through a natural rock pillar formation before slamming into the wall with a screech. Instead of withdrawing and trying again, the creature shuddered with an echoing wail before collapsing in a limp pile across the floor of the gorge. All was silent as 'the lady' dismounted from the head, one slender leg gracefully swinging over the thick neck and joining the other to stand upon the loosely packed sand. She bent over to slide her spear out from behind the wyrm's fangs, belatedly freeing its maw. With an experimental heft, she steadied her grip on the weapon and stared back at the other soldier, who grinned even wider.

"I should have known better than to negotiate with you. Come on, then. Let's get down to business, Anzi."

3

This was unfortunate.

Anzi had expected the wyrm because there had been one when she first ran the Gauntlet herself, but what she hadn't expected was a nearly full-grown beast ready to devour whatever it managed to sink its teeth into. Was the quartermaster insane? These kids were too young, no way any of them could outpace a creature of this size. And the chances of surviving the attack? Laughably low. If she hadn't sneaked down in the first place for other reasons entirely, she would never have been here to stop the beast in time. It had exploded out of the sand like a lightning strike and gone straight for the closest children hanging from the rock wall, and if she had been even a half-second slower in leaping on its head to throwing off its aim, at least one of the recruits would be maimed or dead. On her own First Run years ago, the wyrms in the canyon hadn't been half so dangerous. Idiot quartermaster! She would report this to the colonel so he could go and shred the desert garrison apart for their carelessness.

And worse, all the trouble she had gone to would be for nothing now. Pierro had caught up to her in the chaos, so even after she dispatched this wyrm, she would still have to deal with him. And no doubt everyone else was on their way, too, for their own piece of the spoils. But for now, at least she had this: the spear in her hand was as solid as ever despite having been gnawed on by powerful jaws. Magicked wood was strong enough to withstand the bite of an adult wyrm, a lesson she had not expected to learn today. But against Pierro's brute strength and his steel sword, could it last?

"Come on, Anzi. Have you lost your nerve? You can just lay down your arms and let me take the kids. I'll put in a good word for you when I'm promoted and tell them all about how you took down a wyrm alone. A juvenile one, anyway."

Sometimes, she really hated Pierro. He was tolerable most of the time, reliable, steady, and amusing company, but his habit of trash talking during competitions and spars was one of the reasons she never held back from thrashing him soundly. Today would be no different. She shifted her weight between her bare feet after dismounting from the wyrm's neck. The serpent was out cold, knocked unconscious by a perfectly aimed magic-laced strike from her palm straight to the base of its brain, but how long would it be out for? Hard to tell. She would need to take care of this quickly, which meant no humoring Pierro's theatrics. While he continued to spin his sword, she simply brought her spear back and positioned it upside down in a diagonal stance behind herself, ready to lash out and strike. She didn't like wasting her time with a preamble before the main act.

"Alright, then, come at me—"

He was still in the middle of taunting her when she lunged across the three-meter distance between them, body so low to the ground she looked more like a desert fox streaking across the sand than a human. It was dim down here at the bottom of the gorge, courtesy of the shadow of the cliffs, but there was enough illumination from the dawn light to see the spark of surprise on his face when she was suddenly two inches in front of him.

She couldn't parry his sword with her spear half; his blade would cleave through it from the sheer force of her strength. Magicked wood could withstand ordinary steel, but Pierro had a charmed blade that would snip through her weapon if she hit it hard enough. She had to rely on agility alone to avoid the sword while using her spear to land debilitating strikes at close range. Easily done. She just had to put herself in his face—like this.

"Damn you!"

He only had time for one frustrated curse before she leaped up and rammed her shoulder into his chest, dodging neatly between his sword that had still been mid-twirl and his fist. The upward strike lifted him off the ground, launching him off his feet half a meter. As his body moved backward through the air, she dropped down and twisted her hips so she could lash out with a fierce kick to the abdomen. It connected in mid-air and sent him crashing against the rock wall, and a shower of dust and loose scree cascaded over his head.

"Ugh!"

Pierro shoved himself back onto his feet and narrowly managed to avoid her second kick, a sweeping one that would have arced in from his left and struck him across the jaw. Close, close—she used her momentum to flip over and kick with her other leg in the same motion. He blocked it with the metal bracer protecting his forearm, but her shin found the soft, vulnerable spot right at the inner bend of his elbow. Before he could react, she hooked her ankle over the unguarded joint and dragged him off-balance. The first impact had been hard enough to send him teetering sideways, and this might be enough to put him on the ground—but no such luck. He planted the tip of his sword into the sand, catching himself, and moved behind it to put more distance between them.

It didn't take long for him to pull his weapon back out of the loose earth and point it at her, but he also took several hasty steps back. She advanced and followed, holding her spear out horizontally to guard her progress. Pierro liked leaping face-first; she had sparred with him too many times to be taken by surprise with his favorite tricks.

"Relax," he panted. "Don't waste your strength. The others are almost here."

No, they weren't. If they were, he would have tried to hold out and keep her distracted so they could ambush her. He was stalling for time. But that didn't mean she had all day to waste on him. She needed to finish this leg of the training, herd the recruits away—the same recruits that were currently trying to sneak away while she and Pierro were distracted. She went for his legs with a vicious semi-circle sweep of her spear before hurling the weapon at the opposite wall behind her. The surprised yelp of the foremost girl answered her, an appropriate reaction to the deadly whizzing that had passed in front of her nose by scant inches. A young desert native child, from what Anzi could tell out from her peripheral vision. Was that what she had looked like back then, too, young and determined? The sheer nostalgia almost made her smile, if not for Pierro grinning stupidly at her.

"You idiot," he exclaimed. "You're going to throw away your only weapon for that? For the kids?"

She didn't smile back. "None of you move," she ordered with her eyes still fixed on Pierro. "If anyone thinks I can't catch them"—she threw a fast, hard glower at the black-eyed girl leading them all—"I can. Don't test me."

"And what about me? I'm the one to worry about."

She looked Pierro up and down with vague disgust. "Don't be stupid. You're handled." She didn't give him the chance to take offense. As the last syllable left her tongue, she lunged forward, this time going under his extended sword and burying her shoulder into his abdomen. She felt and heard the pained breath leave his lungs, but he had taken worse hits from her before. This wouldn't be nearly enough. Quick—before she was done driving him back, she grit her teeth and angled her hips to lift him off the ground, arms wrapping around his thighs and unbalancing him.

His elbow came down hard on her back, but she ignored the pain. If she didn't knock him down, he was going to adjust his sword in his grip and swing down next, and she couldn't afford to nurse sliced flesh and still hope to win the Gauntlet. Behind her, several of the children were still going to make a break for it despite her warning words and spear. She had to finish this quickly. Sorry, Pierro, she thought, but not really. He had been asking for this.

"*Oof!*"

She slammed him back into the ground with no mercy. He was still wheezing out his first curse when she released the back of one thigh, leaned over his supine body, and landed a vicious punch right into his exposed underarm. Unluckily for him, that was also his sword arm. A howl of pain and a whole-body later, she snatched up the dropped weapon drew it edgewise against his throat. But he was a trained soldier, so of course he wouldn't go down so easily. His other hand dove for the knife sheathed on his outer thigh—and found nothing. He grimaced, and Anzi tilted her head as she peered down at him.

"I keep telling you those are easier to reach for me than for you," she said. "Too bad." Before he could think of a proper retort, she lifted the sword and brought the butt of the haft down directly upon his right temple. The solid thump of metal meeting bone was loud enough that it made one of the children gasp behind her, but she was already on her feet before his eyes finished rolling back into his head.

She curled her toes into the sand, adrenaline still coursing through her veins as she counted the recruits. Nine. That meant three had done the smart thing and run off, refusing to be cowed by her threat. The rest still needed to be broken in, but their time here on the desert fringes would teach them to be braver. "I didn't look forward to this part," she assured them as she advanced. "But getting beaten is the fastest way to learn."

And she believed that wholeheartedly as she tossed away Pierro's knife and blazed in like a storm, delivering to each young recruit a debilitating blow that either knocked them out cold or had them crumpling to the ground, unable to move. A few of them were moaning, but soon, Captain Sanson of the desert garrison would be sending forth his soldiers for clean up and collection. Any child that had failed to advance in time would be collected so they could be treated for their injuries. But that meant her time was running out—now that the children were immobile, it was time to get to the real work.

Moments later, Anzi stood up after smearing her seal on the last child's forehead with her assigned color dye, a simple circle with a slash through it. All of them, hers. When this was over, she would be standing head and shoulders above the other candidates. But another worry gnawed at her. That wyrm. It was supposed to be a youngling. Those could bruise and slash, but not injure any more grievously than that. And yet the one she had stopped here had been far more dangerous.What in the world had the garrison captain been thinking to allow one of this size to come this far? Was he trying to get the kids killed? Sure, a few small ones were allowed into the Gauntlet every year, and not every recruit survived this part of their training. But this was unthinkable. It was simply too big, too dangerous. Without magic, these children had no chance of fighting back.

Anzi returned to the creature's head and prodded its scaly head with her foot. One this large should have been captured for military use, not left to roam the Gauntlet's course and used to terrorize the kids that came to train here. Would she get in trouble for killing it? Probably. No matter the threat, any this size were protected under Imperial Law as a vital resource, and she couldn't do as she wished to it, not even to ensure the safety of the unconscious children nearby. But she had to go, too; she couldn't wait for garrison officers to arrive and take over. She would fail the Gauntlet. But how could she just leave? What if there were more wyrms? If Captain Sanson and his quartermaster had overlooked one of this size, there could be more.

There was one solution. It was questionable and messy, but it was her best chance at keeping the children safe while also preserving the wyrm's life. And the only way she was going to be able to get away and finish the Gauntlet.

"Sorry," she apologized into the silence, and she hefted Pierro's sword in her grasp as she stared down at the creature's serpentine head. For some reason, she felt guilty even though it was scarcely more than an unthinking beast. She'd never been as fond of serpent hunting as the others in her unit, and even now, she wished she could hesitate. But she couldn't afford to. She had to go. At least she wasn't killing it, she thought. It would survive.

She swung.

4

Anzi remembered this place, every bend, every dip, every shadow. Or so she wanted to think, but that was impossible. This was part of the desert, which changed day by day. Nothing was ever the same, especially not after almost six years.

She had come here when she was twelve just like those recruits. After two years of rigorous training and advancement through the ranks, she had been named one of the dozen most promising and put through her First Run. There it was, the memory of stumbling up and slapping her hands on the tower of circular stones marking the finish point, bleeding and heaving with two broken ribs, a shattered nose, and both eyes so swollen she'd barely been able to see. How she had fought off the senior soldiers chasing her, no one knew, until the four Second Runners trotted out of the gorge with bruises and open wounds. Had they fought between themselves over capturing Anzi, their commanding officer had asked. And they had answered yes, but that Anzi had fought back, fierce and dangerous, even breaking one of the soldier's arms in her violent escape. He had lifted his wounded limb with a sheepish smile to prove it. The girl had clumsy magic, he had said, laughably so, but a powerful body to compensate. Very powerful.

She had become the first and only Runner to make it to the end of the Gauntlet on her first try. They still made her continue to train on the course for months longer, but things were never the same. She made up for her weakness in arcane combat with prodigious fighting ability and advanced year by year, always at the apex.

It was still that way. She was days shy of eighteen but already here. Pierro and the others were a handful of years older than she was, having worked their way to this point in the usual time. But not her. And she didn't want to wait to let them catch up, either. This was the last stretch before she qualified for the greatest honor in Imperial Service.

Becoming a dragon rider. Induction into the Premier Guard, the most prestigious in all the land.

Her heart throbbed violently as she ran on in search of the three missing children. The colonel had explained that to complete this stage, everyone needed twenty-five marked seals, captured targets. Across several tries, the limited points would be distributed among the four Second Runners who caught them, with the task becoming harder and harder over the weeks as the children became more adept at avoiding capture. Twenty five points, twenty five targets was all one needed to complete this stage. The pursuing squad should work together, then split the points equally. Efficient. Easy. Fast. It would take time, but it was the best way.

But she didn't want to split anything. Didn't want to work together. Didn't want anyone slowing her down. She would do this by herself, and she would finish this trial alone. She deserved it, camaraderie be damned. She didn't care about the others and the humiliation they would face. If they weren't good enough to stop her when she was all alone, then they didn't deserve to advance with her anyway. She was already earmarked for final selection—she was the favorite. She was the most promising. If she didn't grind the others into dust and prove here and now that it was a waste of time to dally any longer, it could be months before she got what she wanted. Hence the risky maneuver of sprinting the fifteen kilometers all the way to the other end of the canyon. Instead of fighting over all of the targets at once, she had meant to mark the majority of them here then chase after any that slipped away.

Only she could do that, the fastest out of everyone by far. And she had enough strength in her to fight, too. Dangerously.

She deserved this. She deserved to win.

That left one problem. The escaping targets would be running straight into the arms of the other, and they were already on their way. If she didn't get to them quickly enough, it would be a vicious brawl—not one on one, not even one on two if Pierro regained consciousness in time. He was out of commission now, but he would recover soon. Too soon.

She couldn't lose here. She was here to be a dragon rider, and no one was going to stop her.

Anzi glanced down as she sprinted across the gorge and grimaced at the silver liquid coating her hands and arms all the way up to the elbows. It had been necessary, all the warm serpent blood dripping from her fingers as she splattered it over every child with a swipe. The wyrm was alive, but she had needed its scent to mark the recruits and drive off other serpents. It had been the only way. She wasn't a mage; she couldn't set up a barrier seal to protect the unconscious children. Or Pierro, for that matter. He was an ass, but no one should suffer being eaten alive.

A flash of movement. Finally! She launched herself out of her thoughts as she veered down the left side of the fork that divided the gorge. That was definitely one of the children, light beige desert garb. They would learn soon: the first thing they should have done when they left the starting point was to camouflage themselves by rolling around in the dust and coating their clothes with dust and sand to better blend in with the terrain. But it was too late for this one. She leaped and bounded off a rocky ledge, one arm outstretched to grab the running child by the back of his loose thawb. That was the other disadvantage the little recruits had, loose clothes—

She recoiled and twisted in mid-air, falling to the ground in a crouch with her hand over her chest. Oh, gods, whatever had just struck her had stung deep. She clutched at the bruise she could feel blossoming already where the stone had nailed her right under her leather shoulder guard. Lethal aim. If it weren't for her uncommon resilience, that would have been enough to make her entire right arm numb. As it was, the nerves buzzed up and down from her fingers to her shoulder, protesting with great complaint.

Damn it. The other two were already here, Aimee and Doufan. She hadn't been expecting them to show up yet, but here she had run into them before she was ready. Not to mention she still had to track down the remaining targets. With her hand still covering her sore chest, she lifted her gaze to find the two soldiers waiting for her fifteen meters ahead. Doufan on the left, Aimee on the right. They were too far away for her to leap at them, but close enough for Aimee to lob projectiles at her with irritatingly good aim as she had demonstrated a moment ago. The tall, sharp-faced blonde was impressively magic-attuned with the useful ability to throw small objects around. But that was the only thing about her that Anzi envied. The threat from her paled in comparison to the other soldier, who was already approaching with his halberd pointed squarely at her trunk.

That wasn't good. After Anzi, he was undoubtedly the most dangerous between the four. While he lacked Pierro's brute strength, Doufan's weapon mastery was second to none. He could wield his halberd and the two short swords crossed over his back more skillfully than anyone she'd ever seen, and there was one other crucial difference between him and Pierro: he never sparred with Anzi using his full strength, so she had no idea what he was really capable of. She knew it, and he knew that she knew it. It was a smart move since they were competing against each other. In the end, they might both be called into the elite guard together, but the superior candidate always had the edge which meant it was a good idea to conceal one's hand from the other. Meanwhile, she rarely held back in spars which meant Doufan had seen far more of what she could do than she had of him.

"Fair warning, Pierro won't be coming to help you two anytime soon," she called out as he approached with light, careful steps. "It's just you two against me. No one else."

"That's fine!" Aimee called back. "You just need to go down next!"

Another rock came whizzing toward her through the air at deadly speed, and Anzi ducked just in time to avoid it while keeping her eyes fixed on the approaching man. Trouble. He had closed more than half the distance now. If Aimee gave him another opening like that, he would come streaking in to impale her without hesitation.

Damn those two. Just as Anzi often paired up with Pierro, those two stuck to each other like tree sap. They were rarely apart and always chose each other first when everyone needed to partner up for training expeditions. Now that she thought about it, they probably would have double-crossed Pierro after dispatching her, which was why he had left them behind in the first place. No wonder. At the time, she'd dismissed his recklessness as a terribly executed attempt at a trap, but now she realized he hadn't had much of a choice anyway.

Hindsight. She might have had a use for him after all, perhaps tricking him into turning against the other two and then removing him afterward, but too bad. Now she had to deal with this alone. But there was an upside to the situation: she could see a heap of beige clothed-bodies back there at Aimee's feet even though Doufan was clearly trying to obstruct her view of it by advancing up her line of sight, even shifting to follow her when she tried to lean to the side for a better look behind him. That only solidified her suspicion that Aimee had possession of the last three targets, and she returned her attention to the halberd-wielding young man who looked ready to skewer her.

His dark brown eyes were eagle-fierce and narrowed, head ducked and mouth set in a hard grimace. He was going to give this his all from the very start. One one hand, that was an encouraging sign. It meant that he thought he needed to, if he wanted to take her down. It meant he thought she had a chance. On the other hand, between him and Aimee's troubling ability to harass her at a distance, she would have liked to be underestimated at least a little.

All or nothing, now. She drew her spear from the loop woven into the back of her lightweight leather armor. She hadn't been able to bring Pierro's sword with her. Charmed as it was, it would become heavy and blundering once she carried it too far from him.

So all she had was this spear, and it would have to do.

She hefted the weapon and tightened her grip on it, preparing to clash.

5

The instant Doufan tensed his legs, Anzi followed suit, but she was the first to leap. With spear in hand, she lunged with the tip pointed at his chest. He was too lithe and agile to be struck anywhere else. But he disappeared in a brown leather blur and she reeled back, imagining a blade slicing through her spine already. Disadvantage. Even magicked, a weakened spear wouldn't hold long against his halberd, but she had no choice. He was forcing her hand, and Aimee was in the back still aiming rocks at her with alarmingly deadly aim. They were playing it safe, with her using her potshots to limit Anzi's mobility while Doufan chipped away at her stamina with a rapid chain of strikes from his halberd. She leaped back to avoid a vicious downward stab that would have impaled her foot and trapped it to the ground, but in doing so, Aimee found yet another opening to send a rock flying toward her forehead.

It thwacked her in the face and she staggered back, seeing double from the sheer force. Damn them. If they were alone, she could have taken them down one on one, but like this? It irritated her that they would collaborate against her when she obviously deserved the promotion more. Skewing the odds this way was a disservice to the Empire. What would they do if one of them was really selected for the Premier Guard? They would be less useful than she would be. If they were truly loyal, they would be yielding to her, not letting their greed and personal ambition get in the way of serving the people. But that was all right. It just meant she needed to exceed herself for the sake of the Empire. So long as she got past these two—

She recoiled again from yet another rock and blinked away the blood streaming over her brow to drip into her right eye. Dark hells, this would have been a good time to have a helmet, but none of them had been allowed one. She had to stop retreating. It could be that once they drove her back far enough, Aimee might pick up one of the targets and run off on her own. Anzi couldn't afford to lose even one of them. It would be humiliation, plain and simple. But Doufan gave her no time to contemplate her options. He stabbed forward with the halberd toward her abdomen, aiming for soft flesh with every intent to pierce her straight through. They weren't supposed to attempt killing blows on each other, but this was the Gauntlet. Soldiers died here, and lots of things could happen. No one would know.

And he definitely wanted to *happen* to her. Wise. If he tried for anything less than a lethal blow, she could turn it on him and make him regret it. She didn't like it, but he was making the right choice to go all in —just like she would. Since he was going this far, she had no reason to balk at doing the same. They were supposed to be comrades, but they were competing for stakes so high she could set aside moral hesitations.

When he next tried to jab down at her feet, she danced back and evaded the curved blade by a hair before stomping hard on the weapon's lowered head. It wouldn't break thanks to the reinforced wood and binding of the metal, but there was one thing weaker than the power holding his magicked halberd together: his physical grip on it. If she could just get his hand to slip even for a half second—but he refused to let go even when he was forced to bend his knees and crouch under the force of her ferocious stomp on the blade. How he managed to hold on, she didn't know. She was inordinately strong, even by elite standards, and while Doufan was a fearsome fighter, he couldn't stand against her in a contest of strength. But ah, there! She caught the pained grimace that flashed across his face at exactly the right time. So his efforts had cost him after all. He should have let go or at least let her press the halberd down to the ground and sweep it out from under her foot afterward. Instead, he had hurt himself, but where? His wrist? Elbow? Shoulder? Where was his new vulnerability, his new weakness that she could exploit? She raised her spear and aimed for his right shoulder, his dominant arm, so she could drive it through and pin him.

But two more rocks slammed into her and she cried out with a half-snarl, face and neck throbbing horribly. She hadn't whirled away in time to avoid the projectiles, and worse, she had only managed to nick Doufan's skin and nothing more thanks to the third rock that had struck her hand and sent a crippling wave of pain through her fingers. Aimee! Damn her! Frustration and anger flooded her when she felt Doufan kick at her shin next, trying to bring her down to the ground to his crouching level. Her first instinct was to stop him from knocking her down, but at the same time, continuing to stand over him would do nothing but make her an impossible target to miss for Aimee. She couldn't let him get back up, and yet he was the only thing shielding her from the other woman.

Wrong. Two more thwacking missiles proved Aimee could hit her anyway. None of this strategizing would get her anywhere; she was getting pelted hard enough to collect deep gashes and a ringing headache. She had no choice, then. It would take all the wind out of her for a few seconds, and she hated resorting to this because she was still terrible at it, but she hadn't expected to be so overwhelmed. If she had more time, she could think of a clever and painless counter, but that was beyond her now as she retreated several steps. She had to do it, and now, before either of them pulled another trick. She spun her spear in hand in a blur, attempting to deflect at least some of the rocks that were now whizzing at her in a nonstop stream. Aimee had been hiding her true capability all this time too, it seemed. She had never been this good in the last three months that all of them had begun training together. Sneaky, both of them, holding back in order to maintain the edge. But that just proved how unsuitable they were to advance. A good soldier would give their all, never greedily holding onto what they could offer up instead.

A colossal wave of magic exploded from her body and rushed out in all directions in a perfect sphere, kicking up dust and and a fierce shower of sand. It hurled Doufan back down onto the ground where he let out a surprised wheeze. He had reacted with a psionic shield of his own, nearly in time—but too little, too late. It shattered and dissipated, leaving him with a bloody nose, bloodshot eyes, and a face pale as death. What was this? She had thought he would respond faster; he hadn't been her main object. Aimee had been, who wouldn't have seen what was coming since Doufan obstructed her view. But this was no time for Anzi to worry about others. She stumbled and tripped over Doufan's splayed legs, their shins crashing. With a nauseated retch, she keeled over sideways. Her balance was gone, completely. Panic surged through her when she realized she had both overestimated and underestimated herself at the same time: her psionic burst had been far stronger than she had expected, which meant she was also far more debilitated by it than she had expected, too. She clawed at the sand, desperate to get back up, but all she could do was twitch and writhe as the world spun around her in all directions at once.

How could this have happened? She hadn't resorted to doing this in many months, and even her commanding officer had advised not to practice or otherwise use this ability because of its clumsiness. So how could her magic be so much stronger than when she had done this last?

And for that matter, what had happened to Aimee? Even in the depths of intense vertigo, Anzi was coherent enough to wonder why she could no longer feel rocks slinging into her with fracturing force. Had she stopped because Anzi was no longer a threat, or had she gone down, too? Or maybe she was using this chance to run off with the targets, Anzi thought in a panic, and sudden fear sent feverish energy running through her vein, lending enough willpower to force herself to her hands and knees. When she lifted her head, still dizzy, through double vision she spotted a crumpled form lying in the sand six or seven meters away.

Was that Aimee? The range of the concussive burst should only have knocked her off her feet, not out cold. And yet it had reduced Doufan to a catatonic mess, too. She couldn't pretend to know what to expect anymore. Either way, her confusion, her surprise, both were irrelevant. She was a soldier, and she had an objective to fulfill. She couldn't waste time tottering on the ground like this. She needed to get up and carry on. Both of the others were out of commission and no longer threats, and now there was only one thing left to do.

Oh, no. Her eyes widened as a belated realization dawned on her far too late. The children! She forced herself to focus her vision until she spotted three heaps several meters behind Aimee's fallen form. Had she hurt them, too? How could she have been so stupid? She had only been thinking about how to end the fight, but in the process—! She needed to go, needed to make sure she hadn't...

She fought through the urge to give into the dizziness and collapse again, fighting for every centimeter that her hands and knees dragged through the sand. Her nose was bleeding from both nostrils, and there was still more blood streaming from her forehead and the various other wounds she had collected courtesy of Aimee's aim and Doufan's nicks with his halberd. But finally, she dragged herself the final stretch past the other woman and reached the unconscious children lying side by side.

She breathed a sigh of relief when she felt steady pulses under her fingertips for all three of them. They were a mess and predictably bleeding from several orifices, too, but the medic would take care of that. Maybe having been unconscious beforehand had protected them, who knew? Either way, they were alive, which meant she could go ahead and do what she needed to do. With great effort, she raised her hand and reached for the closest child's forehead first, index finger smeared with her red dye.

A HUNDRED MILES away in the direction of the deep desert, a man lifted his head and stared into the distance. Under the dawn light, his molten gold eyes gleamed brighter than the sky somehow, and a patch of faint, black-tinged scales rippled into existence at his temples under his dark, tousled hair.

He continued to stare until at last, the man behind him asked a quiet question. "Lord, is something wrong?"

Instead of answering right away, he relaxed finally, and nodded to indicate they should continue walking once more. "No," he said.

"Then…?"

He glanced back at the direction he had felt the pulse of energy originate from. Unmistakable. He would recognize it anywhere.

"Nothing's wrong," he said. "I felt her."

"Then should we change our route and go to her instead?"

"No, keep going." He fixed his golden eyes straight ahead toward their destination. "We'll find each other soon."

6

"You look like shit."

Anzi raised her head to see Pierro standing in the hallway outside her open door. She hadn't noticed his approach because of the irritating noise that this barracks building tolerated, the humming of constant conversation leaking through the cabin walls and even occasional shouting. In the Imperial City, noise beyond a whisper was never tolerated in sleeping quarters. If soldiers wanted to socialize and speak freely, they went to the recreational buildings. No discipline here at all. Desert garrisons really were disorganized.

"You don't look so good either," she told the other soldier, making sure to look him up and down with a deliberate, pointed expression from where she sat on her low cot. "You could have left the trash talking behind when I knocked you out, by the way."

He sidled into the tiny room with his hands clasped behind his back, He sidled into the tiny room with his hands clasped behind his back, looking around from left to right and floor to ceiling with casual innocence She stared at him all the while, but he pretended not to notice as he turned to explore the suddenly-very-interesting corners of her quarters.

"If you don't have anything to say, leave."

He threw her a glance over his shoulder at long last. "Oh, come on. You're not mad, are you? That was all friendly banter. I don't know why you let me get you so worked up all the time."

"And why do you try to work me up all the time?"

He rolled his eyes and turned away again. "If you're done feeling disrespected, have you heard anything?"

She pressed her lips together. Of course. Pierro wasn't the sort of person to come back and try to make amends with anyone, even badly. She should have known he had come only to try to find out what was coming next. He had been the most good-natured in their squadron at first, but ever since the group had arrived here last week, his easygoing and playful demeanor had become blotted with a competitive, belligerent streak. It was a shame fellow soldiers couldn't get along. She'd had high hopes for everyone. Too high.

"No," she said. "Colonel hasn't come back from the Gauntlet site. He and the garrison captain are taking care of the wyrm problem."

"Yeah, speaking of which, the size of that thing, right?"

She didn't answer. He was still on her shit list. But yes, he was right. She was still marveling at how one of that size had showed up all the way on the outer edges of the desert. They had only begun reappearing a scant decade ago, nymphs that were a meter or two long at most, no more than that. Who would have thought things could change so rapidly? After two hundred years of tame peace, beasts were reappearing on the Empire's desert doorstep again. Unprecedented.

Well, with the exception of that one time all those years ago. But she didn't like thinking about that encounter. The *incident.* She quickly shelved it away again, queasy at the mere memory of pitch black scales and knowing eyes, flashing golden in the night...

"...llo? Come back to us. Hello, hello."

Anzi frowned and shot Pierro an irritated glare. "We're not talking right now. I want to rest. Go away."

"So even the amazing Anzi needs a breather sometimes. That's incredible, someone fetch the town crier." He waved his hands with mock excitement. "I can't believe it. Next, you'll say you're only human like the rest of us."

"Stop it."

"I'm just kidding. You know I am."

"Are you? Because it seems like you only ever say that when you want to annoy me." She pointed at the door. "Go away. Aimee and Doufan might appreciate your company more."

He turned slowly and carefully until his whole body was facing her. In such a small room as this, his large stature took up more space than it should—not to mention his demeanor had suddenly become frosty and more stifling than his bulk. "You know," he said, "you haven't even asked about the other two at all."

She lowered her eyebrows hard. "They're fine. Just banged up."

"You know that for a fact?"

"If they're not, then they shouldn't have been here in the first place." Did he think he was going to make her feel guilty just because they had done what they were supposed to do? This wasn't a game, and they weren't here to play. She was simply the last one left standing—that didn't make her wrong.

"See, normally..." He paused, holding his tongue in a way she knew was supposed to be at least mildly offensive. "...you would check to see how everyone's doing, just in case. Which is why I came here, actually."

"You didn't need to."

"It's the nice thing to do."

"Then thank you."

Pierro still looked unsatisfied, however, and she was fast losing her patience. She was tired and in pain, even though she had assured the colonel she was fine earlier. But what choice had she had? It would have been embarrassing to request medical attention after all of that, especially since the others were in worse condition than she was. What would be the point of victory if it wasn't graceful? What would be the point in standing out if she was only going to whine about it afterward? Pierro should be thinking this way, too. Or was he not a soldier?

"Another thing," he said in the silence. "Just because you expect it from yourself doesn't mean you get to demand the same from everyone else. You might think you're better than us, but we all came here as equals. Don't forget that."

"Are you posturing on me? I've never said I'm better than any of you."

"But you think it, and you act like it."

"I'm acting the way we all should. We shouldn't be coddling each other."

"And there you go again, being patronizing. This is pointless. You make it hard to be your friend."

Something flared up inside her, hot and hard. "I didn't ask you to be."

"No, because you're too good for that. All you do is try to win, win, win to prove you're more devoted and deserving than everyone else. That's all you do."

"What I *do* is act like a soldier!"

He snorted. "Well, just so you know, one soldier doesn't make an army. See you later, winner."

Forget it. If he wanted to act like a child, that was his choice. She didn't have to humor his bruised pride and pretend to sympathize. Obviously, he was acting high and mighty to disguise his bitterness at his total loss. And the others, Aimee and Doufan, had he already stopped by to see them? Maybe they had all talked among themselves already, and Pierro had come to see her after they had convened and decided to send him to confront her. She wouldn't be surprised. She had never had anyone on her side since the day she entered the Service, so why would that change now? Just because she had expected better from the top echelon of candidates for the Premier Guard? Well, clearly she was the idiot for it. From now on, she would be sure to expect abominably little from the others just like Pierro apparently wanted. She swung her legs up onto the bed, ignoring the throbbing of her muscles as she forcibly settled into the worn dip of her cot. She was going to get her rest while she could. The others would be smart to do the same, even if they were going to be staying right here until they completed their training while she went on ahead of them.

Her fingers dug into the fabric of the scratchy blanket underneath her. Damn Pierro. The Service was no place for soft feelings and weakness. Wasn't he ashamed of himself? So what if she hadn't gone to see how Doufan and Aimee were doing in the infirmary? They weren't dead, and any injuries they had sustained would be fixed by the garrison healer. If they blamed her in any way, let them. She didn't care. She had done what she needed to do and as the training intended. If they held that against her, that would only hinder their own progress. They should learn from this experience instead of being bitter over it.

She lifted then banged the side of her fist down upon the cot by her hip. Damn them.

～

SHIFTING SANDS. The smell of cinnamon. The hot, curling breath of the desert wind against her face. She remembered this. It had been so long, but this was home. She was facing the direction of the deep sands, though, the east. She would have to turn back if she wanted to head home. And she did turn, but too much. Home was due north from here, up the desert fringes, not to the west. The west was toward the Imperial City. She had turned too far. But her body didn't belong to her, and she failed to divert her own course. What was happening? Was she possessed? No, it was more like she was the one trapped inside someone else. She could feel every movement, but none of them were of her own volition, and she struggled inside her mind to try to squeeze out of this uncanny prison.

The body she inhabited paused, and she was forced to stand there in pure discomfort as her disobedient hand rose toward her face. Stop it, she demanded, but she had no voice to speak with. Still, she struggled. Stop! But the hand didn't stop and she glimpsed its shadow just before it began stroking her left temple. The touch stung, and she remembered vaguely that she was hurt there. She couldn't remember when or why, but it hurt anyway, and she thrashed in her consciousness in indignant outrage. Out, she demanded. Let me out!

It occurred to her suddenly that she didn't recognize this touch. These calloused fingers were not her own, and the hand was too large. Masculine. What? But try as she might, she couldn't turn her head to get a better look at the offending hand. Even her eyes were frozen in place, staring straight ahead at the golden dunes touched by the sun, and she was forced to endure the irritating stroking for another long moment.

...Strangely, the pain eased away until only a dull throbbing remained instead of sharp, acrid stings. Afterward, she was left only with confused suspicion when a ribbon of pleased relief spun through her, radiating from the fingers gently running along the side of her forehead.

I'm here, someone whispered. I'm coming to find you.

ANZI AWOKE with a start and a frustrated growl burning at the back of her throat. Awful, awful. She turned her head to check the iridescent time-catcher she had hung by the window, and two knotted threads glowed in the middle of the small circle of netted fabric. It was still half-past eight, barely an hour since she had fallen asleep. What kind of dream had that been? She was more exhausted now than when she had lain down. She threw another glare at the timecatcher, which continued to sparkle faintly in the sunlight that powered its minor magic. She didn't like it, but the colonel had told them all to carry one while they were out here with the desert garrison. He had given her a pointed look in particular, and she'd known there was no point arguing that she didn't like carrying magic trinkets.

Magic. Why was she even more apprehensive about it all of a sudden? It was only a dream. Not real. She rolled her shoulders and settled back into the cot, but her eyes remained wide open and staring at the ceiling. Magic. She had never liked it. Made her nervous. She curled the fingers of her left hand at her side, uncharacteristically hesitant. She didn't like this feeling. What was she, a coward? A superstitious idiot? How could she be so unsettled by a mere dream? Like a child, she was confusing it with reality. But still, she had to be sure. She lifted her fingers to her forehead and pressed the tips to her temple in a cautious probe, testing the ugly, scraped wound that one of Aimee's rocks had left earlier.

Her jaw tightened. The skin had healed over. It still felt heavily bruised and throbbed under her touch, but the abraded surface had become smooth as if it had never been touched.

She let her hand fall back down to her side and continued to stare up at the ceiling, seeing nothing.

7

"**S**ir!"

Anzi shoved herself off the cot and leaped to her feet to stand at attention, arms locked at her sides and back ramrod-straight in military fashion. She faced the doorway where the colonel stood in all his imposing, white-haired dignity. He was clothed in his formal, dark blue and white Service regalia as always—of course he would never strip himself of any of it, even in this sweltering heat.

Colonel Alexandre Bisset, dragon rider, Premier Guard. His bristling white brow suggested advanced age, and yet his face was smooth and unlined. He looked not a day over forty, if that, and yet it was well known that the man had been a loyal member of the Service for over eighty years. This was the youth imbued by a deep bond with an immortal dragon, evidence of his unwavering devotion and prodigious skill.

"Get dressed and prepare to leave," he said, voice curt and raspy as he stared at her with his usual glower. "We're returning to the Imperial City."

She answered with an automatic salute, snapping a hand up to her forehead without hesitation. "Yes, sir!"

And that was it, nothing else. No explanation as to why the rest of her training was being canceled or why they were returning to the Imperial City after just two weeks away. There should be more stages, more trials, but those were questions she was conditioned to not ask. When given an order, she obeyed, nothing more. No wondering whether she was being summoned alone or if the others were coming along, no worrying whether this was a bad turn or a good one. She turned and began to pack, throwing off the last eerie vestiges of the dream earlier. The memory of it had run raw and sharp in her veins, making her skin prickle with inexplicable anxiety and adrenaline every time her thoughts drifted back to it on accident, but no more. *Focus.*

And yet she touched her forehead again despite her better judgment and probed the bruise once more. No. She was overreacting. She had always had an inhuman constitution, something Pierro had hinted at earlier. She didn't like it when it was mentioned, but the truth was out: she was of mixed blood. That wasn't atypical; she knew several other mixed-bloods from her first recruit group who were experiencing something similar. Ironic that she clung to some of the old prejudices even when many others didn't—against herself. It cheapened her accomplishments, and she hated when others used it as an excuse for their failures against her.

"Good luck at the Imperium."

With her bag slung over her shoulder, Anzi turned in the dark hallway to see a familiar hulking shape step out of the next room. Pierro. Had the noise woken him up? It was the middle of the night, and every sound was amplified in this barracks cabin. He must have heard everything. But seeing him like that made one thing clear: he wasn't leaving with her, so she must be the only one heading back to the Imperial City. A cool thrill rushed through her chest. She hadn't dared to hope until now because it was better to expect little than to be disappointed, but now that she knew she was going alone, didn't this mean good news? Clearly it wasn't a military emergency of any kind. Had she really exempted all remaining training? That could mean she was being inducted already. She had to swallow past the sudden lump in her throat and take in a deep breath to steady her excitement.

"Thanks," she said after a moment. "I'll see you when you get back."

"Sure. I'll tell Aimee and Doufan you said so."

She paused. It hadn't occurred to her that she should say goodbye to them too, via Pierrot at least if not face to face. But it was still hard to think of them as comrades when they weren't on the field.

"Okay," she said, well aware how awkward and stiff she sounded, and left without another word.

∽

COLONEL BISSET DIDN'T GIVE her an opportunity to ask what was going on. He hadn't even nodded to acknowledge her presence when she appeared in the darkness, simply turning to climb onto his dragon's back using the multi-rung stirrup that trailed down its scaled side in front of its wing joint. She knew the drill. After he was settled in, she would do the same. But every time, the sensation of the gigantic beast's heaving side under her hands made her shiver so much she could barely hold onto the braided leather ropes. An adult dragoness, grown large and strong over the past century at the very least. Blue scales rimmed in white, like dangerous flower petals gleaming in the moonlight. It took her breath away every time.

This was the only dragon she had ever had the privilege of approaching, much less touching. She and the others had been dumbstruck when they first saw the enormous creature alight upon the ground three months ago. It had been right in the middle of the elite training grounds after their graduation, and at first, Anzi had been terrified they might be under attack. What else was she supposed to have thought? What else was she supposed to have felt except fear and awe at the immense shadow that blotted out the sun above their heads, at least twenty meters long from the head to the tip of its barbed tail? The only times she had ever seen dragons before was from a distance when the Premier went on their aerial patrols, always rising in the air from the closed-off palace court-yard far in the distance. If she hadn't already been determined to be one already, that moment alone would have been enough to make her dedicate herself to becoming a dragon rider. She couldn't have named a reason if anyone asked her, other than the expected response of *for the Empire.* She had simply—felt it. A connection, strong as a storm and just as chaotic, a calling inside her that made her realize she was on the right path.

She wouldn't give this up for anything. Underneath her as they flew through the night sky, buffeted by winds strong enough to topple over anyone else, Anzi reveled in the delight of taking flight. Dragon flight.

She only wished she knew the dragon's name. Colonel Bisset had never said it aloud, never introduced them to her so they could admire her scales and enormous size or her glittering, dark blue eyes that matched the colonel's Service uniform perfectly. Why not? Why hadn't he? She both resented and admired the colonel for it. Such a creature deserved more than silence. If it were her, she would proudly announce every arrival, every departure of her dragon companion, but perhaps that was the point. Maybe that was the wrong thing to do. A dragon was far too dignified to be toted around like a trophy.

Whatever her name, Colonel Bisset's dragon suited her human partner perfectly. Both austere, silent, as solid as three layers of brick and as severe as a a brewing thunderstorm. What would her dragon be like, she wondered. Which dragon would choose her? What part of her would they be drawn to, and she to them?

She was so entranced by the wild, colorful turns of her imagination that she didn't notice until hours later that she felt queasy. Her stomach churned with something like—fear? No, not fear, a vibrating, anxious apprehension. She frowned. She wasn't airsick, was she? She had flown on this dragon's back dozens of times with the others and never experienced any discomfort. But now she felt a niggling urge to put her feet back on the ground soon.

Her eyes widened. Absolutely not. She was not going to develop some inexplicable phobia of flying when she was literally on the brink of being inducted into the Premier Guard. That was absolutely not going to happen. If it did, she would spend her entire life in the air just so she could force herself to become numb to it. Whatever it took. She clenched her teeth and fought back the uneasiness until it was left squashed at the back of her mind, and after a moment, took a deep breath to clear her thoughts.

It had taken two weeks to travel east to the desert fringes from the Imperial City on foot, since crossing rough terrain had been part of the required training. But now they were flying and taking a straight path back. Two nights and half a day, accounting for rest, and then she would be home.

She smiled. Was this her time? Finally, she was answering her calling. This was what she had been meant for all her life. Why else would she feel this way, as if she were teetering on the verge of fulfillment, on the brink of victory?

Two nights and half a day, and then…

She closed her eyes.

"He says he's a chieftain, Your Excellency. I believe him."

"Because of his wealth?" the emperor asked lightly as he leaned back in his chair. He looked around the study as if searching for something, but the only other person in the room was his advisor, who looked at him with a meaningful frown and furrowed eyebrows.

"You know it isn't just that. The jewelry he wore. Dragon claws, Sire. Whether those are old relics passed down from his predecessors or he has access to wild dragons somehow, an ordinary man would be in no position to benefit from either."

"And yet we've never heard of his tribe before."

"That's not surprising. Nomad politics aren't our forte. If they were, we would have been able to take all the lands east of the Adaraat Desert by now. But nomad tribes are enough of a mystery that I can confidently say it would be stranger if we *had* heard of these people."

"Alright. Let him stay in the city. I'll meet with him in two days."

"Two days, Sire?" The advisor's frown deepened. "They've been here a week already."

"Better to let them simmer a bit more in anticipation, don't you think? We don't want to seem too curious, even if we…Never mind. Just do as I say." He waved the advisor away, who stood up from his seat and delivered a deep bow.

"Yes, Your Excellency."

8

T he Imperial City, from whence every good thing flowed. This was the cradle of the nation that had unified every divided territory from the western edge of the Adaraat Desert all the way to the sea. This was the birthplace of all things just and fair, all things meant for greatness. And of course, the seat of the Emperor's power could be nothing less than grand and breathtakingly beautiful. Far below, the colors of the sprawling city blended and rippled into each other like threads in a great tapestry, the red banners of the various districts twining all about with splendid, curated groves of exotic trees lining every roadway. Many generations before, this place once had another name, but the Emperor had decreed long ago that it would simply become the Imperial City. The Empire was therefore simply *the Empire* for that reason as well. Instead of attaching a name to it and making it only one of many, this reign was meant to be the one and only. Not *an* empire, but The Empire.

And that was what it had become. Under its authority, the people thrived. There were no more warlords, no more fighting, no more misery. All of that had disappeared. Even the most destitute of territories that had suffered from the worst kind of poverty and starvation were cared for now. The Empire conquered first the land, then the soul of it: this was how life should be, full of prosperity and peace.

There had been costs, though. The dragons that used to inhabit the land were gone now, and there were no more wild serpents in the skies. The Purge had made sure of that, the difficult decision by the Emperor to wipe out all the wild dragons that could not be tamed. In the final days of the great creatures, the warlords were still fighting tooth and nail over the last of them in the hopes they could still use them to fight back against the Empire, and they all perished as a result. Now the only dragons that existed in the land were those that hatched in the Imperium under the loving care of their human partners. A bloody history, but in the end, this was what it had become, and this was what it had always been meant to be.

Anzi leaned forward and pressed her palms along the dragon's glinting blue scales, marveling at the cool smoothness on her skin. Maybe soon, she would be so lucky...She looked up at Colonel Bisset's back and wished once more that she could ask him all the questions burning on her tongue. But even if it weren't out of line to interrogate him that way, trying to talk would be pointless. High in the sky with the wind rushing in their ears, he would never hear her—

The dragon dropped into a sudden nose dive, and her stomach plummeted like a heavy stone thrown into a pond. She clutched at the knobs on the sides of the leather saddle, fingers wrapping around the hardened protrusions tighter and tighter as they dived toward the ground. Her eyes watered against the wind, but she refused to close them. The descent was the most thrilling part of the flight, and her heart thrummed in her chest with furious gusto as they cut through the sky, down, down, down.

When they finally leveled out, she released the breath she had been holding with a loud exhale. Would there ever be a day when she accepted this as calmly as the colonel did? He didn't look the slightest bit affected. Even his white hair remained perfectly groomed, every strand still in place. That was the kind of poise she aspired to, but for now, she savored the last few moments of being airborne as she imagined riding her own dragon, taking to the skies and venturing forth to new lands, new worlds.

Here they were. Now they soared in wide circles, floating on warm thermals as they neared their destination. The Imperial Palace, right in the heart of the city. It was as grand and fearsome as ever with its gray stone parapets, hexagonal walls, and the river that circled around the entire structure with six stone bridges that led across the water into each gate. A hundred guards were stationed on top of the walls alone while a hundred more guarded the bridges, the gates, and the wide roads that connected the paths to the rest of the city. They looked like ants from this high up. She wished she could stay here forever, gliding on the wind and breathing in the crisp dawn.

When they landed, it was all too soon, but now there were other things to look forward to instead. Her blunted weapons needed replacing, and she needed a refitting for her armor in case she needed to gussy up for official induction. And—well, she ought to send a letter to Oza at the Tower, although she didn't know if she really wanted to…It wasn't as if he would answer. For now, she followed Bisset and slid off the dragon to stand on a grassy, open courtyard in the middle of the palace. It had been difficult to catch the full aerial view of the grand structure from where she had been sitting as they descended, but there would be plenty of other chances to admire the gold, silver, and gem studded scenery later.

"We're to see His Excellency, so make yourself presentable." The colonel hadn't even glanced back at her, but his tone made it clear she expected she was a wind-beaten mess, which she was. "Do what you can with your hair. Unfortunately, we don't have time to cut it."

Her hands jumped to her head, and she smoothed the tousled strands the best she could as she hurried to follow him across the large grassy enclosure. He had a way with words, making her go from exhilarated to ashamed in the span of half a second, and now that he had called her attention to her messy appearance, she felt even more out of place than before.

The blue-and-white clad guards posted between the slender white pillars spaced around the area had nothing to say about it, but as she and Colonel Bisset passed between two of them to enter the palace proper, she could feel their stares digging into her back. When she looked over her shoulder, however, she saw only the colonel's dragon staring after them from the middle of the courtyard. With a rumbling growl-sigh, the enormous creature settled down to rest on the grass, and she quickly faced forward once more, hoping Bisset hadn't noticed her momentary distraction. She had to be perfect in every way now. The smallest mistake could cost her dearly. She was here in the home of the Emperor. This was her chance, her one opportunity. She had worked so hard, given up so much. She wasn't even sure if she could dare to hope.

The white stone reliefs carved into the walls and ceiling of the palace interior told the story of the Empire's history. The beginning wasn't located here, but this hallway that led in from the courtyard told the story of the Emperor meeting his dragon for the first time, a great golden marvel with wings that spanned such a great breadth that it took up the entire wall from one wingtip to the other. Too bad that she couldn't linger long enough to see more; the colonel was striding along too quickly for her to examine anything in depth.

"When you enter," the colonel said, voice echoing between the walls with ominous solemnity, "don't bore His Excellency with any stories. When he asks you who you are, state your name, and when he asks you to speak about yourself, be brief. He has no need to know about your childhood or other useless things. Explain that you're a candidate to join the Premier Guard, and that you would be honored, and that will be enough. If His Excellency attempts to draw you into conversation, don't forget that you are only a soldier. Do not distract him."

"Yes, sir." She didn't turn her head to peek at him, but from the faintly disgruntled edge in his tone, it sounded like he expected the Emperor to be easily *distract*ed anyway. She didn't know how to feel about that. This was the monarch, the head of the Empire. Did the colonel have any right to criticize him, even indirectly? For the first time ever, she felt a trickle of displeasure and dismay at the man's behavior. If it were her, she would never suggest any kind of disapproval over the Emperor, especially not to a subordinate.

So even Colonel Bisset had his faults. She pressed her lips together as they continued to head toward the throne room, and she was glad he had nothing else to say. But with every step she took, something nervous and tight coiled in her belly with increasing insistence, and she quietly wished they could stop a moment so she could catch her breath before the emperor granted them an audience. Stop it, she scolded herself. This was no time to be agitated, no matter how lightheaded her anticipation was making her. This was nothing, just a preliminary step. She shouldn't be so excited when nothing was for certain yet.

Nonetheless, the strangest sensation floated through her. It was the oddest thing, something like—as if she were on the verge of remembering something she had forgotten, or was about to find something she had misplaced. Like the moment a key hovered just before the lock, ready to enter, ready to turn. The inexplicable specificity of it made her uneasy. It was something separate from the excitement, something foreign. What was wrong with her? And why could she feel her knees going weak, her thighs shaking like leaves under her uniform?

"Colonel Alexandre Bisset of the Premier Guard, with Private Anzi from Territory Five. I'm aware he has company, but His Excellency is expecting us."

The two hulking guards standing by moved to open the massive twin doors before them, and her eyes lingered on their craggy faces. They weren't all human, she realized. Was this normal? Hybrids and mixed bloods in the palace? She had never been here before, but that couldn't be right—no. That was wrong. Again, she had to scold herself. Why wouldn't mixed-bloods qualify to be Imperial guards? She needed to put those thoughts away for good soon before she accidentally said something offensive to the wrong people here. Moreover, with things suggesting that maybe she had some inhuman blood as well, she was in no position to keep giving way to old prejudices. She was being ridiculous.

…Maybe it was this boiling anxiety in her stomach that was making her even more irritable. Why, why was she so restless? She could hardly breathe now; it was ten times worse than when she had been in the hallway. She forced herself to stare straight at Colonel Bisset's back and nothing else. With a burst of determination, she shoved down the agitation and resumed walking behind the colonel as they entered the grand throne room. Here, the ceiling arched high over her head in a domed shape and gorgeous reliefs adorned the polished white walls all around them, but she could hardly pay attention to them.

Really, why couldn't she breathe?

"Anzi, to my side. Greet His Excellency, the Emperor Ra-Tet."

Ra-Tet? That was a desert name. Had she heard correctly? She stepped to the side and bowed low at the waist before the monarch on his golden throne. She only had time for a short glimpse, but even that little was enough to confirm the validity of her confusion. The Emperor was pale-skinned and blond with crystal blue eyes. She supposed it was possible he was of mixed ancestry, but with the desert blood being so diluted in him, why would he be given a native name?

Not that it should matter. She swept away the irrelevant ponderings and focused her attention on the privilege of being in the Emperor's presence. That should help her ignore the raging sensation in her belly, too, which had now become almost unbearable. Please go away, she thought desperately.

"It is an honor to be here today," she said. "I live to serve."

She heard a sound like that of a palm striking metal, and she realized the Emperor had just lightly slapped his armrest. "Up, up, that's enough."

His voice was middle-toned, melodic. Graceful. This was the voice of the leader of all men. She took a deep breath and stood back up. But instead of looking upon the majesty of the great Ra-Tet, her eyes immediately gravitated to the white pillar diagonally behind the throne, where another man leaned against it in silence with his arms crossed. Dark hair, black as night, and eyes so piercingly golden they looked as if they were glowing. He was wearing loose white pants in the style of the nomad tribes who wandered the Adaraat, and his deeply tanned torso was bare save the wide, golden collar draped over his shoulders and chest. Various gems studded the article, lapis blue and ruby red and emerald green. And although he was half in the shadows, so it was hard to tell exactly—she could swear those were golden piercings running down the shell of his ear and hanging from the lobe as well.

She almost dropped to the floor. She didn't know why, but as she stared at him, as he stared back—

"Ah, yes, I forgot," the Emperor announced with a flourish of his hand. "This is my honored guest, chieftain of the Mahot tribe, Kaizat-Amun."

She barely heard him. Suddenly, the most important man in all the Empire shrank away to nothing but a speck of dust in her mind's eye, and Anzi thought she could feel her body splitting into a thousand, thousand shards as the room spun around her. Colonel Bisset melted away from her too, becoming nothing but a muddled smear in her vision as she stared and stared. The feeling inside her that had been screaming, shouting—it reared up and exploded, sending fire into her veins and scalding every inch of her soul. The room expanded, the room shrank. The room did not exist. Just him, that man, even though she had no idea who he was. Just his name, only his name—

Kaizat-Amun pushed himself off the pillar, rounded the throne, and stepped off the dais to walk toward her.

9

"Anzi, greet the Emperor's guest."

Colonel Bisset's voice grated in her ear as if he were speaking right into it, and the gravelly anger buried there managed to bring her out of her stunned reverie. Dark hells, what was she doing? Still disoriented, she nearly presented Kaizat with a military salute, only managing to catch herself in time because she saw Bisset's twitch out of the corner of her eye. He was a foreign guest, a chieftain, not an officer. With a smooth flourish, she brought her hand down from where it had been raised halfway and stepped back so she could bend at the waist in a respectful bow. There was no doubt that the colonel had spotted her near-mistake. He was going to have something to say about that later. She grimaced before returning her face to a neutral expression and rising again.

To her utter distaste, however, Kaizat bowed as well. Not at the waist, thankfully, but with his golden gaze fixed on her, he inclined his head as deeply as it could go without taking his eyes off of her. If she were a coward, the intensity of his stare would have sent a shiver down her back, but she forced herself to remain composed. Immovable. He might be an esteemed guest and the leader of his people, but they were both still in the presence of the great Emperor. She couldn't fawn over some foreign dignitary. This was the Empire, and he was on their turf.

"Your name is Anzi," said the chieftain, and once again, she had to school her expression firmly in place. Hearing him say her name was—like brushing against lightning. She didn't know how to feel about that, except on the verge of destruction. "You should call me Kai."

Kai? Call him Kai, like a nickname? Did he think she was an idiot, or was this man really taking her that lightly? She had no intention of assuming even the slightest familiarity with him. She was a soldier, and he had better recognize that...And yet no matter how much she wanted to mistrust and dislike him, all she felt was a growing urge to step forward toward him. No matter how much she railed against his primal, magnetic aura, no matter how much she tried to reject the sickening strength of the sheer attraction she felt toward every part of him, every ounce of him, her heart continued to pound in her chest like a frantic drumbeat, like a thousand warhorses stamping across the plain and shaking the earth down to its deepest roots, its most hidden places...

"It's an honor to meet you," she said, well aware of the audible stiffness of her voice. Better than stammering, at least. Her tongue was so loose she had scarcely trusted herself to string that one sentence together, but Kaizat-Amun was still looking at her as if he were expecting more. What? What did he want her to say? She couldn't think past the swarm of unfamiliar emotions running riot through her: rippling anxiety mixed with a hot, living, blooming dread, and the inexplicable need to get closer, to move forward, to know this man that she felt she should have already known a thousand lifetimes ago.

She was crazy. She was delirious. Or maybe she had been magicked—desert nomads were a suspicious lot.

"Oh, if you like her, you can keep her. I have plenty."

She blinked. What—was that the Emperor? Was that the Emperor's voice?

Kaizat turned to look back at him. She too stared, and there he was, slouched sideways on his throne with one leg thrown over the left armrest. He was the picture of elegant ease, and yet he wore an uncaring, mirthless expression that told her plainly his offer was nothing less than serious. Keep her, he had said, and Anzi was the only woman in the room. She wasn't stupid enough to wonder who he was referring to. But was he giving her away? Just like that? Colonel Bisset had brought her for a personal audience with the Emperor. She was supposed to be a candidate to join the Premier. She was supposed to be...

She didn't dare protest, but a cold sweat threatened to form over her upper lip at the thought of being chained up and given away like a slave.

The last eight years of her life that she had devoted to ceaseless training and patient anticipation all coalesced down to this moment, standing before some strange man she could feel changing her life instantly, continuously, irreversibly. *Kaizat-Amun.* If she hadn't been sure he was a terrible omen before, she knew it for a certainty now. Because of him, the Emperor was about to discard her like refuse. She had spent her whole life dreaming of rising up and finding her calling, and after all this time, she had even made it as far as the Imperial palace and inside the throne room. But now—everything was disappearing from her, and all she wanted was to sink into the ground and disappear.

Because she couldn't say no. It was her duty to obey, without question, without hesitation—

"No. But I want her to keep me company today."

The wave of relief that flooded through her felt like fire and ice at once, and she thought her chest was going to tear open. She didn't even mind that he'd just demanded her *company* as if she were an escort.

"I have a trained harem for that," drawled the Emperor. "They'd be much better. Or you can try the unbroken ones if that's what you prefer?"

"I have no interest."

She was only half-recovered from the previous shock, but she had the presence of mind to glance between them with watchful eyes as they spoke . The chieftain looked angry. Or he *felt* angry. Was it the way his muscular shoulders tensed ever so slightly in front of her, or was it the controlled hitch in the very back of his voice that betrayed his displeasure? Or maybe it was something else, something subtle that her senses couldn't quite catch but that her intuition had.

As for the Emperor, he seemed—unaffected. Bored. She didn't know what to think of him when he was so different from what she had always imagined. She had expected wise eyes, a serene face, the countenance of a patient father who had raised too many children to be surprised by anything anymore. Instead, he'd turned out to look like a young, angelic-looking man with an impatient frown and a sharp but beautiful frown. He looked like he would much rather be anywhere else than here.

Not that she respected him any less. He was still the same guiding hand that ruled over the people, the man who never appeared except from a distance and concealed under a golden veil, like a mysterious god or spirit that would come to visit and watch over them. His appearance had no bearing on his accomplishments and service to the nation, and she was being blind and shallow if she let it color her admiration of him.

Ra-Tet. She was even privileged to know his name now, even though she would never be able to address him that way even in her thoughts. He was the Emperor, nothing less. All a name did was humanize him when he was so much more.

"Well, if you like her that much, all the best. But it seems my man here has something he wants to speak to me about, so if you'll excuse us…"

"Then I'll have Anzi show me the way out."

And just like that, it was over. She was no longer in peril of being carted off like livestock, saved by circumstances as fickle as the tide. From the moment she had walked in, she had endured at least two life-altering experiences in quick succession, and she was wary of yet another—

Something wrapped around her arm, and the contact was like lightning strike jumping under her skin and setting her alight. Hard, callused warmth, long fingers that wrapped all the way around her wrist, thin black markings running up a muscular forearm…She stared. That was the chieftain's hand on her arm. She looked up and held his molten-gold gaze, wondering vaguely whether she was perhaps dying.

"Please forgive me," Colonel Bisset said suddenly, and she managed to tear her eyes away from Kaizat and look to the officer instead. He was paying her no mind, however; it was the Emperor he was speaking to. "Anzi is actually the reason I came to see you today. She's the one I spoke of."

For a few seconds, the Emperor seemed confused and impatient, but a flash of comprehension lit up his face. "Oh!" he exclaimed. "That's her? Oh, no. In that case, my dear friend, I'm afraid I have to permanently retract that offer a moment ago about giving her to you. She represents a lengthy investment, you see. You're free to have her show you around the city, though. I'm not stingy. Just one thing—Anzi, was it?"

She nearly jumped out of her skin. "Yes, Your Excellency."

He tapped his chin and pointed to her with a thoughtful nod. "I prefer speaking to Alexandre alone anyhow, and it's enough that I've seen you like this. You can go and leave us to speak, but we'll call you back later tonight. Understand?"

She bowed her head. "Yes, Your Excellency."

"Also, be a good host. If he asks you for anything, and I mean anything…" The Emperor gave her a meaningful gaze, one that she understood only too fully after the brief mention of harems just seconds ago. "Oblige him."

It was a small thing, she told herself. Dignity and pride were all well and good, but it was better to be humble. She bowed her head again.

"We'll summon you later, but you have plenty of time to get acquainted. And if Chieftain Kaizat doesn't keep you in his room, find a palace servant and they'll find you one to stay in."

Another painful wave of embarrassment. She was still being treated like an escort or common prostitute by the very man she'd spent her life idolizing. She hadn't expected or wanted praises from the Emperor, but when she had learned that Colonel Bisset was bringing her here, she had hoped he would say at least one thing, just one, that would acknowledge how difficult the path had been. But that was conceit. She was in the wrong for that. Wanting recognition when she was only doing her duty— what a disgrace.

"Yes, Your Excellency," she said. "I live to serve."

"Good, good. Then…" He looked expectantly at her, and she turned to take her leave.

A slight pull on her wrist made her slow down after just two paces, and she looked up to realize Kaizat was still holding onto her. She was so disoriented that she'd forgotten, even though now that she'd been freshly reminded, it felt like the entirety of her skin was burning like a bonfire from his touch.

She had to get out of here. She needed air.

"This way, sir."

10

Anzi had never been in the palace before, which meant she had no pass token to flash at whoever might stop and interrogate her. Would the guards at the front gates open them for her so she could leave? They weren't supposed to, but with an important foreign chieftain at her side, maybe they would make an exception. Exiting the palace unauthorized had to be easier than getting in. But lesson learned: maybe she should have thought about that before rushing out of the throne room.

"How long have you been a soldier?"

She looked back at the man and resisted the urge to take a sidling step away from him as they walked down the hallway. She had pulled her hand out of his grasp long ago, but he was sticking too close for comfort. Surely he didn't have to walk so close that their hands threatened to brush against each other with every step, and surely he didn't have to stare at her that way, either. His unnatural golden gaze felt like it was boring straight through her and melting her down like ingots in a furnace.

And as much as she told herself she didn't like it, she knew deep down all she wanted to do was hold his stare. She wanted to memorize every line of his face, the length of every eyelash, the sharp angles of his jaw and his cheekbones. She wanted to be seen by this man as much as she wanted to see *him*.

She didn't understand. All she knew was that this was unacceptable.

"Since I was a child," she forced herself to say, finally. She'd almost forgotten to answer the question, so intently focused was she on resisting his magnetic aura.

"Do you enjoy it?"

She almost stopped in her tracks. What kind of question was that? "It's my calling," she said, making sure her tone was as emphatic as it could be without being offensive. "The Empire saw my potential and set me on the right path. It's all I've dreamed of."

"Is it? Fighting brings you pleasure?"

His voice was resonant, smooth, enchantingly deep. It was almost enough to convince her to overlook his sarcastic question—if that was what it was. When she swiveled her head to look at him, there was no judgment in his eyes, only a mild curiosity and a smile she could have sworn was a little wicked, but that couldn't be right. Chieftain Kaizat-Amun was a serious man, and absurdly dangerous. She knew that for a fact, could feel it in the way she couldn't calm herself as they walked side by side.

Indeed, when she tried to subtly veer closer toward the right wall to put a little more space between them a minute ago, he had mirrored her and came just as close again. Her pulse was still racing. She could feel the heat rising from his bare skin, and she wondered what he wore during the wintry season. Deserts got cold too when glacial winds tore across them. Or did he brave the temperatures and continue about his business bare-chested and enormous, with the gold of his shoulder collar lying flat against his muscular—

"Anzi?"

She was going to stab herself the first chance she got. Right through the gut. She tore her eyes away from him and whipped her head around to face forward again. "I don't fight for myself," she said shortly. "We protect the people."

"From?"

"Anything. The barbarians to the north, west, and south. The growing wyrm population from the east. And when territory disputes arise with other kingdoms, we ride out and resolve them."

"Does that happen often? Territory disputes?"

"Often enough."

"And you've ridden out yourself to help resolve them?"

She smiled despite herself. A real warrior wouldn't bask in her own accomplishments, however, and she quickly wiped it off her face scarcely before her lips even finished curving. "Since I was fourteen."

"Is that normal for this place?"

Ah, right. He was a foreigner. He didn't know the way of things, but he was at least trying…so maybe she ought to be a little more friendly to him, against her better judgment. She glanced at him out of the corner of her eye again to sneak another look, but to her deepest chagrin, found him still staring at her just as intently as before. Shit. "Soldiers must complete basic training by sixteen. From then on, we have the privilege of helping to unify the lands under the Empire."

"Not you, though. You were fourteen when you were first sent out."

"A privilege I'm grateful for."

"You're no ordinary soldier then, Anzi."

She hated it. Hated how she wanted to melt—not at his compliments, but the way he said her name. The back of her head throbbed with something that was on the verge of becoming a splitting headache, and she vowed to meditate this away later on the training grounds. She had a vague idea what this was, after all: the beginning of romantic attraction. She had always thought she was immune as she had never once been tempted by anyone ever since entering Imperial Service, but clearly, she was wrong. It had simply taken her nearly eighteen years to figure it out.

"It's an honor to serve," she said. Her words were too evasive to be polite, but she couldn't help it. If she accepted his compliments, if she was receptive to him in any way or even went so far as to reciprocate his strange solicitousness—it would be the end of sanity for her. To think she was going to be responsible for him all evening…

Finally, they turned the last corner into the wide, short hallway that led out into the courtyard, and a familiar glimmer of blue out on the verdant grass made her heart leap. It was strong enough even to jolt her attention away from Kaizat, and she quickened her pace to get there faster—and froze mid-step. Something sharp and painful blossomed in her gut, and she sucked in a small, silent gasp at the sheer intensity of it. All the excitement she had felt upon glimpsing Bisset's dragon dissipated in an instant, replaced by a foreign sensation simultaneously inside and outside of her at the same time. Her hand flew to her abdomen, pressing against the leather armor and fingers digging in as if she might be able to pry the sudden pain out of herself.

But it wasn't pain. It was—slithering, coiling fury, something venomous like the bite of a cobra if she were the cobra herself. A wall of panic rose up to accompany it like the tide after an underwater earthquake, and she tensed bodily as if to leap away from the threat. Except she couldn't, because the source of it was coming from inside her, not around her.

"Anzi."

And then just like that, it disappeared. Instead, she felt the familiar touch of a hand grasping her wrist and preventing her from pulling away.

"Anzi," the chieftain said again, and she looked up from the strong, veined hand to hold his stare. She was still disoriented, but she recognized well enough the concerned furrow of his dark eyebrows and the lips parted slightly in question. What she didn't recognize was the tightness there, too, as if she had done something to make him angry. What could he have to be angry about? Despite some part of her wondering how the sensation of his hand on her skin could feel so good, so warm and right, she pulled out of his grip and frowned up at him. He didn't take the warning, however, and proceeded to reach for her face.

"What's wrong, you look—"

She leaned away, a quick, deft motion that had saved her countless times on a battlefield when an arrow or spear came hissing toward her. The chieftain froze, hand hovering where her cheek had been less than a half-second ago, and he fixed his eyes on hers for a long, taut moment. The anger creasing his brow disappeared, replaced by something more intense.

He was beautiful. It was a barely audible whisper of a voice in her head, so, so small that she could hesitantly excuse it and pretend she hadn't noticed it. But she did notice, and she wanted to hear more. She wanted to let her mind wander where it shouldn't and ask who this man was that he could make her feel—like this, like someone had reeled in the sun and put her in the center of it, like he was made of fire and she of ice, melting, expanding, floating like feathers released into the wind...

When he moved his hand again, this time, she stayed in place. She stayed even when his fingertips reached her jaw, when it slid up to her earlobe, slow and indulgent, even when they slid back and and began to press ever so slightly into the soft curve of the side of her neck...

"You aren't feeling well," he said. "Would you rather rest somewhere?"

Before she could fully revive and return to her senses, he cupped his hand along the side of her face and ran his thumb over her cheek just under her left eye. The touch was haunting, as strong as it was gentle, and she thought she might fall into the earth if he did it again. But the swipe of his callused thumb along her face was exactly what she needed to pull herself back together. This was unacceptable. She couldn't—no, she *refused* to be taken in this way, like some inexperienced palace maid being seduced by a roguish prince with wandering hands. Maybe she had no choice to accept his advances if he insisted, since the Emperor himself had ordered her to *oblige* him, but she would not let her body respond to him like a mare in heat. No. She was going to lie there like a wooden board and be no better than if had chosen to rut against a training dummy instead.

"I'm at your disposal," she said stiffly, "if you would rather *rest*."

There was another small stretch of silence as he continued to stare at her, then a bright flash of awareness lit up his golden eyes with such a brimming ferocity that she nearly jumped out of her skin. Her, Anzi, the seasoned warrior—frightened by a mere expression? But it wasn't that she was frightened, was it, the voice whispered in the back of her mind once more. More like anticipating—

"That's not what I'm saying," he rasped in a voice that was curiously rough and thrillingly deep. "And you shouldn't offer if you don't mean it."

She blinked. Mean it? What would her *meaning* it have anything to do with whether he accepted or not? The Emperor had made clear she was available to all his demands, including carnal ones. It hardly mattered what she *meant*.

His hand cupped her jaw harder, and her pulse beat faster against her neck when she felt his fingers slide up into her hair behind her ear. She wished she could think properly, but he must have done something sinister to disable her intelligence and amplify her senses instead. He had a faint, almost spectral scent that reminded her of hot, shifting desert sands, of dominant masculinity and solid, heated strength. His voice sent tremors through her down to her core, the center of all she was. And he looked—magnificent. Perfect. As if there had been a blank spot in her memory she had been waiting all her life for someone to fill, for someone to remind her that the place had belonged to them all along. And she wondered what he tasted like, what it would be like to have all five of her senses filled by him and nothing but him.

But it was wrong of her to wonder, she reminded herself. She knew the rules. Base desires had no place in her mind, not when she had already vowed to give herself body and soul to the nation. Kaizat was right, after all: she was no ordinary solder. She was going to be among the greatest, and she had already abandoned all other pursuits for the sake of that dream.

"I'm at your disposal," she repeated, and her voice was stronger this time. Colder. Anything to push back against the deep craving she kept shoving back down inside her. "What I want is irrelevant."

His eyes narrowed. "That's not true."

"It is. I have no objections. Or if you'd prefer one of the harem women, I can ask the guards where to find—"

His hand slid down her jaw, and suddenly his fingers were under her chin and lifting it up. "I don't prefer them."

"Then—"

"Your company is enough for me. For now." His eyes flashed again, and this time there was something that burned even hotter in the sheen of his gaze. "In the meantime, try not to tempt me. It's hard to say no when you offer yourself up to me like that."

"...Of course."

She didn't know what else to say. Clearly, he didn't want to let go of her yet, and he was still watching her as if he hoped she might throw herself onto him and beg him to take her then and there. Well, he was fooling himself. Maybe his scent was slowly killing her in the most agonizing of ways, and maybe his touch was threatening to make her fall apart altogether, but she would never, never disgrace herself by forgetting who and what she was. And what she wasn't. Namely, some common, desperate woman eager for something to fill her between her thighs.

"Then, should I continue escorting you?"

Her cool interruption of the silence seemed to remind him of where they were, and his hand dropped away from her face. Her cheek felt cold, unpleasantly so, but she was an idiot for having liked being touched that way. What was she, a simpering schoolgirl? They both turned toward the courtyard again with nothing further to say—

—and again, she felt something burning inside her once more, just like earlier. She didn't understand why, but she was sure of it now. It was anger, or a vague shadow of it. She glanced to her left and examined Kaizat with a quick sweep of her gaze as they continued onward, noting that his face had taken on that dark look again as well.

Was it...was it possible this was from him? A magical aura, she'd heard of desert nomads who had strange abilities like that. They were mixed-blood, mostly human but with smatterings of non-human lineage. This was why they were dangerous, especially the leaders among them: unlike those in the Capital, those out there in the wild lands considered such things highly valuable. Which was ridiculous. Non-humans ruling over humans? Made no sense at all. Non-humans were inferior.

Except for dragons, she thought with a growing smile as they crossed over the threshold and walked over the vibrant green grass. They continued toward the blue dragon resting in the center of the courtyard.

"This is Colonel Bisset's partner," she said, shining with pride. Wild dragons were nonexistent, and only the Empire could boast of having preserved the existence of civilized ones. Surely, even with whatever treasures Kaizat-Amun might have back home, whether they be gold or gemstones or precious silk, he couldn't claim anything as majestic as this. "They've been together for a hundred years, at least. The immortality she grants him is proof of their bond."

Another sharp twinge inside her had her glancing back toward the chieftain, who was staring at the dragon's massive head where it lay on the grass. The creature's eyes were closed. Perhaps she was sleeping, but more likely, she was ignoring them. Anzi was sure such a magnificent, wise old dragon had no interest in entertaining the admiration of two little humans, but it was enough for her to be in its presence alone.

Maybe not, for the chieftain. She was growing more and more certain he was becoming angrier. Maybe he was envious? In that case, she had better get him out of here before he got any ideas into his sneaky little nomad head. Not that she believed he could ever steal away Colonel Bisset's dragon and not end up roasted to ashes for it, but any disturbance at all would be more than enough to disgrace her anyway.

"Unfortunately, we can't ask her to fly us down to the districts," she said as she stepped away. "But if you don't mind a walk, the Imperial City is the most beautiful in the entire world. There's a lot to see."

The uncomfortable twisting in her gut abruptly faded away, and she breathed a sigh of relief when the man removed his gaze from the dragon and looked at her instead. His golden eyes flickered up and down her body in a way that almost made her forget herself, and as if that weren't enough, he shot her a crooked smile that made her heart jump.

"I'd like that," he said. "I want you to show me."

11

Anzi and Kaizat stood patiently by the enormous stone barrier that made up one of the six massive gates leading out the city. Just beyond the barrier would be a bridge made of the same heavy stone as well, solid and true. The gate guards were the same way. No ordinary beasts, these: while Anzi had her doubts about non-humans, control of the impossibly heavy gates had to fall into the capable hands of the enormous stone golems and no one else. Somewhat man-shaped, just vaguely, while bearing the rippling, coarse texture of rocky earth, the hunched-over creatures stood thrice as high as the tallest human and as many times wide. They had no eyes nor mouth nor ears, but they had a sizable, featureless lump where the head might be on a man along with two arms and two legs as wide around as tree trunks. Mottled gray, black, and white, if they stood stationary, someone who knew no better would mistake them for massive statues chiseled out of a mountainside.

But of course, everyone in the Imperial City could recognize them at a glance. Even the ones who lived out in the farthest rings of the grand Imperium would know what they were the first time they ever encountered one. The dozen stone golems that guarded each gate of the palace, two to a gate, one on either side, were legendary. If the dragons and the Premier Guard symbolized the power of the Empire, then the gate guards symbolized its stalwart sturdiness, its immovable determination.

"The golems dismantle and reassemble the gates as needed," she explained to Kaizat, half because she wanted to distract him from the fact that they had been waiting here for at least five minutes, and half because she was proud to boast of the Empire's mastery over these fearsome beings. As everlasting as the earth itself and strong enough to strike fear into the bravest men, they protected the Emperor unfailingly, protected the heart of the people unfailingly. She waited for the chieftain to say something back, perhaps make a comment about their size or ask how exactly they would dismantle and reassemble a gate, but she was answered only with silence.

Nothing to say? Was he awestruck, goggle-eyed and speechless? She smiled and turned to look at him, eager to see his expression, only to see that tight, dark look from earlier once more. It was more guarded this time, nearly imperceptible. She didn't know how she managed to recognize it so quickly when it was clear he was trying his best to hide it. She narrowed her eyes. Envious of the nation's marvels, was he? Nomad tribes were hardy and strong, but of course there were no treasures hidden in the desert. All they had were their tents and tamed wyrms and little else.

"Where do they come from?" he asked suddenly, and she blinked at the unexpected question. Was he trying to find out their source so he could acquire some for himself? Well, he was out of luck.

"They didn't come from anywhere at all," she said. "The Mage Collective is responsible for their creation. They've existed for as long as the Empire has, maybe even before. No one really remembers that far back, just that the twelve have guarded the Emperor and his home for centuries now."

"The Mage Collective," he repeated, and his voice dropped to a low rumble that would have sent another thrill through her had she not steeled herself just in time. His eyes were fixed on the featureless heads of the stone behemoths, however, so luckily, he missed the way the tip of her tongue flicked nervously along her upper lip. "So the Mage Collective created these beings from…?"

"That's a secret of the masters. I don't know the answer myself, and I'm sure most don't, either."

"And you don't ask?"

"Why should we? They're loyal and true, even if they don't have the intellect to be independent. See there? There's always a soldier to man each one. You can't see it, but they all carry a talisman on their uniform with a certain mark that corresponds to their charge. Together, they guard the gates, and anyone who comes in and out has to go through them first."

"But you never question why the Mage Collective only created these twelve and no more."

"It's probably very difficult."

"Yes. It is."

Again, Anzi sent him a strange look that he didn't catch, as he remained staring up at the golem with an unblinking gaze. Yes, he had said, as if he were suggesting he knew it to be truth rather than simply agreeing with her guess. Curious man.

"Here it comes," someone announced, and the soldier that had been standing behind the motionless stone creature stepped out to rejoin them on the path. Anzi had nearly forgotten about him, and she had only her stupid preoccupation with Kaizat to blame. With one last furtive glance at the chieftain, she turned her attention to the small shadow descending from the sky and watched as the falcon lit upon the guard's outstretched arm. There was a rolled sheet of parchment wrapped around one of the fierce bird's legs, and with a sharp rustle, the soldier detached and read it.

"My apologies," he said a few seconds later, and he rolled the parchment back up in his hands while the falcon made itself comfortable on his silver shoulder epaulet. "Please take this with you. The instructions on it are very clear, and if you present this upon entering through the gate when you return, you won't be stopped."

"No need for apologies. I would have made sure to verify orders, too." Anzi took the proffered sheet and slipped it up her sleeve with a deft twist of her wrist. "Then Chieftain Kaizat-Amun and I will be going."

The guard stepped back with a brief bow toward their guest and made a sharp sound at his golem companion. Previously stationary, now it began to move, and the shifting rocks comprising its body creaked and groaned with increasing volume. Before today, Anzi had only ever seen this happen at a distance from the other side of the gate, and she couldn't help but stare with bright eyes as the creature awakened and began lumbering toward the massive barrier with slow, earth-shaking steps. Far above their heads, she could see the soldiers stationed along the top of the towering palace walls at equal intervals, their tiny forms barely larger than ants against a perfect backdrop of blue, blue sky.

The enormous gate guardian's thundering footsteps stopped, and its thick arms rose into the air. The stubby, finger-like appendages at the ends attached themselves to the depressed stone mass that filled the grand archway , and the solid stone wall that was the gate began to crumble. But instead of boulders tumbling down to the ground at will, the wall crumpled neatly toward the sides, its rocky pieces and slabs sliding sideways with a deafening grind. Anzi held her breath as the golem used its stone magic to dismantle the colossal barrier, faster and faster until an enormous hole opened up in the middle. There. Beyond the archway, through the ten-meter tunnel passing through the palace walls and past the bridge, she could already glimpse the upper districts.

"No one gets in or out of this place without permission," she said, and although her tone was utterly professional, she was secretly glowing with thrilled pride. She had seen all of this happen before, several times, but never from this close. Her heart was pounding even now as she wondered at the inexplicable display, the slow, lumbering movements of the golem and the way it could control the earth with such dignity and steady, earth-shaking power.

She wondered what Kaizat was thinking, too. As a foreigner, he was sure to be even more mesmerized than she was. But a swift examination of his countenance proved her wrong, and she frowned at the dark, haunted shadow that crossed his face. What was wrong with him? Ever since they had reached the courtyard, he had been unhappy and dissatisfied even if he never verbalized it. She wasn't blind; she could see it plainly. It didn't help that his sneaky desert-man aura was acting up, either: she could sense the stirrings of anger inside him along with something more somber, too. Almost—sad.

Well, that was silly, and she refused to pay it any attention. If she was simply imagining things, she ought to ignore them. And if she really was being affected by the chieftain's mysterious powers, whatever they may be, her job was to resist their influence. If he had such inhuman powers, however, it wouldn't be a good idea to take him into the marketplace as she had been planning to do. There were too many innocent people who might be affected by his aura, and it was her duty to keep them out of such danger. Somewhere less populated, then.

With a deferring nod to the chieftain to get him to follow, she guided the way toward the mouth of the tunnel beyond where the stone barrier used to be. With a final glance and a salute to the guard, she and Kaizat disappeared into the dimness, and the rumbling sounds of the gate closing once more echoed all around them.

FOR WELL OVER AN HOUR, Anzi guided him around the grand bridges that went over the Annat River, which circled the palace walls but also branched out to the north, south, west, and east in near-straight lines all the way past the edges of the city, effectively dividing it into perfect quarters. Not only was the four pronged, compass-shaped Annat River beautiful, it kept the land fertile and vibrant, certainly nothing like the uninhabitable desert where the chieftain came from. Beautiful gardens filled with exotic flowers lined both sides of every road and path, and drooping willow trees provided shade overhead with their slender, arching branches that drooped like a noble lady's delicate fingers.

In other words, everything was perfect, and she was well on her way to proving that without ever having to enter the district proper.

"What do you think of the Imperial City so far?"

Shit. She didn't know why she had asked that. The words had slipped out before she realized what she was saying, and now, all of her casual praise for the Imperium would be for nothing. If he realized she was doing her best to impress him with the marvels of her nation, he would surely spite her by pretending to be unmoved by all he had seen. That was what foreign nobles did if they weren't too busy brown-nosing instead. But with bated breath, she waited for Kaizat to reply anyway.

"It's different," he said, and his simple response took the wind out of her sails. She felt rather like the drooping willow branches that they were walking under right now. "But very scenic."

Scenic. She could almost taste how unimpressed he was.

"If this is too quiet, I'll show you to the market soon," she said, although she had no intention of letting him go down there when it was still peak crowd time for a while yet. When there were fewer people, she would chance it, but who knew how many people he could affect with his mood as he was doing with her? Even if it was unintentional—which seemed to be the case? Maybe?—he was still a threat.

"Quiet is fine."

"Then, is there somewhere in particular you want to visit? How long ago did you arrive in the Imperial City?"

He looked at her with a lilting, lazy smile that made her heart flip upside down and retreat to her spine. "It's been a week."

"Oh." She blinked. "I guess that means you've already seen everything."

"I haven't left your Emperor's palace since I came. Today's my first day out."

Your Emperor, he had said, not *the* Emperor. She wanted to bristle at the obvious disclaimer, but there was something about the lovely cut of his jaw that made her forget exactly how to do that.

"But," he added, "I can imagine there's a favorite haunt where you and all your fellow soldiers go to enjoy themselves. Or do you prefer to spend your leisure time alone?"

Leisure time? She had long since left the company of most other soldiers, and the elites whose company she kept only indulged in one form of recreation for the most part: training. Exhaustive, brutal training that involved pushing themselves to the limits for the sheer pleasure of surpassing themselves in service of their nation.

But...as for the rest of the army, they had other ways to entertain themselves. Namely, sex. The most popular place to visit for this was the infamous Quarter Rouge, the place she personally considered the one dark spot of the otherwise glossy and perfect Imperium. Without a doubt, that was a district where a man like Kaizat-Amun would attract a great deal of attention from both male and female soldiers, and countless civilians besides. Indeed, he wouldn't even have to pay for any services. The most beautiful and sought-after courtesans would be all over him in an instant, sliding their soft hands over his bare, muscular chest and rippling biceps, along his thick forearms and chiseled abdomen and—

No. She wasn't taking him there. She would rather stab herself a dozen times than give him a tour that would end with six women moaning and grinding themselves all over his hard, bronzed body. Because that would be improper, not for any other reason.

"The training grounds," she said in an unnecessarily loud, emphatic voice. "That's where we go. All of us."

The chieftain's smile twitched a little wider. "Alright then," he rumbled. "Take me there."

12

She should have known these knuckle-draggers would be here.

"Welcome back, Anzi, didn't expect to see you so soon. Fell off, did you? Passing muster for the Premier Guard harder than you thought?"

"If I fell off, then you should be worried about where *you'll* end up," she said flatly, but she didn't bother putting on a frosty front otherwise. Blunt words were enough to get her point across when it came to this gaggle of malcontent soldiers who thought she was a wise target to heckle. Oscar had never been very smart though, so while his friends would know better than to do much more than sneer in her direction, he was the one who would be raising hell soon enough.

Too bad all the other training grounds were already reserved for drills. She had come up the hill to check with the quartermaster before escorting Kaizat over, knowing there would be trouble-making loiterers about. Like Oscar and his friends. His posse was part of a Service batch three years ahead of her, but when she had been promoted from basic to intermediate training at the age of twelve, she had been assigned to the same squad for two years before moving on ahead to advanced education. They hadn't hated her in the beginning. She had been a novelty, an exotic pet, graduating from basic after only two years of training instead of the typical five, and she had been small and puny compared to the fifteen year olds who were beginning to put on bulk. And for a few days, they had treated her nicely enough.

Until she proved better than them at every exercise and every assessment henceforth. And one day, after she received loud praise from their commanding officer before the entire platoon of trainees, Oscar and his posse of identical blond-haired and blue-eyed minions decided that she would be their undying enemy for all eternity.

To their credit, they did manage to sabotage her several times. If it hadn't been for their repeated antics—usually involving mussing her sheets or throwing her pillow on the floor right before a barracks check, or dropping worms and various insects in her meals whenever one of them was on kitchen duty, and so on and so on—she would have graduated from intermediate far sooner than the two years it took her to get out. To this day, her old commanding officer still thought she was a miscreant, but she had long since put aside her past grievances. That was ancient history.

Unfortunately, Oscar and his posse didn't agree, and they never quite forgot her either. Their parents were also from the glitzy upper districts while she hailed from the humble desert fringes, so their incessant heckling whenever they were out of earshot of any officers, and sometimes even when they *were* within earshot, went unpunished and without comment, even from Anzi herself.

It had been humiliating but necessary. Swallowing insults and training her pride to remain silent when she had been younger had given her the keenness of mind and the undying patience to make it through. And now that she was ahead of the curve, it was that much more satisfying to look back over her shoulder and see how far she had come.

Then again, it was never pleasant spotting Oscar at all, and that included even when he was far behind her.

"Hey, look everyone, Anzi's been sent back. You think she's going to get demoted back into basic while she's at it?" He was still going, and his friends along with several of the other soldiers hanging around the circular training ground chuckled along with him. "Just kidding, just kidding. Hey, why don't you show us how you would have ridden a real, live dragon of your own? Come on, don't be a stick in the mud, come back. You can pull up one of the training dummies and gallop around on it."

She ignored him and strode to the far end of the grounds where the aging quartermaster dozed in his wooden chair. Those were the rules:

without a commanding officer present, the quartermaster of each area decided who came and went. If she wanted to bring Kaizat here, she needed his permission first, chieftain or not.

"Sir," she said, and she leaned over to shake the elderly man by the arm. He awoke with a start, sending his leather helmet askew and nearly sliding off his bald head entirely, and looked up into Anzi's face.

"Wh-whazzat?" he slurred, and she leaned away when he proceeded to spit half-coherent commands to disguise that he had been sleeping just seconds earlier. "Report, soldier! Identify yourself. Whose platoon are you with? Who's your lieutenant?"

"...Sir, I'm escorting an important guest around the city today, by order of His Excellency the Emperor. Requesting permission to bring him here."

At the mention of the Emperor, the quartermaster struggled to his feet, and by the time she uttered her last syllable, he was offering her a sharp salute and a nod. "Of course," he blustered. "Whatever His Excellency commands."

"Then I'll be back in a moment. I think he might be interested in the weapons cache."

"Oh, yes, yes. Have him do that, yes."

Right. She suppressed a sigh and turned with a small grimace. Lack of discipline—she hated that the most, but what could she say about an old man likely nearing the end of his Service? If he had been awarded the position of a quartermaster, then he must have done good during his active years. She couldn't disrespect that.

"What were you whispering over there for!" Oscar asked loudly from where he sat on a wooden block bench with his comrades. Even from this distance, his voice rang loud and clear even though he wasn't shouting, and the thought occurred to her that some people were just especially good at making their voices heard. Vain people. "Come on. Share some stories. Did you get to drool over the colonel's dragon some more? What happened, did he say you were too obsessed and that it would be a bad idea to let you get near one after all?"

Only that imbecile would dare to walk such a dangerously thin line. He was close to ridiculing dragons and the integrity of dragon riders, so very close. If he dared, she wouldn't hold back. Forget patience. He was just as annoying as he had been when she was twelve, and six years later, he was so much more tempting to backhand across the face than before.

...If she didn't have to escort Chieftain Kaizat around. When she brought him up the path and onto the grounds, at least she knew Oscar would have the bare minimum of sense to keep his trap shut in the presence of a foreign dignitary. She ignored his heckling and trotted down the sloping path a hundred feet until she reached the foot of it where her guest awaited her. "This way, please," she said with a polite bow of her head. He obliged immediately, falling into step beside her.

She pretended to not notice how he was walking so close that their hands kept brushing against each other.

"The other areas we passed," he said suddenly. "I saw children. Soldiers?"

"Yes."

"They're very young."

"We enter different fields of the Service when we're ten years old," she said. "Some are chosen to be doctors and medics, some are chosen to become farmers to feed the people. There are a lot of callings that have to be answered, and that means some are Selected to serve in the military. Wherever our talents would best serve the Empire, that's where we go. Why should a recruit start any later than a farmer, or a physician, or a baker? We're all apprentices, and all callings are necessary."

She felt Kaizat's eyes on the side of her head like twin flames. Gods, was she sweating? "That sounded like you recited it out of a book," he said quietly. "Is that what you did?"

For a second, she wondered at his tone. He sounded almost admonishing, and yet pitying at the same time. She didn't like that. Not at all. "We're well educated," she answered, and she allowed an edge to slip into her voice along with it. "Recitations help us remember the important things that shouldn't be forgotten. Ever."

"I see. So you were also ten years old when you became a soldier."

"A recruit," she clarified, although the difference was moot even to her. She just—didn't want to give it to him so easily. Everything he said was beginning to sound like a criticism of the things she held most dear. "It gives us purpose. Most nations' youths are a source of discord and conflict. The Empire is different. Every child has gainful employment and has the means to help their family with their contributions to the nation. It's a privilege, Chieftain."

"I see."

No, he didn't. There was a too-obvious neutrality in his voice as if he were simply obliging her. He didn't actually mean it. She pursed her lips and tried to think of something clever and wise to add but came up with nothing. Unfortunate. Unfortunate that she was so tongue-tied in his presence and even more so under his unblinking gaze. She had never been so unbalanced before.

When they reached the top of the slope, the expanse of the training ground awaited them. So was Oscar, but she noted with great satisfaction that as soon as he saw the man who walked beside her, his mouth snapped shut again instead of delivering whatever witty insult he'd prepared for her imminent return. Try it now, she silently dared him. Do it.

He didn't, of course, and he and his friends watched with wide eyes as she led the way to the quartermaster. That's what she'd thought. This was why she chose to hold back when she could, for the sweet, sweet moments like these when actions spoke so much more loudly than words.

"You're free to take a look at our weapons cache," she said when they came to a stop. "I don't know much about the desert tribes, but you don't use most of these, do you? Wood and metal must be hard to come by."

Kaizat greeted the suddenly-jittery quartermaster with a brief nod before surveying the collection laid out over two wide, wooden tables as well as hanging from several racks. "We have these," he said. "There's nothing I don't recognize."

"What do you normally use when you fight?"

He glanced back at her, golden eyes flickering up and down her form so quickly she didn't have a chance to react. He had already turned back to the weapons by the time she realized he'd all but ogled her. "We try not to," he said in a curiously dry voice. "But when it's inevitable, we use simple blades. Long blades, short blades, either one. You're right about wood being hard to come by; we don't use much in the way of spears or javelins or bows and arrows."

"But you can acquire metal easily?"

"We trade with the lands east of us."

Anzi waited for more, but no further information was forthcoming. Secretive, was he? She too remained silent as she waited for Kaizat to finish looking everything over.

"But we grapple, mostly," he said abruptly, and she looked at him with a frown. "We're always most comfortable when we can use our own bodies as our weapons. It doesn't seem that way for this place. There are more kinds of weapons here than any human can master in one lifetime, and that doesn't leave much room for anyone to master himself."

Her eyebrows furrowed hard at that. Human? Had that simply been a general reference to the short-lived tragedy of mankind in general, or was that a sideways admission that he carried inhuman blood inside him? "We grapple too," she said, feeling both defensive and competitive. Suspicious, too. "We're trained in close quarters combat from basic training to advanced. It's an important part of our curriculum. It's just that all the rest of this is important as well...sir."

He leaned forward slightly and ran his fingers down the flat side of a training longsword lying on the table. "Don't call me that," he said idly. "I told you to call me Kai."

"With all due respect, I can't do that, sir."

"Should I challenge you for it, then?" he asked, and he looked at her with a sharp half-smile that made her stomach do something strange again. "Maybe a contest of sorts. Your friends staring at me from back there must be expecting a show anyway. I don't want to disappoint."

Oh, so he had noticed Oscar's gaping face. That was unfortunate. No matter what he did, he could make her look bad, even when he wasn't intending to.

"...A contest?"

"A spar," he clarified. "You're good at fighting, aren't you? A model soldier?"

She tensed and listened for any trace of mockery in his voice, but she found none. None that she noticed, at least. Somehow, she was sure he was laughing at her at least a little bit. "If you don't mind me asking, sir, how old are you?"

He glanced at her again. "How old do you think I am?"

Answering a question with a question. She didn't like that. "No older than your early twenties. I can't be sure of anything more than that."

He lifted a shortsword this time and held it horizontally in front of his face. His eyes narrowed with a dissecting glare. "That's right."

"And have you trained with blades since you were very young?"

"No, not particularly. I began training with live blades when I was around my early teenage years. Is that what you're getting at, that I lack experience compared to you?" He looked at her again, and this time there was a prowling, almost predatory light dancing in his golden eyes. His faint smile widened into an outright smirk. "I meant it, though. A contest, with stakes."

"Stakes?"

"If I win, you stop addressing me as anything other than Kai."

She would have rolled her eyes if her station allowed her such liberties. "Sir..."

"I look forward to you not calling me that for much longer."

She bristled immediately at the implications. He was confident she would lose, was it? That he would win these stupid *stakes.* He had no idea who he was dealing with.

"It's an honor to meet you, sir," interrupted a familiar voice from directly behind them, and with slow-rising dread, Anzi turned so she could face the unwelcome interloper. "I hate to impose, but I couldn't help myself. My name is Oscar Bedeau. Are you from the east by any chance? Desert region"

By now, Kaizat had turned around too, and he stared down at the other young man with an unmistakably hard expression carved into his face. Great. Dark hells, she had never thought Oscar would be this stupid. But as long as he didn't outdo himself in the next few seconds, Anzi could safely extricate the chieftain and herself from this awkward meeting and—

"If you'd like to be entertained, I'm happy to offer you a spar. I didn't mean to eavesdrop, but I heard you mention something of it a second ago."

Oh, no. Her mistake. Her mistake for expecting anything more than pea-brained antics from stupid Oscar—

"I accept," Kaizat said immediately. "I look forward to it."

Anzi grimaced.

13

"What do you think you're doing." Anzi had no choice but to remain in place since she didn't dare step in front of the chieftain, but if she could, she would have been in Oscar's face in an eye blink. Was he crazy or stupid or both? Didn't he recognize what kind of guest she was escorting by the priceless regalia he wore? Her eyes narrowed to sharp slits as she glared at her fellow soldier, violently willing him to move back.

"I'm just welcoming—"

"It's all right, Anzi. I'm sure he means no harm."

She couldn't bring herself to look over at Kaizat, not even when she felt a soothing hand rest upon the leather guard over her shoulder. This was humiliating. No discipline, she seethed. And what was Oscar's plan, exactly? What did he think was going to happen? Now that he had issued what was little more than a poorly disguised challenge, the honor of the Empire's entire military rested on a pair of shoulders more suitable for posing for portraits than fighting. And yet even if he won, that was no victory, either. A soldier had no right to disgrace a dignitary, whether native or foreign. He had his place.

There was no point glaring at him, though. The idiot was staring up at the chieftain with a serene, innocent smile, utterly oblivious of anything else. So she settled for his friends, and in a rare, brief instant of visible fury, she threw a murderous glare over Oscar's shoulder at the group still seated at the benches. Most of them were wise enough to look away, but as soon as her gaze left them, she could feel their eyes scuttle back once more.

"Where's your commanding officer?" she snapped, trying one last time to salvage the situation. But it was not to be.

"I'm sure whoever it is won't mind." Kaizat looked down and smiled at her. "Oscar Bedeau is being a good host. I accept his hospitality."

A good host...hospitality. More like Oscar enjoyed looking down on desert dwellers including those who lived on the fringes, and his scorn for them had only grown ever since their enmity sprouted. No doubt he thought he was going to have the time of his life disgracing some primitive, sand-rawed warrior of a backwards tribe and implicate Anzi while he was at it. After all, once word got out, she would be the one to bear the blame of failed diplomacy and whatever else resulted from this, not Oscar. She was the one responsible for the chieftain today, and Oscar Bedeau was from a good family. No upper district family would ever let their son take the fall for something when a convenient desert fringer could do it instead.

How many times had he poked fun at her large, pitch-black eyes and gotten others to do the same? Crow's eyes, they had jeered. Fitting, because desert fringers would always have a bit of low-class thievery in them, too, just like crows. She had long since stopped caring, as all soldiers from the desert had to learn to tolerate it, but remembering his ceaseless torment almost made her hope he went ass-up with his face buried in the dirt.

"We don't have to use live blades, sir," Oscar was in the middle of offering, gracious gentleman that he was. He pointed at the leftmost weapons rack next to the nervous, quivering quartermaster. "Those are blunted. Though I don't know if you have blades like these where you're from. These are very heavy, and we're trained to them since we're very young, so..."

Enough was enough. The condescending, indulgent tone he was using, she wouldn't overlook it, not on top of everything else. She opened her mouth, lips twisting into the beginning of a snarl and tongue poised to deliver—only for her to swallow back the sharp warning. Kaizat, who had walked over to join Oscar at the rack, suddenly pulled the single massive greatsword hanging by its crossguard between two wooden prongs with one hand.

Anzi blinked and stared, but said nothing as the chieftain stepped back and deftly twirled the massive meter and a half long blade as if it were as light as a fencing foil. She noted too how silent Oscar was, as well as the faint dread in his eyes. Oh, yes. It was the look he used to wear whenever they were assigned to each other for spars. Satisfying. It almost made her even more eager to see him pummeled to a pulp if it weren't for her reluctance to see the Empire's honor tarnished in the process. But did she even have a choice? There was no one to intervene with a suitable excuse. She was going to have to stand here and watch, even applaud after it was all over.

"Maybe this is too much for you," Kaizat said in a mild voice that made her purse her lips in mixed frustration and relief. Was he going to put it back, then? "I don't think you'd stand a chance of reaching me if I used this."

"...Careful, sir. That does look heavy."

"This? No. Like you, we're trained to this from early on. You understand."

No, Oscar didn't seem like he understood at all. If it weren't for the elegant discipline his posh upbringing had instilled in him, she was sure he would be quivering in his leathers. Someone who could wield a three, four kilogram blade in one hand with such artful, effortless grace—even she couldn't do that.

Or could she? A strange thrum of excitement rose up and filled her like a burst of hot steam. Her hands curled into fists at her side, and for an instant so brief and infinitesimally small that she could forgive herself for it, or pretend she didn't notice—she wished she was the one who could match blades with Kaizat instead. He'd offered, hadn't he? She should have just accepted. Custom, etiquette, surely these were worth slackening for a chance at a clash with a real warrior.

As she watched him replace the greatsword and reach for a shorter blade instead, her eyes were drawn to the flex and ripple of the muscles of his bronzed back and the lift of his golden collar over the jut of his broad shoulders. He was strong, well-trained. That was not the body of a pampered royal, nor was it even remotely close to the stereotype of a starved desert nomad, a homeless wanderer crawling over baked dunes and hunting for his first morsel in days. That was the body of a fighter, a survivor, someone thriving. If she and Oscar could only switch places so she could test her mettle against him—

Her rogue thoughts ground to a halt when Kaizat's head whipped around to face her. He said nothing, but there was a feverish gleam in his golden eyes that hadn't been there just a second ago. What was it? What was it that he wanted to say?

But to her great disappointment, he remained utterly silent, simply staring—and then smiled.

It sent a cool ripple of nervousness through her, seeing him watch her like that. It was almost like he knew what she was thinking, and thought it amusing. Or gratifying, maybe, she didn't know. Either way, the half-concealed, secret pleasure that lingered on the sharp, strong lines of his face made her reel herself in and stand at attention again.

As much as she wanted to believe he was an irritation, that his attractiveness was a horrible inconvenience she couldn't wait to be rid of, every moment she spent in the chieftain's presence dragged the truth out of her a little more…a little more. The truth that she felt as liberated as she felt out of control, that she had never wanted to take her eyes off of him from the moment they met. She could feel his presence under her skin even now, humming deep in her bones and haunting her like a warm breath pluming through a cold dawn chill. Terrifying. She didn't know what to do with these feelings.

"You don't have to entertain him, sir," she said aloud, realizing only too late that her voice sounded thick. She cleared her throat and tried again. "There are plenty of other things to do. Oscar's really not the best host."

Kaizat was still smiling, and he was steadily stealing more of her breath away every time she hit the bottom of an exhale. If he didn't look away, she might die on the spot, blue-faced and clutching at her throat.

"Maybe I want you to watch." His voice was smooth, his tone sincere. And his stare—fire-hot and unblinking. Had she ever seen eyes so hypnotic before? "Anzi, you won't stop me, will you."

Suddenly, her tongue was too clumsy to answer his question that didn't quite feel like a question, but rather a probing tease, temptation. He was luring her in just like he'd done earlier when he had held her face in his hand and trailed his fingers down her skin, sending fire and chills through her all at once. Was there no end to his tricks? Damned mysterious desert man. First chance she had, she would consult with someone from the Mage Collective to make sure she hadn't been bewitched.

"…I don't need to see anything," she mumbled, the words colliding like awkward bricks in her mouth. She barely knew what she was saying anymore. Her wits and speech that used to be so sharp felt as blunt as the hilt end of a blade now instead of the tip. "But whatever pleases you, sir."

"Well, this is what would please me. Come here and find a place to sit where you can watch. If I do well, you can entertain me too, after."

What was that look he was giving her? *Entertain?* He was talking about one thing, so why was she thinking about something else entirely—?

She wobbled.

"Anzi?"

"I'm at your disposal," she said in a controlled monotone. He couldn't tell her joints were simultaneously turning to petrified wood and syrup from the way he said her name, she was sure. No problem. "But Oscar, don't –"

"I'll do my very best," the idiot interrupted, and he flashed another aristocratic smile at Kaizat as he pulled a practice blade of his own from the rack. "I see you've selected a blunted weapon after all, sir?"

"Wouldn't want to accidentally mangle a new friend on my first outing."

"There's no need to fear for me, sir. I'm the sort that never feels complete without a sword in my hand. Very accustomed."

Anzi followed behind them toward the middle of the training area, grimacing all the while as she listened to Oscar's embarrassing half-boasts. But he wasn't lying. He was a skillful swordsman. His wealthy upbringing had ensured a well-educated childhood before being Selected for the military, which meant he had been familiar with bladed edges long before most ever even laid their eyes on a real sword. She was better than him by far, of course, but now she wondered about Kaizat. He was strong, and he had revealed that he, too, had been trained since a young age to the blade. The deft way he had handled the greatsword was proof enough – but wasn't that unusual? Desert nomad tribes were known for their uncanny knack for survival, quick travel, and hunting. Not for their large weapons mastery. After all, that was just extra weight to carry as they wandered the sands. Curious…

No power on earth would make her ask Oscar's friends to scoot over on the bench to make room for her, so when she moved off the dirt area and onto the grass, she took up position a meter away from them with her arms crossed over her chest, frowning. They had better not heckle her. She was stressed, unsettled, and possibly enchanted, too – she was believing that last bit more with each passing second as she found her eyes glued to Kaizat's arms. The way he tossed the blade between his hands with expert grace and precision as if the longsword were as light as a feather – that blade was smaller than the massive one he had picked up before, but it was still a feat of its own to handle such a thing so deftly.

"I trust you'll hold no grudge against me, sir, whatever happens," she heard Oscar say, and she nearly slapped her hands over her face. It was too late to snap at him as he bent his knees and hunched his shoulders in preparation, so all she could do was promise herself that when she next cornered him, she would deliver the punishment and discipline his mother should have given him. What would he say if she told him that Chieftain Kaizat-Amun was no ordinary guest of the Imperial City, that he had had the privilege of seeing the Emperor face to face? Many tribal chieftains came and went especially during the trading season, but none were anything like this man. She knew it. Felt it.

Maybe she should have mentioned that first. As it was, Oscar had better come to regret his choices in the most painful way possible. And if fate didn't take care of it, she would see it through herself.

14

"So you get sent back here, and the first thing they make you do is give a tour to some barbarian nomad princeling?"

Anzi said nothing in response to the haughty sneer that came from her left. She had no idea which one of Oscar's friends was speaking, but it was all the same to her. He wasn't worth responding to.

"Stop that," someone else said. A feminine voice this time, softer but no less lofty. "It must have felt awful coming back like this. It's alright, Anzi...you're five or ten years too early for the Premier Guard, anyway. It would have been ridiculous if you managed it, don't you think? Now that you're back, you can train some more and prepare better. Next time, if you work harder, you'll definitely make it."

The snide, backhanded pretense at encouragement was even more annoying than the outright taunting. If she were allowed to speak of the Gauntlet or the Running at all, she would have shot back with a cold assurance that she had exceeded all expectations, but Colonel Bisset's instructions had been for her to remain discreet. Besides, she still didn't know what was going to happen when she was summoned for another audience with the Emperor tonight. She didn't dare make assumptions and retaliate with a boast, not until she was certain. But after—how sweet it would be to look Oscar and his minions in the eye? Maybe even with her own dragon behind her, she thought with a thumping heart and quickening pulse. The looks on their faces would be so satisfying, so...

Kaizat and Oscar had begun circling each other, but the chieftain swiveled his head to look at her just then as if she had made a noise. She stiffened, eyes widening the instant she met his gaze. What was he doing, taking his eyes off of the enemy!

Oscar darted forward, capitalizing on the opportunity like any good soldier. She didn't blame him. She would do the same if her opponent was so foolish. Her heart flew into her mouth because damn it all, she couldn't bear to see Kaizat lose even if it was dancing on the edge of treason to think that way. And it wasn't just because she despised Oscar, either. No, it was the thought of him inflicting pain, of smashing the blunted edge of his practice sword into vulnerable, bare flesh—she took a compulsive step forward, and it was all she could do to stop from leaping across the distance and knocking the weapon out of his grip. Oscar was bundled in fresh leather guards, too, that were scarcely touched. Meanwhile, Kaizat wore not a scrap of armor, nothing at all that could protect him—and yet, he didn't even flinch when metal crashed against metal in an ear-twisting, nauseating screech. How he had raised his sword in time to parry the blow, she didn't know, but that instantaneous, blurring movement made her suck in a sharp gasp. Especially when she saw Oscar stumble back with a single shove of the crossed swords as if someone had taken his shoulders and hurled him away. He nearly fell, and although he caught himself just in time to stay standing, there was a bewildered look in his eyes that mirrored her own.

This time, it was he who glanced to the side at her, not Kaizat, and she recognized instantly the look of mixed shock and suspicion. Indeed—she knew why he looked at her that way, why he narrowed his eyes and backed away from the chieftain instead of clashing again. Because the way Kaizat moved wasn't normal. She was sure of it, and so was Oscar. He had picked countless fights and accused her of having inhuman advantage more times than she could count. And although she had disbelieved it of herself for years until it became undeniable, she could recognize the touch well enough in others.

Earlier, when he had hefted the greatsword, she had chalked it up to him being a superbly gifted swordsman. Now she knew better.

"Something wrong, Oscar Bedeau?" The chieftain's voice was neither taunting nor impatient, as nonchalant as if he were asking about his day.

Meanwhile, the soldier's eyes drifted away from Anzi's and back to his adversary. But he stayed well away, newly reluctant. "...Nothing, sir," he replied. "Just surprised. You've got a grip on you."

"Would you like to stop?"

Again, not a hint of anything other than casual civility in his voice, but something in Kaizat's words seemed to pluck Oscar's nerves the wrong way. Anzi knew that expression, the tight twitch at the corners of his mouth, the swift downturn of his lips. Even his blond eyebrows rose a little the way they did whenever he was doing his best to hide his annoyance. It was the look she used to see on his face every time she ignored him. Old times...

"Of course not, sir. Here I come."

It was futile. Curiously, Kaizat never displayed that outrageous strength again, but he moved with a dexterity that belied his broad, muscular stature, sliding into vulnerable openings of Oscar's defense and forcing him back step by step. Twice, thrice, and more, he parried a whistling, incoming blade, and instead of shoving him back again the way Anzi knew he could, he simply brought his own sword up with a sliding screech and almost twisted the weapon out of Oscar's hand with a turn of the crossguard. Not only that, but he used every part of the blade like it was an extension of his body. The edge, the crossguard, the pommel of the hilt. If these were live swords instead of blunted for practice use, Oscar would have been dead a dozen times just in the first few minutes.

And, Anzi suspected, if Kaizat were to fight seriously, it would have been far more than that. The way his golden eyes flashed as he moved around Oscar like a circling falcon, glowing only with an amused light, nothing more—

Golden eyes. She blinked and stepped back as if struck, and her heart throbbed once, hard, as if it were trying to wring itself to death. Her hand shot up to press upon her chest, trying to coax it into a normal rhythm and soothe the air back into her lungs.

But golden eyes, flashing in the dim light of the last moments of a sunset far away. Sharp, bright, alive.

Her heart throbbed again, harder this time, and she couldn't even warn Kaizat when he froze mid-stroke of his blade and whipped around to look at her again. Eyes forward, she wanted to shout, but her tongue was frozen and her mouth was numb and she was so close to remembering something she had forgotten for so, so long—

A collective gasp went up from the soldiers that had congregated all around the edge of the grounds. Others besides Oscar's friends had gathered to spectate, and now they all stared as the chieftain leaped to the side, narrowly dodging the blade that came swing toward him from the side. Except he didn't manage to dodge it in time. Anzi's eyes were too sharp to deceive her, and besides, the ecstatic look that exploded across Oscar's face told her he had made contact. Not a small one either, but a full strike. It would surely bruise, and horribly too; the swing had connected hard. Kaizat had been standing nearly stationary when the blunted edge smashed into his upper arm, distracted as he had been.

Why he had turned to stare at her in the first place, she didn't want to examine. How many times had that happened now, that it seemed as if he could sense what she was thinking, what she was feeling, even when she said nothing at all?

Either way, the moment was gone: whatever memory had been at the very precipice of recollection plummeted back into the abyss, sabotaged by the shock of seeing Oscar land such a ferocious blow. And the spar—it needed to end.

"You shouldn't have swung like that," she snapped, and she strode forward with a menacing tightness that she reserved only for when she was angriest. "You've broken bones that way. Step back, Oscar. Right now."

To his credit, he obeyed and scuttled back several steps. He must have sensed her dangerous mood, how furious she was. The little maggot, she seethed, and a hissing anger filled her as she came to a stop in front of Kaizat, who had wrapped his other hand around the arm that had borne the savage strike.

"I apologize, sir, please let me to take you to see a healer."

"It's fine, Anzi. It was a glancing blow."

She furrowed her brow. "Sir, I saw the way—"

"I wouldn't lie to you."

"But I heard it," she insisted, and something reckless and frustrated blossomed inside her. "I heard it when it landed. That was—" Why was she so upset, she wondered. Why did she feel so vicious, on the brink of lashing out. She wanted so badly to turn and wrap her hands around Oscar's throat, bleed the air out of him and hurl him to the ground, except there was one thing she wanted even more than that. Before she could stop herself, her hand shot up toward Kaizat's, and before he could react, she peeled back his fingers several inches so she could see for herself what damage had been done. His shoulder wasn't dislocated, but the skin must be mottled red and broken from the force of the blow. Later, she would allow herself the pleasure of thrashing Oscar to pieces for the first time in a long, long while, something clearly overdue—

She froze. His half-lifted palm only partly shielded from view the unmistakable, shifting black pattern over his skin. The last of it faded from view just before she could lean in for a closer look, but she hadn't imagined it. Couldn't have. And yet now, all that remained was smooth, bronzed skin, marked only by the hard lines of his muscled triceps. She stared for a moment longer, not understanding. It didn't matter how tanned his complexion was; she should be looking at blotchy skin, reddened and slowly swelling. But nothing. There was nothing at all.

Finally, she let go of his warm fingers and stilled, wearing only a carefully controlled, stone-blank expression. Not a sound came from anyone. Not from Kaizat, not from Oscar, not from the soldiers who had gathered around the fringes to watch the spar. Good. She needed the silence. She needed to think.

She hadn't imagined it, had she? Or perhaps it had been a trick of the light. No one else had seen what she had, or else someone would have commented on it by now. After a long, lingering moment, she allowed her gaze to flick up, and Kai stared back at her with an inscrutable expression she couldn't possibly name. But something in his eyes reminded her of the sensation of coasting across still, poised water, right before the crashing rapids of a cascade. Of looking up to see dark storm clouds gathering above, heavy with rain and holding in lightning like a trapped breath. He was watching her, molten gold gaze gleaming with such heat that thought it would melt her through, waiting, waiting...

...Waiting for something she didn't know how to give. She looked away, and with a burst of determination that came from sheer discipline, willpower, and a little thrill of fear mixed in, she stepped back and took in a discreetly calming breath. Slow. Easy.

"Fortunate," she said, and her voice was composed and even. "I'm glad Oscar showed some restraint. We're still going to have a conversation"—she threw an savage glance over her shoulder—"but for now, I'd like to take you away from here if you don't mind. It's more crowded than I expected it would be. And *they* should be training."

She had nothing else to say. Her thoughts were congealing into mush. Words slipped further and further away as she tried to untangle the riot of confusion coiling tight in the center of her mind.

And again, a faint, lost memory whispered to her, beckoning her around one more corner, then another, then another. *Follow me, and you will see...*

She guided Kaizat off the training area without another word. More accurately, she turned and left, assuming he would follow. Hoping he would follow. And as they walked down the slope, listening to the hushed whispers of soldiers fading into the breeze, she let her thoughts drift back to the thing she had seen shifting over Kaizat's arm.

Scales.

15

"The market is still crowded. It'll be better if you wait until closer to the evening to explore the wares."

"That's all right."

It had been quiet between them ever since Anzi led Kaizat away from the training grounds half an hour ago. Since then, they had been walking along the wide, smooth stone path that followed the circular Annat River and bordered the inner edge of the upper districts. Now they approached a divide in the river, as well as in the path. One way would continue leading them around, and the other would take them deeper into the city districts. When they reached the fork, she came to a halt. "What would you like to see in the meantime, sir."

"What would you recommend?"

"There are people who enjoy exploring the Quarter Art, but I don't think you'll be wanting souvenirs."

"How did you know? Do I not look like the sort to collect them?"

She was glad they passed by another soldier just then so that she was obligated to exchange a quick salute. It gave her an excuse to not look up at him even though she could feel his eyes boring into her. But even so, it was clear he expected an answer, a continuation of their conversation. It was too bad. What she wanted was more silence so she could figure out her tangled, confused thoughts. Too late for that now.

"I didn't think desert natives liked carrying trinkets. But I can—"

"No, you're right, I don't want any. But I can admire them."

Alright, then. She would take that as an order to escort him to the Quarter Art. But she had never had time to learn how to properly appreciate paintings or sculptures and whatever else would be there; she would need to look for a tour guide.

"You're from the desert, too," he said as they turned onto the bent path. "I recognize your eyes."

"A number of us come from the districts there."

"And what area are you from?"

She hesitated before answering. After what she had seen earlier—or thought she had seen—she was leery of giving him any more information about herself than she had to. The ever-present thrill of having him close was still there, still humming under her skin, but it was no longer a matter of simple embarrassment and annoyance. Now, it also made her afraid. Quietly, discreetly afraid.

Who was this man, really?

"East and north, some hundred kilometers," she said. "The fringes of the Adaraat."

"Have you been back there recently?"

"I just returned from the desert, a two and a half day flight on Colonel Bisset's dragon. But not my home. It was in the neighboring region."

"Do you often fly with dragons?"

"Only recently. Before this year, I'd never even stood close to one."

"You seem to like them."

Her eyes darted over. He was watching her, unfortunately, and caught her glance. She had no choice but to play it off and look forward again since she didn't dare hold his gaze, not when she grew more and more nervous about what she would find there. She kept—seeing things in his eyes, strange lights and gleams that made her increasingly mistrustful and thrilled and numb all at once. "Dragons are a noble species," she said. "They're respected in the Empire. Greatly."

"Are they? I recall your Empire was built on annihilating them."

A flash of defensive heat passed through her, raising her hackles. "That was a very long time ago."

"Only two hundred years and some."

"That isn't long to you?"

"The dragons must not think so. They haven't come back yet, have they? I would think they're the ones who would decide what can be forgiven, after how long."

"The past is the past," she shot back. "What the Empire did then was in order to keep its people alive. The dragons would have been enslaved anyway by other tribes, other nations, other peoples, and used to massacre innocents. What choice did—"

"So the Empire killed and enslaved them first so no one else could."

"That's not how it happened."

"Neither of us were there, so how could we know?"

She was too overwhelmed by anger to speak. They walked on.

"The Empire preserves the remaining dragons now," she said after a while "The Premier Guard raises and bonds with dragons hatched from eggs that choose them. Whatever happened in the past, we've overcome it. They coexist peacefully with us now. They need us, and we need them. We protect each other, and we protect the people, too. Together."

"It's not the dragons who need you. Before this nation rose to power, the dragons existed since the dawn of time. The Empire is a speck in the course of history. It breeds captive dragons because it can't and never could exist without their power."

"We protect—"

"A nation founded on exploiting one people to protect another is a shaky one."

Her face reddened. How dare he? He was a guest here, privileged with seeing the Emperor himself. What was he here for, then, merely to trade whatever baubles his tribe had brought and to insult the Empire who gave him his means for survival? If he despised it so much, he shouldn't have come here. He could leave and return to the desolate desert, she thought viciously, and the red-hot wound he had opened with his words burned straight through the ever-present, visceral pleasure of being near him.

Good. She didn't mind that. Whatever bewitching enchantment or magic trickery he had cast over her was dimming now that he had shown his true colors, and her anger smoldered and smoked like embers over dry leaves. To come here and insult her home, her people—

"You're unhappy with me," he remarked. "You disagree with me."

Unhappy? Disagree? Did he think this was some sort of civil debate discussing the merits of the weather and other trivial things? "I fight for my nation," she said stiffly. "And I defend it. By blood or by tongue."

"You're very loyal."

"As loyal as the nation is to me. To everyone. I'm proud of it. And I think it's treated you well during your stay here, too. At least, I remember that the Emperor was clear in his orders to prioritize you at all costs..." She trailed off before she had to specify and remind him to what extent, but surely he would get the hint. After all, she had even been ordered to offer up her body for his pleasure if that was what he wanted.

The thought made something throb in her belly, and this time, unlike before, there was the taste of displeasure that coiled with the awkward nervousness there. And instead of wandering to rogue thoughts of what his hard shoulders might look like under his collar or how warm his skin would be under fleeting, exploring fingertips, all she could think of now was how he had insulted her, criticized her.

This was her home. This was her people.

"On that note, I've heard rumors about something," Kaizat said, suspiciously lighthearted. Maybe just changing the subject. "But I wanted to ask and confirm for myself. It's about your Emperor."

"Yes?"

"Is he really the same man who founded your nation from the beginning?"

At that, she smiled, mollified by the sudden, swelling pride inside her. "Yes," she said. "His longevity comes from his deep bond with his dragon. He was a young man when he first rallied the people then, and he looks the same now even though it's been over two centuries since. That's the gift that comes from becoming soul bonded to dragon partners—"

"So," he said in a pondering voice, and she cut herself off so she could hear whatever quiet thing he had to say next. "He's the one who wiped out the dragons then."

Her mouth snapped shut, and she turned forward with a glower.

Conversation over. She would have no more of it.

THERE WERE acrobats performing in the central plaza of the Quarter Art. It was a foreign sight to Anzi since even during the years she had been stationed at the Imperial City for training, she rarely wandered into the upper districts. She was an almost fabled name among her military comrades who had witnessed her meteoric rise through the ranks—even if some criticized rather than praised— but among the civilians, she was nothing more than an out-of-place soldier. Not only that, but she was walking around in broad daylight, and her wide, long-fringed, desert black eyes would draw the attention of anyone who got a good enough glance at her face. There were no fringers here. This was a haunt for the wealthy. She stuck out like a sore thumb.

"Can you do that?"

She heard his voice a little too clearly above the hubbub of the thick crowd congregated in the square. She hated that. Hated how her heart still leaped into her throat at the sound of his voice even though she was angry at him. She wished the crowd would squeeze in around them harder so they could drown him out, but unfortunately, the people had given them a small berth of open space. It had nothing to do with her. Rather, no one wanted to jostle the elbow of someone who was obviously foreign and wealthy, judging by his expensive jewelry. Her eyes darted up to the several small gold bands pinched around the outer helix of his ear. Those alone would fetch a disgustingly high price.

"Anzi?"

"Oh. Uh, what were you asking? Do what?"

He nodded up at the tightrope walker currently pretending to wobble and nearly topple over alternating sides of the line with each sway. The crowd gasped and screamed on cue.

"That," he said.

"That's a performance. Art. We don't learn to do that."

He smiled down at her, and to her utter chagrin, her heart flipped and tumbled into her gut. "I know. But you move differently from the rest. I can tell you're not ordinary."

…When anyone else said that, she always took it as a bitter excuse for their own incompetency, as an accusation. How many times had Oscar and his friends made snide comments about how she must be a mongrel species? But from Kaizat, it sounded like…praise. She shivered.

"You're not ordinary," he repeated, and his golden eyes gleamed even brighter than before. "I've been watching you closely."

She shook her head and pretended she couldn't hear him. It was a poor excuse and she was a terrible liar, but she had no idea what else to do when she could feel herself melting and buckling against his too-honest charms. It was beyond her. She didn't want to stop being angry at him this quickly, didn't want to let him soften her so effortlessly.

She stared hard at the acrobats, promising herself—she would stay cold.

16

Anzi was grateful to finally get away from the chieftain. After spending no more than half a day with him, she was already feeling horribly bereft by his absence, so how much worse would it have been if she had been in his presence any longer? Even now, she could feel the warmth of his fingers trailing along the side of her face, smell the dizzying scent of spice and desert wind rising from his body, hear his voice alternate between smooth syllables and deep, roughened rumbles...

Really, she was grateful they were separated now. Truly.

They had returned to the palace as the sun set even though her summons had not yet come, and they had made it back into the grounds with little disturbance thanks to the letter that vouched for them. After that, she had made sure to deposit him into the care of a pretty palace maid who eagerly agreed to show Kaizat-Amun to his room.

"I said to call me Kai," he had said again with a smile, and Anzi had hurriedly demurred before excusing herself. She shouldn't be doing this, she knew. She should be going with them so she could be sure he had everything he needed, everything he wanted. But the idea that he might look at her and beckon her forward into his room, tell her he had need of her in other ways and reach forward to disrobe her...

She was a soldier. She would not be seduced into the bed of a foreigner and tricked into anticipating it. She would sooner die than disobey the Emperor, but she hadn't accounted for the possibility of being tempted. If Kaizat were cold, if he were cruel, if he were to demand with a sneer that she lie down and accommodate his hunger like a common prostitute, it would have been easy to remain distant while he spent himself with her body.

But the way he had watched her all day, his golden eyes staring as if he were reading her soul. And the probing words he said to her, sometimes easy and smooth and sometimes provocative, thrilling—she didn't know how to deal with that.

Upper Service training included protecting oneself against this. While no one was immune to sensual seductions, soldiers of her caliber were conditioned rigorously against the dangers of emotional seductions, the kind that could slip under the skin and corrupt. Anzi had never been tempted like this before and had simply thought herself a natural resilient, but now she had met an obstacle that was truly her match.

Otherwise, she wouldn't catch herself wistfully thinking what it would be like if Kaizat weren't a foreign chieftain, if he were an official in the Empire instead. Nearly all soldiers went on to form approved families to procreate and strengthen their nation, but the law was clear concerning such unions: Empire citizens were prohibited from mingling with foreigners. If she was eventually ordered to bear children, she would be instructed to couple with a strong, healthy man from within the nation's borders, not Kaizat. Speculating about impossibilities like this was pointless. Besides, she didn't want children anyway, or a sexual partner. Body and soul, she belonged to the Service, and-

"Um, miss, is there something you need...?"

Anzi's head shot up. The palace maid from earlier was still here. "What?"

"I'm sorry, I don't meant to disturb you, but you've been standing there for some time now, and you were pacing back and forth when I stopped by an hour ago. But it's getting quite late in the evening, and you must be very tired."

An hour? She looked around as if she would find a stray timecatcher hanging somewhere in the hallway. That couldn't be right.

"Unless you've been posted to guard the guest," the maid said hastily. "But I didn't think that was the case because you're in the next corridor over from his room...?"

"No need for concern," Anzi said in a stiff voice. "Carry on."

"Of course, miss. I apologize."

The maid left with a swirl of her skirts and disappeared with a blush. Behind her, Anzi stared at the floor, mortified beyond words. An hour! Pacing! Now that she was alone, she was free to slap both sides of her face, give herself a firm shake, and stalk off toward another part of the palace that was nowhere near the room of Chieftain Kaizat-Amun, desert tribe chieftain, foreign dignitary, and utterly untouchable.

Truly, she was better than this—and she would prove it.

...Although she didn't stray too far away. After all, he might need something, and it was her responsibility to tend to his needs whatever they might be...

She gave herself another shake and a pinch on the thigh this time. Enough! She trotted away.

In his room, Kai leaned back against his door, the point in his room closest to her presence that radiated such a manic yet restrained aura. Back and forth, back and forth she had wandered, teasing him with the way she would come closer and closer before fading away again. And then after a while, she had stood stationary some distance away. Was she tired, or was she waiting? For him, perhaps? He kept his arms crossed over his chest and stayed attentive, his pulse throbbing against the side of his neck as he held himself back from doing what he really wanted to do —which was to open his door, track her down to wherever she was lurking, and pull her into his arms the way he should have the first moment he saw her.

But he couldn't. It had been so long since the last time they had crossed paths that she had no recollection of who he was. Not only that, but she had no idea who *she* was either. A soldier for the Empire, that was what she was now...a servant of a nation that had separated them in the first place and kept them apart for so long.

He had waited a long, long time for this. Years of searching, years of patience. Years of an emptiness in his arms as well as the one inside him, he had endured it all because he knew one day, it would come to an end.

She was not yet his. Or rather, she was not yet aware she was his, just as she had no idea he was hers even though he had shown her glimpses of the truth at least a dozen times today. Because until she was ready, she wouldn't understand, wouldn't see. And he couldn't open her eyes for her no matter how much he wanted to.

His eyes slid down to the gleaming, polished stone floor. It was cool against his bare feet, but he barely noticed it past the firestorm brewing inside him. So close. She was so close. He could reach out and take her, take her away from this place. Could take her somewhere far away where he could make her his, once and for all. He could show her and make her understand, a voice whispered inside him. She was hesitant now, but he had felt the way her soul rose to meet his the first time their eyes had locked, had felt it burning bright inside her as they walked together, spoke together, touched each other...

So close. He had waited this long; he could be patient just a little while longer so he didn't drive her away. He wouldn't let her slip between his fingers like this. Like sand held in the palm, he had to be cautious of gripping too tightly. He had to be gentle, calm...

But he was not a gentle man, nor was he a calm one. The tip of his tongue traced along his upper teeth as he recalled the intoxicating scent of her skin, the warmth under his fingers as he ran them down the side of her face. Just as his soul called to hers, whether she sensed it or not, so did his body. He didn't know how much more of this he could endure.

With a heavy exhale between his teeth, he closed his eyes and let the back of his head fall against the door.

Patience. Soon, she would know.

17

"Anzi."

She was on her feet in an instant. Night had fallen hours ago, but the flickering light of the standing torches in the courtyard illuminated every harsh line of Colonel Bisset's face. "Yes, sir."

"You're needed. See the Emperor first, and you'll be escorted elsewhere after."

First? Escort her where? It was already late, and while she didn't dare complain about the hour nor did she have any desire to, the timing was too odd to discount. At the sound of a loud, sudden snuffle, she glanced behind the stone bench she had been sitting on next to the massive snout of the colonel's dragon. She had awoken finally. All this time she had done little more than sleep. Scaly eyelids twitched, then opened to reveal bright blue eyes that sent a tingle down Anzi's spine.

She turned back to Colonel Bisset. "Will I find His Excellency in the throne room?"

"Yes. I won't be accompanying you. You remember the way."

It wasn't a question, but she nodded anyway. "Yes, sir."

"I won't be returning for several weeks. I trust you won't put me to shame."

"No, sir."

"Then that is all."

He said nothing more and strode past her, eyes fixed ahead on his waiting dragon. Anzi turned around in time to see the creature rise to its feet, scales creaking against each other with every lumbering movement. Claws as long as her forearm flexed and dug into the grass, and she stared at the marvelous sight. The dragon had yet to unfurl her wings, but they were beginning to ease apart with a thick, leathery sound. They could block out the whole of the sky from where she stood, she thought wistfully. Truly fearsome, a god of the skies.

It was too bad she couldn't linger long enough to watch the magnificent beast take off into the night, but she had her own duties to fulfill. By the time Colonel Bisset settled into the saddle and glanced back down at the ground, she was already long gone.

"STOP WITH THE SALUTING, you're spoiling my mood. Come here, let me look at you."

Now that she was alone in the throne room in Ra-Tet's company, the sheer strangeness of his appearance had far more of an effect on her than it had earlier when she had been…distracted. Now she noted clearly the emperor's slender figure, how it lacked any of the strong musculature she had expected the great leader of the Empire to bear. And while he was tall, the circumference of his exposed wrists and ankles was undeniably dainty. Built like a reed stalk, long and narrow, he swam in the hitched folds of his voluminous red and gold robe, and it was purely his blade-sharp expression that lent him his dangerous air.

"Closer," he said in a voice layered with the full brunt of his impatience. He hid nothing, she noticed. Whatever he felt, whatever he thought, everything revealed itself in the way he looked, moved, spoke. He was not a composed man. Even in his quieter moments, he appeared indolent rather than simply calm. "That's better. Now turn around. Actually, take off your armor, it's in the way."

In the way? For a moment, Anzi wondered if he was about to order her to satisfy his desires, just as he had told her to do for Kaizat. But the cool light in his eyes was curious and critical rather than hungry, and after she stripped out of her leathers, he said nothing about removing the thin white uniform she wore underneath.

"Hm. You're a mite smaller than I'd hoped, but Alexandre said you're better than any other candidate he's dug up so far. And he's been doing this for a long time."

As the Emperor leaned forward off his throne and scratched his chin, she schooled her expression so it would betray none of the anxious pride threatening to crackle and burst out of her skin. The Colonel had said that? He had given her such high praise before their leader?

"Good stature," he remarked. "But I'll see how you do. For now, just answer a few questions for me. Alexandre told me he brought you here while you were in the middle of some training regimen? Somewhere by the desert?"

"Yes, Your Excellency. We call it the Gauntlet, and—"

"Tell me about the wyrm you found and subdued."

She hesitated only long enough to remind herself she had no right to question the Emperor. If he wanted to know something, then she would answer, not waste time wondering why he was curious about something so inconsequential. "It was about seven meters from snout to tail," she said. "I didn't have a chance to examine it closely, but I recall it was a green variety."

"Green? You're certain? Poor camouflage."

"Yes, sir. I thought it was odd, but at the time, I was preoccupied with trying to incapacitate it. It was aggressive, and there were recruits—"

"Right, right, I heard about all of that already. Now, was there anything else strange about the wyrm?"

"Nothing I can recall at the moment, Your Excellency."

"No? It didn't communicate or...you didn't feel a connection with it...?"

Communicate? Connection? Anzi blinked and considered the question carefully, wondering if she had misheard. Wyrms were incapable of higher function. Everyone knew this. They were animals."No, sir. It was wholly focused on attacking the children. It, ah, there was no communication."

"Ah. Hm. Very interesting. Well, anyway...You have a brother in the city, don't you? Living at the Tower, gifted boy."

A faint hollowness opened up inside her at the question, but she ignored it and responded with a crisp reply: "Yes. Oza, Your Excellency."

"How long has it been since you've seen Oza?"

"A few years."

"I remember he's mute, isn't he?"

"Yes. He's been unable to speak since birth."

"Any idea why?"

She blinked again. A reason for muteness? What was he suggesting, and why were they speaking about Oza anyway? She had chastised herself a moment ago for questioning the Emperor's curiosity, but this was beyond sense. Wasn't she here to be inducted into the Premier Guard? The Mage Collective had nothing to do with that. "There's never been anyone born mute in our family as far as we know, from either side," she said. "He was just born unlucky."

"Unlucky, hm…Anything strange about you, then?"

Ah. So that was what this was about. She should have known it would come up. The newest rumor about her had been flying in the military for a while now. "If this is about the suspicions that I have non-human blood, I can't confirm or deny them. Lineage records on my family only go back four generations, and I thought I was just—suited to my work, until…"

"Until?"

It took her another fumbling second to figure out how best to confess the truth when even she didn't know the extent of it herself. "Over the last year especially, I've become stronger and faster than I should be. If I were human, that is."

"Go on. What else has changed?"

"I was born with innate magic, even though my brother is more gifted. I only ever had the spark, and it never grew as I aged. But I've noticed it's suddenly become stronger of late. More dangerous, I mean, including to myself."

"Oh, no need to worry about that, the boys will take care of you. But this changes things. I never thought I'd find someone with such concentrated wild blood after all this time, and with no warning. You're different from the others before you, but I can see it in you now, slight but growing." The Emperor leaned back in his throne again and tapped his bare foot against the smooth floor several times. "All right, if you know nothing else, then let's not waste time. We might find the answers we want later on, isn't that right?"

She had no idea what he was talking about. "Yes, Your Excellency."

"Good, good. We'll need to take you down to the Cave. The sooner you start preparing, the better for all of us. I'm very, very curious…All right, I'd like some fresh air anyway. Let's go."

He rose from his throne and unfolded himself in one smooth motion. From the top of the elevated dais, he was already standing taller than she was, but now she saw that she had grossly underestimated his height. Slender, willowy—and inhumanly tall. He would stand head and shoulders and even chest above even the lankiest man she knew, easily.

"This way, now. Come."

Anzi was by no means a slow walker, but she had to trot to keep up with the Emperor's long, loping strides. The thought that there was something uncanny and even eerie about his too-skinny, too-tall stature crossed her mind more than once, but she quashed it every time. She really had spent too much time in Kaizat-Amun's presence today if his disrespect for the great Ra-Tet was bleeding over. Focus, she scolded herself. They were heading to the courtyard, though she could hardly guess at the reason. The Emperor had mentioned a Cave, but what cave would they find there?

"Oh, and while we have a moment. Did you entertain the chieftain today?"

"Yes, Your Excellency."

"Did he mention anything about, say, dragons? Even vague mentions."

She swallowed past a sudden lump in her throat. "No, sir," she lied.

"No? That's disappointing…From now on, your job is to keep watch over him, strictly. Understand? You'll be staying here at the palace with the boys for a long time, so in between your other new duties, you'll have to see to it that the guest is entertained and happy."

Other new duties? And keeping watching over the chieftain? Anzi's lips parted in a conditioned reflex to answer with an obedient *yes, sir*, but a hesitant dread coiled up inside her and stopped the words before they could escape. She would never dream of disobeying, but what? She didn't understand. "…Keep watch over him, Your Excellency?"

He waved a flippant hand just as they turned a corner. "He's no threat, don't worry about that. But I believe he has something that would be of great value to me. My people are looking into it. And," the Emperor continued, "see if you can exercise a little, hm, feminine charm with him. I give you full permission to pursue whatever means are available to you to gain his trust. He should feel comfortable here. I want him to know we're all friends. Very good friends."

She nearly choked, only managing to hold herself back from making terrible sounds thanks to rigorous soldier's discipline. "Y…yes, sir."

"Did he mount you? Or do you think it's possible in the near future? Don't rush it, as we don't want to be too obvious and put him needlessly on his guard, but desert folk tend toward the sensual and pleasurable. It would be a good way to establish a healthy rapport with him." He paused and glanced over his shoulder to peer down at her. "Well?"

"No, sir. He didn't mount—nothing happened, sir."

"Hm, that's a shame. Don't forget, whatever he asks of you, make sure you do it well. Consult with some of the harem girls if you have questions about anything. You have permission to pursue every avenue of action necessary to that end, so apply yourself properly and take the initiative when the opportunity arises. Understand?"

"…Yes, sir."

"Actually, I'll have one of them assigned to you so she can instruct you on the methods. I trust you won't let me down. This is very important to me. To all of us. It would be good if you could enter his confidence…Hm. Yes, I think so. I saw the way he looked at you."

So had she. She didn't want to remember it, didn't want to dwell on it, but she most definitely did.

Thankfully, it seemed he had said his fill, and it was in silence that they continued the rest of their short walk to the courtyard. She still had no idea what this Cave nor what her 'new duties' were, but she forced the nervous energy in her stomach to settle. She was beginning to suspect her dreams of entering the Premier Guard were turning to dust before her very eyes, but what could she do but obey?

Finally, they crossed over the threshold that she had already visited several times today, and the Emperor ignored the salutes of the guards who stood at the head of the torch-lit stone path. "I've dispatched all the boys except one, but Bastien is here and will teach you a few things."

"Yes, sir."

"Come on, quickly. Before I get bored." His pace quickened, and a moment later, they were nearing a darkened corner of the courtyard where there were only two guards. No torches, strangely. It was so dark here; why didn't they carry any? But even if she'd had the gall to ask the question, she wouldn't have had the chance. The guards scuttled into action, bending to pick something up. Anzi reflexively leaped in front of the Emperor, alarm and mistrust flaring at the sight, but an impatient command had her falling back once more.

"It's alright," he tut-tutted. "Move aside."

And before them, the guards finished towing away the enormous, woven false grass to reveal an equally enormous hole in the ground.

"Into the Cave you go now," the Emperor announced. "Bastien is expecting you."

18

The slanted, gaping hole in the ground utterly dwarfed Anzi. Five meters across at least, perhaps more, and now that her eyes were finally adjusting to the faint light, she saw it was not a hole at all but a long, long tunnel sloping down into some unknown abyss. The angle was such that she could barely see any illumination inside the giant passageway unless she crouched down and peered sideways. But the Emperor had no interest in her misgivings about entering the darkness. When she glanced back at him, there was a surprised gleam in his eyes, and she realized at once her hesitations were tantamount to disobedience. With a sharp, hasty exhale, she pushed herself off her knee and back to a stand.

"Yes, Your Excellency," she said, and while she remembered just in time that the man disliked being saluted, she couldn't excuse herself from his presence without a bow, at least.

"All right, all right, enough, get up. Don't disappoint me, now."

"Yes, sir."

He turned and left with his long, slender hands clasped behind his back and his red and gold robe trailing behind him. Anzi's cue to go on. Before the cautioning voice of her instincts could grow any louder and make this even more difficult, she advanced into the passageway's giant maw and hurried into the darkness.

And, well—shit. She had been half-expecting it anyway, but when she heard the loud rustle of the false turf being dragged back over to conceal the entrance behind her, she entertained a small inward curse before picking up speed. A lone torch light flickered at the end of the tunnel which was mercifully shorter than she had thought at first glance, and while it was small, it was the only illumination she could glean in the otherwise pitch-black darkness.

With narrowed eyes, she trained her gaze on the walls as she passed them, leery of straying close in case the shadows yielded nasty surprises. Stone, she realized. She had only walked down several meters, but the earthen walls and towering, curved ceiling had become a stone passageway instead. And this was long-weathered, old stone, gray and white rough-hewn surfaces smoothed by the decades. No, centuries. What was this place? It had to be even older than the palace, which had been constructed near the beginning of the Empire's establishment. A secret tunnel that had existed before the Empire, and almost right in the center of the courtyard that existed at the heart of the Imperial home.

A shiver of anticipation fluttered over her skin as she looked around the massive breadth of the tunnel again. She couldn't help but notice it was large enough for just about any creature to pass through. Dragons, even. Could it be...?

"Surprise—*oof!*"

Anzi hadn't hesitated. At the sound of the unknown man's first syllable, she had struck with a lashing sweep of her forearm and elbow, aiming for where she guessed would be the soft flesh of his abdomen. While she didn't find it, she was satisfied to find that her strength was enough to knock aside the man's parrying arm and send him careening back into the shadows of the uneven walls.

"Careful, girl! I'm a friendly face."

The man had a hint of a strange but vaguely familiar accent, and she shelved it for future examination as she leaned back and stepped away. Friendly face, he had called himself, and she gave the man still draped in darkness a critical once-over. The light from the torch down the way was stronger here than it had been at the mouth of the tunnel, and she could see the side of a bald head gleaming back at her at eye level. Small man, shorter than she was, with a compact, wiry frame under his faded leathers. He wore a traditional foot soldier uniform just as she did, which meant he was no officer.

She had expected more. Was this really...?

"Bastien?" she inquired. "That's you?"

"The same, girl. Come on. Every second is precious. Tell me about yourself while we walk, and don't fall behind. We should be able to put your finger on an egg today and see how that goes."

The man's words slammed into her like a searing hot lightning strike made solid. An egg? An egg—hadn't she already suspected just seconds ago that this passageway was large enough for a dragon to pass through? Her fumbling thoughts collided and ground against each other like rock salt in a tin box, and she found herself speechless as she watched Bastien peel himself away from the wall with casual grace.

"What are you gawking at? Don't you know you're in the lair of the beasts?" He grinned, and as he stepped away from the wall and further into the flickering light, she noticed the slight points of his ears, the sharp, delicate angles of his face. But the obvious inhumanity of his appearance mattered little to Anzi right now, far less than it usually would. This was about dragons. Everything else paled in comparison.

Her heart throbbed with a violent twist.

Dragons!

"This way," he said, and his grin grew even wider at her continued silence. "I love this part. The looks on your faces when you first realize what's happening. But we're on a tight schedule, so let's not dawdle."

She followed him the rest of the short way down the sloping tunnel. They emerged into a towering cavern with a curved ceiling full of glistening, crystallized stalactites hanging down like beads of pearls and gems. Crystalline formations streaked the gray and white walls, emerald gashes and ruby veins woven through the pale stone. But besides the natural features of this secret underground world, there was a array of man-made furnishings as well. A grand dining table with more than a dozen seats along either side of it stood in the middle of the hall, and cushioned, luxurious couches and reclining spots peppered the circular cavern. It was still dim in here even if was considerably brighter than the passageway, but no wonder: the torches attached to the walls could scarcely illuminate the darkened center of the massive cavern.

All of this, right under the Imperial palace. How could she not have guessed? She had never stopped to think where the dragons might nest. They were so rarely seen that the thought they might have a central home had never occurred to her. Nor to anyone else she knew, either.

"No one's home today but me, but that's the norm these days. Too much disturbance going on around the borders for one, but we've been dealing with disruptions in the middle of our territories too."

Say something back, she urged herself. She couldn't just stare dumb-struck at everything as he led her into the hall. "The increasing wyrm appearances," she mumbled. "But that's at the edges of the desert, I thought."

"Other problems too, ones that you don't hear about unless we want you to. But you'll learn soon enough. On that note, though—hold on, this way, we're going to the incubation chambers—I heard some story about you and a wyrm yourself, eh? Care to tell?"

What was it about the incident that was so curious? The Emperor had asked her about it too, even inquiring whether such a creature had tried to 'communicate' with her. Ludicrous. That is, the idea was ludicrous, not the Emperor. She hastily banished the thought before it could become any more unruly. "There's not much to tell. I had to disable it, but I know the rules. Preserved, not killed."

"Left a mark on it, though, didn't you?"

"After making sure it was unconscious, I speared it and spread its blood around the immediate area, yes. But not enough to kill it, and only because I needed to make sure that it deterred other wyrms from encroaching on the area. There were recruits there that I couldn't move."

"Mm. I heard. Single-minded, you are."

They turned into another large passageway, and she tore her eyes away from one particularly enchanting crystal gash embedded in the wall so she could look over at Bastien. "I'm sorry?"

"You left the kids there. Didn't think to abandon the objective, huh?"

A rush of hot anger swirled inside her, and it was all she could do to make sure she didn't grit her answer out between bared teeth. "I had a job to do," she said, and even to her own ears, her voice was cold and stiff. "And the recruits had a responsibility to preserve their own lives. I did the right thing by aiding them to the furthest extent possible while not compromising my own duty."

He chuckled, and his lilting laughter bounced around them with a myriad echoes. "Heel, girl. I'm not saying it's a bad thing. As a matter of fact, I rather like it. Shows how important this is to you, for one thing. But also proves you know how to keep a cool head and weigh the costs and the risks against the gain. We do a lot of that, as you'll find out soon enough."

"…Ah." She hadn't expected that. Not that she felt guilty about priori-tizing her success in the Gauntlet over the recruits…After all, she had disabled the wyrm, and she had taken measures to ensure no others would appear to attack the unconscious children after she left to pursue the rest. She had done everything in her power to make sure she did things according to regulation...

So what if she could never boast of such a decision? Some choices were harder to make, less palatable. All she knew was that she had made the right one, so there was no need to feel guilty. Her duties to the Empire came first, her obligations as a soldier. It had been the right thing to do.

And yet...

"Wyrm do anything strange? Try to speak?"

Her uncomfortable frown turned into an outright glare. She was getting tired of this. Obviously there was something being kept from her if she was being asked such ridiculous questions, and while she burned with the need to know exactly what it was, the frustration of being teased so cryptically was even more compelling. "It made noises typical for a wyrm of its size," she said in a crisp voice that teetered at the edge of aggression. "But if you're asking if an unintelligent creature somehow attempted to 'communicate' with me, then no. And if there's something you'd like to tell me, you're very welcome to do that."

"Oho. So you know a little something about it already, eh?"

"His Excellency the Emperor mentioned it. But I assure you there was nothing strange about the wyrm. It was larger than I expected, but other than that, nothing of note."

"Listen to you, going all formal on me just because you're a little upset. That's all rright, you'll warm up to me soon enough. And from what I've been told, you would never lie to your superiors, so I suppose I take them at their word for now. But fear not, I'll help you get to the truth. You might be what we've been waiting for. Better than the others."

"Can you speak clearly for once?"

"Hey, now," he chuckled. "I may not be one of your pretty ranking officers in that gilded military you're part of, but I'm old enough to be your grandfather. You can mouth off to me, but then I'll pay it back in kind once we get into your training. Mind yourself."

Despite his threat, however, he gave her a broad wink, and she stared back at him with a thoroughly mirthless glower. She had no idea who this man was, but he had neither rank nor nobility, which meant they were on equal footing as far as she was concerned.

And yet, he was the man who was going to be responsible for her training from now on, even if he had no officer's uniform and no insignia to back his authority. That meant he must be...

"The Premier Guard," she said. "Does this mean I'm officially inducted?"

"What, were you expecting a ceremony? And don't call us that. Premier Guard, my ass. We're the kings. The dragon masters. You'll learn."

The pounding of her heart at the confirmation was enough to silence her for now. Yes, gods, this was what she had been striving for all her life. The pinnacle of honor, the Emperor's First Guard, the dragon riders—

Except he had said something different, this Bastien. Dragon masters, he had said. She had never heard the term before, and she didn't know if she liked it. Not at all. It sounded—cruel, somehow. But that was a matter to inquire about another time, not now.

"Here we are," he announced after they passed by several branching corridors. "The greatest treasure in all the kingdom. Come and see."

She stepped forward at his behest and entered the dim chamber. She could hardly see anything until with a wave of his hand, Bastien lit a fire in the cast bronze brazier in front of them. It roared to life with a echoing rush, flames roiling out in every direction and spitting sparks as it cast its brilliant light all around them, red and yellow tongues licking out past the metal strips like groping hands.

Anzi stared and stared. In utter silence, she took in the sight before her, eyes roving around the room from wall to wall with her mouth agape.

"Incredible, isn't it? What do you think?"

She couldn't speak, couldn't answer. This was beyond everything she had ever believed was possible. Lining every centimeter of the natural stone shelves and buried in straw and hay, dozens of them, maybe even hundreds, entire piles shoved together to make room—

Dragon eggs!

19

This was impossible. Dragons were all but extinct; everyone knew that.

Following the great Purge over two centuries ago, only the scant few taken in by the Empire had survived. The Imperial dragon bonded to the Emperor along with those partnered to his four generals—those were the only ones that had made it safely through the catastrophic war that decimated their population. After that, the only dragons eggs in existence had been those produced by those survivors, and that was why the Premier Guard only numbered so few, less than a dozen.

But all these eggs. In two hundred years, had five dragons really multiplied into this unborn horde? She couldn't hope to count the number crammed into this chamber. From wall to wall, some eggs were as long as her forearm and wider around than her waist while others could fit in the palm of a small child. Eggs scaled with rippling, iridescent patterns, eggs bearing feathers, eggs with fanned fins and horned spines—Anzi's eyes burned as she strained to take in the entirety of it, every implication of this discovery. And it was that unspeakable mixture of numb shock and paralyzing confusion that rendered her deaf to Bastien's question, until he elbowed her in the side and brought her back to her senses. She jerked and nearly struck him for the second time if not for his quick reflexes.

But too quick. Yet again, as she stared at him with the heat of the blazing fire warming her face, she made private note of his inhuman traits. She had heard rumors before that the prestigious Premier was more diverse than anyone realized, but hardly anyone paid attention to such talk. It had always been easier to assume they were all pure. Human, that is. They were the ones who had cleared the land long ago and claimed it from the savage races that used to roam it, after all. Humans should champion humans.

But Bastien wasn't human. Neither was the Emperor if his strange stature was any indication, and now Anzi had no choice but to face the truth of her own questionable roots. Had this been deliberate? Had she really been sought out because of the 'wild' in her that His Excellency had mentioned?

Everything was wrong. Different. Confusing. Nothing was the way it should be.

"You're in a room full of treasures, each of which great men would pay entire kingdoms for, and you spend your time admiring me?" Bastien chuckled, and the points of his ears twitched as he laughed. "I'm flattered, girl. But go on. You can ask your questions, I know you have them."

She did. But there were so many that she didn't know where to start. Not only about the eggs, either, but also—

"You said earlier you were old enough to be my grandfather. That wasn't a joke, was it?"

"No. I've been around for a long, long time, one of the earliest to get blooded in after the first wars ended. I never flew much because I always preferred staying here, so I became the egg keeper. And there's no one better at it than I am."

Egg keeper? "You watch over them. You stay behind and protect them."

"No, girl. They don't do anything after they're popped out—that's not the real job." He let out another braying laugh. "Breeding the dragons every time they return home is the hard part. Figuring out which ones we can put into heat and trying to make better, stronger eggs each time— that's why I'm so invaluable. And I get better every time, too. We've had some accidents along the way, but the little people are none the wiser for it. Free rein to wreak havoc with the spawning cycles and see what kind of masterpieces I can cook up, what more could I wish for?"

Anzi had never been a coward in her life. She had never been afraid of anything that couldn't reach out and strike flesh, had never wanted to shrink away from mere words when she knew they couldn't draw blood or break bones.

She would not start now. Not even if the things he said chilled her to the bone. With her mouth set in a hard line and betraying nothing of her growing horror, she turned and fixed her eyes along the back wall. The natural stone shelves and steps that furnished the chamber were steepest there, and in the dark shadows they cast, there was something peculiar. The sight of it jarred her out of her discomfort, and she grasped at its opportune timing like a starving urchin. Anything to distract her from the troubling thoughts brewing inside. "That one over there. What's wrong with it?"

"Nothing to worry about, just something I've been fiddling with to pass the time. I call that one Prince Bastard."

"Prince...Bastard?"

He laughed yet again. She was getting the feeling he was the sort to find humor in things he shouldn't. "Tet's dragon sired that one long ago. Ra is the big, meaty type, as the dragon king should be, so he makes big, meaty spawn, too. But none of them ever come out quite right, which is usually fine because we have plenty of others to choose from. But it sure would make me proud to get something good out of Ra."

"Ra? And Tet? I don't understand—"

"Ah, don't worry about it. You'll pick up these things. All you need to know now is that Tet and Ra really are bonded, not like the rest of us. Even took the beast's name. You won't find any of us doing that.."

With a sickening lurch, she realized at last that 'Tet' was the Emperor, and Ra the Imperial dragon. She had wondered at the strange composition of the name, and now she was learning that there were stories stranger still behind it. But what did Bastien mean when he said that the rest were not bonded that way? Goosebumps rose all along her skin in an icy wave, and she crossed her arms to hide them in case the man noticed.

"Anyway, Prince Bastard's never going to make it. At this point, I'm just waiting to see how long it lasts before it starts rotting in its own soup. The shell's defective. Far too thick for the hatchling to break through and come out on its own, and the whole thing's so sopped in magic we can't try to force it open from the outside like we sometimes can. Little Bastard's been fighting his way out for years now, which is why the egg looks like that. He's growing and growing on the inside like any good dragon should, but the shell isn't too good at keeping up. Think he's reaching the end of his rope. Give it a few more years and he'll crush himself to death."

...Nauseating. Trapped and doomed to meet a torturous, repulsive end. Her heart sank and twisted into a horrific knot. "There's nothing we can do?" she asked. "There has to be something."

"Nope. Usually, we put defective hatchlings out of their misery so we can make more room, but the Prince is a fighter. Even if we had the ability to break through his shell—which we don't—I want to see the end of it. I've put too much time into him not to. I'm attached."

There was a wistful fondness in his voice that made her hesitate. She had been on the verge of lashing out with a furious tirade about cruel games played with helpless lives, but as she watched Bastien stare at the misshapen, scarred, black-and-silver mottled egg with a strange affection in his eyes, the words died in her throat. She knew so little, she told herself. No matter how shocking and confusing the things she learned tonight, she had to swallow her protests and try to understand. She was stepping into another world now. The old rules no longer applied, and she had a duty to fulfill. Surely the things she found repugnant at first glance had a hidden nobility behind them, a truly just and good reason for their existence.

This was the heart of the Empire, the source of its strength. Dragons and their riders protected the nation and saved countless people daily from the onslaught of barbarian tribes and greedy foreign kingdoms. There was a system here that had been in place since before her grandfather's grandfather, and she would be an idiot to judge it. Her small view of the world and its workings couldn't possibly compare. All she had to do was put her trust in the authority that bound them all and devote all her strength to it. In time, she would understand. She just had to try harder, that was all. Her lack of sufficient devotion was to blame here, nothing else.

She forced her gaze elsewhere, anywhere. "Am I going to meet my partner here, then?"

"Meet? Farm one, is what you'll do. We'll have you pay a visit every night, and I'll see which ones are the most receptive. We know you've got a strong spirit, and you handled a wyrm all on your own—I'm thinking we'll see good things. And don't let me make you nervous, but we're expecting great things from you…On second thought, never mind."

He flapped his hand at her with a knowing smile, and she knew better than to try to fish for the rest of what he held back. Bastien was an infuriating mystery who thought everything was merely great fun and mischief —no doubt he had cut himself off purely to stoke her interest.

Well, this was not a game to her. This was the most important thing she would ever do in her life, and an unimaginable weight was settling on her shoulders now. The nights she had spent dreaming of touching open sky, of feeling the beat of leathery wings carrying her leagues and leagues, of feeling the rumbling strength under her hands as they breached the clouds...All gone. Childish fantasies, now replaced by the brutal reality of the Premier Guard's true nature.

They were still the protectors of the nation, though. They were still the heroes and champions who guarded the countless souls of the Empire, warriors and healers and mages all, the last hope of everyone in the direst straits. This was not the dream world she had hoped for, but...it was what the people needed.

She didn't want to be afraid. She didn't want to be weak. She didn't want to be the coward who, upon the threshold, ran away and proved herself too weak to carry the burden. What would everyone say? They would nod and speak among themselves, say they had seen it coming. That she hadn't been meant for such honor.

But it wasn't about the honor anyway. It was about duty, offering up her body and her soul to protect those who couldn't protect themselves. It was about sacrificing her small self for the sake of the greater good like she had always been taught. It was about shoving aside her petty misgivings and falling into the rhythm of the way things were done, of giving herself over so she could be put to the greatest use.

And that was why she had no right to feel this way. She shouldn't feel —horrified, angry, disgusted. Just because her little girl dreams had been forced to face reality didn't mean she had any right to judge and condemn the truth.

"What should I do now?" she asked and turned her head to pin Bastien with an unblinking stare. "Tell me what to do, and I'll do it."

He smiled and shook his head. "So quiet you had me worried," he chided, and he raised a knobby hand to wag his finger at her. "I thought you were going to bow out on us for a minute there."

Us. Us, she repeated inwardly. That was right. She was not alone, not anymore. The Emperor's Premier Guard, the First Guard, the dragon riders—they were her family now, even if she had yet to meet the rest of them aside from Bastien. She couldn't let them down. They had been waiting for her just as she had been waiting for them, and this was—this was the way she could best serve the people. This was how she could best protect everything she loved and cherished.

She had promised herself she would never stop until she reached this place, this pinnacle at the top of the mountain she had climbed all her life. She would not stop here.

"Never," she said, and her voice was loud and hard enough to echo around the chamber several times. "You're underestimating me."

"Oh!" A delighted smile spread across his narrow face in a flash. The outer corners of his slanted green eyes lifted with it, giving him a fox-like look of glee. "Now that's what I call a war face. Come on, then. Let me introduce you to the family, and then I'll send you on your way."

Hours later, Anzi was perched outside on the balcony of her room back at the palace. Her fingertips and palms were still buzzing after having touched countless eggs, many of them much rougher than she would have ever expected. More than three hundred viable eggs, he had explained as he led her around the chamber, all carrying a sleeping dragon inside. She would awaken one soon, and he would be strong and swift and fearsome.

There had been no talk of bonding, no mention of chosen ones, nothing. The stories were all make-believe; there would be no magical moment of riding off into the fading sunset with her destined partner, no cosmic connection forged between their souls.

"You'll tame it and master it," Bastien had said. "You're a king, now."

The bite of the cool night air reminded Anzi with a vague throb that autumn was fast approaching. She looked down at the ground far below with her legs dangling over the carved railing. She should be happy, she thought dimly. She should be ecstatic.

She shouldn't be—like this.

A sickening shame rose up inside her. She had never doubted like this before, not once in her life. She had always believed. Always had faith. How could she be so weak now, and why did everything feel so wrong when she knew it was right, that it had to be? The Empire had thrived for two centuries. She was just a small thing, nothing more. She wasn't meant to change a thing, only to preserve it.

She pulled her feet up on the railing and buried her face in her knees.

20

"Y ou haven't slept."

It was only thanks to years of rigorous discipline that Anzi didn't leap out of her skin. Instead, she reacted the same way she had when Bastien had surprised her earlier, lashing out with her arm at the source of the unexpected voice while simultaneously sliding backward off the stone railing. But a spark of something indescribable exploded under her skin when she struck warm flesh, and she nearly stumbled. Head reeling, she retreated several swift steps toward the doors before she finally realized who it was before her.

"...Chieftain Kaizat?"

"Do I have to get on my knees for you to stop calling me that?"

She stared in silence at the darkened silhouette half-straddling the balcony wall. She hadn't bothered to light a candle before coming out here, and with the clouds muffling the faint light of the moon, all she could see was the tousled, almost shaggy black hair curling over his ears and eyes—eyes that gleamed a little too bright in the darkness to be normal. It was him, without a doubt. Even if he hadn't given himself away already, his voice was unmistakable. And his presence...she crossed her arms to suppress the goosebumps that raced over her entire body.

As bewitching as ever. Barbarian magic, obviously, now that she thought about it. The Emperor had mentioned earlier in the throne room that desert folk were more sensual...carnal. Combined with the obvious inhuman lineage Kaizat bore, small wonder that he could play tricks on her mind like this.

But even knowing that there was something sly at play, she couldn't help the way her eyes darted over his form. One leg was folded up with the foot braced upon the top of the wide stone railing, while the other leg dangled carelessly over the other side. He was leaning forward just a little too haphazardly, balanced a little too perilously...One false move and he could go plummeting over the edge. The casual grace, the effortless poise was—captivating. She wanted to reach out, to rest her fingertips and feel for herself that masculine certainty he carried himself with. He still had no shirt, murmured the small voice in the back of her head, and even in this darkness, she could see all too well every strong, sure ripple of muscle along his frame.

"...Hello," she said, because what else could she say? She was too numb to put together a proper greeting, especially when his eyes flashed hot and golden through the murky night at her. "Have you rested well?"

"No."

Oh. She stood stock-still, unable to move. Unwilling to move, too. She didn't know what to do, whether to move closer or step farther away to invite him off the balcony edge. And there was that irritating, irrational fear trilling inside her that if she made the wrong move, he might disappear and leave without another word. Not that she wanted him to stay. No, wait, she did. But only if that was what he wanted. Because her duty was to make sure all his needs were met, and if he had come to find her, there must be something he lacked.

...She wondered what that was. Her eyes dropped from his gaze and almost dropped down the hard lines of his body before she could stop herself. Luckily, she caught herself just in time and forced herself to hold his stare.

"Aren't you going to ask me why I haven't been able to rest?"

It was still too dark to tell, but she could swear he was smiling. "Why is it you've been unable to rest, sir."

"Because I was thinking of you."

Her stomach dropped. "Oh," she said. "That's..."

"That's what?"

She floundered for far too long. Why couldn't she simply steel herself and get her act together? She had never been like this until him, just him. With other soldiers, with her superiors, with anyone else, she was as sharp and efficient as a well-honed dagger. Even the Emperor hadn't driven her to speechlessness like this.

"That's…something I don't know how to help you with," she lied. A lie, because she was fairly certain where this was going. Her skin buzzed in anticipation. No, wait, apprehension. Obviously. "If I may ask, how did you get here, sir?"

Kaizat pointed up, and she followed the direction of his finger until she was staring up at the bottom of the balcony on the next floor. "My room is up the way. So I came and the room was unlocked. I went in, I saw you, I dropped down…and here I am."

What a coincidence to find her simply by wandering around. She banished the thought before it could turn more troublesome. "Is there something I can do for you?" she asked, very much against her better judgment. "There are calming teas I can request from the kitchen," she hurried to add. "I think there are also the springs somewhere nearby. Hot springs. I passed by several harem girls earlier today while they mentioned them."

"Harem girls?"

Her throat bobbed. She hoped he didn't see it. "Yes. Harem girls, sir."

"How many are there?"

"Many. I saw two dozen or so today alone in one of the lounging rooms, all of them sitting together." Her answer was swift and short, but her heart steadily hammered its way higher and higher up her throat. Why was he asking about them? Why was he so interested? Was he playing games with her? He had tried several times today to seduce her, hadn't he? So was he trying to make her jealous by expressing interest in other women now?

No. She couldn't think like that. Kaizat didn't need to seduce anyone at all, much less her. She was freely available to him whenever he might wish it. If he told her to bare herself or to fall to her knees, or to turn around and let him 'mount' her…there was nothing to do but oblige and obey. Her throat bobbed again. His hands looked especially large, suddenly, and she wondered if the cool night air had chilled the warmth from his body yet.

"I pity the man who can't find the one woman to satisfy him," he said. "And I think he would be even worse at being the one to satisfy. Two dozen women and more, all between his governing? He won't even know their names, much less how to give them pleasure."

Her mouth was dry, but she had to respond. He was insulting the

Emperor again, wasn't he? Subtly. Or maybe not so subtly. It was hard to process exactly how impudent Kaizat was being when her legs felt more and more like half-empty waterskins wobbling about.

"His Excellency...doesn't need to know how to pleasure them," she managed to say. "That's their job, not his."

"A man should take pride in his ability to please his woman. You don't think so?"

He was definitely propositioning her. Just do it, she wanted to snap... or suggest, possibly. But only to get it over with, all the suspense. She didn't like wasting time, after all. If he had come here to find his satisfaction with her body, then he should just come out and say it plainly. They were both adults, and she was a more than competent, highly loyal soldier. She would have no issue obeying the order of her Emperor and agreeing to whatever carnal demands Kaizat made. Because she was loyal. And followed directions well. She could be very good at that. She was, already.

Her gaze dropped to the floor. This was mortifying. War and violence weren't nearly so traumatic.

"What are you thinking about, Anzi?"

"Nothing, sir. Should I be thinking about something."

"I was hoping you were."

If ever she had hoped to die, this was it. The sky could open up and strike her down with lightning, and she would praise every storm god for it.

"...About what? Sir."

"This, maybe that. Lots of things." He abruptly swung his leg over so that he was facing her now. "You should stop calling me sir. Not like this. I'd rather you call me Kai."

So he had said many times before. But—"I can't do that," she said, as stolid as ever. Bewitched or not, she had her head on straight enough to know elementary rights from wrongs. "It's not right."

"Why isn't it?"

"We have our places. Being so careless will only confuse everyone."

"What's there to be confused about? They can call me one thing. You would call me differently."

She shook her head. Either he truly didn't understand and it would be futile trying to explain, or he was playing games just to rib her. "There's an order to things. A proper place and arrangement, that's all. Please understand."

"Then do this for me. When we're alone, call me the way I want you to. No one else would be around, so there won't be any confusion or misunderstandings. It would only be you and me. No one else." He slipped off the balcony to begin crossing the short distance to her with slow steps, and she stood rooted in place as if someone had shackled her down. She thought she could feel his warmth seeping through the space between them already. "Would you do that, Anzi?" he asked—and was she imagining it, or was his voice a little deeper suddenly, more quiet, more guttural?

"I…" What had she been about to say? "Why is it so important to you?" she blurted before she realized what she was saying. And after that, it was too late. Her mouth snapped shut, and she sucked in a sharp inhale through her nose as she waited for him to retaliate. She'd asked that so insolently, so rudely. She hadn't meant to, but she was growing more frustrated and defensive by the second. The sharp, insistent words had slipped out on their own.

But instead of snapping back at her or calling out her slip of the tongue, he said nothing as he came to a stop mere centimeters away. He was too close, she wanted to say. Or—not close enough. Did he want to hold her? Touch her? Did he want to use her the way the Emperor had told her to oblige if he demanded it? She thought she could smell his scent, laced with spice and desert and hot sun…

"Did something happen tonight?" he asked, and his voice was even softer now, so quiet it tempted her to lean in so she could hear him better. And for no other reason, of course. "You can tell me if something's wrong. I can help."

She stirred. What was he talking about? As far as he knew, she had been in her room all night. When she had left earlier to meet with the Emperor and Bastien, it had already been late enough that no one else would be outside, and no windows or balconies faced that direction. Kaizat should have been in his room the entire time. But then again, he had managed to slip out and find her here. Who knew what other trouble he had been up to in her absence? But—how could he possibly know she was troubled?

Bluffing. There was no other explanation. Other than her foolish clumsiness around him, she was sure no other weakness had slipped out and betrayed itself. He couldn't possibly know what was on her mind, couldn't possibly know she had spent the last several hours alternating between wanting to bash her fists into the nearest wall and running far, far away where she could forget everything she had learned tonight.

Maybe he was fishing for information. He was a foreigner, after all. Foreigners were spies, looking to profit off the secrets of the Empire's success. No matter how drawn she felt to Kaizat, she had to remember—in the end, he could be the enemy.

"I don't know what you mean," she lied. That was the second time she had said an untruth to him tonight, and it felt just as terrible as the first. It felt...wrong. But that was his kooky desert magic or inhuman blood working its charms on her. She had to remember that. No weakness, she told herself sternly. No wavering. "Or maybe there's something bothering you, not me?" she suggested. "It's very late and you're here. Is there something I can do for you? Other than the matter of your name."

She knew how damning the words were even as they left her tongue—practically propositioning him—but she had no choice. She needed to steer the conversation away from herself and back to him, even if that meant he might take advantage of the opening she had left him. Even if that meant he might...

"You look like you want me to be bothered, all of a sudden." His serious grimace disappeared, promptly replaced by a crooked half-smile that made her want to throw herself over the balcony. "Anzi? Are you all right?"

"I'm perfectly fine, sir."

"Sir, again. I thought your orders were to...please me. Call me Kai when we're alone, at least. Or are you no longer going to agree to please me now?"

"That's not what the Emperor meant—"

"Oh? So what did he mean?"

He was too close. She wanted to close her eyes and fall into him, or let him fall into her, she didn't care—

"He meant—he meant that—"

"Yes?"

"...For me to oblige you whenever possible," she finished, and she knew her voice had come out far weaker than it should have. Damn it. Damn everything. She was a soldier. She was one of the greatest soldiers in the entire Imperial Army. She was a Premier Guard now, even, one of the greats. She was not someone to melt and titter because of some hard-bodied, fire-scorching man with eyes that were swallowing her up and hands she could almost feel sliding over her skin, pressing her down, down, down—

"Then you should call me Kai," he said, and his voice was so sly and smugshe could have sworn he knew what she was thinking. "Because that would please me. There are other things that would please me even more, but I think this is enough for now."

For now? Please him even more? Her stomach flopped, then flopped again. "Yes, sir."

"What was that?"

"Ah—yes…Kai."

The name was syrup on her tongue. It tasted so—good. Was she going insane? How could names have a taste?

But the world wasn't done turning over on its head. Kai reached up to push a lock of her hair behind one ear, and he let his thumb caress her on the cheek just below her eye in the same movement. It could have been an accident if it were anyone else, but no. This had been deliberate.

Anzi was burning. Melting.

"I like that," he rasped, and his whisper stabbed through her a dozen different ways. None of them hurt, though. Not one. "Call me like that from now on."

"…When we're alone, sir."

"Then let's make that happen more often." His eyes flashed. "A lot more."

21

"**A**re you Anzi?"

She leaped to her feet and reared up like a serpent about to strike, only to realize the voice belonged to none other than a pretty girl wearing a pale pink chiffon gown and bedecked in numerous small articles of silver and pearl. Loose blonde ringlets fell about her pale face, giving her an innocent yet womanly look, but the pale blue eyes that stared back at Anzi were more alarmed than sweet. Her hands were clasped and folded in front of her chest, and she stood half-turned away from when she had jumped in fright.

One of the harem girls. Anzi relaxed and made sure her relieved exhale was slow and silent. No need to reveal her agitated state this morning to anyone. "That's me," she said. "Are you the one His Excellency sent to see me?"

"No, but she's fallen sick this morning, and all I know is that I'm to see you instead. I was hoping you could fill me in on what I'm to do."

Anzi blinked. She hadn't been told? Even if an emergency had arisen and they had hastily sent this substitute, this was the Emperor's orders. Had no one taken the time to inform her? Apparently not, going by the young woman's hesitant expression, which presented a dilemma. Anzi would sooner drop dead than say the truth aloud, that she was supposed to teach her the sensual secrets of plying a man so she could seduce her way into a desert chieftain's bed. Was there a way to say it that wasn't mortifying? Worse, she hadn't expected someone so young for a teacher. Surely there was an older woman far more experienced in matters like these? This girl looked scarcely older than her.

"Your name?" asked Anzi. "And how long have you been in the harem?"

"Violetta. I've been here for a few months. How old are you?"

How old? Why did that matter to her? She was here to help Anzi, not the other way around. Regardless of age, she needed to do what she had come here to do...as soon as Anzi gathered up the nerve to tell her what exactly that was. "I'm turning eighteen soon," she said, relenting only because she was tired and didn't want to be roped into a useless conversation full of pointless niceties. "I—"

"Oh? How soon!"

She hid her grimace. Harem girls were to be treated gently, she reminded herself. Easy. "In three days."

"Oh, my goodness! A birthday celebration, what will you be doing? Is that why I'm here? To service you?"

What in hell? "No," she said, perhaps a little too forcefully to be kind. "No, not me. You're—not to be servicing anyone at all, actually."

"Then why am I here?" Violetta asked, utterly nonplussed. "I don't mean to discount whatever other good qualities I might have, but there aren't many other things I'm more qualified at than others. Except this."

This? This, she had said. It made Anzi queasy that the girl could speak so casually of things like—sex. In the military, such talk was heavily punished if a commanding officer overheard any of the soldiers discussing it, even in the privacy of the barracks. That was why the Quarter Rouge was so popular. Perpetually repressed while on duty, soldiers on leave streamed to the sleazy district both to satisfy their desires but also to revel in the atmosphere itself.

She had never gone there. She had never had any interest. And now she and a harem girl were standing outside her room about to engage in tutorship of pleasuring someone for the sake of political stability.

How had things come to this?

"So...what you'll be doing today is—" She paused and tried again. "The reason you're here is because..."

Violetta watched her with what looked like bated breath. Really? Couldn't she stare at her a little less enthusiastically? Anzi was about to break into a sweat as flashes of images trickled through her mind. Kai, with his bronzed skin and taut muscles, watching her as she tried to exercise all the things she was about to learn now. What—what would that even be like? How would that happen? Would she be lying in bed and giving him come-hither eyes, or would he be the one to order her there to join him?

"...Anzi?"

"You're supposed to teach me how to pleasure a man," she blurted before she could lose her nerve. "Tall, built heavy. Desert nomad, a chieftain. He's wealthy enough to own expensive jewelry beyond most citizen's means ten times over. He appears sexually comfortable enough to make suggestive comments and would likely be receptive to advances as well. I can acquire more information on him if you need it to pinpoint his vulnerabilities." She stopped to take a breath, but decided against continuing when she saw the half-amused, half-alarmed look in the girl's eyes.

"...That's...very nice," said Violetta. "But, um...Listen." She reached forward and patted Anzi on the shoulder. The gesture was so unexpected and foreign that she didn't think to step away and dodge it. "So, I know you're a soldier. They told me about that. But this isn't...fighting, you know? It's not war. It's like fishing, you have to relax and flow with the current, or else you'll be fighting the tide all day and no fish will bite."

What? Fish? What was she talking about?

"I was also told this was a long-term assignment, and since Berenice will probably be out of commission for a few more days, we can take our time with the basics. The foundation is the most important, you know? Here, let's go in your room. I wish you'd waited inside, you shouldn't have been sitting out here waiting for me where it's so uncomfortable."

Anzi let Violetta herd her back into the room through the door that was slightly ajar without argument, mostly because she didn't want to explain that she had only been sitting against the wall outside because being alone in her room had been unbearable. The memory of Kai's hand on her face, his thumb brushing her cheek, the powerful grace of his movements as he came closer—all of it had tormented her ever since she awoke this morning.

No. It was better not to mention any of that. It would only make everything more complicated and humiliating. As far as Violetta was concerned, all she had to know was that Anzi had a mission assigned to her by the Emperor himself. So there was absolutely no need for her to know that Anzi was foolishly being seduced by the one she was meant to be seducing.

"Wow, what a nice room! And made for one, too."

The girl flounced on the bed, the chiffon of her skirts rustling as she wiggled her rear end on the mattress then crossed one leg over the other with an exaggerated motion. She bounced several times on the down-cushioned bed with experimental intent. "We have to share one big room," she explained to Anzi who remained by the door. "It builds camaraderie. I always wanted one to myself, though. That was the hardest part about moving to the palace, losing my room. Nineteen years of living in solo luxury, and then suddenly, poof! I have to share everything now, which is awful. But I will say that the beds aren't as soft as ours. Yours is a bit hard, isn't it?"

Anzi didn't think so, but then again, she was used to sleeping on the ground or wherever else she needed to lay her head while on the march. Barracks beds were the pinnacle of comfort for her after eight years of that life. These, the ones in the palace—they were too soft. It was like sinking into mud that sucked her down into its depths. She had woken up this morning molded into the mattress.

"Am I talking too much? Sorry."

Oh. She hadn't said anything in response. She sighed and shook her head. "No, it's fine. I was thinking."

"About what? Your man?"

"He's not my man!" she exclaimed. "I've been assigned to him."

"…That's what I meant. I didn't mean anything silly by it."

At the sudden mischievous, knowing smile that spread across Violetta's pink lips, Anzi was tempted to recoil. Shit. "Ah," she said, forcing her voice back to a cool, composed tone. "I misunderstood. Then, let's get to work. What would I need to learn first in order to…" Just say it, she told herself. She was a soldier. She had *killed*, what was this in comparison? "In order to seduce a man like the one I described?" she finished. "His Excellency told me that the desert tribes are more sexually liberated. I'm assuming that means their practices are going to be different from ours, and thatI should adjust my tactics to suit that."

Violetta was still smiling. Damn it. "Listen," she said. "Seduction is not all about sex. Have you ever been in love, Anzi?"

…What? "No. I don't have time for that."

"No, no, it's not about time. These things don't happen because you make room in your schedule or because you have a few extra minutes at the end of your day. Come here, sit next to me, let's get to know each other. If you want me to teach you the real secrets of how to make a man yours, I have to learn about you a little, and the same for you but with me.

After that, I'll be able to tell you the best…what did you call it? Tactics, right? I'll be able to tell you which tactics are the best for you to use on your man. Or your assignment, whichever description you prefer."

Okay, now the harem girl was outright teasing her. Anzi considered refusing the invitation, but that would be entirely too petulant. Besides, the sooner this was over with, the sooner she could send her away, she thought sourly. She was a soldier. She shouldn't have to waste her time being lectured on the finer points of 'real seduction' by an inexperienced woman scarcely older than she was.

And it wasn't as if she were completely ignorant. She knew about men's bodies and how they functioned. The Imperial Army was made up of more men than women, after all, which meant that her barracks had been comprised of mostly men, too. She knew about their bodily functions and the ways they would satisfy themselves when there were no accessible women to use instead.

Yeah. That was right. She knew men's weaknesses, or at least some of them. That was the point of seduction no matter what Violetta tried to tell her, no matter how romantic and fancy she tried to make it sound. Seduction was down to skill and observation.

"I'd rather we get to the point," she said coolly as she moved forward to take her spot at the foot of the bed. "I don't think it's necessary to get into any extraneous details. His Excellency would agree."

"Just trust me. A little time is all I need, and you'll see. First, tell me about what you really think of this chieftain…"

22

"I don't think about him at all. Except the things I told you about him. That's it."

"Oh, don't be like that. I want to help. Trust me, I know I said I've only been here a few months, but I'm very gifted at this sort of thing. You can ask any of the other girls when you see them next. They'll tell you. I've been training for this since I was fifteen, and I know how to read people when it comes to those syrupy sweet feelings they try to hide."

Anzi leaned away. She most certainly did not like that. As a matter of fact, she felt threatened, as if Violetta was saying she could look right through her down to where she tried to quash the wild, twitching spark that was her attraction to Kai. So what? She was human. It was only natural that she would appreciate a fine musculature and handsome face. It didn't mean she had things like *syrupy sweet feelings.*

This was annoying. And humiliating.

"Well, I guess this isn't working, huh?" asked Violetta.

"No, it's not."

The harem girl abruptly flopped back on the bed and fanned her arms out. Her delicate, flowing dress billowed up with the movement, and Anzi stared at the gossamer material wrapped around her skirt. She had never worn such a thing before. Leather armor and military-issue clothes had been her whole life ever since she had been Selected. Powders and rouge and sparkling gold and silver dust, women in the Imperial Army never touched these, not even those who had been born into upper class families before being placed.

Would she have to wear something like that when she went to approach Kai? Something soft and revealing, she thought as she glared at the cleavage-revealing. Breasts—instead of tightening and holding them in place with a band under her armor, she imagined she would have to flaunt them. She had hardly ever paid attention to hers except to make sure they were well bound and wouldn't hurt when she ran. But the chieftain was a man, so of course he would be easily distracted by breasts. Cleavage. And leg? Showing leg? What next, was she to bare her rear end and bend over with a coquettish smile?

She buried her face in one hand. This was beyond humiliation. It was utterly degrading, taking lessons in how to bat her eyelashes and lure in some foreign princeling when she was supposed to be the newest inductee of the most prestigious order in the entire Empire, a Premier Guard, someone who vanquished foul enemies and defended the virtue of the people.

Yes, this was her, sulking in bed next to a silly harem girl. How had things come to this?

"So, this is discouraging," Violetta murmured. "I was hoping things would go better, but I guess you hate me already."

What? Anzi twisted around to look at her. She was still lying back on the bed, painted eyes closed and her hands folded primly over her abdomen. Hate her? What had she done to make her think that way? They barely knew each other; she couldn't hate someone she'd just met a minute ago.

"No," she said. "I don't hate you. Why would you think that?"

"Because I'm a harem girl, and I know what people think of me before I even open my mouth. The same way you think of me."

She stared back, wordless, and the moment stretched itself thin. *The same way you think of me.* Had Violetta really said that, and so wryly? Where had the flowery and perfumed disposition gone, the charming sparkle in her voice and dainty, pink-lipped smile that could put any courtesan in the Quarter Rouge to shame?

"I don't..."

"When I said I could read feelings, I meant it," said the woman. "It's a skill I've mastered as I grew, and it's not just the sweet feelings I can read. It's all rright, I'm used to it. Harem girls, we're not worth much more than moments of fleeting pleasure for the guests we entertain. I mean, it's not like the Emperor ever comes to see any of us, so we can't even boast that we service His Excellency. There's nothing to be proud about when all we do is give our bodies and make men feel good about themselves. That's what everyone thinks, anyway, even if they don't say it or even realize they're thinking it. It's enough that it shows in their actions, the way they treat us."

Anzi stood up from the bed and turned to face her, and the sudden movement made Violetta lift her head. There was a surprised look in her eyes as she stared up at Anzi. A brief pause later, she planted her hands in the mattress and sat up, although she remained leaning back on locked elbows as if she were wary of coming too close.

They stayed like that for a moment, neither of them speaking.

"I'm sorry," said Anzi. She kept her gaze steady and firm. "You're right, I disrespected you. You have your duties just like I do, even if you serve a different way. I hope you accept my apology."

Because Violetta was right. From the moment they had met, Anzi had been denigrating her in her thoughts—perhaps not maliciously, but she had dismissed her as a mere harem girl just the same. All morning, she had dreaded this meeting and moaned to herself that this was below her, that she was a soldier with dignity who shouldn't have to stoop to this. The resentment must have shown in the way she had treated her, with brief moments of condescension and impatience that she hadn't even noticed herself until now.

Seconds passed, and then several more. Anzi held her breath, wondering if this was pointless. Forgiveness was something she had never been good at herself. Instead, she simmered and carried grudges, vowing to defeat everyone who looked down on her by rising above them and putting them to shame. She was in no position to expect anyone else to forgive her disrespect. But at last, after a long moment, a sweet smile grew on Violetta's lips, and the pretty glimmer of impish joy returned to her eyes.

"When you're so earnest, you leave me no choice but to accept your apology. I like that. I like you. Come, sit back down." She patted the spot on the bed next to her. "I'm sure you have lots of things you'd rather be doing, so let's just make this morning comfortable for both of us. What do you say?"

Anzi pressed her lips together as she lowered herself down to the bed. She was still embarrassed at having been confronted with such bold gentleness and by someone she would never have expected such assertiveness from. But she was relieved it had ended so cleanly, and she would remember this lesson in humility. She refused to become the kind of person she hated, the ones who had always looked down on her, too. "That's good," she said slowly. "I'm fine with that."

"Oh, don't be so stiff. We've put it behind us, right? Don't worry, I'm not upset."

She should be. Anzi grimaced, thoroughly subdued.

"Fine, I guess it'll be a bit awkward for a while between us. But I meant it, I like you. It's hard finding people who are any good at saying they're sorry, much less ones who actually mean it. So—here, let's meet in the middle. Today, we'll have fun. I have you for the whole morning, right?"

She wavered. Yes, she regretted behaving like an ass, but that didn't mean she wanted to devote several hours to this, either.

"Don't worry, don't worry. How about we go exploring so we can get familiar with each other? I have my monthly allowance that I haven't touched yet, so we should go down to the market district and browse. Usually, we're only allowed to leave with permission from our seniors and with a guard, but if you escort me, there's nothing they can say. I'm fairly certain you outrank all of us anyway since we're only lowly harem girls, right?" She gave a broad, playful wink, but when Anzi's mouth tightened into a guilty line, her hand came up in a disarming gesture. "That was a joke! It was supposed to be funny. I guess that's something else we might need to work on."

She couldn't say no, lest it cheapen the sincerity of her apology seconds before. "All right. But is this really going to be any help?"

"It sure will. Come, I'll show you to our rooms. You'll have to vouch for me to the guards before I can leave. The good news is that the Aunts are gone, and most of my sisters, too. So we won't run into too many nosy people who talk too much like me, if you were worried about that. Promise."

Damn it. It was like she could read minds. Anzi pushed back her hair and coughed to cover the silence before getting to her feet once more. "Well, let's go, then," she muttered. "And I wasn't worried about that."

"Sure." Violetta winked again. "Just let me get changed into something more suitable once we're there. I don't want to tear this while walking around in a crowd."

And she was right: after ascending one floor and arriving at a grand, open chamber, Anzi could see a only a few girls lounging about inside. She wasn't curious enough to try to walk past the two guards and inspect the sight more closely, but it was odd that the place was so deserted. There were supposed to dozens of women in the Imperial harem; surely they weren't all out wandering the palace grounds at the same time?

But that was none of her business. She would do better to worry about what she was doing now. Was it really all right to escort someone out like this on the basis that it was for the sake of her task from His Excellency? Well, it seemed so, since the guards nodded and handed over a slender golden token without argument. Violetta, now wearing a humbler dress of green cotton under a cloak of a darker shade, accepted it with both hands and a wide smile.

"That's it!" the woman said cheerily. "We're going to have so much fun."

ONE GOOD THING resulted from the hectic pace of their morning: it distracted Anzi from obsessing over Kai and his visit last night since she had to devote her energies to shouldering apart the crowd and clearing a path for Violetta to wriggle through instead. She really should have stayed in the expensive attire she had worn earlier. Even if she were afraid of damaging it, the people would have parted for her upon seeing that she was from the palace. Concubines would never be regarded with the admiration that nobles of the upper class received, but they were still women with the privilege of living alongside the Emperor. Even the wealthiest of the city's citizens couldn't boast such a thing.

She noticed something peculiar, however. There were numerous other harem girls out and about too. Their expensive dresses and accessories were unmistakable even at a passing glimpse through the crowd. That must have been why the room at the palace was empty, but it was strange that Violetta seemed to veer away from her sisters whenever they were about to cross paths. Almost as if she were avoiding them and trying to go unseen, but that didn't make sense. Unfortunately, the woman's surprising agility and talent for escape made it so Anzi could hardly spare a moment to ponder the mystery.

"Violetta, we can't be separated," she snapped when the harem girl manage to slip away for the tenth time to admire some brooches displayed in a market stall. "I need to know where you are at all times."

"Sorry, sorry. I'm not trying to get you into trouble—just, look! Aren't they gorgeous?"

"…Yes."

"Oh, no. You don't agree at all."

Anzi frowned. "I think they're pretty."

"No, you don't. You hate them. I can tell."

"…Imperial soldiers aren't permitted any jewelry."

"But you're still allowed to admire beautiful craftsmanship! Come here, let me find one that suits you. Your eyes are so pretty, I bet a nice emerald will really contrast them."

Anzi reluctantly obliged with a small snort and smiled despite herself. Pretty eyes? That was the first time she'd ever heard such a thing. Crow's eyes were a mark of the destitute. No one ever complimented a fringer's pitch-black gaze. She really was something else.

"Just buy them for yourself, Violetta. I'm not interested."

"Call me Letti. Also, wow! Look at that, see? It's stunning."

"I don't want it."

"Then I'll buy it for you."

"I won't use it, either."

"Then I'll hold onto it for you until the day you change your mind. Who knows? Maybe you'll find a dashing man you want to dress up for."

Anzi sighed. There was no winning against her. This was the problem with keeping the company of anyone who wasn't a soldier; she couldn't just settle this with an intimidating glare or, in case of emergency, a swift punch to the chin.

Violetta handed over several coins to the vendor and dropped the brooch into her coin purse. "For later," she chirped. "If we have time when we get back, I want you to try on a few dresses so I can see how they look on you."

"For the task?"

The harem girl blinked at her. "Task?" she repeated, slender eyebrows furrowing inquisitively. "What do you mean?"

"You're asking me to try on dresses to seduce the chieftain, yes?"

"…Right, right. Yes, that's, mhm. Anyway, let's look at those shawls—"

Strange woman. But to be honest, it wasn't so bad…True, Anzi would rather have spent the morning training instead of chasing Violetta from stall to stall, but somehow within the span of just an hour or two, the woman's incessant chattering became almost adorable instead of irritating. Even if she was terrible at following orders and kept slipping out of Anzi's sight.

"Oh, that's fantastic, sir, what a bargain! But I need to shop around first, so hold that thought and I'll be right back."

"Violetta, wait, I need to go with you—"

Too late. Violetta was gone in an instant, weaving through the streaming crowd to the opposite side of the street where a vendor proudly displayed too-expensive earrings and other gaudy accessories Anzi would never wear. Damn it. But at least those blonde ringlets were still within view between everyone's bobbing heads. With a sigh, she waited a moment for a particularly thick gaggle to pass long before moving to cross the street.

There she was. She had lost sight of the woman for a second, but that bright golden hair was unmissable. She pushed past the last clot of civilians in her way—

—just as someone delivered a vicious backhand to Violetta and sent her crashing brutally to the ground.

23

Nosy passersby chose that exact instant to cluster around the scene, and now Anzi was on the wrong side of the circle of murmuring civilians forming around the disturbance. Not for long. She forced her way through with savage shoves, earning strings of filthy curses, until finally she caught Violetta's gaze over the last several shoulders. The woman was still on the ground, kneeling in the dust and twisted to the side as she shielded the lower half of her face with a dainty hand. A thick drizzle of blood dripped from her chin, and Anzi's face tightened in hot anger. Who dared? Violetta was her responsibility. Whoever was stupid enough to lay their hand on her was going to lose it. She wouldn't even give them a chance to apologize, neither to Violetta nor to the Emperor whose charge she was.

But before she could charge in, the woman sent her an almost imperceptible warning, a quick shake of her head and a bright, frightened look. It stopped Anzi in her tracks, and instead of leaping forward to grind the offender into the stones, she remained stock-still and stared back at Violetta in stunned silence. What? She wanted her to stay away, but why? Anzi turned her glare on the culprit for a clue, and it was then she realized the reason.

Three harem girls in shimmering, slender dresses and veils stood before Violetta, looming over her with their hands on their hips and their stances haughty and insolent.

"So you're told to stay inside, but you sneak out anyway?" the middle concubine sneered. "I can't believe you had the nerve. But then again, you *are* stupid."

"Noemi, I can explain—"

Before Anzi could step forward, the one called Noemi lashed out once more with a another slap across Violetta's face. And again, as she fell back down, she caught Anzi's eyes and shook her head ever so subtly. Why! Why was she tolerating this? Fight back, she wanted to hiss, but when Noemi reached back to deliver yet another slap with an ugly, sharp smile, Violetta did nothing but close her eyes and brace herself for it.

No. Unacceptable. Anzi didn't care if there were mysterious rules in the hierarchy of the Imperial harem. Right now, she was the one in charge of Violetta's safety, and if that meant she needed to protect her from her own so-called sisters, then so be it. Before the third slap could make contact, Anzi was standing in their midst, and Noemi's hand landed on her arm instead. She didn't even twitch.

But all three harem girls gasped aloud at her appearance as if they were the ones who had been struck. Anzi was reminded of a covey of pigeons when they all simultaneously raised their hands to their mouths over their veils and made sharp, high-pitched noises of disbelief. Pretty pigeons, though, with their powdered faces, rouged lips, and decorative flecks of paint on their cheeks. They were dressed as if they were at a festival, not indulging in a humble shopping trip, and she let her disapproving grimace show plainly. Such luxury shouldn't be wasted on mundane activities.

"How dare you!" the girl on Noemi's left exclaimed. "A dirty soldier touching us! We'll have you lashed a hundred times!"

"Lashed! You mean executed! Look at Noemi's hand, I bet it's bruised!"

"Then we'll have her hand cut off before they execute her, dirty rat—"

"Cut off both of them!"

Right. Squawking pigeons. She was done listening.

"All three of you need to leave," she ordered, her voice icy as a northern wind. She didn't care about treating these women with any delicateness, not after what she had seen them do and say. "I can't help but notice you're without a guard escort. That's against the rules, last I heard."

But instead of confessing their error and hurrying off to do as she said, all three of them proceeded to shoot her with even nastier scowls. Their painted lips twisted in near-identical snarls as if they had practiced this routine before, and Anzi let her eyes glance over each of their faces again so she could commit their furious countenances to memory. Now that it was obvious that they were willfully disobedient instead of wandering lost, she would report them to the head of the Imperial Harem. Their veils made it difficult to pick out identifying marks, but she would remember the loose, elegant braid in a ruby clip on the one and the mass of tight blonde curls on the other.

Noemi, on the other hand, had a far more distinct appearance. A small beauty mark by her upper lip and dark, sharp eyebrows framing bright green eyes. Her dark tresses cascaded over her shoulder in graceful waves, long and thick. Definitely easy to remember. Once she found out who their chaperon was supposed to be, she was going to give him a sound wallop for having lost his charges. How did a man lose three harem girls when they were all decked out in the most luxurious, eye-catching attire possible?

"Now would be a good time to leave," said Anzi. "Before you make me go report you. I don't think any of us want that."

"Shut your mouth. And then get on your knees and apologize to me, you stupid bitch. Do you know who I am? Do you know who you're talking to right now?"

…Stupid bitch? Get on her knees? Had she heard that correctly?

She stared at Noemi, the apparent ringleader of this trio who had just spat such venomous words at her. She had the haughty voice of an upper class woman, and she was several years older than everyone else in this unruly mess. Her middling twenties, perhaps? That would explain her evident seniority and self-important delusion. But even so, how could Violetta allow a fellow concubine to hit her like that?

"I know who I'm talking to," said Anzi. "A runaway harem girl who must have gotten lost in this great, big market district. Go find your escort."

"Go on. Your impudence will just make it all the sweeter when I watch the guards flay you alive right here in the middle of the street. But if you get down and lick my shoes clean, maybe I'll let you keep your miserable, worthless life. So what'll it be?"

Were all harem girls this vicious? She had never thought such dolled-up denizens who lived soft lives in the luxury of the Imperial Palace could speak this way. But it was nothing compared to the kind of insults soldiers flung around at each other. If anything, Noemi's sneering threats were embarrassingly juvenile. But Anzi still had to watch her mouth.

These were the Emperor's concubines, even if these ones were no better than wild animals off their leash.

She opened her mouth to deliver a sharper, more menacing retort this time, an order to return to their chaperon or else she would drag them off to receive punishment per Imperial code—when she felt Violetta's hand tug on the back of her leather jerkin, a silent plea to hold back.

What in hell? Why was she defending these women who had struck her so hard they had drawn blood? Why was she saying nothing at all in her own defense, and not only that, but asking Anzi to leave off as well?

...Fine, she would compromise since she had a niggling feeling she didn't have the whole picture here. It was better to exercise caution when she knew so little, and there might be a reason indeed for Violetta's confusing patience under her sisters' abuse. The last thing Anzi wanted to do was get her into more trouble, although she couldn't for the life of her understand why she was being subjected to such treatment.

In any case, the most important thing to do now was defuse the situation. And after all of this, she knew exactly how to go about doing that.

"Before you go off and fetch your guards to flay this miserable, worthless servant of the Empire alive," she drawled in the voice she used to reserve only for Oscar's most annoying moments, "you should know I'm chaperoning your sister today because she's to assist me this morning. A task, actually, assigned to me by His Excellency himself. Should I take you to request an audience with him, so you can properly ask permission to punish someone for obeying His Excellency's orders?"

As expected, Noemi's two companions promptly lost all the color that remained in their powdered-pale faces, and they stared at Anzi in undisguised shock. She reveled in the pleasure of having terrified them; moments like these were what she used to live for back when she endured the torment of her peers. She was half-tempted to milk the opportunity and force them to apologize to Violetta, who had yet to make a sound.

But this wasn't about herself. As much as she craved the satisfaction, it wasn't hers to take. This was about Violetta, and the hasty interference might make things worse for her in the long run. Saving her from a slap or two in the present was nothing compared to what might happen behind closed doors, and Anzi had no authority beyond them. If, by some chance, the harem girls decided to punish Violetta when they were alone in the palace, there was nothing Anzi could do other than report it to someone she hoped would listen. And who would want to insert themselves into the politics of harem girls? The only reason she was willing to wade into the mess now was because she couldn't stand to see such blatant, shameless abuse happen right in front of her.

"If you're really here as her escort, then I want to see proof. Let me see, right now." Noemi's eyes were narrowed to snake-like slits, and she stuck out her hand with an imperious shove. "Show me!"

Interesting. She didn't seem nearly as afraid as her two companions. Was she stupid, or was she simply that arrogant? This was about the Emperor's authority. Who did she think she was? Anzi never broke the stare as she reached behind her, and with a flick of her wrist, presented Violetta with an upturned, demanding hand. There was a brief hesitation she didn't miss, then cool metal pressed into her palm, slow and careful. She could sense the woman's apprehension, and an angry, indignant curiosity burned inside her. The hold these women had over Violetta—it was abominable. It made her want to slap them all across the face and see how they liked it. If ever she were allowed the opportunity, she would take it in a heartbeat.

"Here. Can you see it?" Instead of handing it over and placing it into Noemi's waiting hand, Anzi reached forward and dangled it in front of her veiled face. "That should be close enough. But seeing as how you're without a guard, maybe I should be the ones asking you for your pass tokens." Another tug on the back of her jerkin. Damn it all—fine, then.

"But," she added, "instead, why don't we part ways peacefully here, and you handle your business while we handle ours. Yes?"

A long silence boiled between them, and the sudden quiet reminded Anzi that they had an audience. The crowd of passersby who had stopped in their tracks to see beautiful concubines arguing with a soldier were still watching with rapt attention. That wouldn't do. So many eyes on them was no good for anyone involved. Thankfully, Noemi seemed to arrive at the same conclusion, judging by the way her poison-green eyes darted around the numerous faces gathered about. She reached up to adjust her veil with a delicate touch and licked her lips before giving her reply.

"I'm tired of standing around anyway. The girls and I will...go find our chaperon." She turned with a whirl of her skirts, but before taking her first step, she looked over her shoulder. "Oh, and Violetta...we'll see you when we get home."

And that was that. Scarcely before the last word dripped from her venomous lips, the woman flounced off with a jaunty step, her two companions trailing behind.

24

Anzi said nothing after that, neither when she picked Violetta up from the ground nor when she helped clean off her bloody face nor even when they returned to the palace. Whatever the reason for Violetta's willing subjection to such mistreatment, it was up to her to confess it. She was an adult. They were both adults. And they were neither friends nor each other's confidants.

"I lied to you," Violetta blurted. She had whirled around to face Anzi with clear, stubborn eyes, and her hands were clasped together white-knuckled-tight over her chest. A semi-defiant incline raised her chin.

"Lied?" Anzi repeated. "How."

"I told you the girl who was supposed to teach you is sick. Berenice. She is, but what I didn't tell you is that today, everyone else planned to go out into the city. But someone has to stay behind to entertain any unexpected guests, and that's me. It's always me, every time. I stay behind and mend their clothes and clean and whatever other tasks they decide to make me do while they're gone. That's why I had to show up to meet you in Berenice's stead, too. But I was sick and tired of it, so I lied and told you that going down to the market together would be useful. It's not. I just wanted to go, that's all."

Anzi listened to the rushed confession without making a sound. Even when it concluded, she said nothing, and the silence continued.. There was no one else in this stretch of the hall to interrupt it, and they stayed that way for a long moment. Until at last, the harem girl sighed, took a deep breath, and pressed her hands down the front of her dress.

"Anyway," she said in a far more subdued voice. "I just want to say I'm sorry. You'll probably report me, I'm guessing."

"Do you want me to?"

"No, obviously. But it would be the right thing to do. And you're going to do it anyway."

Anzi fell quiet. She was right. Reporting her would be the right thing to do, especially since she had dared to waste His Excellency's time by toying with his assigned task. It would be an easy, simple thing. All Anzi had to do was take her back to the harem quarters, find the head guard, and inform him that one of his girls had engaged in gross misbehavior.

Because in the end, that was what it was. Anzi wasn't allowed to care about the extraneous details like how obvious it was that Violetta was the outcast of the harem, or at least its most popular doormat. She didn't know why or even if there was a reason for it in the first place, but that had nothing to do with Anzi. It wasn't her responsibility to assign sympathy for unfair troubles. She'd had a job, and she still did. They both did. That was all.

And yet—

"I don't know why you think I'd report you for anything," she said coolly. "I trust your judgment implicitly. If you thought at the time it would help, that's your prerogative. Your harem politics have nothing to do with me, so whether you broke some rule or not is irrelevant when it comes to my responsibilities."

As she spoke, Violetta's stare lost its defensive gleam, and by the time she was done, her eyes were shining with quiet amazement instead. Again, another bout of silence fell over them, but this time it lasted only briefly before the harem girl smiled.

"You're doing it again," she said softly.

"Doing what?"

"Talking all formally. It doesn't suit you, you should be more relaxed."

"All right."

"I mean it. You'll never seduce a man if you're that stiff and uptight."

When Anzi tilted her head up with a sharp, indignant breath, Violetta's smile broke out into a wide, beaming grin. It was enough to make her pause and swallow back the sharp retort she had been about to deliver, which gave the harem girl yet another chance to ruffle her feathers.

"Anyway, if you really mean it, let's chalk today up to a much-needed learning experience in fashion and charm. You really do need to do something about your clothes, don't you think? I don't know what barbarian chieftains like to see in a woman, but I bet they'd rather peel back a nice cleavage-baring dress than…leather bits. But baby steps. We'll get there."

Anzi rolled her eyes. The woman had recovered fast as lightning from it all. Maybe she had been too quick to forgive? "I have things to do," she said. "Go in and clean yourself off. Your clothes are stained."

"Blood will do that, I suppose. Good thing I changed before I left."

Blood. That was right. It was the nosebleed from the slap that had soiled the clothes. "Are you going to be all right?" she asked. "Tonight. When the others come back."

Violetta's smile never faded, but clearly that was an act. A hint of a wan quality entered it, so slight Anzi nearly missed it. "You mean Noemi and the girls. I'll be okay. This is just how things go…All I have to do is make it through the next few months, and it'll be someone else's turn. This is how it's always been and always will be. No real harm, not really. It's like a ritual of sorts."

"A ritual?"

"You know. Knock down the new girl and kick her while she's down, beat the system into her. I was already prepared for it before I ever came here, so don't worry about me. Though to be honest, it feels nice to be worried about. And it feels even nicer that you're going to lie for me."

Anzi twitched. "Lie for you?" she demanded. "Excuse me?"

"Well, you said you weren't going to report me, right? That's pretty naughty of you and—well, never mind. I don't want to accidentally convince you to change your mind." Her smile flashed wider once more, exposing a glimmer of straight, perfect teeth. "I'll be going then. You don't need to walk me the rest of the way, you should go and rest after all this excitement."

"So…you'll be all right?"

"Of course I will. It's a harem, not a jungle. There are still rules they have to abide by. So don't worry about me, go on and take care of business. I'm going to spend the rest of the day relaxing in bed, I think. And checking on Berenice. See? I have a full schedule. Now leave me alone, shoo!"

Anzi rolled her eyes again at the woman's exaggerated wink. "Then I'm leaving. If you're seeing me tomorrow too, then you'll find me at my room."

"Sure. But one thing, just one thing. A small favor?"

Oh, brother. What now. "What is it."

The girl tapped her on the nose with a playful finger. "Call me Letti from now on."

SOMETHING WAS DEFINITELY wrong with her. Not with Violetta or Letti or whatever she wanted to be called, but herself, thought Anzi. In the span of two days, she had undergone life-altering trauma. First in the form of meeting a desert prince who could drive her into existential confusion, then the discovery of the truth behind the dragons of the Empire, and now this. Blatant rejection of duty, this was. Nothing less. She shouldn't have hesitated even for a second as soon as she and Letti returned to the palace. She should have marched over to the head harem guard and informed him that the woman had schemed to the Emperor's injury on the basis of her petty selfishness.

But she hadn't. Even now, she had no desire to do such a thing. Inconceivable. Since when had she become such a flagrant violator of the rules? The Anzi of three days ago would look upon her with nothing but disgust. Cutting corners because of something silly like sentiment and sympathy, harboring borderline-treasonous thoughts just because reality didn't meet her expectations, and even wasting her time accidentally daydreaming about a foreign chieftain when she could be doing something productive. All of this, everything, it was ruining her life.

She was so unbalanced. Unsteady. All she wanted to do was forget everything that had happened to her since she arrived and throw herself into her training like before.

…And maybe see Kai again one more time. Just to get it out of her system, that is. It wasn't because she missed him and his too-knowing eyes or anything. It was because he was objectively handsome, that was all, and was it unusual to be attracted to good-looking men? She couldn't be the only one. She'd bet any of the harem girls would agree.

At the thought, she stopped in the middle of the hallway.

The harem girls. They entertained important guests. In fact, if what Letti had said this morning was true, then that was their primary responsibility since His Excellency the Emperor never went to see them himself. Did that mean Kai had been offered their services already?

Another faint memory rose to accompany the sudden thought. Kai had mentioned yesterday that he had already been in the palace for some time, and that he simply hadn't left it to explore the city yet. But what was there to do in the palace, what entertainment could he possibly indulge in for days at a time?

Other than the company of the harem, that is.

Her pulse throbbed in her neck as she struggled to control her thoughts. What business was it of hers, anyway, if Kai had already availed himself to the services of nubile girls and women? He was a nomad, a desert dweller, and His Excellency had said such people were more carnal than most. It made perfect sense, and if not for that, what else was Kai supposed to have done to occupy himself while waiting in the palace? That promiscuous man, with his big, muscled chest and rippling arms and bronzed skin.

None of her business. It had nothing to do with anything at all. With a furious exhale, she stalked off to her room.

25

K ai came to her first. He wasn't supposed to. She should have been the one to go to his room an hour from now, according to the timecatcher hanging from the window in the sunlight. But for some reason, he was standing here and looking at her with a slow, lazy smile that almost made her close the door in his face in the compulsive need to escape from it. He was too much. She couldn't do this. He was too early. She had needed the extra time to steel herself so she wouldn't do idiotic things in his presence, but now he had stolen that from her.

"Anzi."

She hated how he said her name. It made her bones shake and her eyes hot. "Yes, sir."

"Come walk with me. I'm lonely."

"Weren't you with His Excellency and his advisors just now?"

"I was. But talk of business and trade doesn't warm a man any." He extended a hand to her across the threshold, palm up, and she dropped her gaze to it with a look that was both apprehensive and inquisitive. What was he doing? Well, she knew what he was doing, but why? She wasn't an upper-class lady who expected her arm to be taken by her gentlemen company wherever she went. It would be laughable if she put on a pretense of it even to humor him.

"Your hand," he said. "I want to show you a place."

Her hand? She reflexively balled hers into fists and pressed them harder into her sides. She didn't care how tempting it was to give in so she could feel the warmth of his touch again. She was not going to hold hands with him while they walked down the halls for anyone to see. Or in private, either. Not a chance. She could give her body over to him for his pleasures if that was what he wanted, but letting him hold her hand crossed into the territory of the sentimental.

"Anzi?"

"Sir, I'll just follow you if that's all right."

He cocked his head at her, and strands of his dark, tousled hair fell over one golden eye. "Sir?"

She sighed. "Kai," she amended. "I meant Kai."

His answering smile was too much. Did her knees just go numb, or was that her tormented imagination? "I missed you. I want to feel you. You don't want to let me?"

What kind of bold, shameless question...She stuck her head out past the doorway and glanced left and right to make sure there was no one eavesdropping in the corridor. Luckily, they were alone, or else she might have marched over to her balcony and dived headfirst over the edge like a graceful porpoise and it would have all been Kai's sole fault. How could he say something so...sickly sweet without looking bashful about it? She was on the verge of blushing merely from having heard it.

"Kai," she said sharply. "Please."

"Please, what? What is it you want me to do?"

"Not this. It's embarrassing."

"Not for me. I couldn't think of anything all morning except you, and I spent every minute of the talks wishing I could just leave." He stepped forward, moving closer to her and into her room. "I missed you," he repeated, but his voice was lower suddenly. Deeper. There was even a guttural undertone in it that had the hairs on the back of her neck standing on end, and a rush of adrenaline flooded her from head to toe when she realized he was looking no longer into her eyes, but down at her mouth. Why was he wearing that expression now, staring at her lips with his eyes half-lidded, and his own mouth parted despite no other words slipping out...and was he coming even closer? He was. Another step, and suddenly she was nearly pressed to his very bare chest-

Her hand shot out to take his even though he had lowered it by now, and she wrenched it into a solid death grip as sheHer hand shot out to take his even though he had lowered it by now, and she wrenched it into a solid death grip as she nearly crushed his fingers between hers. He could have what he wanted then, she snapped privately. Never mind that she had to fight hard to still her pounding heart and work to convince herself that she didn't find any pleasure in this at all. None. This was solely to keep him from doing anything even more embarrassing and juvenile like —like kissing, and someone as serious as she was would never lose her composure over something so silly. Holding hands! Really. Like children at play, honestly.

"Your hands are warm," he said, and his voice, all but purring, made her twitch. Even worse, he noticed, and she immediately released him and tried to snatch her hand back with a defensive scowl curving her mouth. Damn it all—

But he caught her before she could get away, strong, rough fingers wrapping around her wrist so swiftly she almost gave in to the conditioned reflex to twist herself out of his grip. She didn't—managed to hold herself back instead of lashing out. Or was it something else that made her still? Was it the strange, buzzing warmth that filled her, the breathtaking energy streaming into her from where they touched? She stared at it, half-petrified by the sheer intensity of the rising tide inside her that yearned to answer, to touch back, to hold.

"Not like that," he said. "Like this."

And as he stared into her eyes, he slowly released her wrist, but only so he could slide his fingers down to hers with a keen slowness like a blade being unsheathed in a graceful, languid motion. And one by one, he laced their fingers together, sliding along her knuckles with tantalizing yet assertive strength, tempting and demanding all at once. With his other hand, he folded her fingers down the same way against his, leaving her to stare at their joined hands.

"How does that feel?" he asked. "Do you like it?"

"No," she lied.

He smiled.

"I don't," she insisted. "With all due respect, this is ridiculous."

His smile grew. She died a little more. Why did he have to be this way?

"Why are you doing this? It's not needed. I'm already at your disposal if you want to have me, you don't need to play games and pretend to seduce—"

He leaned forward and stopped her mid-sentence with his other hand cupping her jaw and his thumb brushing her lips, half-rough and half-gentle. She froze, thoughts blanking with a white, bright buzzing that expanded and occupied her mind in a flash like an explosion of woolen tufts. She forgot everything she had been about to say, and the world narrowed to a pinpoint tunnel of light that illuminated only Kai and nothing else.

He was moving. Coming closer. Leaning, leaning. She couldn't breathe as his thumb pressed against and then between her lips, before parting them with an insistent pull along the bottom one. She could taste him, almost. He smelled of cinnamon and other spices, warm and baking in the sun as their scent wafted toward her on a lone desert wind. And still he came closer, head lowering as his gaze remained fixed on her mouth that remained parted under his touch as if in passionate expectation. He nudged it open a little wider, moved a little closer—

—and pressed his lips to her forehead.

Then again. Twice. And this time, he lingered, slowly running them over the delicate ridge that was her brow, coming perilously close to kissing her eyelid. His breath felt warm on her cheek, on her nose, against her mouth. He was so close. He was so—here. Her body, tense as taut wire pulled from both ends, thrummed with such wildfire agitation that she thought she might collapse against his chest. He was so big, the only thing in the room, the world. Did she even exist anymore? She had strong doubts, especially when his lips slipped down from her forehead and he lifted her chin up with a nudge. His other hand tightened around hers, their fingers still laced together so firmly she wasn't sure where he ended and she began.

"You misunderstand me," he murmured against the corner of her mouth, so, so close to her lips. "You really do."

What? What was he saying? She didn't even remember what he was talking about. Wait, had they been talking? She didn't think so, but then again, she wasn't aware of much outside the way he pressed forward little more with each passing second. She didn't know if she wanted to melt or to explode, but she would have accepted either. The horrific mixture of exhilaration and disappointment ran raw inside her like a raging water-fall, or like frantic rapids as the rowboat of her sanity tried to navigate them with a single oar.

"Anzi."

"…Y…es?"

"What are you thinking."

"I don't know," she said honestly. She was no longer even aware that she wanted him to kiss her anymore. All she knew was that they were standing so close, the heat of his body was sinking into her and touching something that had been asleep for long, long years. Something heavy and cold that had been locked away, that she had forgotten about.

She knew this feeling. She knew she did, or at least she recognized a little of it. She just didn't understand why or how, but it was so real and present that she could hardly breathe. What is this, she wondered. Why do I remember this.

"You're so beautiful," he murmured, his voice a low, resonant rumble against her mouth. "I could kiss you. I want to."

Then do it, she wanted to say, but she was petrified that the slightest movement of her lips now would bring them together with his. The scent of warm cinnamon swirled around her again, making her wonder if perhaps she wasn't imagining it at all.

"Anzi?"

"Ha?"

"I'm going to save this for later. I hope I can change your mind and make you understand."

And that was it. He drew back and stepped away from her, although his fingers slipped down and lingered under her chin a second longer. His eyes flashed hot and molten at her when she stared up at him, and he twitched as if he were about to change course and lean in once more. But he didn't, not even when her lips remained parted after his thumb left with one final swipe against them.

No? He wasn't going to…? But why—

He turned away, dragging on their joined hands so that she stumbled out of her room and into the corridor. She didn't have the sense to close the door behind her, but thankfully, Kai was far more present than she was. He reached around her and did it himself as she stared open-mouthed at him, and again, his golden eyes flickered down to linger on her lips.

"I'll make you see," he said. "You'll know."

See what? Know what? What did it all matter, anyway. He had been so close and she would have let him, so why hadn't he…

"I want to show you. Come."

As he towed her down the way, she mindlessly obeyed and followed his light, his warmth, drawn like a moth to flame.

26

H e was going to have to let go of her hand eventually. Anzi glanced down every hallway they passed, heart pounding harder and harder with each one. For a short while, she had been too entranced by the sensation of his fingers intertwined with hers to pay any attention to the rest of the world, but after narrowly dodging a few giggling maids who were luckily too distracted to notice, Anzi had realized this was too outrageous to continue.

She would not be seen holding hands with a foreign chieftain like they were lovers. Maybe she was still officially only a foot soldier, but she had a reputation to uphold, a reputation arguably as fearsome as any officer's —more than most, if she set aside modesty. Not only that, but once it became public knowledge that she was the newest member of the Premier Guard, she refused to let it be marred by shallow rumors about illicit affairs with exotic men. It was hard enough being a woman in this world, sometimes. She just wanted...

"What are you thinking about?" he asked.

Instead of answering, she tried to tug her hand out of his grip just as they passed by another bustling pair of maids, but he held on tight and pulled it closer to his chest. Her knuckles brushed against warm skin, hard and muscular, and her ears promptly decided to burn like wood stoves with too much kindling.

"Kai."

"Why are you angry?"

"I'm not angry, what do you mean—" she began to ask, but when he brought them to an abrupt halt and pulled her off to the side until they were standing by the wall, she forgot what she had been about to say as she looked up into his eyes. What was he doing, she wanted to snap, but his sharp brow was furrowed with such violent concern that the urge disappeared as quickly as it had come. Now she said nothing.

"You are," he said. "You're angry. Tell me why."

But she wasn't, she wanted to insist. Why did he think she was angry? Because he was forcing her to do such childish, immature things just to make him happy? Sure, it was annoying...sort of, but she hadn't said a word. Because as much as she hated her weakness, the truth was that the heat of his skin against hers was making her feel like she was floating off the ground.

He pulled her close and let his breath whisper against her forehead. For a second, she was so tempted to close her eyes and fall into him that she had to grope sideways until her hand braced itself against the wall. Unbelievable. She was going to discipline herself with extra training every day as soon as she was no longer stationed at the palace.

"Do you want me to stop this?" he asked quietly, and her eyes widened at the slow, careful question that hummed across her cheek. He was holding her close with their fingers still laced together between them, and now he pressed the whole back of her hand against his chest until his warmth sank all the way down to her bones. "Because I'll stop if you want me to, Anzi. If that's what you really want."

Her lips twitched. What—where was this coming from? Where had the infuriatingly self-assured man gone, and who was this man who pressed her against him with such tender caution, yearning but hesitant? No, not hesitant. Questioning. She didn't recognize him at all. The surprised thrill of it had her staring back at him in silence, forgetting to reply. It was another moment before she realized he was waiting for an answer, and she immediately cursed herself for being so entranced that she had simply been waiting for him to say something else. Anything, just more. His voice, soothing but rough underneath, like crystal formations glassing over rough stone...

She tore her eyes away from his and shook her head, scowling. How was she supposed to answer that? Of course she didn't want him to stop. Wait, but of course she did. Well...

Damn it, he knew what he was doing to her. There was no way he didn't. She was supposed to hate this and turn her nose up at it, scoff at something as trivial and meaningless as physical attraction. But every time he drew close, every time he touched her, and now every time he would be holding her hand like this—she would turn a little more into a sentimental, helpless sap with no independence, no strength at all.

"Let's just go," she grumbled, suddenly in a far more sour mood than she had been before he pulled her aside. She still wasn't angry like he thought she was, but how could she not be embarrassed and frustrated at —how affected she was. If anyone else could see her right now, they would laugh themselves sick, holding their bellies and cackling at her soft mind.

But she couldn't help it. This man she had met for the first time yesterday had become...something immense, terrifying yet captivating, intimidating yet irresistible. She didn't want anyone to see her so weak, yet right now, she wanted nothing more than to splay her fingers against his chest and feel his heart beating there She didn't even know him, how was it she could crave him as if she'd been waiting for him for a lifetime?

"Anzi?"

"I'm fine. I just want to go."

Instead of relenting and moving them away from the wall, he reached up and brushed his knuckle against her cheek, her jaw. His thumb ran a slow, gentle line down the side of her face, too, and she almost leaned into his touch. "I'm still learning you," he said softly. "I'm sorry it's taking me longer than I thought it would."

She was hypnotized by every little thing he did now, by his voice that hid something she didn't quite understand but whose secret undertones she could hear, by the way his eyes looked so starved and sated and bruised all at once as he swallowed her up in his golden gaze, by his touch that somehow felt so good and right and yet not enough as he trailed callused lines down her jaw, to her neck, to the curve of her shoulder just before it disappeared under her leather guards.

But she heard what he had said, and she paid attention to the strange words. Her eyes narrowed in questioning suspicion. "Taking longer than you thought it would?" she repeated. Some might have thought the words innocuous, meaningless, full of soft feeling but nothing substantial. But there was something buried inside them that he wasn't showing her, a corner of a hidden chest. She was missing something. Something important. "What are you talking about?" she demanded. "What do you mean?"

But he didn't explain. He lingered for a moment longer as she breathed him in, uneasy and ecstatic and yet somehow blissfully blank. And here was more proof she had become weak in the head thanks to him: she was too afraid of repeating herself and insisting on answers lest she lose the moment. Lest she lose—him.

And then it was over. Without another word, he stepped away from the wall and pulled her along behind him. And this time, she only tried half as hard to hide their joined hands.

Maybe a little less.

THIS WAS the rear of the palace. The last two days were the first she had ever spent within the walls at all, so this was also the first time she had come out here. And gods, was it beautiful. The decorative stone walls lining the massive garden full of strange, beautiful flowers; the man-made stream rippling and burbling out of a spring in the center; the flat, circular stones tracing various paths through the maze of clustered, slender trees with leaves that glowed various soft shades even under such bright sunlight—enchanting, all of it.

But none of that was what Kai had brought her to see. She knew it as soon as her eyes fell upon the wooden cart off to the side, parked on the grass between four guards who looked ready to tear apart any man who dared approach. That was probably the point, of course, but Kai moved toward it with no hesitation. He was still holding her hand, too, but thankfully, the guards seemed to take their jobs too seriously to pay attention to that.

It must be some rich merchant's cart, Anzi thought, until she drew close to the side of the cart and stood there in stunned, paralyzed amazement. Impossible. Unthinkable. She had to be imagining things, utterly. But if she wasn't—these were no mere merchant's riches. Not even a king's riches. These were beyond anything she could have ever imagined.

Dragon mementos!

Full claws, both rough and polished. Scintillating scales of every shape and size. Bony spines that might line a dragon's neck frill. Dragon mementos—but how! Entire kingdoms would go to war for even a fraction of these priceless treasures, the Empire included.

But it wasn't admiration she felt as she surveyed the trove. It was dull horror and a creeping dread, a sickness in her gut that threatened to make her retch. "Are...are these yours?" she asked. She didn't dare look up at Kai as she continued to stare at everything, eyes wide and unblinking.

"Yes."

"You...hunt dragons? They exist in the wild somewhere, still?" A faint memory tickled at the back of her mind. *Remember,* something whispered to her, *remember.* But she had no idea what it was she was supposed to recall, and more than that, she was afraid to. Afraid to think that at long last, she had finally seen something of Kai that made her want to run away from him instead of moving closer.

Hadn't he criticized this nation, her people, for their hand in the extermination of the wild dragon? Hadn't it been just yesterday that she had been angry, defensive—and guilty, yes, she would finally admit it— because of his accusations? But here he was, and these without a doubt belonged to him as he stood there surveying the pile. Souvenirs collected from dragon remains, from every part of their body from spines to bones to claws to teeth...

"I'd sooner die than ever harvest a dragon." Kai's voice was flat, hard, unforgiving. It wasn't aimed at her, and yet she inhaled sharply at the hostility simmering under his words. "Just as soon as I would kill a man for attempting it."

Relief flooded her like an ice storm, chilling the hot dread that had been pooling in every part of her. She still didn't understand, though, as she continued to stare at the contents of the large cart. "So, then...where did these come from?"

"Passed down in my family. There are no more dragons in the wild, not like before. These are...precious."

His hand twitched around hers, a compulsive jerk that had her turning her head to look up at him. And there, she saw something shining in his eyes that made him look—haunted, as he stared at the contents of the cart. Pain.

"Are you trading these to the Empire?" she asked. "All of this?"

"Not yet. The Emperor wanted proof we have dragons. We had already brought these with us out of the desert, knowing it would come to that."

"He wants to introduce these to the market here? There'll be chaos. It'll be out of control. We have discipline, but this will drive people insane."

"And yet he wants it all anyway."

The reply was so sharp and cold that she floundered for a brief moment, taken aback by the simmering anger she sensed in his voice. She didn't understand. Didn't understand anything, not even a little. But then again, it wasn't her job to understand. She was to listen, obey.

Was this why His Excellency had asked her to keep watch over the chieftain? To seduce him and make him pliable, manipulable? Kai's fingers were still tangled tightly with hers, giving her no hope of escape, and the sickening sensation in her stomach grow tenfold.

Maybe what she was doing was wrong, a small voice murmured inside her. Maybe she should just tell Kai. Warn him that her duty was to capture his mind, turn him toward the Empire's interests. Before, she had thought perhaps there was some greater purpose behind it all, but if it was all purely for luxuries and riches and nothing else, treasures for the wealthy who already had so much more than the poor, what good would a mountain of dragon remains do for those who had nothing?

The dead should stay at rest, she thought. In peace.

Wait, what was she thinking? She blinked and shook her head, knocking away the swirling doubts. Gods on high and dark hells, she had nearly lost her mind for an instant. With a quick stiffening of her shoulders, she straightened her thoughts, her back, and most importantly, her priorities.

"I hope you and His Excellency can come to some agreement," she said, voice firm and final. "Something that will help both of you, I mean."

He turned his head to meet her gaze, and a lump rose in her throat at the long look he gave her. What was that expression he wore? That dull sheen in his eyes that made her feel—guilty?

She looked away. She had a sneaking suspicion that the thing she was seeing in his face was none other than disappointment. And somehow, that cut her more deeply than any insult, any wound. The silence stretched on, and she withered bit by bit—

"Your Emperor is hosting a grand gala in three days," Kai said, breaking the quiet at long last with the abrupt announcement. "I want you to come with me."

She stirred. He wasn't angry? She could have sworn... "I haven't heard about it, but I'm sure I can. His Excellency tasked me with guarding you whenever you aren't in his company."

His grip tightened around her hand. "Not as my guard," he said simply. "I want you to come as my companion."

Companion....Companion? What—

"I'd like to see what you look like out of your armor for once," he added, and she caught a hint of a terrible, terrible smirk teasing at the corner of his mouth. "Anything besides that. Something that will let me see a different side of you."

A different side of her? Ha! She only had one side, how laughable—

"...or at least something that will let me see...a little more of you."

All lingering worries evaporated in an instant, and with an indignant noise, she tried to tug her hand out of his grasp again to no avail. "Kai! You're being very—" She struggled to find the right word that would encapsulate his outrageous brazenness without being overtly insulting.

"Yes," he said with a slow smile. "Yes, I am."

Anzi looked elsewhere with a huff, and as she turned away, missed the pained light that flashed in his eyes.

27

"You're late."

"I'm early."

"Not to me." Bastien pointed down the Cave's sloping passageway. The scant light of the moon faded as the woven grass cover rustled into place, and the growing darkness made his sharp smile look even more sinister.

Anzi followed the direction of his jabbing finger without another word. She had no time to waste on him. She was here on a mission, one more important than any argument no matter how irritating he was, especially since Bastien had laughed in her face last night when she spoke of soul bonds and a singular *meant-to-be* waiting for her in one of the dragon eggs. He had said she was being ridiculous, but if it made her feel better to think that way, he didn't care so long as they found a good steed for her. *Steed,* as if dragons weren't noble creatures with great intelligence even if it was different from that of humans. She knew it. She saw it in Colonel Bisset's dragon every time she found herself at the center of the creature's heavy gaze, something in the energy behind its eyes. A mind as great and massive as a force of nature with a reach that exceeded any mortal man's, something grand. Irreplaceable.

"I'm telling you that you've got it wrong," Bastien hummed when they reached the egg chamber. "Look at all of these beautiful beasts-to-be.

You're telling me that you'd be satisfied with just one? No, girl. Open your mind."

"What? What are you on about."

"Well, when your dragon dies, what's your plan, my dear Anzi? Are you going to give it up and throw yourself on the pyre? Die with it? Give up everything you've reached, the pinnacle of the mountain you've spent all this time climbing."

She scowled. "I haven't even found the one that will hatch for me yet, and you're already thinking about its death," she snapped. "But when we go out into battle, I'll be fighting alongside him. I won't let my partner die so easily. I'll put my life on the line to protect his, just as he would do for me."

He laughed again, even bending over and leaning against the wall as he wheezed. "Oh, dear girl," he gasped. "I'm not talking about death in battle. How many men do you know who can defeat a dragon, much less one with a rider to control its power? I'm talking about when it ages and withers, which will happen no matter what. And when it dies, you'll be left standing alone. What'll you do then? Hm?"

She stared. "Dragons are immortal."

"Not these. We're the immortal ones, Anzi, not them."

Her eyes narrowed when he burst into another peal of echoing laughter. "Explain," she demanded.

He wiped a tear from his eye and straightened his back. There was still a chuckle trailing from his sharp mouth, little breathy whistles that made her hair stand on end. "Later, you'll know. But we have work to do now and an egg to charm."

No matter what she said, he remained immovable, insisting only that in time, she would learn. The sooner she found a dragon to hatch for her, the sooner she would get the answers she wanted, he said, and made a sweeping gesture at the room and its unborn inhabitants. "You pick. Follow your instincts. The ones that are receptive will grow on your magic, and the one you favor most, you'll keep."

"My magic?"

"Your essence. Your spirit, the wild blood that flows in you. That's what it takes to master a dragon, girl, haven't you figured it out yet?"

No, she hadn't. And she still hadn't even now. Wild blood a requisite for bonding with a dragon? Ridiculous. Everyone knew mixed-bloods had always been on the lower rungs of society and still were even after the passage of the equality laws. It made no sense that being one was a requirement of joining the highest echelon of the Imperial military. The prestige of the Premier Guard would never have become so lauded if the people had known.

"You'll pick these things up," Bastien assured with a pat on her shoulder. He let his hand fall away when she responded with a belligerent one-armed shrug. "Just know you're here because you're meant to be, and in a few weeks, you'll be carrying a reptile vassal in your arms. Come on."

He gave her no room to argue. With a sudden shove that she failed to dodge, he made her stumble toward the closest egg. "Look for the power inside, keep at it with each one until you feel it. If anything tirs, tell me, and I'll set it aside. Remember, you have to wake it up—the sleeping energy that holds still until it's called."

Sleeping energy, she scoffed inwardly. That sounded like harebrained kook magic, romantic and mysterious and nonsensical, the sort she especially distrusted. No, this should be about soul bonds, the deep, primordial thing that existed under the soul and inside it. But of course there was no point saying so. Bastien wasn't a believer.

And common sense said he was right. He was the one who bred the mighty dragons of the Premier Guard, the secret keeper, the one who had spent two centuries on this mission and hid in the shadows while the rest of his comrades took to the skies. She still couldn't wrap her mind around it, the amount of knowledge and wisdom he must possess, the perpetually laughing Bastien. How could someone like him be so privileged? All his disparaging talk of dragons who no longer possessed the immortality of tales of old, of riders who mastered their dragons rather than becoming one with them. Pets, beasts of burden, weapons. That was all he treasured them for. His fondness was patronizing and superior, not respectful. Not honorable. He was wrong. Everything about it was wrong.

So maybe it was wishful thinking that made her disbelieve him so passionately. But if it was, so be it. She didn't care what he said. She knew deep inside what she believed, and that if she searched carefully and listened inward, she would find the fate that had been waiting for her. This was what she had been striving for all her life, to find her dragon, to answer her calling. Ever since that night—

"Not like that, girl, focus. Focus! Of course you won't be able to feel anything if you don't put your back into it. Are you a soldier or not?"

He had never been so stern, and she unconsciously obeyed his sharp command. And then it happened: when she wrapped her hands firmly around the shell, palms pressing in and every finger molded to the hard surface, a spectral warmth rushed into her skin. It sank deep, deep, until it dived down and touched the very center of her like a seed sprouting under the sun. It happened so fast she didn't realize it at first. She simply stood in place, staring at the egg until the man ordered her to move on to the next one.

Wait, she was tempted to say. This one. She had felt something. Could still feel it now. Maybe this was the waking of the *sleeping energy*. But just to be sure, she obeyed and moved on without a word to the next egg. It might have been a fluke or a figment of her overexcited, hopeful imagination.. The chances that the first egg she touched was receptive were ridiculously unlikely. Bastien had explained yesterday that he expected no more than a handful at best out of the hundreds that littered the room. It would be an arduous process to find them, he had promised. This must have been a mistake. Just to be sure, she would try the next before she said anything.

Except something was wrong. Something was wrong and strange and incomprehensible. Because as Bastien babbled on about each egg and its particular breeding and what kind of wonders he expected from the dragons that lay dormant inside them—Anzi progressed from one to the next, heart thundering louder with each egg she lingered over.

Because the soul-touching energy, the waking flicker of faint life inside, the seed of power and passion and a living urge...She could feel it from them all.

Every single one.

She remained silent. Instinct commanded it even though she didn't know why. There wasn't a single reason she could justify it with, not a one. And yet her mouth remained tightly shut as Bastien continued to prattle on at her side. *Tell him,* she tried to order herself. *This is your duty. Your responsibility. This is a good thing, something to be glad about. Why are you afraid?*

And yet her pulse throbbed with such ferocity every time her lips twitched that she gave up on the third try. So she said nothing as she moved from egg to egg, silently marveling at how each life inside felt so astonishingly different. Some seeped into her skin like the rays of a rising sun, warm light cutting through morning mist and drawing up the dew from the grass. Some lanced into her like needles of ice, whipping through her veins and filling her up like a biting, glacial wind. Still others dripped under her skin and flooded it like a thin film of rainfall over stone paths, like shadows spreading through the wood on little pitter-pattering feet as the sun set over the horizon.

All this, and she said nothing. Not one word.

"Nothing yet?" Bastien asked after she had acquainted herself with every dragon egg in the chamber. "I didn't expect much, but to not find even one is a little disheartening. No matter. We have plenty of time, they won't be going anywhere. Tomorrow night and every night after that if needed, we try again."

She didn't know why she said what she did next. "Maybe I'm not right for this. Maybe you have the wrong rider."

But at that, all he did was laugh, and loudly. "Don't be dense. You have enough wild blood in you to drown me twice over. You'll see. I suspect it's because you're young—never had a child in here before."

"I'm not a child."

"You are. Anyhow, go on back up and see yourself out. No time to babysit."

It was probably the first time since they had met that she had failed to rise to his baiting. She realized only too late her mistake when he narrowed his eyes at her.

"You look sick," he remarked. "What's the matter with you?"

"This was tiring. I still think you're wrong, you know. One of them will choose me in the end, not the other way around."

"Sure, sure. Believe what you want."

Relief flooded her in a tidal wave when he rolled his eyes and turned away. She was so tense she could hardly breathe, but this was what she excelled at, what she prided herself in. Control. Composure. Stability. She needed time to get away and think, that was all, and then everything would become clear to her. But just as she began to move back to the chamber's entrance, her gaze fell on the giant, misshapen, mottled egg settled into the far corner by itself. She'd nearly forgotten about it, the so-called Prince Bastard.

"That one. Why didn't you have me try to wake it?"

Bastien turned to her with curious, raised eyebrows before transferring his attention to the thing in question. When he saw what it was she spoke of, he snorted and shook his head. "Don't worry about that. I already told you it's a lost cause. Besides, even if it makes it out of its shell somehow, it'll be a freak of nature. Better off dead, girl. Leave it be."

"But—"

"Go. I'm tired of you." He waved her off and she had no choice but to obey. With a grinding of her teeth and one last glance back at the Prince, the lone dragon egg cast off and languishing in the dark corner, she beat a reluctant retreat.

But there was something about it, she thought to herself later in bed. The dragon egg Bastien dismissed as an abomination, the Prince Bastard that was so large and strangely shaped. He dismissed it, mocked it. But if every egg large and small could have a presence, a life, a soul that sang or whispered or shouted, why not that one? How lonely it must be, a voice murmured inside her, to be damned to rot and die because it was unlike the others. Bastien with his disdain for the ugly and his obsession with creating the perfect specimen, the perfect dragon, when hundreds of his so-called creations lay dormant underground, likely never to hatch for hundreds of more years.

Anzi turned over in her bed, too agitated to sleep. There were only a few hours until dawn, and she hadn't slept the night previous, either. She should rest. She needed to. But as the moon slowly disappeared in the lightening sky sliver by sliver, all she could do was stare at the ceiling and think.

Dragons. Dragon riders. Immortality, immortality lost…Sleeping energy and souls waking up like a breath blown upon a dim ember. Touching each egg and sensing the life inside, every single one—and moreover, her instinctive reluctance to admit it.

What was happening to her? What was happening to the world that she thought she knew? She barely recognized either one anymore. She could almost believe that if she tried to take a single step outside, she would find the earth had removed itself from her feet, replaced by a hanging emptiness like a gaping gorge. Things were changing so fast she couldn't keep up. She—was afraid. In a swift motion, she dragged the covers over her head and stared out at the fuzzy silhouettes that seeped through the fabric like faded ghosts. It was almost morning, she realized suddenly. When had that happened? When was the exact moment that night turned to day, and how could it have happened so quickly, without warning?

Sleep was lost to her anyway, so she jumped up and headed for the women servants' baths. It was early enough that it wouldn't be crowded yet with the palace maids, so she took a little extra time to try to wash away all her anxieties. It was a new day. She had responsibilities. So for now, she needed to keep a clear head and handle them. When she returned to her room, she found a familiar face waiting for her already.

"Letti? Why are you here? It's too early."

"It's never too early to come see my savior," the pretty harem girl said with a pout and gestured at the door with a graceful flourish. "You won't make me leave, will you? Not after I came all this way."

"You're only one floor up."

"But…"

Anzi rolled her eyes. "Get in, then," she said and pushed open the door. "But no visiting the market today."

"The thought never even occurred to me! Really, I mean it." Letti blinked at her with wide, innocent eyes as she stepped inside. "You look exhausted. Would be a bad idea."

"Hm."

"…Are you all right?"

She frowned. Just get on with it, she wanted to snap, but she held herself back. She had vowed just yesterday to treat Letti with respect from now on, and her terrible mood had nothing to do with the woman now looking at her with growing concern and eyes that were becoming more sympathetic by the second. Damn it, but Anzi didn't need sympathy, and she didn't want it either.

"I'm fine."

"Are you?"

"I don't want to waste time. What are we doing today."

Letti gave her a long, silent look, so probing it almost made her break the stare. "Well, first of all, this," the woman announced, and took an abrupt step closer before enfolding her in her arms. Held captive in a sea of coral chiffon and lace, AnzI stood like a plank of wood, thoroughly stunned.

"…You're supposed to hug me back. Go on, you hopeless dolt." While still draped over her, Letti proceeded to reach down and pick her wrists up so she could wrap it around her own waist. "Like this."

What in dark hells—

"You've got on a face that says you're hurt," the woman said, quiet and soft, "but it's the kind of hurt that's secret and can't be shared. So this is the next best thing I can do for you."

Anzi sighed.

28

For the next three days, everything was an uncomfortable blur. For one, Anzi had let slip to Letti that there would be a gala or some such thing happening soon, not realizing that it would promptly send her into deep, long-lasting convulsions. Secondly, she was still diligently pretending she could sense no life in any of the dragon eggs whenever she and Bastien made their rounds. And there was the matter of Kai, who had unfortunately noticed there was something wrong with her and refused to leave her alone until she told him exactly what it was.

She couldn't tell him, obviously. Couldn't tell anyone. She had to keep this secret and guard it closely until she could figure out what to do next, until she figured out why she couldn't expel the lingering dread that plagued her from morning to night. Was it shock at all the gruesome things she had learned over the last several days? Maybe that was what it was. Poisonous disappointment, the sinking of her optimistic ideals into a miry swamp.

So she hid from Kai whenever she could. She couldn't avoid him during the afternoons after he concluded his trade negotiations with the Emperor and various advisors, but as soon as evening fell, she claimed fatigue and retired to her room. After that, even when he came wandering over and knocked on her door, she faked illness to could cut short their interactions as much as possible. That was an egregious violation of her express orders to get close to him, but sleepless nights and stressful days made her insubordinate attitude feel less criminal and more numb. She did the same with Letti, too, but the difference was that the harem girl got the message. Kai...didn't.

"Anzi."

His voice slidalong the walls of the hallway behind her, and she suppressed a wince before turning to face the chieftain. Letti had just left her room after a fruitless tutoring session on how to seduce men using suggestive body language, and Anzi had been hoping to sneak down to the baths for a relaxing soak before Kai came to find her. No such luck.

"Anzi," he said again upon reaching her. "Where are you going?" His voice was strong and soothing in equal parts, and something in the careful way he touched her shoulder made her ache deep inside. She didn't know how to describe it, didn't know if there was a way at all. But the gentle pull as he tried to bring her closer was as painfully sweet as honey taken raw, and she didn't know if she could withstand it.

She hated this. She hated that she didn't hate it.

She was exhausted, frustrated, and paranoid that at any moment, Bastien or the Emperor would send someone to behead her for deliberate sabotage. She was angry at herself for being so duplicitous and sneaky when she knew that wasn't who she was, and she was ashamed that instead of the strength she had always relied on, all she had now was a pathetic urge to keep her head down. Forget modesty—she had known from the beginning she was meant for greater heights. So what in hell was this? Slinking around like a guilty creature, no longer knowing what to believe or what direction to turn like a naked idiot caught out in a blinding blizzard. She'd never been so pathetic before. It made her furious.

"Going to the baths," she said. "I didn't realize you would be done so early."

"Tonight's the gala. Everyone wants to prepare."

"Are you going to prepare, too?"

"I already have everything I want."

When he cradled her face with his warm, strong hand, the heat of his palm sank deep inside her like a blade slicing to the quick. It was so sweet it hurt, the way ice could burn. And yet she couldn't step away. She didn't dare let this go, this pain that tasted so close to pleasure that she couldn't tell what it was she felt anymore.

She'd lost so much already, a faint voice whispered in the back of her mind. She'd given everything up to get this far. Her family, her friends, her happiness...Oza, too, whom she had sworn never to abandon. She'd given all of them up only to end up lost and alone. But Kai—he was with her still. He was holding her like this, close, warm. Tender and strong.

She didn't want to lose this too, even if she couldn't possibly understand how he made her feel this way. If only she could go back to the old days, simple days. Days that hadn't made her ask questions as painful as the bite of a knife.

"Come," said Kai, and he ran his thumb along her cheek before letting her go. He took her hand instead and pulled her along the corridor. She had no choice but to follow him. She had no desire but to follow him.

Just this once, she would let herself have what she wanted.

"Where are we going?" she asked, half-mumbling. She was so tired her mouth refused to move properly. Or was it because she was drunk on the guilty pleasure of his touch?

"My room."

Despite herself, her pulse quickened. "Why?"

"You don't want to?"

"That's not—I just want to know why."

"But you don't want to?"

"Don't ask me that," she said, and it wasn't until the words were out of her mouth that she realized her tone had betrayed an aggrieved, frustrated edge. She hadn't meant to let that show. With a hasty twitch, she tried to pull her hand out of his, a defensive reflexshe couldn't have explained even if she wanted to. But he held tight, fingers intertwining with hers so tightly they might as well be tangled.

"You're unhappy," he said as they walked. "And you've been more unhappy each time I see you."

"I have a lot of responsibilities."

"They make you miserable."

"They're still mine."

He said nothing to that, and was it shameful that she felt a rush of disappointment press into her from every direction? It was almost as if she had wanted him to disagree. Almost as if she thought he could relieve her of her burdens with a single word, a single defense. But of course that wasn't how it worked.

When they reached his room, a grand guest chamber with double doors, he shouldered one open and pulled her inside. Her heart throbbed in her chest with a little too much interest when he closed the door behind them, but strange: the electric thrill she knew she should be feeling wasn't there. Instead, it was replaced by something cooler, heavier, tainted with something tired and worn. That was what it was, she thought. She was just—tired. Too tired for all of this.

Her rambling, stumbling thoughts came to a sudden halt when she suddenly fell into all-encompassing warmth, and it took her a few blinking seconds to realize Kai had pulled her in and was holding her in a tight embrace. She was pressed against warm skin, hard muscle, and the smooth metal of his golden collar, and—oh, but they made all of her thoughts freeze in place, even the most terrible ones.

He was holding her, and she was standing there and accepting it. She blinked again.

"Do you trust me?" he asked, and his voice rumbled through his chest and into her body like heat waves shimmering off desert dunes. "Anzi?"

What was she supposed to say? The answer that would make him happy? She closed her eyes. "No," she said honestly. "I don't."

A twinge of pain stung her somewhere in the center of her chest, and for some strange reason, it felt—foreign. Like it came from both inside and outside of her at the same time, but that made no sense. She ignored it.

"I want you to trust me," he said. "I want you to need me."

Again, another twinge. She stirred in his arms, embarrassed by his words but also intrigued. No one had ever said these kinds of things to her. Why was he being this way? She had done nothing kind for him. Or was it because he knew she wanted him, too? Was it because she was already half-won over? She would slit her own throat before she asked, though. Even numb and exhausted and furious, she was present enough to control such stupid whimsies.

"What—Kai!"

He didn't stop. He continued pulling her toward his grand, plush bed, towing her along by the wrist despite her strangled protest. Was this happening? Now? She wasn't ready! In her head, she had been prepared for something like this, but wait—

No. No waiting. She couldn't and shouldn't object. This? This was easy. She had already done things so much more difficult, so much more unimaginable. She had lied to Bastien, put her life on the line by rebelling against the Emperor's wishes. Not just that, but now she was questioning everything around her from beginning to end, its fables and myths and legends that had always sparkled under the sun. Now that she knew the

Empire had a pitch-dark, chaos-seething underbelly, everything seemed tinged with rot and disappointment…

She said not a word as he peeled off her shoulder guards and the rest of her leather armor. Fine. This was fine. She was attracted to him, right? That would make it all the easier. It didn't matter that she wasn't ready for this. That wasn't important. She ought to consider herself lucky she was going to be bedded by the first man she had ever felt attracted to, which made her luckier than harem girls and most other women, too. This was fine.

This was fine…

It was strange, though, that he left her in her uniform, and even stranger that he did nothing but guide her onto his bed with careful but insistent, guiding hands. She sat back, silently obedient, but now she watched in undisguised curiosity as he pulled the covers away and positioned her bodily until she was completely under them. Then, to her amazement, he shucked off the golden collar around his shoulders and tossed it down the ground with a heavy clink. What! That was a priceless article, worth more than the value of most people's entire livelihoods. And he had just discarded it like trash.

The wonders continued when he slid under the covers next to her, and said nothing still even when he pulled her back against his chest and wrapped his arms around her. Her eyes remained wide open and fixed on the curved dome ceiling, wondering what was happening.

…And wondering how this could feel so right.

He was warm. Solid. Strong. It didn't cut through the suffocating fog blanketing her mind, but it took away the restless buzzing that had made it impossible for her to ever rest. The sharp sensation of pins and needles that had stolen sleep away from her every night dripped away like melting icicles, until soon, she was left only with deep, ocean-like warmth surrounding her on all sides.

"Rest," he murmured in her ear, and the deep rumble of his resonant voice was impossible to resist. "You need to rest. So rest."

She shouldn't. Rest was for the weak. She didn't need rest. She needed to figure out what to do next, that was what she needed to—

"Rest, Anzi."

Enfolded in his arms and pressed against his body, at long last, she finally let her eyes flutter closed.

29

When Anzi awoke, it was in utter confusion that she found herself wrapped in hard, solid arms and pressed back into a very bare chest. For several seconds, she had no recollection of how she had ended up in this unfamiliar bed with a man's face buried in her hair and his hands perilously close to dropping below her hips. But she certainly knew who said man was in an instant. There was no mistaking the intoxicating masculine scent she could never get out of her head.

Oh. Oh, that was right. He had pulled her into his bed and all but forced her to fall asleep against him. But how long ago? What time was it now? Her eyes widened in unadulterated shock when she realized it had to have been hours since. She was far too well-rested and soothed, and struggling still to rise out of the comfortable depths of delicious sleep even now. Wake up, she ordered herself, and she tried to pull out of Kai's embrace so she could jump off the bed and onto her feet. Sleeping in the middle of the day when she had no battle wounds or anything else to justify the greediness—when had she become so lazy!

"Go back to sleep."

Kai's voice, sleep-rough and deep, sent an involuntary shiver up her spine as he murmured into her hair. And of course he felt it—how could he not when he was so close? A fiery flush came over her cheeks when she heard—and felt—him chuckle, and it worsened when he pulled her back even harder against himself and began moving his lips against the back of her head.

"How long has it been?" she asked, voice tight as he shifted against her once more. "How long have I been sleeping."

"Not long. A couple of hours."

"Hours!"

"And still a few more before we need to leave. This is our time, remember? What does it matter if we spend it exploring the city or in bed?"

...He had a point, not that she would admit it aloud. Where they went every day was up to him, and if he chose to stay indoors, then she was supposed to guard him even still. Although lying together in bed with his fingers tracing sly circles on her arm did not constitute 'guarding' in any way whatsoever in her humble opinion.

"It bothers you," he said after a long moment. "You would rather not be here?"

She refused to tell him the truth, but if she said she would rather be elsewhere, he would know she was lying. Just knew he would. "I don't like sleeping during the day," she said instead. "It wastes daylight, and we have less of it every day the closer winter comes."

"Have you never relaxed like this?"

"Only when I need to?"

He chuckled. "Why does it sound like you're asking a question? And anyway, don't you feel better now?"

She didn't know what to say to that, so she chose that moment to gather all her willpower and wriggle out of his arms, ignoring the grumbling urge to stay exactly where she was. She had never been lazy in her life, and she had no plans to start now. He let her go without a fight this time, surprisingly—disappointingly?—and she was reattaching her shoulder guards a few seconds later with deft, practiced fingers. Nothing strange about putting her leathers back on, she wanted to think, but somehow, doing this in some man's bedroom felt so illicit. And all she'd done was sleep...

She decided then and there to say nothing of this to Letti. There would be no point explaining that nothing more questionable had happened. The woman would lose her mind anyway.

"Then where do you want to go today?" Kai asked behind her, and the rustling of sheets told her he was sliding out of bed as well. Her eyes darted to the ground where his shoulder collar lay in a heap, and she hesitated before bending down to pick it up. The instant she turned around with it in hand, however, she promptly regretted it. The way he stared at her with that lingering, knowing smile made the innocent, even helpful action suddenly feel terribly intimate.

She hastily reached over to place it on his side of the bed. "I don't have a preference. It's wherever you wish to go."

"Maybe I wish to go where you want."

"I've lived here long enough to know every part of it already," she said. "There's no particular place I want to explore. But if you're not interested in visiting the Quarter Art again or the central plaza, there's another place visitors like to stop by. Animal trading is prolific here, and—"

"I'm not partial to animal zoos. But now that I think about it, I remember seeing a spire in the distance. Very tall, gray. I couldn't make out much else. What is that?"

She knew immediately. Her stomach twisted. "That's the Tower. The mages live there."

"Your magic practicers live separately from everyone?"

"For everyone's protection, theirs and the people's. And the isolation helps them focus without distractions."

"Distractions," he repeated as he dropped the collar over his head. "I guess that means we wouldn't be welcome if we tried to visit."

She hesitated. She didn't want to go, but the truth was... "You're an important guest of the Emperor. There's almost no place in the city you would be unwelcome. And most visiting dignitaries from both annexed and unattached kingdoms do go to see the mages at some point."

"Unattached? Interesting way of saying 'free.'"

"We don't enslave them. A number of domains even joined us willingly."

"But some didn't."

She turned back around and pretended to adjust her guards a little more to hide her discomfort. A few days ago, she would have been seething at the not-so-subtle, critical observation of the Empire's practice of military conquest, but something had dulled inside her since then. Instead of righteous fury, she felt only a rumbling unease, and she could think of nothing to say in defense. She was even more tired than she had thought.

"Will you show me to the Tower?"

Her gaze fell to the floor as she finished tugging on the last strap. That bothered her even more: he had clearly changed the subject to spare her.

It stung to think he might even feel sorry for her now when not a week ago, she had been vehemently insisting the Empire was faultless in all it did. "We can go," she said. "They'll likely put on a show of some sort for you. They're always ready to entertain."

"Entertain? Are they performers?"

"It's...a demonstration of their capabilities."

"Ah. A show of force, is it?"

She patted down her leathers one last time and turned around. "That's right."

"How long has it been since you were there last? Do you normally escort your 'dignitaries' there?"

He sounded almost teasing now, and she rolled her eyes. "I've never escorted one before," she said. "But it's been—"

"So I'm your first."

She shot him an unimpressed look. "Sir."

He grinned. "You look especially beautiful today. Please don't be angry with me."

She shook her head. It was hard enough reconciling his important status with the casual informality of their strange relationship. Figuring out how to navigate his nonchalant flirtations and playfulness made her head hurt. "I haven't been there in a long time," she said loudly while giving him a pointed glower to make sure he knew she was changing the subject back on purpose. "But I'm happy to take you there. Seeing as how you're an especially valued guest of the Emperor, I'm sure they've actually been waiting impatiently for you. It's just that they're not allowed to ask anyone to visit."

"Interesting. Am I so special?"

She gave him a long look. "I can name on one hand the number of people I know of who have ever been in his direct presence, excluding his advisors." And the Premier Guard, she supposed, but she didn't want to think about them right now. "You've seen his face, know his name, and have spoken with him on equal terms. That's more than most anyone will ever achieve in a lifetime."

"His name? It's secret?"

She had to remind herself that this was a man who had no knowledge of their ways. Not only that, he was cooped up in the palace whenever he wasn't with her. It shouldn't be surprising he knew so little. "Kai, when we met in the throne room, that was the first time I'd ever seen His Excellency's face, heard his voice, and learned his name. You knew him well before I did."

He stared at her, and she stared back. "I've never known a leader to keep himself a secret from his people," he said. "You have a strange way of doing things here."

She shrugged and gestured at the door. "We protect our treasures. And the Emperor is the greatest of them all. Would you like to go see the Tower now?"

He must have known she had changed the subject yet again on purpose. But all he did was give her a small smile, and the tight, surprised expression on his face softened as he continued to watch her.

"Of course," he said. "And tell me more on the way."

PEOPLE STARED, but that was unavoidable. Anzi drew eyes with her distinctive fringer features, but that was nothing compared Kai's reception. From the moment they left the palace—with an official letter vouching for passage this time—he was subjected to dozens of stares at all times. Several people even changed direction just to follow them, and Kai threw brief half-glances over his shoulder whenever someone tagged along a little too closely on his heels. But he didn't care, it seemed, or at least not enough to demand they all scatter.

And if he wanted to, he could have. As she walked on the stone path alongside him, she was all too aware of his imposing stature, the broad physical presence of him that she hadn't truly appreciated until now. It bothered her that she hadn't noticed it, not fully, but it bothered her even more that she did notice it now. Especially since that awareness heightened every time she peeked at him out of the corner of her eye and glimpsed his wide, strong shoulders. The memory of being pressed into him in his bed kept resurfacing like a stubborn piece of bobbing driftwood. He saw it, too, which was the worst part, and he would try to catch her gaze every time he caught her. She spent the entirety of the walk in a cold sweat.

Anzi breathed a sigh of relief when they finally reached the outer perimeter of the Tower. She had offered to call up a rickshaw so they could ride the rest of the way to their destination, but Kai had declined with a slow smile and a remark about how he was enjoying the scenery. The way he was staring at her, she decided it was better not to ask him what 'scenery' he was talking about, and so she had been forced to endure the entirety of the boiling tension between them while they traveled on foot.

But they were here now, so she could breathe at last. Kai turned his attention away from her and to the tower reaching into the sky on the other side of the grassy courtyard. "I thought so," he said. "That's heat-glassed stone. The base, at least."

Anzi turned to him, surprised. "You know it?"

"Of course. Before the dragons were wiped out, it wasn't so rare. Now, you can only acquire them from the volcanoes to the far south."

Dragons again. She nearly winced, reminded afresh of everything she had wanted to put out of her mind. But there would be no avoiding the subject with Kai, not forever. Now that she knew his ancestral roots had valued dragons so much that they had entire treasure troves of their bejeweled remains, she could understand his passion for them.

Didn't make it any easier. After the time she had spent with Bastien every night this week, listening to him speak of fearsome, noble dragons as if they were no better than livestock to be bred, she now struggled with the guilt of knowing Kai had been right. His criticism of the Empire and its cruelty to the once-prosperous, powerful species, the eagerness to destroy those they couldn't subjugate—it was true, wasn't it?

Maybe not all of it...she hoped. Hoped she wasn't simply closing her eyes to unthinkable things so she could keep believing only what she wanted to believe. Just like everyone else.

And even now, she hid. She wasn't ready. Not yet.

"Anzi?"

She pretended she had been staring at the Tower's base across the way and jerked her chin his way. "Legend says that dragons made it," she said. "Or the obsidian and other glass-stone portions, at least. And then the Emperor had his men build the rest of the Tower on top of that."

"This was before the dragons were killed? They were alive?"

She shook her head. "The dragons that survived the Purge. There were four of them that the Emperor's First Guards bonded with. That was the first name of the Premier Guard, by the way, before they became known as riders. Those four dragons and His Excellency's, it's said that they gifted the base of the Tower here to show their gratitude to their human partners."

"What a story."

She had nothing to say. The sarcasm in his voice as loud as any bell, and he was right. It was condescending, patronizing, an utter lie. Everyone knew it was untrue, but everyone chose to pretend to believe it because—it was nice. Ever-so-grateful dragons bequeathing a work of art unto the Empire's people, a gift. "Not a good one," she said in a low voice, but she hastened to change the subject when Kai's gaze sharpened on her face. No doubt he was surprised at her remark, but she didn't want to confront that right now. "Look, one of the mages, there."

Perfect timing. An old man with a long, white beard trailing from his chin to his chest hurried across the grass to meet them, blue and white robes billowing with each step. There was a staff in his hand with a ruby-red sphere embedded in the top of it, glinting in the afternoon light.

"The Magisien Abelard," she began to say in the way of both a greeting and an introduction, but the elderly mage had no interest in her. With a rude, dismissive nod and flicking gesture, he turned with eager enthusiasm to Kai instead.

"Gods be praised," he proclaimed in a quavering old-man voice that had somehow become even more grating than the last time she had seen him three years ago. "The man of the dragon hoard himself. Come, come. We have been expecting you."

She was about to cast Kai a meaningful look—*I told you so*—when a sharp, searing sensation cut straight through her chest. With a flinch, she clutched at it in a reflexive attempt to stop whatever it was that had just pierced her, only to find nothing there. She made sure of it with one more pat. Nothing. And yet she could feel it buried inside her still. What was this?

"The dragon hoard?"

Kai's voice brought her to her senses. Her eyes darted back up to his face at the frigid words, and the expression there reminded her of the very first day they had met. It was a little like the one he had worn when she had shown him Colonel Bisset's dragon, and come to think of it, she had felt this burning sensation then, too, several times. But Magisien Abelard noticed nothing at all, and he released a screeching peal of laughter as he gestured back toward the Tower. "You're quite famous already among my esteemed peers!" he exclaimed. "Oh, yes. One of us was there at the palace a few days ago when you brought in your treasures among treasures, truly a marvelous sight if he can be believed. I only wish I could see it with my own eyes! And have a claw or two, perhaps."

Kai's face became even more rigid, and he fell into a storm-dark silence.

Anzi stared, wondering if the mention of his 'hoard' alone had really made such a change come over him, and so swiftly. But Abelard was already turning to leave, so she clamped her hand over Kai's wrist and tugged on it in a silent urge to follow. He turned his head and looked at her, golden eyes lingering a touch too long. But the uncomfortable shiver down her back was well worth the trade. The dangerous shadow of quiet wrath melted from his face, twitch by twitch, until he sighed and surrendered. Without another word, he moved to follow the chortling, oblivious mage toward the Tower's grand entrance.

Once through the heavy double doors between the posted guards, Anzi hesitated and let her hand slip away from his wrist with an uncomfortable grimace. Just before she could escape, Kai caught and captured her fingers between his with a squeeze. He gave her a sidelong look, a curious one, before pulling her along behind him. It happened so quickly she didn't have a chance to give him a warning, wide-eyed glare; she had to follow him if she didn't want to fall on her face. But this wasn't like back at the palace where there were empty hallways to take refuge in or in the market where the crowd was too thick for anyone to stare. Here, any milling mage loitering inside their tower home could espy Kai's brazen displays of affection.

At least the corridors were mostly deserted for the moment. She hadn't been here in a long time, but she knew well their routines. It was still the afternoon, and the mages would be in classes and training. But it wouldn't be long before they filed out, all of them.

Her stomach lurched, and Kai glanced back at her again with a worried expression. Seriously, could he read her mind? Ridiculous. With a quick twist of her wrist, a maneuver she usually reserved for disarming opponents, she wrested her hand out of his grip and looked away, none too eager to catch his gaze.

She had been nervous about this. She hadn't wanted to admit it. Not to him and not to herself. But now that she was here on the Tower's doorstep with Abelard ordering the heavy doors open, she could no longer avoid reality.

"What's wrong?" Kai murmured. "Tell me."

No. She shook her head, unwilling. How could she? Oza—he might not even come down from his quarters in the upper spire anyway. She hoped not. They hadn't spoken in years, and they led their own separate lives. Too separate. It was enough for her to look in the direction of the Tower's silhouette in the distance and send letters letting him know what she was doing, where she was going. Even if the last time she had sent one was...

She quashed the guilt as hard as she could. She shouldn't worry about coming face to face with her younger brother right now. If anything, the Magisien body had wanted to keep them apart for years and probably never even let him know she had come today.

"This way," said Abelard. "Do you enjoy great and wondrous magics, O Chieftain Kaizat-Amun of the desert?"

A theatrical streak. Anzi sighed while Kai rolled his shoulders in a shrug. "I'll have to see it to know," he said, and smiled down at her with a question in the curve of his lips.

She didn't answer.

30

"This is where the understudies train the apprentices," said Abelard. "There aren't enough masters in the Magisien body, so we delegate what we can."

So many explanations. After the latest long-winded speech from Abelard in front of several dozen adolescents, by now, Kai must have mastered the art of tuning him out, a vital skill Anzi too possessed. She believed in the great strength and glory of the Imperial City—even now despite recent doubts—but she didn't put on performances for its sake. The elderly mage, on the other hand, had waxed poetic about the storied history of the Empire's mage class and its renown throughout the land for the last half-hour.

No one liked his speeches. Anzi was an outsider, but the practiced, dead-eyed stares of all the students at their desks were proof enough. Oza hadn't liked him either. At least, he hadn't...the last time they had spoken.

"And for the chieftain's pleasure, we will be going down and doing some demonstrations. Up, everyone."

Kai looked like he was about to say that nothing would bring him greater displeasure, but Anzi shot him a knowing look that stilled him. Abelard was powerful but even more sensitive. Kai wouldn't bear the consequences of offending him—she would. Abelard might even try to strip her of the assignment of being Kai's personal guard and have someone else escort him instead.

For reasons that only partially overlapped with a sense of duty, Anzi did not like that idea.

Several minutes later, they were back on the ground floor and in the courtyard, on the other side of the Tower now. The students had all filed down the steps and onto the grass in their white-trimmed, dark blue robes, looking truly like an army as they arranged themselves in formation on the grass. Their right forearms were folded over their left as they stood, silent and still.

"What are they doing?" asked Kai.

She leaned over, voice low so as not to disturb the ceremony. "They're about to do the salute. You'll notice they're facing the direction of the Imperial Palace."

"The salute?"

She wouldn't have to explain. Just then, every one of the mages opened their mouths and began reciting the Oath as one. The words were so ingrained in her memory from her own years of schooling that she couldn't help the nostalgic smile that curved her mouth.

...to serve is freedom...

...forever loyal, forever true...

...Fealty to the Empire and all it means for the great people of...

...joined to the spirit...

...we live to serve.

Patches of the Oath trickled into her ears while the rest floated on the breeze like a fluttering leaf. When they finished, their arms were down at their sides again, and now Anzi could see some of them beginning to chatter, excited. They liked demonstrations. Most of them were children or adolescents, some barely older than toddlers, and they relished the opportunity for play. Forever cooped up in the Tower, this passed for entertainment.

"What was that?" asked Kai.

"What was what?"

"The chanting."

"Oh, that's not chanting." She shook her head. "The Oath of the People, or just the Oath. It's something children learn to recite from when they're very young."

"Children?"

He looked stunned. Why? "It's not as long as you might think," she told him and crossed her arms over her chest with a smile. "It's harder *not* to memorize it when you hear it so often. Every day at minimum and sometimes more—like these demonstrations in front of foreign dignitaries so they can impress. And you'd have years to learn it properly, anyway. Even as a fringer, when I moved to the Imperial City, I started formal schooling at the age of ten. The rest who live there and in other sanctioned cities would already know it by heart by the age of...five? Six? The younger, the better."

She watched his face, wondering why he looked so appalled. What was wrong with him?

"You have...children swearing fealty to the Empire," he said slowly. "Children who don't even know the meaning of what they're saying."

"Of course they know. They're children, not animals."

"They don't know what it means to swear fealty," he insisted as Magisien Abelard began lecturing again somewhere behind them. "You have children making an oath when they have no idea what they're even making the oath to."

She knew this tone. Instantly, she bristled, but kept her voice calm and controlled. "Does that bother you?"

"It explains a lot."

"And what's that supposed to mean."

He didn't answer, and a hot prickle of defensive anger crawled over her skin. He hated everything. He hated the Empire, hated the Emperor, hated the people, hated everything that wasn't his. Well, not everything was about him.

"It's a show of solidarity," she said. "What's the alternative when they grow up? Are they going to desert and defect to some other kingdom? Showing and professing loyalty now does no harm. Children go on and grow up just the same as they would anywhere else, except with more discipline...because of things like this. Like I said, solidarity. And discipline. It prepares them for when they're Selected to go into their respective lines of Service."

"So those are their only choices. Either chant their undying servitude to a kingdom they don't even know, as babes, or don't and become traitors?"

"What's so troubling about this?" she demanded. "Even if you take issue with training young children to pay their respects to the kingdom that brought their families prosperity, these mages are in their adolescent years. They've been serving it for years now. They know the land and its people and what it means to be loyal. "

"Do they? Do *you* know your Empire?"

She recoiled. This was what she had been dreading to hear for more reasons than he knew. She didn't want to hear it, didn't have time to hear it. "Just enjoy the show, Kai. This isn't the place to argue. Look, they're starting."

She pulled away just in time to see the mages shout as one and raise their arms to the sky, where a giant sphere of rippling orange flames began to grow, grow, grow...

"...and as you saw, we have the perfect coordination and power to siege any city and penetrate its defenses," Abelard said proudly a little while later. He led them back into the Tower behind the three perfect columns of students filing back inside. "Anywhere we go, we have the advantage. Intelligence, of course, but also discipline and strength and..." He twirled his white beard with a preening finger. "...a certain strategic intuition."

He didn't seem to notice at all the stiff tension between Kai and Anzi and pointed back out at the courtyard with a vague gesture.

"Now, I know the Empire has had its differences with the desert tribes throughout the decades. I must say, it is very hard to fight against a nomad people who have no fixed stronghold. And I've seen from all the history texts that desert tribes will often split their forces and infiltrate the land of the aggressors, engaging in various methods of petty warfare there so that the main forces are handicapped. It's all very genius indeed. I hope we can discuss the..."

Kai was long gone. He was here, physically, but there was a shuttered, faraway look in his golden eyes. Well, shit. Coming here had been a bad idea. He was hating this.

"So you sequester your mages here," he interrupted in a voice that was more than a little displeased, and the Magisien made a rumpled *harrumph*ing sound in response.

"For everyone's safety, including theirs," said the elderly man as he led the way down the curved stone hall. "Magic is unpredictable when untrained. Keeping them away from the people ensures that even if there are accidents, civilians are unharmed. And in this environment, they learn much more quickly to control themselves than they would otherwise. They can focus here with no distractions. When they arrive, we isolate them from any part of the outside world for at least five years, ten or more if needed. Not one step outside."

"They're imprisoned here?"

Again, Abelard snorted. "Dear sir, you may not agree with our practices, and you would not be the first nor will you be the last. But may I remind you the Empire spans a dozen former kingdoms and still expands to this day. We are strong because of what we do."

"Do they at least get to see their families? Surely they must be visited if they aren't permitted to leave."

"That would be unacceptable. Those of the mage class must learn to forge loyalty to the Empire over all else, so all traces of other burdens must be removed while they are learning to do this properly. With…rare exceptions that I never recommend."

Anzi pretended not to see the darting glare the mage shot at her, but Kai certainly noticed. Something sparked in his gaze, bringing back life, and his golden eyes shone bright in the darkness. So they *did* glow, she thought absently as she did her best to avoid his stare. She'd suspected as much.

They toured the great library that held all manner of valuable scrolls, almanacs, and texts that examined magical theory as well as artifacts behind spelled barriers to protect them. They toured, too, the armory Abelard was so proud of despite the admission that mages were no longer trained in physical combat for a few decades now. After that, the conservatory, the common hall where everyone ate, and various other places. There were more that the Magisien wanted to show them, but apparently to Kai's undying relief, someone eventually came springing up the way to the mage, wheezing and hacking.

"There's been an accident in the living quarters," the young man said. "We need you."

"Oh, gods damn the troubles of youth," Abelard grumbled, and he turned around with a deeply affected and apologetic expression. "I'll be back in moments," he promised. "Please, relax here. This is where my peers and I usually lounge, but you will have it to yourself until I return."

Anzi waved him away on behalf of Kai, who was probably going to tell him not to return at all. It really had been an awful idea to come here, but how could she have known he would take offense with such harmless things? He was just too different. He couldn't reconcile the ways of the Empire with his own. And so what, if she had a few doubts about certain things? This wasn't one of them. Children learning to be loyal to their Emperor and everything he had built for them over the last two hundred years—that was good. It was right. They didn't have to understand everything at first. They learned, always. She had turned out just fine, after all.

"You have family here," Kai said suddenly, and she swiveled her head around. He was staring at her, hard. "Tell me."

"I don't want to—"

"I want to know."

How? How had he known? Had he deduced it solely from the look Abelard had given her? "It's got nothing to do with anything," said Anzi.

"It has to do with you. That's enough for me to want to know."

"I don't *want* you to know. That's my business."

"So you won't tell me?"

Her expression sharpened, bordering dangerously on anger. "Are you going to make me? Are you going to report me to my superiors if I don't?"

He crossed the distance between them in two long strides, so quickly she didn't have time to react. Or had she? She saw him coming, saw him staring at her with his fire-intent, bright gaze eating her up, but her feet remained glued to the floor, trapping her in place. And when he lifted her chin so that she had to meet his eyes squarely instead of glaring at him from under her eyebrows, her stomach twisted with something that was weaker and more pliable than the anger she wished she felt.

"This isn't about that," he said. "You've been unhappy for days, and now this. I knew when we came here that something wasn't right, but I won't let you do this to yourself anymore."

"Do what?"

"Do things that make you unhappy just to prove you're strong enough. Making yourself suffer doesn't mean strength. Stop testing yourself like this."

She almost reared back, stinging at his words for reasons she hadn't yet deciphered. Just words, she wanted to tell herself. There was nothing to be defensive about. She could calmly reject what he was saying and assure him she would never be so dramatic, and that if she did anything, it was only ever because she had to, nothing else. Testing herself? Making herself suffer? Ha! Small things like these didn't bother her at all...It was only because...

"All right, then," she said. "Let's leave. I don't want to be here, and since you don't want me doing things that make me *unhappy*, that means we should leave."

"You can leave, but I'll stay."

"What!"

"Because I need to know what it is you're trying to hide from me. You've been wanting to leave since we came here, and you've barely paid attention more than half the time. Why? If you have family here, why are you trying to escape instead of going to them?"

"And I said that's none of your business!"

"It's either because you don't want me to see them or because you don't want to see them. Which is it?"

"Kai!"

"Am I wrong?" he demanded, and she nearly vibrated in frustration at the wall-like stolidness in his eyes. It wasn't even emotion she saw there anymore, just a hard, unyielding intent to do according to his own way regardless of what she wanted. "Tell me I'm wrong, Anzi. If I am, then I'll leave here with you right now, and we won't look back. But look me in the eye when you try to lie to me."

She should take him by the arm and pull him right into a headlock, she fumed to herself, but as he continued to force her chin up so she couldn't look away, she found no strength at all to push him back or otherwise extricate herself. Her arms hung useless at her sides as if he had weighed them down with stone blocks and chains, and all she could do was glare up at him like an enraged animal stuck in a trap. And she felt just like one.

"That's what I thought," he said, and his eyes glowed a little brighter just as they had earlier in the dim hallway, although it was harder to tell this time under the light that warmed the lounge. "You can hide so much from me, but not this. Let me in."

Let him in? What kind of poetic nonsense was that? And hiding things from him? What, was he her keeper? Was he her house shrine, sitting there in readiness to listen to her secrets as she confessed them over the altar? He didn't need to know anything. She didn't *hide* things form him, she was just—just—

When he wrapped his other arm around her waist and yanked her to him, she let out a half-furious, half-surprised sound just before feeling his lips on her forehead. He stayed like that, holding her to him and pressing that long kiss near her temple as if they were lovers instead of unlikely companions pushed together by the Emperor's ambitions. Because that was what this was. Whatever connection he sought, she had no way of fulfilling it, she thought with a heart that simultaneously sank and soared, twisted and unraveled. She almost brought her hands up to rest on either side of his waist, and gods forgive her, she wanted to so badly, but she was still angry, still wounded, still defensive.

"I will you would stop hiding from me," he whispered. "I've waited so long…"

"It's been less than a week, sir."

"Sir? You're angry with me."

"...Yes."

"I wish you weren't. You don't understand how much I wish you weren't."

She grimaced, but despite herself, felt her eyes fluttering closed as he began to run his lips along her forehead and down to her brow. How could he do this to her? Make her furious one moment then so weak in the next? She was a soldier, one of the greatest, able to tear down all enemies and obstacles in her path without blinking an eye. And yet when he held her like this, one hand splayed along the small of her back and the other cupping her face, caressing her chin, her jaw...

"Why do you have to do this to me?" she asked in a voice so small she barely recognized it. But she couldn't help it. If he would just—hit her, shout at her, threaten her into submission, she could rise up and give back tenfold what he delivered. No longer would she care about propriety and duty and rank; they were too far past that for her to care right now. So what if he was a foreign chieftain with secret riches expansive enough to topple the very peak of the Empire, so important that even the great Emperor Ra-Tet demanded that his every need and desire be satisfied? Right now, it was just Kai and her, no one else, and she wished he would lash out and cut her.

But he didn't, and he wouldn't. All her life, she had learned to fight back and parry against every kind of assault except this kind: tender, slow, strong yet smooth, unsubtle yet gentle. If he wouldn't properly fight her, then how was she supposed to fight back?

"You have no idea what you do to me," he whispered back, and a hot shiver ran down her spine at the joint longing and greed in his voice. "I can only do to you a fraction of it in return."

"What does that even mean!"

"Anything you want, Anzi. I'm tired of not knowing what that is. So just tell me."

"What I want is for you to stop talking in riddles."

He pressed her harder into himself, and for a second, she thought she felt a different kind of energy surge through his veins. How she felt it in her own body, she didn't know, or maybe it was just so potent that it infected her through the intimate contact of their bodies pressed together. Something scorching hot and powerful, wanting, needing—

"I could," he said, "but you would run from me in a second if you knew what I really wanted."

She was not a coward. She had never been afraid of anything in her life. Wary, yes, but afraid? Terrified? Ha! She never retreated unless it was strategic, never ran unless it was toward victory. Who did he think he was?

And yet when she felt the thrum of inexplicable but all-consuming energy course through him, like the ripple of a heartbeat strong enough to topple her if he weren't pressing them together, she did. Want to run, that is, and she had never been so terrified. Like standing on the edge of a precipice and hearing a voice urging her to fall in, the unknowable, terrible, but irresistible temptation to let it happen, and damn the consequences.

Unacceptable. She would never let that happen. She was a warrior, and she was stronger than any enemy she would ever face, and that included strange men who made her feel like she was standing on the summit of a towering mountain she hadn't known she'd climbed just by looking at her. Ha! Weakness and shame, that was what it was. With titanic effort, she slid her hands between them and planted them on his bare chest, fingertips brushing the bottom of his drooping golden collar and sending shooting pains up her arms. Pain? Or was it some kind of thrilled pleasure, she didn't know, but even if it was the latter, she would reject it nonetheless. Pleasures, how stupid, how shallow, how weak. She wasn't like everyone else. She was different, better.

She pushed him away, hard. She shouldn't have. She shouldn't have, and she knew it, but this wasn't about her orders to satisfy him and the Emperor's desire for the chieftain's favor. This wasn't about any of that at all. And so what if she saw something jagged and hurt flash in Kai's eyes like she had just torn open a gaping wound inside him? And so what if she thought she could feel it, too, a hint of unimaginable pain streaking through her body from head to toe at lightning speed, so fast she would have missed it if it didn't cut her to the quick in her spirit?

"I don't know why you keep doing this to me," she said, knowing she sounded every bit as angry as she felt. "You should know I'm not some skirt to chase. I don't know what you do with women back home in your free time, but I don't have enough of it to entertain you like this forever."

And again, she felt that searing promise of pain wash through her like an ice bath and a firestorm all at once, making every inch of her skin prickle with unnameable dread. Why? Why was this happening to her?

But it didn't matter. To prove she was above its influence, she had to keep going, she had to stay the course. She was better than this, and she would show it to him.

"If you want to keep acting like you care about me," she continued, "if you want to keep trying to whittle me down because you think it would be funny to see someone like me shrink down and crawl at your feet, you're in for nothing but disappointment. And let's say you really do care —then, you won't touch me anymore. You won't look at me like that anymore. And you definitely won't say things like that anymore. I don't want to see it, hear it, nothing. That's what I really want, Chieftain Kaizat-Amun. Just because I haven't said so doesn't mean it isn't true. I have to keep my mouth shut because you're an important man, but don't act like you know what I think just because I tolerate everything you do."

He looked—cut, and for a second, she was so terrified she had done something irreversible that she almost choked. But they were just words. It didn't mean anything. She was just protecting herself and making sure he knew she wasn't one to trifle with.

"Anzi," he said after a moment, still staring at her, still cut. "You and I are—"

"What?" she challenged before he could finish. Why she felt such a panicked urge to interrupted him, she didn't know, but since it happened anyway, she was going to ride it to the end. "What is it? You and I are what?"

His mouth twitched. There it was. He was going to answer with something ridiculous, something unbelievable. And if he did, she should leave him, orders be damned.

But something cool, calming, soft came over him, gently creeping across his expression and down every muscle in his body as she watched. She could see it. She could see the way he chased out the tension in his body, the loosening of every taut sinew. Stop looking, she warned herself. Before she forgot what she had just told him.

"Anzi," he said again, but this time, his voice was less raspy, smoother. "You really don't know what you do to me."

He sounded calmer, and yet something in how he spoke sent terrible dread pushing into her veins, coursing through her blood. And for a terrible, torturous moment, she wanted nothing more than to step forward and fall into him, to wrap her arms around him and apologize and take back what she'd said. But she was strong, so of course she didn't.

Of course.

"If you're that curious, I'll humor you," she said flatly, using every ounce of her training and discipline to make sure her emotions didn't slip through and spill all over the ground between them. "Yes, I have family here, you're right. A younger brother I haven't seen in years. I send letters that I'm sure never make it to him, and maybe he's sent letters to me that I never received nor asked after. But other than that, I've had no contact with him, and I've left him to his education here, alone."

A compromise. She could do this much. He was—he was putting on a fair show, a persuasive performance that she'd really hurt him, so she could do at least this much in return. She might as well, since it didn't matter anyway. Just like she had sacrificed everything else in her life already, neither would Oza sway her from her duties. And she could prove it by giving Kai what he wanted, and she wouldn't even care. Not a bit.

"He's a gifted mage, and even at his young age, he would more than qualify to be a Magisien's understudy here. But he's mute, and his sickliness has endangered him since he was a baby. Undue strain could kill him. So they keep him in the upper quarters and take care of him there, that's all. Anything else you would like to know?"

She had told him too much already. Why was she offering more answers if he wanted them? She should have ended it there.

"I want to see him," he said in that same cool, composed voice that a secret part of her knew was entirely false. "Let me meet your brother."

"I can't. It's not up to me."

"You know where he is, don't you? You said he was in the upper quarters. Is he a prisoner, unable to—"

"I've returned!" an appallingly familiar voice announced from the doorway, though out of breath and quavering more than before. Anzi turned her head to see Magisien Abelard at the lounge's entrance, mopping the sweat from his forehead with his flowing sleeve. "Apologies for the delay, I—"

"I want to see the boy named Oza. Take me to him."

At Kai's rigid command, Anzi's head whipped back around so she could stare at him now instead, and she knew Abelard was doing the same. She could hear the elderly man adjusting his robes with a slight rustle, no doubt a nervous movement.

"But, Chieftain Kaizat-Amun, there are surely much more interesting—"

"I want to see the boy. Or I'll leave since there's nothing else I'm interested in."

Abelard looked as if he were about to pop open like a stretched waterskin, and he frantically waved his hands before stationing himself right in the middle of the doorway as if he could stop Kai from shoving past him if he chose to walk over and do so. "Wait! Wait, I'm very sorry, I shouldn't have presumed to know what would please you."

"You shouldn't have."

"Then—then, please allow me to do according to your wishes. Yes, yes, we are so honored, so privileged—please, come this way."

Stunned, Anzi watched as Kai strode across the room without a backward glance at her. She tried to glare at the back of his head and make him turn around with the sheer heat of her anger, but he ignored her completely. She knew he could feel it. She knew it for a certainty—though how, she didn't know—and yet he pointedly ignored her as if she weren't in his sight at all as she hurried after him and Abelard both. She joined them in the hallway, strides long and quick, every step angry.

How dare he? She had told him what he wanted to know, and now he had the nerve to demand to see him? She tried to get his attention with discreet glowers and twitches of her head as they climbed the spiraling stone steps running along the outer edge of the tower, but as the stairs curved more and more tightly with their ascension, he still refused to acknowledge them even after several minutes.

They couldn't do this. He couldn't. They were almost there, and she didn't want to see Oza. She didn't want *him* to see Oza. She didn't want anyone to see him at all.

"Here he is, just beyond." Abelard hurried up the topmost step and unlocked the lone door there. He disappeared inside, and Kai followed in short order. Left with no choice, Anzi did the same, and she cringed upon entering the plush, padded room full of red and yellow tassels everywhere, tapestries hanging on the wall, soft rugs laid out over the stone floor, a warmth that shouldn't exist this high in the tower…

And there in the back of the room, sitting at a desk far too large for him, was a young boy with black hair. He had his back turned to them, but he twisted around in his seat when Abelard made a clicking sound with his tongue. "Oza! At attention."

And slowly, he rose from his chair and turned to face them, eyes as black as night. Crow's eyes.

"Hey, Oza," Anzi said in a near-croak. "Long time no see."

31

He was so much taller now than when she had last seen him. Anzi's stomach lurched for the hundredth time since she had come to the Tower, but this one was the final one, the real one. She was here, looking Oza in the eye and coming face to face with the boy she had left to fend for himself in a world she had known would be too cruel to him.

And yet he looked healthy, or as healthy as he could ever be with his frailty. Still as skinny as she remembered, though. He positively swam in his robe.

"You're not wearing initiate's garb anymore," she said, partly because she was proud of him but mostly because she didn't know what else to say. "Congratulations."

He raised one shoulder and made a twitching gesture with his opposite hand, but made not a sound. He blinked, long lashes somehow making his eyes look even darker than they were. Did she look like that, she wondered. She couldn't remember the last time she'd looked at herself, and fringers didn't often pause to examine each other's appearances the rare times they passed each other on the streets.

"Your sister did not come here to see you, mind you," Abelard said suddenly. "Chieftain Kaizat-Amun is the one who wanted to meet you. He is from one of the tribes of the Adaraat desert region. You remember from your studies, don't you?"

Oza nodded, a quick jerking motion.

"Good boy. Now, as you can tell, there isn't much to see. Very quiet boy, a mute. Now, we should let him return to his work—"

"Let's not," Kai interrupted. "It's been a while since my friend Anzi has been able to see her brother. It would be a shame if they couldn't make good use of that time now."

"A-ha-ha, but Private Anzi has not been to see him for a long time now, and of her own free will. I'm sure she is just as busy today as she usually is…And Oza is doing well. His condition need not be inspected, especially not by an outsider. That is—I do not mean you, of course, Chieftain, but rather the soldiers. They know nothing of our world anyway, so there would be no point."

"Anzi? Do you want to see your brother?"

When he turned and asked her the question, she had not been prepared. She stood there and stared back at Kai in stunned silence, every muscle in her body slowly tensing with each second that passed. Abelard was sending her death glares behind Kai's shoulder, bushy white eyebrows slanted and knitted together like hairy caterpillars fighting to the death, but still the words refused to come out. It would be so easy. No, she could say. It was fine. She didn't need to see Oza any longer. She had already seen him, so it was done, over with.

That would be the right thing to say. Besides the terrible wisdom in angering a powerful member of the Magisien body, she had already been exercising the good decision of staying away from her brother all these years, hadn't she? In the beginning, she had fought for the privilege to see him, even patiently waiting months in between. But once she had been sent on her first march and exposed first-hand to the real world, the battlefield of blood and violence, she had realized that distance was the best thing for both of them. She couldn't be the best soldier she could be with her brother on her mind, and Oza—he was a gifted magic user. Without her distracting him, he would excel and be of greater service to the Empire than all the rest of his peers.

And he was being treated well here despite being a fringer. That was something about the Tower's internal hierarchy, that everyone's status was almost solely determined by their magical prowess and little else. No one had riches inside the Tower, after all. Magic-gifted children were taken away from their parents as soon as they were found, and they lived in the great spire castle with no contact with the outside world. Wealth, friends, possession, all of these things disappeared. They were like ghosts entering into another realm. So of course Oza would make friends and be happier there than with her. Of course. He didn't need her.

So then she had stopped going to visit him. Started sending her letters less and less frequently. And despite knowing the Magisien body would never deliver those letters, she continued anyway,pretending obliviousness because it was just...easier that way.

But now? What now? If she bent, then all these years would have been for nothing.

"Maybe it would be better if we were left alone," Kai suggested, and she shook her head, knowing what Abelard would say even before he said a word.

"I would be happy to oblige your honorable presence any requests you desire—except the ones that violate the rules we cannot cross." The mage bowed his head and made a flourishing gesture with his arm. "Please forgive this old man. But the law is that young master Oza never be left alone, for both the sake of his protection and that of others."

Kai narrowed his eyes. "For the protection of others?"

"He's a very powerful, gifted boy, but he's not in his right mind. He is normally an obedient one, but occasionally..."

Anzi had to bite her tongue to force herself to stay quiet. Not in his right mind? They were wrong. They kept saying that, kept insisting he was crazy when he just thought and acted differently from others his age. They made sure he was pampered with all the material things he could desire, but did they not yet respect him?

"Then, so long as you're here, Anzi should be free to speak with him over there, with due privacy. You don't have laws about that, do you? Or is he some kind of prisoner without the privilege of speaking to his blood relations? Or is Anzi not a loyal servant of your Empire to be trusted?"

Abelard looked like he had just swallowed a fly, and she felt like she'd done the same. Why was Kai doing this? ...But then again, he was powerful enough to get away with it, and he'd proven again and again that was all the reason he needed to do anything. He was a foreigner in this land, but he was a foreigner who had the favor of the Emperor. No one dared cross him except Anzi alone, and that was only because she kept forgetting herself whenever she was in Kai's presence.

This was terrible. Once he was gone from her life, he would leave everything in shambles, and she had no idea where she would even begin to pick up the pieces.

"Your brother looks like he's waiting for you. You should go to him."

She stiffened. No, Oza didn't look like he was waiting for her, what was Kai talking about? But the way he stared down at her as if he couldn't get enough of her, as if he wanted to reach out and grab every part of her for himself like an insatiable fire hungering for the wood, that was even more nerve-wracking. Why was he like this, she wanted to ask. Why did he have to be so…

If only he hated her. She knew how to handle things like that, how to protect herself and fight back. But what was she supposed to do about someone who thought—or pretended—that he cared so much? It was like trying to fight the wind; all Kai did was wrap around her and strangle her even more. If strangling could feel so harmless, even tempting.

She moved away from him just to get away from the aura exuded like flames licking her skin. And since she couldn't retreat and leave, she had no choice but to move forward, taking steady, slow steps toward Oza who watched her with blank eyes from the other side of the room. And then too soon, she was standing in front of him.

"…You're taller," she said, and the words left her mouth before she realized how plain and dumb they sounded. But too late. It was true, anyway. He stood level with her chest now, and he had always been on the smaller side. She'd missed his growth spurt sometime in the last few years. "Studies going well?"

He nodded. His arms hung by his sides, straight and unmoving. He had never been the type to make gestures or otherwise communicate with his hands, which was why he had never picked up on speaking through signs, either. But that had been all right, at least before. Anzi had always done her best to understand, and most of the time, that had been enough.

But not anymore. She could hardly tell what he was thinking, what he wanted. She used to be able to look him in the eye and understand what went on behind them, but now…

"You should eat more," she added. "You're skinnier. Are they giving you enough?"

Out of the corner of her eye, she could see Abelard bristling at the somewhat-accusation, and decided to lower her voice. Not just to keep the mage out of her damn business and conversations, but to make sure Kai didn't pick up on anything she didn't want him to, either.

"You've been staying busy, right?"

He nodded.

"Any episodes?"

He nodded again.

"Bad ones?"

A shake of the head this time. She breathed a relieved sigh.

"That's good. Stay indoors as much as you can. And up high, where the air is better. Does that window open?" She pointed at the square depression set into the stone wall on the left side of the room. There were no drapes, but there was something shuttering it closed from the outside.

He shook his head again, and guilt stirred in her gut. Cooped up in here without even a window he could open for fresh air. Things she took for granted, being able to step out into the open almost whenever she wished. But Oza—did they even let him outside at all yet? Did they ever let him see anything that wasn't within these walls? Parades and celebrations were out of the question, but at least the odd outing or two...

He really was a prisoner, she thought with a jolt. All this time, she'd thought of it as protection, but if it were her, if she were trapped in this dead place full of silks and wool and candle light, she wouldn't know how to live with it. With herself. She was about to ask something else when he turned and sat back down in his chair. A hurtling, sinking feeling dropped her heart into her stomach like a heavy stone, until she saw him pushing aside several large parchment sheets in search of something. Oh. She had thought for a second he was dismissing her.

Moments ago, she hadn't even wanted to see him. Now, she was afraid of ever leaving again. What had Kai done to her? What doors had he forced back open in her mind, doors she had inched closed with all her strength over the years on the things she knew she couldn't have, couldn't keep. Not if she wanted to achieve her true calling. Something always had to go. Would she have to choose all over again?

Oza found what he was looking for, and he pushed his messy black curls from his forehead with an impatient jerk before standing again. After shaking out the parchment sheet three flicks the way he always did even though there wasn't a single rumple in the paper, he presented it for Anzi to take, and she received it with both hands to examine it.

A translation of something. While she had never learned any of the old scripts, it was just one of many things the Magisien body had schooled Oza in since toddling days. But she soon understood that the scribbles— his handwriting had never been good—weren't the things he wanted to show her. He reached around and jabbed at the bottom of the page, where there were sketches of a dragon's gaping maw, fangs and all. Ah, so the translated piece had to do with dragons. Made sense, considering that it was such an obsessive topic among the Empire's academics. He jabbed at it again, nearly pushing the parchment out of her hands, and a slow smile crept onto her lips. It was funny how things had come to this. She had been away for years, but the first thing he wanted to know upon seeing her again was if she had—

"Yes," she said. "I did it. Just inducted. I'll have a dragon partner soon."

He nodded, and although he could not speak, she thought she could sense the excitement in him that he kept buried so deep underneath his serious exterior. Not like old times when she understood every twitch and exhale of his emotions with all the sensitivity of a weather vane in the winds, but...a little. With some hesitation, she let go of one of the sides of the parchment and held out her hand to him, palm up.

Her heart thudded in her chest when he reached up to tap her fingertips three times, then withdrew. It really was almost like old times. She smiled at him, and while he didn't give her one in return, that was normal, too. His sharp face had lost so much of its childishness in the time she had stayed away, and she wondered for a moment what he must have looked like between then and now. He had been only seven when she had last visited, when she had been sent away to fight in a real battle for the first time. She'd been fourteen. She had wanted...she had wanted to do things right, and to walk the path she was meant to.

Back then, she had been so sure of it that she had been ready to give up everything else.

"Don't let them bother you," she said softly. "If the other kids or teachers mess with you, you show them you mean business. Got it? You're important, and you've worked hard to get here. So don't waste it."

He nodded, and he reached up to tap her fingertips again. After that, she let her arm drop and smiled down at him. It was hard, though, to look pleased. She wanted so badly to apologize, but no matter how many slow breaths she inhaled, exhaled, she couldn't. It would open her up too much and she wouldn't be able to reverse what it did to her, like kicking down a door and letting the light stream through a mangled doorway. She wasn't sure if she could take responsibility, be accountable.

The way he stared back at her made it even worse. Because there was nothing expectant in his eyes, no waiting for the apology. He was simply...there. And he didn't want her to leave. Despite how much he had grown while she had kept away, she could read at least that much. If he wanted her to go, he would have turned his back and made it clear they were done. But he hadn't, and instead, they were standing here together and meeting at the line where she had built a wall, brick by brick, until they couldn't see each other anymore. With one fell swoop, Kai had knocked it down, and now...

"I'm sorry," she said. "I should have come to see you. But it was too hard. I'm sorry."

He considered her words for a few seconds before nodding. Her smile faded. Hesitation meant he was angry. But of course. She'd known he would be. And hurt, hurt beyond the words he couldn't even speak. She should have known better to deal such blows when he couldn't even protest them, when al he could do was stand back and watch.

She should have known better. She should have *done* better. Especially when he turned again and reached for something behind a different stack of parchment sheets in the opposite corner of the large desk. He scooped it into his palm, and she took it into hers when he shoved it toward her.

Cool and smooth, but with sharp edges around its many surfaces. Between two fingers, she lifted it to eye level so she could properly see it in the bright candle light, and crystalline shimmers of blue and black glinted from the diamond-esque, marquise shape of the gemstone. She had no idea what it was. She had never seen a gem like this before, but then again, magic tended to wander into the realm of the fantastic, even little baubles like these.

"Thank you," she said. "You remembered my birthday."

He raised and lowered one shoulder, and she thought with another surge of twisting guilt how he couldn't have possibly known she would come again. It had been four years, and her birthday had already passed a few days ago. Had he hoped she would at least visit for his in a few months, even though she had kept away all this time? Or maybe he had summoned and grown this crystal long ago and had simply kept it to give to her when she eventually came. Maybe he had wanted to give her this years ago. If not, where were the others that he had made, the ones he always crafted meticulously over months for every one of her birthdays? And where were the ones he had already given her before? She couldn't believe it. She must have left them someplace for safekeeping, but to think that she couldn't remember exactly. They were probably long lost by now.

"I'll be back," she said. "I can't stay long today, but I'll come visit again."

He nodded.

"Then I'll be going."

Abelard was furious when she swooped past him and descended the steps. After closing the door to Oza's private room, he chased after her—

with a respectful series of hasty bows to Kai as he passed him by—demanding to see what she'd been given.

"A gift," she said breezily. "Nothing to concern yourself with, Magisien Abelard, sir."

"You are not allowed to take any possessions of the Tower outside."

"Just a soulstone." She flashed the gem between her fingers at him before shoving it back into the pouch hanging slightly open on her belt. She never stopped walking all the while. "The last time I checked, these passed approval from the body so I can receive these from him. That hasn't changed, has it? Or are you all concerning yourselves with harmless trinkets now?"

"Not harmless baubles, I'll have you know Oza's handiwork is—"

"Gifted. I know. But it's mine now. If you would like to discuss revoking the approval you gave eight years ago, then be my guest, but until I have the order in my hands to surrender it, I will hold onto it, thank you." He made an angry, frustrated sound that sounded like it was erupting from the bottom of his lungs, but she paid it no mind. "Chieftain Kaizat-Amun, have you seen enough of the Tower?"

He picked up on the cue. "I think I am. I'll retire from here now."

It happened so fast Abelard could do nothing, and some minutes later, Anzi and Kai had crossed the courtyard and returned to the wide path beyond the Tower's borders. It was evening now. With winter approaching, darkness fell so quick that the moon was visible high in the clouds already. Anzi looked up with a smile. What a day. It had been like a storm, fast and strong, moving over a meadow then sprinting out after leaving everything soaked and windblown in its wake.

"Are you feeling better?"

She turned back to Kai with the wind on her face. He was smiling, the irritating…irritating idiot of a chieftain. She could hardly stand it. "I won't say." She whipped back around and began marching away without him.

"Anzi, wait for me—"

Ha, she thought, but she was smiling too, now. Her, wait for him? Not a chance.

But if he was quick enough, he just might manage to catch her.

32

"I'm not wearing that." Anzi pointed at the door with a commanding finger. "The thought's appreciated. But no, thank you."

"You don't mean that."

"Yes, I do."

"I'm talking about you saying you appreciate it. You don't." Letti planted her hands on her hips, eyebrows furrowed hard like two swords on the verge of a violent clash. "Why don't you like it!"

"Because."

"Give me a reason. A real one!"

"The list is so long you could make new dresses and wraps out of it for every girl in the harem. Take it as it is. I'm not wearing something that clumsy to the gala."

Letti looked like she was going to explode. Her fabulous blonde ringlets bounced along her bared shoulders as if they had a life—and anger—of their own. "But I saw it! That man, the one with the wonderful back and beautiful chest, him—he said, he said he was looking forward to escorting you there!"

She hated how fate had arranged things. The woman had apparently been hiding around the corner when Kai had walked her to her room against her objections, and heard his every word, too. She had then promptly lost her mind after hearing whatever flirtatious things he had said that she could no longer remember, and proceeded to flee back to the harem quarters to fetch a ridiculous red thing with lace, satin, silk, and strange accessories that were completely unacceptable.

"I'm going as his guard," she said crisply. "I don't care what he thinks I'm going to be wearing."

"But why! If you've been given permission to go as his companion, then surely you don't have to wear that ugly, hideous uniform—"

"I happen to like it, Letti."

"—and you certainly don't have to go in all that armor! How old is that leather, anyway! It looks so worn I can hardly believe any of it would protect you."

"Believe me, it does. And I'm choosing to go like this. The Emperor won't mind, and the chieftain won't mind, and those are the only two opinions that matter. That means yours doesn't, in this case."

"How awful! You have such lovely arms, I can't believe you're wasting the opportunity and not showing them off—"

"I'm guessing you're going in that, then," she interrupted and pointed at the slim, elegant pink dress Letti had on. It accentuated her gentle curves, the narrow waist and slender hips looking impressively beautiful under the modest fabric. "But don't you think it'll attract a little too much attention? Very pink."

"Don't be silly! I'm not wearing this to the gala." Letti snorted and made a sharp gesture down at herself. "Something this plain? Have you ever seen any of the harem girls wearing anything like this?"

Anzi squinted. "Dresses become hard to tell apart when they're good for little but pleasing the eye."

"Which is important! Incredibly important. My goodness, you poor, deprived thing. No wonder you're so dry and un-fun all the time, you're basically a domesticated cactus. Well, still wild, but clothed…Fine, I won't fuss at you about your armor, but you should at least bring me with you so I can come meet your new man."

"Those two things have nothing to do with each other, that's not a compromise. Also, he's not my new man. Stop calling him that. I told you."

"Anyway, I have to go back now so I can get my makeup on, which will take at least an hour. I'm so, so, so late. But promise me! Come pick me up so I have permission to go with you. Please? Oh, Anzi, please, you know the other girls can't stand me."

She batted away Letti's pleading, groping hands. "Fine! I said fine. I'll come find you in an hour and a half. But don't forget I can't entertain you tonight, and I won't help you befriend whatever important person you set your eyes on. I have a job to do."

"You think I'm trying to—no! I just want to meet your tall, dark, and handsome chieftain friend...And I want you to wear this. Remember? Remember this little thing? It would go so well with your eyes, I mean it." Before Anzi could beg off of whatever ordeal this was about to become, a familiar pouch appeared in a flash in the harem girl's hand, and a sparkling emerald brooch came out of it. "From back when we went to the market! This would go so well with this nice dress I found for you..."

"Absolutely not."

"But this brooch was so expensive. I'll cry if it never sees the light of day."

"Then you wear it. Wear it tonight with whatever monstrosity you're going to dress yourself in."

"Oh, really!" Letti's hands flew to her chest, and alarmingly, tears began to brim with perilous speed in her pretty eyes. "This is so perfect, we're already borrowing each other's things, I knew we had a real connection...I'll pin it to my hair. That way, you won't lose me in the crowd in case we get separated, but of course we'll be holding hands the entire time so neither of us get lost because that's what best friends should do, anyway—"

It took another several minutes to get her out of her room, which she managed by pointing aggressively at the timecatcher dangling by her open balcony door. After that, Letti had promptly fled, gasping about how the minutes had flown by, and Anzi was finally able to secure a little peace and quiet. She sat down at the foot of her bed, gaze fallen to the floor as she contemplated her day.

That damned Kai. Always used to getting things his way, was he? She couldn't believe the nerve of him—demanding to be let into Oza's quarters and forcing her to see him for the first time in years when she had been too guilty—and yes, she could admit it—too afraid ever since she had abandoned him. How dare he presume to step into her life and try to set things aright as if he knew what she needed and wanted. He didn't know her. He pretended to, but he didn't, and he certainly didn't know what was best for her.

And yet she was happy. It was like a great weight had been shoved off her shoulders, and for the first time, she thought she could sit up without feeling it crushing her down. She had borne it so long she'd stopped noticing, but after today, after Kai had barged into her business and refused to leave until he left his mark on her private world, her personal realm where she never let anyone tread...She couldn't stand him. Not even a little bit. Her heart pounded as she flashed back to the moment he let her push him away back in the Tower, the way he'd looked at her like she had grabbed hold of him and ripped his chest apart with her bare hands. And yet he'd come right back and insisted on doing something that he thought was best for her. Which—he was wrong, of course, because he was a stranger and strangers shouldn't act like they knew her so intimately, but...

They hadn't said anything about that on the way back to the palace. Not a word about the harsh words she'd given him, not even a wary glance. It was as if they had never argued at all. Was it because she was always like that, rejecting his advances over and over again so frequently that he was now committed to taking it in stride?

But she'd seen that look in his eyes. She remembered it still, burning and hot and burst with pain, like looking into the eyes of a man impaled.

She shook her head. Ridiculous. She was thinking too much into it. In the end, it didn't matter if his feelings were genuine or if they were all just an elaborate performance. He was a visiting dignitary; she was a soldier of the Empire. He would be leaving sooner or later and she would not be going with him, no matter what. If he really had taken some kind of stupid liking to her —though what was there to like? She was strong and rough, had none of the soft, lush curves that ordinary, pigheaded men wanted with their slobbering denseness—then he was foolish and shortsighted. Or if this was all a trick, then...well, she would still come out the winner, because she had no intention of letting him make an idiot out of her. She would humor him as far as the Emperor ordered, and no more. He could have her time and her body if he eventually demanded it, but she was fast and bright, too clever to be taken in by attractive looks and low, deep voices that felt like they were vibrating straight through her bones.

Either way, what a waste of time. Whether he was a fool or a trickster, he wouldn't be getting what he wanted.

A hard knock at the door pulled her out of her musings, and she rose from her bed. She stood to the side before opening it, per her typical cautious ways, but the man waiting in the hallway was but a messenger with a rolled-up scroll, already presented before she finished opening the door. "A message from the Emperor," he announced. "He requires your presence immediately after you have read the contents."

So much for peace and quiet. But her pulse quickened as she took the scroll with a nod. It seemed that whatever doubts and tormented questions she had about the Empire's dark, secretive practices, she still couldn't banish her eagerness to serve. In the Emperor's very presence, being spoken to, given direct orders—she hadn't even dared to dream of this when she was younger. Being a dragon rider of the Premier Guard would have been enough. She would never have been presumptuous enough to expect the most powerful man in the land to ask for her presence. No matter how...unexpectedly casual His Excellency was, his demeanor changed nothing about his accomplishments, after all. He was still the immortal Emperor who had pulled and threaded together his kingdom from nothing, driven out the barbarians and made a safe home for his people who had spread far and wide under his wise leadership. He was still the man she had always striven to serve. A privilege. And now, to properly show her appreciation for it, she needed to get to work right away. She closed the door after the messenger and began poring over the scroll's contents, still standing—

Her eyes widened.

~

"I TRUST you've caught up on everything?"

"Yes, Your Excellency."

"Unbelievable, isn't it. But every word of what you read is true. There are still dragons alive and well in the desert, hidden away from my eyes all this time. Imagine!"

Anzi didn't know how to respond. She was still reeling at the revelation, and the scroll that was now rolled back up in her right hand felt more like the stuff of dreams than reality. How could it be? And yet she had read the report, or rather the transcription penned by the scribe assigned to record the negotiation session this morning between the Emperor and the Chieftain Kaizat-Amun.

Dragons. In the transcription, Kai hadn't said outright that he possessed them, but...

If the kingdom is hospitable, I will bring back what has been lost. The dragons live on, like shoots who have survived the storm...

The words had been almost ominous, but the implications could be nothing but stunningly glorious. Live dragons in the wild! Among Bastien's ramblings had been the frequent complaint that the bloodline of each egg could only be so varied, no matter what season, temperature, moisture, or any other condition he induced. There were only so many adult dragons to breed, and after two hundred years, the possibilities were running thin. But dragons in the wild! He would be ecstatic. And Anzi, too, desperately wanted to see them.

After that first day when she had shared bitter words with Kai about how the Empire had destroyed the legacy of the dragons, she wanted so badly for him to be wrong. Could it be true? After all his talk, could it be true he had been hiding the surviving wild dragons all along? Could it be possible that some had escaped the Purge two centuries ago?

"I understand that look on your face," continued the Emperor. He was standing before his throne instead of sitting upon it, and he now descended the dais with a wide smile on his strangely beautiful mouth. Grinning, even, from ear to ear. "Mind you, I'm not one easily impressed since I've seen about all there is to be seen, but you've truly outdone your-self. Whatever you've been doing to the chieftain, keep doing it. I knew you had promise all along, very good."

Wait, what? Her? She hadn't even done anything. Why was she being praised? But she dared not speak out of turn, and he went on as he approached her with slow, ambling steps.

"Tonight's event will be extremely important. I expect you to go all out, as this is the final impression we'll be leaving on him so he can make his decision. It would take too long to force him to comply, since we have no idea where in the Adaraat he's hiding the dragons, and I don't have time to send men to root around in the desert, not when most of them will die before they search even a tenth of it. So you'll need to impress him. Thoroughly. But you've already been marvelous, so have confidence."

"Yes, Your Excellency."

"I'm assuming he'll want to lie with you again if you do your job well, so you have my full permission to leave the gala with him whenever he wishes, and wherever he wishes. Wear something nice. I'll be providing rooms for anyone who wishes to couple with their chosen partners or with those in my harems, and keep a sharp eye out so as to select the best conditions to satisfy him. Make sure he knows he's the most important man in the room at all times, yes?"

Aside from the Emperor, of course, she wanted to add, but His Excel-lency seemed far too excited to be accepting mild assurances of his signif-icance. But more than that, what did he mean! Did he really think she and

Kai had been sleeping together all this time! "I—Your Excellency, I think it might be prudent to let you know he hasn't...gone so far as to use me," she said, making sure to keep her language appropriate. "Not in that way."

But it didn't matter to him, evidently. He flapped his hand at her, long red sleeves billowing with the motion. "Maybe not yet, but certainly tonight. He made it clear to me that's what he intends, either during or after tonight's events. Just make sure you're prepared. And feel free to direct him to the private springs, I'll put out an order to keep everyone else away in case he takes a fancy to mounting you there. I heard it's almost like bathing in an aphrodisiac, really."

What! What in dark hells—

"I'll put it simply. Do whatever it takes to keep him under your spell. I always said there would be other unexpected good uses for a woman in the ranks, but stupid men will continue in their stupidity and stick to their stubborn ways...That's no longer a concern. This will prove it to the rest of the silly Guard. Tonight, if the chieftain's sufficiently satisfied, I'm sure we'll see results. Oh, and another thing."

Something else this time! Anzi could hardly believe what she had heard already. What now?

"I've decided to publicly elevate you and your rank or whatever all of the fuss is. I've been told by my advisors that your, hm, current status leaves much to be desired. I don't want anyone ridiculing you behind your back at the gala tonight while you accompany the chieftain. Nothing good will come of that, since either he's so bewitched by you that he'll be horrifically offended on your behalf and throw a tantrum, or he'll draw away from you if he thinks you're too below his station. Can't have that."

The criticism didn't sting at all. If anything, His Excellency was doing her a favor by being so blunt without being cruel. But still—so sudden!

"I'll be announcing you as an official First Guard tonight to mark the beginning of the celebrations. I was looking for a plausible reason for all of this anyway—it's better not to let it get to the chieftain's head and make it obvious everything is to impress him. With your appointment to the Premier Guard, it's most definitely a cause for ruckus. Plus, I'm sure it'll make him happy that his woman is being put on a pedestal. Yes, good idea."

His woman! And an official announcement! Anzi's head spun. But the Emperor wasn't done speaking, and he paced back and forth, nodding as he rattled off instructions.

"You'll have to assert yourself more. I understand the attack dog routine where you only have a mind to serve at my whims, and really, I appreciate it, sort of—but tonight, you need to focus on exciting him. So be exciting. Make him feel important, and that means you have to flaunt yourself. It's a shame you couldn't hatch an egg yet so you could bring your dragon with you, but a week was too short a time to expect that to happen anyway. No matter. The point is, you're a First Guard now, and your foremost duty tonight is to make sure Chieftain Kaizat-Amun is happy. You have to make him bring back the dragons. Understand?"

She didn't. She really didn't. But she had no choice but to say—

"Yes, Your Excellency. I understand."

33

Anzi couldn't believe the one time she wanted to see Bastien, she couldn't. Did he know? Did he know about the possibility of surviving wild dragons yet? It would send him into a raving-mad, delirious fit of ecstasy, but she had to ask him how it could even be possible. He had been there during the Purge, hadn't he? Despite his looks and his immature, irritating personality, he was an old, old man who could shed more light on the subject than nearly anyone else in the entire Empire. And yet tonight she couldn't go to see him. No egg-searching, not when she had to accompany Kai all night and entertain him.

Entertain. Had the Emperor meant it? Had Kai really told him he intended to couple with her tonight? Maybe he had changed his mind after everything that happened during their afternoon together; he hadn't told her a thing about it. But wait, he had dragged her to his room and put her in his bed this morning, had even slept beside—around her—for hours. Maybe that was supposed to be the warning, the harbinger of his intentions for tonight.

She desperately wanted to ask Letti for her well-versed opinion on these matters, but she couldn't. The woman would become feral if she found out anything about it. Or maybe she could ask in a roundabout way, in a hypothetical way that wouldn't raise suspicion. Either way, she was going to the harem quarters now to pick her up. Once she was there, she could make her decision. Except when she arrived, Letti was nowhere to be seen.

"She's supposed to come with me," said Anzi. "She knew this."

Both guards answered with small simultaneous shrugs. "She's not here," answered the one on the left.

"Then where did she go? If anyone comes or goes, you know it."

"Not tonight, fringer. The harem girls have been in and out all evening. They wanted to see the wares being put out on display before the gala begins tonight."

Fringer, he'd called her, and while she sensed no malice in it, he would never have dared to address her so casually if he knew who she was. Not that she minded. If anything, it put her at ease. He looked friendly and relaxed, not combative, and she enjoyed the strange, wistful sensation that swirled around her. After tonight, she would have to carry herself differently. She wouldn't be allowed to tolerate such familiar address. The other soldiers would have to speak to her with the respect they'd always withheld, all because she was a First Guard now.

It stung that her official induction could be so messy. She should be able to present with her dragon, newly hatched. This would be the first time in recorded Empire history that a Premier would be revealed to the public without one. No proof of her back-breaking efforts, no evidence of anything. There would be talk.

She wished it didn't have to be like this, officially inducted only so she could be more appealing to Kai, to make her more important, more impressive. A thin tendril of resentment against him rose inside her, but she couldn't stand here being bitter about it. It was as good as done, on the Emperor's orders. Who was she to feel dissatisfied?

"Can you check again?" she asked. "I can't come back. I'm supposed to escort one of the guests soon—and also, I need Violetta's help putting some dress on. It's some harem girl special. Complicated pieces."

The man rolled his eyes. "Tell me about it, like fisherman's knots sometimes. All right. I guess if you twist my arm like that, I have no choice but to go in and look for her one more time." He winked , and Anzi couldn't help but roll her eyes as well with a wry answering smirk. Of course a young man like him wouldn't pass up an excuse to go wandering inside where the beautiful women all congregated, even if half of them were already out roaming the palace grounds already to explore the sights. "I'll be back in a minute. Hang on."

She liked him. Didn't know who he was, and he was a bit of a pervert for wanting to go in and mingle with the nubile young ladies of the harem, but he had an honest, harmless way about him. Plus, he was doing her a favor by running back there and checking for Letti a second time without a fuss. She was running out of time. If she really wasn't there and had run off without her, then she needed to hurry back to her room and figure out how to get into that stupid dress. On her own, she had no idea how long that would take.

The guard returned. "Sorry, friend, I don't see her. Her name is Violetta?"

Damn it. "Yes."

"What does she look like? I'm a new post, don't know them all by name yet."

It was likely he never would. Anzi had known a few comrades to get sent up into the palace, and as far as she knew, guards weren't allowed to keep this post for very long since it encouraged...ill-advised attachments and secret rendezvous in the middle of the night with their charges. He would be rotated out within the year. "Blonde hair, twirly little curls that come down to her shoulders. She usually has her hair up in the back. Blue eyes, very, very light blue. You'll know when you see her. She's a pretty girl."

"They're all pretty." The guard grinned at his partner, who ignored him.

"No, she's...very pretty. You'll recognize her."

"I don't know, I prefer nice chestnut hair myself. But all right, then. What's your name, so I can tell her to find you?"

"Anzi."

The name made him take pause. Both of them, actually, and she could see them racking their minds for why it sounded familiar. It was a fringer name, of course, but they would have known that just by looking at her.

"Anzi?" he repeated. "You wouldn't happen to be the...never mind. That's stupid of me, be like one of those idiots who think all fringers look alike." He laughed aloud, and she snorted at his carefree attitude because he was right. Her face wasn't so recognizable to anyone she hadn't served with, but her name was a different story. Not that she would correct him. She rather liked that he was so casual instead of wary. That would change if he learned she really was the half-renowned, half-notorious soldier that he'd thought she was for a second.

"What's your name?" she asked. She didn't care about his friend who hadn't said a word, but this one was interesting. Likable.

"Julien Blaise." He stuck out his hand, and although she'd had no intention of being so familiar, decided it was fine to shake it once. Quickly, though. "I'll send her to you as soon as I see her, this most beautiful girl you say I'll recognize the instant I lay eyes on her."

She thought of the too-bubbly girl's demeanor, how she flounced around while blending perpetual cheerfulness with elegant flair. However annoying she could be, her charm was undeniable. "Oh, you'll know."

"Good luck, then."

Back in her room, she sat at the foot of her bed and stared at the blood-red mess of fabric in her arms. Damn it. She had no choice but to struggle into the dress on her own if Letti wasn't here. She wasn't about to go ask some other woman to get her sorted out like some kind of lame animal limping around with a trap closed around her leg. Or maybe she didn't need to wear this ugly thing after all...?

She recalled the prying expression Kai had worn when he'd first suggested he would enjoy seeing her in different attire. It had annoyed her then, but she had dismissed it because the thought of wearing a cumbersome dress had been laughable. But now she remembered, too, the mildly repulsed, pitying look the Emperor had given her armor when he'd surveyed her appearance in the throne room earlier. Well. She had gotten the message. If she went in the 'hideous' uniform and armor, it would be tantamount to slapping His Excellency across the face. She could never willfully defy him just because of her vanity.

Still, it wounded her pride. She was a soldier, what was she doing prancing around in this like some kind of show dancer? All to impress Kai, who was after all but a man. It hurt to think that to her public induction, she would be wearing some frilly nonsense instead of standing tall and true in her war attire. They would never ask a man to do this.

Her heart ached. She'd spent her whole life looking ahead to this moment, and now everything was in ruins. She would go down in history as the only First Guard wearing a dress, and the only one presenting without a dragon partner, too. This was humiliation, not a celebration.

She bowed her head and tried to still the throbbing of her heart. This was all right. She couldn't let this hurt her. In the end, her service was what mattered, not what people thought of her. And neither her desires, her pride, nothing. The work she accomplished with her own hands, that was what she needed to worry about, not whether she would finally have the respect of those who had sneered at her all her life.

But still. Presenting as a First Guard in *this*? Her heart sank for the dozenth time, and her stomach churned with a sickness hot and sour. Embarrassing. This was supposed to be her night—in name, anyway—and yet she would go out looking like some kind of painted clown. She wouldn't look like a warrior at all. She would be remembered as the woman in the red dress who didn't look like she could fight her way out of half a dozen layers of silk, much less the armies of their enemies.

With a sigh, she stood up and stripped off her leathers, her mind going blank as she dropped the pieces onto her bed covers one by one. She had draped the dress over the sheets further up, and she stared dead-eyed at the blood-red silk that made up the body of it. There were other layers sewn into it as well, such as the straps that would fall off her shoulders as well as the sash that would circle around her waist and trail down the skirt. There was also some kind of strange sheer material sewn over the waist, something stiff that surrounded it all the way around in graceful ripples. It looked like the chiffon fabric that Letti so loved, but this was stronger, more stubborn. It gave way when she poked a finger into it and rose back to regain its shape when she removed it. Interesting. If only its sheerness weren't combined with the irregular hemline in the front that would reveal some of her right leg in flashes as she walked.

Alluring. Sensual. This was a dress that could tempt and service a man according to his desires. But this was not the garb of a soldier. That of expensive prostitutes, perhaps, from the Quarter Rouge, who lay on their backs with their legs spread for wealthy customers, their own way of servicing their nation. And that was what she would look like when she presented before the crowd, not a dragon rider ready to sweep away every foe from their midst. After tonight, no one would respect her at all.

She slipped the dress on and fastened the sash, staring down at her abandoned leathers and uniform.

This was going to be a long night.

THE ONE MERCY of wearing a dress like this was that there was no end to the places she could hide weapons. On her uniform, there weren't many secret spots she could hide a blade, but already, she had discovered that a holstered leather strap around her thigh was easily accessible because of the irregular hemline and slight split in the fabric. There was also the wide sash around her waist that hid a narrow dagger behind it as well, not to mention the surprising usefulness of having a plunging neckline that revealed cleavage she hadn't even known she had: laid flat against her sternum was a tiny blade the length of her palm. It was a needle-thin dagger that might seem inferior to long swords and other flashy weapons, but a man's jugular wasn't so deeply buried, now was it? Along with all the other important arteries such an unassuming blade could easily reach.

This was better than she had expected. While it was still cumbersome and felt strange on her body—did silk normally feel like this? So slippery smooth and wrong, like it would slide right off her body if she didn't hold it up—at least she could move her legs more freely than she had assumed. There was some kind of fashion trend going on with restrictive skirts that squeezed the thighs to show them off; good thing Letti had known better than to pick something like that for her. Still, Anzi couldn't bear to see the look on her face when she saw her wearing this. That would be the most bitter *I told you so* in all of recorded history.

Except she never appeared. Anzi rushed back to the harem quarters just in case one last time, but Julien had shaken his head. All the harem girls had left already, he said, when they were summoned together so they could prepare to entertain the guests. There was no one remaining. And indeed, Anzi insisted on checking herself, but when she stepped past the doors, all of the beds in the group chamber were empty and made. Where had Letti gone? How could she have disappeared in the short time they had been separated? With a shake of her head, she vowed to scold the woman for her flighty ways. No doubt she would end up finding her by the merchandise stands set up outside the palace, admiring the expensive goods with sparkles in her eyes.

Anzi shook her head again. Time to go.

Kai wasn't in his room when she went to go find him. She narrowed her eyes. First Letti, now him? He had been the one to ask to escort her to the gala, but he was nowhere to be seen, and she was standing here like an idiot in the middle of the hallway.

"Miss?" A young palace maid with a streak of soot on her cheek appeared in the hallway. She held a rag in her hands along with a bucket. She must have been in and out of the rooms in this corridor to clean them. "If you're looking for the gentleman foreigner, the Emperor sent for him a little while ago. I don't know much else, I'm sorry."

"Thank you. I would have kept looking for him if you hadn't told me."

The young girl beamed. "You're very welcome, miss."

Miss. She'd never been addressed so reverently in her life. No doubt the maid thought she was one of the harem concubines.

A part of her was was relieved Kai wasn't in his room. It gave her a little more time to gather her nerve before she let him see this monstrosity she'd stuffed herself into. She didn't look forward to seeing what anyone thought of her in her dress, especially when she knew that many of the solders garrisoned in the Imperial City would be seeing her later tonight, too. They would all have a grand laugh about it, sneering at how she'd gone from soldier to whore, dressed like a courtesan with none of the trained grace.

She sighed again. Kai was but a man after all. He had said it, hadn't he, with his own tongue? He had wanted her to wear something that would let him see *a little more* of her. And she shouldn't be surprised, so why did she feel such crushing disappointment at the memory? All men were the same. Women in revealing dress, that was what they wanted. They didn't care about how strong or skilled she was. All they wanted was a warm body to fantasize about taking to bed, and that was it.

So maybe she had hoped Kai would be different. He had seemed so genuine in his affection that she had almost started to think it was something other than her body that he desired. But after her conversation with the Emperor, now she knew his intentions. She wondered how things would change after tonight. She really wished Letti had hurried up with her lessons in sensual pleasure instead of preaching to her about flirtatious looks and come-hither flourishes. That, and talking non-stop about clothes, makeup, and whatever exotic luxuries had enchanted her for the day. But too late. She would have to make do tonight and hope Kai found her performance satisfactory. If she did well, then…

Dragons. She could hardly believe it. And the more she imagined seeing them in the sky, throngs of them wheeling in the cloudy skies over the Imperial City, the more she could forgive the chieftain for being an ordinary man after all. Dragons…

But now she had to go and track down Kai and the Emperor. The gala would start in a little over an hour, and she needed to find her place soon. With a rustle of her dress, she whirled away and trotted down the hall.

34

They were in the throne room, and evidently, his Excellency was in grand spirits. The faint laughter filtering faintly through the doors made her pause. Had she ever heard the man laugh like that? It startled her to think that Kai—because he was in there too, as confirmed by the Emperor's personal guards before her—would be the reason for such joy.

Ah. Because of dragons. Of course. Kai was perhaps the *only* person in all the Empire who could make His Excellency so joyous now. Ironic, considering that Kai blamed the Emperor for the massacre of the dragons in the Purge. How surreal to think that Kai would now offer to bring back those dragons as a gift for the man he had scorned before. Then again, it was hard to defy the will of the most powerful monarch in the land.

"I need to go in," she said. "They're waiting for me."

The guard looked her up and down with a skeptical eye. "You?"

She refused to clarify further, and he looked away first, as he should.

She slipped in without allowing him to open the doors for her and announce her arrival. By now, she knew to forego the formalities per the Emperor's preference. Instead, she stationed herself just past the threshold with her hands clasped behind her back and her shoulders rigid, standing at attention and waiting to be acknowledged.

The Emperor was not sitting on his throne as she had been expecting, and there was someone else standing next to the grand, ornate chair, leaning on it over a bent forearm braced on top of the backrest. Kai. He must have been speaking to His Excellency before she came in, and yet he was staring right at her as if he had somehow known she was on the other side of the doors before she ever entered.

Their eyes met. Clashed, more like. Despite no one saying a word or making a single sound, her blood began boiling inside her as if some unknown flame had been stoked in the deepest parts of her. She didn't have the chance to question where the sensation had come from because the next thing she knew, she was trapped in Kai's molten stare. He stood on top of the dais across the throne room, and yet it was as if distance between them vanished. It was like the first time they had met when he had cast that spell on her, the one that had nearly driven her mad, but this was heavier, more suffocating...more scorching, thrilling.

His gaze fell from her face and clawed its way down her body, slowly, deliberately. It rested on the cut of her neckline that plunged between her breasts, lingered at her waist, then dropped to the hint of her knee and shin that she knew were peeking out between the draping folds of her dress and behind the stiffened sheer fabric over that. He stared hard there in particular as if he might be able to pry apart the slit and expose her thigh, and maybe more. She knew that look, had seen something like it in the faces of many men, certainly. But something about the way he wore it made her entire body feel hot and cold and electrified all at once. Different.

He drew his forearm away so that his hand clutched at the top of the throne, fingers digging into the plush fabric cushioning the backrest. She could see it, every tensing sinew in his bare arms, the way his breaths grew deep, the way his shoulders spread and widened as if he were about to rear up and stalk toward her. His eyes gleamed bright, hard and hot, and the heat of his whole being flared through her like a volcano erupting and-

"Oh, there you are. Good timing, I say."

No, bad timing! Or was it? She didn't know. Couldn't tell. Her head was full of raging winds that had come from nowhere, and Kai's stare was making her want to draw closer, closer, to meet him halfway. She knew he wanted to come to her, too, and if the Emperor had just held back for one half-second, that was all, a half of a half-second, Kai would have come down the steps and bore down on her like a furious storm.

But...that wasn't right. It wasn't. She swallowed hard and forced her dizzy mind to rightagain, tearing herself away from the confusing tangle

of fire-lit urges threatening to burn her to cinders. Urges to what, she didn't even know, except that she wanted to touch, press, move, scream-

She blinked hard. This wasn't right. These thoughts weren't her own. She had never been half so impulsive, but besides that, she knew instinctively it was something else, too. They felt too different. Not quite foreign, but they didn't feel like they had come from within her, either. Kai with his strange aura must be doing this, she realized. Whatever strange magic he wielded, whatever it was that he did to infect her with his emotions, this was it. A rush of self-conscious heat flooded her from head to toe at the implications, but she didn't want to think about that right now. If her suspicions were correct, then it meant he did lust for her, that he wanted her body under this dress that suddenly felt too exposing, too naked.

Away, she scolded her thoughts. Away.

"How may I serve, Your Excellency?" she asked, forcing her voice to come out flat and unfeeling. Stone. Steel. "Would you like me to escort you to the great hall?"

The Emperor had noticed nothing of what happened between his favored guest and his soldier. He stood by a table full of various plates of fruit on the side of the room, and after popping a final grape into his mouth, gestured with a sweeping motion as he walked over. "No," he said, still chewing. "You and I need to have a word, briefly. My good chieftain, do you mind giving us a moment? I'll be sure to surrender her to your capable hands afterward so she can take you to survey the sights."

Take only Kai, and not the Emperor? She had been under the impression that she would be staying close and guarding both of them until the gala officially began. She said nothing, however, because even if she'd dared, all the strength to speak suddenly left her when Kai began descending the steps of the dais. He came straight for her with long strides that were too quick, too slow; she couldn't decide. Closer, closer he came, and she didn't realize she was holding her breath until he came to a stop in front of her.

He smelled—good. So good. That scent of spice, of warm cinnamon and clean fire, hot like the desert and sharp as the wind. He smelled so good and she had no idea why because he definitely hadn't smelled like that when they parted ways just a couple of hours ago. The rough fingertips that came to rest on her bottom lip scalded her—intoxicating. Fingers pressed ever so slightly into her lip before tracing the shape of it. He touched her like that only for an instant, a teasing flash of desire, hunger, setting aflame her skin with a raging heat that shocked her into paralyzed confusion.

And then it was gone. He dropped his hand, and she watched him out of the corner of her eye as he moved past her and headed out the doors. Even after they latched shut with an echoing click, her legs refused to move, and she remained planted exactly where she stood for a long, silent moment.

"Oh, well done, my dear. Excellent choice, you have him wrapped around your little woman finger. Very good!"

What? The Emperor? When had he gotten here? "Thank you, Your Excellency." Her voice was thick. Was she even speaking? She was so dizzy she couldn't recognize her own voice, or maybe something had taken possession of her body and was speaking through her like a puppeteer. She had no idea what she was saying anymore anyway.

"What's wrong? You look sick." Ra-Tet stood in front of her now, looming over her with his inhuman height casting a strangely heavy shadow. He was frowning. She tried to meet his gaze, still lost and stumbling after having survived the cataclysmic collision that had been Kai's molten gaze on her body. "You need to be in top form tonight, Anzi," he admonished. "No weak spells, no fainting. Is that understood?"

"Yes, sir."

"And don't forget what I said about asserting yourself. Look strong. Be strong. He's attached himself to you and not any of the harem girls, so I'm assuming he'd rather rut a woman who's a bit dangerous like yourself."

"Yes, sir."

"Good, good. What else. Remember well anything that he says about the dragons, Anzi. See if you can loosen his tongue. We have plenty of wine and other things that should help. But that will only work on the body—you'll have to find a way to get through that stubborn mind of his." The Emperor tapped his temple with his forefinger. "He's very secretive, and he's managed to keep hidden every hint that might help us track down where his tribe comes from in the Adaraat or how he kept the dragons alive and unseen. But where I failed, you might succeed. Anything can be valuable, my dear woman. And if you can't acquire those secrets, then at least try to discover his weaknesses, anything I can use against him. Lovers, family, anyone that can give us some leverage, all of that is good. Worm into his head and crack it open, understand?"

"Yes, sir, I do."

"Then that's all. I'm to discuss a few things with my advisors before I go down to oversee tonight's celebrations, so go and soften him up while we still have time. Take him to see the dancing girls, that might put him in the mood."

The thought sent a twisting sharpness through her gut like a fist full of blades, but she nodded and bowed her head.

"Good, then go. Remember everything I said."

THEY WALKED side by side through the palace, heading for the growing sounds of clamoring people at the front. Anzi trained her eyes forward, refusing to even glance at Kai out of the corner of her eye even though she knew he was staring. She couldn't look at him. Not when she could still feel the warmth of his fingertips on her lip and remember wanting nothing more than to taste him, to let him taste her.

"You make this hard," he said, breaking the silence, and his words came rumbling from deep in his chest in a way she'd never heard before. "But maybe I asked for it when I suggested you wear something different tonight."

Her face heated up like a geyser. She still hated this dress and what it meant, how it degraded her life's work and reduced her to nothing more than a showpiece, to bait. But she wondered exactly what it was that he saw when he looked at her in this thing. All she could imagine was that she looked like a red blob, more a bloodstain than a person. But his eyes when she had come through the doors into the throne room—he'd seen something else.

It made her want to ask, but she didn't know if she wanted to hear it. Men hid their desires so poorly. And it injured her pride that this was all he could see now when he looked at her, breasts half-exposed and skin flashing, sensuous silk and satin replacing the hard leather of her usual attire. She wasn't quite so desirable when she was ready to fight and protect, was it? How typical. The women fell over themselves for the soldier men in their armor, but men preferred their women in limp, vulnerable things that exposed as much as they hid. Her chest squeezed with a strange pain. She pretended it didn't hurt.

"I was told my normal choice of wear is hideous," she said coolly. "I'm sure this makes me less unpleasant to look at." Because now she was all walking cleavage and a pair of swaying buttocks. Her mouth tightened into a thin line.

"Whatever you wear, I would watch you all day and do nothing else if I could. There's not a thing about you that's unpleasant."

"Really? So my wearing this dress doesn't change how you look at me?" She couldn't stop the edge of anger that seeped into her voice. Why was she being so defensive? Why was she so disappointed when she had already known? She had already expected him to turn into a drooling, shallow man anyway, with thoughts only of groping soft curves and—

"It changes nothing about how I see you. The only thing it does is make it harder for me to hide it."

She twitched at his reply, and her surprise cut through the growing anger and dissipated it like morning dew. She fumbled for something to respond with, something clever and sarcastic, but all she could do was shrug and pretend she thought nothing of what he said. Pretend she wasn't repeating the words over and over in her head at lightning speed, trying to dissect every deep meaning hidden inside it. "Well," she managed finally. "Try harder."

"Try what harder, Anzi?"

She hated it. Hated it! How could he sound so suggestive and yet so serious at the same time? And how could he say it like…like *that*, and make her feel strange and raw all over, when she knew full well that if any other man dared, she would break them into pieces without a second thought? It was like she wanted him to. Wanted him to push his way to her, to change her mind and convince her he wasn't so bad, that this irritating routine he inflicted on her day in and day out might not be so irritating after all…?

"Hiding it better," she snapped, although her syllables came out the slightest bit more slurred than she intended. "If you keep looking at me, you're going to walk straight into a column."

"If you won't let me look at you, you should at least let me take your hand."

"Not a chance."

"Would you let me kiss you?"

She whipped her head around and stabbed him through with her most powerful glare—only to find him smiling. It was the kind of smile that disguised a laugh, and she narrowed her eyes. "Are you having fun?" she griped. "Is this funny to you?"

"It's fun. The way you have no choice but to understand what I'm saying. You're so good at ignoring me that this is what passes for pleasure for me now. See what you've done to me."

"I've done nothing!"

"Which is torture all the same. I mean it. If you'd let me kiss you, I would. This instant."

She almost told him to. Almost. It was at the tip of her tongue, and there was such a perfect excuse for it. Get it out of the way, she could grumble, so he could stop mooning after her. It would be so easy to say that, and she could roll her eyes just before they collided and he drove her up the wall, lips on her neck like she'd seen several of her soldier comrades do when they reunited with their sweethearts after a long march. It could be so easy...

But she wouldn't, because she knew herself. She was in danger of tumbling over the line that she needed to stay behind. He was a mission, she reminded herself, or was she about to let the hunted become the hunter? Not a chance. She needed to hold the upper hand.

"I said you'll run into something if you keep looking at me." She jerked her chin forward a little to indicate the entrance of the enormous hall they now approached. It was so loud now that she had to raise her voice to make sure Kai heard her. "I'll take you out to the grounds so you can explore."

"There's only one thing I have any mind to explore, and it's right here with me."

"Kai!"

"I meant your conversation and good company, Anzi. What were you thinking about?"

She hated him. She hated him so much, so much! How dare he make her face feel like someone had lit a bonfire under her cheeks? Without another word, she picked up her pace and marched through the growing crowd of wealthy socialites, all the way until she reached the other end of it. If Kai wanted to keep up, he had better focus his efforts on that instead of trying to trick her into...anyway, yes! She hated him.

Outside, the darkness of near-wintry evening was falling fast, but there were standing torches planted in the grass along the stone paths to light the way. Displays were already up from wealthy traders to sell their expensive wares, silks and gemstone jewelry, satin imported from the south, even some captured exotic animals in cages. The crowd wasn't too thick yet, but that would change soon. The people of the Imperial City would never miss such a chance, and while only the upper class would be allowed inside the palace itself, the grounds were open to all citizens. It would be chaos here in just a little while-

In the failing light, a familiar green glimmer skirted across her vision like a dancing moth. She didn't know why it was familiar. Didn't know what was so compelling about it that she simply had to chase after it when it disappeared, either. But just as Kai caught up to her, his voice snaking through the sounds of the crowd to reach her ears, she slipped away from him once more to follow the light.

She tailed it through the people as it bobbed this way and that, and it took her a moment to realize it was something glinting in a woman's hair. A piece of jewelry. She kenw it. Oh, yes, she knew it well.

She was in front of the woman in an instant, blocking her path. There were others flanking her on either side, but Anzi had no interest in them. Just this one. "You," she said in a loud, flat voice, and she stood nearly toe to toe with the woman to ensure they could hear each other past the noisy clamor all around them. "You have something that belongs to me."

"Excuse me? Get out of my way."

"I don't think so. Because that's my brooch keeping your hair together."

The woman's hand flew to her tresses. "You're mistaken, I have no idea who you are."

"I'm not, *Noemi*, and I don't care if you remember me or not. So I'm only going to ask you this once…"

She paused, taking in how the harem girl narrowed her eyes, slowly coming to a belated realization. Too slow, though. She didn't have time for this.

"Where is Violetta?"

35

She wasn't mistaken. This was Noemi, the woman who had slapped Violetta that day in the market district. Her black hair was done up in elegant style with delicate silver links decorating her tresses, but there was no mistaking the poison-green eyes and the beauty mark by her mouth, nor the sour, sharp expression creeping into her gaze. Evening darkness had fallen, but the torch light was plenty enough to see by.

Anzi knew. This was her. And for some reason, she had the emerald brooch in her hair that Violetta had bought for her and held onto. Anzi could believe that young harem girls were forced to lend pretty baubles over to their senior sisters on demand, but something was wrong. Not only was Letti nowhere to be seen, but she had disappeared from the harem quarters altogether. After another fight—or more abuse, rather—had she run off somewhere so no one could find her? If Noemi had slapped her again and left another mark, Letti would hardly show herself in public bleeding and bruised. She was too prideful for that, too vain. But she wouldn't have hidden from Anzi.

"Are you going to make me ask again? You're an adult. You understood the question. Answer it."

She didn't know why she was being so aggressive to Noemi, either. Harem politics were beyond her reach; that was a world with rules unto its own. No one interfered with them, least of all a soldier girl who'd just been stationed at the palace a week ago. But there was something about the woman that made her angry, that made her want to feel dangerous. Like she was out there fighting someone on the field.

"I can't believe it's you," said the woman. "The little soldier bitch with crow's eyes. It's so dark out that I could hardly see them on your face." The girls gathered around her tittered. They didn't seem like the same ones from last time, but who the hell knew? "You traded out the disgusting leather for something like that, I see. Too bad, might as well wrap a pig in silk. Here, why don't I feed you some slops? You can follow me around tonight, and I'll give you my leftovers to keep you happy."

Anzi barely heard her. Blabbering idiot. "I warned you. Before I do anything else, though, I'm going to take that back." She reached for the brooch in Noemi's hair, only for her arm to be slapped away with an enraged squeal.

"How dare you! Keep your filthy fingers off of me. Disgusting fringer trash, I can feel my skin crawling just from the way you look at me. Look down at the ground, or I'll tear them out of your head. Now!"

"Very funny. Now stay still."

This was reckless. Harem girls were the Emperor's property, denizens of the Imperial Palace. And yet Anzi was so cold and composed about confronting one face-to-face and even—

"You can't have it! Get away from me! Get!"

Too late. Anzi ripped the brooch out of the woman's hair with a flick, sending black strands flying out of the fastened clip to droop down the side of Noemi's face. "Now that that's taken care of, I'm going to get some answers out of you. Now."

Noemi was desperately trying to refasten her loosened tresses and her glare intensified tenfold. "Shut your disgusting whore mouth," she hissed. "I can have you killed anytime I want. Do you think you can do anything to me? Do you know who I am, who my father is? I'll have the nearest guard cut out your black tongue and feed it to the dogs. And Violetta? Ha! Go and play with her. You two are just alike. I can see why you two are together so much."

Before Anzi could inform her that she didn't care about all the useless lip-flapping she had in store, the woman was letting loose with another barrage of insults and threats.

"Common bitch thinking she can put a finger on me and get away with it. This is twice now. There won't be a third, one way or another. Get on your knees and lick the ground right now, and maybe I'll let you off easy unlike Violetta. She's regretting talking back to me right now, and she won't think about trying to crawl her way into another gala for a long time yet, either. But you're lucky. You're just a dirty soldier, so it doesn't matter what I do to your face, unlike her. So I can do this—"

She reared back, and Anzi knew what was coming. It would have been so, so easy to stop it, to smack away her hand with a roll of her eyes, but in that instant, she saw something behind her and the other harem girls that made her freeze.

Kai. It was Kai, staring at the women, but it was the murderous light in his golden eyes that made her heart skip a beat. That was the look of a killer, a predatory animal protecting its territory from intruders. That was a look absent of all anger, emotion—just an intent to hurt, and hurt badly.

That instant of hesitation was Anzi's gravest mistake in a long, long time. Noemi's hand landed on her cheek, and while it wasn't even strong enough to make her turn her head away, she saw what it did accomplish: Kai now strode forward through the crowd, pushing, shoving his way forward, glaring at Noemi as if ready to tear her head off her shoulders.

Oh, gods. She knew, *knew*, that if he reached her, there would be blood, and worse. She had seen that kind of expression before all too often in her life of violence, but never had she seen it so deadly—even terrifying. If she were anyone else, she would have been frozen to the spot despite it not even being aimed at her.

She couldn't let it happen. Noemi was an irritation and even a pain, but she couldn't let some harem girl fall into Kai's hands over something so minor. Instinct told her there may well be a dead harem girl splayed out on the ground tonight, right in the middle of a gala-to-be.

Unacceptable. There was only one thing to do.

The slap from Anzi was so merciless it sent Noemi crashing to the ground in a twisted heap. There was no preamble, no winding back of the arm, just a flash of movement and Anzi's hand slamming across her face hard enough to break the skin. She felt a wet spot on her palm, a spurt of blood from Noemi's nose.

Had she really hit her that hard? No matter. It had accomplished what she intended. Behind the stricken harem girls who stared at her in horror, Kai stopped short, momentarily mollified. There was a flicker of surprise in his golden eyes behind the fury, and she held back a sigh of relief before it could give her away. Good. She had him under control again. Noemi, on the other hand, was still a floating question. Anzi looked down at the fallen girl, who had yet to pick herself up from the ground much less clean off the streaming nosebleed dirtying her dress.

"Get up."

No response.

"I said, get up. Or do I have to slap you the other way this time?"

Even still, the woman said nothing as she continued to fix her fish-eyed stare on Anzi's face, and it took the help of all her whimpering friends to get her to stand back up. Noemi stumbled when their grip slackened on her arms, and Anzi shoved her backward into her friends with the heel of her wrist on her chest.

"If it won't be Noemi, then someone had better tell me where Violetta is. Breaking only one nose tonight is a bit of a disappointment, and good things come in threes."

"She's—she's back in our quarters," one girl sobbed. "Please, stop. Please..."

Gods, she hated when people begged. It grated on her nerves to no end. "I already checked there."

"She's in the bath basin. We—we put her there."

Anzi narrowed her eyes and stepped forward. Everyone drew back, scrambling to keep their distance from her. "Explain," she snapped. "Now."

"N-Noemi gave her a reed to breathe through, she's not drowned! I'm sorry, we're sorry—"

A reed to breathe through, underwater. Anzi's blood boiled. That was a torture method reserved for criminals, what did they think they were doing? But there was no time. If it was true, then Letti could be dead already. How long ago?

This time, when she advanced on Noemi, she meant it. She meant it brutally, with no compassion, no pity, only anger and an urge to make her eat her own medicine. Her left hand clasped the woman's shoulder, holding her in place, and the other went up, up, up—

The girls screamed at the almighty crack of the slap, and something flew out of Noemi's mouth, but all Anzi did was grip her in place for another strike. By the time another tooth hit the ground, she was already wiping the blood on her palm off the woman's dress. And then she let her go, but with one final glance around the gaggle of girls sobbing openly in front of her. Four of them, she noted. And this time...

"I'll remember your faces," she said. "You'll wish I didn't."

And then she was gone, leaving a mess of weeping harem girls and a stunned audience in her wake.

SHE DIDN'T REGRET LEAVING Kai behind, and when she found Letti at the bottom of the filled bath basin, trussed up tight in what looked like braided silk so that she was bent backward with her hands tied to her ankles, she knew she had made the right choice. They had left her naked as well, and when Anzi hauled her up from the bottom of the water, the bruises all over her skin mottled nearly every inch of her black, blue, and purple.

She didn't understand how this could be overlooked. She didn't understand how this was allowed, as if harem politics was a real tool to control the hierarchy and not simply a creature that had been left to fester and rot for too long. Letti didn't even have the strength to sob as Anzi pulled the hollow reed stalk from her mouth and hit her on the back with rhythmic beats to get out any water that had made it into her lungs.

This was something soldiers did to each other sometimes if they thought they could get away with it. Tying someone up and forcing them to stay underwater and breathe through a narrow reed, a torturous deed that used to be reserved only for criminals before it became a hazing routine. Anzi couldn't believe such a practice had made its way to the Imperial Harem.

She had never been forced to endure this in the bunks. She had always been strong enough to beat back whoever crossed the line and tried to hurt her. Words, taunts, insults, those she let go until the time was right because she enjoyed anticipating her eventual victory, but this? She had never allowed it.

But Letti wasn't like her. Letti was weaker, defenseless. She couldn't fight off half a dozen other women on her own, and she couldn't slap someone so hard they lost a tooth. She couldn't protect herself the way Anzi could.

"It's all right," Anzi murmured in as soothing a voice as she could manage. She was still furious, still bone-cold with such piercing anger that it felt like icicles stabbed into her body all over. "I've got you. Just breathe, slowly."

It wasn't long before the palace physicians arrived. There were two of them, which went a little way in mollifying Anzi. When she had barged into the harem quarters past Julien, she had shouted over her shoulder to fetch them, and that he had, in record time. She would have to thank him later once she was sure Letti was safe.

She didn't let the physicians try to carry her, though. They were scrawny and weak-looking; she didn't trust them not to drop the hacking harem girl on the way to the bed. And it wasn't Letti's bed she took her to, the one placed with all the others' in the main room, but to one in the back with a lock. She didn't care that the room belonged to one of the harem's so-called reigning Aunts. They should have kept a closer eye on their charges if they didn't want their private rooms commandeered as a consequence. They weren't even present, anyway, although Anzi intended to come back and find them. Someone was going to have to answer for this. Not just Noemi and her friends, but every single person who had let this happen. Every single one.

She watched the girl shiver under three thick blankets as the physician measured her pulse and checked her eyes and mouth. They observed the marks all over her body, too, and Anzi stood by with a cold glower until they were done several minutes later.

"She needs rest most of all," the first physician said. "I gave her something to put her to sleep so she's not in quite so much pain, but she wont be able to walk for a few days. It seems she had some severe muscle spasms in her calves and feet from the way she was tied up, and..."

"I know what happens with these things," she interrupted. "How long will she be asleep for?"

"Until the morning, at least."

"I know a young man who stopped breathing in the night after this happened. Will that happen to her?"

"We'll stay by her side until she's awake again to make sure it doesn't. In the meantime, I'm very sorry, but the rules are that you must be escorted out...You can't stay here, unfortunately."

"I'm the one who found her!"

"Yes, but...the rules..."

Anzi seethed. How dare they. "I can't trust anyone in this place to keep a single harem girl safe," she snapped. "If nothing else, where is the respect for the Emperor? If she'd died, someone would have to answer for it. Tell me that isn't true!"

"Please, miss. Please understand, these are the rules..."

Damn the rules! Damn the rules that let this happen, and damn the rules that probably meant Noemi and whoever else had been a part of this to get away with it! Most of them were the daughters of wealthy nobles, and even if upon entering the harem, they lost all their status and influence in the outside world, they were still powerful within the Imperial Palace. The richer the families they came from, the more powerful their fathers were in the city, and the more atrocious things they could do with impunity.

Anzi's fists curled at her sides. She'd had enough of this. Letting them bully Letti with strikes to the face had been hard enough, but this? They should all be punished for conspiracy, for a malicious intent to murder.

"Please, miss. You shouldn't be back here."

She had no choice in the end. She brushed Letti's hair from her forehead with a clumsy touch, a gesture both unnatural and unfamiliar but necessary nonetheless, before stomping out of the room and then the harem quarters. Julien was waiting there, straining his neck to try to see and hear what was going on. Unlike her, he hadn't been reckless enough to charge in on his own without permission, and now he stared at her with an obvious question for an explanation pasted over his face.

She didn't want to explain, though. What she wanted to do was tell him what came next.

"My name is Anzi," she said coldly. "I'm a First Guard, inducted to the Premier as of last week. I'm glad you were here when I came."

"W-what?"

She didn't care to repeat herself. "Violetta is the harem girl I told you about earlier. I know you aren't allowed to interfere in whatever happens beyond these doors, but I need you to do me a favor. Keep an eye on her. Make sure you see her every morning, every evening, when she comes and goes for every meal. If you peek in and don't see her in her bed, take note and have a messenger sent to me. I want to know everything that happens in relation to her inside this place, as far as you can manage it. Can you do that?"

He was still bewildered. She could see it clearly in his eyes that he had no idea what was going on, but there was a gleam there, too, that told her he understood the seriousness of her request. She didn't know if he believed what she'd said about being a First Guard, but he certainly believed the implications that someone was in danger, and that Anzi needed his help to keep that one safe.

"Her name's Violetta," she said. "Remember it."

36

"Anzi?"

She looked up. "Yes."

"I'd like to sit with you."

"It's not comfortable."

"I'm not looking to be comfortable."

She scooted to the side and made space for Kai on the stone steps that led out to the rear of the palace grounds. This area wouldn't open up to the milling citizens just yet, not until the gala was truly underway and all the wealthy elite decided they wanted to admire the beautiful scenery here. But she had bullied her way past the guards with a cold look, and surprisingly, they had let her go on through. She wondered if they knew who she was somehow.

Kai settled down next to her, but she said nothing to him as the silence stretched on. It was dark now, so she could pretend she didn't see him staring at the side of her face as if she had the map of the world on it. She didn't want to talk. He should know that just by looking at her.

And he did, it seemed. He remained quiet too, until finally she began to wonder if perhaps she did want him to speak after all. It was just too silent. And she could still remember the light in his eyes earlier when she had spotted him coming toward her, and the fire that had burned in them when he saw Noemi hit her.

That rage she had seen in him, had she eaten it up herself instead?

Because beneath her iron control, her bones crumbled under the intensity of the sheer fury she tried to bottle inside. She wanted nothing more than to stand up and track Noemi and her friends down, grab them around their necks, and throttle them all until they were all choking and wheezing on the ground with crushed throats. How could they do something like that. What kind of evil spirit went into any man, any woman, that made them so gleeful at the prospect of making someone suffer just because they could? What kind of terrible soul did one have to bear to take pleasure in tying up a defenseless girl and nearly drowning her for tiny perceived insults and the rampant desire to beat her into submission? What did they get out of it that made them so willfully cruel?

She wished she could do to them exactly what they deserved. Letti couldn't have been the first, and because nothing would change, she wouldn't be the last, either. Hell, they would come for Letti yet again, even, because Anzi knew as soon as she was on her own, the other harem girls would go after her like chicken to scattered feed.

"Who was that back there?"

She shrugged. "Someone who didn't deserve to be let off so easily. But I had to be someplace."

"Would you like to tell me about it?"

"...Not now."

From him came a low rumble of assent, and before she could react, a strong, muscular arm was sliding around her waist and pulling her into his side. Her dress rustled against the stone, the stiff material veiling it making an especially loud noise, but he noticed neither that nor the sour look she shot him. "Stop that."

"You could have stopped me yourself if you'd wanted to."

She pursed her lips. That was true; she couldn't deny it. She could have moved away from him if she really couldn't stand being pressed into him like this, but she was staying where she was and soaking in his warmth this cold, cold night. She wished she had her armor. It wasn't good winter wear, but at least no breezes sneaked its way down between her breasts when she was in her uniform. This stupid dress was making her life all sorts of miserable.

"You're wet," he said. "Don't tell me you went for a sudden swim."

She glanced down at herself and noted the dark discolorations on her dress, only just visible at the edge of the nearest torch light's range. He had sharp eyes. Or maybe some stray drops had made it onto her side where his fingers traced up and down her waist in soothing strokes. Was he trying to seduce her, she wondered dimly. Right now, when she would rather walk barefoot on hot coals than even think about entertaining him by jumping into bed and shimmying under his body? But no. No, it wasn't like that, she realized as she felt his hand stay exactly where it was on her hip and stray nowhere else. In truth, his touch was comforting, and all her tension began to unravel and melt away in response. Why? Nothing had changed. Everything was still unfair, still broken. Just because he was warm and strong and solid against her body didn't mean anything was actually better.

"Those damned snakes went and tried to drown Letti," she growled, and Kai settled in closer so he could lean in and hear her quiet words. "I should have known there was something wrong when I couldn't find her earlier, but I can't believe…"

"The one who hit you? She was a part of this?"

"If you could call that a hit," she snorted. "I gave it back tenfold and should have gone for a hundred."

He relaxed against her, and something tight and hard left his body at her words. Fingertips stroked along her side, each caress gentle and soothing. He had still been angry, she realized belatedly. And he likely still was, but now it was leaving him, bit by bit.

She felt gratified. Not that she needed anyone to be furious on her behalf, but it felt good knowing she wasn't alone in this wrath. Maybe their targets were different, but sitting here together like this, working through their turmoil, it felt…right.

"We could run away," he offered. "You wouldn't have to come back. You could come with me and we'll go someplace where this doesn't happen anymore."

She said nothing. Was she supposed to be tempted by that? Even as a joke, had he meant that to give her a bit of wistful, dreamlike hope? He didn't understand, then.

"It won't matter if we go somewhere else. Because I'd know that back here, everything is still exactly the way it is. And next time, Letti drowns."

"She must be important to you."

"Even if she wasn't, I'd still want to scalp Noemi with my bare hands anyway." She shifted and showed them to Kai, palms up, as if she meant the sentiment literally. Because she did, by the gods. She did mean it. "I hate her. I don't know if I've hated anyone in my life before."

"Never?"

"Most people are annoying at worst. I stop thinking about them as soon as they're out of my sight, and they're not a problem until the next time they appear. But with her, I can't stop thinking about how much of a waste it was to not hit her more . You should have seen Letti's body. There were marks all over her, some old and a lot of them new. All this time, she's been hiding them. I saw her every day this week, and I never thought for a second that…"

"It's not your fault."

She snorted. "I know it's not. I'm just saying I can't believe I missed it. And I can't believe Letti would let this happen to her. Why didn't she tell me?" She clenched her fists in her lap and bowed her head. "If she had said anything, just one thing, one hint, I could have made it right before this ever…"

"Maybe she didn't want to trouble you."

"Well, I'm troubled now!"

He tightened his arm around her waist and pulled her close again, and with his other hand, he took hold of her chin and turned it toward himself. She found golden eyes staring back at her, warm and heavy. She was floating in them, just a bit—

"I'm glad you're troubled," he said softly. "It means you feel, you feel for others so deeply that you want to change the way things are."

"Well, I can't, so there's no point."

"There is. I promise you, there is. Keep trying, Anzi. Keep going. Never stop being who you are."

Promise? What a thing to say. She shrugged and did her best to look away before he could say something else that made her heart throb. Nonsense words. Nonsense feelings. All of it, purposeless and ridiculous. "Let me go," she grumbled, even though a part of her was becoming a little too interested in the way the rough pads of his fingertips scraped ever so gently against the curve of her jaw. And was he leaning closer? Closer, closer…

He hovered just over her lips, and his warm breath rolled across them just as she was sure her own did to him. Well, if he was going to kiss her, then he ought to get a move on and do it. What was he waiting for? So warm, so strong, so-

"Uh—excuse me…"

At the unfamiliar voice behind her, Anzi jerked away from his touch and shot up to her feet as if she'd been scalded. Kai reacted far more slowly, and instead of looking around at their unexpected guest, he kept his eyes fixed on her as she dusted off her dress with hasty, frantic pants.

"Sorry to disturb you," the young man squeaked. "But we've been looking for you for a little while now."

Her mouth was dry, and her heart hammered so hard against her ribs she could hardly get her words out at first. Calm. She'd done nothing wrong, nothing at all. "Looking for us? Is it time already?"

"Yes, miss. Please allow me to escort you back to the main hall."

She wasn't ready. She wasn't ready at all, not when her dress was still damp to the touch and the anger beneath her skin yet simmered and hissed like angry serpents coiled to strike. Bu it was His Excellency who summoned her. She took a deep breath, willing her pulse to slow and her fury to subside—and found it far easier than it should have been. A cool layer of calm had come over her, something she could drape over the cage of her body and calm the wild emotions churning inside. Settle, settle….calm.

Strange. This felt foreign too, a little like the flashes of anger that had come over her time to time in Kai's presence. And now his scent floated around her like a warm cloud clinging to her skin, soothing the leftover tension in her muscles even though he was no longer touching her. She could even remember the sensation of his fingers stroking her side still, slowly, softly…Indeed, she remembered it a little too well. She really, really wished that this messenger hadn't just caught her and Kai necking on the stone steps as if they were actual lovers.

It had been comfort, that was all. If she had leaned into him at any point, if she had fallen for his deep, rasping words whispered into her ear and the way he touched her so reverently, so possessively, then it was only because she had needed a little comfort. She should be allowed to be a little weak sometimes, she argued against no one. Besides, Kai didn't mind anyway.

"All right," she said after a brief pause. "We're ready. Take us there."

She ascended the steps only for Kai grab her wrist from behind. The sudden motion was fast, too fast, and it took her by surprise when he folded her fingers down and pressed her knuckles to his lips. He laid a lingering kiss there as he stared up at her, and a rush of hot confusion and embarrassment swirled through her once more. Damn him, now she was agitated all over again…but this was a different kind of storm inside her now, much more preferable to the wrath she had been struggling to contain.

Would he really have kissed her if the messenger hadn't interrupted them? What would that have been like, his mouth on hers and drinking in her every breath? Would he have kissed her light and quick, or long and deep, and what would she have done in return? Sit there and stolidly take it all, or would he have coaxed her to respond? Because he made her want to. She didn't want to admit it, but yes, it was the truth—he made her want to rise up to meet him, to answer his intensity spark for spark and flame for flame. She had never felt like this before, simultaneously calmed and thrilled by his touch, comforted and agitated in the same breath. He made her feel too much. She couldn't stand it.

"We need to go, sir," she said. "I'm needed."

"Yes." Kai held her hand tighter. "Yes, you are."

Later, when she stood at the very head of the great hall with one of the Emperor's advisors making the official proclamation of her new status—His Excellency sat high up in one of the balconies with a veil concealing his face from everyone—it occurred to her that everything felt like a dream. She had been so upset earlier that this night would be marred forever, that her reputation would crumble beneath the underwhelming weight of a legacy in a red dress and a shallow presentation before the people of the Imperial City. Now, it barely bothered her.

So what if they didn't respect her? So what if they didn't recognize her as the warrior she knew she was? It didn't matter. She knew herself. She knew what she could do, and what she had done with these hands. She could protect; she could fight for others. And maybe if she tried hard enough, she could change the way things were.

She caught Kai's gaze as thunderous applause erupted all over the great hall and outside on the grounds. He was there at the foot of the dais, smiling up at her as if he could read her thoughts. Damn that man, how she hated his knowing expressions. But his gaze was the one she held as she stepped down to join him, and his gaze was the only thing that reminded her that all of this—was unimportant.

Later, she would go and check on Letti one more time, physicians' warnings be damned. That was final. She had done something good tonight, and she was going to be glad she had been there to do it. She was going to feel happy and relieved and a dozen other good things.

Because tonight, she had done something good. And tomorrow...

Tomorrow would take care of itself.

37

When it happened, there was no warning.

"You're leaving?" Anzi demanded. "Now? But you never said—"

Kai's hand rose to cradle the side of her face, and for once, she didn't shoot him a glare or make a single complaint to keep up appearances. She was too stunned to remember to, as he stood there with a small entourage of similarly dressed men standing behind him, all of them waiting in silence. No, two of them were women, now that she looked more closely into the darkness, all various shades of bronzed skin with their heads and shoulders wrapped in the style of the desert nomads. Bodyguards? They had weapons at their hips and slung on their backs. She had never seen them before tonight. Where had they been all this time?

When her narrowed eyes continued to dart around at his companions' silhouettes over his shoulder, he turned her face back to him with a gentle nudge. He only stared at her, nothing else, and for a moment, she almost forgot there were others with them. For his part, he didn't care about them at all; the way he looked at her was as if they were alone as they stood over the water on one of the arched stone bridges past the palace wall.

He had been waiting for her here. As soon as she had gotten the message upon returning from the Cave, she had hurried out to meet Kai, mind whirling and thoughts ablaze. *Leaving*, the message had said, in slanted script. *Meet me where you took me to see the city.*

Leaving. It was just last night that she had been publicly inducted into the Premier, so she had spent all of today being fitted for new armor and uniforms as well as commissioning new weapons to be smithed for her personal use. She had been so busy that she hadn't spent a single second with Kai today, and she had never thought for a second this could happen so suddenly. Shouldn't the Emperor have warned her? He had wanted her to get close and fulfill her mission. Wasn't that what the Emperor wanted? Then why, why hadn't he told her Kai was leaving, she wasn't ready at all—

His thumb stroked along her cheek, warm and slow. She could feel a sleeping strength in his touch the way she always did, something he held back, kept hidden. She could feel—him. "Will you miss me?" he asked, and in the light of the flickering torches placed along the sides of the bridge, his golden eyes glowed bright and hot. They shone brighter than the fire around them, reminding her of molten metal flowing in the belly of a furnace. "Will you think of me when I'm gone?"

Her lips twitched, and she could think of nothing to say. Not at first, anyway, but when he smiled, the words came tumbling out in a rush as if they had a life of their own. It was a visceral response, wild, hurried, pure reflex. "Where are you going? When are you coming back? What happened?"

His fingers drifted back to push her hair behind her ear, then traced down to rest behind it. His thumb ghosted across her cheek once more, then twice, and he stepped forward to erase the space between them. They were so close she could feel his breath warming her chilled lips when he lowered his head, and she thought she could feel the drumming of his heartbeat under his bejeweled collar. Or maybe that was her own, fast and hard and frantic with some emotion she didn't want to name.

"Back to the Adaraat," he murmured, and his voice slipped over and around her like the lapping of waves against the shore. "I'll be back as soon as I can."

"But why? Why are you leaving?"

"To bring the dragons." His smile widened a little, tugging more on one corner of his mouth than the other with a lopsided tilt. "Your Emperor's in a great rush, so I thought I would return the favor."

"You—you found dragons that have survived until now? Dragons that escaped the Purge?"

His palm was under her jaw again, fingertips pressing against it and stroking softly. "Dragons are a resilient kind. They aren't gone yet. They fight."

"You...you didn't tell me."

"Maybe not outright. But you knew already, didn't you? I imagine that's why the Emperor was so eager to have you attached to my side all this time."

Her face burned, and she didn't even have a way to hide it. He was so close that even in the dark of night, he could probably see the reddening of her cheeks courtesy of the flickering flame beside them. "You knew," she said. "You knew all this time but you still let me..."

"There was no *letting*. I would have razed cities to have you by my side. I don't regret a single second of it."

Every inch of her body tightened, coiling with a terrible heat under his gaze. He inched closer, closer, until the tips of their noses grazed one another.

"Will you miss me?" he asked again, his voice quiet and yet somehow loud, too, grinding through her like the rumble of a landslide down a mountain slope. "Because I'll miss you. I'll miss you every second I'm away. I'll miss you like I missed you every time you had to leave my side while I was here."

"Kai."

"Won't you say it?" he whispered, and she could hardly breathe, her chest rising and falling faster, faster. "I wish I could take you with me. We shouldn't be apart. You should be with me, always."

"Kai—"

There was no warning. Fine, yes, there was, but she had pretended not to notice even though their lips were only a hair's breadth away and she could feel them brush with every word he spoke. And now—now he was upon her, their mouths melding in heat and desire so thick she was aware of nothing else. His other hand was behind the small of her back suddenly, yanking her to him so that their bodies pressed together from lips to hips and more, and his iron-hard fingers kept her locked against him as he consumed her with a wild kiss that set her entire soul alight.

She had never done this before and certainly didn't know how, but somehow, they fit together in a perfect way no matter how they moved. His lips on hers, moving and pressing and roaming with a hunger that she could feel down to the smallest parts of her, his tongue in her mouth and coaxing hers to life with nudges gentle then strong then gentle again. He tasted her everywhere, dipping her head back so he could explore every part of her mouth, her lips, and every so often under her jaw where he pressed sharp teeth to skin she had never known could be so sensitive.

He was making sounds that made her burn, low groans that made her heart throb and her pulse race. And she was making sounds back that would have embarrassed her if she were anywhere in her right mind. But she wasn't, and all she knew was heat and hard strength, passion made flesh as he crushed her against him and moved as if he were trying to possess her, body and soul.

He felt like light, darkness, fire, time. She lost herself, hands pressed to his bare chest that felt so warm in the middle of this cold, cold night. She hadn't known until now that this was what she had wanted from the instant she saw him, to touch the whole of him that he had extended so willingly but she had refused forever. She didn't understand it and wouldn't pretend to. The only thing she knew was his mouth on hers that drank her in with such possessive, desperate fire.

She clutched at him, fingers clawing down his chest, and he crushed her even harder against him as he kissed the breath out of her. Until finally, he drew back, their lips still brushing each other and the taste of him still lingering. She stared at him, every kind of stunned and stricken and still floating in the mindless rightness that had been his kiss.

"The sooner I go, the sooner I can come back to you," he murmured. "But I'm already a thousand leagues away just thinking about it."

"Kai..." She didn't know what else to say. Every word left her like sparks fleeing into the sky.

"We'll find a way. I'll show you, and you'll understand. I've never forgotten you, Anzi. Not a day passed that I didn't wait for you, not one second. I waited so long..."

"Waited for what?" she whispered and gasped when he took her bottom lip between his teeth. He nibbled her briefly before swallowing her up in another kiss, shorter this time but no less desiring, no less heated or passionate.

"You know me," he said. "And when you're ready, you'll remember. You will."

When he left her, she felt stripped and see-through like a column of smoke rising into the night. Silent, faded, and tasting the bite of a fast-cooling fire on her tongue, she could still feel every part of him around her. It was the scent of warm cinnamon, faint gusts of hot wind, the scraping of sand against her skin...

"SHE'S ASLEEP AGAIN," Julien told her. "I swear I saw her up and about, though. The doors were open early this morning, and I was just trying to have a little peek, that's all, you know how it is, right? She was trying to come down the stairs on the left, but those physicians came chasing after her and caught her when she fell."

"Fell!"

"Only the last few steps, and not hard enough to split anything, I'd say. But you were right. I could tell she was a pretty thing even from here. My jaw dropped, first glance, didn't know what hit me."

She shook her head. This Julien fellow was a good-natured one as she had thought, but he was more driven to admire women than focus on his duties. And right now, she wasn't in the right mood to humor him. "They're still not letting anyone see her, then?"

"Probably not. One of the Aunts was steaming mad that she couldn't use her room still, and some of the girls were complaining about how she gets to sleep in a private quarter all by herself. As far as I can tell, no one's seen her since she got put up there."

It was nearly nightfall again, three nights since her public induction and two since Kai had left. It still didn't feel real. If she turned around, she should see him there, standing behind her and staring with that enigmatic smile that she never could deduce. If she took a step back, she should feel his warmth, his hands always eager for an excuse to stroke her shoulder, her back, her face, anywhere he could reach. She should be able to hear his voice in her ear, murmuring things she didn't understand, hovering close so he could kiss her once more...

It was too late to deny it anymore. It had taken his leaving to make her realize she was beyond hope. Somehow, without her knowing, she had fallen for him.

"Anzi?"

She disguised her startled jerk with a short cough. "That's all. Just wanted to be sure no one is trying to get to her again. And don't forget what I—"

"I know, I know. If I glimpse anything strange or suspicious, I'll send word. Now go ahead and take care of those mysterious Premier Guard duties, hey? Hey?" He adjusted his shoulder guards with a grin. "Can't believe it. I mean, you're serious enough to be the type, but you're so young. You look like you should still be finishing up your time in Advanced."

"That was a long time ago, Julien."

"So I've heard, girl genius. Anyway, don't let me keep you since you said you were in a rush. Unless you changed your mind, in which case you're welcome to occupy me with some stories about—"

She left. She was not going to let him get into the habit of being so familiar with her. Not him, and not anyone else. He was a good man, lighthearted and sincere, which meant she needed to be especially careful about getting attached like she had with Kai. She was a First Guard, and despite the questions and doubts and fears that came with all the terrible things she had learned ever since she came here, she still had her duties. And that included putting them first.

Kai had never said how long he would be away, and the Adaraat was vast. It would be at least weeks. Months, maybe. It wasn't so long ago that she had been at the desert's fringes for her Second Run, and it had taken her and the others two weeks to travel there from the Imperial City on foot. He would be gone so much longer…

"Oh, girl, you look so glum tonight. That won't do. But I have just the thing for it, wouldn't you know." Bastien waved a hand in front of her face before jabbing his finger down the sloping entrance of the Cave. "Do you want the good news first, the better news, or the best news?"

"…Whichever order they should be told in."

"You're not very fun, but you weren't hand-picked for your sense of humor, I suppose. Let's see…the good news is that you've done it. You can really start dreaming of flying high in the skies, ah? Yes?"

Anzi glared at him. "Get to the point, old man."

"You are terrible, just terrible. I'm saying that your egg is hatching."

What? Hatching, now? Her heart slammed into her ribs with a singular thud so hard she lost the ability to breathe for several seconds. "You said—you said it was going to take a while."

"That was when I thought you weren't doing such a spectacular job. I figured you'd be the one to know best and was going off of that, but unbeknownst to you, you've stirred up life without knowing it. And not just that, but here's something even better. Not just one, but two eggs, girl. Maybe more. Never been done before, mind you, never this quick, but you've made history. We knew all that wild blood had to be good for something, and your way with wyrms, too. The wyrms always know."

She stepped away from him, the movement involuntary. She needed space to think, to understand. "Two," she repeated. "You said, two eggs."

"Well, you'll only be favoring the one, of course. No sense in hogging both for yourself, ah? But what it means is that we can have a, say, auxiliary rider accompany you, a bit like a squire from the old times. Imagine that, the first one out of the entire Premier to have your own servant follow you around on a second dragon. You won't just live like a king. You'll be a king among kings. It's the funniest damned thing I ever did see."

And he laughed. He laughed as if it truly were funny instead of petrifying, and Anzi stared at him while hiding her horror. She stuffed it back down deep inside herself so he couldn't know that she had been trying desperately all this time to stall, secretly shying away from connecting with the dragons inside their eggs. Because she still had questions that needed answering, doubts that had pulled apart her faith that used to be so unshakeable.

"Look at you, all frozen. Don't worry, it'll be a cinch once you get it down. You've already proven yourself adept at putting down a serpent hard when it needs to be disciplined, and that's all it really takes. Control, power. Never let them forget who is their lord and master. And with all the magic singing inside you, two should be no problem. Besides, they'll hatch at different times since one is further along than the other. You'll have time to stagger the strain a bit, so have no fear. Come on, then. Let's get to it."

She had no choice but to follow. Deeper into the Cave she went, trailing behind Bastien while he whistled merrily all the way. He was bouncing with every step, overjoyed, but all she could feel was the rising dread inside her at the thought of bringing two innocent dragons into this cruel, ruthless world that saw them as nothing more than pets, as symbols of power.

"Faster, Anzi. What are you dragging your feet for?" He flashed her a toothy grin over his shoulder. "You're about to change the world."

38

"Go in and look. I've got everything prepared for you."

Anzi hesitated outside the chamber. This one was different from the ones she had seen before, but then again, she had only been to the main hall, the egg chamber, and the small sleeping quarters so far. With how cavernous and extensive this underground system had to be, she knew there was much she was missing. This would be one of those things.

"Something wrong, girl? You nervous?"

How could she not be? There was a dragon egg hatching in there—two—and she wasn't ready. Not with all her doubts. She couldn't do this knowing she would have to train her dragon into absolute submission as Bastien had made so clear. A dragon, noble, thinking, feeling, reduced to a pet. She couldn't do this.

Not that he knew what she was thinking. He was no doubt chalking her hesitance up to nerves. She hated that he would think so lowly of her, that he would use this opportunity to condescend to her as if he knew everything and she was nothing more than an inexperienced child. Any second now—

"Ahh, the softness of babes. Have no fear, little one. Go in and meet your new friend." Bastien's chuckle echoed around them, bouncing against the bumpy cavern ceiling and curling around the corridor like a slithering snake. "No need to be so scared. It's just a dragon, you'll have plenty more. Though I guess there's something special about your first."

She clenched her jaw. Insufferable. Maybe in another world, she might have found him entertaining and amusing enough to befriend him, but knowing that he was a rampant breaker of dragons and saw nothing wrong in glorying in their plight made her want to turn around and smash her fist in his face. It hadn't been so bad when they first started, but every time she had to listen to his proud sermons about breeding dragons and finding the *perfect* egg, the one to lord over all others, she had to stop herself from wrapping her hands around his throat and throttling the life out of him. Who did he think he was to speak disparagingly of the 'inferior stock' that failed to meet his presumptuous expectations? Who did he think he was to treat them as if they were but cattle, without thought, without awareness, without minds of their own?

Maybe dragons couldn't communicate the way humans did, and maybe they didn't experience life the same way either, but that didn't mean they were inferior pack animals to be put to use like warhorses.

"Oh, don't get mad, girl. I'm only joking around. Go on in, I'll show you your clutch. Still blown away by how you've managed to stir awake not one, but two of them in so short a time. If I'd known you had this much promise, I wouldn't have been so against recruiting a young doe like you. I almost convinced them to wait until you were older. That would have been so much wasted time. At this rate, a year or two and you'll be ready to give me your dragons for breeding."

She was done listening. She swept into the dark chamber, knowing Bastien would light the torch fastened to the wall. When it flared to life behind her with a hiss, her eyes darted to the back wall where two eggs lay in a messy nest of sticks and leaves. One was small, small enough to fit comfortably in one hand from wrist to fingertips. It was a reddish color reminiscent of a sunset over the dunes, a burnt sienna hue over its shell that bore a patchwork of hexagonal cracks. The other egg was larger, not in length but much wider around, with a shell of a frosty white hue like half-translucent ice. She couldn't see much more than that from the entrance.

"Do you think staring will do the job? Get in there."

A few seconds later, she was hovering over the nest resting on the wide ledge that jutted out from the wall at waist height. She didn't like it here, how the flicker of the torch at the entrance made her cast a long, jagged shadow that trailed over the nest and up the wall like an ominous apparition. How heavy must it be, her weight that lay over these eggs, dark and cold. She wished she could do better. She wished she knew what to do to make things right.

But there was no such thing. Bastien chuckled next to her and prodded the eggs with spindly fingers until they lay separate in the nest instead of leaning against each other. "Looks like these ones prefer to stick together," he said. "I know I settled them down separately earlier. It's better to keep them apart even when they're still in the shell. You don't want them bonding together. You want to be their one and only friend— for both of them. It can get messy if they compete for your attention when they're hatchlings, but that's why we'll be raising up one at a time until they're under control and heel on command. Got it?"

"Bonding together? What do you mean?"

"What do you think, girl? Not all, but some dragons are pack creatures. If you include Tet's dragon, that's three of the original surviving five that weren't solitary. Well, his was a hybrid type, so he's half-solitary and half-pack, I guess, but that's besides the point. Since all the eggs are incubated together, some things leak over, can't stop that. Keeping them apart works only half as well as you'd think, and that's how you get hatchlings that are the product of two solitaries but can't seem to survive without a pod to cling to. Poor bastards."

"I don't understand."

"Just know that sometimes, we have to put down the damn dragons because it's not worth it. For us, because we have to waste all that time trying to train the bad traits out of them, but for them, too, since you're so keen on feeling for them. Dragons be fickle creatures, and sometimes, they just aren't meant to live long."

Anzi, brave, fearless Anzi who never cowed from the enemy, dreaded hearing whatever he had to say next. So instead of pressing him for further answers to her questions, she hastened to reach for the two eggs in front of her.

"Ah, ah, hold it. One at a time."

"Does it matter which one?"

"The one closer to hatching is the more promising one. Testing time, can you tell which?"

She squinted at both eggs, hands hovering a safe distance away. She didn't want to jostle them; who knew how fragile they might be? Cool wisps of air billowed under her right palm from the white one, as if it were truly as chilling as its frosty appearance made it look. It felt alive, but..."The one of the left?" she asked, and turned to inspect his expression. He was standing on her left, watching her progress with wide, eager eyes. She'd never seen him half so agitated before. "This red one. It's cracked all over already."

"Appearances are deceiving." Bastien wagged a finger at her before pointing down toward the nest. "Dragons have magic. They *are* magic. Their essence reveals itself in the shell, too, especially the closer they are to hatching. You can never tell until you touch, so go ahead and do it. Go on."

She didn't like this. If anything, she wished she was alone so she could figure this out by herself instead of having Bastien babble next to her, no doubt ready to launch into another tirade about good breeding stock. She wanted help, she wanted guidance, but not from him. Not from someone who was more excited about new hybrid breeds than he was about a new life, another bud slowly unfurling in a long-dead rosebush.

"Can I do this by myself."

"Not a chance. I'm here for every hatching, so get used to it, girl."

She didn't waste time arguing any further. The sooner she got this over with, the sooner she could tell him to piss off and stop breathing on her arm, and she lowered her hands so she could wrap them around both eggs as he instructed. And it was instant: the swirl of energy inside both of them, the life awakening, surging, blossoming in response to her body and her magic and all her hopes, her fears, all the dread she harbored about bringing them into a world that would never give them back their rightful place—

Bastien tugged her away by the back of her collar. "That's enough. Damn gifted you are, let's not speed awaken them too quick. Not both of them, anyway. Now, that should have been enough to tell: which one's further along?"

It had been. The one she had thought was closer to hatching wasn't close at all; those cracks all along its shell were part of the egg pattern and nothing more. The white one, ice-cold to the touch though not painfully so, was a different story. "This one's almost ready," she muttered. "Can't believe it's really..."

"Take it, then. Couldn't help but notice, no cold burn on your hands?"

Was it supposed to have hurt her? She examined her palm, noting only a faint pink dusting on the skin. She had assumed it was purely a magical sensation, an illusion more than anything else, until Bastien showed her his palm as well. It was a shiny, smooth red from top to bottom as if he had been gripping an icicle barehanded for hours.

"Just from trying to hold it long enough to settle it on the nest. I keep saying it, but you're one of a kind." He tucked it away under the hem of his tunic to press it against his abdomen for warmth. "I know these eggs well enough to know which I need gloves for. Or at least I thought I did. Learned my lesson, hey? You're all sorts of mystery, and now you're opening up a brand new world. I get to be surprised now, thought I was too old for that. You're changing them, the eggs. I feel like a new man, a babe born into a strange world. It's everything I've dreamed of."

"Stop talking and tell me what I need to do next."

He wagged his finger at her again instead of acquiescing. "Lived two hundred years and get talked down to by a wet puppy. But believe it or not, I like that too. Young, scruffy thing, you put a fire in me I didn't realize I'd lost until now."

"…Step back."

"All right, all right. Go on, pick your egg up so we can leave."

"And leave the other?" She pointed at the reddish oval that would lie alone there in the dark once they departed. The thought sent a rush of displeasure through her. "By itself, just like that."

"Well, sure, girl. Remember what I told you about keeping your dragons separated while they grow up. You need them dependent on you, not each other. Or eventually, you'll have a regular riot on our hands since they get all sorts of bad ideas if they're invested in each other…Had an issue with a rebellion a little over a hundred years ago, never again since. We learned our lesson."

She didn't want to hear about it. She already knew how that had ended, after all, if Bastien was still here and dragons were still being forced into bondage. "I want to raise mine *my* way," she said after picking up the ice-cold egg and cradling it against her chest. "You can tell me the basics of what I need to do, but don't think these dragons are your newest playthings. They're my responsibility. I'll take care of them and decide how to do that on my own, aside from the essentials."

He rolled his eyes and pointed at the chamber's entrance. "Ah, the naivete of youth. You're the worst I've had so far, but then again, you're all but a babe. Bit cute, though. Hurry up, let's go."

She wouldn't get an acknowledgement out of him. Not today, maybe not ever. It was ingrained into his mind that dragons were cattle, livestock, nothing more, and in the end, he held more authority and influence than she did over these things. If he really was as old as he said, then he must have been serving the Emperor faithfully for two centuries, supplying all the dragons His Excellency could want whenever a new rider was inducted. She was nothing. She was a new recruit who hadn't even yet learned to harness her scant magic, lost in a civilization that was slowly becoming more unrecognizable day by day...

But she wasn't trapped. She wasn't weak, either. She was who she had always been, even if she'd been wrong about what she had thought that was. She would make it work, and even if she dreaded failing, she wasn't afraid of the future. She wasn't afraid of the world.

Because who was to say she couldn't change it?

"Hello," she murmured to the egg cradled in her elbow as she followed Bastien to the main hall. Frost smoke rose from its surface, thicker and thicker, and she thought she could hear the sound of snow crunching underfoot as she moved along. She could smell northern snow, frost on the pines in mid-winter, the sensation of walking over the frozen Annat River in the wintertime, compass-point tributaries webbing throughout the Imperial City...

"Talking to it already, are you? Don't get whipped by it. That's what happens with half the people I have to train up, very annoying. You'll only break your own heart with what you have to do later."

"Excuse me?"

"Never mind. Just go and sit there at that table and put the thing up. I can hear it trying to get out already, your wild blood is something else."

She wanted to ask him why he kept talking about her *wild blood* without ever explaining it, but she didn't want to hear the answers from him. Not from someone who had so little respect for anything except power and control, and certainly not for dragons or the other *common* people of the Empire. Damned rodent of a man.

"You really do look sour today. Come on, girl, cheer up."

"Why the raw meat?" she asked, ignoring his patronizing and pointing at the thick, glistening slabs on the tin tray waiting on the long table. "Dragons can only eat live prey."

"You still believe everything you heard growing up? Get it all out of your head. This is our world, no one else's." He settled next to her on the wooden bench, slouching sideways on one bent arm planted atop the table. "You were taught we only have one dragon partner for life because we want to foster the idea of destiny. You were also taught dragons are still immortal because we want our strength to be seen as everlasting.

That's just the beginning, and this is one of those things, too. Dragons don't only eat live prey. Not ours. We taught that because it makes them sound fiercer, but most dragon species are capable of scavenging carcasses if need be. Oh, don't look at me like that. It was a necessary ruse. For a long time, people of the annexed territories hated the dragons enough to try to protest riders coming around, so we had to make them more afraid than they were angry."

"They hated the dragons?"

Bastien snorted. "Well, of course. Think about it. You have the five dragons that we owned at the time coming around to burn entire cities down and siege them. Roast fields and women and children alive for weeks and months, non-stop. The shadows of their wings brought terror and agony and death for those people. Dragons are the symbol of our whole power, the Empire's identity. You don't think the annexed peoples hated them to death? They still do. You've never been garrisoned in a conquered city yet, but when the time comes, you'll see it in their eyes. They'll stare after you like you're evil incarnate. Bit funny because they'll never have the seeds to say anything aloud—but when they do, you get to have your fun."

She stared. "None of that ever happened. The Empire fought in civil warfare in its crusade, and the warlords surrendered once they realized they were beaten and and that the Empire could care for their people better than they ever could."

"Ye gods, Anzi. Don't tell me you actually fell for that. Even the other recruits figured out that was all crockery."

How? How could—burned alive? Women and children. Terror. Death.

"But history lessons are for scholars. You, girl, are something infinitely more important. Now, eyes on your egg, can't you hear your new friend chipping its way out? It can't wait to meet you."

Her blood rushed in her head like the roll of deafening thunder. Her vision swam. She could hardly see, and she thought her eyes might be burning with tears as if she were some stupid child and not a strong, seasoned warrior who had fought all the way to the top for the privilege of serving her nation. Stop it, she told herself. Now—was not the time. She would think about all of this later when she was alone. Right now, there was something more important.

"Ah! Hold it. Make sure it calls for you first before you help it get out of its shell."

She froze, holding her hands away from the egg as she watched it rattle around on its base with small jerks. It drummed the wood underneath with its efforts, but the shell had stopped cracking. The hatchling was not going to be able to make it out on its own. Her chest burned. She needed to help. It needed her help, it needed—

"Why does it have to call for me first?" she demanded, annoyed enough to raise her voice in a snapping snarl. "Why are we wasting time? What is this ritual?"

"Ritual?" Bastien laughed. "No, not a ritual. It's your dragon's first lesson. It must ask to receive, and you are the master. If they want something, they need to beg first. It'll teach them submission from the very beginning, very good for your relationship."

Silence.

The egg swayed a bit more, and Anzi heard the slightest rustling from within.

"So," she said slowly, dragging each word with a cool, deadly composure. "I sit here, knowing it needs help, and don't give it until it's crying for me?"

"Well, in nature, I believe the sire or the dam would help them out, but this way is better. You're not its natural parent, so you have to force that bond in a more—"

"Go fuck yourself," she said calmly and pried open the shell.

39

Bastien had no authority over her. He was neither an officer nor did he hold some bloated rank in the Emperor's court, and his only purpose here was to acquire dragons. An old man with a young face who fancied himself an innovator, a laughing jester who thought himself so high above everyone else just because he had been gifted with immortality obtained from dragons. And where was his dragon, anyway? What noble creature was so unlucky to be bonded to a man like Bastien? She ached for whoever it was, felt their pain as real and sharp as if they were shackled and bound before her very eyes.

To all the burning, dark hells with him. He might have gotten away with tormenting innumerable others, but he would not lay a hand on the ones she was responsible for. Not on her life.

When he reached over to stop her from opening the egg, she shot up from her seat and lashed out, hard and fast. But he was quick and agile, so she was already swinging with her other arm to deliver a second blow when he stayed her fist with his palm. She went for the side of his head, not enough to knock him unconscious but certainly enough to beat any further stupid ideas out of him, and her fist made contact with soft hair, hard skull. Too hard, actually, and ridged underneath his curls, the sensation distinctly inhuman just as his mixed appearance had always suggested.

But inhuman or not, she him hit hard and true, and there was no escaping the consequences. Bastien had risen half-off the bench and now went flying off the seat entirely. He landed on his back a full meter away with a sickening impact that echoed through the cavern a dozen fading times. He rolled twice from the force of her strike before coming to a stop, half-curled on his side, and Anzi stared down her nose at him with her head tilted back at a defiant angle. For a moment, there was no other movement, and she waited until he slowly unfurled, sat up, and turned around on the floor to look at her.

She spoke first. "I don't care what you've seen or what you are," she said, and she could have sworn the words were cold in her mouth, like ice chips crackling against her teeth and tongue. "But this is my dragon. Not yours. You might be here to guide me, but until someone tells me differently, I don't answer to you and you certainly don't put your hands on any dragon I'm responsible for."

He wiped the corner of his mouth with his thumb, and she saw it come away with a glimpse of a red smear under the torch light not too far from them. He must have bitten his tongue. Maybe he should have thought about doing that a long time ago, instead of spouting all the disgusting things she'd been forced to listen to.

He said not a word. No protest, no threat, nothing. Instead, a slow smile crept over his thin mouth, pleased and curious. Something about it made her skin prickle in defensive alarm, although she didn't know why. Was he about to leap up and come for her without warning? Was he going to use his strange magic that she had yet to understand or know how to counter? What was he going to do now, and what was it about him that was making her muscles twitch and tense in eager anticipation of a bloody fight, fast and brutal and full of violence—

"Careful, girl," he purred from the stone floor. "Those are the territorial instincts coming through. That's good news. I didn't expect it to be so pure, though. Looks like we're going to have a real ball of a time getting you trained up."

"I don't care what you're talking about," she said flatly. "I'm done with riddles and I'm done with you. I'll respect you in the capacity you fill as the resident *expert* on dragonkind, but beyond that, nothing."

"Nothing at all? Really?"

He was still teasing, still thinking this was nothing but play. Did he not realize she was on the brink and not the slightest bit sorry about it? She wanted to climb off the bench and teach him a lesson, a real one, never mind who he was. It had become apparent to her long ago that all the hopes he had in her made her far more valuable than she had first realized. Well, now she had a vague idea, and she wasn't going to hesitate to exploit it. Too many people these days wanted to step on her toes just because they thought they could. Who said she had to tolerate it?

Besides, it was as the Emperor himself had said. She was a First Guard now, a member of the Premier, the highest echelon of military authority in all the Empire. She had to assert herself as his Excellency had advised, as befitted her station. And when it came to Bastien, he was no real dragon rider even if he kept company with the Guard and tended to the dragons' eggs in this hidden cave system. When it came down to it, she was willing to gamble that she could go toe to toe with him in any dispute, not just physical ones.

"Problem?" she asked, still staring down at him, half-wishing he would get up and charge at her. Her blood was singing, shouting in her veins. She wanted to hit something. A cold whisper of a gust whipped around her, making her twitch in growing anticipation.

"Not from me," he said with that same shit-eating grin he refused to wipe off his face. "For now, at least. What I'll say is that you need my help, and eventually, you'll accept it. You don't have a choice. It's what they all do in the end, if that makes it any easier for you."

"I don't need your help if I don't want it. And all I want from you is the basics, no more. How to keep it alive and how to care for it, except I get the feeling that you only know how to do the first half. So I'll figure out the rest on my own."

"That would be a waste of time, girl. You need someone who knows what he's doing. That would be me."

"You're not the source of all knowledge on dragons."

"No, just what's left of it."

She bristled, and yet she knew he spoke the truth. It was the reason why no one in the Empire truly understood dragons, and why the city's people admired yet largely ignored them otherwise. They were mythical beasts, spotted in the skies every so often, but too mysterious. The same went for the Premier Guard. There were no books written on them by scholars even to memorialize their names and their service, and with half the civilian population barely literate, who could pass down any kind of knowledge about them anyway, rider or dragon? There was no one who could help. No one but Bastien.

A high pitched cheep from the table made Anzi glance at it out of the corner of her eye, and the tip of a blueish white snout poked out of a tiny hole in the dragon egg. A small, sharp, tooth-like nub wiggled futilely against the thick shell, and a wisp of cold steam circled around it before enveloping the egg in a see-through mist.

Her dark eyes darted back to Bastien in case he tried to pull anything while she was distracted, but all he did was slowly raise his hands as if to show he was unarmed and meant no harm. "Do as you like," he said with a wink. "But wait any longer and you'll end up doing exactly as I say, anyway. I still suggest you wait until it starts calling to you for help before you go and jump to its aid. Makes it easier later."

Damn him. Why was he provoking her? Surely he could surely sense the hostility rising in her like a voracious animal. Every word he said, every sound he made had her wanting to hurt him the way she had Noemi so she could beat the humanity back into him.

She hadn't felt this kind of anger in—years. It was foreign in its familiarity, like an ancestral memory she couldn't quite grasp. All this time, she had lived on pure determination and spite and devotion to what she had thought was her calling as if they were her bread and water, but now... now, she wanted more. Had more. And she would fight tooth and nail to protect it.

"Don't touch me or the dragon," she said, letting slip a snarl. "I'm not afraid to hurt you if it's necessary."

"As you've proven, girl. But like I said, beware your wild blood. It's made you a little *too* wild. Don't you feel it, the way the dragon's changing you, manipulating you? This is part of the process. You need to dominate it in every way, make certain your power and mastery over it."

"I feel nothing except the need to stop listening to you. I can make that happen one way or the other."

"So fearless." He got to his feet, slow and steady, with his eyes fixed on her and never blinking even once. Why there was such an excited, pleased expression on his face she didn't know, especially since she had just walloped him hard enough to knock the wits right out of an ordinary man. "I've never had a recruit bursting out of their britches like you. They're usually fawning at my feet...This is a nice change. You've got me shaking, I'm so excited."

"Keep your excitement to yourself."

If he provoked her again, she would lay him out flat, caution be damned, but there was a more important matter to handle. Urgency filled her mind with swirling haste, nipping like a winter wind through an open door. The hatchling, she realized. She was feeling its presence, its power. Could Bastien feel it too, or just her?

Anzi didn't even bother sitting back down on the wooden bench before nudging the snout tip back into the egg with her thumb. The infant dragon chirp from inside, a disgruntled sound, but she continued to push it back until her nail was resting against the cracked opening in the shell. And then with a mighty crunch, she crushed the hole open and tore away a section of the hard encasement. When the pieces fell onto the table, she thought she could hear an icy clinking hidden in the clattering sounds, but she paid it no mind and tore open another section, then another until the shards were an uneven heap.

There. Curled up inside the egg but now wriggling free, a beautiful white creature tinged with frigid blue. It was wet, and yet by the time she grabbed for one of the linen napkins next to the tray of raw meat by her elbow and turned to wipe it down, the moisture had frozen into perfectly clear residue all over its skin. Still, she tried to wipe it away, only for the hatchling to tumble out of the shell's remains onto the table and narrowly dodge the cloth. She caught it before it could fall off the edge, but a lancing pain up her palm had her clenching her teeth as she eased the small dragon back onto the level surface. Cold. Freezing, in fact, as she had suspected, but the frosted rime that formed over her skin where the hatchling had touched melted into droplets a few seconds later. No harm done. In fact, when she nudged the hatchling again away from the table's edge, there was no pain this time. The creature crawled around on its belly, dragging its slender form around the table and shaking off icy crystals with every movement.

Gods, it looked so fragile. Now that its tail had unfurled, she could see it was bigger, or at least longer, than she had initially thought, but even then, it was scarcely as long as her arm from fingertip to elbow including the flexible tail now swiping from left to right. Its scales were so small she could hardly tell where each individual one began and ended, all of them an almost translucent blue-tinged white that shimmered under the torchlight's flickering illumination. There was a shifting light underneath them, too, that reminded her of a frozen waterfall trapped in motion, gleaming under moonlight.

With a rattling shiver, the hatchling loosened the short spines that she hadn't noticed were lying flat along its back. There was a main ridge of themtrailing from the top of its head down to the tip of its tail, long then short then long again at its end. An auxiliary line of pure white spines jutted out on either side of those as well. They were much shorter, the smallest of them little more than tiny nubs poking out from the scales. A moment later, all of them folded down and lay flat again.

Incredible. Beautiful. Unbelievable—a live dragon right in front of her, still shaking off flakes of ice from its scales and leaving them to melt into tiny puddles as it rubbed itself clean on the table's surface. Anzi watched eagerly, mouth open, marveling in the silence—

—until it let out a high-pitched screech that made her wince and draw back. Then again, a whining scree that sounded like the tip of a dagger dragging down the length of another blade. Angrily.

"It's hungry, girl. Feed it."

Damn him, she could have figured that out on her own. The hatchling was flaring its spines again—the tallest of them were about the length of her finger, she noted—and opened its maw in a gaping cry with yet another wail. Easy enough to tell what it wanted. She dragged the tray closer and hurried to grab the smallest chunk of raw meat she could see before bringing it over to the infant's mouth. It must be terribly hungry.

As evidenced by the way it swallowed not only the meat, but also tried to take off her fingers. Luckily, it wasn't strong enough to relieve her of them even if the small teeth sank deep enough to draw a few thin rivulets of blood. This was nothing, no more painful than being bitten by a small dog, and a rush of fond affection swirled inside her in response.

But Bastien leaped forward as if to snatch the hatchling away, and Anzi planted the heel of her wrist into his chest hard enough to send him reeling back with a wheeze. When they locked glares, gone was his eerie smile and the twinkle in his eye, replaced by sharp panic and angry alarm. "Idiot girl!" he snarled, his once-smooth voice sharp and hurried. "Get it off of you! I already warned you about your wild blood, you don't know what it'll do to creatures like dragons."

"Let me handle it."

"You want her to get a taste for it?" he demanded. "You don't know how many I've had to put down because they decided they liked biting off a chunk of human flesh. Get your hand out of its mouth!"

"It's teething," she snapped. "And it's hungry, but not for me. Calm down." She was sure of it, especially when the hatchling gave up exploring her fingers with its teeth upon realizing she was hiding no more meat between them. It let go with another wail, tail flicking out with a snap that had it dragging its extended spines along the tabletop. See that, she wanted to snip. Harmless. She fed it another strip, more cautiously this time, and then another when that disappeared in a flash. Then another, and another.

Would it ever stop? Scarcely larger than a street cat and it was eating more than its own weight. She was almost afraid it would hurt itself or burst open in its sheer greed, but when no warning was forthcoming from Bastien—because fine, yes, she was waiting for his cue in this regard —she continued feeding its hungry mouth, enduring nips and scrapes of sharp teeth and the occasional eager swipe of its spined tail.

Until at last, she noticed it was struggling to swallow the last chunk of dripping meat, scaled throat bobbing as it tried to work it down from its half-open maw. "All right, that's enough." Without hesitation, she pried open its muzzle and reached in with her other fingers to pull the chunk back out. The hatchling screamed, furious about being deprived of the last morsel, but she held on tight with a stubbornness and strength far superior. It had had enough. Its belly was so distended that the formerly slender, lithe looking thing was now unrecognizable with its fat sides, and while she found it terribly endearing, she was not going to watch it choke itself because it had no self-control.

"And there you go." Bastien's voice was smug she would have swungg at him again if not for the fact that she had to continue restraining the hatchling. "Congratulations. You're a regular dragon tamer now, Anzi-girl. It'll go to sleep soon, all they do at this age is eat themselves to death then sleep it off. Give it a name before you leave for the night so I can report the good news to Tet."

Tet. His Excellency, he meant. She would never become accustomed to the casual way he referred to the Emperor, but that was none of her business. "She has a name," she said coolly and lifted the now-heavy hatchling to cradle it in the fold of one arm. As Bastien had said, it had fallen asleep within seconds even though just a moment ago, it had been screeching its head off and angrily demanding more to eat.

"Fine, then, what'd you name it, girl?"

"No. I mean she already has a name, not one that I'm giving it."

"That bite must have addled your wits," he chuckled, but she narrowed her eyes and stood up from the bench, maintaining her glare. She knew she was right. She had felt it earlier, a whisper of a sensation. And what had been but a frost-kissed suggestion in her mind had grown, solidified, taken shape in her thoughts until she knew exactly what it was.

"You can think what you like," she said and turned to walk toward the hall's exit. "But her name is Netra-hau."

40

A nzi didn't stay at the palace. She returned only for a quick bath and a woolen blanket that one of the palace maids had left in her room when the weather took a turn for the frigid. When she departed and reached the wall, she flashed her vouch token at the guard who didn't seem to recognize her.

"It's too late to go through the gate," he said. "It'll wake up everyone with the tremors. Go up the wall and they'll show you how to get down."

She nodded and followed the direction of his pointing finger. The guardhouse wasn't far; she had already been expecting to be sent there. For officials and important guests, of course the stone golems could open the rumbling gates in the middle of the night, but for a single soldier? Never. Maybe if she had revealed the sleeping Netra-hau inside the bundled blanket in her arms and informed the guard who she was, he wouldn't have hesitated to afford her the courtesy, but she didn't want that. She wanted discretion. She wanted peace. The last thing she wanted was for someone to know that a First Guard was leaving the palace and report back to someone who might try to stop her.

She needed time and space to sort things out in her head. She had a sleeping infant dragon in her arms, the first of a new generation, and she couldn't bear to think that its first sunrise would be from the bosom of the Imperial Palace. Not when she knew what she did now. Not when all she could think about was how Kai had been right, that the Empire had wiped out dragonkind then preserved the last traces of it for itself with sinister purpose and practice. Everything Bastien had said to her, every dark and depraved thing he had tried to teach her, she needed to get away from it. Netra-hau deserved at least that freedom, however fleeting.

She loved this land, she assured herself as a swinging rope ladder fell down the towering height of the palace wall. She loved its people, how there was so much good in them, thriving and beautiful. She loved even those who had treated her with such disdain over the years. They had grown up in the arms of this nation just like she had, this strong kingdom that had brought peace and stability to this side of the continent after centuries of bloodshed between countless warlords all vying for cruel domination. The Empire had paid a heavy price and demanded heavy sacrifices to make that possible, and now, what used to be blood-soaked territories now mingled together in peace, in prosperity. She loved this land. She loved the things in it in all their abundance.

But she couldn't pretend to forget the repulsive mire that hid below it all, the foundation of dark and terrible things that held up the house of the Emperor. She couldn't forget Bastien's laughter as he spoke of reducing the last of the dragons to mere pets, controlled and mastered by the will of their riders as if they were nothing but pack animals. She couldn't forget what he had said about immortality, of kings, of glory.

She could hardly understand it. No, she did—she just didn't want to. But hiding from the truth couldn't shelter her conscience for long. Soon, she would have to reconcile with it and step into her rightful place.

The climb back down the wall was long and perilous, or would have been for anyone else. Not for Anzi. She lashed the opposing corners of the blanket around her neck and made sure Netra was completely concealed within it against her chest. And then she descended, hand over hand, the rope ladder swaying with both the shifting of her weight and the stiff winds that blew against her. Cold, refreshing, with a painful enough bite that it distracted her from her other worries. When she reached the bottom, they pulled the ladder back up, and she left without a backward glance. When she returned, she could enter through one of the gates; she didn't intend to make her way back until after sunrise, after all.

Netra stirred within her swaddle, and Anzi quickened her pace. She didn't want the hatchling squirming out in view of anyone, even if the city was nearly deserted this time of night. There were still guards on patrol and the odd civilian wandering around, usually lovers looking for a quiet, private moment just as she was. Luckily, she wouldn't get in their way since she was headed for the lower districts where no one would pay her any mind. She would be safe in her anonymity since few there had the luxury of worrying about anything that wasn't their business.

It was a long walk even though she set a brisk pace. If she were to run, she would have reached her destination far sooner, but with Netra so close to waking already, that wasn't an option. A too-swift pace would have her clambering out of the swaddle and screeching again for sure.

The Imperial City was vast and sprawling, but with a population in the hundreds of thousands, it was a miracle there was part left in it not crowded by life. Thankfully, there were just such a few spots left, one halfway out toward the direction of the Tower rising like a dark needle in the distance, shining under the moonlight that beamed down to glisten along its narrow sides. Anzi slowed her pace and wondered if she might visit Oza again soon—today, perhaps. She didn't want to draw undue attention to him in case anyone got any strange ideas, whatever they might be, but of course he would want to see Netra.

She settled down by the riverbank in the deserted swatch of land surrounded by several drooping willows. No people, decent privacy. She could do nothing about it if someone happened to trudge down the path close by, but it wasn't long before sunrise. She would have to leave again soon anyway if she wanted to make it back to the palace before anyone realized she was missing, and she wanted to see Letti, too, if the harem girl was in any condition to receive visitors.

Anzi didn't miss her, of course. It was because she felt responsible for her safety, that was all. Admitting to that kind of sappy sentiment would be as ridiculous as saying that she missed Kai, that smug know-it-all chieftain who'd dared to kiss her as if they were lovers. If he tried that again, next time, she wouldn't be taken unawares. She would grab him around the waist and throw him over her shoulder, show him she meant business. How dare he.

She touched her fingers to her lips, still marveling over how presumptuous and pompous he had been to kiss them as if he owned them, tongue moving against hers with such ferocious want that he had left her heaving for breath after they parted. Half-controlled, half-wild, it had been so astonishing she hadn't even thought to resist. Heat, strength, a possessiveness that had had her wondering how he could be so confident and demanding when he knew nothing about her other than the little glimpses he'd stolen of her life over the course of mere days. He had no idea who she was or what she had done in her life. Those days they had spent together in careless leisure as she showed him the city, her life, her world—that was only the barest speck of her true existence.

She was a soldier. She fought for the Empire. She had left her mark on dozens of battlefields, wiping out barbarian tribes and destroying rebellions scarcely before they could even begin. She protected this land both from within it and on its fringes, wherever she was called. That was her life, to fight and be fought and see that the peace of their world lasted for as long as she could protect it.

She had killed. Did he know that? How could he not? The Empire was a warring one, after all, and even if she didn't like to think about the inevitable violence that came with every annexation, that was something she couldn't deny anymore. The things Kai had said, the things Bastien had said, they came and swirled together in her head like storms crashing in from different directions. The world beneath the world, the hidden one she had never spared a thought for. And now it was being shoved before her on a platter she couldn't refuse.

With a start, she looked down at the squirming swaddle hanging from her neck. Netra was awake, and judging by the sounds she made, distinctly unhappy. Anzi undid the blanket with deft fingers, detaching it from herself and releasing the hatchling from its confines. And just as she had guessed she would, Netra began screeching anew as loud as she had the first time when she had crawled out of her egg.

"Patience," she muttered under her breath even though it was futile. How nice it would be if dragons could understand human speech. "Hope you like fish."

The Annat River flowed fast and strong, and this particular bend in it was full of life since few ever came out this far to fish in it. Seconds later, Anzi had taken off her leather guards and rolled her pants up to her knees so she could stand in the cold water. She was bent over, hands hovering over the surface while Netra perched around her shoulders, talons digging into her skin deep enough to leave marks, maybe even draw blood. And that was all right, honestly, if she would just stop screaming so angrily to be fed.

Cold. Cold enough to hurt, but it didn't. The fast current that splashed around her legs and wet her clothes should have her shivering, but it was little more than a nipping coolness against her calves. Numbness spread up her knees and to her thighs, body tightening and tensing to try to conserve its heat, and yet it was—nice. Soothing. Around her neck, Netra quieted too, softening her enraged shrieking. At least until she spotted a fish wiggling below the crystal-clear surface.

Who would have thought Anzi would ever start her morning with fishing? Much less to feed a dragon. It was both unimaginably mundane and fantastic at the same time, like daring to step into the Emperor's presence in the throne room with nothing but her smallclothes on. How strange, how uncanny, how marvelous. Sitting now with the dragon between her knees and gorging itself on whole, flopping fish, fins and bones and all. Anzi dried her hands off with a corner of the woolen blanket as she watched in wonderment and in sadness. Such a small thing, no larger than a house pet, hungry and craving. How long it would be before she grew up to be as big and strong as Colonel Bisset's dragon? How long it would be before they had to fly out together to suppress rebellions, raze foreign cities, blaze the path forward for the Empire to spread across the land...

This was the life she was destined for. Had always been destined for. That was why her path here had been unswerving and true from childhood until now. If this wasn't what fate had in store for her, then why had it had led her here? Why had everything she'd done, every step she had taken, end with her in the heart of the Empire and dragons hatching under her hands?

"We have a connection," she told Netra, who was now lying haphazardly on the grass with her belly looking like someone had gone and inflated it. "I knew your name and I don't even know how."

She noticed a small twitch on the hatchling's side and leaned closer to inspect it. The wing, she realized. It was so small, though—a single slender ridge for the bone and the gossamer skin flap folded underneath. So fragile it looked like it could snap easier than a twig. A rush of protectiveness surged through Anzi, and to the dragon's complaining dismay, she scooped her up in her arms. The hatchling hissed like an angry cat, jaws clacking menacingly at her forearm, but she didn't care.

"Bite me, then," she said. "You're going to be trouble as it is. I can tell."

Netra clicked her teeth again with her small fangs half-bared.

"It would be easy if you could understand me, but we'll make do." Anzi sighed. "I'll make mistakes. I'll make a lot of them. But we're together, and I'm going to do right by you. So you have to do your best, too."

That was how it was. A new, vulnerable shoot sprouting from barren ground, small and breakable, and Anzi was responsible for it. She had to protect it, cultivate it, teach it how to survive and thrive with or without her. Because she wasn't going to raise Netra the way Bastien insisted, breaking her like a common horse with no spirit, no soul. Dragons were people. Dragons lived, dragons felt, dragons were more people than humans were. She didn't know how to put into words how she knew this to be implicit truth, but she did, and from now on, she would protect that knowledge with her life.

Netra, for all her cold, ice-white scales and fragile wings, was still so weak and small. She had no one to protect her in all the world except Anzi and Anzi alone, and by the gods, she would do it right. She would do this for Netra, she would do this for the other hatchling she hadn't met yet, she would do this for any dragon she brought into this world. If only she didn't have to expose them to the caprices of the Empire. If only she could keep them hidden away and safe until—until things were different, or at least until she wasn't so confused about everything in her life that used to feel so right and permanent. She wished she could wait until she was ready, but it was too late. It had already begun. It was only Netra now, but soon, there would be more, and she still remembered how it felt to have connected with every single dragon egg in that chamber down in the bowels of the Cave. She'd stirred them all awake, she now understood, and it was only a matter of time.

She might have made a grave mistake, and yet it was one she could never have prevented. She'd been brought here for this reason by the machinations of the Emperor, the Empire, and she had fallen into a mold of their making. But from here on out, she would strive to carve out one for herself. The things she knew to be wrong, depraved, immoral, she would reject. She would find another way. There had to be something she was meant to achieve in his lifetime that she could be proud of, something other than bowing her head and joining with the secret, ugly decadence that hid in the Empire's shadows. She had to be meant for something more.

She knew she was on the right path, at least. How could she not be? She had found Netra and soon, other dragons would come crying into life as she fed them, raised them, made them strong. But maybe—maybe becoming one of the Premier wasn't all she'd been destined for. Maybe it was just a stepping stone on the way, and her calling was something beyond this, beyond what she was able to see right now. Something hidden behind the veil, deep in the mist that shrouded the world she used to think she knew.

Or maybe destiny had no plan for her. Maybe it was up to her to make her own way.-

She let Netra go, who scrambled down and began scolding her immediately with furious hisses and raised spines. "You're like a cat," she told the hatchling. "But a bad-tempered one."

The infant dragon hissed again, talons leaving scratches in the dirt as they stretched and flexed.

"But it's almost time to go back. His Excellency might call for us since he'll probably hear from Bastien in a little while, if he hasn't already. And you'll meet Letti. You'll hate her, she's even more handsy than I am."

Netra looked doubtful, if dragons could do such a thing. Her wingtips shifted again.

"And...eventually, you'll meet Kai. He's a terrible person. He only speaks in riddles, and he thinks he's irresistible. He even kissed me, can you believe that? Like I'm his woman. Please." Anzi reached for the hatchling and beckoned it over. "And you'll meet my brother, Oza. You might like him, he's a bit like a cat himself."

It took some coaxing, but finally Netra plopped herself down on the grass with a demeanor that struck uncannily of a temper tantrum. She remained utterly stiff and motionless as Anzi wrapped her back up in the swaddle, although she clacked her slender jaw a few times when the flap came over her head. "It's better if you stay hidden," she told the dragon. "Or else you'll have all sorts of people trying to pet you, not just me. Or do you like being touched and handled by strangers on the streets?"

She hadn't expected any reasonable reaction to that; she had mostly been talking to herself. But as if she understood, Netra lowered her spines and ducked her serpentine head with what Anzi could have sworn was reluctance, as if she had understood. But that was impossible, so she put it out of her mind and finished securing the concealed dragon to her chest as she had before. Damn it, but this would be so much easier if she could just ask Kai what to do. She was still wary of him and all his secrets, especially now that she knew he had been concealing the survival of wild dragons all this time. But as disappointed as she was that she had never suspected him for a second, she wished he was here to help with his secret knowledge of dragonkind.

But all she had was Bastien, a twisted man who raised them like livestock, and her own wits. Nothing else.

"I hope I'm doing this right," she whispered. "I hope you don't hold it against me if I'm not."

From within the blanket, Netra wiggled in her arms before falling asleep with a snuffle.

41

"How are you feeling?"

Anzi needn't have asked. Letti's sunken eyes and inability to get up when she had entered was indication enough, but on the other hand, she looked far better than she had before. Just yesterday, there had still been hints of bruises around her arms, but they were now as pale as ever as they lay folded on her chest over the sheets. Indeed, she looked almost at ease if not for the more obvious signs of her condition, and the harem girl sent her a beaming smile so sweet it hurt her heart. Too bubbly by far for someone who could have died just days earlier.

"Anzi! You're here."

"I was here yesterday, but you were sleeping." She grasped the back of the wooden chair by the wall and dragged it over on its rear legs to Letti's bedside before sitting on it. "You don't look well."

The girl clucked her tongue. "Never tell a lady that," she scolded. "That's just another way of saying they look terrible. Which means they look ugly."

"You did almost die."

"A lady taking her beauty to the grave is the best way. But also, I didn't almost die. Thank you for what you did, though."

"You were definitely almost dead, Letti."

"Then a third of the girls here would be dead, too. I'm not the first and I won't be the last. It's not unusual, you know."

She had suspected as much, strongly enough to rant to Kai about it that very same night, but the truth remained that there was nothing she could do. As a First Guard, she had no business with the inner workings of the palace. Her newfound authority was shaky as it was, with barely anyone recognizing her despite her public induction—without her blazing red dress, she looked like any ordinary fringer, she supposed—but even if she were able to exercise it, it would never extend to the harem.

She had no way of protecting Letti. All she could do was wait until something happened again, until someone as stupid as Noemi dared to tread on her toes so she could retaliate tenfold. All she could do was wait until they hurt Letti again.

"Can't anyone do anything?" she asked. She leaned forward with her elbows on her knees, hands clasped. "They can't get away with this. Have they even been punished at all?"

Letti giggled. "Of course they were. Their allowance for next month will be confiscated. No shopping for them."

"That's all?"

"Well, it could have been worse. But when they asked what I would like to have done to them, I told them that was enough."

Anzi leaped to her feet. "What!" she exclaimed, eyes bulging. "You did *what!*"

"Calm down, sit. Trust me, this is the way. I have reasons for this, and good ones. I haven't gone soft in the head."

That was exactly what she was about to accuse the harem girl of. She'd been beaten, strangled, nearly drowned and whatever else they had seen fit to do to her—and her answer had been allowance confiscation? Of course Anzi was going to question Letti's sanity, but a knowing glint in the woman's eye that made her swallow her next retort.

She settled down in the chair again and adjusted the swaddle over her chest. "What's the reason, then. Better be good."

"You shouldn't doubt me. Most of us in the harem come from families who've had their share of brushes with the court, including mine. I know my way around politics." Letti winked and shifted more cozily under the covers. "See, it always comes down to how valuable we are. I'm new and unpolished, and they're—well, they're them. Especially Noemi, she's a favorite of lots of visiting dignitaries, so they'll never do anything that matters to her. A few whippings will fade in days, and she already half-starves herself so rationing won't do anything, either. So this was my chance to change her mind, or at least make her indebted to me, and I chose to lighten what I was due because I have nothing to lose from it. And maybe something to gain."

Anzi pursed her lips. "You thought of all this while you were recuperating?"

"The secret is to never stop thinking ahead and to be sharp to everyone's scheming. That's how you make it in this world. But hey, what's that you're carrying around your neck? Almost looks like a baby, but I don't think anyone would trust you to be tender with one..."

"A baby," she snorted. "Well, I guess it's a baby of sorts...Here." With a hidden smile, she reached up to undo the knot around her neck, and after carefully placing the bundle on her lap, unfolded the flap over the sleeping dragon's head. "Her name is Netra-hau. Hey, careful! Lie back down."

But there was no stopping Letti, who clumsily scrambled to throw off the covers and sit up with a strength she hadn't had just moments ago. After a few tries that involved swatting away Anzi's hand, the harem girl threw her bare legs over the side of the bed so she was sitting knee-to-knee with her and stared at the hatchling with wide eyes.

"Wh—is that—that's a—no. It is a wyrm? Are you—"

"A dragon," Anzi corrected. "She just hatched last night. You've missed a lot, Letti. I had a feeling no one told you about any of it."

"Told me what! What happened while I've been cooped up in here!"

It took a while to get through the recounting of everything that had occurred, mostly because she kept interrupting to ask questions and to demand more details. And when Anzi made the mistake (mistake-not-mistake?) of mentioning Kai and the sheer audacity he'd had to kiss her the night he left, Letti screamed like a hurt pigeon and clutched at her throat, grasping a necklace of invisible pearls.

"He *what!* And he's bringing dragons, too! Oh, what a world—"

"Calm down. Things happened but everything will be back to normal soon."

"Normal! You're joined the Premier Guard, which you never mentioned even once to me even in passing, and you have a dragon, and you managed to seduce your lover without flashing a single breast—"

"He's not my—"

"—the same lover who's now gone off to bring wild dragons back to the Empire—"

"I said he's not my lover!"

"And you kissed! You kissed, I never taught you how to do that! I thought we would have more time, so I was just going to teach you how to flirt until you were confident first—"

"Letti!"

This was a mistake. Anzi now regretted saying anything, but as she felt sorry for the harem girl's still-weakened condition as well as the apparent real hurt she felt in having been excluded from all that had happened while she was recovering, she could hardly do anything except sit back and wait for the wailing to be over. It seemed that even worse than the near-death ordeal she'd suffered only days ago was this newfound misery, and Letti ended her heartbroken complaining several minutes later by burying her face in her hands.

"This is a disaster," she moaned. "I've missed all the excitement!"

"...There hasn't been much. The gala's probably the loudest thing that's happened, and it wasn't even that enjoyable."

"Maybe not to *you*. But social events are everything to us. Besides, it's not just that! I wanted you to introduce me your chieftain—"

"Not my chieftain—"

"—and I wanted to see what all the fuss is about. He's the reason we met, don't you remember? And if Berenice hadn't been sick that day, we'd never have crossed paths."

Anzi paused. It was true, what she said, even though it felt like it had happened so long ago she could barely remember it. What happenstance, what twists of fate. She had lived an entire lifetime in less than two weeks, and the insanity showed no signs of stopping. She looked down at the sleeping Netra on her knees, wondering how long it would be before she had two dragons clambering over her instead of one, then three, then more..

She dreaded it. She had no way of protecting them, not unless she was crazy and foolish enough to run off with them. Maybe that was possible with one or two, but even that would only last for as long as they remained small enough to stay hidden. She had no idea how much time she had before Netra was too large to keep concealed like a swaddled baby, but even if she were to leave now, what of the others? The ones she had stirred awake without even meaning to, the eggs slowly hatching down in the Cave. She would have to leave them all behind, and whether it took a week or a month or even years, they would come into the world without her to protect them.

She couldn't do that. She couldn't abandon them all just to save the one, no matter how fiercely her heart burned at the thought of Netra suffering in the hands of anyone who dared to touch her. None of them were safe from Bastien or even the other riders she was sure to cross paths with sooner or later. And—even the Emperor...

Her pulse throbbed in her neck. A month ago, she would never have dared to entertain such thoughts. But everything had changed since she had come here, ever since she had met Kai and began to doubt. And the things she had learned from Bastien, the terrible things she had never imagined—but above all else, it was Netra.

She had to find a way. There just had to be one.

"What's wrong?" Letti waved a shaky hand in front of her face. "Have you fallen asleep sitting up?"

She moved the woman's hand away with a sigh. "No. You should lie down."

"Then let me see it! I want to hold it—"

"She's a her," said Anzi, eyeing the harem girl's eagerly clawing hands. "And she's not all that friendly."

"She's the most gorgeous thing I've ever seen. Let me hold her."

"You should know better than I do that being pretty doesn't mean you don't bite," she muttered, but nonetheless, she reluctantly—and carefully—held Netra out for the woman to take. Her heart fluttered uncomfortably at the thought of someone else touching her, but Letti could hardly do anything to hurt the hatchling. If anything, it was the reverse she should worry about. Should Netra wake up and bite her on the finger, Letti wouldn't take it nearly as well as Anzi did. "Careful..."

"I'm being careful, I'm being careful." The woman set the infant dragon down on her lap over her white nightgown and stroked its scales with her fingertips. "Ouch. Cold."

"Very."

"So little." Letti stroked the creature's head, tracing the lowered needle-thin spines there. "I thought they would be bigger..."

"She will be. She's just a baby."

"I know, but still. So, what now? You raise her here until she's big enough to ride into battle? Does that mean you can stay here until then? How long would that be?"

The question Anzi didn't dare answer—the one about the inevitability of plunging Netra into war. "I don't know," she admitted. "I'm learning as I go."

"But the others of the Premier, can't you ask them what happens now? They're your seniors."

"They're not around, Letti. How often do you see them in the Imperial City? Besides my superior officer who left the day he dropped me off here, I've met none of them...except this man named Bastien, but he's not a soldier like I am. I thought he was a member of the Guard, but all he does is stay down there and talk my ears off."

"What?"

"Nothing. Just, there's no one who can give me answers. No one I want to ask, at least."

"Well...what about the Emperor?"

She shot the woman a sharp look. "I'm not going to ask for an audience with His Excellency for a few questions."

"But aren't you curious? And besides, you're a First Guard now. If anyone has the luxury of doing that, it's you."

Anzi frowned and reached over to take Netra back, ignoring Letti's mumbled protests. "I don't want to do that. I'll wait until things unfold on their own. My job is to take care of Netra, and that's what I'm going to do until the time comes to..."

To what? She paused, dropping into an abrupt silence. To what? To bend and consign Netra to unending violence, unwittingly fighting for the kingdom that had wiped out her kind? Could she bring herself to do that to her? She was innocent. She knew nothing. And all she would ever know was nothing.

"Anzi?"

"I should let you rest." She began lashing the corners of the blanket around her neck again. "But I'm glad you're doing better. Rest and don't do anything dumb."

"I'd never—"

Anzi shot her a look.

"Ugh. I won't. But just so you know, I only do questionable things because I get so bored. Visit me more, come play with me...I haven't been able to wear anything nice or eat anything besides that disgusting gruel the physicians keep giving me. It's driving me crazy. And I want to see Netra again. I can't believe you have a dragon. She's so beautiful."

"I'll stop by tonight. Are the others leaving you alone?"

"Considering that I'm not even allowed to leave the room except to bathe—with supervision from the Aunts, don't look at me like that—I can promise you no one has bothered me since. And besides, I told you I had them go easy on Noemi and her girls. They owe me now. It'll be fine, really."

She didn't think so, but there was no point in disagreeing. Letti's over-confidence was insurmountable. No matter what she said, the harem girl would never admit the truth.

"Then I'll be back later. I have things to take care of today."

"Don't forget to bring Baby. Do you really have to cover her up all the way like that, though? What if she can't breathe?"

"She likes it like this."

"Really?"

Anzi paused again just before the impatient *yes* could leave the tip of her tongue. Her eyes flicked up from where she had been adjusting Netra's blanket to Letti's inquisitive gaze, and she wondered how exactly it was she could be so sure. She hadn't questioned her intuition even once. At first, she had only wrapped the hatchling up from snout to tail to keep her out of sight, but then...

"Yes, I'm sure," she said. "I need to go now."

"All right, all right, since you're in such a rush to leave me. Sneak me in something to eat when you come by, okay? I would kill a man for a grape."

"Absolutely not." Anzi was utterly devoid of any sympathy. "You're going to eat the porridge five times a day like the physicians tell you to until you're well enough to eat solid food again. No exceptions."

"Ugh. It was my mistake for even asking."

"Yes, it was. Now get back under the covers. All the way, Letti."

It took several more tries to convince the harem girl to cooperate, but at long last, Anzi marched out of the harem quarters. No sign of Noemi anywhere, incidentally, nor of the other women she'd seen that night. Just as well. She might have felt compelled to start some yrouble if she saw them now, consequences be damned. Instead, Julien waited for her at the doors—and looking very different today. His brown hair was combed perfectly in place, and his uniform under the parts of his metal half-armor had not a single wrinkle or rumple. Not to mention the eager, spirited look that flashed across his face when he saw her approach.

"How's she doing?" he asked as soon as she came within earshot. He hovered dangerously over the threshold, a hair's breadth shy of trespassing. "Is she better today?"

Anzi raised an eyebrow. "Much better."

"That's good. That's good."

"I take it you think she's as pretty as I said," she deadpanned. "Don't even think about it. You're setting yourself up for a world of hurt no matter what happens. And maybe no one's told you yet, but you'll be rotated out before long. Don't get attached, Julien."

"I'm—listen—"

"No. Goodbye."

She didn't wait to listen to his injured protest or the beginning of a shameless request for her to introduce them ("You should bring her out with you next time!"). With Netra slumbering so deeply, it was a good idea to set her on the bed so she could be comfortable. In the meantime, she would wait on a summons from the Emperor, assuming he had the time to see her today. Secretly, she hoped not. She still had yet to decide what exactly she thought of the fabled man, the one who had brought all the warring peoples of this land together in peace and harmony—but at such a terrible cost that continued to be paid in blood even now. She didn't know how to feel, how to reconcile the visceral horror of it all with the reality that her world, her life, everything as she knew it, wouldn't have been possible without such a colossal price.

The ghost that haunted the Empire's underbelly, the ghost no one knew about and never would know about. The countless happy children who would grow up to become happy men and women raising children of their own in peace, in prosperity, in this unending golden age that had brought so many good things into their lives—none of them would ever know. Maybe it was better that way...

And yet Anzi could never regret knowing the truth. If she hadn't come face to face with its grisly existence, Netra wouldn't be in her arms now. Those eggs in the Cave—even if she hadn't been the one to awaken them, someone else would have, and then...

"A message from His Excellency," a young man announced when she neared the door to her room. "You're to see him immediately. Alone."

He probably didn't know the full import of the stipulation that she come 'alone', but she certainly did. It meant without the hatchling. With a nod, she dismissed the messenger before entering her room and settling Netra on the bed. She wouldn't awaken for hours yet, gorged full as she was. After settling her in a makeshift nest of more soft wool, she left, closing the door behind herself and feeling strangely naked without the dragon's weight against her chest.

When she arrived at the throne room, the guards allowed her in without hesitation, and the Emperor welcomed her with open arms. "My dear! I've heard the good news. How fantastic, how spectacular."

She gave him a small bow, a quick one to avoid irritating him. "Yes, Your Excellency. I'm glad things are going according to your wishes."

"Oh, yes. Just wonderful. Well, all except one thing, but it's only a minor problem, really. Nothing we can't fix?"

The lanky, too-tall man closed the remaining distance between them with slow, languid strides. His arms were still spread open, vibrant gold-trimmed, red sleeves trailing below them in majestic fashion. There was a wide smile on his slender face, an affectionately impish expression. No. Couldn't be. He wasn't about to do this...really? She braced herself, hoping it would be over quickly. How did one respond to being embraced by the most powerful man in all the land?

When he came to a stop before her, however, his arms lowered no further fuss, and she held back a relieved sigh. "Bastien tells me you had a disagreement," he said with the same mischievous smile.

"...Yes, sir."

"Was it very awful?"

"No, sir."

"You care very much about your dragon," he remarked. "Do you know that you've exceeded my expectations?"

"Thank you, Your Excellency—"

"Especially in that you laid hands upon Bastien so fearlessly."

There was no warning. No change in the air, no whisper of an instinct to save her. One second, she was standing with her hands clasped behind her back and shoulders squared as she answered the Emperor's questions, and the next, something cracked against her jaw and sent her hurtling across the throne room. Her body had already smashed horizontally against a thick stone pillar and tumbled to the floor in a heap before she even realized she had been struck.

Numb. Pain, such pain, but numb at the same time. Anzi tried to stand up but stumbled back down on one knee. The world spun, faltered. She was half out of her body and half inside it. With bleary eyes, every inch of her body shaking as if reverberating from the impact, she looked up to see the Emperor walking toward her.

"My dear Anzi," he said. "We are going to have to do something about that."

42

Anzi's chin jerked up when the Emperor grabbed a fistful of her hair, but when another blow smashed across her ribs, she doubled over again with a loud wheeze and stumbled back against the pillar once more. She didn't get the chance to straighten up on her own before a fist came crashing into her face in a swooping upward arc, the force of it so great it lifted her off her feet and sent the back of her head crashing against the stone. She didn't know if her skull had caved in, but it felt that way as she gasped for air past the thick streams of blood dribbling from both nostrils and her mouth. The skin on the back of her head had broken as well; a wet sensation spread across the rear of her scalp and began to clump her tresses.

"You're still standing! They did tell me you're a hardy one."

She didn't know what he hit her with this time. A punch, a kick, it could have been either, but it was so fast her eyes interpreted it as nothing more than a red blur. And then impact, crushing impact that blew the strength out of her in an instant. She felt two of her ribs give at once when he sent her hurtling to the floor, bone snapping inside her like brittle twigs. She curled up with a hacking groan, every part of her body shaking as it tried to comprehend the sheer brutality being inflicted upon it with strength impossible.

She had never been struck so hard before, never. It felt like her lungs had been torn out of her body, every joint wrenched out of place. She had never imagined agony so crippling as when he kicked her in the ribs over and over again, driving her body back until her spine cracked against the column once more—and even then, he continued. With each savage, ferocious kick, her body lifted horizontally off the floor and slammed into the pillar again and again until she could feel her legs no longer. Her head, too, was filled with only a half-conscious buzzing, but maybe that was the blood seeping out of her ears drowning out everything else.

And then for a blessed, dull moment that had her mind sliding into a different kind of awareness, it stopped. It stopped as suddenly as a storm vanishing into thin air, a fire swallowed up and sent fleeing into a disappearing wind. Anzi opened one swollen eye—something was wrong with the other one, she didn't want to stop to think about what—to find the Emperor crouching on the floor next to her.

"I didn't want to do that," he said softly. "But there are consequences when you make certain choices. I shouldn't have to tell you not to put your hands on your friend. You know better than that. I want you to all get along."

He reached down and brushed her blood-clotted hair back over her torn ear. She shuddered. Even that light touch was agonizing, sending new fire searing every part of her like lightning blackening a tree with an all-consuming crack of light and heat.

"So here's your first lesson, now that we've made sure you're going to remember it: no fighting. Not among yourselves, at least. Feel free to do whatever you like to anyone else, I won't hold anything back for my most treasured servants." He ran his long, twiggy fingers through her hair from root to tip by her temple, and when he pulled his hand back, there were feather-light streaks of red on it. "That means the world belongs to you. Anyone you take a liking to, you can kill them, maim them, tear them limb from limb in front of a crowd, and you know what? I would be proud of you. I like surrounding myself with strong-minded people, it's very satisfying. But you never, ever lay a hand on each other. Not only Bastien, but anyone else like you. Understand?"

She couldn't move. There was something wrong with her body; all she could do was blink. A dribble of blood mixed with saliva seeped out of the corner of her mouth and pooled on the floor under her head.

"Now, don't think I'm angry with you, it's not that. No need to feel guilty. But this is discipline, and when you misbehave, I have to take you to task. It's the way they all learn, and now you. I want you to think of me as a friend, no mistake about that...Just as a friend who can break you into pieces, put you back together again, and do it all over on a whim if I feel like it. Remember that at all times. See, I think the main reason you felt emboldened enough to attack him was because you forgot there's someone to fear. If you had remembered to be afraid of treading on my toes, you would never have done something like that. But you forgot yourself. Your place. And the fact that above all, you need to think—will what I do offend Tet? Will he be angry with me? What should I do instead? And you should be thinking that every second of your life. It's very simple once you get used to it, and it makes things much easier for the both of us."

Anzi struggled to breathe. Every inhale had her snapped ribs stabbing deeper inside her, tearing into things she dared not contemplate. Even the stuttered beating of her heart exhausted her, each painful, laborious throb sending another pulse of blood pulsing through her veins and out of her wounds. She still couldn't feel her legs.

"I won't ask you to answer me or anything petty like that," he added. "I know you'll agree, since you don't have a choice. Now, I know you're a tough nut to crack since both Alexandre and Bastien have said as much, but here's the thing. You're loyal to me. Always have been. I'm your everything, and I'll stay that way because, well, I'm the light in your heart, aren't I?"

He adjusted her uniform by the blood-stickied collar. The mild jostling felt like all of her bones were being crushed anew, and twitches ran down her limbs in uncontrollable shivers. She couldn't control them anymore. Not just her legs, but her arms.

"It's all right. You don't have to speak, like I said. I understand everything. Now, there's also the other matter—about the dragons. Bastien mentioned you're very, very attached to them, is that right? He laughed about it, but you see, that worries me. He might not think it's serious, but I've run into my fair share of devout zealots who think they have some kind of say in how things are done here. They don't, but the ideas they get in their heads about it, those can be dangerous. And what I mean is, it makes them dangerous to themselves. Because it confuses them. It makes them think I'm the enemy."

More blood dribbled from the corner of her mouth. Her eye hurt too much to stare up at the Emperor out of the corner of it, so she let it flutter shut as she dropped her gaze down to his feet.

"You're not the first who's had these thoughts, my dear Anzi. Surely you must know that. Bastien thinks it's all a joke, but it breaks my heart.

Because when we get a bad egg—so to speak—we have to crush it before it becomes a problem. Goes for both the riders I choose to grant privileges to as well as the dragons… Bad eggs, crushed. But there's not a one that I've forgotten. Everyone stays in my memory forever whether they disappointed me or not, and Anzi? It hurts me. It hurts me to hurt you just as it hurt me to hurt them, because you're one of my favorites. Out of the million useless souls in all the land, I've chosen so few. So don't disappoint me. Be happy. Be good. Be kind to yourself. You don't need to worry about useless things, just yourself for now along with your friends and me. Don't get attached to the dragons and start thinking you have some moral obligation to bring things to rights. Because, Anzi, in the end, I will do what I have to do. I've come too far to let you stagger me."

He was talking, still talking. She was vaguely aware of how strange it was that she was still conscious after everything she had endured, how strange it was that she could pay attention to every word he said enough to remember it for later.

"You're the kind of power I've been seeking for a long time," he said. "But I also know that eventually, someone else like you will come along again. That's the advantage of age, Anzi, I have the wisdom to play the long game. I also have wisdom that tells me when someone's going to be a problem too, though, and it's giving me little warnings about you. Can't have that. It's why I've beaten it out of you. Put away any mischievous thoughts and dedicate yourself to me as you always have." He chuckled and tucked his flowing sleeves back, long fingers rolling them back to one elbow then the other. "Always remember. I overlook your transgressions for as long as I'm too impatient to look for your replacement. You're valuable, so I'll be more lenient than I would with others—including even the rest of our Premier friends, just don't tell them that, darling. But no one is irreplaceable, and I have all eternity to wait for someone more palatable if you end up being too sour on the tongue. Understand?"

He patted her on the forehead. His fingers came away with a red smear.

"And not that I think you would be so stupid, but just in case you hold this against me instead of taking it as a valuable lesson learned, don't forget: those dragons you adore so much, they mean nothing to me. I only need enough to keep the status quo, not all of them. So I can always punish you and your soft little sensibilities. Do you know I can kill all of them with a thought, especially when they're still defenseless in their eggs? I'm the master of a dragon king, make no mistake. His little lizards belong to me as much as he does, slaves of a slave. But if that isn't enough to convince you, I'll have to resort to something truly horrid, like cracking the softer ones open and making you eat their half-formed flesh with your bare hands, I don't know." He flapped his hand in a dismissive gesture. "I'll think of properly terrible things later when I'm in a better mood. I'm too worried and afraid you'll turn out like the failed ones I had to put down for thinking of turning on me."

With a final sigh, he stood up and wiped his hands off his robe.

"Well, that's it. I'll see you very soon, my dear. In the meantime, don't go anywhere. I'll have the best healers tend to you, and you'll be back on your feet soon enough. Make sure the next time I see you, you have a sweet smile on your beautiful little face to put me at ease. Really, I'm so lucky. To think that our first surviving woman warrior of the bunch is so good-looking. If I still had the urges of ordinary men, I might have taken you for a wife! So very beautiful, really. So don't be upset with me, darling. I favor you more than you will ever know! Now, I'll be off. I hope you feel better soon."

The heavy doors to the throne room closed behind him a moment later, and a wet breath gurgled out of Anzi's throat. To anyone who stumbled upon her, she would look pitiful, broken.

But a twitch, there, in her fingers. Next, a slight movement in her toe as she fought to regain control of her body. A sound, a murmur...and a burning darkness in her good eye that glared down at the floor.

No, she thought. He had nothing to fear. Because she would never forget.

SLEEP CAME FITFULLY and only in the dead of night. Hours of enduring painful healing magic from the palace's best physicians meant she could find no rest until it was well into the darkest hours. Even then, she woke up every few minutes thinking about Netra in her room. Someone had gone to feed her at Anzi's choking insistence, but what if something happened? Tet's threats weighed heavy in her gut, and and she well knew they extended to Netra.

She couldn't let that happen. She couldn't. And yet she was unable to even stand. In the morning, she might be able to eat, and then the day after, to walk slowly and carefully...And she would make sure she was soon strong enough to protect her own again.

Now she saw. Now she knew. The Emperor was nothing like she had thought, like she had always believed. If he had only beaten her to within an inch of her life, she might have explained it away as necessary though brutal discipline, but he had gone so far as to make such a disgusting threat against the unborn dragons hidden in the Cave. Weren't they in his care? Did he feel no responsibility for them?

There was no point bemoaning his evil. She would simply have to recover, and recover quickly. She closed her eyes and allowed the potent herb mixture to sap all of her remaining strength and sink her into a healing sleep.

SHE WAS in the middle of the desert. At night, though, so instead of brilliant white and red-tinged dunes of sand under the sun, it was dark, utterly still…and cold. Ah, that was right. It had been years since she had gone into deep desert, but now she remembered it could become chilly in the nighttime after sunset.

But what was she doing here? And why did she feel so, so tired…

I was calling for you. I'm coming to you, Anzi. Don't go-

She wriggled in place. What in the world? It was like she was trapped in a body that wasn't her own, and hearing thoughts that belonged to somebody else, too. She was so drowsy she couldn't even remember whose voice it sounded like, if thoughts could have a voice, but there was something familiar about it.

Anzi! Wake up!

Her eyes eased back open. But this was a dream, it had to be. She could remember falling asleep. But why was she so tired even in her own dream? And more importantly, why did everything about this feel so uncannily familiar? Not just the disembodied thoughts running around in her head, but this…this body. This strength that coursed through her, masculine, broad, burning…

No. It couldn't be….Just a few weeks ago when she had completed her Second Run of the Gauntlet, after everything had gone to hell. That afternoon, she had fallen asleep and had a vision. She'd had a vision just like this one.

I didn't want to do it like this. I wanted to wait until you knew, until you understood—but I had to. Anzi, who hurt you. What happened?

Oh, dear gods. All the fatigue left her in a flash, and she hovered in the dream-state without making a single sound.

"Kai?" she demanded, the single syllable starting as a croak and ending with a sharp, upturned question of disbelief. "You—I—magic!" she accused. "You've magicked me, I knew it, I knew it wasn't my imagination, you—"

Anzi, calm down. Tell me what happened to you.

"Absolutely not. You explain to me how to reverse this right now, or I'll..."

It was the Emperor, wasn't it. I could feel him, his twisted...I could feel him when you were in pain. I'm on my way back, Anzi, I've turned around and I'm coming for you-

"No, you're not. You're going to tell me how to get out of this enchantment, or I'll find a way to—I'll do something." She paused. "Is this your body? Am I inside you?"

As you always have been.

"Don't talk like that. I don't like it."

Anzi-

"Dark hells, I'm fine. And don't come back. Not like this, anyway. There's...something wrong with the Emperor." She frowned inwardly, still floating in her consciousness but now more aware of her own autonomy. She could still feel and radiate emotions of her own despite being trapped in Kai's body, it seemed. That was a relief. Except why wasn't she more alarmed? She'd reacted appropriately at first, but her shock and anger drained away far too quickly to be normal. More magic! He was bewitching her!

What do you mean, there's something wrong with him? I don't care what his reasoning is, or if he's gone mad. He hurt you. I'll-

She shushed him with an irritated scowl. "This isn't a dream, then," she interrupted. "This is you, and I'm..."

With me. But we'll be together again soon in more than just spirit. We're only resting briefly, soon we'll be turning and flying back—

"Don't," she warned. "Don't do it, whatever it is. Trust me. I could feel it when I was with him, the Emperor...something's different. I don't know if he's gone mad, but he's acting deranged for sure. The slightest thing will set him off, and to see you returning without a wild dragon as you promised—bad things will happen."

The hatchlings. She didn't know if she could trust Kai yet, or if she could, whether he would be able to help rescue them. She would think about that in the morning when she wasn't so exhausted. But what she did know was that she had to keep the Emperor happy at all costs, to keep him calm with an outward appearance of obedience while she put together a plan. She knew better than to think he had merely been bluffing even if he might have exaggerated the ease of it. Somehow, the Emperor could harm the dragons.

She couldn't let that happen. She needed time to figure out how to stop it, even if she had no idea how.

Anzi, you're not making any sense.

"Well, too bad. I—maybe I'll explain to you later. How long is the journey? Six months? Would you be returning before summer?"

...If I were to go, it would be three weeks, maybe a month.

She snorted. "Don't be silly. How long, Kai."

Like I said, it would be—

"You can run as fast as the wind now?"

Flight is a wonderful thing.

She paused, then swallowed hard. Ah. Flight...right. Because dragons. He could return on their backs instead of having to travel on foot. "Then...anyway, let me go. And don't come back now. If he sees you and knows something's wrong, there's no telling what he'll do. I won't let you do it. So go and turn back around and keep on the—"

I'm coming to get you, Anzi. I won't leave you alone with him.

"The sentiment's appreciated, but I'm more than—"

And when I see him, I will tear him to pieces! he snarled. A pulse of fury, energy, magma-like wrath flowed through him—through her—and she recoiled from the sheer force of it. It took her a moment to regain her bearings.

"No, you won't!" she snapped. "Not until I'm sure that the hatc—I mean, no, you won't! Damn it, Kai, just trust me and do as I say instead of wandering around according to your own whims for once!"

His spirit stilled, and she felt herself settle alongside it. Oh...This felt deceptively nice. Not that she liked magic and the resulting synchronicity of their emotions. At all. Damn him. "Let me handle this," she said. "I can't risk you accidentally causing damage we can't reverse. Please, Kai. I'm begging you."

She felt the rush of cool shock as if it were her own. *But-*

"Please."

Silence. A long silence. She thought for sure they would be here the entire night before he answered. *I want to be with you,* he murmured. *I couldn't do anything. I'm so far away, Anzi...I couldn't-*

"I can take care of myself. Just a few bruises," she lied. "Now go. And let me out of this...you're too big. I feel like I've been wrapped up in a loose sail. Let me out! You witching abomination."

His small chuckle sent a warm shiver of pleasure through her, not that she would ever admit it. Sneaky black magic things, it wasn't her fault.

I miss you.

"Well, the faster you go, the faster you come back," she said, and it wasn't until she'd finished the thought that she realized it was what he had said to her before he left the Imperial City...before he had left her.

(And then there had been that kis-)

"What are you waiting for! Go! Go."

I don't want to leave you.

"Well, you already have, and you need to get used to it."

Then at least let me do this...

Something warm and good pulsed through her, a billow of air, of energy. Suddenly, she was aware through the tenuous strands that connected her to it that her body was in less pain. Just slightly, but the difference was noticeable.

I wish I were closer, he murmured. But we can heal like this. It would be faster if I were there, and if you would let me in, but you're so stubborn...

Gods. More suspicious magic. And suddenly she remembered again this sensation—that night in the barracks when she had envisioned Kai just like this, before they had ever met. It had been him; she knew that without question now. And he had healed her then too, the wound on her forehead. But how? How could he have done that when they hadn't even known each other, when they...She wanted to ask. Wanted to know. Needed to.

But she was afraid of the answer. Afraid of what he might say, of what she would be forced to hear-

She awoke with a start, shoved back to wakefulness by her own force of will. She didn't have the strength to sit up, so she lay there in bed and stared up at the ceiling, chest heaving and sucking in breaths as deep as her injured ribs would allow. Gods. She had no idea what was happening anymore. She was so confused, so on edge, ready to fight but knowing one misstep could cost her everything.

She closed her eyes and forced herself to fall asleep again, and this time, kept her spirit grounded in her body.

That was enough magic for one night.

43

The healers were inadequate, making excuses that her injuries were too extensive and greivous for her to get up and move around on her own. They also claimed she needed to waste several more days lying in bed and doing nothing at all. And these were supposed to be the best in all the Imperial City? Pathetic. It was the only time she wished she were surrounded by those more adept in magic.

Damn them. She had expected to be back on her feet already. Experienced healers, her ass. Two more days! Two, even with her constitution, they said, and she was going to have to continue relying on others to care for Netra. Whoever was responsible for the task had not revealed themselves, nor had they brought the dragon to her. But she couldn't be surprised. Netra was probably terrorizing them according to her ways and would scarcely tolerate being toted around by strangers. All the more reason that she needed these healers to do their job. But on the sixth morning after her bloody encounter with the Emperor, she began to suspect the healers were deliberately dragging their feet. She had been treated often enough after battles, and it had never been this slow. Was it possible they had been told to extend her discomfort to keep her down longer?

Well, if that was the case, she had a secret edge. One they knew nothing about.

"Just so you know," she announced as she bumped around in Kai's consciousness and did everything she could to demonstrate how uncomfortable she was, "this is not going to be a thing. I'm accepting your help for now because I don't have a choice, but as soon as I'm able, I'm going to the mages at the Tower to cleanse me of your magic. I thought you should know that in case you were underestimating me."

She bristled at the low, rumbling chuckle that reverberated through her chest, her entire body. Well, not hers, but his...Oh, this was so unnerving. She especially hated how it made her suspiciously warm and bothered in a way that had nothing to do with the hot sun beating down on her skin. *His* skin. Damn it.

Tell me more, he said. I missed you.

"I still don't understand what it is you miss about me." Especially since she had been spirited away in her sleep to him like this every night for almost a week now. It was the same each time, a few minutes of her giving him sharp reminders that this was not a permanent arrangement and that she would never let her guard down around him, and then floating off again after he bathed her in unknown healing energy that soothed her entire body so. With how prickly she had been, he should be sick of her.

But if anything, her objections only delighted him. Indeed, she could feel him smiling in the movement of the muscles of his face. And—laughing! Now he was laughing. She scowled.

"Let me go!" she demanded. "I'm tired of this. Like I said, I'm only tolerating whatever spell this is because it's helping me...for now. Once it's served its purpose, you'll never be able to do this again, I promise you."

He laughed again. *But Anzi,* he said, and she could hear the roguish grin in his voice despite not being able to see it. *I'm not the one bringing you here.*

"Excuse you?"

I can't make you do anything you don't want to. I never have. You're here every night because you come to me first...just like how you can leave me anytime you wish. But I see you choose not to leave me, so despite all of your threats...

She exploded. He was wrong, she was about to shout, and she most definitely was not choosing to stay here as a disembodied spirit possessing his form. It was his doing, not hers, and it was outrageous to think otherwise. Because no matter what he said, she did not, *not*, want to be here at all-

In a flash, she was catapulted back into her own body with a furious impact, and she jerked under the covers so hard she nearly threw the blanket off. In the darkness of the palace infirmary, she breathed hard, sweating from the sheer shock of how swiftly she had been launched out of Kai's body...or rather, how swiftly she had launched herself out of it. There could be no mistake. As soon as her mind had filled with the stubborn, determined thought of *I don't want to be here*, she had disappeared, leaving him behind in the desert once more.

A few seconds passed, and then a scorching heat flooded her face with such intensity she had to open her mouth and heave in a cool breath to keep from melting on the spot.

You're here every night because you come to me first.

Absolute nonsense. She squeezed her eyes shut and determined to forget everything he said, immediately and forever.

"Please, you should stay in bed until we examine you again. Please..."

"No." She shrugged on her clean pair of leather shoulder guards that someone had delivered to replace her ruined and bloodied pair, at least until her new custom uniform was ready. "I told you I feel fine. And one of you just examined me this morning."

"Oh, yes. But—it's just we weren't expecting you to be feeling so...fit again already. We thought you would need to rest for another few days before you were in any condition to rise."

Anzi shot the physician a glare. "You sound disappointed."

He stopped wringing his hands and waved them in a frantic motion. "Oh, no, not at all! Not at all..."

Right. She let her cool gaze linger on him before returning her attention to the last button on her uniform, which she resumed fastening with weak, still-shaky fingers. It seemed her suspicions had been correct. The physicians weren't trying their utmost to return her to full health after all, judging by the reluctant expression the man failed to hide. Well, if the Emperor wanted her to stay down, perhaps he should have beaten her a little harder. She jerked on her collar to straighten it with unnecessary force, channeling her spite into it the way she couldn't upon the real object of her frustrations.

"I'm going out," she announced. "It'll be good exercise. Staying in bed for much longer will ruin me."

"But, but—"

"I'm leaving. I'll return soon. Goodbye."

Even to her ears, her farewell sounded like a threat, and the physician shrank back against the wall with wide eyes as she passed him by. She managed to hide her limp until she was alone in the hallway, but she couldn't go much farther without holding onto the wall. She glanced back over her shoulder to make sure the door was closed and the physician wasn't peeking out to spy on her, and with careful, measured steps, began the trek up to her room.

Everything hurt. Her joints shrieked, her skin crawled, and her pulse throbbed furiously in her throat with every small movement. She had to stop too many times to count on the winding steps that took her three floors up, leaning against the stone railing or the wall with panting breaths. At least the scenery wasn't bad, she thought with no little sarcasm as she glanced around at the meticulous craftsmanship of everything in sight.

She used to admire all of this. The marble, the granite, the carved reliefs in the walls that detailed the glorious history of the Empire. Now, all she could see was the hidden truth underneath it of which she had dug up only a small portion. How many other atrocities drenched the earth on which the Empire stood? What else was she blissfully unaware of as she went on, fulfilling her duty as a loyal soldier?

How things could change in so little time. Now, everything reminded her of defenseless dragon eggs waiting in the Cave and of the Emperor's eerie, serene smile as he battered her senseless with no mercy. Something had lifted from her eyes, a veil she had never noticed before. With it gone, she could see everything just a little more clearly.

It hurt. It hurt worse than the pain that racked her body, that scored her bones and scoured her flesh. It hurt and it hollowed her and she knew she would never, ever trust anything or anyone so implicitly ever again. She knew it as if she were a seer looking into her future, reading the portents with a too-wise understanding. That trust, that devotion, the way she had put every ounce of her being into following this path because she had believed in it so faithfully. She had left her brother, mother, father, her home, everything she had known behind so she could pursue it. And it was all false.

With a sharp exhale between puckered lips, she forced herself to straighten and ascended the stairs once more. Fine. So she had learned her lesson. The Emperor was not the man she had believed he was, and his true legacy, not the one shaped with lies and misdirections, was repulsive and hideous. There were still the last vestiges of hopeful desperation lingering inside her, the parts of her that still prayed she hadn't wasted all her life until now chasing after something rotten and horrific, but this was reality. She had to face it, had to make choices—choices that might get her killed if she wasn't careful.

Choices that might get her killed no matter what.

She remembered the nauseating, world-shattering pain of each blow Emperor Tet had rained upon her, every cursedly calm, condescending word he had spoken over her bleeding, quivering body. She remembered his threats, his promises. And yes, damn it, she was afraid, because who wouldn't be? But she wouldn't let it stop her. She had never run from the enemy before. She wouldn't start now. But what she needed to do was bide her time and tread carefully. One mistake, and she could end up killed. Who would save the dragons, then? And she needed to be especially careful when Kai returned...If he really brought back a wild dragon, then she was sure she would need to find a way to rescue that one as well. Tet so loved treating dragons as possessions to be hoarded. Who was to say he wouldn't try to wrest that one away, too?

She was still deep in thought when she opened the door to her room, so much so that she didn't realize she had arrived at her destination until Netra hissed at her from the floor. The sound snapped her back to the present—and she gasped at the sight that met her eyes.

"They didn't!" she snarled as she strode forward. "They didn't—"

But they had. Whoever had been responsible for feeding Netra had apparently found it a task too daunting to do in any decent way, and they had shoved her into a cage that looked like it was built for something no larger than a canary. Tiny and cramped, it didn't even have enough room for the slender hatchling to turn around in. With a furious noise, Anzi miraculously forgot every screaming pain in her body to drop to her knees and twist off the metal latch.

Netra tore out of the cage door as soon as it cracked open, and in the next eye-blink, Anzi was holding the trilling, shrieking dragon in her arms and doing her best to console her with soft strokes along her scales and raised spines and gentle words. But all the while, she burned, boiled. Who had done this? Who had dared to cage Netra, not even affording her the barest dignity of one large enough for her to lie comfortably in the way they would for a prisoner? She was just a baby, a baby-

"I'll never let them do that to you again," she muttered as Netra buried her snout in the crook of Anzi's elbow, hiding against her belly as her tiny white scales twitched and flexed with small tremors. It hurt her ribs unthinkably, but the thought of moving the hatchling away never even occurred to her. "I'll be careful now. I'll watch my every step and make sure I stay ahead. I'll make sure I win—" If only so this would never happen again. She bared her teeth and glared at the unseen enemy, full of rage but with no one to inflict it upon.

Forget the meaningless idiot who had done this. The one ultimately responsible was Tet. The so-called Emperor who cared for nothing but himself, who thought only of conquest and not a whit about his people. He had said so, hadn't he. He had said they were all hers for the taking if she so wished, all the people who pledged their fealty to him and his kingdom.

Ungrateful. Traitorous. In her arms, Netra stirred and made a half-snarling, half-yowling sound, and it was almost as if she could feel Anzi's emotions. That wasn't it, of course, she knew; it was simply that the hatchling was still rightfully upset about her humiliating, tortuously cramped imprisonment. But the incidental symmetry of their emotions soothed her anyway. She felt less alone.

She wouldn't let this happen again. She would make sure of it.

"Let's get out of here," she murmured. "I hate this evil place."

～

SHE FELT dirty using the vouch letter now, but she had no choice if she wanted to leave the palace grounds. And the temporary freedom was well worth the indignity. Hours later, she was at the river bend again where she had fed Netra not too long ago. Strange how it felt like a lifetime had passed since then. She had learned much. Too much to not let it change her.

A month ago, she had never dreamed of such thoughts. She had believed with all her heart and every ounce of her living soul that she would go on to serve the Empire for all eternity if the monarch permitted her the immortality to do so. She had thought that was her destiny. Not for a second had she ever wondered if she might grow restless of duty and service. Not for a second had she ever considered whether she might chase her own desires out there in the world she didn't know.

She still didn't. She believed in duty. She believed in service. And yes, she wanted to believe she was promised to something greater than herself so she could dedicate the whole of her spirit to something good and true…but if it existed, this wasn't it. She treasured the peace the Empire had brought to so many people, but the cost that had made it possible was unthinkable. She was done trying to justify it to herself. She was done trying to reason that it was all part of the grand tapestry of things, of fate, of higher design.

It wasn't right. None of it was.

"Oza could help," she whispered to Netra, who lay curled between her legs on the grass like a sleeping cat. "I know he can. He's so clever, and he must know things about dragons since he was translating those texts when I last went to see him. But I can't risk it. I know he's going to have the mages report me if I show up at the Tower, and if he uses Oza against me..."

Just when she had reunited with him after all these years of her stupid, greedy stubbornness. She had been so blind. And now she might lose him forever if she wasn't careful.

"I can't believe I left him all alone. I wasted so much time. He's half-grown up, and I missed everything. In a few years, he'll be as big as I am."

She didn't even think of Mama and Baba anymore. But Oza, poor Oza. She had vowed to protect him all her life, and what had she done? Abandoned him so she could go on to give both halves of her spirit to an Empire grown in atrocities unspeakable. How could she have been so blind?

"I'll do this on my own, at least until I know it's safe to approach anyone else. I know he's watching, always, so I'll have to stay my hand for now. I'll let him think he's won. Until the time's right." She stroked Netra's back, tracing her fingertips down flattened spines and collecting the frost that gathered at the tips. "But I won't roll over and die. I've got to take care of you, and I've got to take care of the other dragons. I've got to take care of all of you and..."

She looked up at the sky and took a deep breath. Winter was fast approaching; the chill in the air bit hard enough to flood her lungs with an icy sting. But that was good. It made her more alert, made her brighter and sharper and more ready. And Kai's healing magic from afar had done her a good turn; she was in far better shape than she would have been otherwise. Despite her mistrust and fear of his power, she had to acknowledge the debt between them that had allowed her to return to Netra more quickly. She would pay him back twofold. How, she didn't know, but she would.

So what now? Where did she go from here?

"I'm going to start training again tomorrow," she murmured as she rubbed the top of Netra's slender head. "The pain doesn't matter. It'll make me stronger. And that's what I need to be so I can protect you. So I can..."

Kill him, a voice whispered in her thoughts. You know that's what this comes to.

She did know. Not yet, not when she was still uncertain whether he could truly kill the dragons with a thought, he had said, like black magic. If he could, even in the moment of death, she knew he would do it out of pure spite if nothing else. The way he had patronized her as he bashed her to pieces, the melodic sing-song condescension as he tore her apart. He was that type. That sort of monster. She knew it, and she knew it well.

The bigger problem was that he was so much stronger than any foe she had ever faced. No enemy on the battlefield or jealous soldier in the ranks could compare. His strength was superior, his speed, his agility. If she wanted a fighting chance in the future, she would have to rely on the one thing she had never trusted...

"My magic," she said with a displeased curl of her lips. "I have to learn how to use it. Properly. Netra, there's no stone I'll leave unturned if it means I can keep you safe."

Magic and deceit. She would hone the former while she exercised the latter at the same time, putting on an obedient front so that Tet suspected nothing. She had never thought she would stoop to eagerly utilizing either, but she had no choice. She had to do everything she could, even everything she couldn't, if that was what it took.

So this was what it felt like to be changed, to be transformed. She could hardly believe that all this time, she had kept her eyes squeezed shut against the world. But not anymore. She gathered the hatchling up in her arms and held her to her chest with her mouth set in a vicious line. She was one of the greatest soldiers in all the Empire, a prodigy warrior from birth. Fighting came so easily to her, and now that she knew who the real enemy was, now that she saw him standing in front of her in all his radiant glory, hiding every dark and twisted thing under those voluminous robes and behind that false, wicked smile—

She would do what she did best, and *fight.*

44

Every part of Anzi's body still ached, but she had no regrets about remaining firmly grounded in her own body last night. After Kai told her that it was her doing and not his, she made sure to remain especially vigilant so she wouldn't make the same mistake again. Her? Wanting to see him? If that was what he thought, then she was only too happy to prove him wrong. From now on, she would stay well away and deal with this on her own. If things became so dire that she needed his help, or that of his strange distance-healing magic, at least, she would consider compromising—but as it was, it would be suspicious if she recovered too quickly. Especially since she now knew the Emperor had instructed the physicians to delay her recovery.

She could never let him discover the extent of Kai's magic. If she were ever forced to ally with him against the Emperor, she needed his advantages to remain a surprise. Tet was strong, stronger than she was. She needed every advantage she could get.

...Incredible. She was really doing this. She was really harboring treasonous thoughts and plotting against the Emperor just days after her induction into the Premier. Not once in her life had she thought she would ever end up this way, never imagined doubting the nation or the man who presided at the very peak of it. But this was it. If she were to save the dragons, this was what it took. Iron will—iron strong enough to crush and grind other inferior irons. That would be her. Forged in the hottest fires and alloyed with stronger metals, a surpassing weapon. She would have to be keen, quick, and strong to not only survive, but also to lie in wait and seize the perfect moment. Her mouth ran dry at the very thought of it, especially when flashes of the memory of her savage beating returned in pulse-like waves. She looked down at her fist and closed then opened it several times, remembering intimately every ounce of her agony. She would never forget.

Good. The memory would make her strong.

"I'll be back soon," she announced as she wobbled off the foot of the bed, but when she turned around, Netra was lying on her back with her forelimbs and backlimbs splayed out, utterly vanished into a deep slumber. Her distended belly had put her to sleep so quickly. Maybe she was feeding her too much?

She left the room, but slipped a piece of parchment against the bottom half of the frame as she closed the door. If anyone came in, she would know by the displacement. It was her hope that no one was snooping around in her room in her absence, especially since that meant they were far closer to Netra than she trusted anyone to be. But she had to find out, and carrying the dragon around all day would not only highlight her distrust but also impede her in other ways. Namely...

"What happened to you? Fail your first mission as a First Guard and got kicked around?"

The words didn't even sting. If anything, being referred to as 'First Guard' instead of 'fringer' felt more the insult. She turned from the weapons rack to find Oscar Bedeau standing behind her, and she narrowed her eyes when she saw he was alone. Unthinkable. He never went ten feet without his posse, and when she had shown up here moments ago, she had made out at least three or four companions. Where had they gone? She got her answer when she looked over his shoulder and spotted familiar figures retreating from the training grounds.

"What's this," she said and let her gaze slide back to Oscar's face. "You want to stir up trouble but you don't ask your friends to help. I'm surprised."

He crossed his arms, holding her stare as fearlessly as ever. A long time ago, she used to give him credit for standing up to her despite knowing she could whip him seven ways into next month and all his cronies too, but it had been a while she'd been so generous. Now, she barely deigned to pay any attention to him. Her eyes raked him down from head to toe with a critical half-scowl, and he answered in kind.

"Stir up trouble," he repeated. "Funny, coming from you. Considering that I figured out you were waiting for me to come to you about five seconds after you got here."

She crossed her arms as well. "Was I?"

"You were parading yourself. Getting my attention isn't half so hard, fringer. You could have flaunted yourself a lot less obnoxiously and still had me take the bait."

"And yet here you are, taking the bait anyway. Couldn't resist?"

"You might say that. Also, congratulations on presenting without an actual dragon."

She'd known he would bring that up. Why wouldn't he? "You've been privileged to see a public induction in your lifetime. Maybe you'll see the next one in your children's generation."

He smirked. "No need to drop such a heavy hint that I won't ever measure up. I've known that for a long time. I don't have fringer magic to compensate for my inadequacies, sadly...but luckily, you have that advantage. Must be strange representing your people from such a place of privilege while they live in squalor in the sands."

"Definitely. It makes us wonder what went wrong with all the pedigreed soldiers who come from the upper districts and fail. Lots of gifted lineages of their own, but so few with potential."

His smile disappeared, and he rolled his eyes with a dismissive snort. "All right, enough games. We've done the obligatory exchange of insults, so what do you want from me. Get to the point, and maybe I'll indulge you."

She uncrossed her arms. "You were curious enough to send your friends away to approach me, and jealous enough about what it might concern that you didn't want them to share in it. You're not indulging me. You're dying to know why I would come and rile you up on purpose."

"Do they teach mind reading to First Guards, too? That's fantastic. Something else to add to your repertoire, congratulations."

"Keep your congratulations to yourself. What news have you gotten about your cousin?" His cousin being-

His eyes gleamed. "Pierro's coming to the Imperial City earlier than planned. I was at Uncle's estate when the news came. Colonel Bisset sent word of it."

"They mentioned nothing else?"

"Maybe. You'd have to convince me to remember."

She grit her teeth and mulled over her options. But no, telling him about multiple possible dragon hatchings and inductions of so-called auxiliary riders was too much. She had too little to gain in exchange. "That's all, then. I'm not that desperate; you've given me the answer I wanted most anyway."

"What if I told you there's news from the Adaraat-bordering territories? Probably including yours, if I cared which one you came from. And it's news you won't hear anytime soon except through me."

She narrowed her eyes again. She had thought this conversation was over, but if Oscar was volunteering information first, then she would be an idiot to turn it down without at least considering its import. "I'm not interested in gossip," she said stiffly, pretending heavy disinterest. "Not all news is valuable. Whatever you and your friends talk about—"

"It's about the wyrm infestations, but I can shut up if you want me to. Oh, look at that. Interested suddenly, are you?" He smirked once more, confidence returned. "That's right. Wyrms. I received a letter from him yesterday about it. He wrote it the day after you left, and a lot of things happened without your knowledge since you happened to leave too early. So how about that?"

After she left? Wyrms, she thought. Wyrms—like the one she had stopped from attacking the children recruits on their First Run in the Gauntlet. There had been something strange about it all from the very beginning. An adult wyrm on the desert fringes was unheard of, and when she had returned, the Emperor had asked her such strange questions about it. It had been so absurd that she had chased it out of her memory until now, but…

"I know how to keep my mouth shut when I need to," said Oscar. "Tell me yours and I'll tell you mine."

Anzi chewed on the words several times before reluctantly letting them go. "…More dragons," she said. "Pierro might be inducted into the Premier soon. And the others who were training with us too, Aimee and Doufan."

"Doufan? Who's that?"

"Immigrant from the northern Feng lands, from the Qin principality."

"An immigrant," Oscar repeated, voice twisting in incredulity. "An immigrant training to be a First Guard?"

"He's a good fighter. Best technique I've seen yet, he just hasn't gotten used to countering our native styles. But he'll get there soon."

"You would compliment an outsider, seeing as how you're one, too."

"The infestations. Tell me about them."

"Whatever happened while you were up there, it's not an isolated incident. Pierro didn't tell me much, but he said it's 'happening'—that he overheard a report come in about not one, but three wyrms appearing in Territory Three. All adult. Then one in Territory Six, but this was an elder one, took out half a patrol before they managed to kill it."

Kill it! It must have been dire indeed for them to be forced to kill something so valuable. Half a patrol could be any number of lost lives depending on how many were assigned in the first place, but the rules were clear when it came to these things: preserve the wyrm if at all possible, and capture.

To think they had been forced to kill it...but that was for the better, she now acknowledged. The Empire's practice of taming such creatures for the Imperial Army to terrorize other nations with was barbaric at best. With her heart growing stonier against the kingdom's darker practices, she was willing to admit that now.

"And he overheard all this the day after my departure?"

"Seems so. Lots of things happening at once, aren't they. That unplanned gala even though you haven't hatched your dragon yet, I knew something was strange. And there was that nomad chieftain wrapped around your neck and all but inside you already, I know he's no ordinary human—"

"Keep talking that way and I'll relieve you of some of your teeth. You'll have a hard time finding them again for a healer to reattach."

"Why? Sensitive? Did you finally give it up to some foreigner with a nice chest?" He chuckled and looked her up and down. "I really thought you were going to wait to let the Emperor himself fuck you."

She stilled, jaw clenched.

"Or not? I guess you have your limits after all." He flashed her another smile before pointing at the rack. "You should pick up something and spar with me. It'll be suspicious if we part ways this peacefully, and my friends are known to gossip. Give them a show, and they won't bother mentioning to anyone the little side details like how we were conspiring together beforehand."

"Who's conspiring?"

"I'm not as stupid as I let you think all this time, Anzi. I know that unless something drastic happened, you would never look twice at me, much less seek me out or wait for me to come to you. And asking me for information on top of that? You're a First Guard, nothing should be off limits to you. You're keeping secrets."

She revealed nothing. She wouldn't let him see the growing apprehension that crawled all over her skin as she stared back at him, wondering at how different he seemed suddenly. There was a sharp light in his eyes she had never seen before, something sly and satisfied. And although he was as vain as ever with his groomed hair and the expensive accents he added to his uniform, he exuded a strange aura of mature insidiousness she could have sworn he had never possessed until now.

"I waited all this time to see when it would happen, when the perfect Anzi would finally break cover and show her true colors. Glad I was around to see it. I'm so happy, in fact, that I'm going to do you a special favor and help you out, as far as it benefits me."

She forced her lips to move. "Benefits you?"

"Entertains me. Whichever. And you're in no position to deny me if I want to meddle. I only have a year or two left in mandatory service before I go through second Selection and find something else to do, which means I'll be trained to take over the family. If you're finally being greedy enough to follow your own ambitions, you'd do well to make an ally out of me."

She paused…smirked. Aha. Now she saw. "All your casual posturing doesn't fool me. You just want to keep Pierro where he is, and making sure he ends up inducted into the Premier is a sure way to solidify your spot in the family. You're the next oldest after him, so if he's obligated to Service indefinitely as a rider, you get to reap the windfall. I bet you were wetting yourself when you saw me return, then. Thought he'd failed, did you?"

"That sharp fringer mind is so dangerous, Anzi. I love seeing it at work."

That made her pause again. What was with him? She didn't like these sarcastic compliments…too lilting, a tad softer than they should be. She much preferred his outright insults and taunting, and she didn't like this other side of him. She had always known he was sneaky and vindictive, but now she detected a scheming mind she feared she had underestimated to her injury. How had he hidden it all this time?

"You have a look in your eyes that says you don't trust me," he said. "Good choice. But I'm afraid it's too late. You've given me a scent, and I'll follow it until the trail's dead. I expect you to let me meddle without fuss whenever I feel like it, or else I might go and spread some rumors, fast as lightning, about how the First Guard Anzi is sneaking around and scouring for information through strange channels…"

Damn it. She wasn't all that sure his threats held much water since he had a reputation for harassing her for years—who would believe him if he cried wolf for the thousandth time?—but she couldn't risk even the slightest suspicion falling on her. Not yet, anyway. Until the bruises Tet had left on her faded and so had his guard, she had to keep a low profile.

"Don't try to screw me over," she said softly. "I'll make you regret it."

"Ah, I love it. Just like old times. Are you ready to spar now? I won't go easy on you since it looks like I might take a win this time, with the miserable state you're in."

"You're dreaming if you think you can take me as I am. As long as I have even one hand—"

"And overconfident in battle as always," he interrupted. "You and cousin Pierro are so alike in that respect, even if he's a far more advanced asshole when it comes to taunts."

"You two share an uncanny resemblance in that. Nearly everything you two say pisses me off."

"Then maybe you should take it out on me while you have the chance. Or are you going to beg off of it since you're in a delicate condition today?"

That was it. She didn't often rise to the bait whenever Oscar shoved it under her nose with such obvious flair like he was doing now, but he had a point. She didn't want anyone mentioning that they had spoken at length and done nothing else before parting ways. If they fought and made it long and harsh and worthy of attention, that was all anyone would remember.

"Get ready," she said. "I'm going to enjoy every moment of this."

"Don't try to put on a sadist's act, Anzi. It's not suited for you. For me, yes, but you'd find the greatest pleasure in knocking me down on the first try and getting me out of your hair immediately." He ambled forward to peruse the available swords on display. "But that won't be happening today. I can tell you're in bad, bad shape. If you win, I'll be making you work for it."

She bristled. He was right, and while that bothered her, that he had noticed it at all alarmed her even more. She had been certain to hide her limp as she arrived at the training grounds even if she could do nothing to hide the faded bruises on her face and the other exposed areas of her body. He couldn't know how seriously she was hurt. He had to be bluffing.

"You have no idea how long I've been watching you," he said and slowly extended his blunted sword so that the tip hovered close to her chin. She didn't move away. She could dodge him even at this distance with ease, and he knew that too. He had to. He didn't think this was actually going to intimidate her, did he? "I know you a lot better than you think I do. Been reading crow's eyes fluently for a long time now. I can tell when you're pleased, when you're angry…when you're worried, like now. Do I worry you, Anzi?"

All right, she'd had enough. Without turning her head, she reached over to tug off the closest blade on the rack and spun it to knock his weapon away. He let it fall, but continued watching her with that same irritating smile she was looking forward to wiping off his face.

"Enough talk," she growled. "You better fight well enough that I won't be disappointed. Not after I've had to listen to you babble your head off."

"Go on, then," he said in a lofty tone that made her simmer even more. "Let's see if today's the day I can live up to your expectations."

He didn't, but that didn't mean the spar wasn't hard-won. Anzi was slower and clumsier than she ever should have been, even taking her injuries into account, and she earned several fresh marks and bruises from Oscar he wouldn't stop gloating over. Half an hour later, she managed to sever the brutal, dragging spar by slamming him into the dirt bare-handed after they both tossed their weapons away on a synchronized whim. The sound he made like air rushing out of a burst hole made her feel wonderful.

She didn't say a word before departing. She was still uneasy, especially now that she had confirmation Pierro and the others would be joining her soon. Her auxiliary riders that Bastien had mentioned…and while they hadn't been able to quite match her zeal at its peak, they were all loyal to the Empire, unquestioningly. Even if the Emperor didn't specially task them to spy on her, keeping discreet in the company of four partners was going to be difficult. Maybe even impossible.

"I don't know what to do," she muttered to Netra as she stroked her back. The dragon lazed in Anzi's lap as she sat back against the bed on the floor. "I had a suspicion, but I was hoping it wouldn't be true. I need to plan. I need ways to get around without any of them noticing." She continued stroking the hatchling, who clicked her scales and flexed her talons in growling contentment. "Not to mention that I don't trust any of them with caring for dragons until I know they're not going to abuse it the way—"

Hungry.

Anzi looked down at her lap where Netra stared at her with belly upturned, scaled eyelids blink-blinking in expectation. What. No. That had to have been her imagina-

Hungry! Hungry! Hungry!

The dragon reared up and snapped her snout dangerously close to Anzi's face, and she leaned back, stunned. Oh, gods. No one had mentioned anything about dragons talking. Since when!

HungryhungryHUNGRYHUNGRY!

Netra took up screaming with her hissing, snarling cries and clawed at the floor hard enough to leave gouging marks. With a sigh, Anzi consigned herself to helpless acceptance and stood to go and fetch the reigning queen her next meal.

Well, she thought. All right. This might as well happen.

45

S he had *talked.*

When was anyone going to tell Anzi that not only did dragons speak, but they could also barge into someone's mind to do so? She had thought before that a rider and their dragon must be able to communicate, but she hadn't dwelled on it ever since learning the Premier enslaved dragons rather than truly bonding with them.

Speech! Real speech! Bastien had said nothing about this. Or maybe it was just Netra who was special? She was more clever than full-grown humans by half even though she was still so small. That must be it.

Or maybe it was something else entirely. What was it the Emperor had asked her about the wyrm, again…? Whether she had communicated with it. Her heart fluttered as she stared up at the ceiling with the hatchling splayed out next to her, not quite touching but close enough that she could feel each breath Netra took. She'd spoken. She'd spoken in her mind, clearly, unmistakably. Incredible…She wished she could tell the whole world.

But that would never happen. She clenched her teeth and balled her fists. She couldn't tell anyone at all, couldn't trust Bastien and the Emperor with this knowledge. Rather than celebrating, they would want to stamp it out to maintain their dominion over dragonkind. Speech, intelligence, the ability to not only understand but also to make others understand them—those two would consider it a privilege, not a right, that dragons should never be able to exercise.

And they might take Netra away. They might consider her too dangerous to let live, and as they had done with so many other hatchlings they'd deemed unfit to bloat the so-called Premier Guard's legacy, they might kill her. Anzi's fingers twitched as she resisted the urge to pick Netra up and bury her in the crook of her arm. Take her away? Kill her? Anzi's blood boiled at the mere thought, and she sank her fingers into the mattress since she had nowhere else to channel her savage frustrations.

Not in hell. She would tear apart anyone who dared. But for all her determination, the surest way to keep the dragon safe was to remain quiet. Not even Letti could know just in case someone happened to overhear it.

The most pressing problem was whether the hatchling could speak to others, not just her. If that were the case, she might scream at a passing palace maid or another soldier or, gods forbid, Bastien or the Emperor directly. She was a baby, after all. What did she know? She couldn't let that happen. Maybe if she kept Netra fed at all times so she would spend her days sleeping rather than harassing anyone who passed by.

Carefully, *carefully*, she slid off the bed toward the opposite side, almost sweating with the effort of not waking up the sleeping reptile. She had just finished eating only minutes ago, so she would be fine for another few hours. In that time, she could return to the training grounds and find a more private spot than the one she'd chosen earlier so she could start figuring out how to exercise her magic properly. Without anyone to guide her, it was going to be disgustingly difficult, but who could she turn to? She was no longer among her old comrades, so she couldn't approach her old superior officers for instruction. And Colonel Bisset was nowhere to be seen, either, despite having been gone for weeks already.

Bastien was out of the question. He could drink out of the shattered end of a broken glass bottle before she asked him for help. The less influence she let Bastien have over her, the safer Netra would be. Maybe she could go to Aimee. She hadn't gotten Oscar to say exactly when Pierro and the others would be arriving, but it would be soon.

And when that happened, she would be dragged back down to the Cave and forced to hatch more eggs for them. Dragons...vulnerable, helpless hatchlings dropped into the hands of those who would end up hurting them. It burned to think she could do so little to stop it. Even bound and gagged, she was sure her presence alone would suit their insidious plans. The unborn dragons, all of them stirring little by little in their shells...One way or another, whether she wanted to or not, she would be meeting more of them soon.

When she passed by a giggling group of harem girls, Anzi paused in the hallway and thought of Letti. She hadn't been to see her as promised because she hadn't wanted her to see what a terrible state she was in. There would be no hiding the yellow-purple bruises mottling her face, her neck, even her hands. And despite it being the truth that Oscar had managed to mark her afresh a few times as well, Letti would never believe it if she tried to pass off a simple spar with a lesser soldier as the reasons for her condition.

Letti wouldn't be able to do anything anyway, so sparing her was the wise choice. Besides that, Anzi dreaded admitting it was the Emperor himself who had inflicted all of these wounds on her, half because she had no idea where the harem girl's loyalties truly lay and half because it was— humiliating. She would never speak of it to anyone if she had the choice. Not to Letti, not to Kai, no one. She vowed to bury it inside herself until the day she inflicted the indignity tenfold...

And there was another reason to avoid seeing her. Just like with Oza, she couldn't let anything happen to the woman in connection to her. The best thing she could do for Letti was to simply stay away. If the harem girl came to the conclusion that Anzi had abandoned her, or that she no longer wanted to be friends, then fine. Even if she became angry, at least she would be safe.

...So long as Noemi and her dolled up friends stayed away, too. But with Anzi no longer there, who would protect her?

Damned either way. She shook her head with an angry snort, frustrated and furious at her own helplessness. Never in her life had she felt this stupid, this useless, this vulnerable. If only she had opened her eyes earlier. If only she had been prepared. With a scowl, she stalked off and headed toward the palace exit so she could breathe in something that wasn't infected with the corrupt air that swirled between these walls, stagnant and mired.

Soon, she would find a way to get Netra out. Soon.

She was in no better condition when she reached the training grounds than she had been earlier when she sparred against Oscar. Clumsy and slow, she struggled to go through even the most basic exercises against the wooden dummies, wincing with each strike. She grunted and swore under her breath as she labored to drum up the arcane energy she had always tried so hard to keep buried inside. It used to be a brand against her pride, something to scoff and turn her nose up at, but now she wished she hadn't been so vain.

A white flame enveloped her fist at last, only to fizzle out as soon as she looked at it. Still, it was the only progress she had made in hours, and she grasped at the thin straw like a starving man to bread. Twice more she managed it, a little longer each time—but whenever she so much as tapped the dummies to see what damage her magic could do, it sputtered to nothingness again. She couldn't even drive it to combustion the way she had during the Gauntlet against Doufan and Aimee; her body was too weak. This was all she had.

Could she really be so terrible? After all the praise that had been heaped on her about her wild blood and her strong magic, after everything Bastien and Tet had said, she had assumed it would amount to something impressive. More than this. She had thought the only thing holding her back was her own reluctance, and that if she got past it, she would achieve something great. Vanity. Pride. She had been so certain.

She couldn't ever remember struggling before. Not like this. If anything, the more desperate she became, the more pitiful the results. Indeed, now she couldn't summon even the brief bursts of magic at all, and after failing a dozen times, spun away from the dummy at last. One step, and with a furious scowl, she delivered a brutal horse kick that tore the wooden stand out of the ground and sent it flying away.

But she received no satisfaction from that, either. A second later, she was hobbling away with a pronounced limp as a heavy cramp threatened to swallow up the tendons in her leg. Damn it. Maybe it was because she hadn't let her body recover first, she reasoned as she settled on the stone bench and nursed her twitching calf. But she couldn't let that excuse hold her back. No matter what drove her into a corner, she had to be able to retaliate, to bite back harder than she was bit no matter how injured she was. What was the point of having magic otherwise? If it didn't strengthen her, if it didn't make her more dangerous in the direst of circumstances, then what good did it do? If she could only access the power of her *wild blood* when she was already healthy and strong, then what a waste.

She tried one last time, flexing her fingers hard while glaring at the tips. Ah! A glow on her pointer finger. But aside from that...nothing. She gnashed her teeth and punched down on the bench next to her thigh, not caring that it only hurt her more. If only she could cow her magic into submission the way she did with her body. That was how she always used to do it, by treating herself as the enemy, pushing herself viciously onward until she teetered at the edge of a cliff. And then it would be do or die, fall or fly.

But trying to choke the magic out of herself was accomplishing nothing. Surely this was unusual. The other few soldiers she knew who possessed inhuman abilities, especially Aimee with her telekinetic power, seemed to always instinctively know how to utilize them. Maybe they weren't very good at particular complex maneuvers and struggled to train in them the way anyone would with a new physical regimen, but they never had to stop and *try* to summon up the power. They simply...did it, like breathing.

And yet here she was, with magic that wouldn't *magic*. What good was any of her wild blood?

"You should stick to what you know," a cold, gravelly uttered behind her, and she leaped to her feet and spun around.

"Colonel Bisset!" She straightened, saluted. "I wasn't aware you would be here today."

"Obviously. I came on short notice. Get your dragon and receive your provisions from the maid that will be waiting at your door. We leave in half an hour."

Leave? Where? "Sir, may I ask if this has anything to do with the auxiliary riders?"

He glared at her, expression as cold as ever. Colder, in fact, or was it her imagination? "I would rather you not waste my time," he barked. "But since you've already asked, no. We have a situation brewing at the edge of Territory Five. You're needed, and quickly."

Territory Five! Home. Not that she would get the chance to visit Mama or Baba—or if she even should, given that Tet might get the idea to use them against her as well—but still. Home...after so long. But she didn't even want to go back to the village, she realized. There was no one there waiting for her.

"Yes, sir," she said and turned on her heel to hurry away. The colonel was not a man to keep waiting-

"Anzi."

She stopped. "Yes, sir."

"I understand you've already been insubordinate in the short time you've been here. I'm disappointed that you've embarrassed me."

At his words, the bruises on her face ached, reminding her of the consequences of said insubordination. But she wasn't ashamed. She wasn't remorseful. Not one bit.

Because knowing what she knew now, knowing that the Colonel Bisset she had so fiercely respected was just like Bastien deep inside made her so much less eager to please and impress him. He was just like the other riders after all, wasn't he? Someone who had subjugated his dragon with such brutal methods…stripped his partner of all dignity, all freedom. And to think she used to be so envious and dream of the day she could fly high in the sky on the back of her own enormous dragon.

Now, it was all she could do to conceal the snarl that curled her upper lip as she received his cold glare. And—his poor dragon. If only she could help.

"I sincerely regret my actions," she lied. "I've learned my lesson. I'll tread more carefully from now on."

"See that you do. Now go."

46

Netra remained sound asleep as Anzi carried her in her arms down to the palace courtyard. A fortunate thing, since she typically screeched at disturbances that dared wake her from her post-gorge slumber. And doubly lucky since Anzi had yet to find a way to keep Netra from speaking. Better for her to sleep and remain silent while Bisset was around.

The man was waiting for her on top of his dragon when she arrived. As she crossed over the grass, the enormous creature extended her wing and blanketed the ground with a rumbling, leathery sound. The clacking of heavy scales made Anzi's hair stand on end, and although she never slowed her stride, her gaze fell away from the colonel's stern face to land on the dragon's head.

What a truly massive leviathan. Her twenty-meter body lay flat on the grass, but the relaxed stance did nothing to make the dragoness look any smaller. The dark blue, white-rimmed scales were each larger than her hand, and the reptilian eyes that stared at Anzi as she approached were as wide across as her arm was long. Unbelievable. Every time, her sheer size drove Anzi to stunned silence.

Would Netra grow that large? She had only ever seen the other riders far in the distance before, and it was hard to gauge the size of the creatures they flew on from the ground. But Netra was so small, how could she possibly grow to such a length? It didn't seem possible.

But all such wandering thoughts fled her mind when the dragoness's eye began following her. Eerie. Desolate. It was the sensation of abruptly staring down into a dark abyss that she hadn't known was even there. Empty and utterly devoid of light, of life.

She looked away and suppressed a shiver. What had that been? She had seen the colonel's dragon many times before; this was hardly the first time she'd seen her eyes. Why was it so unnerving now? She did her best to put it out of her mind and appear unaffected as she made the long climb up the massive wing with Netra tied around her neck in her blanket. Ignore it, she told herself. She needed to handle what was in front of her first, and Netra's safety was her priority. It hurt to be so callous, but she couldn't afford to worry about Bisset's dragon when she had one hatchling to worry about already.

…Even if she knew the man must have victimized the creature as surely as Bastien would have.

She closed her eyes as a deep rumbling began underneath her, louder and louder until it was joined by a deafening wing beat that gloved the air on either side of her—it was like sitting the middle of two brewing storms. The ground fell away, heavy and slow. Oh, she had missed this. Flight. At least they could never take the love of it away from her. Even if she never flew on a dragon again, she would always remember it this way.

Except something was different. A strange energy reverberated through her like someone pounding on an enormous drum skin. Each beat shook her to the core, but when she opened her eyes, neither Colonel Bisset nor the still-sleeping Netra reacted to the immense pulses of unseen energy. But it was there, she knew it. She wasn't imagining it. Every rhythmic throb was earthquake-intense now, threatening to drive her right off the dragon's back and send her hurtling to the ground.

Her heartbeat, Anzi realized with a start. She knew what this was even though she couldn't explain how. She was feeling the heartbeat of Bisset's dragon, the pulsing of the blood that ran through all the veins and arteries hidden deep within massive flesh and scales. She could feel it as if she were touching it with her own hands, could feel the life that flowed there, strong and explosive like massive cascades.

This had never happened before. What was this? What was happening to her? She tightened her grip on the leather saddle and closed her eyes again, willing herself to block out whatever insanity had entered her mind to swirl through her body, lighting up every part of her with a fire she had no idea how to put out.

Act normal, she thought. Stay calm. Betray nothing.

As they rose higher into the sky and left the palace grounds, a faintly familiar sinking sensation pooled in her stomach. The discomfort pulled her into the present, and as the nausea thickened, it replaced the pulsing sensations completely. She breathed a sigh of relief when the last of it slipped away… and wondered if Bisset's dragon had felt it, too. Whatever the explanation, their senses had tangled together for a moment. Could it be the connection had gone both ways?

The gradually worsening roiling in her stomach forced her to stop her pondering. She was grateful that it grounded her, but where had the nausea come from? She had felt sick the last time, too, when she had first arrived at the palace, but it was so much worse now. Why? Why then, and why now?

It couldn't be. Fate wouldn't be so spiteful as to make her unfit for flight, would it? Not when she had just found Netra. How ironic. She stroked the hatchling's head inside the swaddled blanket with a sad smile, thinking back to when she used to dream so fervently—flying off into the sunset to save a village from barbarian raiders and marauding bands, heroic feats and cheering crowds. Glory, triumph.

She knew the truth now. Being a First Guard meant worse than nothing. It meant terrorizing the weak and upholding the cruelty of the mighty. And romantic fantasies were so pointless now when she had a new mission, a new cause. In that case—she held a hand to her stomach and took solace in the discomfort. At least like this, she would never become like the others. She could hardly become a scourge of the sky if she couldn't even hold onto her lunch in the air.

The thought even made her smile.

~

"Leave it with me."

Anzi's hold tightened on Netra. "She'll be hungry soon, sir. Should I feed her before I go?"

The colonel's stare sharpened. "I said, leave it with me. Go see the garrison captain and get your instructions."

Damn it. But the quicker she obeyed, the sooner she could come back and remove the hatchling from the man's care. She didn't trust him, not for a second. "Yes, sir. I'll return as soon as I can."

He didn't even answer her that time, turning away and heading for the desk in the small private cabin they were in. With her eyes on his back, she lowered the dozing dragon in her arms onto a pile of old blankets someone had left by the door. And then she was gone, heading back out into the midday heat at the edge of Territory Five.

The trip had taken longer than expected, a little more than three days with fewer rests in between. Anzi had been horribly tempted to demand that Bisset let his dragon rest, especially when twice more, she felt the creature's heart pumping and straining against the unfavorable winds that buffeted them halfway through the flight. But he had been utterly callous to the dragon's difficulties, even when it became physically evident that she needed rest by the unmissable, titanic heaving of her flanks.

Of course he was that way. Of course he wouldn't care. If there was anything Anzi had gained from seeing witnessing such awful treatment, it was her amplified distaste and scorn for the man she had once respected the most, second only to the Emperor. Forcing the drago on and on until she was so exhausted that she nearly crashed into the sands when she landed, and then not caring at all for her welfare—he had simply greeted the waiting garrison captain with a sharp nod and disembarked.

That was it. Nothing, no soothing of the dragoness's pain and fatigue. Maybe it was possible they were speaking to each other in their minds, like how Netra could, but she doubted it. All Bisset had cared about was getting what he wanted. The indifference sickened her even more than the flight had.

"Captain Gorien, sir."

A man with badly cut, short brown hair turned to look at her. He was standing next to another man, likely his adjutant, and they had been staring out at the deep desert just before she arrived. What were they looking at?

"Good timing. It's a privilege to have you and your fellow First Guard here." The captain stuck out his hand and withdrew it after a cursory shake. "I understand the colonel's not briefed you on anything, but it's just as well. Circumstances have changed drastically since our last report anyway."

"Sir? Is there something wrong?"

"Sure is." He pointed out at the desert. "We've gone from having one attack perhaps every few days or so to having small swarms assaulting us multiple times in a single day. We don't know why. None of my men stray too deep in, so there's no chance they could have agitated the wyrms and provoked them into attacking us. But here they are. We try to keep a lookout and a constant patrol so that we have an early warning when they appear, but they've already taken ten of my men just in the last six weeks. Good men, fathers, brothers, sons...It's too much. I can't send my men out there knowing that it's likely they won't return. And yet I can't leave it unpatrolled. We're the only thing standing between the wyrms and the villages."

The villages. Her home wasn't too far from here. If the wyrms were becoming aggressive and invaded, even a juvenile was capable of killing children easily. "Have any gotten past you?"

"Not yet, but I have too many wounded. Just a matter of time now. I need your help, desperately, but I have almost no resources to spare. I don't even have enough men remaining to send with you."

She glanced behind them. Was he asking her to go out there alone, then? Not a chance. She would report back to the colonel and let him know, and they would go out and beat back the wyrms together. It wasn't a one-person job, nor was it even for two, but she was sure they could manage it between them. The colonel might be a dragon-enslaving monster, but he was the most fearsome fighter she had ever encountered in the Imperial Army.

"Any adult wyrms?" she asked. "There's been trouble with those lately."

"I've seen three just in the past week. You may not believe me, but something's going on, madam, and we have no idea what. But we don't need to know. We just need it to stop before they break through and get to the civilians. You must have seen how close they are; the nearest one isn't but three kilometers from here. It'll be a massacre."

"Understood. I'll report this to the colonel immediately."

Just as she turned, however, Captain Gorien made a staying gesture, a hurried wave of both hands. "Yes?"

"Ah...Colonel Bisset is already aware. He ordered me to tell you what the situation is so you can resolve it."

Her eyes narrowed. "Alone?"

"...Yes. I'm sorry I can't be of more help. He told me to supply you with some provisions, but he made it clear he had no interest in joining himself."

She blinked. She was supposed to go handle this kind of problem alone, all because the colonel had no *interest?* How? Even a group of juveniles were dangerous, but to face what might be a swarm of adult serpents....The colonel's dragon was in no condition to help even if her massive girth didn't handicap her against her more agile enemies already, but she had expected the man himself to be the one leading the expedition.

Maybe this was another test. Maybe he was spiting her. "Are you sure?" she pressed. "He—"

"Yes. Those were his exact instructions."

She gnashed her teeth as she adjusted her uniform and leather armor over her various bruises and aches. She was going to get plenty of work out of them today. She just hoped they would keep her alive.

It wasn't long before she returned from the quartermaster fully outfitted. She had also been given three days' provisions which she would be need to stretch for twice as long. Generous, considering how she knew this mission would be over long before that, one way or another. More importantly, she had been given her weapons, and she stared down at the lethal swords in her hands. They were charmed to cut deep, nothing fancy but singular in purpose.

"I'm to kill them," she said. "Not capture?"

"Colonel Bisset's orders. But I admit I strongly recommended it."

"Are you insane—"

"I know it sounds outrageous, but when you see them, you will understand. These cannot be captured and tamed. They have only one desire and it is to kill. And I don't mean for the sake of survival."

"You're making it sound like they're lusting for blood."

"I can't think of another reason why they would attack en masse out of nowhere. This stinks of predation changes—could be they've developed a herd's taste for human flesh. Seems like it, everything from their sudde numbers and behavior changes and—"

"So killing them is my only option."

"I assure you, you have full indemnity for your actions even if you weren't, well, a First Guard. I don't think anyone will question your decisions on that basis alone, frankly."

She sheathed her swords and unhooked the scabbards from her hips, busying herself with placing them more comfortably so she could avoid the captain's gaze. First Guard. Being addressed that way out here for the first time sent an unpleasant shiver down her spine. The admiration, the adulation in the man's voice as he said it—*First Guard*—disgusted her as much as it made her pity him. If he knew the truth, would he take it all back? If he knew the truth, would he curse the ground she walked on and tell her she was complicit in the darkest evils?

She wouldn't be able to deny it. She was complicit. But only because she was too weak and unprepared to change the way things were...for now. But not forever. And if she meant to stick around and last long enough to leave her mark, she needed to outlast this ordeal first. At least she had regained some of her strength the last few days.

"What can I ride out with? Any sand horses?"

"Yes, one's on its way now from the stables. Our best, never shies from the wyrms or whatever else you might see out there in the deep. A fantastic stallion who'll do as you say, even to the death."

"It won't come to that." She abhorred the idea of sending any animal to their certain demise. She especially hated that Captain Gorien thought it would please her to hear such a thing. Then again, blind loyalty all the way to the grave was exactly the kind of trait bred in every soldier. She had been the same way until not too long ago.

"Of course not. Ah, here he is now. If there's anything else you think you may need for your supplies, please say the word."

"This is plenty," she lied. Rope, provisions, the swords—no, it wasn't plenty, but her chances of survival and success relied on how light she traveled since she was doing this alone. She still couldn't believe it. No longer did she wonder if this was a test of any kind—it was retaliation, pure and simple. The report of her behavior and Tet's punishment must have angered the colonel a great deal if he was going this far. Maybe he had reasoned to himself that she was only worth keeping around now if she could prove her mettle with this. Did he have that authority, though? Hadn't Tet himself emphasized her value?

Either way, Bisset could slip into a dozen dark hells because she would see this to the end. She didn't know how she was going to manage it, but she would come out of this alive because she still had work to do. Netra and the other dragons, they needed her protection. They needed her scheming. They needed her fury and her rage.

"I'll send word to the colonel that you've departed, madam. I thought he would be seeing you off."

She almost snorted, but she concealed it with a clicking command to the sand horse under her to have it face the desert. She had already guessed Bisset wouldn't show. "Don't bother," she said shortly. "He'll only be interested in my successful return."

"All right, then. We'll hold the line here for any wyrms that slip past you. Good luck."

Luck. Luck against a swarm of reptiles with an inexplicable drive to kill for killing's sake, if the captain's words could be believed. Anzi doubted *luck* would budge any part of the fate waiting for her in the sands. Just her skills, her wits, and her fortitude.

"Thank you," she said anyway. "Good luck to you, too."

47

Before departing, Anzi had changed into lightweight desert garb in anticipation of boiling heat, but the sunlight that streamed down over her was more comforting than hot. It had been a long time since she had last trekked this far into the desert, although this wasn't anywhere near the true deep sands at all. They'd gone no more than twenty kilometers, roughly, and the stallion was still trotting comfortably over the dunes with no signs of tiring. Large, fanned ears flicked this way and that, and over Anzi's head, the creature's long, tufted tail did the same, providing both of them shade.

Captain Gorien had been telling the truth. This stallion was a remarkable specimen. Well-trained, intelligent, strong, and possessing even greater stamina than its kind typically had. Anzi was sure they could go another twenty kilometers before they had to stop for a rest, and that only because of her own limitations, not the sand horse's.

At least her bruises were nearly healed. Not only that, but she felt—energized. Strange. The three-day flight had been grueling and exhausted her to the bone, but all alone in the blazing desert after a two hour trot, somehow she felt far more refreshed now than she had the entire journey to Territory Five. Probably all in her head and just the product of no longer being airsick, but still. Strange.

"Let's stop here." She tapped the horse with her reins to signal for it to halt. There was no cover in sight as they were in the portion of the desert with only loose sand under their feet, but that was the good thing about a steed like this, a sand horse—the ultimate desert-adapted creature. She nestled against the beast's side after it lay down, avoiding the large, flat hooves tucked under its body, and took refuge under its fanned, curved tail that hovered over them both. And despite the hostile conditions, in all honesty, it was the most peaceful she had felt in days.

She reached back to grab one waterskin secured inside a saddle pocket and offered it to the stallion, who seemed disinterested. Of course. Before departing, the stable master would have given him all he would need for several days' time. More for herself, then. Anzi took several rationing swallows before putting it away again.

"No wyrms," she said aloud and patted the stallion's flank. "Better be careful. They'll come out in a flash and eat you up."

Not really. Sand horses were notorious for being unpalatable for any predator, given their stringy flesh, the tough fat gathered in their tufted tail, and not much else. Anzi, on the other hand, would make a perfect snack for a wyrm. She ardently hoped Captain Gorien had been wrong about the appearances of adults, but after what she had seen only a few weeks ago on her Second Run, she couldn't discount anything.

Those kids. The recruits. Were they all right, she wondered suddenly. She'd left them all alone in the gorge after rendering them unconscious, and with a live wyrm, no less…what had she been thinking? She had cut into the reptile's body in non-lethal spots so she could spray its silvery blood all over the area to ward off others, but she had done nothing else besides that. She hadn't even asked after their safety after everything was over.

She looked down at her lap, stricken. All she had been thinking of was herself. All she had been aware of was her desperation to succeed, her beast-like need to win at all costs so she could reach her goal. She hadn't thought for a second about anything else.

That was what Pierro had been criticizing her for when they had argued afterward.She had assumed he was envious, that he resented her, but…he had been right. No wonder the others had hated her. She would have, too. Was that why she had been hand-picked for elite training, besides her so-called wild blood? Because she had been willing to sacrifice everything and everyone else to get what she wanted?

She cringed. She had been just like them. Bastien, Tet. Bisset, too, she suspected. How could she have thrown away her family, her only brother, innocent children recruits, and everything else she had stepped on to get as far as she had? Was this how every First Guard was chosen?

She regretted it. She regretted every terrible choice she had ever made. But at least her path, terrible as it was, had led her to the dragons. Now she had to make up for everything she had done. Every mistake, and every malicious not-mistake she had made. Maybe she didn't know where to start, but she knew exactly where all of this had to end. Tet needed to disappear, and all the Premier Guard, and every tenet of their Empire that she had discovered to be rotten and festering on the inside. Everything she had believed in but had never been true. Somehow.

She was still simmering in her anger when the stallion tensed against her back. She stiffened too, knowing to trust the animal's instincts. Sand horses weren't nervous beasts, but they were sensitive ones. She leaped to her feet and drew one sword as the horse scrambled up to trot away at the same time. Anzi considered following, but she had to stay far away enough so that whatever spooked the horse wouldn't get to it nor the supplies stored on its saddle. As long as she kept her distance, any predator would choose her over the stallion, and after she dispatched the threat, she could continue unimpeded.

Assuming she survived.

It happened so fast she had no time to dodge, only block. Something long and serpentine shot out of the ground, sending a shower of hot sand spraying all over her. She threw her forearm up, presenting her leather bracer just in time to catch gnashing fangs that dug vainly into the hard-ened material. Good—she was stronger than the slender sword in her hand, and she couldn't afford to let her blade snap against a sheer force it might not be able to withstand.

Before she could slash at it, a bone-jarring force crashed into her, and her feet ground and slid back through the loose sand. Before her, a large, hissing serpentine head as long as her forearm thrashed against her, desperately trying to dig its elongated teeth into her flesh through the bracer.

It wasn't alone. To her left, something else leaped at her, and another from her right. She dropped to a crouch just in time to let them collide over her head and collapse on the sands, nearly hitting her on the way down with their heavy, banner-like bodies. She slid back and swiped up, down, short but swift strikes meant to cut deep into vulnerable flesh unprotected by scales.

But they kept their distance as soon as they saw the twin steel blades flashing in the sun. With angry hisses, they wriggled back until they were several meters away. Anzi narrowed her eyes. They weren't adult wyrms, but they most certainly weren't immature nymphs. The smallest of them was well over three, perhaps three and a half meters while the other two were far larger, even if she couldn't tell how long they were from tip to tip because of their coiled stances.

More concerning than their size was that the one farthest to the right was dripping something from its extended fangs. Its maw was wide open, prepared to deliver a crushing bite, and snake-like, vertical slit pupils trained unmistakably on her as it drooled a gleaming, clear. Venom. She pressed her lips together, too tense to afford herself the liberty to curse.

The upside was that all three paid no attention to the escaping horse, only to her in synchronized unison. The downside was that this only confirmed every one of Gorien's dark suspicions. Wyrms were supposed to be mindless. With their diamond-shaped heads and legless bodies, they were little more than giant snakes with intelligence to match, and they were ruled by the urges of their nature the same as any species. They had no concept of planning, of advanced strategy. They were just—animals. They couldn't speak, couldn't think, could only chase their primal instincts and no further.

So why were they now circling her in equal intervals, as strategic and cautious as human soldiers circling a dangerous foe? They shouldn't be able to do that. Even in crazed swarms, the most they were capable of was ganging up on a single threat and slashing and biting all at once. But this? Three of them? They should be fighting amongst themselves over her. She circled with them, keeping the one with the dripping venom in front of her at all times while trying to maintain the others within her periphery.

But it was impossible. They were somehow intelligent enough to ascertain exactly what she was doing and how to counter it. In keeping her attention on the most dangerous one, the other two were free to slip behind her and lunge. She ducked only in time to avoid one, and the other sank its fangs through her outer desert attire and her leathers. She felt it break skin before reaching back and wrenching its head with an iron grip around the vulnerable, unprotected ear hole on one side. With a grunt, she dragged it around herself, using all her strength to fight its thrashing and slash at its neck right under the frill for a clean kill—

Green. Vibrant, breathtaking green, a cross between the hue of a pure emerald and the green of verdant grass and clovers in the lushest of meadows.

Then clear blue water, sparkling under the sun, a whole pool of it under the shade
of drooping palm trees with fronds as large as she was tall—

She was still trapped in the vision when she stumbled to the side just
in time to avoid a lunging attack from one of the wyrms, but half-blinded,
she came away with an open gash over her collarbone and up to her
shoulder. The fang had dragged over the leather guard and sunk into her
collar, and she hoped frantically that it wasn't the venomous one that had
landed its mark. Sand sprayed under her feet as she dragged the wyrm in
her grip with her, and it wasn't until she had retreated at least a frantic
five meters that she realized she was still holding onto its head. She had
paralyzed half its body with her fingers pressing punishingly deep into
the base of its skull, accidentally targeting its weakness with lucky accuracy. With all the flashes of color and images still flooding her mind, she
had forgotten what she was doing in the middle of trying to kill the
captive reptile. Instead, with convulsive strength, her hand had squeezed
around its neck and head, and now it writhed with weak movements as
its long body trailed before her through the shifting sands.

What had that been! And why could she see the vision even now! This
was no mirage in the distance; it was like something was fighting to
possess her mind. She gritted her teeth and tried to drive out the thoughts
with violent force of will, but they didn't disappear, only receded. At least
it was manageable now. Now she could focus. She raised her sword again
to stab into the back of the wyrm's head to end it quickly—

They're harmless, leave them be. You've scared them enough.

She nearly choked. What was this? A voice in her head? It wasn't Kai's,
and besides, she wasn't sleeping, wasn't spirit-walking in her dreams. She
was wholly awake, outraged, and terrified at the foreign presence that had
entered her mind so effortlessly. It took up residence inside her thoughts
with no difficulty at all and-

Didn't you hear me? Let them go.

Whoever was using their black magic to take over her mind was not
only dangerous, but insane. Let go of the wyrm when it would twist right
around and attack her?

They didn't know what you were until it was too late to retreat. Now they
know. So release them, and they'll leave you.

Insane. Insane-

You don't want to kill them, anyway. You could have already. But you
stopped, and it wasn't only because of me.

The voice made her want to tear into her skull and dig the invading presence out. The only thing that made it even remotely bearable was that it was the voice of an old woman, gnarled but spirited. There was nothing malicious in it despite everything, and just like that, she found herself releasing the reptile's neck as ordered and flinging it away. In a flash, it wriggled away over the sand toward the other two—and disappeared. All three, burrowing into the sand with a grinding whisper of the grains against their scaled bodies until only a glimpse of their vanishing tails remained.

Then, nothing.

Anzi stared, stricken silent except for her uneven panting. At the height of her fight for survival, she hadn't noticed the renewed pain from the sudden movements straining her weakened body, but now, with the wyrms gone, her ribs throbbed anew and made every breath feel like a punch to the stomach. She dropped to one knee and caught herself with her free hand over her thigh. Shit. Everything hurt. Badly. With a wince, she sheathed the sword and adjusted the scabbard of the other so she could rest more comfortably on the sand. But she couldn't relax now. Not with an unwelcome guest in her head.

"Who are you!" she demanded aloud. She didn't know what the rules of possession were or how to communicate with the old-woman-voice, but talking out loud was easier than forming coherent sentences in her scrambled mind anyway. "How are you in my head. Also, get out."

I knew I would like you. Your spirit is strong. That's good. You'll need that.

"You're a witch. You—"

Ah-ah-ah. Careful, now.' A knowing, smug chuckle echoed inside her and made her twitch. We're two of a kind...or will be, one day. You're a little too green for that yet. But still, insult me, and it returns on you twofold, little bird.

Little bird! Whoever this woman was, Anzi was going to find her and make sure she realized she was no little *bird-*

You should do something about how you're bleeding magic all over the sands, it'll draw every unkind thing to you if you don't staunch it.

Anzi clapped a hand over her wounded shoulder at the amused warning, clencing her jaw at the way it stung under her palm. Damn it. The supplies were with the horse. Now she had to go and run it down, because the voice was right. If she continued to allow herself to bleed like this, every water-hungry creature within a ten-kilometer distance would be able to smell it and come chasing the precious fluid. And then she would have worse than wyrms to contend with.

The first in a generation. I didn't think you would be so fierce, but I suppose that's what it takes to blaze the path for the ones that come behind you.

"You can't bewitch me with strange talk. I know someone who's even worse than you are when it comes to that."

Oh? Someone worse than I am...what a fearsome thing that would be.

Anzi bristled. "Enough. Tell me what you want or get out of my head."

The unreasonable courage of youth. Endearing. What isn't endearing, though, is the situation you're in. You came this far to stop the wyrms from encroaching on human territory, but you can neither kill them nor can you let this continue. What to do, little one?

Little one? What was she, a house pet? A toddling child? "How do you know what I'm here for?" she challenged. Her hands itched to draw her swords despite the enemy's presence being only in her mind, and to suppress the urge, she turned and began stalking off toward the sand stallion resting a ways off with its white tufted tail visible against the sandy dunes. Maybe getting a move on would put distance between the old-woman-voice and herself, too.

But no such thing happened, and an echoing chuckle mocked her efforts.

Once you treat your injury, go back. Leave this place. It's dangerous for an untested one such as you to travel alone. There are things moving in the desert in ways men cannot even imagine...And nothing can be done about the wyrms. The ones that invade are the ones that have been chased out from the deeps. They're smarter, stronger, faster than the ones that grow on the edges of the desert. They will not be so easy to contend with, and they will come and come and come. The most you can do is warn them off while you are here since now they know who you are, but once you leave the humans, the wyrms will attack again. They will only be obedient for as long as you are present.

"What kind of nonsense are you—"

Oh, my...Have I said too much? Shall I let you learn alone?

The chuckling again. She really wished she could punch whoever it was in the throat, elderly or not. "Tell me what's chased them here, then. You mentioned that. What is it?"

I did say that. Hm...you will see soon enough. Now go. You will find no more wyrms now. They've tasted you, they won't come within a league of you anymore. Neither them nor the others.

"What even are you? How would you know all this in the first place? I won't believe anything you say without proof."

The proof will be in the way you will be as stubborn and fierce as I can feel you are. You will wander here in search of more wyrms no matter what I say, and you will find none. They will flee from you. Your efforts will be in vain. Just a little bird you are to me, a green shoot. But to them...

"...Yes? What am I?"

You'll know that too, soon.

"Why go to all the trouble to bother me like this if you aren't even going to do anything? Just riddles and play."

It's no trouble at all. I haven't had this much fun since before that abomination of a king rose to power with the humans...but a story for another time, perhaps when we next meet. Until then, fly high, little bird...just not too high. Those like us need to stay close to the earth.

Anzi blinked.

Gone?

She checked again, stopping in her tracks so she could close her eyes and focus inward, explore every crevice of her mind in search of any trace left behind by the infuriating foreign presence whose identity remained an utter mystery. But she was gone. The old woman along with her taunts, both. What in dark hells?

Fine. Who cared? Not her. She was on a mission, and if that enchantress or demon or whoever it was wanted her to go back to the outpost so badly, she wouldn't play its game. She would stay out here and complete her mission, whatever it took. Little bird, her ass. And she'd called her green—a green shoot, even. Who did she think she was. After Anzi reached the stallion and dug out the medical supplies to seal up her wound, she lay an energetic slap over the horse's rump.

"Let's get to it," she said. "We're going to go find those wyrms."

48

Anzi lasted all of three more hours before her spite-fired endurance ran out. Searching for dangerous serpents in the Adaraat's sands with not a hint of a scale or tail was fast becoming torturous. She wanted to go back. Netra would definitely be awake now, and she would be hungry. Anzi had already guessed Bisset wouldn't lift a finger to feed her and had asked the guard on duty to tend to her instead, but she dreaded to think what the colonel might do if the hatchling irritated him with her insistent screeching in the meantime. Or spoke.

She should go back, but she hadn't decided whether to report the encounter with the old witch crone in her head along with what she had learned from it. Should she? But if she did, that would be one more reason for Bisset and everyone else to keep an even closer eye on her. She didn't want to attract more attention. She needed to fade. But if she didn't report the incident, she had no excuse to return to the outpost early. She was supposed to be traveling at least a day and a half's journey both ways, and if she returned before that...

This was hard. She had no interest in slaying wyrms when she knew there had to be some other way that didn't involve slaughtering them the moment they crossed paths. Maybe it was the lifelong conditioning to capture rather than kill them that made her so reluctant, or maybe it was that they looked so much like dragons that she couldn't stomach the idea.

But there had to be some way, she thought for the hundredth time, something that would both protect the village and outpost while minimizing the bloodshed.

She didn't know how she heard it. One second, she was deep in thought about the mysterious cause of the wyrms' outward migration and the annoying old woman who'd invaded her mind earlier, and the next, she was pulling the stallion to a halt and straining her ears for whatever she had detected. Or maybe she was hallucinating? The horse hadn't sensed anything, and its hearing was far better than hers. She waited anyway, hands grasping the reins tight and her eyes darting this way and that. A whisper...the hushed spilling of sand, there had to have been something. But no, only silence.

There! Again! Except now that she was alert to it, she realized she hadn't heard so much as she had sensed it. A twisting in the back of her mind, a word on the desert wind, like someone tapping her shoulder for her attention. She slid off the saddle and drew her swords, both this time. Whatever it was, she had no idea which direction it would be coming from nor even what it might be. What could be so stealthy that even a sand horse couldn't detect it, and how was it that she alone had heard it?

...Anzi.

She shoved her swords back into their scabbards so hard they nearly fell off her hips, then stomped back to the horse to climb back up on it.

Anzi?

"No!" she snapped, loud enough to startle the stallion. It let out a gentle, questioning wicker before pawing the sand with its wide, tufted hoof.

What do you mean, no? Anzi, what are you doing here?

"Leave me alone!"

Saying no won't-

"We are not doing this while I'm awake! Or ever again for that matter," she shouted at nothing, and again, the horse craned its neck to look back at her with a wary stare. Did it think she was crazy? Maybe. Was it right? Possibly. Because that was the only reason why she would be hearing Kai's voice in her head again right now. He sounded faded and distant, but there could be no mistake.

You need to get out. Go back. It isn't safe.

"I'm never safe," she grumbled. "And I don't need to be. I'm on a mission, so leave me alone and don't ever do this again. Because I don't care what you say, I wasn't even thinking about you, so don't go blaming this on me and saying that I came to you first or whatever it—"

I'm sorry. Don't be angry, Anzi...I thought something was wrong. I would never do this if you didn't want me to otherwise.

She let loose a noisy, relieved sigh. Oh, good. In truth, she had been worried that she *had* inadvertently done something...because yes, maybe the thought of him had crossed her mind more than once in the past few hours because the desert reminded her of Kai and his bronzed skin, but if he didn't know it, no harm done. "Well, I'm fine. Go away."

Please. You need to go back.

"Does this have something to do with the wyrms?" she demanded. "I already know the ones that are attacking the outposts along the fringes are those that are being pushed further outward from the center of the Adaraat. Why? What's happening, and what's responsible?"

She swore she could feel how startled Kai was. *How did you know that?*

"...Because...I could tell they're different from the usual ones."

Not to the naked eye. And I can feel you lying to me. Don't, Anzi. I'm trying to help.

"Then help me by giving me some answers. Believe it or not, I want to head back too, but I can't without something to give them. As if I would rather be here when I need to be with—" She stopped. She couldn' mention Netra now. He would find out when he returned to the Imperial City, but it served no purpose to treat the chieftain like a confidante. She still didn't know how far she could rely on him when her situation was so unsteady. "Anyway, trust me, I want to go back, too. But without a solution to stop the attacks or at least slow them..."

There's nothing you can do. We're waking up the sleeping ones...go back. This will all be over soon. Wait for me.

The words were ominous enough to send a shiver down her spine. Just as she opened her mouth to demand an explanation, his presence disappeared, sliding out as smoothly as it had entered her mind. There one second, gone the next—was everyone treating her head like a common inn now, sauntering in and out as they pleased?

"Bastard," she muttered, and only felt a little better for it. The sleeping ones? What had he been talking about? Surely he wasn't speaking of the wild dragons hidden away wherever he'd gone? Hibernating species... could it be? Goosebumps rose all over her arms at the very thought of it. Truly, surviving dragons in the wild in all their glory of old, what would it be like to see them?

She shouldn't be so excited at the prospect. Bringing them to the Imperial City, possibly into the clutches of the man responsible for their extinction—the thought was enough to make Anzi's lips curl into a fierce scowl. But why was Kai doing this, then? Why would he bring them where they were in the most danger—for what? Prestige? Wealth? He didn't seem the kind of man to care about either.

...But what did she know, anyway? They weren't friends. They weren't comrades. A kiss meant nothing, even if she could remember the heat of his lips and the warmth of his arms and chest even now. She didn't know him, and he didn't know her, either. Maybe prestige and wealth were enough to convince him after all. Certainly, Tet would treat him gloriously in return.

With no answers, Anzi had no choice but to go further into the desert, plunging inward into deep sands as far as her provisions would last for the return trip. The horse never tired under her, but she too stayed awake through the second day. Strange. She had always been of superior stamina, but she felt even better after skipping an entire night's rest than she had the day before. Why? She pulled back the billowing sleeve of her desert robe and inspected one arm, noting with narrowed eyes how the last remnants of her bruises had disappeared. It had only been a week since the incident, and the mottling of her flesh had still been visible yesterday. Had her communication with Kai sped up her healing once more? Maybe. She wouldn't pretend to understand his strange, suspicious magic. But something told her it was something else.

"This is pointless," she growled on the second night. "Come on, back the way we came." She twitched the reins against the horse's tufted mane and turned him around. He seemed to like that idea; his speed increased from the steady trot to a swift canter across the shifting sands. He was eager to get out of this place too, which was odd since it was a well-known fact that sand horses preferred the kind of terrain their name implied. They had no fear of enemies when they could detect and escape them easily, even if they had any natural predators in the first place that wouldn't gag on their naturally desiccated flesh. They had no need of water or food for long stretches, either. They adored the desert. So why?

"You know it too, don't you?" she asked. "Whatever he was talking about. Him and the crone. Something's happening, something you don't want to be here for. That's no comfort."

...Worse, why was she talking to a horse? Raising Netra had done something strange to her; she found the need to babble to everything now. She shook her head and clung tight to the stallion as he sped up to a steady gallop over the sands.

～

WHEN ANZI RETURNED to the outpost, her report was lackluster: she had seen only three wyrms, and although she had subdued them when they simultaneously attacked, she had been unable to capture or kill and therefore had allowed their escape. She was prepared to receive whatever consequences her inadequacy had earned, she told the impassive Colonel Bisset, and bowed her head to emphasize her cool subjection.

Except he had no judgment to render. If anything, he looked pleased.

"You saw no wyrm activity at all?" he repeated. "Except for the single encounter, and they retreated after you wounded one of them. You're certain you saw nothing else?"

"Yes, sir. I suspect they went under me in the sands. They were the burrowing kind. If these are the sort that have been attacking the outpost, then I have to confess I have no idea how to stop them. I apologize for being unable to stave them off."

"No matter," he said gruffly. "There have been none since you left."

"Sir?" What? But the attacks had been happening mightly up until the day she left. "I didn't realize. That's good news."

He ignored her optimism. "That wound was deeper a half-hour ago."

She looked at her shoulder where the collar of her uniform had been punctured and torn. The leather shoulder guard was decidedly more ragged than when she had left for the short expedition, too. "Yes, sir. Drew blood, but no venom. I was fine after standard treatment from the medic."

"Drew blood. I see." He stared at her for so long she could feel the muscles in her neck tightening. She didn't like the way he was looking at her. There was no malice, because Alexandre Bisset was capable of no emotions other than cool disregard and disappointment, but she could swear he was pleased about her being wounded. Was it spite? Was he really that angry she had earned 'discipline' from the Emperor Tet and disgraced the colonel? She might have thought so if she didn't have the vague notion that it was something else. Something stranger, more sinister. Either way, if it pleased him, it could mean nothing good.

"Your wound must not have been deep," he said. "It's almost healed."

"I have a healthy constitution. Flesh wounds rarely linger."

"I can see that. Especially the injuries you bore before you left. They've disappeared."

She was tempted to tell him that her ribs soundly disagreed, but in truth, even she had to admit her recovery had been abnormally swift. Its pace had stalled during the three-day flight here, but she had come back from the desert feeling not just better, but *good*. Bisset was right to be pry. She had questions too.

"I've become hardier in the past year," she said. "It improves as I age."

"That'll be useful. And it'll serve a use now as well. Bastien has suspicions that we are going to explore before we leave for our next destination. Out. *Now*."

The order was so abrupt that even with the added encouragement of a cold glare on top of the crisp command, it took Anzi an extra fraction of a second to act on it. Her eyes slid over to where Netra lay sleeping in a heaping pile of what looked like uniform shirts with rags to soften the makeshift nest. She was loathe to leave her again when she had just returned. But she had no choice. She had to remember her mission. Obey, she reminded herself, and gain their trust. Later, her chance would come. Netra was fine.

She exited the small lodge with Bisset following close behind, and they headed for the edge of the outpost that faced the desert. Her heart throbbed with sudden alarm at the thought that they were going back out there. She was still armed since Captain Gorien had insisted she keep the twin swords on her person as a precaution, but she didn't trust Bisset not to try to strand her in the middle of the desert to satisfy whatever deep-seated resentment he held against her. She could withstand the conditions for at least several days no matter how punishing, but it meant a longer separation from Netra. Her pulse pounded frantically-

"Bare one arm."

They'd reached the edge, and she obeyed without question, knowing whatever came next, it was better to get it done quickly. She undid her bracer and rolled her uniform sleeve back up to her elbow.

"Mark this area," Bisset ordered. "Enough that any wyrm who comes close enough will catch the scent."

Mark? Her gaze moved down to the pale underside of her forearm that she presented. He wanted her to spill her own blood? And from the sounds of it, a lot. Was he insane? This sounded like a magic ritual, a blood ritual. And yes, she understood that dragon riders seemed to all possess some degree of magic, and indeed, that it was a condition of their selection in the first place, but she wasn't a mage. Whatever magic she possessed was instilled deep in her bones as a passive force, not a channeled one, other than the occasional burst of power she could summon forth.

But damn it, she knew this wasn't the hill to die on. When the time came to cut her losses, she would recognize it. Bisset ordering her to harm herself to invoke strange magic wasn't it. Before she could convince herself otherwise, she drew one sword, held it in a reverse grip with the tip pointed downward, then sliced its edge along her extended forearm to send a rivulet of blood dripping into the dirt-and-sand mixed earth below.

"Fifty meters that way, again," said Bisset. "And then fifty meters more. Be liberal. Then return here."

The silent *I'll be watching* didn't go unheard. She masked her displeasure with a sharp, obedient nod and did as he said, and some minutes later, she returned before him with her arm now dressed in three long gashes dripping blood that trailed down her fingertips. She didn't ask for an explanation. Would Bisset tell her even if she did? But she had a sneaking suspicion now what this was about even if he gave no justification for this odd demand. This was no ritual, and neither was it a show of force, of authoritative superiority. There was purpose behind it, something that had to do with Tet's obsession with the wyrms...Tet's and everyone else's in the First Guard.

She was blood marking. The thing she had done back when completing her Second Run when she sprayed the unconscious wyrm's blood to ward off all others, that was what Bisset was telling her to do now. For some reason, he believed that *her* blood would accomplish the same thing, keep the reptiles away from the outpost and the villages behind it. Incredible. What was it with these people and their stubborn belief that she had some strange connection with wyrms? Her blood would do nothing.

You will find no more wyrms now. They've tasted you, they won't come within a league of you anymore.

The sudden memory of the old crone's words rushed into her head with no warning. Her mouth tightened, and she did her best to hold her neutral expression before Bisset as he continued to stare at her. Damn it. Hurry up. Whatever he was doing now, he needed to get it done more quickly so she could go back and take care of Netra while ruminating over everything she had been through in the last few days. The wyrms, the crone…and Kai. How was that even possible? She wanted to bash her head into the closest wall so she could strengthen whatever part of it was so weak that the latter two could enter and leave her mind as they pleased. And after that, she would punish herself for missing Kai's presence after he disappeared, too.

"Whatever the nature of your blood," said Bisset, "Bastien believes it affects dragons and like breeds. We will be testing this further, but he believes you are still growing into it. It will take time."

She'd thought he would say something like that. "Yes, sir."

"Report to me any strange incidents that would shed any light on the matter. Is that understood? Without exception."

"Yes, sir." She wondered if he could ever believe she would be so disobedient, in vengeful secretiveness. No, she was not going to tell him a thing if she didn't have to, not unless it benefited her more than it did him to do so. She had a purpose now that exceeded and surpassed the interests of the Empire.

"The suspicion is that your blood will keep the wyrms away from this area for a time. We'll know whether it proves true soon enough."

"Will you be stationing me here during that time?"

"No. You're needed elsewhere. We're going there now. Captain Gorien will send reports to the Imperial City, and Bastien will study them while he waits for us to return."

"Yes, sir." Damn it. Moving again, and she had no idea where. She knew better than to ask, too. "Would you like me to go pack now?"

He seemed to detect that perhaps her facade of immediate obedience was only veiling her true intentions. Namely, her desire to get back to Netra. Even so, he gave her a brisk nod. "Feed your dragon and meet me where we arrived. Be ready to depart in half an hour, I'll be speaking with the garrison captain first."

Finally. Anzi had no doubt she was headed for more trouble whatever it was that Bisset had planned, but at least she would have a moment to herself first. She saluted him and hurried away.

49

Netra was furious for a week. She ate well enough, but every time Anzi reached over to pick debris between her scales or examine her claws for chips, she snapped at her, teeth clacking furiously and head twitching this way and that like an angry bird. There was no soothing the young dragon and even when Anzi and Bisset arrived on the back of the colonel's dragon outside the city of Lumenera, Netra was still refusing anything but the most necessary of handling. There was no way for Anzi to explain why she had had to leave without warning for the desert expedition. It was one of the few times she wished the hatchling would communicate again despite the risk of alerting the colonel.

She and Bisset stood at the front gates of the city before a small retinue of men who had come to receive them, mostly soldiers wearing the colors of Lumeneran scarlet. The elderly man at their head wore military garb as well, making her narrow her eyes in skeptical question. This was an annexed city, the home of the once-sovereign Lumenerans who had fought hard for years until their conquest three decades ago. A coastal city to the west, they were a naval power to be reckoned with but had fallen to the forces of the Empire that came from their east. There were occasional rumors of rebellions that seeded this place, but she had never been stationed here before.

"We're honored by your visit," said the elderly man, and she instantly recognized the diplomatic veil that half-hid his lie. His tone was neither disrespectful nor disinterested, but there was a formal falseness in his sandpaper voice that seeped into her skin. "We look forward to offering you the utmost hospitality."

"Governor Hosef." Bisset stared down at him, a full two heads taller. "I've received reports of seditious activity. I expect full compliance as I get to the bottom of this. No one in my way and no one protecting the guilty."

"We sincerely hope you find it to be a baseless rumor, Colonel, as you did your last several visits."

"I'm sure you do."

Anzi absorbed every word. Sedition. So Bisset had brought her here to help root it out, or perhaps to teach her how to resolve such issues for when she was inevitably sent on similar missions. And Lumenera, unsurprisingly, had been inspected frequently enough that the governor recognized the colonel on sight and vice versa. It was odd that a man more youthful and more sympathetic to the Empire hadn't been assigned to the post, though. It was clear that this Hosef had no true affection for his city's conqueror.

And for good reason, no doubt. After everything she had learned, she knew that awful things must have happened here to quell the once-proud people.

"We don't have a stable large enough to house your dragon, unfortunately. Will you be leaving it here? Our streets are narrow and unwelcome for something of its size."

Anzi started at the governor's question. A stable? For a dragon? What a degrading...

"I'll decide that for myself," Bisset said, utterly dismissive. She noticed the lack of any insulted tone in his voice, only irritated impatience. She shouldn't be surprised. It was too much to expect anyone in the Premier to stand up for their dragon partners, wasn't it? "Put out the notice that Lumenera is now under martial law. Everyone is to proceed indoors immediately. I'll be personally punishing anyone I find out of doors at sunset."

For the first time, the elderly man's expression broke. A flash of alarm creased his weathered skin, and the top of his bald head twitched as his bushy white eyebrows flew up. "Sunset! It's already nearly time."

"Then you should get going, shouldn't you."

For a tense moment, Anzi thought the governor and his escort of half a dozen soldiers would unleash violence upon them. She wouldn't have blamed them, either, but a handful of increasingly tight inhales later,

Hosef bowed his head. "As you say. Please excuse us." They retreated through the large, wooden gates in unison, armor and weapons clanking in a rush. She watched them go without a word, knowing that neither her opinions nor questions were welcome. If Bisset wanted her to say anything, he would have said so.

Two guards stood at either side of the gates, staring at her and the colonel through the visors of their helmets. No movement. She stared back until she heard the colonel speak.

"Lumenera has always been overtly religious," he said gruffly, and a gleam of disgust entered his eyes. "It fuels their rebelliousness since they consider themselves beholden only to their gods, and they think their freedom is a birthright. That ouldn't be further from the truth, but it being a port city, dangerous ideas flow in and out of this place almost unchecked. We routinely exert pressure here to make sure they remember why they should be afraid."

She didn't like the sound of that last bit. Not at all. Her fingers twitched at her sides, and she had to force herself to keep them from clenching into fists. "To stomp out whatever rebel groups we find?"

"If we do find real evidence of rebel activity, then good. But we're here to make sure it doesn't become a problemto begin with."

So it was fear? Fear was the reason they were here, to intimidate and bully citizens to make sure they stayed in line? He wasn't actually acting on reports of seditious activity at all? "I misunderstood," she said, voice cool and level. "From the conversation, I thought we were going to be overseeing an investigation, and helping enforce martial law to enable it."

"Imposing martial law reminds them who they submit to."

"...Of course."

"A problem, Anzi?"

She shook her head. "No, sir."

"Then go tend to your dragon. She's shedding, so gather up the scales so you can dispose of them off the harbor later. If you leave any behind, there are scavengers in Lumenera who will collect and sell them for profit. Even the scales of juveniles can sell for an exorbitant amount overseas."

"I'm sorry if this is a shortsighted question, but I got the impression earlier that the people here don't think highly of dragons. Is it possible we can change their perception of them if we encourage trade of dragon remains and relics to bolster their economy?" She pointed back at Netra who was currently biting at her loosening scales. "It costs us nothing, and maybe it'll encourage a more favorable reception next time."

The look Bisset gave her was a mixture between pity and amusement, both things she had never seen him exhibit before. It gave her goosebumps. "What do we need a 'favorable reception' for?" he asked. "They can do nothing either way. You need to adjust your thinking, the sooner the better. Do you enjoy catering to the whims of the lesser because you're afraid of treading on their feelings?"

It wasn't even cold, the way he spoke. He spoke as if it should be obvious, some undeniable facet of common sense, a callousness that was not only blasé but sensible, logical. Anzi was seized by the sudden urge to pick the man up and hurl him upon the ground and ask if that had *trod on his feelings,* and she had to refocus her attention on Netra's sudden squeaking to pull herself out of the moment.

"Yes, sir. If you could excuse me." He gave her a brief, dismissing nod, and she went off to collect the complaining hatchling crawling around on the ground back near the larger dragon's snout. Bisset's dragoness was already sleeping, hot breath billowing out and rustling the blades of grass as well as raising thin clouds of dust. The colonel had pushed the massive creature to her limits again. A week's flight only—and Anzi was finally beginning to understand that more so than typical dragons, this one's size made it difficult to maintain stamina. She wondered again why Bisset was incapable of valuing his dragon partner at least for her incredible strength, or even her usefulness if nothing else. Fine, so the Premier were full of exploitative slavers who subjugated dragonkind for their purposes, but it was inconceivable to Anzi that they couldn't even respect the sheer power that resided within those scaled bodies, within their spirits.

"You're going to have to make a decision," she snapped, though quietly, when she reached the still-struggling Netra. "You can be angry at me all you want, but I had my reasons for doing what I did. And to be honest, I think you *do* understand, you're just stubborn and spoiled. I know you listen, and I know you get more than you let on." She glanced over her shoulder and saw that Bisset had left to speak with the gate guards. She pitied them. "And you—yes, you! Netra-hau. You haven't spoken to me since that one time back at the palace. You had better not do that to anyone else. You don't know what they'll do to you if they find out you can speak, and neither do I. Understand?"

The hatchling bared her teeth at her.

"So you'll be that way, then? I guess that's your decision. I'll feed you, but nothing else. No grooming, either, so forget it. You can try to shake off those loose scales by yourself and see where that gets you." Netra's snout twitched. Then twitched again. Finally, she growled and settled back down on the grass, and Anzi sighed as she sat down to join her. "Stay still, I'm going to clean you up."

The colonel waited what might have a half hour then beckoned her over. "Come with the dragon," he called, and she hefted Netra in her arms.

"Damn it, you're fat now," she grumbled again, and the hatchling pecked furiously at her collarbone, yet again demonstrating that she understood perfectly what Anzi was saying. Figured. Whenever she said something Netra didn't want to acknowledge, she suddenly had no comprehension of human speech, but when it suited her... "Yes, sir," she said when she reached Bisset. "Is there something you need?"

"You're to go in first. Walk the streets, make your presence known. The governor will have put out the order by now, but you'll be encouraging swift obedience."

"Am I to...enforce it?" she asked cautiously. "It seems a bit early to be heavy-handed, with all due respect. It hasn't been long, and with a city of this size, I expect there will still be a great number of people who are unaware."

It was probably an awful idea to outright question him this way. Her abdomen tightened with remembered pain, every one of her ribs recalling Tet's vicious kicks against them, but she couldn't let fear and caution rule her every moment. Fine, if the colonel wanted to report her for being insubordinate so that she earned another instance of body-shattering abuse. But she was not going to unleash on innocent citizens.

Luckily, Bisset only waved at her, a gesture of boredom rather than irritation. "As you will," he said before turning away to walk toward his dragon. "If you feel the urge, you have every authority to act as you see fit. I ask only that you execute no one who matters."

Bile rose in her throat. Easy, easy. Now wasn't the time to make waves. "Yes, sir," she said. "Then I'll go patrol."

"Make sure they see the dragon. It's important to reinforce these people's fear."

She gnashed her teeth as she watched him walk away, utterly at ease. Repugnant. Amoral. Not just him, but everyone who gleefully joined in and reveled in such corrupted, rotten ways. Bastien with his sick obsession with turning the dragons into nothing more than breeding stock, Tet with his enthusiastic willingness to destroy dragonkind and use the remnants to satisfy his greed for more, more, more, and Bisset with his unfeeling, stone-like way of using dragons to instill terror and subjection as if he deserved to exercise such power, as if he were a god reigning over insects.

How could she ever have admired them?

No one came within a meter of her. Even in the thick of a crowd, the people of Lumenera parted for her as if she were a goddess or perhaps a demon, eyes glued to her face and form as she marched down the street and headed for the opposite end of the city. She hated it. She hated how she could feel the terror thick in the air, the fury, the bitterness. Netra was quiet in her arms as well, unusually tense and quiet as if she too were uncomfortable with the attention. As she should be. She was the source of their hatred, after all.

As Anzi walked on, knowing what effect she was having on the populace and despising every second of it, she realized for the first time how big the hatchling had gotten. Compared to how small Netra had been when she first hatched, she was at least twice as big now, maybe more. She was spilling out of Anzi's arms, and her wings were no longer gossamer-thin and fragile. She had yet to fly, but that was probably for the better. At least for now.

Anzi just wanted this over with. This show of gratuitous, domineering force and the part she was playing in reinforcing it. The staring, the whispers, the way she knew that everyone who looked at her wished she was dead and gone.

"Filthy snake queen!" someone shouted, a young boy's voice, before being muffled and dragged away. By the time Anzi looked over her shoulder, there was no sign of the culprit, and she felt at the same time the intuitive sensation that everyone here protected each other. No one would claim to know anything even if she had even the remotest interest in demanding that someone drag the boy out.

Good for them. They were all they had. She moved on.

The dead silence unnerved her the most. A crowd of this size back in the Imperial City would have been deafening; there would have been no way to hear the words of a friend shouting in one's ear. But not here. Her skin crawled, chilled in frigid apprehension. She hadn't done a thing to these citizens, and yet they feared and abhorred her nonetheless. This was what it meant to be a First Guard, then, something to be hated. And to think she had believed she would be received in cities with great fanfare and adulation. Only in the Imperial City, it seemed, and even then with some reservations.

She passed by two news criers eventually, both of them calling out as they rang a bell in their hands, informing every citizen they needed to proceed indoors immediately. Again, silence besides their voices—no one else's. Could the news have already spread so quickly? There was no grumbling, no shouting, no complaints within earshot. Swiftly, the crowd thinned and disappeared. Self-preserving obedience.

"I'm glad we found you, young miss," a familiar voice called behind her, and she stopped in her tracks to turn around. There, the elderly man from before approached on horseback, hooves clip-clopping along the stones that made up the road. "I'm ready to escort you to the Governor House if you're unoccupied, or wherever it is you wish to go first."

Hosef. From his tone and the empty, cool look in his eyes, he knew she wasn't exactly 'unoccupied' and knew what she was truly doing: simply walking around to inflict fear wherever she went. Her stomach twisted at the realization that he thought she was happily complicit in all of this, in the mindlessly cruel and ruthless abuse of power over his people. But she couldn't defend herself. She *was* complicit. She was letting Bisset making her do this, wasn't she? Her excuse of saving her wrath for the bigger picture only meant that she considered the Lumenerans too insignificant to break ranks for, after all. In her arms, Netra stirred, spines rising and flaring on her back to stab her under the chin. She wasn't screeching yet, but she certainly wasn't liking the mood, and Anzi lowered her arms so she could shift her downward and away from herself.

"I don't need escorting anywhere," she said. They probably thought the stiffness in her voice was haughtiness, not regret. "The colonel sent me ahead to…begin patrolling."

"Indeed."

Her eyes counted the five guards who accompanied the governor, all on horseback as well. They were well-trained, not a sign of hostility on their faces. "So I'm…grateful for the offer," she added. "But I'll be doing as I'm ordered. I hope you can understand."

That was probably a little too on-the-nose, but the compulsion to justify and defend herself was too strong. She wanted them to under-stand, even if it had to be in coded, indirect talk. She wanted them to know—if she could help, she would. Maybe that would soothe her guilt.

Sure enough, a strange flicker ran through the governor's eyes, and his mouth tightened into a thoughtful grimace. Not a kind one, but at least it was better than a violent response. Being hated by a wizened old man was the worst.

"We all have our orders," he said finally, aged voice grating like sandpaper. "We are here at your service, of course. May I ask when your fellow dragon rider will be joining us."

"I couldn't tell you, sir. His intentions are usually a mystery to me."

He lifted his chin and observed her. "I see. As to us. But we are happy to oblige."

"How many times has Colonel Bisset been here, if you don't mind my asking, Governor?" She glanced around in the short lull that followed her question, noting how the street had suddenly become nearly deserted in the last few seconds. She looked back up. "Or any of the Premier, actually."

He was watching her with that same hard, guarded look tinged with wary receptiveness. "Too many times to count," he answered. "We've been so blessed as to receive the colonel's personal visits at least every other season. The others come and go as they please. We never go more than a few weeks without such an inspection of our status."

Every few weeks! That explained much. No wonder the Lumenerans responded so swiftly. They had been through this countless times. "I wasn't aware he was so attached to the city," she said, keeping her voice carefully modulated as she let slip an incredulous note. She wanted the elderly man to know she was on his side...or would be, if she could, but she couldn't afford to give him any ammunition to use against her, either. The last thing she needed was for him to make remarks to Bisset later about how *different* members of the First Guard could be.

"Perhaps you're too young to remember, though it's improper of me to assume your age." The wide smile that split his face held not a hint of mirth. "But the colonel was personally responsible for bringing this place and its people into the bosom of the Empire. Thirty years, it's been. I remember every moment as if it were yesterday."

Until recently, she would have insisted that such an annexation would have been carried out with all dignity and humanity. Now she knew better. "It's not improper at all, sir. There's much I don't know. I've had... my eyes opened to a lot of things lately."

His eyes remained fixed on her. It felt like they were looking down into her soul. "Oh, yes," he said, and a note of affected loftiness crept into his tone. "The colonel and I have had a great deal many disagreements in the past. But I'm an old man...it's difficult to keep up. And after he appointed me governor of this place, I could hardly refuse, now could I?"

"I suspect not."

"Especially since he had the previous one executed."

She'd figured as much. The reigning monarch of an enemy stronghold couldn't be allowed to keep ruling, after all. But then, why had Bisset installed this one as governor instead? He wasn't an enthusiastic supporter of the Empire-

"My son, that is," he added. "Along with the rest of my children and grandchildren. There was no one else to do the job, of course."

Her stomach twisted, hard. "Ah."

He gave her a long look, then snapped the reins against his horse's neck. "Please come with me," he said. "I'd like to show you something."

50

Anzi had the distinct feeling she wasn't supposed to be here, but she hadn't been about to reject an explicit invitation from the man who'd just told her that her traveling companion had been personally responsible for the death of his entire family. Colonel Bisset could discipline her later all he liked, but she was not going to look Governor Hosef in the eye and pretend her suffering would be greater than his had been.

She couldn't begin to imagine. She had never been close to her family, partly because she'd left them at a young age and partly because she had fostered that distance herself in her determination to follow what she'd thought was her destined path. But this…She didn't need to have experienced fellowship in pain to sympathize. And blame. This was the kind of carnage the Empire wrought, the kind that no one spoke about back in the Capital because everyone was taught that the annexed lands all held hands and danced around in a ring together.

"I'm a very old man now," Hosef announced when she reached his study. They had entered his mansion at the heart of Lumenera, a pretty, three-story structure lined with numerous columns and coastal foliage decorating the beams. "I don't have many years left in me. I'm expected to name a successor, which I've put off for a long time."

"That's a weighty responsibility."

"Not really." He settled into a high-backed chair and sat at the oaken desk before a large window, facing her. "I'm only choosing in name. The Empire will decide."

"I see."

"You seem very young. Something drastic must be happening that the Premier would be recruiting youths such as yourself. And of course, no one has seen such a…an immature dragon before, either. I didn't know one could be so small."

"I hadn't either."

The elderly man raised a bushy eyebrow. "Yes. The ones we're used to seeing are far larger. They put fear into the people far more effectively than a little youngling would."

She shifted her weight between her feet. She didn't know where to steer the conversation. In the face of the things this man said as well as the further implications buried within, it was hard to pull any kind of small talk out of thin air. She felt like she deserved to hang. "Can you expect all the people in the city to be in their homes by sundown?" she asked. "There wasn't a lot of time."

"We've had some practice. The panic that comes with the promise of death or mutilation generally has my people running faster than they would otherwise."

Wrong question. She was too hardened to begin sweating merely because of an uncomfortable exchange of dialogue, but she was starting to wonder if she should look for an excuse to take her leave again. She had thought the old man had invited her to show her something significant, but maybe this was all he had. His study, and a stream of deadpan responses to remind her of the vile company she kept. Through it all, she had to mask the secret that she would sooner stab Bisset in the chest a dozen times and end his tyranny than to help him with any part of it, because even if she revealed the truth, the Lumenerans would never believe it, least of all this man who had lost so much in his long, hard life. They wouldn't be so reckless as to jump on her supposed sympathies. They would suspect her of trickery, perhaps even report her to Bisset for dissenting speech in the cold hopes that they might gain a little favor from him.

If that happened, she might well be dead. Or worse. She looked at Netra in her arms, thinking back to Tet's casual threats back in the throne room. She was valuable, but not indispensable. They would do terrible things to get what they could out of her before they consigned her to dust.

Caution. Discretion. She needed to be patient.

"The people here hate dragons," she said. "Down to the children. Dragons have shaped the...terrain of your city thoroughly. Is this normal?"

"Normal?" Hosef leaned back in his chair. "I don't understand your question, madam First."

Madam First. It must be a regional form of address; she'd never heard it before. "I mean to ask if every city on this side of the continent regards dragons the way the Lumenerans do. And if—"

"And if those cities bear the weight of enforced rule as heavily as we do," he finished with a wry smile. "I see you are very new to this."

She said nothing.

"...Yes," he said. "I have more pity for my own subjects than for others, but our experience isn't unique. We are always under the shadow of dragon wings, madam First. It colors everything we do, everything we say, everything we dare to think. It has shaped us for two generations now. It surprises me that you would ask."

She didn't miss the hostile undercurrent of resentment that rumbled under his words. "I'm ignorant in a lot of things," she said in a low voice. "I'm learning every day."

He narrowed his eyes. "So it seems."

"...But I hope to keep learning from you during my time here, even though I don't know how long that will be." Her pulse quickened. This was risky. And yet it was nothing that Bisset could take her to task for even if Hosef turned on her and reported her strange words to the colonel. "Maybe you can give me some insight that I wouldn't discover otherwise."

He gave her another long look. "Perhaps.But I think you will get plenty of that tonight while walking our streets with your comrade. Colonel Bisset never shies away from teaching a sound lesson."

There was bitterness in his voice, roughened by grief. But there was an ominousness too, a promise of something dark that made her skin crawl. She'd only been under the colonel's instruction for a scant few months before she was taken to hatch Netra—in truth, she barely knew the man aside from the cold, unfeeling demeanor demeanor he presented to the world. No. That wasn't true. Just outside the city gates, he'd said things about the Lumenerans that had made her blood curdle in her veins. The casual intention to terrorize, to subjugate. That he could appear cold and unfeeling didn't mean he was any less insidious than laughing, jeering Bastien or petty, long-winded Tet.

"You must be the type to learn quickly," Hosef added when she failed to respond. "Frankly, I don't see why someone like you would be brought here otherwise. This is unprecedented in my lifetime."

"Someone like me?"

"Yes." He lifted his chin, eyes narrowed. "Someone unhardened."

For a second, her pride reared and threatened to revolt. She had been sympathetic toward this man because she knew he was in the right, that what the Empire had done to the city and its people was unforgivable, but to be called *unhardened* rubbed her raw in all the wrong ways. She was strong even if maybe it wasn't in all the right ways. To be called weak stung every sensibility she possessed.

"I don't mean that as an insult, madam First," he said. He must have seen a flash of her discontent before she forced it back down. "I mean to say that you are not what we've come to expect. You are unhardened —malleable."

It sounded like he thought he was giving her a begrudging compliment, but *malleable* was a strange one. Like an easily manipulated metal, untested and soft-

"Because perhaps something of us will mold you well enough to stay with you," he continued, still staring. "Maybe you will learn more than an old man like me should hope."

Ah. They were both talking in code. They could hardly trust each other given the circumstances, not fully. But maybe this was a start.

SHE HAD to be back out on the streets and asserting her presence before Bisset came back, lest he discover that she had spent time engaging in questionable discussion with the governor of the city. It was a valuable half-hour of learning that Governor Bantan Hosef came from a long, previously uninterrupted line of kings that ruled Lumenera and the waters that nourished it. He had already passed the crown onto his heir back before the proud city lost its sovereignty, but when it finally fell to Empire forces, the crown was ripped from his beheaded son and returned to him. He had already been in his fifties. He was an old man now, and with only human blood running in his veins, he had no exotic stamina to sustain him for much longer than a decade more, perhaps. Less, probably.

Bisset had been the one to personally carry out the massacre. He and three other dragon riders had converged on the city thirty years prior to lay waste to Lumenera so horrifically that it had made history:. After suppressing the defending mage army and laying siege to the city for two weeks, the walls fell and blood ran in the streets. Even the mighty city by the sea couldn't hold back the wrath of four dragons.

From every household, Bisset had ordered one child be killed, or if the parents begged sufficiently, enslaved along with their mothers. The fathers were spared, but only so far as they vowed to devote their lives to the service of the Empire instead, disowning their loyalty to the city of their birth for all time. To spare the remaining children, most had no choice but to agree, and mothers and one offspring from each family had been taken away in chains to be sold into prostitution and slavery. Most were never seen again. Others were eventually glimpsed at one time or another, sometimes pressed into the service of lecherous foreign dignitaries coming to visit and ogle the Lumenerans' fall from grace, other times on the road, imprisoned in brothels and forced to serve every filthy customer who stumbled in with grubby hands and dirty jowls.

The city fell. It fell and fell and fell again, unable to rise. The rebuilding of the city walls alone took twelve years, and of course, the Empire banned all attempts to rebuild their army. All mages, even those with the barest slivers of magical potential, were taken away and sent elsewhere. The Lumenerans stopped celebrating magic and began hiding their children who had the gift.

And to this day, Governor Hosef had said, there was a population crisis in the city. Too many men and not enough women after thirty years, especially since many of the widowers of the previous generation decided to take far younger wives to replace their stolen ones. And that had introduced a moral decay that rotted the city even further: the sale and trade of girl-wives, child brides. Kidnapping and rape became prevalent both within the city and without, as slavers and traders of women began frantically gathering 'stock' to sell to desperate men. And all the while, Bisset watched and did nothing. He oversaw the city but only in silence and inaction, watching impassively as Bantan Hosef toiled to reclaim the Lumenera his fathers and forefathers had built...the Lumenera that his son had tried to preserve. In the end, the people never recovered. Crime remained rampant, and everyone lived in fear of the violent packs that roamed the streets. The only thing that curbed those was the fear of something even worse: dragons.

Because no one could forget the way the dragons had soared over the city, burning, searing, melting the barriers that the city's mages cast. Flesh blackened and burned, children weeping, children screaming, children dead...

"Your report?"

Anzi stood before the colonel in front of the city gates. "All is quiet," she said. "Everyone's indoors now."

"That won't do. We'll have to look more carefully."

"Do you think they're brave enough to disobey?" she asked. "They seemed terrified."

"Not brave enough." Bisset walked past her, leaving his dragon to sleep on the grass some distance away. "Foolish enough. Reckless enough. Stupid enough. Yes, to all of that. We find several to make an example of more often than not."

"Maybe they'll be obedient this time," she pressed, pitching her voice with a casual lilt as if she didn't care one way one the other. "It would be less work. I hope that's the case."

He gave her a withering glower. "No. We'll find someone to punish regardless. We came here to carry out our duties, Anzi. Don't shirk them. If they won't produce wrongdoers to make examples of, we will create them."

She knew better than to wonder if he really meant that. Create them, he had said. Create wrongdoers to make examples of. She had no respect for the name of the Premier anymore.

"Lumenera has been hiding mage activity," he told her after he beckoned for her to walk at his side. "It's well known that this city's population produces more gifted magic users than most, including the Imperium. We took measures to both exploit and mitigate that some years back, but not enough to stifle it."

Her breath caught. Measures to mitigate the birth of magic users? Was he talking about the mass killing and capture of women and children that Hosef had told her about when Lumenera first came under Empire rule?

"But we knew it would be wiser to let this place maintain at least some steady supply of mages," he continued. "Tet has expressed concerns about how dry our own wellspring is becoming, so we will need to pull from magic-rich city populations. Especially once we finish preparing to advance northward. The terrain isn't conducive to marching, and foot soldiers will keel over by the hundreds if we rely solely on mundane means to take those strongholds."

She had to say something. Anything. Whatever it took to mask her horror. "We have dragons," she said. "What's stopping us?"

Bisset scoffed. It was a small sound but no less derisive for it. "We have no strong winter breed of dragons, none who would be resistant to the cold. Yours is the first one that has hatched alive in our climate and survived this long. It remains to be seen whether she will last until adulthood, though even if she does, she will never be of large enough size to be a credible threat against the defenses of the north."

She had no idea how the man could possibly know what size Netra would become, but then again, he was an old man despite his youthful appearance. No matter how much she disliked him, his attitude, and his words, she had to defer to his experience when she couldn't rely on her own. "Yes, sir. May I ask what defenses we're concerned about?"

"Basilisks, primarily. Once the mages devise some plan to keep them at bay, we can move. Until then, we wait and grow our strength. We'll have no foot soldiers to absorb losses and exhaust the enemy; Tet will likely send a half-dozen of us to siege the first city to gain a foothold in winter country."

She had no idea basilisk lived that far north. Toward the Feng lands, yes, but winter country? Suddenly, Bisset began climbing up on stacks of wooden crates by a building and left her on the ground. "Sir?"

"You will patrol on foot," he told her before disappearing over the eaves. The sun had already nearly sunk over the horizon, and the growing darkness draped him from head to toe as he stood up on the roof. "When you find the first curfew violators, assess who they are. Street urchins and others of no consequence, you may punish as you wish including execution. Just don't waste time. We're not here for the street urchins, Anzi. Keep searching until you find evidence of any hidden mage enclaves. Once you do, neutralize them, then wait for me to find you."

"Execution, sir? Of street rats?"

"You may."

He'd mistaken her question as a request for permission, not an expression of disbelief. It turned her stomach thrice to hear such a casually indulgent reply, as if he were doing her a favor by doling out the privilege of taking defenseless lives. If she weren't carrying Netra, she would have had to restrain herself from taking hold of her sword hilts...despite knowing the colonel would win if she dared to go against him now. Any common soldier, Anzi was confident she could sweep, but she had seen the colonel in action before. Only once, but that had been enough.

She needed to wait. Patience, she told herself. Patience. If Governor Hosef could stamp down all his rage and grief and withstand violent occupation for thirty years for the sake of his people, then she could do this. She could hold it in.

"Would you like me to make my way northward as I patrol?" she asked, training her voice to pinpoint neutral precision. "Will you be moving southward at the same time?"

"Yes. Sweep your half overnight, and I will do the same on this side. You'll find that most streets aren't worth your attention, but keep your eyes open. We need of fresh blood at the Tower, and the Magisien body would like children. The younger the better. So be aware, and...Anzi."

"Yes, sir."

"Don't underestimate the Lumenerans. They are a desperate people."

She swallowed back hateful words. "I understand."

"Then check your supplies and go. Meet at dawn and report."

51

"**S**top *squirming*, Netra."

Netra, of course, didn't listen. With a furious clicking of her talons and a raising of her spines, she fought her way out of Anzi's grip and leaped to the ground, leaving the soldier rubbing her scraped chin. The dragon immediately trotted off to inspect the market stalls, tail swishing behind her like a cat's.

"Those things need a trim," Anzi muttered. "And you need to stop eating. Gods, you're fatter than a palace pet."

She was. It had been adorable at first, and Anzi had been powerless to resist over-feeding her whenever the dragon screeched and wailed for more (what if she really was starving?). But the gluttonous habits were clearly too much. Instead of walking, the reptile wobbled and waddled on her clawed feet, belly hanging down between her legs with an almost comedic curve. But she was longer, too, and stood taller at the shoulders. Anzi had been toting her around in her arms every day since she had hatched so she had missed it, but she had finally noticed Netra's growth during her absence for the three-day desert expedition. And now that she thought back, freshly hatched, she had only been about as long as her forearm from snout to tail. Now, the little dragon was more than twice that, and she had been growing even faster ever since shedding her scales. Unfortunately, all that led to even more ravenous behavior, and Netra had no qualms about scavenging or stealing food.

"You know you're not supposed to do that," Anzi hissed. "Come here." An answering hiss and a series of angry clicks. "Netra! Now! That's dirty."

She was never going to have children. Being responsible for a moody, spiteful, spoiled little princess of a dragon was infinitely worse than being responsible for any squadron or even entire platoon of soldiers, no matter how undisciplined or inexperienced. And if she didn't get back here...

"That's what I thought," she said darkly as Netra dragged herself over with bared teeth. "And you're going to stay next to me. You think you're so terrible, but what are you going to do if you run into a pack of strays who want a piece of you?"

The little white dragon clacked her teeth.

"Don't you talk back to me—come back here!"

Unbelievable. She looked around to make sure Bisset hadn't followed them in secret before running after the unruly dragonet. The empty market stalls themselves were bare; Netra must have caught scent of something in the warehouses where the sellers kept their wares overnight. But they were not going to pillage Lumeneran goods today if Anzi had anything to say about it, even if that meant prying open the little dragon's jaws and extracting every bite she stole.

It was strange, how still everything was. Sure, all the people had fled indoors under threat of lethal consequences for violating the sudden curfew, but a large city like this couldn't possibly be so quiet and peaceful, even in pretense. The stray dogs she had threatened Netra with earlier were nowhere to be seen now, and animals didn't understand curfew or martial law. They should still be out here, digging in the wooden waste bins or following behind her at a safe distance for scraps. She looked over her shoulder as she walked, wondering if she was simply missing them, but nothing. Her eyes narrowed. Everything was too quiet.

...Quiet?

"Netra!"

Quiet Netra was bad. The click-click of talons on the ground and the occasional complaint meant she was only slightly misbehaving, and Anzi had learned to tune it out. But silence? Disaster. Anzi sped up, looking frantically around. Netra had better show herself and scamper out of the darkness right now.

"Netra!" she hissed again. "Come back here!"

Her heart dropped when she received no response, not even the typical annoyed screech that roughly translated to *shut up*. Nothing at all. She looked left and right, noting the tall stacks of wooden crates on either side of the narrow street she'd turned onto. Behind them, maybe. She hoped. She peered over and around them, searching for a telltale flicker of a shadow, listening for the unmistakable sounds of greedy eating, the flick of an impatient tail in the corner of her vision. Her stomach turned when several minutes later, she had yet to find her. With a burst of panicked determination, she leaped up and grabbed hold of the over-hanging eaves of a one-story building roof before pulling herself up in one smooth motion. It vaguely occurred to her that she had grown stronger in the past few weeks than she had ever been before. Namely, besides the lingering pain and occasional cramp that plagued her ribs, she was faster and more agile, more sure of her strength. Whatever damage Tet had done to her with his brutal beating, she was well on her way to full recovery and more besides.

Too bad she couldn't appreciate it as she trotted over roofs and climbed higher onto taller buildings, searching the streets below for movement. Netra had never wandered off like this before, and even if she was disobedient, she had never let Anzi call for her more than several times before showing herself. There were limits to her unruliness and spite. But still she failed to appear, and a flash of ominous comprehension seared through Anzi when almost a half-hour later, the dragon was still nowhere to be seen.

Shit. *Shit.* A sickening heat filled her throat and dropped into her stomach as she grasped the hilts of her swords. If only it weren't so dark. But even without the illumination of sunlight, Netra's glimmering white scales should stick out like a beacon in the gloom.

"Netra—"

There! She was still mid-call when something darted along the next street down. She couldn't make out anything through the murky dark, but that had been movement unmistakable. Maybe it was just a stray, but it was all she had to go on. With a flying leap, she abandoned the rooftop and landed on the ground below, not even noticing that she had just fallen two stories for the price of a petty bruise on one knee. She took off at a flat run, body stretching out over the ground as her legs kicked up dust and dirt behind her.

She found nothing. Anzi glared at the doors to the warehouse that had been left ajar not far from where she stood. Ordinarily, she would exer-cise caution, but she wasn't afraid of anything that might try to corner and capture her here. Not like this, when she had her swords drawn and ready. But even so, something wasn't right. It wriggled underfoot like a worm, the call of intuition. That warehouse...Maybe it wasn't an ambush, but a diversion. Could be someone wanted her to enter it so they could sneak out of this alleyway while she was distracted. Too convenient.

Netra. She had to find her. That she hadn't heard her screeching yet was a terrible sign. She had never been so quiet except in her sleep. And that little flurry of movement she had spotted could be no coincidence. If it wasn't Netra, something was following her, keeping to what they must have thought was a safe distance. Follow then, she thought. She sympathized with the Lumenerans who had been oppressed and tormented by the Empire for decades, but if someone hurt Netra, she was going to carve them to pieces.

There, again! This time, she moved even faster with no regard for quiet and discretion. She crashed through the tower of crates stacked along the wall and lunged with such swift violence that she surprised even herself. Wooden splinters went flying as she charged and toppled barrels next, following the now-visible scramble of something grey and brown just up ahead. Got you, she snarled inwardly and rushed forward, eyes glued on her quarry.

But it was no dragon—it was a child. She kept up the hot pursuit anyway, and while he was fast on his feet and knew the terrain of his native city far better than she did, a mere kid couldn't possibly outrun her. With every rushed corner and every cramped alleyway he tried to lose her, she only drew closer, closer, closer. He slipped away twice. She didn't know how, except perhaps by her own excessive haste, but that only made her all the more determined. She didn't know if he had anything to do with Netra's disappearance, but if he had been tailing them, he must have been watching closely. That meant he had seen and knew something, and she was going to get it out of him if it was the last thing she did.

She didn't bother with threats. With a fierce clenching of her teeth, she resorted to her last option, one she might regret but did anyway. A blast of spectral force left her body and her outstretched hand with mighty, concussive force, radiating from her in an intense corona that rushed outward in every direction. But most importantly, straight into the back of the fleeing child. With a pained yelp, he went flying forward off his feet and landed on the ground a few meters away, catapulted by both her attack and his own speed.

She was on him before he even stopped sliding. He was small and skinny, but she refused to underestimate him, not when he might know where Netra was. Her casting hand was blistered and throbbing with white-hot pain, but that didn't stop her from kicking him back down to the ground and pinning him there.

"I won't hurt you if you cooperate," she growled with a bent leg resting on the child's back and the other knee on the ground. She had sheathed one sword and kept the other in her good hand, but the tip was planted on the ground to support her weight, not angled at the boy. She didn't want to hurt him. She just wanted him to talk. Fast. "Understand?" she demanded, leaning forward. Her eyes were still darting this way and that in case there were others around, but she kept half her attention trained on the child for any sign of trickery. Lumenera was a magic-rich city, she remembered, even if the Empire insisted on kidnapping mages away to fatten its own forces. That could mean any number of the street children had escaped detection and were magically endowed. She rapped the child on the back of the head with a tap of the sword hilt, not too roughly but with no excess of gentleness, either. "Answer me!"

"Yes!" the child half-shouted, wheezing into the stones. But his little voice was neither helpless nor afraid. Wary, bitter, disappointed, but there was no weakness in it. She would have respected it more if her heart weren't threatening to beat right out of her chest.

"I'm going to turn you over. If you try to run from me, if you try to fight me, I will put you down."

It was a threat she would make good on. She didn't like bullying children, but gods knew she'd done it before. The faint memory of her Second Run slipped through her thoughts, the frightened faces of the young recruits as she wrangled the wyrm then fought with Pierro... She took her weight off the child's back and flipped him over before pressing her fingers into his skinny chest.

"Why were you following me?" she demanded. "Who put you up to it?"

The boy couldn't be any older than perhaps ten, maybe. He looked about the age she'd been when she went into Service, a blend of youthful immaturity with a budding touch of adolescent awareness. "You've got money," the boy snapped. "I'm hungry."

She pressed her fingertips harder into his chest, making him struggle. "Don't lie to me. I'm not here to play games, and I didn't catch you so you could feed me fibs and run right off. You weren't trying to pickpocket me, not when the streets are deserted and I'd have been able to chase you down anyway with no crowd for you to hide in."

"I'm hungry," he repeated, little mouth turned down in an angry snarl. "Or you think starving's got a bedtime? Curfew, my ass."

She was no stranger to children swearing. It had been severely punished in the barracks when she was his age, but everyone did it. Still, it was unsettling to see it come from the kid's mouth with such conscious venom—with an adult's bitterness. "Where's my dragon?" she asked. "I know you saw something. Or maybe you're the lookout and were part of it. Who put you up to it?"

"No one! You crazy hag."

Hag. She was only eighteen, the youngest hag in written history, then. She dug her fingertips even harder into his chest, making him squirm again. "I'll dangle you by your toes from the highest building I can find," she warned. "I'll keep you like that 'til morning."

"And then kill me? Go ahead. I'm not afraid, you snake-kisser."

Snake-kisser. If she weren't so desperate to get Netra back, she would have paused to admit that was a good, memorable insult for a dragon rider, she presumed. "I'm not going to kill you," she snapped. "Just tell me where my dragon is. She's done nothing to you."

"It's already done enough just being alive!"

Hatred. She'd never heard such vindictive strength in a child's voice before. "That's enough. Stop wasting my time."

"I told you, you can kill me." The boy grinned, white teeth gleaming in the dark under the moonlight. "I'll never tell."

She narrowed her eyes. There was no fierceness in his voice, only a smug, accepting ease that disquieted her. It was the voice of a soldier dying in captivity, bleeding out and refusing to give in to the enemy. "I told you I'm not going to kill you," she repeated. "But you do need to tell me what I want to know before I get angry."

"I don't care. Do what you want. You must think I'm stupid to not know you'll string me up and cut the skin off my whole body soon as I say anything." He smiled wider. "But that's not gonna do much for you, snake-kisser. I'm not afraid of anything anymore."

"Stop talking like that. You're a kid. Just tell me what you know before I put you over my knee and spank it out of you."

"Go ahead and try it, old hag."

She really was tempted. But there was a crazed look in the child's eyes that told her it would be futile, and despite his suspicions, she wasn't going to flay him alive for the truth. "In any case," she said, "you just as good as admitted you know something. You're with others, then. I can easily go see Governor Hosef and have him give me his hunting hounds, and they'll track your scent to the others fast as lightning. That's right, I know about his hound kennels. I also know they can track anything with a scent within thirty kilometers, and I doubt your friends are that far away. There's no place within the city they can get to from here to slip out of that range, and the moment they step out past the city walls, trust me, I'll find them that way, too."

Bullseye. The child's grin faltered. It didn't disappear completely, but she could see something like horror blossom in the back of his gaze. She hated that he could be so terrified for the fate of his comrades when she hadn't even outright threatened to do anything to them yet, but if fear could serve her purposes…

"You won't get all of them," he said, but there was the barest quaver in his brave declaration. "We'll never stop. We'll go down to the last man and you'll still never win."

…Words that didn't suit a little kid at all. It was like he'd heard them from someone else, an adult, someone older…An impassioned leader of a rebel gang, perhaps. Her mouth thinned into a hard line as she stared down at him. What could she possibly say to convince him he was being stupid? It astounded her that such a youngster could be inducted into the goings-on of sketch, underground Lumenera, besides the fact that he looked homeless and probably orphaned, too. She couldn't imagine parents letting their little one run around and volunteer himself as a martyr for a cause.

"I'm not your enemy," she told him. "I don't care about curfew. No one's getting hurt, and all I want is Netra back safe and sound. I don't want trouble, and since you don't either, help me fix this so I don't have to involve anyone else. I'm not even going to go to Governor Hosef, so stop being stubborn and help me make this right."

He spat at her, and she grimaced before wiping away the one fleck that managed to reach her chin. "Go to hell!" he raged. "And kiss my—"

She sheathed her other sword and smacked him. Not on the face, but across the top of his head, and although it was far too light to actually hurt, it made him stop short before he launched into a full spiel of insults and challenges. With a warning finger, she jabbed at his face. "Enough swearing," she said sternly. "You don't even look old enough to wash yourself."

His face twisted into a furious scowl that reached all the way up to his eyes. "I hate you!" he shouted. "I hate all of you, you're all dirty, filthy foreigners who couldn't hold your own against us if you didn't have a demon king who makes pacts with evil spirits—" She smacked him across the top of his head again, and he rubbed his hair and shielded it from her. "Stop it!" he snapped. "You're so—annoying!"

"Then stop being a little brat of a boy," she fired back. "You've taken my dragon, who's done no wrong, so you're the one who needs an attitude adjustment."

"I'm a *girl*, you idiot hag!"

"All right, then. Stop being a little brat of a girl."

The child immediately began to struggle in earnest now. A moment ago, she had been eager to sacrifice herself just to spite her, but now she beat on Anzi's thigh and knee and every other part of her she could reach. Interesting. Short, dark hair cropped nearly to the head in tiny curls could indeed belong to either a girl or a boy, Anzi acknowledged. Her mistake for assuming.

"Stop that," she ordered. "You're not going to get anywhere like that. I can wait here all night until you're done with your tantrum, but we are going to settle this. Understand?"

All of a sudden, the girl's struggles stopped, and she stared up at her with a smug grin. "Good luck with that. Bye-bye."

She had tensed as soon as she felt the shift. Not just in the kid's demeanor, but in the very air. She was too battle-hardened to be taken by surprise so easily, and she ducked the hissing swing of the keen blade that sliced through the air above her. In a flash, she rolled off the child and was on her feet, both swords out and one in front of her, one behind. Finally, she thought. It had taken them long enough. Her blistered casting hand was going to be a bitch to peel off the hilt, but it would well be worth it-

She froze. Two men stood in the darkness of the alleyway, and the urchin girl jumped up to her feet and scurried behind them, all bared teeth and narrowed eyes. Anzi looked from one to the other, jaw tight and hands clenched so hard around her sword hilts that she thought she might dent them.

"Calm down, dragon rider," one of the men murmured, his gravelly voice just loud enough to slip through the space between them, nearly whispering. "Or you can guess what happens."

Anzi's eyes slid back over to the second man, who held something limp in his arms. Gleaming white scales, slender neck, limp wings dragging down her body...Netra. The man's gloved hand was wrapped just under her head at the base of the dragonet's skull.

"Hesitating? Then, shall we...? You should know better than anyone that we have nothing to lose. Your decision, dragon rider."

Her heart skipped a beat when the second man's hand tightened with a leathery sound. "Stop," she snapped. "Tell me what you want."

"I'm glad we could come to an agreement. This way, then. Follow me."

52

Netra had yet to stir. Whatever they had done to her, she wouldn't awaken anytime soon, which was just as well because her furious screeching would have only made things more perilous. And in this cramped run-down stable she had followed the men into, there was no room for sudden movements and ill-advised sounds. Her eyes darted between them both, watching their hands and feet as she kept her hands close to her sword hilts.

"You're not going to cut us down before I crush this one's neck," the man holding Netra assured her. "Wyrms and dragons are the same when it comes to this. She's small enough it makes no difference. One good wring, and…"

She knew it. He didn't have to remind her. Her eyes rested on the limp dragon's form that trailed from the man's grasp, and she had to swallow back a hissing command for him to hold her up properly so as to not strangle her. With his hand gripping around the base of her skull like that, she feared they would hurt her, but there was no reasoning with these men. The dragonet was still breathing, at least, a testament to her captor's precision.

"Talk," she said stiffly. "If you're going to make demands, do it."

The man on the left looked like the one in charge. Grizzled and gray, he wore something that looked like a cross between cobbled-together, bandit-style leather gear and typical traveler's garb. Likely an underground revolutionary. Who else would be desperate enough to kidnap a dragon and threaten a First Guard? If she were to die here, if Netra met any harm, surely these two men knew what end awaited the city. She didn't condone it, but that was how it was. Neither Tet nor any of his Premier would ever forgive so easily an insult to their dominance. And besides, it was hard to remember to sympathize with them as she watched the younger man on the right hold Netra up by her slender neck like a dead goose. Her fingers twitched.

"Ah—careful, now," the older man warned. "Don't be reckless."

"Then at least have your friend hold her right so I know she's unharmed. You're pushing me into a corner I don't want to be pushed into, and you don't want that either."

A low chuckle reverberated through the barely-lit gloom. The moonlight filtering down through the warped space in the rafters gave both men an eerie halo of silver that made them look almost like apparitions. "You don't need to remind us to be nervous, soldier woman. I'm not ashamed to say I'm too frightened to be cowed any more than I already am."

"Are you done mocking me? Say what it is you want."

"No mockery. You don't understand that I'm only standing here because I'm in too deep already, soldier woman. So understand when I say we're already as afraid as we'll ever be, and you can't persuade us from our intentions."

"Then *say* what those are," she retorted, voice flat. "If you're going to speak only in half-threats, I'll remind you that the only hold you have over me is that dragon. If you do anything to her, I will hurt you. I will hurt you badly."

Their eyes gleamed in the dark. They really were afraid, but the knowledge did nothing for her. Not when the younger man refused to adjust the way he held Netra. She wondered if she could behead him quickly enough to loosen his grip without his ever knowing it before he died.

"I can't guarantee nothing will happen to her since I don't know what you'll do," the first man rumbled. "But I can say if you don't startle us, your dragon lives a little longer, moment to moment."

She pressed her lips together, thinking of a safe response. "Whatever you're doing, you're still plan to kill me. You have no way of knowing I won't retaliate against the city for what you did here if I make it out. So as frightened as you claim to be, I have less to lose than you do. I already know your intentions, and I'm not stupid enough to think I can convince you otherwise. You're going to try to silence me here, no matter what."

"We're not here to kill you, soldier woman, and we aren't underestimating your wits. You're a dragon rider, aren't you? Of course we knew you'd piece that much together."

"So why?" she shot back. "What's this you're doing here. And what's with that little girl who was following me? You're making a child do your dirty work?"

"She's no mere *little girl.* You should know that already."

She bit the inside of her cheek. Yes, she'd figured. The kid had slipped away from her not just once, but multiple times. Ordinary humans couldn't surpass her agility like that no matter how small and spry. "Doesn't matter. She's just a child. You shouldn't have put her in danger that way."

"There it is, the reason we came to you—to wit, we know you have secrets." The man flashed her a grin. "One of them being something like a conscience, and we know dragons and those who make pacts with them should have no such thing."

"A conscience? If you want to keep playing games..."

"Let me be clear, then. You plot against your own ilk, soldier woman. For reasons we aren't interested in but are happy to take advantage of. We know you were with the traitor governor and asking questions, all sorts of them. Not much of a First Guard if you start taking an interest in the ones you're supposed to be breaking, are you?"

A long time ago, she would have hurled herself at him for daring to stain the honor of the Premier and speaking so derisively, but she could only press her lips together, mute. He was right about that. Still, she had no idea who these men were or what they wanted, and Netra was in danger. "Make your demands. There are only so many times I can repeat myself before I figure out you have no intention of acting with integrity."

"Integrity...I'd laugh, lass, if I didn't realize you have some humanity in you. Let's see, then. The girl's been watching you all day, and someone else has been, too. Let's make a deal. Get us the dragon, soldier woman. The big one. And help us get rid of your companion, too, natural-like, so the Emperor doesn't send down the rest of his reptile flock to roast us alive."

She froze. Until that last demand, she had been ready to dismiss everything the man said, knowing it was all just a desperate clawing of rebels driven to madness. But what was this? He was insane. Not only did he want a dragon, but he wanted her to help kill the colonel? "You're crazy. You have no idea what you're saying. Do you not know how dangerous he is?"

"Eh. I've fallen this far. I'll take the chance of grisly death."

"And you're trying to threaten me into rebelling. Do you think I'm stupid?"

"You're already rebelling. Up here." He reached up to tap his forehead, and for the first time, she noticed something about his left hand: he was missing three digits, leaving only his thumb and index finger. "Lookin' at my hand? I'll tell you. It happened when I was a young man, newlywed. My wife was taken from me, and when I tried to hold onto her, they chopped half my hand right off. Won't ever forget the look on her face, it was the last glimpse I ever got of her."

Her stomach turned, but she couldn't spare all her sympathy for him when she could still see Netra dangling helplessly.

"Pick the snake up, son," the man said suddenly, and without argument, his companion scooped the dragonet into one arm and held her that way instead. "There, now. I had to wait until you heard me out before I proved I can be reasonable. You understand."

She bristled and stepped forward. "I don't, actually."

"Then I suppose we both die, eh? But I don't think so. See, I didn't expect you to catch the girl, and even if you did, didn't expect you to go so easy on her. Your fellowman, the other First, he would have sliced her apart soon as he figured she was useless. But you didn't. I knew I had you, then."

"...You used her as bait?"

"No, of course not. I'm not like you...well, like your friend, rather. But when you had her in your clutches, I thought that would be the last we saw of her alive."

"You weren't even going to try to save her?" She thought back to when she had the little street urchin trapped under her knee. She knew she'd never be able to kill a child, but how could these two men have known that if they judged her by the company she kept.

"Have to do what we have to do." The man wagged his finger at her, and again, she found her eyes drawn to the maimed hand. "See, we've been waiting for a sliver of a chance for too long, too long. That means when I see it, even just a flicker of a flicker, I know. I know in a flash, soldier woman, and when I heard about you lingering a little too long with the governor and how you didn't kill a single soul to punish anyone when some brat shouted out of the crowd at you. You not killing the girl, either—that confirms it."

She thought back. Yes, she remembered the boy who'd called out to insult her when she walked the streets earlier in the day. It hadn't occurred to her to ever retaliate, but she supposed that was a far cry from what Bisset would have done. He would never have overlooked it. But still-

"You're insane," she insisted. "You have no idea who I am or where my loyalties lie. You're grasping at straws." But even as she spoke, there was a rising light in his eyes, both fleeting and long-burning like a sputtering flame resurrected from the same embers too many times; snuffed out then re-lit, snuffed out and re-lit again. That was the look of a man who'd suffered too much, a man now careening in any direction that gave him momentum. Meaning. She pressed her lips together. "Don't be reckless," she said quietly. "I won't admit to whatever you're accusing me of."

"Not accusing, soldier woman. Praise. You're not one of them, is what I'm saying, you're different, I swear it—"

"But!" she snapped, cutting him off before he could continue. "If...If." She paused. "...If I were to say I might...help you in some way. You would need to follow my lead."

"I knew it, I sensed something had changed, I knew it in my bones."

"Stop. I said, stop!" She glared at him until he stopped laughing, focusing the whole of her razor-sharp attention on him. "You need to follow my lead, if you do anything. I mean it. I won't see Lumenera burned to a crisp while I have anything to say about it, but what you did tonight—it was reckless and wild. If you'd miscalculated, if you'd been wrong...you would have brought hell down on the heads of all your people."

"My people?" The man's eyes went wide, and his brow flew up into his long, unkempt hair. "You really do mean it. You fear for them like your own."

"People are people. Now, listen to me. I know you're itching to make your move. But listen!" She jabbed a finger at him. "Let's say for a second I might support your cause. But now isn't the time to move. There's going to be a chance soon, but it's not now."

His face contorted into a furious grimace. "You protect them?" he demanded. "What do you mean, stalling for time like this? I don't believe it. I know what I saw, what I felt. You're different from them. I know it—"

"Shut up," she snapped, her patience now grown too thin to humor any further outbursts. "You're not going to hijack a dragon, kill the colonel, and fly off into the sunset, victorious. Neither of us will get far. What, do you think I can just sing to his dragon and get him to listen to me? That's *his* dragon, not mine. And even mine doesn't listen to me properly, as you've learned." She nodded in Netra's direction. "Whatever beliefs you have about dragon riders, get rid of them now. I might... Listen carefully, *might,* be able to help, but I need proof we're both—"

Both what? What should she say? Both willing to conspire against the Empire, signing their death warrant in doing so? Maybe this was all a trap. Maybe this was Bisset's game, a twisted trial to test her loyalty. In that case, she could simply say that she'd played along purely to preserve Netra's life. That would be her only excuse oif this all turned out to be a deceit.

"Need proof we're both committed," she finished. "I need to know whether I can really trust you, and the same with me for you."

The man seemed to fight with himself for a long, tense moment, muttering something under his breath and breathing hard. He hadn't seemed nearly so unhinged moments ago, was he actually unstable? That didn't bode well for her. But at long last, he shared a look with his younger companion and shifted his weight around on his feet with a shuffling motion.

"Proof we're committed," he repeated slowly and rubbed his thick beard with contemplative fingers. You mean proof we both have too much to lose if we turn on each other. Fine. Then how do we do that?"

"A trade. In information. We talk."

53

Five minutes in and they had made no progress beyond introductions. This was going nowhere.

"The Emperor's weakness."

"I don't know. Pass."

"The secret to taming a dragon."

"Obviously, I don't know. Pass."

"The names and abilities of every dragon rider?"

"I already told you I've only been at this for a month," Anzi snapped. "I haven't met but one actual rider, and as for the Emperor, other than finding out he's not one to trifle with, I don't know anything substantial about him."

"This is useless." The bearded man paced back forth across the stable. "I've asked you a hundred questions you have no answers to!"

"Ask the right questions, then!" she fired back. "You're looking for a magic potion to fix all your problems. It's not going to happen. I can't fight back yet, probably not against Bisset and certainly not against the Emperor. *Yet*. You need to wait, and you need to plan. Jumping in headlong will do nothing but get you killed."

"How could you not be able to able to stand up against even one of the riders! You're supposed to be one of them. Are you the weakest, or just the most frightened?"

"You listen to me, *Isvan*." She was in his face with three swift strides.

"You're the one who came to me. I didn't ask for your help, you asked for mine. I don't care how clever you think you are for kidnapping my dragon and using her against me, it doesn't change the fact that you need me more than I need you. Curse me for being useless or being cowardly, go ahead. But I am not going to go against someone who's been around for a hundred years along with a dragon massive enough to crush a small village flat without even meaning to. If we do this, we do this to win. Or are you going to be throw yourself at their feet just to prove how good a martyr you can be?"

Isvan's unkempt beard bristled as his lips twitched this way and that, wrestling with the sour words she knew he wanted to snarl. But despite his zealot-like, crazed demeanor earlier, she knew he yet retained enough sanity to accept bare logic. He narrowed his eyes, holding her glare as they stood nearly nose to nose. "Then when?" he demanded. "You can't wait until they move north like you say they will. The Empire has been trying to take the winterlands since before they ever set foot on this coast. You don't know when that will be, if ever!"

Maybe it had been a mistake relaying to him what Bisset had said about Tet's intention to push north. Instead of being relieved at the implication that pressure would lighten on the coastal cities, Isvan was even more agitated than before. "It'll happen *soon*," she insisted. "Change is coming. Things are moving faster than they ever have."

"How! Speak, woman."

"I agreed to give you information. I did. Now it's your turn."

He yanked at his hair in savage frustration, another sign he was more unhinged than she wished he was. But she couldn't afford to pity this man or be cowed by his feral intensity. She had given him slivers of information, not enough to completely damn her in the event that it turned out Isvan was a malicious trickster spy and not an actual rebel, but enough to have her punished for loose lips no matter what excuses she gave. It wouldn't surprise her if she found out at daybreak that this was all an elaborate ruse to test her loyalty. Even so, she had to try. This could be the opportunity she had been waiting for, and if it passed her by, she would have to return to the Imperial City empty-handed and consigned to her assigned fate. She would hatch more condemned dragon eggs, create a new army for Tet to ravage the other nations. She would spawn more ruthless riders to raze cities and massacre innocents.

"Fine," growled Isvan. "What do you want to know? All our names? What we've lost? Or maybe you want to know how we train using wyrms to take down dragons." A wide grin split his face. "Your little one has yet to wake."

She wanted to smash her fist into his face for gloating, but it was futile. It wasn't out of hatred for her that he did such a thing but rather hatred of dragon kind. There was no reasoning with him. He was convinced they were evil and capable of nothing else. But she supposed after what he had gone through, she couldn't fault him. He was at least half-crazed from grief.

"Yes," she said. "Tell me how you disabled her. Do wyrms and dragons have the same vulnerable spots?"

He wagged a finger at her. "We'll tell you later on, soldier woman. You might double-cross me, and snake-wrangling would be our only weapon left. Even if you take me to be sliced apart and hung, I'll keep that secret hidden so the rest can fight on without me. We will rise."

Damn him. She only wanted to know so she could use the knowledge for herself when the time came and stand a fighting chance against the other riders, but Isvan's caution was sensible, even if it was highly inconvenient that he chose this moment to be appropriately shrewd. She glared. "You weren't afraid of me double-crossing you when you brought me here, you two-faced son of an ass."

"I surely was. But I had to take a leap of faith. I'm tired of waiting."

Thirty years. Thirty years of waiting, of mourning not only his wife but the daughters taken from him and sent into slavery as prostitutes as punishment for his resistance. He had been struggling for longer than she'd been alive. Almost twice that. Whatever she thought of him and his messy, foolish, reckless ways, she had no choice but to respect his pain.

"Fine," she said, echoing his impatient, bitter surrender back at him. "We'll discuss that later. For now, tell me what you know of the dragon riders, the ones that come and...do what Bisset does. Inspect annexed cities."

"And terrorize the people?" His upper lip curled up in a scowl.

"Even so. How many are they, and what do you remember of the ones you've seen? Or heard about?"

His sneer melted away into confusion. "Ten or so, including the Emperor. Everyone knows that. There's the dragon who breathes fire hot enough to turn sand to glass and the one-eyed rider who flies with it. There's the dragon who has shield plates all over itself, natural protection of bone you can't slice through." He continued to name several more, until finally she held up a hand and stopped him. He frowned.

"The ones we see on our side of the continent are different."

His eyes squinted even further. "What's that mean, woman?"

"It means we may have a lot more than just the supposed ten or however many to contend with."

"What!"

"I'm sure there's been changes in the ranks of the dragon riders that neither of us know about or understand." She paused. She wondered if she should tell him...yes. "Hatching a dragon isn't as difficult or rare as they make it out to be," she said in a low voice. "The truth is that new riders qualify into elite Service a lot more often than I ever believed, but not all of them pass the...tests. Of loyalty. The ones who don't fall in line are eliminated. And while I can't say how many are the ones who've fallen like that, I can guess it's been many. The Emperor takes care of that personally sometimes."

"Eliminated," Isvan repeated. "Then—are their dragons preserved? What happens to them?"

"I told you, hatching dragons isn't as rare and precious to them as you think. They have hundreds of eggs all hidden away, and the Emperor doesn't value them nearly as much as everyone else does."

"*Value*," he sneered. "I'd rather smash them all open and rid the world of them."

Calm, she told herself. He was blinded by hatred. He didn't know what he was saying. "Either way, I don't know what happens to the dragons, but it's a possibility they're killed with their riders." She glanced over at Isvan's younger companion who had remained silence. He was still holding the sleeping Netra, but it was clear her weight was tiring him. He leaned against one of the stable posts for support. "You may not believe it, but my dragon's attached to me. The ones who proved unsatisfactory in the Emperor's eyes might have had similar bonds with theirs. And if the rider's disobedient, the dragon might be a problem, too."

"So—you mean to say they'll kill a dragon?"

"Get used to the idea. Dragons mean nothing to the Emperor. I can already confirm the riders regularly outlive them. That could be part of the confusion—when a dragon dies, the rider needs to raise a new one, and what are the chances it looks identical to the previous?"

It felt surreal to be sharing such privileged information with an outsider. Lumenerans were annexed, not Empire natives. But this wasn't treason, she reminded herself. This was freedom, and redemption.

"We need specific information about all the riders in every region," she said. "It might be that the Premier deliberately downplays their number. There's a tactic in the Imperial Army's counter-scouting division. They feed false numbers to the enemy, make them think we're few and weak and that the odds favor them. And when they lose, it's all the more demoralizing because they believe we're simply that much stronger, soldier for soldier. It could be the Premier wants to seem omnipresent. Say a rebellion starts; maybe the ten closest riders stationed around that region respond. With numbers like that, it would look as if all the riders spread across the entire continent moved perfectly as one, a uniform unit. The speed, the coordination."

"Damn it all," Isvan swore. "More deception."

"I'm only guessing. This is why we need to work together and gather information first. Imagine if we attacked and found out in the middle of battle that we have twice as many dragons to contend with than we'd thought. All resistance would be wiped out. It would set a revolution back by decades. Don't forget the Emperor's been in power for two hundred years, he's not new to this."

"Well, you'll just have to betray them from the inside and whittle them down to numbers we can handle. We can't wait another thirty years for a chance at freedom."

"I'm not saying you will. But as I said, I need time. Not thirty years, but I can't do this at the drop of a hat. You say a lot of fighting words, but in the end, I'm the one who has to go in alone and do the bloodiest, most dangerous work."

"If you're afraid…" he began to taunt, and she jabbed a finger in his face.

"Don't push me," she warned. "Unlike you, I have something to live for. That's right, I know you have a death wish. That's why you were so reckless and threw yourself at me, not knowing for sure whether I might be ally or enemy. But I'm not like you. I'm going to survive, or at the very least, if I have to die, I'm going to use my life to secure the future I want and not throw it away on pure spite. Understand?"

He pushed her hand away. "What now, then? Speak. If I like what you say, I'll tell my men the good news."

What now, indeed? Because a dangerous idea, a horrific idea was blossoming inside her. It was insane. She knew it was, but… "If I procured dragon eggs for you, if I could do this, I would need a guarantee that whoever—"

"Dragon eggs! You're saying you can bring—"

"I would *need*," she hissed, "a guarantee they will never be abused. That they'll be respected. And that means you are never going to get one because I know your hatred blinds you. But you can find others who aren't so embittered by the past that they can't look to the future. I need riders who will take care of my dragons like they would their own flesh and blood."

"If you do that, we could fight back! With dragons, if we had dragons, we could—" He floundered, beads of spittle flying out of his mouth in his excitement as he stammered and sputtered. "You mean to say you can bring us dragons that can go head to head with—"

"Not head to head," she said swiftly. "The riders are dangerous, and both they and their dragons will be faster and stronger and better in every way. But this is a start. This is what I meant, Isvan. We need a plan. And time. Don't forget you're trying to go against a force that has subdued the better part of the entire continent for two centuries. Or did you think this would all end with fairy tale ease just because you feel so passionate about it?"

But he wasn't listening. He was beyond reason. Excitement shone in his eyes so brightly she could see them gleaming like cat's eyes in the moonlight that dripped down through the stable rafters. She couldn't fault him. But hope, she thought, was so dangerous and fragile...

"I don't know when Bisset and I will leave, so if you're willing to trust me, you need to do one thing for me right now," she ordered. "I refuse to entrust dragons to anyone I haven't met myself. I'll make that decision only when I look them in the eye and swear I'll hold them accountable for all they do."

"What do you want then, soldier woman?"

"Bring me the ones who can get the job done." She fixed him with a smoldering glare. "Bring me my soldiers."

54

The coastal cities had always been more diverse than landlocked ones, but Anzi's knowledge of the various cultures within the continent was stunted by the degree of their relevance: if it didn't help Imperial soldiers fight and defeat their enemies any better, they never learned it. All she was certain of was that in seaside Lumenera, humans still reigned at the top of the hierarchy while inhumans took up their positions at the foot. At least in the Imperial City, outright discrimination and abuse of the mixed-blooded was outlawed. Here, they had no such protection.

So why was this girl so fiercely loyal to the men who cared so little about her?

Anzi stared down at the urchin from earlier, unimpressed by the ferocious scowl on her pointed face. She was skinny and small, swimming in the gray and brown rags she wore, and her badly cut dark hair was cropped so close to her head it couldn't even curl. Dirt smudges and bruises all over, too. She might have passed for any scruffy street urchin if not for the leathery texture that had appeared on her skin. Sometime in the last hour, the girl's appearance had changed—*dried up* might be the more accurate description—and there was no more hiding the inhuman touch.

"What're you staring at?" the girl growled. "They should've just sliced your throat. Snake-kisser." She hacked up a wad of spit and aimed it at Anzi's boot.

"You shouldn't be here. You're going to get yourself killed."

"Like I care what you say. You have something to hide? Too bad, I'm not leaving. I'm staying right here and watching you."

Anzi knitted her brow in a scornful expression. "You're not here to *watch me.* They told you to stay behind because they don't want you tagging along with them. Isvan and his friend would just as soon be rid of you. Why are you throwing in your lot with them when it's so obvious?"

The girl bared her teeth. They were all pointed. So that glimpse she'd caught earlier hadn't been a trick of the light, after all. "Like I'd listen to anything you say," she sneered. "You hag. Boot-licking Empire scum."

Anzi was used to *fringer* or *crow* being thrown in there somewhere, but maybe this region was too far away from the desert to be familiar with those kinds of names and insults. Honestly, being addressed as a hag felt novel more than anything else. "Yeah, sure," she said. "But I'm not the one they left for dead. I could have cut you into ribbons, and they had no interest in stopping me. You're no better than bait." A small fist darted out to punch her in the stomach. She could have stopped it. Didn't care enough to bother. "Look at that," she said with no little disdain. "You can't even hit someone right. Take my advice and respect yourself a little more than Isvan and his friend do."

"Respect! Like a stinking snake-kisser knows what respect is." She spat again, and Anzi pulled her boot away and knocked her knuckles into the girl's forehead.

"Watch it. I don't care if you're a kid, I'll smack you upside the head if you keep annoying me."

All right, fine, so she'd never been great with children. Maybe it was because she had spent the first ten years of her life only picking fights with them instead of making friends, but that couldn't have been helped. She had no regrets about bullying right back the ones who had mercilessly teased her brother, and to this day, they would probably flee from her in tears.

The fleeting memory of Oza made her almost homesick, but she shoved away the distracting thought and focused on the scowling girl before her. "Keep looking at me like that, and I'll blacken those eyes, too," she warned, suddenly far crosser than she had been before she'd remembered her brother so suddenly. "What's your name, anyway. And how'd an inhuman like you get mixed up with Lumeneran rebels? You have nothing to gain from being their errand rat. They'd sooner chase you out than trust you with anything more."

"Shut up! You don't know anything!"

"Fine. Do as you like." Anzi turned away and faced the stable entrance again. What little interest she'd taken in the urchin girl's circumstances evaporated in an instant; clearly, the child was too stupid to listen to sense. And here she'd even begun to feel sorry for her.

"Acting all high and mighty like you're better than everyone." The girl stomped around to stand in front of her again, eyes flashing. "Well, you're wrong! They trust me. And I do all sorts of things for them, things no one else can do."

"Like?"

"Spying! And stealing when I have to."

"Stealing. You mean from the citizens, probably. Let me guess…food, armor, other supplies that they need but have to be careful gathering because they don't want to attract too much attention. So you do the work they don't want to be caught doing, and you get the bad reputation for being a little monster thief while they reap the benefits. Smart girl! I should never have doubted you."

She looked like she wanted to sink her teeth into Anzi's flesh, but good luck with that. She shoved her back with another swift knock, this time against her collarbone.

"I don't have time to entertain kids," she added. "Just take my word for it and see yourself out of this business. It's between adults."

Another punch to the stomach. This one was marginally stronger than the last but still futile. The girl was even weaker than a child her age should be, far weaker, and Anzi suspected it had less to do with being a hungry street rat and more to do with her natural physiology. She really was skinny. What species was she mixed with—or so she would ask if she were interested, which she wasn't. She made it a point to look over the girl's head at Netra, who was currently lolling against the foot of the wall as she recovered from her unconscious spell. As if sensing her attention, the dragonet turned her diamond-shaped head and caught her foreboding glare, only to answer it with a rebellious hiss.

Honestly. She had learned nothing from nearly dying. After this, Anzi was going to make sure they had a good, long talk about wandering off-

"Stop *annoying* me," she snapped when the girl tried to punch her again. Seriously, what was wrong with her? She should just scurry off before she got hurt. She had no place here, and even the men who—what, hired?—her didn't want her around. It was painfully obvious they had no special affection for her despite her devotion. She was a kid. She deserved better than that.

"You're the only one who thinks I'm a monster," the girl half-shouted. "I'm one of them, they trust me!"

Anzi slapped her hand over the girl's mouth to muffle her rising voice. "Do you really need me to tell you to shut up? I'll leave if you expose me, and then you can explain to Isvan why I disappeared instead of waiting for him to come back."

Instead of calming down, the girl wrenched herself away and stood back with her fists clenched at her sides and her chest heaving. "You're the only one," she said again. "You're the only one who treats me like that. You wouldn't talk to me like this if I were all human. You wouldn't talk to me like I'm nothing but a stupid idiot. You're the one who wants to get rid of me, not them."

Anzi opened her mouth to deliver a stinging retort, something along the lines of how she didn't care enough to want to be rid of her in the first place-

"Because at least they don't say it to my face. Not like you."

...Anzi's mouth closed, and she stared down at the girl with the pointed face, the strangely narrow chin and reedy body that hid under the baggy rags of her clothing. The sinister-looking, weathered, stretched texture of her skin as if someone had tanned a patch of deerhide and pasted it over her face and arms. So...inhuman. So different. Was it so wrong of Anzi to have noticed? She was only saying what was already obvious, only telling the truth. She wasn't the villain for pointing out what both of them knew already.

Unbidden, the vague memory of her first meeting with Letti brushed against her mind.

I know what people think of me before I even open my mouth. The same way you think of me.

She almost recoiled at the humiliating recollection. That had been the moment Letti had confronted her about her disrespect. The memory still burned, and for some irritating, infuriating reason, she was reminded of it now now as the mixed-blooded girl glared at her. *At least they don't say it to my face,* she had said. *Not like you.*

"I'm probably not all human, either," she said after a long pause, half-angry and making sure it showed in her voice and her stance. "So I don't have a problem with you because of that. You just annoy me."

"Yeah, right. You look human to me and everyone else, and that's all they care about. And by the way, that's even worse if you're like me. You're a—you're nothing but an asshole for talking down to me if we're the same. You asshole, asshole hag."

Her gut reaction was to snap back that they were not the same and never would be, but the searing heat boiling up from the pit of her stomach made her pause. Why was it she felt so insulted? No, it wasn't like that, she told herself. It wasn't like that at all. She was only...

No. It was true. She'd always been against inhumans the same way she had been against magic in all its forms. She'd hated anything that wasn't the norm, had mistrusted it even more than her peers did. It wasn't so long ago that she would resent everyone who dared to suggest that her advantages came from a sullied pedigree. She'd hated it. She still did. The silence became decidedly more uncomfortable, and Anzi hurried to take back control of it.

"What even are you?" she asked suddenly, her voice still rough but ever so slightly more subdued."Where'd you come from, and why do they keep you around?"

A childish sneer accompanied the girl's smug reply. "I'm a piscin," she said. "Half, and I don't mind it. So long as I'm in the water every so often, I can stay on land for half a day at a time."

Pis-kin, Anzi thought to herself, mulling over the vaguely familiar name. Piscin—those were water dwellers.. She couldn't recall anything else except that they were somewhat amphibious with their tails that could temporarily split into legs. The lack of knowledge suggested they were no threat, then, if her Service education hadn't taught about them. Shame. If she could at least grow to become a promising fighter, then maybe Isvan and the other Lumeneran rebels would value her more, but she was barely...

Enough. That was none of her business. Deriding a child in her thoughts was not only pointless but stupid, and maybe her prejudices were seeping back without her noticing. She pursed her lips and stepped around the girl, but the latter followed her with a persistent sneer.

"I'm right, aren't I?" she jeered. "I know your type. You have to be extra nasty to us to cover for yourself. You're the worst of them, pretending so hard because you wish you weren't like us. Like you. Well, too bad. You have to deal with it. You've got that dirty blood, and nothing's going to fix that."

She shouldn't have said anything about herself, Anzi thought with gritted teeth, but it had been a knee-jerk reaction to being accused. It was the only defense she'd been able to think of. "Get away from me," she snapped before bending to pick up Netra. "If you're going to keep *watching* me, you better keep your voice down. I have no problem leaving you and going my own way if you keep being a pain in the neck. Explain that to Isvan when he comes back, bet he'll be happy with you then, won't he?"

...Silence, at last. Anzi didn't know how long the temporary peace would survive, but at least the little *piscin* girl was shutting up long enough for her to focus on shaking Netra out of the lingering vestiges of her stupor. There weren't even any muttered insults and curses about snakes and snake-kissers, either.

"What's your name?" Anzi grumbled after standing back up and straightening her back.

"Me?"

"Who else would I be talking to?"

"I don't know," the girl snipped. "Maybe someone who's all human, since you only like those kinds of people."

"Fine, I don't need to know your name. I'll just call you piscin from now on—"

"Rania."

That had been fast. For a kid who'd been almost gleeful about her so-called dirty blood a second ago, she'd reacted quick as a rat to the threat of being addressed as 'piscin' indefinitely. "All right, Rania. I'm going to treat you the way I would anyone else if that's what you want. But that means I'm not going to go out of my way to help you out anymore. So—"

"That was you trying to help me?"

"Yes. Yes, it was." She narrowed her eyes. "Considering that I was tired of seeing you pant after them like a dog if they so much as twitched a finger in your direction. They're taking advantage of you. And I still don't understand why you're helping them when they'll probably kick you out the second you're no longer useful. But that's not my problem, and I won't care anymore."

"Good. I don't need some lady who thinks she knows everything feeling sorry for me."

"Fine."

"Fine!"

Another bout of silence. This one felt pettier and that much more infuriating. How could a kid be so irritating? But she was not going to let

some twiggy idiot of a vagrant child get the best of her patience. She
turned to the stable doors again, determined to say nothing else until
Isvan returned-

"What?"

Anzi narrowed her eyes and glared back at the girl. "What do you
mean, what. What do you want now."

"What do I want? You're the one who just said something to me."

"No, I didn't. Now, be quiet—"

"You just did it again! How did you do that!"

Anzi's scowl deepened when the girl clutched at her head, palms
pressed to both temples. "What's wrong with you? I don't have time to
play nurse for..." She trailed off when Rania's wide eyes dropped from
her face and landed on Netra in her arms, who was staring back at the girl
with all the stock-still intensity of a cat waiting to pounce on its prey.
Silence, again, but it was a different sort this time, as if Anzi were sitting
on the outside of it, watching. Waiting.

It couldn't be, she thought, but in that very instant as if to purposefully
contradict her, Rania's eyes bulged in horror. The girl proceeded to
scramble back and all but leap into one of the stable stalls, skinny limbs
wheeling and sending hay flying into the air. "What is that!" she half-
screamed from behind the wall. "Your dragon is in my head! It's gotten
into my mind! Oh, bull's balls—"

Bull's balls, truly. Anzi tracked back all the way to the opposite wall
even faster than Rania had made her escape. Her heart pounded so hard
against her ribs she feared it might crash right through, but she forced
herself to remain quiet as she whipped around and stood with her back to
the girl, hiding Netra from her sight and holding her even tighter. The
dragonet immediately attempted to clamber up out of her arms and perch
on her shoulder so she could keep watching the urchin girl.

"Stop it," she hissed. "Leave her alone. Don't *ever* do that again, understand me?"

But Netra was a bad listener. That, or Anzi had about the same
authority over her as a slab of raw meat would.

"Oh, gods, get her out of my head, get away from me—"

And in the middle of that chaos was the moment Isvan chose to shove
open the stable doors and stride in to join them, his companion from
earlier at his side and several other new figures in tow as well. Rania was
still babbling when he made an angry, throaty sound, which finally
quieted her. "What's this mess?" he demanded. "I could hear you from

outside. What are you thinking? You were the one telling me I was being reckless, dragon rider."

She didn't know what to say. Didn't want to tell him, rather, both because it made no sense that Netra was *speaking* to Rania of all people and also because, yes, she would admit it right out, it hurt that the dragon had chosen to communicate with someone else so abruptly when she had only ever spoken to Anzi once, just once. And she had raised her! Hatched her from her egg and fed her five times a day and groomed her scales and...

"I have good news, at least," she muttered darkly as she finished wrestling Netra down against her chest. "Looks like our tentative plan is making headway already."

The man was so confused even his beard looked inquisitive. "What? What are you saying."

She held the wriggling dragonet tight in one arm and jabbed her other thumb over her shoulder, indicating the still-hiding Rania who had yet to say a word since she'd stopped screaming. "Her," said Anzi. "That's our first rider."

It took a dozen tries to get Isvan to stop cursing at her, and by then, Anzi was two seconds away from taking his head off with no further argument. She was the one taking on the greater risk. She didn't care if he thought she was insane for resting even a portion of their hopes on a child, and on an inhuman child with no innate loyalty to the Lumeneran people, no less. Or so he said. She saw the flash of hurt that bathed Rania's face when he spat the words as if she weren't right there listening to them in subservient silence.

She ignored it. Soothing the pains of children wasn't her job. And right now, she needed to get it through the man's thick skull that she was going to be the one in charge when it came to selecting their rider candidates. What did he know? Even she wasn't confident about what she was trying to do, and she had hatched a dragon with her own hands and was due to hatch countless more if the Emperor and his faithful Premier got their way.

"You don't have a choice," she snarled, though she kept her voice low and let her eyes dart up to the bent and warped rafters every other second in case she spying eyes appeared there. "I decide this. What do I care about your grudge against inhumans? All I'm interested in is accomplishing what I set out to do, and if you don't want to have a part in it, then that's your choice. I've made mine."

"I have four men in good health right here. Pick them! What will she do that they can't."

"Get a dragon's approval, first of all." She shot him an even dirtier look than the one she had been giving him already when his gaze dropped to the dragon in her arms. "And no, I'm not choosing your men. I saw the way they looked at Netra when they walked in. I specifically told you I'm only trusting those who will respect the dragon in their care, at least more than they would hate it. I saw none of that in their eyes."

"And you say you'll choose the girl! She hates dragons even more than they do."

"Maybe, but haven't you noticed?" She pointed back at Rania, who cowered behind the stable wall that she had been peeking over for the past minute. "Now she fears a dragon more than she hates it. Netra took care of that."

"I won't accept—"

"I said it's not up to you!" She had to keep herself from bellowing in his face. That wouldn't do. She had no idea what time it was, but at least half the night had gone by. Bisset had said they would meet at dawn, but it would be just like him to come looking for her a few hours early with no warning. Her blood ran cold at the thought of him stumbling upon her and discovering what she was up to. "And raise your voice at me again. Go ahead. I won't let you compromise me."

He narrowed his eyes. "Threatening me already. I thought we would get along better than this."

"I didn't." She fixed him with an even more vicious glare to make sure he understood she was playing no games. Not now. "Everyone you brought me is unfit. I don't have time to wait for you to round up more, so here's what happens. I'm going to go on patrol the way Bisset thinks I am, and you're going to take Rania and get her cleaned up and clothed properly. I don't care whether that offends your sensibilities or not. Come dawn, I meet with the colonel, and I'll do what I can to draw him out of Lumenera without incident. My guess is that we head back to the Imperial City afterward. And when that happens, you wait for me. No secret messages smuggled back and forth, no secret rendezvous until I'm ready, until I initiate. Got it? I'll take the colonel away and find an excuse to come back in two, maybe three months. By then, I want you to have trained Rania in the basics. Teach her how to hold her own in a fight, put some meat on her bones. I'll take care of the rest when I return."

He looked like he was going to explode. Go ahead, she challenged silently. She wouldn't miss him at this rate. She'd find someone else to conspire with.

"…This is too fast," he muttered. "Doesn't make any sense."

"Then I'll explain it to you like I would a child since you're so determined to not understand." She pointed at Rania again only to see the girl shrink back once more. Netra made a sharp clicking sound, a sign she was fast becoming too furious to be controlled. She must have been trying to communicate with the urchin girl again all this time, Anzi realized, while she had been busy arguing with Isvan. Sour resentment filled her stomach at the thought that Netra had developed a sudden attachment to someone else, and a stranger no less. But what could she do except go along with it?

"The dragon's decided," she said. "Simple as that. Now, are you in or are you out?"

55

Anzi wasn't used to giving orders, but that didn't mean she lacked the ability. She was firm, cold, and gave away no uncertainty. And while she had lost all respect for the colonel upon learning the truth, she mimicked his countenance and sophistication now because if there was anyone who could exercise authority with immaculate precision, it was the colonel. She would leave no room for Isvan and his men to doubt her, not when she was the one shouldering the heavier end of the yoke.

She didn't like Isvan. She didn't like any of them. They were the exact opposite of what she needed, made passionate by their bitterness and acting on the suppressed, violent wrath of a generation trod on by outsider overlords. What she needed was determination and cold composure, patience and frigid logic. How could she work with men like these?

She had no choice. This was all she had. And the farther out from the Imperial City and the cradle of the Empire she went, the less likely she was to find allies willing to overlook their hatred and terror of dragons, ones willing to trust her despite her seeming allegiances. And conversely, the closer she looked toward the Empire's stronghold where the abhorrence for dragons was replaced by admiration and adulation, the more staunchly loyal people would be to the kingdom.

She had no choice. She had to ally with this ragtag band of rebels who dreamed of cleansing Lumenera of all foreign influence—including even ones that meant no harm. Like piscins, for instance.

Her stomach churned. The longer she thought about it, the more she realized the girl had been right. Anzi had spoken out of her own scorn for mixed-bloods earlier even if she had thought she was only being honest. Her callousness had been unneeded. And now that Netra had evidently gone over from her side to the girl's, Anzi was more aware than ever that she was more poisoned in the head than she wanted to admit.

The girl. Rania. She was going to be important. She already was important. It didn't matter than her leathery, dry, stretched-skin appearance sent an uneasy tickle down Anzi's spine. Netra had fixated on her and refused to let go. Even now, the dragonet was struggling in her arms and attempting to get closer to the piscin girl, who had finally begun inching closer over the last half-hour.

"Just do it," Anzi snapped. "The worst she can do is bite your fingers off, and there are healers who can fix that."

"I don't have any money for healers, snake-kisser."

And no one in Lumenera would willingly treat her, she realized belatedly. All right, fine, so she had a point. "I've got her, so stop being a little chicken. I know you want to come closer, so just do it. Isvan and the others are gone and won't come back until I tell them, so do it now before I leave and you lose your chance."

She was bluffing. She couldn't leave without doing this, without being sure. Her heart still throbbed with painful wrenches at the idea of losing Netra's attachment so suddenly, so…without warning, but if this was the way it went, then it was the way it had to be. She couldn't forget the resolve she had committed herself to, and she couldn't forget the hopes she had carried this far. She didn't want to be like the others, binding dragons to herself out of pride and cruel ambition. Dragons had minds of their own, a piercing intelligence that surpassed humans' by far. She knew it. She'd seen it. Netra was only weeks old and understand human speech well enough to speak it even if she rarely deigned to. She was conscious, thinking, even as a little one scarcely older than an infant. Frankly, it terrified Anzi that the dragonet was already so independent, the little thing that used to scream to be hand-fed and hissed whenever Anzi left its sight for any longer than a few hours at a time.

But she knew the old stories, the legends. Dragons chose their own warriors. She couldn't interfere.

"See?" she said waspishly when Rania finally came to a creeping stop in front of her and Netra. "You could have saved us a lot of time by doing this in the first place. Is she talking to you?"

The girl swallowed hard, and her skinny throat bobbed twice. "...Yes. She's—in my head."

"You know her name?"

"She—she said it's Netra-hau."

"Well, introduce yourself back, then."

"...I did."

In her thoughts? Anzi stared, startled at the implication that the two were communicating telepathically already, both ways. Jealousy pooled in her chest again, and she had to fight to push it back so she could exercise her authority with the coolest composure. "Good," she said. "You're going to have to hold her."

"What! No. I'm not touching some no-good, stinking—"

The dragonet hissed, a savage sound that made both of them jump. It was the most vicious that Anzi had ever heard her sound, and even her scales vibrated, emitting a rapid chain of small chinks as they rattled against each other. A chilly aura covered Anzi's forearm bracers with a layer of frost, and she narrowed her eyes at Rania, whose face visibly paled even past the now-darkened color of her cheeks. "I suggest keeping your insults to yourself for the time being. You can hate the Empire all you like for what they've done, but dragons were never complicit in it. They were the ones wiped out, and the last of them enslaved to the will of people who care about nothing except conquest. Or are you going to keep acting like that and treat Netra like she's done something wrong, the way the Lumenerans treat inhumans? Hm?"

The girl stiffened. "It's not the same."

"Isn't it? Netra just hatched several weeks ago. Where was she before then? Did she play a part in whatever reason you have to hate dragons?"

"It's not the same!" Rania insisted as she stared hard at the dragonet. "You can't change my mind."

"I don't have to. Netra doesn't either, because whether or not you like her, she's going to get what she wants in the end. I know that better than anyone else." She stuck her finger in the girl's face, capitalizing on the sudden intimidation that flickered in her eyes. "Because you don't say no to dragons."

To her credit, the girl stuck her bottom lip out in one last attempt at a stubborn display. "I'll say no if I wanna say no. No one's the boss of me."

"Except Isvan, apparently, who can't wait to get rid of you. Take my word for it. You won't get anywhere sticking to his shadow. Whatever the reason you want his approval so badly, some people just can't and won't give you want you want. Ever. So make your own path."

There, perfect timing. While the girl was cowed into silence at her stone-cold words, Anzi took advantage of the momentary submissiveness and shoved Netra forward. A second later, Rania was struggling to keep the dragonet steady and holding her away from herself, but at least she was obediently holding onto her instead of hurling Netra to the ground. Progress.

Anzi's stomach twisted again when she caught the way they stared at each other, no doubt communicating in silence through the linking of their minds. The girl, the piscin girl—there was something special about her that Anzi didn't have, and that was that. She would have to make her peace with it no matter how crushing it felt. Dragons were their own, and just because she had hatched Netra didn't mean Netra was hers. Not even in fondness. When she had hatched, she'd already known her own name and asserted it in silence, letting it drip into Anzi's mind, proof that she was sentient, intelligent.

She'd made her decision. Anzi would just have to live with it.

And when the time came—she would let Netra go.

～

"You're up early this morning, Governor."

"Almost sunrise, madam First. Not very early for an old man like me who can't sleep through the night anymore."

"You should still be careful. I don't know what the colonel's definition of dawn is, exactly. If he catches you out here too early…"

They were in front of the governor's estate by the gates. Bantan Hosef had appeared seconds ago, pushing open the wooden door and walking out alone through the archway of the facade to join her. He was even more haggard than he had been yesterday, but that was likely the absence of his armor. He looked so small in his official red robe.

"Dusk to dawn," he said, and she thought she could detect a hint of bitterness in his gruff voice despite his nonchalant demeanor. "I'll have a defense ready in case he wants to sentence me. The first break of light no matter how faint should count as dawn, hm?"

Anzi didn't bother to answer the question; it was clearly a sarcastic one. They both knew the colonel wouldn't care about pleas and appeals. "I can't stop you if you want to be reckless. But it would be a shame if Lumenera lost you before your time."

"I won't last much longer, anyway."

"Not with that attitude."

The elderly man crossed his arms and scoffed, sending a narrow plume of white fog spiraling up over his head. "If I'd had any remaining doubt there's something strange with you, it's gone now. Never have I met a rider so eager to tell me to live on." He gave her a mocking look when she made no reply. "What? Nothing to say? Not going to defend yourself and claim dragon riders are decent men beneath it all?"

Not in the least. "Sir, dragon riders are worse than you know."

"Hm."

"Hm."

He understood she was different from the rest of the Premier, that much was evident. But she couldn't explain to him how much. She couldn't risk it, not with the situation with Isvan's rebels and the hatred they had for the old man they considered nothing but a whimpering collaborator. And one thing was true enough: she suspected Hosef might betray them all if he ever became aware of what was happening, of what was being planned. He was the caretaker of a city of tens of thousands, and he couldn't afford to throw in his lot with a half-baked, wildly unprepared band of revolutionaries who had nothing to fight back with. He would be an idiot to trust them. If Anzi were in his place, she knew what she would likely do. Report the brewing rebellion and potentially gain the temporary favor of the Empire along with its trust. Buy time for something better, something smarter. It was far safer than writhing and flopping to the rhythm of a doomed effort that would only lead to more draconian oversight and oppression, once caught and punished.

She couldn't let Governor Hosef do that. He was an effective leader, but he was too scarred from the terrible losses he had had to endure already. When the revolution came, let it be a surprise. He could claim innocence that way whether the attempt crumbled or succeeded.

They stood in silence as the sun's first rays continued to creep across the sky, dripping through the heavy cloud cover that had moved in overnight. It was cold, and the air was wet. Rain, probably. Anzi rolled her shoulders back and earned the heavy, vocal scorn of Netra who had draped her serpentine body around the back of her neck. She was getting too big for this. Already was.

"Colonel." She stood at attention several minutes later, clasping her hands behind her back when a familiar blue-and-white clad figure approached. "Reporting."

"Go on."

"I found no one out past curfew. There were several street urchins, but they were inside one of the open stables attached to a tavern. I thought that should count as being indoors."

"You could have punished them. I wouldn't have disciplined you for it."

She was already standing up straight, so he didn't see how she stiffened. Horrifying. He was speaking as if she wanted to do it, as if he were obliging some naughty blood thirst of hers like a parent buying a treat for a begging child. And right in front of the governor, too, although the elderly man expertly hid whatever he must have felt at such cool words and presented only neutral ease. She would have envied his control if she didn't know exactly how he'd learned it: through pain unimaginable.

"I didn't think it was necessary," she said. "I thought that might give the wrong impression as to who we are."

The colonel's thick eyebrows came down in a frown. "And what would that impression be?"

"That we're unreasonable. If they obey, it seems right that we hold to our end as well."

Bisset's next words were abrupt and unexpected: "Governor," he said flatly. "Leave us. Now. I'll be seeing you inside in a moment."

She braced herself, wondering if she had crossed the line with her half-cautioning statement. To dismiss the governor meant he was going to say—or do—something he didn't want anyone else to see. Was he going to discipline her for her backtalk, do to her what Tet had done not so long ago? Her ribs seared with remembered pain, and she tensed despite her every effort to remain calm. Her pulse thrummed even harder in her throat when she heard Hosef's shuffling footsteps disappear with a whining creak of the manor's gates.

"You still think like a commoner," said Bisset. His voice was hard, cold. "Fix that."

"Sir?"

"You answer to no one except the collective of the Premier and to Tet. No one else. Certainly not to Lumenerans."

"I'm not understanding, sir."

"You held back when you could have made an example of the street urchins you found. They're of no value to the city or to us, so that would have been an efficient and uncostly way of reminding Lumenera who rules them so that they will be only afraid instead of resentful. You did this because you worry about our...image. Reputation." He chewed the last two words out as if they were bad-tasting morsels of spoiled food. "But you have nothing to fear. You are a First Guard. You answer to none of them."

That was what he thought? That she abstained from killing children only because she was afraid of being called to judgment? Did the colonel have even a shred of humanity in him? How could he not understand? Fine. If he wanted to reduce this to cold, soulless calculations, then she would stoop to his level and justify herself the same way.

"It's not about the fear, sir," she said crisply. "It's about efficiency."

"What was that?"

She lifted her chin. "You mentioned that we want to rout more resources northward soon. That means we'll have to thin our forces here, won't we? Sir."

"Eventually."

"Then it would be good to establish real order here. Not one reinforced by constant fear. Because once we remove that fear, they have no more reason to obey. They'll feel emboldened by our shrinking presence, and right when we least need it, they could slip out of the harness and make trouble. We would have to fight on the northern front while trying to bring the Lumenerans back to order at the same, then. And it wouldn't just be Lumenera, sir. It could spread like an infection to every seaside city here, the spirit of rebellion. I hate to think of what would happen if news of that spread across the sea, too. There's a lot of water trade coming and going from Lumenera's ports..."

The final part of her defense was a bluff more than anything, but an educated one. It was easy to guess that with Tet's greed, he would want to expand his conquest to continents past the wide waters, too, the oceans and seas that separated this one from the rest. Surely the colonel agreed. Everything she had said made perfect sense from a military perspective even without accounting for sympathy, for basic humanity—

"I don't care for speculation," he said, and she swore he sounded *bored*. "We're here to reinforce Empire authority, nothing more. We don't need to be creative when we already know what works."

She opened her mouth to reply, but no sooner had she sucked in a breath to deliver the words bubbling up on her tongue, the colonel moved on. Just like that. No argument, no debate. She had spoken, and he had ignored it.

"Wait out here," he ordered as he moved past her to enter the estate. "I'll bring the governor out, and we will take him to the central plaza. We will be choosing a successor there."

"I—sir?" What? All of a sudden?

"A successor," he repeated, visibly annoyed as he shot her a disapproving glower over his shoulder. "The governor will die soon, and we need to ensure a reliable transition of authority before that can happen. So obviously, we need to be present for the appointment of the next."

When had he decided this? Bisset had never mentioned it. Her pulse quickened, and her skin prickled in cold apprehension. Yes, Hosef had mentioned the inevitability of being replaced, but something didn't feel right. There were motives behind this other than seeking reliable transition of authority. There was scheming behind this, dark and sinister.

"Be ready to leave," he said as he turned back to face the gates. "It won't be long."

56

The central plaza. It was a pretty sight, or must have been before it became the chipped and shattered ruin it was now. White stone blocks made up the bottom, rimmed with opalescent stones that went around it in a wide circle. In the middle of it all was a broken fountain, flowing with water but half of its upper stone tier sheared off.

And that was it. Nothing else. Besides the gentle burbling from there, Anzi heard nothing else, not a whisper nor a breath. Of the hundreds gathered around the plaza and hundreds more trudging forward to join the crowd from behind, not a single person made their voice heard. It was so eerie a shiver trickled down her back. Never had she encountered such a silent crowd. There was only the distant sound of stray dogs barking, a rustling of the wind against cloth awnings set over market stalls, the rush of the waves against the sands along the far pier…

"Your governor is being retired today," Bisset announced. "We appoint his successor."

It was the loudest she had ever heard him raise his voice, and it rang out over the heads of the assembled crowd. Standing next to him, she could not only hear but feel every ounce of the cool disdain in his voice. It made her skin crawl.

"Governor Bantan Hosef. You're welcome to nominate whoever you find favorable. Do so now if you wish."

Anzi didn't miss the fearful gleam that flashed through the old man's eyes as he shook his head. Wise choice. After everything she'd gleaned about Bisset's brutal methods just in the last day, she knew without a doubt that if Hosef took him up on his invitation and did indeed 'nominate' anyone, they would meet a sickening end at the edge of the colonel's sword. It would be a terrible but effective way to assert utter dominance and remind the people how helpless they were. Of course he would never allow anyone, much less the presiding ruler, to dictate their own fates. Dull horror echoed inside the hollow space she felt expanding under her skin, between her bones. She was beginning to understand Bisset's barbarity so well she could understand his reasoning without him saying a word. Like a vine growing and shoving into the cracks of her mind, dark and twisted and creaking. Understanding him was poisoning her, clouding her with something ugly and rotten.

"Then I invite someone to nominate himself," the colonel announced. He looked out over the crowd, flat blue eyes casting over their heads without actually looking at anyone. He was bored. He wanted this over with. "Anyone is welcome. Man, woman, child. Respect the will of the Empire while controlling your people, that is all that is required. You will be the wealthiest man to walk the city for decades to come, so long as you obey."

This was his strategy to choose the next successor? Then again, it made sense. Choose someone drooling and incompetent, someone who wanted only the gilded life of a pet ruler. Of course Bisset didn't want someone intelligent and capable who might inspire the city and instill within it any hope for the future. He wanted them to despair. Better if they drove the city to ruin.

Or maybe he just wanted to kill whoever dared to volunteer for the vaunted position. That seemed like something he would do, too, and judging by the continued silence, the crowd agreed. The Lumenerans must have learned well in these last few decades that any offer of seeming generosity was the exact opposite. In the eyes of everyone close enough that she could see their expressions, there was only fear.

"No one?" Bisset demanded. A note of anger crept into his voice now, and it grew louder with each word he ground out: "Step forward now. I'll only ask once more."

No one. Anzi's heart constricted when he drew his sword and let it slant downwards toward the ground, the hilt tight in his fist but not yet pointed at anyone's throats.

"I'm disappointed that no one seeks to serve their fellowmen," he said calmly. "I offer, and you all disregard the merciful hand. Let me emphasize the importance of this arrangement and my impatience with you all."

She didn't see it coming. Not for a second, not until she saw the blade swing through the faint morning mist. She had thought he was going to intimidate the civilians standing closest to the plaza or threaten to kill them if no one stepped forward. But not this. Not this—there was no time to react. No time to think. A splatter of blood landed on her uniform and armor in the next instant, and she stared in muted horror as she watched Governor Hosef crumple to the ground. Blood fountained out of his slit neck and pooled under his head, red and vibrant and terrible.

Her heart stopped, and her blood froze in her veins as she stared down at the lifeless body of the old man who lay face down on the flat stones. The governor. The governor who had been alive just a second ago, living, breathing—now murdered with a single stroke. It had happened so fast that half her mind had yet to catch up. The dull thump that had sounded when his corpse hit the ground, had it even been real? She looked up, searching for Bisset's gaze as if he might assure her that it was an illusion, that he hadn't just done that. But he wasn't even looking at her.

"Now you have no one," he announced past the several sharp screams that came from around them, and the thread of anger multiplied in his voice, strand by strand. He sounded as if he were the one slighted, as if he hadn't just slain a man in cold blood for no reason at all like a mindless beast. "I suggest someone take his place before I decide it would be a better idea to raze this city and burn everyone in it to ash and dust. Or is that what you all want?"

But his words did nothing except to terrify them further. Although some still looked too terrified to shout aloud, most of the ones closest to the plaza began scrambling back, shoving past the ones behind them in their panicked haste. Someone cried out and fell, but no one helped him back to his feet and he fell between a flurry of frantic bodies, arms and legs disappearing as they began to trample over him.

"Stay where you are, or burn!"

The sheer scorn in the colonel's voice stopped even Anzi. She had been in the middle of rushing forward to do something she could no longer remember, and now, she stared at him just as everyone else did. Cold sweat gathered on the back of her neck. Her tongue was too thick in her mouth to manage a single sound, much less a word. That is, if she was even permitted to speak. There was something manic to Bisset's energy now that hadn't been there before—or perhaps she'd merely missed it—and she knew instinctively that a single wrong word, a single wrong sound, even, would tip him past a line she dared not see him breach. Between them on the stones of the plaza lay a corpse he had just laid waste to with a single thoughtless slice of his sword, blood pooling and running down the cracks, spreading along them like a blooming labyrinth of red…

She could feel the terror of the crowd rising on every side of the plaza like tidal waves rearing up from the north, south, from the west and east, everywhere she looked. It threatened to crash over her and drown her thoughts, sickeningly thick and viscous. No wonder. No wonder these people despised dragons and their riders. This was their reality, the world they'd been born into and lived for the last thirty years. Degradation without reason, without justification. And the governor was dead. At the single whim of a First Guard, not even the Emperor, the ruler of Lumenera was dead, and now Bisset sought another.

"I'm still waiting," he said, and although his voice was now lowered from the furious roar he had used to quell them all, there was still a murderous lilt, something made of cold rage ready to snap. Anzi discreetly pulled her hands up to the hilts of her swords, keeping her eyes fixed on the colonel. Her snarling impulses demanded she attack and subdue him, but the wiser instincts in her warned her she would lose if she tried. His changed aura chilled her down to the soul. Magic, she realized suddenly, he was using magic even if she didn't know exactly what he was capable of, and she would lose if she confronted him now. But even so, she couldn't let him cross the next line. It was too late for the governor, but if Bisset truly meant to massacre these people, he would use his dragon against them, and they wouldn't stand a chance.

She couldn't let that happen. Even if it meant foiling her careful plans for the future, she wouldn't stand by and watch him char thousands of corpses and leave smoking ruins in his wake. She would make him run his sword through her first.

But as her hands tightened around the hilts, she had the feeling that was exactly what was going to happen. Her skin prickled with a primal fear as every inch of her body, every twitching sinew, warned her to stay quiet and stand by lest she become caught in the rage of a superior predator. Didn't she remember, a small voice demanded, what had happened with Tet? She had been outclassed then in every way, and the same thing would happen if she tried to face down Bisset. There could be no doubt about it. There was power in him she couldn't match now. Maybe not ever.

...And yet it didn't matter. She wouldn't watch and become a part of this, silent and accepting.

"I'll do it."

Her head whipped around at the sound of the familiar voice, and this time, a different kind of horror bloomed inside her. No. It couldn't be. But it was: standing there was a man who had pushed through the crowd, craggy, grizzled face set in a defiant grimace. Her chest expanded in an involuntary breath as she drilled Isvan with a half-panicked glare, one she hoped was strong enough to send him running. Get out, she wanted to shout, get away! What was he thinking-

"I'll do it," he said again, and this time he was close enough that his voice rang out loud and clear. "I'll take up the governorship."

Anzi almost tackled him to the ground. He was insane, exposing himself. The leader of the ragtag rebel force of Lumenera standing before two dragon riders, striding into the light. Had he truly lost his mind?

"Excellent," Bisset said before she could do anything. "Then come closer. All that's left is to pledge your loyalty to the Empire, and you can make arrangements to move into the newly vacated governor's estate." He nudged the corpse next to him with his boot and added, "And your first exercise of authority can be to have this cleaned up."

Don't, she warned as Isvan approached, stepping up onto the raised plaza stones and glaring straight at Bisset's face. Don't—

She knew what was about to happen and yet couldn't bring herself to stop it. He was going to make his approach, but only to get close enough to draw a blade and try to kill the colonel outright. Of course he would try, he had no self-control and was barely sane enough to hold himself together. His fevered devotion to liberation was the only thing that kept his leadership over the Lumeneran rebels intact, nothing else.

He didn't have the restraint. He'd already proved that by stepping forward to answer Bisset's threat in the first place. Now, it was too late. With every eye fixed on him from now on, with no way to move about in secret and foster the rebellion. And he was going to go out as a martyr. Of course he was. Nothing less would satisfy the stupid man who thirsted for revenge but couldn't keep himself together long enough to properly carry it out.

But he came to a stop before the colonel and simply stood there in silence. No shouting, no snarling, no lunging with a drawn sword. He simply...waited. Anzi stared at, disbeliving This was the man who had spent every spare second of their meeting last night ranting about the evils of dragons and dragon riders. This was the man who had lost his wife and his children to the very dragon rider standing before him. This was the man who had cost him his hand, too, maiming him for life and leaving a physical mark to last for all time, something to match the gnarled scars inside. But at last, he was holding back.

"I pledge...loyalty," he said, voice rough with barely bridled emotion. "To...the Empire."

"To death?" Bisset pressed.

"...Yes."

"And what is your name."

"Isvan."

The colonel nodded, slow and dignified. "You're a brave one. A particular breed. The only one of your stock to understand what was at stake."

Anzi's gut churned at the self-satisfied voice. This man...how could she have ever admired him? How could she have ever idolized him, dreaming of the day she could follow in his footsteps-

"Unfortunate that I reject your pledge."

This time, she saw it coming. This time, she saw, she knew, she felt it—

And yet could do nothing *again* as Bisset's sword whistled through the air and found flesh for the second time. No, everything was wrong, twisted. The rebellion, the alliance, the secret dragon riders she had intended to raise up within Lumenera with the help of this man who had given himself up so stupidly-

"Your reflexes are admirable," the colonel murmured as a fresh wave of screams began to erupt from the crowd. "It almost compensates for the idiocy in approaching me when you can't even conceal your true emotions."

On the ground, Isvan held a hand to the thickly flowing gash on the side of his neck as he scrambled to crawl backward off the plaza. But Bisset followed him with slow, deliberate strides, sword pointing down toward the ground and thin rivulets of blood trickling off its tip.

"You have the look of rebelliousness. I will snuff it out." The tip of his sword rose, hovered, and Anzi gritted her teeth. He had signed his own death warrant, and it wasn't worth sacrificing everything in a vain attempt to save him. Someone else would rise in his place to lead the fight, all she had to do was stay calm and maintain the cover. So she had no choice. She had no choice but to watch.

"No! Get away from him, you snake-kisser!"

Anzi's body reacted before she knew it. In a flash, she was standing in front of the colonel, blocking the swing of his sword with her own. The grinding of the steel sent a shudder along her entire body as she realized instantly that yes, her judgment had been correct: Bisset was far stronger than she was. It had taken all her might to intercept his casual swing. And while she had succeeded for now in stopping him from cutting through both Isvan and the screaming Rania who had thrown herself over her leader, she knew it wouldn't last.

"Anzi. What are you doing."

His low snarl promised pain. Much pain. But she had to stop this.

"Please forgive me, Colonel. If you'll let me explain—"

"Move aside."

"The girl is special. I need her."

"I don't care."

There wasn't a hint of curiosity in his voice. Nothing but flat denial and imperiousness. He hadn't even asked her to explain herself, and he was ignoring the way Netra had leaped down, half-flying, to crouch before Rania and began snarling and hissing at everyone in the vicinity. "Colonel, you can see for yourself. My dragon has an interest in the girl. If you make the decision to spare her, I think it'll do us good to—"

The scream of metal clashing for a second time rang through the air, and it took everything Anzi had to keep from grasping her shoulder and twisting away to safety. The reverberation of the horrendous impact felt like it was going to tear right through her joints, but she couldn't let the colonel move her a single step. If she did, Rania was dead. Isvan was dead. And even Netra, too, because the flat brutality in Bisset's eyes promised exactly that. He didn't care.

So there were no more words to say, no more begging for him to listen and give her a chance to speak. The only thing she could do was block every vicious slice that came her way, desperately angling her swords in the nick of time but slowing down more and more with each swing. And now he was forcing her back, back, back—her forearms were numb, and her shoulders were screaming in pain as she stumbled again and again.

Somehow, she stalled long enough for Isvan and Rania to disappear. She didn't know how they had managed it, but when Bisset lashed out with a swing of his sword that knocked both of hers away and sent her sprawling over the ground on her belly with a savage kick, she lifted her bleeding face to find nothing remaining except some splatters of blood on the stones where they had been a moment ago.

And then there was Netra, crawling back up onto the plaza. She must have gone with Rania to make sure she would be all right. But here she was again, returning to Anzi in the end. It almost made her smile—just in time for her to howl in shrieking agony when Bisset impaled her calf with his sword and pinned it to the stones. She writhed, thigh and foot seizing with crippling pain as she screamed and screamed.

"You've made a mistake," he said, and his voice was calm, dead. Like the still air that sat heavy over the desert right before a lethal twister. "A shame you'll have to learn the same lesson twice."

57

She didn't see Rania again nor Isvan. There was no opportunity to sneak even a single final instruction their way before Bisset dragged her slumped body by her hair, although she did her best to try to spot them among the screaming people of the fast-scattering crowd. All chaos, all fury, all terror—it was so overwhelming even Netra's first-ever display of dragon magic went largely missed: she let out a terrible, ear-piercing screech that rent the air and ejected a stream of white fog straight at Bisset's back. White crystals solidified and formed over his shoulders and the back of his arm, coating the upper right half of his body and locking his neck so the couldn't move his head.

But the only thing he had done was grunt, tense, and wrench free of the ice, sending broken, sparkling shards down to the ground where they evaporated into misty plumes. And that was that. Netra tried again several more times, but he hardly seemed to notice. When she gave up the attempt and chased after them both so she could snap at his legs, he kicked her aside hard enough to send her flying.

That almost broke Anzi's stone resolve. It certainly bent it. Despite the horrifying state of her calf, the rest of her body tightened and coiled, trying to spring up and lunge at the colonel even though she knew how that ended. But hold, she commanded herself. Survive. But this was true hell, watching Netra cry and limp after her while Bisset dragged her along the ground behind himself. Hell, and rage, boiling rage that baked her from the inside out. If she hadn't already been determined to see him in ruins, that was enough to make up her mind. For what he did today—not to her, but to Netra—he would pay.

And she had already made sure of that, halfway. She allowed herself a fleeting moment of gloating satisfaction. Since Tet and the Premier treated the rest of the world like a personal plaything, like a game-

Then she could play, too.

And she would win.

SHE WAS CRIPPLED. After a week and a half of no treatment aside from the rudimentary measures Bisset had permitted to avoid infection, she knew that even if she sought healers now, she might bear a limp for the rest of her life. Even her inhuman body had its limits, and she had borne an injury most men would never recover from. She had to be prepared, mentally. Because with a limp or not, crippled or not, she she had to keep going. Having her leg stabbed through and the vital tendon in the back of it severed had not been part of the plan, but it was too late now to have regrets. All she could do was take care of her leg the best she was able and hope that the palace healers could do her another decent turn again.

When she and Bisset finally arrived at the Imperial Palace, she was carried off the instant her condition was discovered. She made no mention of the circumstances surrounding her injury no matter how insistently the physicians asked, only admitting the bare minimum in order to facilitate their work. And for three days, they labored to heal her leg the best they were able.

The colonel never came to see her, of course. It would have been strange if he had. No, she thought as she stroked Netra's back and straightened her spines, he would be far too busy reporting her failures to Tet. Maybe he would recommend she be disposed of, consigned to the refuse heap like the rest of the candidates who'd failed to live up to expectations. Her situation would be peculiar since she had already been presented to the public, but after a few years, no one would remember her anyway. She would fade into history, a small speck in the annals of Empire history.

Her leg burned under the covers, still twitching and trembling from the forced healing it had undergone over the last few days under the palace healers' magic. But instead of subduing her, it only raised her anticipation. She was waiting, watching. Holding her breath.

When the door opened with a terrific bang three days later, she knew who it had to be. No visitors were allowed to see her, not even Letti who had reportedly been demanding entry into the infirmary since the morning Anzi arrived, and the physicians would never make such a ruckus. That meant it could only be-

"My dear Anzi, we've come to see you at last."

She made sure her face betrayed nothing but pleasant surprise as she pulled herself up to sit on the bed. Her reflexive reaction would have been to recoil and grimace at the sight of the Emperor barging in with a wide smile, but she had been preparing for this moment in her head ever since Lumenera. She hadn't expected this inevitable moment would occur while in bed, true, but throne room or infirmary, it didn't matter.

She had a plan. A scheme. She was ready.

"Your Excellency," she greeted. "Please forgive me. I can't stand at the moment."

"Oh, no. Rest, my dear." Tet stood at her bedside with Bisset next to him. The colonel's face was stone-blank, hinting at nothing. His gaze slid down to Netra who lay curled into her side, but other than an initial bristling from the dragonet, she too was remaining calm. Good. Exactly as arranged.

"You look much better than you did when you came," Tet remarked. "That's good."

"You saw me when I arrived, Your Excellency?"

"Oh, well, no. But that's what I've heard, and I'm sure they're right."

Figured. Of course he wouldn't have deigned to check on her; did he care about anything other than himself? "Is there something you need, Your Excellency? Whatever it is, I'll do my best."

"Good girl. You know, this is why I like you. So very helpful. The others might make fun of you and call you a bit of a lapdog, but you're a priceless find. Talented, bright, strong, and so eager to please. I'll take good care of you." Tet wagged a finger at her, his long red sleeve billowing slightly with the movement. "But only so long as you're useful, yes?"

"Of course."

"But that leg isn't looking so good, and you do need that. To think you might lose it! Unacceptable. We'll wait for you to be stable again, because we care. See, that's the arrangement I have with all the Premier, or whatever you all call yourselves. The prestige, the privileges, the pomp and fanfare of ceremonies and such—those were never my idea. I just wanted a close-knit family, if you get me? Someone I know will always get the job done so I don't have to worry about it myself if I don't feel like it."

He called that a family? Sounded more like he wanted a close-knit ring of capable cronies and nothing more.

"And see, family looks out for each other. Or at least that was my vision. It's nice not to have to ask for every single thing I want or order this and demand that. Do you understand? I want a family that will give me what I want before I can ask for it, before I even know I want or need it."

Right. So he wanted a ring of cronies and nannies, too. She nodded.

"I never wanted mindless servants from the very beginning. Well, I did at one point—but that was before I knew how exhausting it is to control everyone all the time. Now, I don't want to control anything or anyone. I just want them smart enough to know to obey me without question."

A warning thrill swirled in her gut, but she forced herself to keep calm and continue listening. Her body was reacting of its own accord, remembering the horrific abuse he had laid upon her only a few weeks ago. But there was no need, she told herself. This was within the realm of her preparations. Calm. Patience. Endurance. "I understand, sir," she said. "I agree. I think this is how all the Premier should be, if you'll forgive me for being so forward."

Tet smiled and flapped his hand at her. "Smart girl, of course there's no need for forgiveness. Do you know why I'm telling you this?"

"I do, sir. It's about the incident in Lumenera."

"And? Tell me your side of things. Alexandre let me know what happened already, but I find it a bit peculiar. I want to hear more, and from you."

Yes. Yes, this was good, what she had been hoping for. She would still have carried out her scheme even if Tet had chosen to beat her first and ask questions later, but her guess that his curiosity would momentarily outweigh fury had been right. After all, she couldn't possibly be so stupid as to disobey Tet again so soon after her last disciplining. He had to be in sheer disbelief and wondering what exactly he was missing.

Still, some humility would tilt the odds in her favor a little more. "I don't want to bore you," she said demurely. "I realized my thinking was incorrect, and Colonel Bisset's discipline taught me why. I wholly accept whatever other punishment awaits me. It won't happen again."

The Emperor's head tipped back, chin rising minutely. Something sharp gleamed in his eyes. "Discipline, is it? And punishment."

"Yes, sir."

"Explain. Why aren't you defending yourself? Thought for sure you'd try."

Her skin prickled, not with apprehension but anticipation. This was it. She had to use the right words here, the perfect combination to tip the scales. The look in his eyes combined with the strange speech he had given her about family and control, including the fact that he hadn't started thrashing her the instant he entered the room with Bisset at his side—it all pointed toward one thing. He wanted to know *why*.

"I shouldn't defend myself at all," she said. "I was presumptuous and thought I could help prepare for our northward invasion that Colonel Bisset informed me about. It was wrong of me, but I thought at the time it was worth the extra effort. I wanted to try to establish a positive rapport, something we could use to train the Lumenerans into willing obedience to spare us trouble in the future."

"Interesting? Go on."

She brushed her hair back behind her ear, a subdued gesture. Measured, of course, with care. "I'm embarrassed to recount it," she said, faking contrition. "But if Your Excellency is willing to tolerate it..."

"I said go on."

The impatience in his voice almost made her betray her pretense with a smug smile. "When Colonel Bisset let me know he would be appointing Hosef's successor—"

"Hosef?"

"The governor of Lumenera, sir."

"Ah, all right."

...He hadn't even known something like that. Decades of terrorizing the city and he didn't even care enough to know the name of the man left in charge of it. The man who had lost everything he ever loved, the man who had been forced to take up the mantle left behind by his beloved son and try to protect the burning remnants of everything he'd once had. "Yes, sir," she said. "Him. We convened in the plaza, and things devolved in such a way that the colonel deemed it necessary to execute the governor. And unfortunately, the man who answered Colonel Bisset's call for a replacement was unfit. So he moved to execute him as well—which is where I erred."

"Mhm. Keep going. Tell me why you interfered."

"There was a girl," she said. "I'd seen her lingering near the edge of the plaza for a while. She jumped up to try to intercept the colonel, and she would have died alongside the man. Ordinarily, I would never cross Colonel Bisset's orders, and I apologize again, sir"—she made sure to twist at the waist and present the other man with a deep bow of her head —"but there were two reasons I thought it necessary. I know I was wrong now, but first, my dragon was drawn to her, I don't know why. I understand it's irrelevant now, but I thought then it was important to find out why. Just in case there was something strange either with Netra or the girl, or in case it was something we could use to our advantage. Bastien has told me before I can do things no one has done before, so I also thought this might be another unprecedented incident I should examine more closely."

"Hm. True, true. And what was the second reason?"

She bowed her head even deeper. "That was my most egregious mistake. I had the wrong understanding at the time that I should be thinking ahead and trying to manipulate things in our favor for the future, instead of following orders as they are given. I thought the killing of a little native girl would create trouble. I don't have the experience that the colonel does, of course, so I must have been wrong—but I was concerned that killing her would trigger rebel retaliation."

"Rebel retaliation," Tet repeated. "So you interfered to save her."

"I had been meaning to suggest to the colonel that fostering a more positive relationship with Lumenera would work well for us," she continued. "Especially after they've been pressed down heavily for so long. If we relaxed our stance even a little, they would be ecstatic about it—and I thought, maybe, some leniency would lead to them being more passive and cooperative in the long-term, even when we have no choice but to thin our forces in that region and reduce our presence. But now I know better. Your Excellency, I don't deserve to ask for your forgiveness or the colonel's, but I hope you both decide to overlook my ignorance one more time. I understand now. It's more important to obey orders as they are given instead of being so presumptuous as to try to be useful to you."

She bowed her head in deceptively calm subjection, but her blood surged like magma spilling out of a volcano, bubbling hot and dangerous, partly because of the adrenaline flooding her entire body and partly because she couldn't help but recall the last time she'd stirred Tet's wrath. Pain. Unending pain. Pain every part of her could still remember and would continue to remember for a long, long time.

But there was another hidden part of her, well-buried and kept secret under the layer of false subservience, that reveled. Because she knew. She knew from the instant the light in Tet's crystal blue eyes flashed—that she had won.

When the crack of his knuckles against Bisset's face pierced the silence, she had to fake her surprise and recoil in a believable way, pushing herself back up toward the head of the bed as if scrambling to escape the range of the Emperor's sudden violence. Netra drew back as well, letting out a low hiss and raising her spines along her back while sticking close to Anzi's side. Good. Excellent. Anzi stared in false shock as Tet struck at the colonel again, sending him into the wall so hard she heard the audible crack of bone striking stone.

"Look at that," the Emperor said, his voice deadly calm. "You've almost ruined her. I had a feeling you've been overstepping, but I ignored it because it was too much of a bother. But now, I see."

He left her bedside to walk over to Bisset, who had grabbed onto the wall to pull himself up. The colonel made not a sound, however, when Tet struck him again for the third time, and even when the latter held him up against the wall with a long, twiggy hand wrapped around his throat, he offered no protest. His boots dangled completely off the ground as the Emperor used his uncanny height to lift him half a meter up the wall.

"I knew you were leaving something out. Why would she make the same mistake twice? She would only do that if she forgot to be terrified of me, which makes no sense." He bashed the colonel into the wall again, and a shower of stone dust billowed from the ceiling. "You're supposed to know better," he chided. His back was turned to Anzi, but she could imagine all too clearly the serene smile he must be wearing. He liked doing that, especially while hurting someone. Oh, yes. "See, Anzi and I had a conversation about this not too long ago, but I guess I should have given you a fresh reminder, too. You're free to take whatever spoils you want, chase whatever tail you want, eat, drink, fuck as you like. But what's the one thing you need to ask yourself before you do all this, hm? Anzi, tell him."

She was ready. "We need to ask ourselves if it's something *you* would want."

"Explain it to the nice man, would you? A little more clearly."

"We need to think about whether what we do will offend you. Or make you angry."

"That's right. And the opposite! You need to ask yourselves if what you're doing is in my best interest, if it will make happy. Because that's all

I want. I don't think that's too much to ask. Because we're family. What do you think, Anzi? Seeing as how you haven't even been serving me for very long but know to look ahead and live on my behalf...to *my* benefit. Obedient, but also thoughtful. Intelligent. See, this is what I want, Alexandre. Not mindless dogs slobbering all over themselves, drunk on their own power. And look what you've done—you say you had the gall to 'punish' her? To me, you and Anzi are on the same level, little one. I told her that already. Both of you are insects to me. You two and all the others. My favorite insects, but insects nonetheless. And you have the gall to punish each other? In front of *me?*"

She suppressed a smile. There. That had been the linchpin.

Because Bisset had never deemed it punishment. He hadn't called it that even once.

She had.

Every word she had said a moment ago was carefully placed, edged with a half-lie she knew would irk Tet past his endurance. There was a man who couldn't bear the thought of sharing authority and respect, there was a man who would resent every bit of it that went to someone else in the room other than him. And her show of fawning subjection to the colonel standing right next to him—her talk of discipline and punishment at his hands as if Bisset had been the one to feed her those words, that would have wounded Tet's ego.

And besides, she thought smugly as she continued to watch the Emperor strangle Bisset against the wall, hadn't she learned? The very first lesson she'd been taught by Tet's fists and feet, through pain:

No fighting. Not among yourselves.

Bisset had wounded her back at Lumenera. If she had fought back, if she had left a single retaliatory mark on him even in her own defense, she would not have been able to do this. It was only because she had surrendered utterly in that moment that she could be victorious now.

Finally, Tet dropped the panting, twitching Bisset to the ground, leaving him in a heap at his feet. With a sniff, the Emperor clasped his hands behind his back and turned to look back around at Anzi.

"Dear? I have something to say."

She straightened her back, putting on her best show of paralyzed fear. "Yes, Your Excellency."

"Don't call him *sir* anymore. And definitely not in front of me. Very annoying. Understand?"

"Perfectly, sir."

58

"You did great this morning," she murmured to Netra. "I'm proud of you for not flying off the handle."

The dragonet let out a sound like a cross between a purr and a snarl before lowering her serpentine neck and sunning herself on the broad rock by the water.

"I see you're still not talking to me. Considering that I know for a fact now that you can talk, that's hurtful." Anzi ripped up several grass blades and tossed them in the reptile's direction. "You talked to that piscin girl instead. So either I'm just a chump, or she's extra special. Either way, it means you don't like me very much, huh?"

She should have known better than to try to play the pity card with Netra. Not only was she terrible at it in the first place, the dragonet had no pity to spare. She only opened one scaly lid to give Anzi a contemptuous glance then rolled away again.

"Fine. But...I mean it. You and I are going to have to figure this out. I don't know why you won't talk to me when it's clear you can, but with everything that's going to happen very soon, we need to be on the same page. We're going to keep inching closer to Tet's right hand, but that puts us both in more danger than before. We need to work togeth—are you sleeping?"

She was. Anzi sighed and adjusted the wooden splint attached to her leg before lying back on the grass as well. They were out by the river bend again where no one wandered, and for a single wistful moment, she wished she could fall asleep and enjoy the peace. But of course she couldn't. After her latest incident with subtly arranging for Bisset's subjugation at Tet's hands, she needed to tread even more carefully than before.

The colonel wouldn't be able to prove it, but he would have begun suspecting now that she was no longer the obedient little soldier she'd been before and coming into an unexpected talent for scheming. And he had plenty of soldiers at his command, ones eager to please and ready to spy on all she did. Tet had made it clear once again that the members of his Premier Guard weren't allowed to have altercations with each other, but that didn't mean the colonel would leave her alone. Especially when it was so clear that he considered her his personal responsibility and every one of her failures a black blemish on his record. Little did he know that she was planning on making sure by the end of all this, his ledger would be dripping in mud.

"You—slattern!"

She had been expecting the voice, so she didn't startle at the noise. What she wasn't expecting was for Letti to come crashing into her with a wracking sob, sending her sprawling on her side and her leg seizing up with a terrible cramp. "Ah—ow! Letti, get off me!"

"No! How dare you! Why are you always hurt? And why do I have to hear about you from everyone else first? Do you not want to see me anymore?"

"Stop it, Letti, sit down." Anzi straightened her splint and gave the harem girl a stern glare. "Where's Julien."

She didn't look pleased about it, but the woman settled down next to her on the grass with careful movements, arranging her dress so as not to wrinkle it. "Over there by the other bend, behind the trees. You were right about him. I didn't believe it when I got your message, but he really did jump up and say he'd escort me around today the second I asked."

"I know a whipped one when I see him. And he has your token? No one suspects anything?"

"They shouldn't. As far as Noemi and the girls know, I'm only escaping from the quarters today because they've been absolute bitches to me lately."

Anzi narrowed her eyes, momentarily diverted. "What have they done?"

"Oh, nothing like you think. It's just sneaky things, things I can't whine about or else I'll look like the one being awful."

"…They—"

"You've already scared them witless. It's fine, it's fine. Now tell me what's going on. Something's obviously turned upside down if you're sneaking around passing me messages through harem guards and asking me to meet in secret—and in disguise, too. I look like a…a…common housewife."

Anzi looked her up and down. Even in the drab and ugly gray cloak Letti had thrown over herself, she most certainly did not look common. "You covered that too, right?" she asked suspiciously, pointing at her face. "If you didn't, someone will have recognized you."

"Of course I did! And Julien did, too. Someone even stopped us and tried to sell us flowers from her cart like we're lovers. I promise, no one knows a thing."

"Good. We can't stay long or else people will get suspicious, but listen carefully." Letti straightened at her sharp tone. "And wipe your face. You look like a mess."

"Excuse me! That's what I get for being worried about you, is it—?"

"Even so, there's no need to cry like a baby. Anyway," she continued when it looked like the harem girl was puffing up with an explosive protest, "this is important. It stays between us and only us. You know there are ears everywhere in the palace even better than I do, so aside from when we have complete privacy like this, we never speak of it. Understand?"

"Oh, get on with it! I'm dying. What are you asking me to do?"

Anzi fixed her eyes on the woman with a hard stare. "I need you to spy on the other harem girls. Information on all the dignitaries who come to visit the Imperial City, other kingdoms, annexed cities, what relationships they have with the Empire, everything. Can you do that for me?"

"Of course, I can. That's all we talk about." Slender eyebrows furrowed in a pretty frown. "But why? What's going on? Don't do anything danger-ous, I already know you were avoiding me before you left on that sudden trip, wherever you went. Because you were trying to hide your wounds, weren't you? I know about them, they said it looked like you'd been dragged behind a horse for miles."

People gossiped too damn much in the palace. "I can't tell you every-thing. The less you know, the better. If it were up to me, I wouldn't involve you at all, but I know you'll stick your nose in where it doesn't belong and get it cut off at this rate. I heard you've been asking Julien about me every day. You're lucky he doesn't have a big mouth, or someone might have been sent to watch you already."

"What? But why!"

"Because I'm in deep shit. Or was. Might still be. I need you to be careful, and if possible, to listen well. That's it. It's bad enough I'm asking you to do this."

"Spying is easy," Letti scoffed. "What do you think our real purpose is? To be entertainment? Just another warm body? Our main job is to collect information and report it. I may not be a veteran, but I've already been doing that for a while."

Anzi blinked. Harem girls?…Spies? What was terrible about the revelation was that it made perfect sense. Her stomach churned with uneasy heat as she wondered if she was doing the right thing. And to be honest… "I'm lying. I'm lying to you."

"What? What do you mean?"

"I have no idea what I'm doing," Anzi clarified. "And I don't know who to turn to. I don't want to put anyone important to me in danger, but the only ones I trust are the ones important to me in the first place." She dropped her head and pressed her wrists to her temples, fists clenched. Her chest felt tight with everything she had buried, all the outrage, the fury, the horror of things she almost regretted learning. "I can't…do this alone. I don't know who to turn to."

"Oh…Oh, Anzi."

She looked up, irritated at the syrupy-sweet rise and fall of Letti's voice. She was doing it on purpose. "Why are you saying my name like that. I don't like it."

"Because you're being so sweet. I can't help it. You're going to make me cry."

"What? When was I sweet," Anzi demanded. "What do you mean."

"You just said I was important to you."

"No, I didn't."

"Did, too."

"No. I definitely didn't."

"Yes, you did. Come here, I love you too."

"What the hell—get away from me!" But it was futile. Her agility was at an all time low thanks to her maimed leg, and Letti took full advantage by clambering over and wrapping her up tight in her arms. "Get off me!"

"Never. Muah, muah, muah—"

She struggled to dodge the harem girl's sloppy kisses all over her cheek. "This was a mistake," she growled. "I shouldn't have asked you to meet me. Never mind, forget everything I said."

"Then I'll just have to keep following you around and asking everyone about you until you stop avoiding me. I'll bring you all sorts of attention so you can't sneak around and get up to whatever mischief it is you've got going on."

"Letti!"

"That's what I thought. Now let me hug you."

She'd made a mistake. She had thought Tet was the most dangerous, ruthless person she'd ever met with no trace of a conscience, but it was clear the harem girl currently holding her prisoner was far worse. Threatening to expose her unless she humored Letti's annoying affections? What kind of remorseless...

"So are you going to tell me about what happened to you before you left?" the woman asked after Anzi finally managed to peel herself away. "They told me your entire face was black and blue. And they said you were in the palace infirmary for days, and no one was allowed on that side of the wing the entire time. You had all the best healers, too."

"...An incident. I can't say."

"Can't, or won't?"

"Both. I'm serious, Letti. I know I'm asking you for help and it makes no sense that I won't tell you these things, but it's because knowing them will change the way you act toward certain people. It'll change the way you talk, think. People will notice, and then you'll be in more danger than I've put you in already. That's why I'm asking you to trust me, at least until I know you won't get kidnapped in the night and interrogated in the dungeons for something I did."

"...You're really in trouble, aren't you?"

"Something like that." She dropped her gaze to the grass between her spread legs and frowned. "Or will be. I don't know how soon, but it'll happen. I have to be ready."

"And how do you know that I agree with whatever trouble you're putting yourself in, then? What if I think you're making a terrible mistake?"

In the silence that followed, she realized Letti was right: she was plotting to commit treason, and even if the harem girl would ever agree to become an accomplice in such a crime, Letti's loyalty to the Empire might be as unshakable as her own used to be. Just because they were friends didn't mean the harem girl would agree with her newfound beliefs.

Indeed, the only reason Anzi's had changed at all was because she had been taken into the confidence of the Premier Guard. That was where she had learned. Things that no one knew, not the civilians, not harem girls, no one. For all Letti knew, the Empire was still the golden kingdom of the heavens, blessed by the gods and magnanimous to the people, meant for glory forever. Even in the face of proof and brazen confessions posed as boasts, it had taken Anzi far too long to accept the truth, and that only after she had suffered immensely for it. So how could Letti possibly understand? If she ever realized what Anzi was doing, would she turn on her? Tell her she was insane, evil, all the things Anzi would have accused a traitor of being not too long ago?

"Oh, don't look like that. I'm not going to leave you in the lurch."

She stared. "You don't know if you'd agree with what I'm doing," she said. "You just told me that."

"Maybe. But I can trust you. You saved me once, I can't believe you'd abuse my trust for something all that bad. Besides, you're a lot sweeter than you let on." The harem girl patted her cheek and smiled. "I just wish you'd trust me back."

"I do. That's why I—"

"Trust me to take care of myself, I mean. Which, to be fair, I haven't done a good job of, so I guess I can't really complain. You're just looking out for me, that's all."

Anzi shifted. Was she really doing the right thing? If she really were 'looking out' for Letti, she wouldn't be pulling her into danger. But...she couldn't do this alone. She used to think she could. All her life, she'd wanted to be the only one who helped herself up so she could look down and proudly say she'd done it all alone. She used to think that was the only way to prove she was worthy of what she achieved. But now...now, she couldn't bring herself to think about *worthy*. She couldn't think about achievements and pride and every other petty thing that used to matter so much. Now she was in a world where everything was so much bigger than she was, and she had no choice, no choice but to try to change it. She didn't care about glory anymore and never would again. How could she when she knew all she did?

So she had to try. She had to try because she could, because she had power when others didn't. If she could change even one thing, just one...

"I'm sorry," she said again. "I hope when I can tell you about this, that you'll understand why. I hope you believe me when I..."

"Shh, it's okay. Come here. It's all right."

From the rock, Netra peered over at them under scaled lids, reptilian eyes blinking slowly under the sun.

~

NIGHTTIME.

After the incident this morning with the colonel, neither man had called on Anzi again. No surprise there. Bisset was Bisset, and that the Emperor had left the throne room for her at all was a miracle. Someone must have cleared out the hallways beforehand so none of the staff could look upon his face.

And after all that fuss, all she was left with was this. Trapped in a room she had come to think of as 'hers,' permanently, with heaps of luxurious food set on tables around her bed that servants had brought in earlier. It seemed Tet was so pleased with her that he had ordered the most grandiose treatment for her, usually reserved only for the wealthiest of foreign dignitaries. Good. No matter how stupid and hollow all this was to her, it meant her real goal was in sight: gaining the Emperor's trust. From his right hand, she would have the highest vantage point. She just had to keep working, keep deceiving, keep cutting down everyone else around him until she got there. And when she did, she would make sure they all fell in shambles. But getting closer to Tet meant more than privilege, more than advantage. It meant danger. Because she would be close enough to kill, too, if she ever slipped outside the lines of his favor. One wrong step, and she wouldn't have the safety of distance between them. A wrung neck, gasping her last breath on the stone floor as he stood over her. Mangled, broken...

A thin layer of cold sweat formed over her brow as she fought back the terrible memories. She could still feel the unending pain that refused to leave, the taught fear she didn't think she could ever un-learn. He had dominated her utterly, and even if her mind retained its sensibility, even if she had the strength to rail against him in her thoughts, it was impossible to make her body forget. Every shattered bone would remember what he'd done forever and tremble at it. Maybe in the distant future, she could overcome him, but she couldn't wait that long. People were dying. Dying, she thought as she clenched her fists on top of the covers, just like Hosef. A man who hadn't deserved his end. How many? How many like him?

She couldn't wait. She had to act. And since she couldn't do this alone, she had no choice but to ask for help. From Isvan, from Rania, from Letti, even from…

Out of the distant darkness, a flame roared to life, and her chest tightened with all the crushing emotions suddenly sweeping her up, emotions that were too intense and foreign to be her own. Cold. Hot. Anger. Panic. Relief. And something else beneath it all that blossomed like a wildfire consuming dry wood, terrible and addicting and so fierce she couldn't even begin to understand what it was.

But that wasn't what she was here for. Not that.

"Hello, Kai. It's been a while."

59

nzi!

She pushed out all of Kai's emotions. She couldn't handle them. Too intense, too heavy, too much. The way his mind tried to swamp hers the instant she stepped into his mind—she wasn't going to deal with it.

Anzi, what's happened to you? Why are you-

"Hurt? Because that's part of my job. If you keep asking me why I'm hurt every time you see me, I'm going to start wondering if you know what a soldier actually does."

Don't do this now, he snapped, startling her. He sounded terrible. She didn't know how an inner voice could sound as fatigued as a physical one —but no, it wasn't mere fatigue. It was rough and hollow like a boulder chiseled out from the inside, full of crags and brittle spikes. *I'm coming to you. And you won't stop me this time. I'm coming for you.*

"Careful, sounds like a threat," she said, light and sardonic. Could she calm him? She hadn't expected him to be so angry. "Maybe I should come back later. You don't seem like you're in the mood for visitors."

The whole world plummeted downward, and she reeled from the sudden vertigo of the abrupt plunge. It took her a second to realize Kai had shot to his feet. He must have been sitting on the ground. *Don't leave me,* he growled, voice raw and twisted like braided leather. She shuddered. Why was he being like this? All she'd wanted was to talk. It had been a mistake to reach out no matter how desperate she was for allies.

"I'll come back later," she lied. "Maybe tomorrow night—"

You won't let me in, but you let me feel it every time you're hurt. Every time someone hurts you!

She recoiled at the guttural edge of his voice. He sounded—so different. His voice, his presence, everything was different. There was something terrifyingly primal creeping out and seeping into her from him, dark and heavy.

No more. If I have to stand here one more time and do nothing while you— He broke off with a snarl that made her shrink back, except she had nowhere to go. She couldn't even withdraw and escape his mind anymore. He was holding her fast somehow so that she couldn't fade away. Panic simmered, then streaked out in every direction from her core, burning and bright—

Don't, he said. *Don't be afraid. I would never hurt you. Anzi, please-*

She struggled, fear killing her senses one by one. She couldn't get out. She was trapped, tied down and staked all the way through. It was just like when Bisset had impaled her leg with his sword and pinned her to the ground, and although there was no pain, the cold terror of feeling her connection with her true body dissolve and break slashed her open deeper than any corporeal weapon could.

She couldn't make a single sound, couldn't scream. She lashed out, trying to break free of the suffocating darkness that closed in around her, but soon she was borne down into the depths of it where she twitched, desperate for freedom far out of reach. She'd made a mistake, a voice screamed inside her as it thrashed and ripped itself apart over and over, drowning in panic. This had been a mistake-

Don't, she heard Kai groan, and he sounded as if he were dying. Something echoed back to her, the sensation of jagged pain that wasn't hers. *I have to. I can't let you go. I can't.*

Him. So it was him, he was admitting it outright. He was the one trapping her here, severing her ability to return to herself. Her heart swelled, cracked, tore open. "You said you couldn't!" she cried, barely able to string together the right words past the sheer animal terror threatening to swallow her entire soul. "You said you couldn't make me do anything I don't want to." Yes, he'd said that to her, he'd even told her—"You said I can leave anytime I want!"

I can't let you go, he said again. *You keep doing this to yourself. I won't let you. Stay with me. Stay with me, I'm coming to you and I'll never let anyone hurt you again-*

"Let me go!" she shrieked. She had never begged like this before. Had never been this helpless, raging against something hopelessly immovable. Had she ever met an adversary she couldn't fight? Even breathing was becoming too hard. Her heart pounded harder and faster with every second until she could feel it about to explode out of her chest-

Stop! she heard Kai shout, but his voice was tinny and distant in her ears as if he were suddenly a thousand miles away. *Stop, you're killing yourself, don't fight me, Anzi, please-*

She didn't know if she fell unconscious or if it was simply the blind terror that blacked out her memory. Maybe it was both. But when her eyes shot open and she felt bunched covers under her hands instead of the numb blankness of the void, she let out a choked sob before scrambling to sit up. A second later, she was doubled over the side of the infirmary bed and vomiting with hacking coughs and wheezes. Her eyes burned, and the acrid taste of bile climbed into her throat and her nose as she struggled to catch her breath.

From the dimly lit corner off on the far side of the infirmary, someone shot up from the table and hurried over. The physician's journeyman assistant, she thought, still half-numb but now present enough to process her surroundings. "I'm fine," she croaked when he brandished an ugly plant stalk. "Just a nightmare."

"No, no, I was warned about this. It's magic overflow, you've had to absorb so much so quickly from the healing. They said you need to take this when it happens."

"It's not magic overflow," she said and even managed to insert a sneering scoff in the middle of it somewhere. Maybe on the wrong syllable, but she was too drained to care. "Like I said, a nightmare."

"But—"

"Go away. I'm not vulnerable to overflow. Don't you know who I am?"

She hated forcing attention toward her status as a First Guard—how could she possibly be proud of such a title now?—but it was the only way to bring the overenthusiastic journeyman to heel. She didn't want him touching her, didn't want anything at all touching her, and he was far too close for comfort. Even the faint sensation of his body heat made her shudder, and her overactive senses twisted and writhed.

"Just leave me alone. I'm tired. Going back to sleep."

"I have to clean this up first, I'm so sorry. I'll do it right away."

Sudden guilt washed over her. Shit. That was right, she had vomited. Somehow she had forgotten. It was like her head had been reduced to wet parchment, stretched and soggy and falling apart. A single botched encounter had reduced her to a squirming, cowardly worm. She clenched her teeth, resisting the urge to shout and scream her frustration until her lungs withered. How could she be so weak? She hated it. Hated herself.

As for Kai—she had no idea how to feel about him. What he had done was unthinkable. He had lied to her, held her captive. And maybe he had let her go in the end, but even as she struggled and demanded her freedom, he had refused to let her go. How could he?

She would not go to him again. She had made a grave mistake in trusting him. Yes, the terrible emotions she had felt spilling over their connection had been genuine, had been real enough to make her want to stop whatever it was she was doing to make him feel such transcendent pain and suffering. And yes, deep down she knew he must not have meant to do this to her—but there was the rub. He hadn't been able to restrain himself. Until tonight, she had never seen him lose control, had never seen the foreign, beastly nature inside. He had been like darkness drowning out her single candle flame, violent, hard, overwhelming.

Whatever it was, she couldn't trust him anymore. Maybe he hadn't meant to hurt her, but reality came before feelings. Came before faith. He was out, then. She couldn't ask him for help. Not now, maybe not ever.

She gave the journeyman healer an apologetic look when he stood back up. "Sorry," she said. "I didn't mean to take it out on you."

"If you're very sorry, perhaps a little nibble of medicine…"

Her gaze sharpened. "Not *that* sorry," she corrected. "Go back and do whatever it was you were up to. I'll be fine. I'm just going to wash up and be right back."

"I should go with—"

"Try it. See what happens."

All right, so she was still too testy to maintain a civil conversation. Damn Kai for how much he had rattled her, body and soul. And damn herself for being so weak that her body yet quivered in muted fear of sleep. She couldn't get any rest like this. Not when her heart twisted and lurched at the thought of accidentally falling into Kai's grasp again. And even after a half hour of soaking in the hot medicinal bath the palace maids set up for her, she still had yet to shake it off. It couldn't be helped. Netra was still dead asleep in her nest back in the infirmary corner, but she was sure to throw a fit if she woke up to find Anzi gone. She might as well climb back into bed and pretend to sleep.

And until the sun rose, she did just that.

～

"Anzi, dear, is that you?"

"Yes, sir."

"Oh, good. One second, I'll be there soon."

"Please take your time, Your Excellency."

"Yes, good, yes, follow me out—what was that you said, Anzi?"

She pressed her lips together, affording herself only a split second of annoyance while he was still out of sight. What was he doing back there past the drapes behind the throne? "Nothing, sir."

"Hm, thought you said something. Never mind. All right, are you ready? I've prepared a wonderful gift for you."

She frowned. A gift? What was he talking about? Ah, her custom uniform, perhaps, along with her weapons. Those had been commissioned before she left with Bisset for the impromptu trip to the desert outpost and then to Lumenera. It seemed too soon, but maybe the commissions had been rushed. Small pleasures—she hated the circumstances, but she had always loved new weapons. "I wish you hadn't," she said, making sure to pitch her voice just so with the optimal intensity of guilty shame and modesty. "I haven't done anything to deserve a gift of any—oh."

She heaved in her next breath so sharply she almost choked. The only reason she didn't was because the sheer shock of the sight that met her utterly paralyzed her throat.

"So? What do you think? You like it, eh? The other boys all loved getting gifts like this, so I just adjusted it for your type, I think." He made a flourishing gesture...at the line of several nearly-nude men who filed out behind him and stood at attention before Anzi. "I didn't have much time so I couldn't pick out more than a handful, but you are privileged to receive this personally selected gift basket from me." Tet reached down to tweak her nose. "The loin clothes were a last minute addition, but I thought it would suit your tastes. You're a desert dweller, right?"

"...I am."

"Perfect. Now, I give you these on one condition. Go on, ask me."

"...What is your condition, Your Excellency."

"That should be obvious! Why are you asking that." He tweaked her nose again. "When Kaizat comes back, he's not going to be very happy that he has to share you. So...?" He looked at her expectantly, and she had no choice but to swallow her dull horror and answer.

"I should be discreet with...your gift, when he returns."

"That's right! But until he comes back, you get to have as much fun as you like. And yes, while he's here, I expect you to reserve your body exclusively for him, but after he leaves again, tada! I know you'll enjoy yourself immensely. And I have even better news for you, my dear. I'm going to keep you close by in the palace so you don't have to spend your time flying this way and that, at least for a while. You see, I have need of your talents besides the situation with Kaizat-Amun. How long has it been since you were last in the Cave? Have you gone to see Bastien yet?"

"No, sir."

"Well, why not!"

She tore her eyes away from the scanty white loincloths the men wore and looked down at her leg instead. Tet followed her gaze and made an amused sound.

"Ah, that's right. Forgot Alexandre skewered your leg and ruined a perfectly good conformation. Very disappointed in him, still, by the way"

Another expectant look. She bowed her head. "I'll be sure not to make the same mistakes he did, Your Excellency. If nothing else, I hope you can look at it as a learning experience for me. I'll remember it for life."

"Is there anything you want from him? Payback, revenge, anything?"

She had been expecting this. Had even been hoping for it, for him to test her with a probing question. "Of course not, Your Excellency. He's my comrade. As you said, we should all get along. Whatever his misstep with you, you've resolved it, sir, and I hold nothing against him."

"Oh, good girl. You always know what to say to put me back in good spirits. Now, I'll have your new boys sent to your room so you can have your fun before you go down to meet Bastien tonight, but let's see...Ah, that's right. The reason I'll be keeping you here is because you're going to hatch more eggs for me, how does that sound! Exciting, right?"

He was talking to her like she was a puppy, or perhaps a child. But as degrading as it was, it was better than being hurled into the wall and strangled like Bisset, or being kicked until her ribs were in pieces. She could tolerate this if only because it meant she was alive and not in miserably agony. "Yes, sir."

"And to be specific, you'll be hatching eggs for...what did he call it?"

He snapped his fingers and nodded. "Auxiliary riders! That's right. I think it's a fine name, a bit pompous, but then again Bastien's the one who came up with the name for the Premier Guard back then, too…Predictable. Anyhow, I've been told you already know the ones we'll be bringing in for training. They served with you before?"

She paused, uncertain whether to pretend ignorance. Yes, she knew— it would be Pierro, Doufan, and Aimee. But she only knew because Oscar had told her, and she couldn't risk casting even a shadow of a suspicion upon him. "I've served with many soldiers, yes," she said. Maybe he would think she was an idiot, but it was better to err on the side of caution.

"I mean the ones you last trained with, dear. Before you came here."

"Yes, sir. There were three of them in particular."

"That's them!" He snapped his fingers again. "Another woman and two men. Interesting, actually, I wonder if we can have the four of you breed in the future and breed some children compatible with the eggs…Hm, I'll have someone look into that, don't know why it didn't occur to me until now. But anyway! That's that. You've got your gift and your mission. That is, you'll be hatching those eggs and training up the three of them to serve under you."

"Serve under—won't they be First Guards as well, Your Excellency?"

"Ah. No. We've tested them, and they're no good. I've an open mind, but I have my favorites, and then there are the rest. They can't hatch their own eggs which annoys me, so they go into the latter group. And you'll be the one in charge of them! You get to do whatever you want, by the way. They don't count so they're expendable." He patted her on her head. "I'm sure you have a lot of pent up frustration to let out after everything you've been through. Which is why you'll love your gift! Go ahead and enjoy your concubines. I wanted to present them personally since you've been such a darling."

"I—yes, sir."

"And don't forget! I know it's easy for your sort to get lost in the thrall of a very sound and enthusiastic fuck, but I really do need you to show up to help Bastien tonight. I want three eggs hatched and sorted out by the end of the month, no exceptions." His smile disappeared, and she drew in a sharp inhale at the sudden chill he exuded. "You can do that, can't you, Anzi."

"Yes, sir."

"Wonderful! Now go and busy yourself. Ta, Anzi dear."

60

The entire way back up to her room, all Anzi could think about was what Kai would do if he appeared this very second. She didn't know why. She was still jarred by what he had done to her last night, and her skin crawled at the memory of being trapped under the strength of his presence. She didn't know if she would have died if he'd held on any longer, but it had certainly felt that way. Even now, her heartbeat quickened, and her pulse throbbed in her neck with remembered fear. Maybe he hadn't meant to, but the damage was done. She couldn't even fall asleep again lest she accidentally transport herself to him and end up imprisoned once more.

So why was she still thinking about him now? If she could drive a hammer into her skull to knock out her wandering thoughts, she would. She'd promised herself she would stay away from him no matter what, regardless of the suspicion she had that he hadn't been in his right mind when *it* had happened. If anything, that was precisely the reason she couldn't trust him.

She closed her eyes and paused before her door. She had never been the sort to pray, but she begged the unanswering void for a sliver of guidance as to what to do now. Her mind was stuck on Kai and the terrible, primal energy he had released last night that she could still feel washing all over and straight through her. Meanwhile, four men in loincloths were waiting patiently behind her for her to let them into her room. How had this happened. Was this the cost of gaining Tet's favor? Maybe it wasn't worth it after all. The one thing she was grateful for was that Letti hadn't wandered over to find her and run into this latest disaster-

"Anzi? What's—what's going on?"

Shit.

∼

SHE HADN'T KNOWN what to do. She didn't want them in her room, but she had no idea how to go about asking if they could be put in their own so she could have her space. Letti, on the other hand, seemed to think she was both insane and stupid for even considering such a thing. She also made no attempt to hide this opinion.

"Are you blind?" the harem girl demanded. "Or are you neutered. Do you not see how beautiful they are?"

"I'm not interested in oiled legs and chests, Letti."

"You can't tell me you didn't catch a glimpse behind those flappy little cloths—"

"I said I'm not interested! End of story."

The woman rocked back on the bed with a sudden knowing look. Her eyebrows came down hard as she stared at Anzi, who narrowed her own eyes and slowly turned to face her. She didn't like the look she was wearing. Not in the least. "I know what it is," the woman announced. "You're pining after the chieftain! I knew it. Woman, I hate to break it to you, but a kiss does not mean he owns you! You're a free animal, so do as you like."

Anzi choked. Hard. It took her several tries to speak past the knot in her throat, and even then she stammered. She never, ever stammered. "Y-you don't know what you're talking about. I wasn't even thinking about him! Why would I. He's just a mission, and I already succeeded!"

"Succeeded in what, falling head over heels for him? Please, I know that look on your face. It's the look the girls get when they fall for marks whose pants they're supposed to be wriggling into so they can get information. The ooey-gooey eyes as they think about, ooh, what if things were different and they could run away together to another kingdom where no one will recognize them. Ooh, and marriage, and ooh, babies—"

"Babies! Letti, I swear to every god if you don't be quiet—"

"Ha! Try me. I've seen straight through you. You're thinking about tall, dark, and handsome as if he's already got you with what's behind *his* loincloth—"

"He doesn't wear a loincloth!" Anzi raged, shooting to her feet. Letti did the same with a triumphant smirk.

"I bet you wish he did!" she shouted back. "I bet that's why you won't even bother peeking at the ones standing out there with those firm buttocks you could crush rocks between. You're already hypnotized."

There was no point arguing with the harem girl. For all Anzi's fearsome determination to win the argument and prove her wrong, Letti was still the better speaker by far. She had Anzi stammering again in fury within seconds, until at last they were both glaring at each other with their fists clenched at their sides and breathing hard.

"...Truce, then," Letti offered. "I know I'm right, but I'll let you off the hook for a little bit since I came to see you for a reason. It's important."

...Fine. She felt as if she'd been losing the fight anyway, so it was good that they could end it like this. Damn Letti for being so good at talking. "What is it," she snapped, using her strongest irritated voice to conceal her relief. "It had better be good. You shouldn't be seeking me out like this if you don't want to attract attention."

"Oh, please." She flapped her hand with a dismissive snort. "Sneaking around is my forte. They don't even know I'm gone yet. I'm still in the springs, in case you wanted to know what the guards and the girls think."

She was good at that, Anzi had to admit. "Fine. What is it."

"Well, rumor is that wyrm attacks have crippled the trade routes by the desert, all the way up and all the way down. And they're advancing inward, too, more and more. All except one place. That one's been completely free of the wyrm attacks, and they've actually been able to send out more soldiers to other outposts instead. Curious."

"Where? Which place are you talking about?"

"Somewhere near Territory Five or something. I don't remember the names of the villages they were talking about, but the outpost is manned by a Captain Gorien. His name sounds ghastly, doesn't it?"

Anzi said nothing. She was too stunned to comment. Letti took advantage of her silence to deliver the rest of her news at whip-crack speed:

"There are also other rumors about dragons. It's been all over the continent, not just here. Word is that there's going to be a huge parade, a celebration the likes of which has never been seen before. It's going to be right here in the Imperial City, all to celebrate the return of the dragons. I remember what you said, Anzi, but I can't help but think this isn't what it seems. I just don't understand how your chieftain can have anything to do with them. They're been gone forever. Everyone knows. The last of the dragons are with their riders in the Premier, and no one else has—"

"How much did I tell you?"

"About what?"

"Kai and the dragons."

"...Why are you asking me that, and why are you looking that way at me?"

"Because," Anzi said honestly. "I'm trying to figure out how little I can tell you without you knowing I'm withholding information."

"How dare you!" Letti's hand shot forward, and she pinched Anzi on the underside of her breast.

"Ow! What the—don't do that!" Shit. That had actually hurt. What the hell? Was that some kind of secret harem girl maneuver to disable their enemies? That hurt worse than being kicked in the back of the knee. With a grimace, she rubbed at the sore spot and stabbed Letti with a venomous glare. "This is for your own good. I'm trying to protect you."

"Well, you should change your tactics," the harem girl shot back as she fixed Anzi with a fierce glare of her own. "Because from where I stand, it looks like you're the one who could do with some protection."

Indignation flared through her. "Excuse me?"

"You're not excused. I'm going to tell it like it is. You're always getting into trouble and getting hurt every single time I hear about you or see you. Obviously, you're doing something wrong."

"I fight! It's what I do!"

"And yet I don't see this happening to anyone else."

Maybe it was because what Letti said reminded her a little too vividly of Kai's words, too, but she was fast crossing into the territory of Anzi's anger. She set her mouth in a hard scowl. "I'm in a different position from everyone else," she said coolly. "I won't be compared to people who don't have to risk what I do. I can handle anything that comes at me, whenever and wherever."

"So you invite being hurt just to prove you can *handle* it?" Letti waved her hands in a mocking gesture of astonished fear. "Oooh~ That's so impressive! Listen, Anzi. Do you know what's really impressive? Do you want to know what's a real demonstration of skill? It's being able to do something without being caught. It's doing something without getting hurt. It's being so good you make it look easy. But you—you're always bleeding and bruised and getting hurt. Stop it! Stop doing that."

For a moment, Anzi struggled to hurl back a fiery insult just as prickly, a difficult feat because she had no idea what Letti's weakness was, while her own couldn't be more obvious—her pride. But then she recognized the gleam in the harem's girl's eyes, recognized the way her face scrunched up with words she had held back. And that was when she realized—Letti was afraid. Afraid for her.

It stunned her to silence once more, and she floundered for words when none came. Damn it. *Damn* it. "I'll...be more careful," she grumbled. "But some things are unavoidable. I have to do what I have to do. Even if you think I'm unskilled for it, or whatever other criticism you have. I'm doing the best I can with what's at my disposal."

Letti's eyes glimmered brighter. "All right. Just...don't forget that I care. You can be a warrior all you want and smash things with your sticks, but you should know that whenever you disappear somewhere, I'm always waiting. I'm always hoping you come back safely."

"...All right," said Anzi, with difficulty. "I'm sorry."

"Don't be. Just please, be more careful. It's harder to be the one waiting, Anzi. You never stop for long enough to know that, but one day... You'll understand."

She hoped not. It sounded horrible.

❧

"Long time no see, Anzi."

She came to a stop. The main cavern was half-dim and gloomy, the same as ever after weeks away, and the man's voice echoed in eerie fashion as it bounced all around the craggy walls before pooling at her feet like a fading ghost.

"Hello, Pierro," she said.

"And Doufan, and Aimee," he added. He jabbed a thumb backward over his shoulder in the direction of the two sitting at the long table. "I can see you haven't changed much except for that nasty plank you've got strapped to your leg. Wouldn't happen to want to give sparring a try, would you? Bet I'd lay you out flat now. Might even straighten that leg out for you. How about it?"

She didn't react. Once upon a time, she might have chosen between firing back with a cutting remark or ignoring him and rolling her eyes instead, but she hardly had the energy for it. Just looking at him exhausted her. Was this what she had been like when she first stepped into the Cave? Had she looked so excited and thrilled? Of course she had.

Maybe even more so. At least Pierro was doing his best to keep his composure and be his suave self, and Aimee and Doufan were silently watching, absorbing everything with caution. She hadn't been nearly so cautious. She had been overjoyed, brash. Besides the annoyance that Bastien had been, she remembered nothing but sheer happiness and wonder and gratitude for having been privileged to come so far.

And now, this Cave meant nothing to her except as a symbol of the things she hated most. The sanctuary of the dragon riders, Tet's hideaway for murderers, thieves, monsters. That was all this place was, a massive nest of them. The only thing that redeemed it was the existence of the dragon eggs hidden deep inside, the hundreds of unborn lives waiting. Waiting. Waiting to be freed and rescued.

And yet...here she was. Standing in the Cave with no choice but to quicken the hatching of three more dragons who would have to live out their lives in the cruel, ruthless service of humans who would dominate them as if they were nothing more than common animals. She didn't even know how to stop it. If she could, she would at least pretend uselessness and beg off of the task, but every egg responded to her mere touch, her presence. It was too late. From the very night Bastien had led her around the nest room and had her put her hands on them all, she had stirred them out of sleep. Now she knew. Some had more time than others, but the rest...the unlucky few, they wouldn't escape this fate. Her stomach churned.

"Guess this life is more dangerous than I thought it would be," Pierro said. "I never thought I would ever see you hurt like this. How'd you get it? Fighting in the winterlands, maybe? Or did you run into a pack of wyrms and fight them off single-handed? Or wait. Maybe you conquered a city all on your own with only that one injury to show for it, I bet."

He was mocking her now, openly. She couldn't tell if he was doing it out of malice or simply bored. And then she realized—she didn't care. His insults were sliding past her like slippery feet on a frozen lake surface. He used to be able to rile her up so easily, and he was saying the same garbage now—but what of it?

"Bastien," she said flatly. "You're here."

From behind Pierro's hulking figure, the other man popped out and sent her a mischievous smile. Gods, she hadn't missed that. She wanted nothing more than to plant her fist in his face, and he wasn't even trying to provoke her the way Pierro was. "Nothing slips by you," the man said with a wide grin. "But you're late, so I already introduced myself to your friends."

Not her friends, she almost snapped. "I'm not late. I'm on time."

"Hm, so you always say. But no matter, you're here to hatch eggs and to whip these little idiots into shape. You three, you understand the situation, don't you? Turn around and look at me so I know you're paying attention." He waited until they obeyed. "From today onward, you answer to this lady here, the one who whispers to dragons. Fancy, no? I agree. But she's more than fancy. In order, the masters of your fate are thusly: the Emperor, and then Anzi. She owns you from here on out. Yes? Easy to grasp?"

He didn't wait to hear their answers, and truthfully, neither did she. She didn't want to. She'd never asked for this. If she could, if she could have anything she wanted, she would leave and never look back, never remember any of this. But that was impossible. She was here, and this was happening.

"You know what comes next, don't you, Anzi?" Bastien beckoned her forward with the same terrible smile she had come to hate so much. "Dragon time. I hope you remember that second egg you were about to hatch. I notice you didn't bring Netra today, but you should have. This will be her first brother. And I hope for so, so many more."

She wanted to vomit. She had no way of stopping this. Even if she fled, they would drag her back and bind her hand and foot, press her up against the eggs and force her to hatch them that way against her will. No choice. She fought so hard, so hard—and yet impossibly, inexorably, horrifically, the miry swamp pulled her in.

"That's right, keep going, girl. You're doing wonderful."

Stop, she begged her magic. Stop, she begged the dragon stirring inside the burnt-red egg she held in her palms. Stop, everything…

But it was futile. She stared down at the broken remnants of the egg and the dragon that sat on her palms on top of them. Dark red scales, horned frill, scaly gaze watching her…

"Congratulations, Anzi. You have another dragon."

61

Was-Serqet was her name.

This time, it wasn't a whisper of a suggestion from an unknowable, outside force. The name came from inside her, welling up like a spring breaking through the earth for the first time to bubble out in a stream flowing downhill. It was there, it was alive, it had power. Snakebite-quick. Strength. Resilience. This was Was-Serqet.

From her bed, Anzi watched as Netra raised her spines and crept around the new hatchling on the floor. Serqet followed her progress, turning in place with slow shuffles as her wide claws clicked against the wood. Dark red, compact, covered in segmented armor from behind the frill all the way down her flanks and rump. An also-segmented tail that unmistakably resembled a scorpion's, right down to the coiled curl and what could only be the nub of a growing stinger at its tip. It twitched and hovered over her back, staying pointed at Netra as the latter circled the younger dragon with a growing growl.

"Behave," Anzi warned. "I don't care whether you like her or not. You're going to get along, understand?" The white-scaled dragonet made an angry hissing sound like a rattlesnake whose tail had been stepped on, but Anzi was having none of it. She was tired, sore, frustrated, and now more sleep-deprived than ever thanks to returning late from the Cave last night. Bastien had insisted on getting Serqet acquainted with all three of her 'auxiliary riders' to see who was most compatible with the hatchling, and no matter how many times Anzi had insisted it was impossible to tell, he had made her stay anyway. All of them. It had been the most irritating, fruitless exercise of her patience in a long while, arguing back and forth with the man who thought he knew all there was to dragons.

Although in truth, she had been lying, so there was that. She hadn't known for certain whether Serqet would attach herself to anyone so soon and therefore had no idea that she wouldn't, either. Even Netra's decision to attach herself to Rania the piscin girl had been completely unexpected. Anzi knew absolutely nothing.

Luckily, she had spared dramatics last night. Pierro, Aimee, Doufan, all three of them had watched in rapt attention as the little dragon hunkered down and waited on the stone floor, twitching every so often toward the pile of raw meat waiting for it an arm's length away. So different, so foreign, nothing like Anzi had expected: she had been waiting for it to begin screeching and dive into the food as Netra would have, but it seemed not all hatchlings were created equal. This one wasn't hungry enough to take her dark, glittering eyes off anyone in the vicinity, choosing instead to remain as still and patient as a stone. Cautious and quiet, Serqet was nothing like Netra.

That was another peculiar thing about her—her eyes. All-black, round and beady and unblinking. They might have been sinister if they weren't hooded by double-layered eyelids that flickered open and closed. They shone with a luster like obsidian glass, and upon seeing their color, Anzi had been reminded abruptly of the mages' Tower and its black-glassed base. And of Oza. She wondered whether he was still waiting for her to visit again, unaware she could do no such thing. Not yet. Not until she was sure she wouldn't be putting him in danger.

Even though he would be ecstatic if he could see her now, watching over two live dragons right in her very room. Months ago, the thought of hatching even one had been a scintillating dream, beyond her reach but craved for still, but two? Two! And if Bastien and Tet had their way, there would be far more. Yet, instead of exciting her, the prospect made her sick to her stomach. This wasn't fair. None of it was.

A knock on the door shoved her out of her angry thoughts. Quick as lightning, she shot up from the bed and turned toward the door, eyes honing in to glare at the rattling handle. Excuse them? Trying to enter before she had even invited them in? Her first thought was that it might be the Emperor, presumptuous as he was, but he wouldn't have bothered to knock in the first place even as a formality. Letti would have put her cupped mouth to the door and begun nagging her already, so it wasn't her. So who had the gall to—

"Hey, shut-in, let me see you for a minute."

Her glare sharpened further. "Not now, Pierro. I'm tired."

"Sounds like a personal problem."

She really hadn't missed what he tried to pass off as banter. Now that she had spent some time away from the egotistical bastard, she could appreciate how nice it had been to have him and his constant provocations out of her hair. "Have I told you that you and Oscar are more similar than I thought?" she asked through the door. She had yet to move any closer to it even though the rattling of the handle was growing louder and louder. Try it, she thought. Break it. She would make sure he learned the price of his meddling and subsequent vandalism.

"Oscar can't hold a candle to me. Come on, let me in before I break your lock."

"You're not going to like what happens if you do."

"Don't be an asshole, Anzi. I thought some time apart would mellow you out. Anyway, I'm coming in whether you like it or not."

Her lips curled up into a sneer even though the last thing she wanted to do was smile. From the floor, Netra stopping slinking around Serqet and stared at the door as well, slender, cat-like body vibrating with a warning growl. "Whether I like it or not," Anzi repeated. "All right. So long as you know what happens when you walk inside without my permission."

The rattling stopped, and in the abrupt silence, her eyes remained narrowed in displeasure. She had never really compared him with his younger cousin before, but now that she considered Pierro's traits from a respectable distance, it wasn't so difficult to see how they both harbored an overbearing streak with their pompousness. They both liked to shove their way into spaces they didn't belong in and shoulder their way to the top, or others out of the way. Well, that wasn't happening now.

"You're really going to be like that? You're going to pull rank on me and try to scare me into submitting?"

"Having my permission to enter my room has nothing to do with rank." Her voice was even colder now. "I don't care what you want with me. Unless someone is dying or the Emperor himself tells me to mind you, I'm going to rest. And you aren't going to bother me."

"Damn you, Anzi. You're the same stuck-up ass you were when we met."

"I don't mind the insults so long as they don't wake me." She sat back down on the bed. "Whatever you came to talk about can obviously wait, or else you wouldn't be wasting time trying to fight me about it."

"Yeah, because no one would ever win in a fight against you."

"The sarcasm is pointless unless your only goal is to make me want to humor you even less. Later, Pierro. I mean it."

A brief silence. Then: "My grandparents have invited you for a formal dinner tonight. I wanted to give you a heads up."

She rolled her eyes. Upper-crust denizens of the Imperial City did like their useless frivolities. Stupidly fancy table settings and political ramblings shared over sips of soup more expensive than the entire annual wages of a foot soldier in the army. "We don't have time for dinner invitations," she said tightly. "There's training tonight."

"Not until late. You should just get it over with, they won't let this go. The sooner you make them happy, the sooner they'll get off your back."

"What is it they want from me? Your family's notorious for hating anyone who hails from anywhere further than the Imperium's walls."

"Joining the Premier changes a lot of things for you, in case you haven't noticed. You're sought-after now. A real princess."

"But what do they want."

"The usual. More connections. More power. Oscar's going to be there. I'm guessing they want you to find a way to get him in the Premier, too. Like us."

Like us, he said, with a note of confiding smugness as if they were in an exclusive club too good for anyone else. What did he know? What did he know of the rotten putrefaction that existed below the Premier's gilded exterior? And even if she did tell him, would he care? He had never been in it for the glory of anything except his own. A lover of fighting, of winning, of women, of pleasures unattainable for others, 'lower' others—how was it that she had tolerated him for as long as she had? "You know I'm not going," she said. "We don't have time for socializing."

"It's not socializing. It's my family."

"And you have time to share meals with them? Instead of training?"

"Not all of us fill every hour of our lives trying to prove we're good enough. Or that we're better than everyone else."

No. Because Pierro already believed that of himself. "I'm not interested."

"What? I just told you Oscar's going to be there. What other excuse do you need to see him?"

The note of surprise and disdain in his voice was so genuine she had to stop and process it for a full, extended moment. She blinked, several times. "What?"

"Oscar. He's going to be there."

"And…this changes my mind, why?"

"Knock it off. He already told me what's going on. You two sneaking around trying to see each other and shit. I know all about it."

She blinked again. In the distance, a cat yowled. "I *what?*"

"Whatever. He already told me everything. Anyway, I thought I'd do you a favor just this once, but seeing as how it's unappreciated, I'll leave you alone. Oscar's going to be pretty disappointed. He was telling me that's why he would owe me one if I managed to get you to come over, but having him under my thumb isn't worth the effort of trying to place nice with you when you're being an asshole. Later."

All at once, a flash of understanding seared her confusion and alarm. Of course. Code. Oscar must have something to tell her per their agreement, information she couldn't get anywhere else without attracting suspicion. With how difficult it had been lately to find excuses to meet, he must have engineered something to their benefit. Or maybe his and Pierro's grandparents had proposed the idea of an invitation on their own and he was simply taking advantage of it. Either way, now she knew what was going on.

"Fine," she said, knowing the other solider was still waiting on the other side of the door despite his flippant farewell. It nauseated her to think that he truly believed she and his cousin had something going on between them, but it wasn't a bad idea. She had to admit that much. "I'll be there. What time."

"I'll come pick you up in about four hours."

"It's still morning."

"Early dinner. We have training tonight, remember?"

Damn him. She was frustrated, exhausted, and more than ever, she wanted to shut herself away and take a long, long break that no one would disturb. Her leg was still killing her, too. "Fine. Don't be late."

"Of course not, lord and master. I would never dare."

…One day, she would get another chance to drill Pierro into the dirt and adjust his attitude. Maybe even tonight. She looked down at Serqet and Netra on the floor and noted their stares, how they watched her without a sound. How long it would be before she had three, then four dragons in her room—that is, if she didn't have to surrender them. Her gut churned at the thought of entrusting any of them to her so-called auxiliaries. They knew nothing. Even when she used to train with them, she had always mistrusted them all on the basis of their ulterior motives, their unclear purposes. It was good for her that they weren't loyal unto death to the Empire the way she used to be, but that didn't mean they would ever be on her side. If anything, they would the ones who wanted most to tear her down because once she was gone, logic dictated one of them would take her place. They were the other candidates, after all, that she had competed against to get here. She doubted any of them had the specific traits Tet was searching for—his preoccupation with wyrms and the domination of dragons spoke of something more pointed and sinister —but they didn't know that. All they would know was that she was the one who had gone ahead of them and carved out a place for herself in the Premier, had found fame and glory and dragons.

That wasn't how it had happened, and she had neither fame nor glory. But what did they know? They were her most dangerous enemies now. She needed to tread carefully even as she pretended to train them, needed to keep them at a disadvantage without being suspected. She had to come out on top.

"We're going to have a time of it," she told both dragons. "Both of you better be on my side."

DINNER WAS A DISGUSTING AFFAIR. Not only did she not know how to eat most of the elaborate dishes laid out on the banquet table that seated more than two dozen of the frilled Bedeau dynasty, she had no idea what to make of the stupid table manners they all prescribed to with their gloved hands and simpering laughter. To pass the salt down the wrong side meant garnering wide-eyed looks and anti-hex hand signs (as if those even worked when they weren't magically gifted), and three times, Oscar kicked her under the table when she picked up the wrong fork. What the hell was the meaning of all this anyway when the food was supposed to end up in their gullets in the end? And worst of all was the continual cramping of her bad leg in these damned fancy chairs.

"Fucking brilliant idea," she hissed to him when he invited her out for a walk and a private conversation (to his grandparents' delight and Pierro's unimpressed rolling of his eyes). "You make a public spectacle of me instead of finding a way to take me aside without drawing attention. It had better be worth it, Oscar."

"Save it, gimp-leg. Do you have any idea how hard it is to get a hold of you? Do you realize that I had to jump through a thousand hoops just to end up spinning a wild story about how I'm courting you so I can have a few minutes to tell you something you wanted to know in the first place?"

She narrowed her eyes and glanced around. No one. The estate itself was small since property space was at a premium everywhere in the Imperial City, especially the upper districts, but the groundskeeper was trimming the hedges on the opposite side and there was no one lingering by the stone bench Oscar sat on.

"Sit next to me and act like we're talking about something stupid and shallow," he suggested. "Don't smile or laugh, since that'll give you away immediately. You'd never laugh. Or smile."

He was right. But she wasn't going to sit next to him. "Just spit it out. I'm busy."

"I bet. I heard about your new male harem, guess I should be glad you didn't bring them with you. Anyway, you should take the time to listen to everything I've learned while you can. I'm not going to be able to pass on anything else for a while."

"Just find a way to send a spell-sealed letter to me," she snorted. "Your family has connections with the Magisien body. They'll help."

"That's obviously not an option or I would have done that already. My grandparents couldn't even get approval to borrow you for one meal until they bribed the Emperor's advisors to allow it."

She stared. "What are you talking about. I'm the one who accepted the invitation."

"And we weren't allowed to invite you until we had permission." Oscar's blue eyes glittered at her. "You don't understand yet how difficult it is to even lick your boots now. It galls me to see you so ignorant of it that you aren't even taking any enjoyment in it."

She shifted. His words made her uncomfortable. She'd never asked to be so exclusive and elusive. "I was away for weeks," she told him. "That's why you couldn't get approval or whatever."

"No. It's not just that. But think what you will. Anyway, here's what I've learned. Whatever you and my cousin are up to, they're not satisfied. The Emperor's advisors, I mean. My best guess as to what they want to do next is get your loyal chieftain dog to 'donate' his dragons to the cause."

Her heart lurched. She had no idea what he was talking about. No, she did, she just didn't want to believe it. "They're going to force him to give up the dragons? The ones he's bringing now?"

"That's the idea, I think. From what I understand, he was only supposed to be bringing the wild dragons as proof they still exist and that he has them. Proof to the people. Performative grandstanding to get everyone excited about our prospects for further expansion."

"To the north, you mean."

"Yes. You know it's not a popular idea. The last time we sent forces up was before we were born, but my grandfather talks about it all the time. Decimated. It's the one time in our history that we've been so miserably defeated."

"So they're going to force Kai to give him the dragons to supplement our forces. Because I'm not working quickly enough."

"Kai? You call him Kai?"

She ignored him and paced to and fro with her hands clasped behind her back. Damn it, she should have known. She should have guessed her stalling would have consequences, but honestly, what was Kai thinking in cooperating to this extent? Why would he be bringing dragons to show them off when he so clearly despised the Empire for its role in nearly eradicating them? Or maybe she was the only one who knew his true feelings on the subject. Maybe he hid them from Tet and the advisors, maybe they had seduced him with promises of rich trade, money, power, influence...

But he wasn't like that. She was an idiot to pretend to know Kai any more deeply than she might a casual acquaintance, and yet she had sensed no greed for gold and glory in him. Especially the last time they had met...A flurry of goosebumps rose up all over her body at the memory of it. Past her terror at being trapped, she had felt such primal, elemental energy from him, something beyond, something animal. No hunger for prosperity, there. He would never bend to such promises.

So why? What was he up to? She dragged her hands down her face and glared hard over her fingertips at a nearby hedge. Kai, the ever-mysterious, when he wasn't being outrageously forward. A man full of contradictions she couldn't even begin to untangle.

"Oh, and mage scriers say he's only a day's journey away, so I'm assuming he's flying those dragons he's bringing. Which indicates he's tamed them. Take that as you will, I don't know anything beyond that. But something is happening, something big. You should be prepared."

She turned to look back at Oscar. Damn him. They used to be mortal enemies, or at least they used to treat each other that way, and here they were now...semi-plotting and on the brink of treason, if she were being honest. She never would have thought this egotistical idiot would ever throw in his lot with her. She still had to be careful, but...

"Thanks," she said, voice thick with a reluctant shade of gratitude. "I appreciate the trouble you went to."

"It's all right. You'll pay it back tenfold one day. You can't stand being in my debt."

She scowled. He was right. "You said he's a day's journey off?"

"Hard to say. Apparently we're not very good at estimating how fast dragons fly, but he's not far.

"I understand. If you hear anything else about the invasion or any movement in the troops—"

"I'll get it to you if I can. But it won't be easy."

"No. It won't be."

～

As it turned out, she had no opportunities to thrash Pierro for all his provocative talk. Bastien had her trying to hatch more eggs all night despite her protests, and Serqet and Netra watched from the corner where she had planted them with a firm command to stay where they were. Even Bastien hadn't dared to contradict her. In her towering mood, she was in no mood for arguing.

When her leg buckled from underneath her, that was that. She'd had a long day, and to her utter—though concealed—terror, she felt one particular dragon egg stir beneath her hands. Her magic was acting too fast, too compellingly, and although Bastien had missed it for now, there was no way she could hide it if it happened again.

"I'm going back," she announced. "My leg is killing me."

"Oh, Anzi girl. We're so close—"

"Then it won't matter if we wait another day," she snapped back. "Just leave me alone. We'll be back at it tomorrow anyway."

She hadn't waited for a dismissal. Why should she? She was starting to understand at long last her place in the hierarchy, especially after the incident with Bisset and being elevated to Tet's special favor. She would use it to her advantage now and make it clear to Bastien she would not be yanked around. Not tonight. She returned to the palace and threw herself into bed, ignoring Netra's occasional hissing and answering clicks from Serqet's claws and scorpion tail...

It was the middle of the night when the knock came at her door.

Her eyes flew open, and in an instant, she knew. She *knew.* Lnew it, felt it, saw and heard and sensed it in every way she couldn't explain. And in the darkness, she waited, stock-still...

"Anzi," a familiar voice murmured through the door. "Please, I need to see you."

She waited another moment. Then another. Until finally, with a determined inhale, she pushed herself up out of bed. She hesitated one final time for a single heartbeat, but her mind was made up already despite herself. Damn it. No willpower. She strode over to the door, squaring her shoulders and making sure her face was set in a hard grimace.

She opened the door.

"Hello, Kai."

62

He shouldn't be here. Not so soon. Oscar had told her only this past evening that the chieftain was still a day's flight out. Then again, he had also admitted to the general ignorance surrounding the average flight speed of a dragon, so perhaps she should have been prepared well ahead of time.

Because that was Anzi's most pressing problem. Unreadiness. Unreadiness for the shadow of terror washing through her and the lightning-hot thrill that ran over the entirety of her body like a wave of static at the same time. Unreadiness for both the simmering, fast-rising anger that made her clench her fists, and the sheer, inexplicable relief of seeing him standing in front of her unharmed all at once. She wasn't ready at all. She had thought she would have more time.

"Anzi," he said. "I'm sorry."

Under the light of the flickering torches along the hallway outside, his dark, shaggy hair seemed to glow with a yellow-orange halo. It was far longer than when she had last seen him, but it didn't make him look unkempt even as the tips of his unruly hair brushed the wide, golden collar that sat upon his shoulders. Just—wild. Ah, but one thing was the same. Winter was here, and yet he wore nothing but the same harem-trouser style pants the desert folk favored so much. Wasn't he cold?

"You haven't cut your hair," she remarked. "If you were a soldier, you would have been whipped raw for looking like that."

He looked startled. No doubt he had assumed she would confront him about the other night, about what he had done. So had he been expecting cold words or hot ones? Had he been expecting a hissed stream of invective or outright shouting? She would give him neither. He looked terrible, eyes full of every kind of dread as if he were standing on the crest of a bubbling volcano ready to burst over him, or as if he were standing on a precipice, seconds from plummeting. Something dark brewed in him. What was it? And how was it that she could feel it as surely as if it roiled and tumbled under her own skin?

"Well? Is there something else you wanted to say?"

His lips parted, but no response came. For a long moment, they stared at each other. His golden eyes glittered with a hard, craggy gleam while she knew her own were blank, neutral. She would give nothing away because the silence between them would say more than she could. This man standing before her from the wild desert where no civilized men dared to tread, this man with all his secrets and sinister magic, this man who made his home in endless sands under hot desert sun—she didn't know if she could trust him anymore. Didn't know if she should forgive him. Not after she had seen evidence of how horrifically he could hurt her—and almost had.

…And yet she had no choice. Because she had to save his dragons.

"Are you alone?" she asked. "Where's your entourage?"

With his eyes still fixed on her, he shook his head. "Outside, in the city. I slipped past the guards."

"A palace maid might have seen you."

"No one saw me."

She pursed her lips, wondering if she could trust even that. Hasty and unstable as he was, would he have even noticed if someone followed him? His hair was wind-ruffled, his eyes burning through her too intently to be seeing anything else. But what choice did she have except to believe him? She couldn't afford to argue here of all places where the walls had so many ears. "Did you bring the dragons with you to the city?" she asked. "How many, and where are they? Have you posted guards? Did the Emperor send any of his men yet—"

She was still rattling off more quiet questions when Kai stepped forward. She stopped immediately and drew back, every inch of her skin prickling, and her mouth clamped shut so hard her teeth clacked together.

"Anzi—"

"I'm very tired," she interrupted. "And I had plenty of reason to turn you away when you came here. The reason I didn't was because there's something important enough to me that I have to overlook what you did. For now. But it doesn't mean anything else. Because I don't trust you. You're at least a little insane to have done what you did, and I don't know when that's going to rear its head again next."

"It never will," he promised. "It was an accident."

"An accident is slipping on a grease spill. An accident is dropping a milk pail. What you did—"

"An accident is falling down a cliff and not finding anything to catch myself on, too." He stepped forward again, and this time, he came so close they were standing nearly chest to chest. She felt suddenly naked without her armor on, without her weapons. All she had was the dagger strapped to her thigh where she always kept it when she went to bed, but the thought of using it against Kai—it sickened her. How weak was she, she cursed herself, that even after he had proven what he was capable of, she still couldn't bring herself to hurt him? How weak was she that she was more wary than angry—more hurt than vengeful?

Why did she feel this way at all?

"It happened before I knew what I was doing." Although his voice was quiet, it set every bone in her body resonating with each syllable. The heat of his body sank into hers across the narrow wedge of space between them, and his breath ghosted across her lips. "I couldn't catch myself. I was afraid. I thought..."

"You thought what?" She shouldn't have, but the words were off her tongue before she could stop them. "What was it that made you think you had any right? I trusted you enough that I did something I never thought I would, because I was desperate for help I couldn't find anywhere else. I came to you willingly because I never thought for a second I was in danger. I—"

"I thought if I let you go again, I would lose you." He was holding her face suddenly, warm palms cradling her jaw and his fingers sliding along her mussed hair. "I already let it happen once. Then twice. I thought—I didn't think. I left you when I shouldn't have, and you've been hurt. Again. And again. Every time I see you..."

The rasped pain in his voice stunned her. No mere sentimentality, this. However it was that he knew she had been wounded, it was as if he'd felt it, had lived it. Mystical arts she couldn't possibly begin to understand, she was sure, and the very idea that he was in her head even when she was fully awake and conscious sent a stormy streak of apprehension through her.

"How did you know?" she demanded. "And how do you keep doing that? How is it you can tell whenever I—listen, you need to tell me what you've done. What you've done to me. Because this has been going on longer than I've known you, I'm sure of it now. It was you that time in the barracks too, before we ever met. I was with you back then. You spoke to me. And then you…"

One of his hands slid up the side of her face, and his fingers threaded through her hair to push it back from her forehead. His thumb brushed along her temple, and she shivered when a ghost of a memory slipped right through her like a sharp wind.

"You were hurt here," he said softly. "I helped you heal it. That was the first time you ever felt me, after all that time. That was when I knew all my waiting was finally coming to an end. That was when I started believing, not just hoping…I knew."

She reached up to yank his hands away from her face, but she faltered just before she could do it. All the strength sapped out of her body as if it were draining from a ripped sheet. "We hadn't met yet then," she said. Her voice was hoarse even to her own ears, weak, maybe horrified. She didn't understand. "You didn't know me. I didn't know you."

"We did meet. You know me, Anzi. You've known me for years, ever since you were that little girl who came out of the night and saved me, then sent me on my way. You know me." His thumb brushed her lips. It was so warm it nearly singed her. "I would never hurt you. I was afraid. I thought if I let you go, I would never see you again. I can feel it whenever someone hurts you, whenever you fall, whenever you bleed, whenever you pick yourself up and do it all over again. I've had to let it happen too many times to count because I didn't know who you were or where you'd gone, didn't know how to find you. And when I finally did, I thought I never had to let it happen again. But I keep…losing you. I keep losing you and you keep fading from me, and whenever I reach out, you pull away until I can't catch you—"

It happened then, fast as a snakebite, quick enough that she could pretend she hadn't known it was coming: he kissed her. He kissed her as if she'd been brought back to life, like a lover waiting by a graveside. His mouth on hers was hot and demanding, yet pleading, eternally grateful. He kissed her as if she weren't supposed to be picking him up and hurling him to the ground, kissed her as if he owned her and she owned him, body and soul. She couldn't breathe except for the scant instants their lips slid sideways just enough that she could suck in a lungful of priceless air, and then he was drinking it right out of her again.

He pulled her close with one arm that she hadn't noticed snaking around her waist, and just like that, he was stroking her tongue with such insistence that he coaxed it to life despite her initial misgivings. Warm and fire-bright, gods, it really must be magic to make her feel this way, she thought distantly. She had promised herself she would be colder and stronger if he ever did this again, had promised herself she wouldn't crumble the way she had on the bridge when he'd kissed her the first time before his abrupt departure, but now...

"If I tell you, you'll push me away," he whispered against her lips an eternity later, but he caught her in another deep, burning kiss before she could reply. And then again, when she had forgotten what she had wanted to say. "But I want you to know. I need you to understand why I need you, why I can't let you..."

Her head was swimming. She couldn't remember anymore what they had been doing before this. Couldn't remember why she was supposed to be livid with him. "You're making no sense," she said, half-panting and struggling to make her knees stay locked. "I can't understand you. Explain to me, and make it simple."

He pushed her hair back behind her ear and pressed a kiss to her forehead, then over one closed eyelid, then the other, and a final one on her lips, chaste but no less desperate...

"You're my fated mate," he said. "You are my destiny."

WHEN ANZI AWOKE, the first thing she realized was that there was someone large and warm wrapped around her. Arms around her waist, face buried in her neck, fingers perilously close to the bottom of her shirt hem—oh, there they went. That was what had awoken her, the sneaky way they were tasting the jut of her hip.

But it wasn't sneaky at all. She turned her head to find exactly who she expected behind her, a sleeping Kai breathing slow and deep into her hair. He wasn't faking it. Somehow, she could tell. The fingers creeping under her shirt were far from decent, but he could truly blame it on the oblivion of sleep if she shook him awake and confronted him about it now. And, in truth, it was cause for relief. The fact that she had a shirt on at all—as well as the rest of her clothes—meant things hadn't gone too far off the deep end after he made that ridiculous, nonsensical declaration right to her face. Following a short, sharp argument and his insistence that he would do whatever it took to prove it to her—*you're my mate, Anzi*—she had finally managed to calm him down by inviting him to sleep with her. Only sleep. As in, resting. Not a euphemism.

And yet it had satisfied him nonetheless. He had crawled into her bed and proceeded to capture her in his arms as if she were a stuffed toy for a child—well, all right, so the way he'd held her hadn't been like a child at all, but very much like he was ready to prove exactly how much of a grown, virile man he was. And that was how they had ended that 'discussion.' With a lot of unanswered questions.

Mate, he had said. Fate. Destiny.

…Hogwash.

She rolled her eyes and scowled. She didn't dare to move yet, knowing he would wake the instant she tried to slip out of the cage of his arms—and legs, because gods smite him, his knee was wedged between her thighs from behind in a way that was decidedly suggestive. But she didn't feel steady enough to try to stand on her feet anyway. Her head was throbbing, her vision swimming. And even worse, her leg was no longer so sore.

Yes. It was less sore. That was a bad thing. It was bad because there was absolutely no plausible reason for it feeling so much better than it had a scant few hours ago, unless Kai had something to do with it. Damn him. She hadn't asked him to use his mysterious desert magic to help her. And no, she wasn't going to believe his wild claim last night that he was able to heal her at all only because of their bond, that he could imbue her with his own strength so as to accelerate her healing. First of all, that made no sense. But secondly, as she had had to remind him, she had no magical core. It didn't matter that she was a mixed-blood—the human side always won out in hybrids. They still had a capacity for magic, but humans couldn't bear a magical center. And without one, there could be no such thing as a 'mate.'

It sickened her that he believed it with all his might. Not because she disliked him—far from it, she was beginning to suspect with a sinking heart—but because she had no choice but to pity him. The way he had held her, the way he had kissed her, the way he had insisted over and over that they were meant to be and always had been…it was real. His belief, his faith. He truly believed what he had told her last night.

She had been raised in a human society, so she would never truly understand the mystical concept of true mates. But what she did know was common knowledge: mates of a magical species bonded instinctively. They knew. It was an animalistic thing, primal and beastly. Something she didn't possess.

And neither could Kai. Because as strange as he was, as strange as his magic was—he was human, too. Maybe his tribe thought otherwise of themselves, but reality was that they were little closer to magical beasts than she was. They had hands, feet, five fingers, five toes. Fine, so there were a few things about him that made her extra wary, inexplicable things, but *wyrms* had magical cores. *Dragons* had magical cores. *Sirens* had magical cores.

Not. Humans.

It had to be a culturally ingrained thing. His tribe likely passed down legends that encouraged their members to believe they were something more than they were. That they could have mates, that they had magical resonances with the denizens of the old world, the world before humans. It wasn't uncommon. There were plenty of barbarian tribes that believed they were direct descendants of gryphons and unicorns and phoenixes, among many others. Primitive religion and spirituality played a heavy part in such deception, and Kai must have been indoctrinated in these teachings to truly believe she was his mate. He was mistaking his magic and its effect on her for something else entirely, and his attraction to her was only making it worse. And he had all the proof he could want by now that she was drawn to him as well, but didn't he realize? Didn't he realize it was purely physical? Well—maybe she was attracted to his deeper qualities. Maybe there was something magnetic about his rawness, his unhesitating certainty, his determination to pursue what he wanted and the way he could be gentle and strong at the same time where she was concerned. But that wasn't the draw of fate or destiny or whatever he called it. That was just...

"Anzi?"

She closed her eyes. Damn it. "Yes?"

His lips moved along the side of her neck with such horrific, lazy grace and terrifying seductiveness that her toes curled under the covers. Shit. Right when she had been scheming up ways to break the truth to him as gently as she could. He was a good man...Or so she wanted to believe. He had crossed a line the other night when he had trapped her spirit within him, but in the end, he had let her go, hadn't he? And he had at least tried to explain himself. Maybe she was being too easy on him, damn it, but if she could avoid hurting him, she had to try. And she could keep telling herself it was only because she still had a job to do, and she needed his help to finish it. If she told herself that enough times, she would be able to train her mind into remembering that physical attraction meant nothing, no matter how paralyzingly good it felt to have him press up against her like that-

Hungry! NOW!

She surged out of Kai's arms and off the bed, and after a pause, he too slid out. One moment, they had been curled against each other with the covers tangled over and between their legs, and the next, they were staring at the foot of the bed where Netra had unfurled her wings and was glaring at them with bared teeth and flexing claws. On the wooden floor on the other side of the bed, Kai's side, another set of clicking talons tap-tapped closer and closer.

Oh, shit.

"You...Dragons," she heard Kai say, and it was the first time she'd ever heard him speak in such a voice. Wonder mixed with disbelief, utterly stunned. "Hatched—"

"Right!" she interrupted, already starting to break out in a cold sweat. "Yes, dragons." Shit, how had she forgotten about Netra! And Serqet! They had been in the room the entire time, and she had let a pair of muscular arms and a hard chest make her forget—"Good timing," she added in a voice as convincingly casual as possible. "I was going to bring something up about them in a minute."

"Two dragons—"

"It's urgent," she interrupted once more. "So I'm going to be blunt. Are you listening? Kai, look at me, please."

She felt marginally less like a babbling idiot when he finally tore his eyes away from Netra to look at her. She saw her chance and leaped for it.

"We need to take the dragons you brought out of the city again," she told him. "Because Tet's going to try to steal them."

63

How to explain what she knew? How to convince him her information was good? How to make him see that bringing the dragons here had been a terrible idea no matter what his reasons? Anzi was still scrambling to put together proper responses for when he inevitably demanded answers and explanations. She didn't want to give everything away, a conditioned cautiousness that she saw no reason to do away with, but in order to persuade him to go along with her wild plans, Kai needed at least some justification to cling to.

But he said nothing. The silence stretched on as she waited for him to explode in either anger, outrage, or fear, but all he did was stare at her with a—what was that, a secretive expression? Slowly, her hackles rose as her gaze turned from stern to suspicious, and it wasn't long before she pieced together what he wasn't saying.

"You know already," she said. "You knew before I told you. You know that Tet's going to do something."

He said nothing still. Her stare sharpened into an undisguised glare, and she turned to face him properly across the bed as if they were enemies on the battlefield. All she needed was a pair of weapons in her hands and they would look the part. Because what was this nonsense? The look on his face said he was concealing things from her while she was here trying to help him. And help the dragons, which should be reason enough for him to cooperate even if he wouldn't do it for his own sake.

"Kai," she said sharply. "What are you looking at me like that for?"

He dropped his gaze to the floor to observe something at his feet. Serqet, if that swaying telltale stinger waving over the bed was any indication. "You brought dragons of your own," he said evasively. "You'll be hard pressed to take care of them. I'll take care of mine in the meantime."

"Don't give me that vague talk." She anchored her hands on her hips, fingers digging in so hard they hurt. Ignore it, she told herself. Ignore the irrational anger swelling inside her, which in truth only masked the real culprit: the mortified hurt that Kai was hiding things from her. She shouldn't be wounded. She hid things from him all the time. And yet it was different when he did it because she had thought he… No. She was being stupid. This was what Kai did to her, made her act like an idiot. His presence always amplified her emotions tenfold, a hundredfold.

"Don't worry, Anzi. I'm prepared for whatever comes."

Wasn't he listening? Or was he putting on a manly front of indifference? "I don't think that's true. From my side of the fence, I can see a lot that you can't."

"I'm the same way."

"Except you're on my turf, far from home. Things are happening here that I can't begin to explain because even I'm in the dark about most of it." She pointed first at the growling dragonet still perched on the covers, then down at his side of the bed, indicating his feet hidden from view behind it. "I've been taking care of Netra—be quiet, Netra, stop that—for weeks. And Serqet too, now. They won't be the only ones. I'm going to be hatching dozens more. The Emperor wants every dragon he can—"

She stopped when Netra's serpentine head cocked to the side before craning backward at the door. Her hearing was brighter than Anzi's by far, so if she was paying attention to something beyond the wall, Anzi trusted her judgment. She held up a warning finger at Kai, both cautioning him, and sure enough, a knock sounded at the door. She breathed a sigh of relief, recognizing the sing-song tapping on the wood in an instant.

"Coming, Letti." She shot Kai a meaningful glance and pointed at the corner parallel to the door, silent instruction for him to retreat there so the harem girl wouldn't see him. Not that the other woman couldn't be trusted, but she already knew what would happen if Letti discovered him. A perpetually half-naked man with chiseled muscles and a physique that would make even the most veteran of Quarter Rouge courtesans salivate, in her room at the crack of dawn. Anzi wasn't ready to deal with that this early. Maybe not ever.

"Hurry up," Letti complained in a hushed voice. "It's urgent. I only have a moment."

"I'm here—" She cracked open the door and wedged herself between the space, poking her head out into the hallway rather than letting the harem girl enter the room. "What is it?"

"Are you crazy? Let me in. We're supposed to be doing this all secretively, aren't we? Palace maid is going to come around the corner and spot me any second."

She floundered. Letti was right, but... A thin sheen of sweat formed on the back of her neck. "Uh, then let's talk later. It's not a good time."

"Oh, quit it. Let me *in!*" With a hiss and an exasperated shove, somehow the woman managed to squeeze her head in through the door before Anzi could react. "Oh. Oh!" Then: "...Oh..."

"Not a damn word," Anzi was still struggling to get Letti's head back out without hurting the woman. Her hand splayed over the wide-eyed harem girl's face in a vain attempt to simultaneously blindfold and shove her away. "Get off me! Out! Move!"

"Hello!" Letti exclaimed anyway as she smushed her own hand back into Anzi's face and defied her eviction. "Hello, Chieftain. I've heard so much about you. My name is Violetta, but friends call me Letti and since you're very, very close with my best friend Anzi, I'll have to insist you call me Letti as well. It's such a pleasure to meet you—"

"Get *out!*"

"Let me *in!*"

Wisely, Kai said nothing as the two women scuffled in the doorway. When Letti let out a yelp of pain, Anzi had no choice but to yield lest she seriously hurt her. But the devious harem girl—liar!—dropped the act and flounced into the room a heartbeat later. With a flourish, she slammed the door shut in a way that was decidedly provocative and threatening at the same time and dropped into a too-elegant curtsy in Kai's direction. She was wearing a silvery thread-laced black dress today, winter wear, along with an expensive shawl Anzi hadn't seen before. When Letti flicked the end of it at the chieftain in a smug, knowing gesture, Anzi's dark eyes narrowed in a glare.

"You shouldn't be here," she grumbled. "I don't know why I let you in."

"Because you love me, hush," Letti murmured back out of the corner of her mouth. "Chieftain! It's been so long. You're even bigger than I remember!"

Kai's eyebrows came down in confused grimace as he watched her giggle behind her hand. "Have we met?"

"Oh, I've seen you coming and going. Quite a stir when you left so suddenly a month ago. You're very famous!"

His golden eyes darted to Anzi, who slapped an exasperated hand over her face. "That's enough. Leave him alone. We're...discussing something serious."

From the bed, Netra hissed and flexed her claws on the covers. The sound of fabric tearing scratched through the silence of the brief lull that followed Anzi's evasive words.

"...Serious how?" Letti asked. She stared at her with an expression that was suddenly stone-hard, suspicious. She glanced between Kai and Anzi several times, a cold gleam of infant understanding lurking in her bright blue eyes. "Serious," she repeated when no one answered her, and looked between the two dragons in the room as well. By now, Serqet had crawled around the bed and was staring up at everyone from the floorboards, the membrane of her inner eyelid clicking as it opened and shut. Letti looked back at Anzi again. "What are you two doing? What are you hiding?"

Anzi's gut clenched. There was a growing shadow of a horrified question in the woman's eyes. Suspicion, disbelief. And deeper than that, a solidifying determination to stop whatever was happening in front of her.

"Wait," she urged. "I can explain. I have reasons. I didn't tell you because I didn't want to put you in any danger but I was always going to explain what I found out, the Empire isn't—"

"I knew it," said Letti. "You're pregnant."

"How was I supposed to know?" the woman cried. "You were being so dodgy, it's exactly what the girls do when they find out they're with child. They act like you, all sneaky and asking you for help but won't explain what they need it for."

"And you thought it's because I'm *pregnant!*"

"What other explanation was there!" Letti threw her hands up, aggrieved. "It's not like you're the most transparent person! You keep to yourself so much and have all these secrets that I have to connect the dots myself. You did this! It's your fault. If you'd only trust me, then this would never have happened."

"Or you could mind your own business!" Anzi snapped, but even as she spoke, she knew that was an unreasonable request.

"Uh-huh, and that's why you asked me for help, because it's none of my business. Also, only in your wildest dreams will I stop being nosy." Loose blonde ringlets bobbed as Letti swung around on the bed to stare at Kai. "If she won't tell me, then you should. I don't understand how she can trust some desert stranger over me, even if your bare nipples do look very fashionable. I think the gold draping over your chest accentuates them very well. Whoever arranges your wardrobe has talent."

The chieftain, still banished to the corner where he stood, inclined his head at her in a small, modest bow. She bowed back.

"Stop!" Anzi raged. "Stop doing that. This is not a game. I already explained to you it's something that has to do with the dragons, I'll tell you the rest when I know for sure—"

"Tell me everything *now!* I'm doing my best to help where I can while you keep me in the dark. Why! Is it because you think I'm stupid and can't be trusted with my big, fat, gossiping mouth? Is it because you think I'm going to sabotage you because I'm just a ladder-climbing socialite who'll use anything to get ahead? In case you haven't noticed, I'm willing to risk whatever it is you think I'm jeopardizing by associating with you. I'm ready! I can do what you need me to do! I'm here, so what are you waiting for!"

She had been trying to appeal to Letti's affectionate nature by sitting on the bed next to her, but now she shot to her feet and glared down at the stubborn woman. "First of all, lower your voice. The last thing we need is someone sneaking over and listening to us, and you're being so loud even Netra wouldn't be able to hear if someone's approaching."

"Fine. But no changing the subject. What are you hiding?"

When she caught his gaze, Kai gave her a minute shrug of his shoulders as if he didn't care, but there was a dangerous sheen in his golden eyes that told her it was only a superficial pretense. There was a prowling energy in him like a tiger lying in wait behind the tall grass. Well, she wouldn't let him pounce. Letti was reckless sometimes and gave no thought to what she was doing if it meant temporary enjoyment, but she was a good woman, sharp and bright. She could be trusted.

"There's something going on with the Premier," said Anzi, but how much could she reveal? What if Letti didn't believe her? What if she chose loyalty to nation over wild conspiracies? "And there's something going on with the dragons. Nothing is like we thought, Letti. And things are changing even more for the worse."

"Is that why you have two dragons?" The harem girl jabbed a finger at the floor. "I don't understand how that's even possible. I thought you're only supposed to have one."

"It's all lies. All the stories, all the things they tell us, false."

"But it's always one man, one dragon. Or, well, one woman."

"Just make-believe, lies to hide the truth." Anzi sat back down on the bed and slapped her hand on Letti's knee. "Things aren't how we've been taught. There are..." She stopped, tried again. "The Empire's not what we've been told. There are people being massacred out there, crushed under our weight. We've been treading on them without ever knowing, and now we have to make it stop. It's not *our* fault, but we have to take responsibility. So that's what I'm doing."

"Anzi, stop looking so serious. You're scaring me." Letti press her handed to Anzi's cheek. "Whatever's going on, don't be hasty. Wait and see. That's one of the first things we learn in the harem, so even when we learn something crazy and terrible from any of our marks, we make sure we know everything first. Not everything is black and white."

"Some things are. Some things are unacceptable no matter what. You can't take the time to look at it from every angle until you find the right one to blind you." Anzi encircled Letti's wrist with a careful grip and lowered it. "I need to make things right."

"You're making me nervous. Whatever you're doing, don't." The woman's eyes darted back over to Kai in the corner, who was now staring at them with no trace of his former smile remaining. He looked dangerously tense. Anzi gave him a warning look to dissuade him from doing anything, although she couldn't be sure that would be enough to stay his hand if Letti's words became any more skeptical. "Are you two planning something together? When did you start...doing this? What are you going to do?"

"What I've been doing has nothing to do with him. It's separate, it's...I learned the truth on my own when I started training with the Premier. Letti, listen to me. Look at me." She waited until the woman acquiesced. "Things are going to get dangerous. More than they already are. Do you remember when you told me I always end up hurt, or something like that —you asked me, remember?" The harem girl nodded, and from the corner, Kai stirred as well. Damn him. Damn both of them. Anzi's heart throbbed like a clenched fist. What right or reason did they have to care about her, a common soldier who'd just gotten in over her head? What right did she have to command their concern, their fear, their loyalty? She couldn't begin to understand it. "The truth is the Emperor nearly killed me. Because I tried to…" She shook her head. "They don't care about the dragons. They don't care about the people. Letti, if you had heard the things they say, if you were there…"

"So, what? Are you trying to revolt against the Emperor?"

"I wouldn't do anything if I thought it was going to hurt innocent people. I'm not leading anyone into war to get slaughtered, I don't want to see children losing mothers and fathers to some madness they have no control over. So I'm trying to make things right my own way."

Letti stood up from the bed and turned to face her, skirts rustling as she spun around. "You're insane. Do you have any idea what you sound like? That's exactly the way men talk when they're plotting treason. And even if that's not what you're doing, that's exactly what they'll take it as. Don't you know people have been executed for less? You're a soldier! You should know this!"

"Yes, I do know. That should tell you how serious I am."

"Serious enough to get yourself killed! The wrong person sees you, hears you, and they'll give you up to be skinned in the blink of an eye. You're out of your mind, Anzi. And you!" Letti stabbed an accusing finger at Kai. "You put her up to this. None of this happened until you got here, I bet. She made it all the way to the Premier, to the Imperial Palace right under the Emperor, and then…you!"

"Letti, stop. It wasn't him, I told you. Trust me on that, at least."

"Trust! I recognize crazy talk when I hear it. And there's only one person who'd benefit, an outsider, an outsider like *you!*"

Anzi yanked her down with a grip on both of her wrists, and the harem girl turned her wide-eyed, startled gaze on her. Their foreheads were nearly touching, and they were close enough that Anzi could whisper instead of speaking aloud. "I haven't told him everything either," she snapped, or as much as she could snap while whispering. "He only knows some of it. I still don't know who to trust and who I can afford to put in danger. I'm alone, Letti. I'm doing this on my own."

Silence. A long one, fraught with palpable fear from the harem girl and frustration from herself. There were so few words she could say to convince anyone she wasn't out of her mind, that all of this was the inevitable culmination of every rotting evil that had festered in the heart of the Empire for two hundred years.

"They stole the dragons," Anzi murmured. "Dragons aren't rare. Not their eggs, at least. There were hundreds down there in the Cave, that's where they keep them. And they bring candidates into the fold to see how well they do. Whether they break their dragon well enough, whether they fall in line with the rest of the Guard and play along. If you don't, if you're different, if you try to stand up for something, if you try to protect the dragons or suggest that it's wrong, that it's *all* wrong..."

"I don't understand. If that's true, then how could we not know? The Premier's been serving the Empire since the founding of it. They—"

"They've been serving the *Emperor* since the founding of it. And serving themselves. Do you know why we never see the dragon riders anywhere near the Imperial City? Do you know where they are most of the time?"

"They're protecting us. Putting down threats to our way of life."

"They're out there slaughtering and terrorizing anyone in the annexed cities who try to rise up. Some of them are still resisting. And do you know what the riders do when they find resistance? I've seen it. I've seen the colonel open up the throat of an old man who had already lost everything he ever loved just to make a point, just to show everyone he was in control. This is what it's like outside of the world we know, Letti. There's so much I could tell you, but what will that accomplish? I only need you to trust me. That's all. I'll take care of the rest."

The harem girl looked sick to her stomach. Anzi had never seen her look so terrified before, so frozen. Had this been a mistake? Was this the breaking point, the thing that would sever their friendship? Was it over now?

"Promise me," Letti said suddenly and pressed her forehead against Anzi's, eyes squeezed shut. "Promise me something. You have to."

"What is it."

"Promise me you won't get yourself killed."

64

When Anzi at last convinced Letti to leave before someone noticed she was missing, the harem girl shot the chieftain a sharp glare before stepping out through the doorway. It was an expression Anzi had never seen before, like she was a breath away from running right past her and clawing Kai in the face. Not even when she had been slapped by Noemi in the street—twice—had she looked so vindictive.

One final encouraging push and shutting of the door later, Anzi and Kai were alone again. That is, save for Netra, who was now sulking in the corner, and Serqet, who was flipped over onto her armored back on the floor close by, tiny legs wheeling as she struggled to right herself.

"Netra! Do that to her again, and I will swing you around by your tail! Understand?" Anzi hurried over to pick the hatchling up while Netra hissed at her from the wall. "Don't talk back to me!"

The dragonet lay her head down, still glaring.

"Stay there until I say so. On the gods..." She turned around with Serqet in her arms to find Kai staring at her. He had been silent all this time, but there had to be something he wanted to say. After all of that chaos, who wouldn't? "Well?" she demanded. "Are you going to help me save your dragons or not? Because if you won't, I'm not going to bother trying to convince you anymore. I have too much to do to harp on you alone."

He took so long to respond she almost gave up. "They're already here," he said. "Whatever you have planned is going to be futile. Your Emperor's posted guards all over the city, not just along the palace walls. Mages, like the ones you showed me living in that tower. Probably to make sure I don't go anywhere, and that I don't try to fly the dragons back out. I don't doubt they'll be ready to attack the instant they sense something's wrong."

"You figured all of this out and still aren't worried?"

His eyes narrowed, but into a thoughtful expression rather than an angry one. "Are *you?*" he asked. "Are you going to move against your Emperor when the time comes?"

"What kind of question is that? I already said I'm trying to help you."

"Helping me is one thing. You can even get in his way and stall him. But are you going to move against him?" He came closer. One slow step first, then another. A pause. "How far are you willing to go?"

"I'm not going to discuss treason with you. We barely know each other. I'm still figuring things out, so you need to—"

"You know that's not true. You know me. And I know you."

"Since when? Since I started walking in my dreams and finding myself in your head? Since you kissed me on the bridge for the first time? How about when you had me come to your bed and sleep next to you? You already told me before you left that you knew the Emperor was only using me to get to you. I don't understand why you're keeping up this facade when it's obvious that..."

"Obvious, what? Tell me."

"That it's not even real! It was planned. I came to you because I was told to, and I accepted everything you did because those were my orders. I'm trying to make this easier for you, Kai. Now that you know, there's no point in playing the game anymore. I don't have time for it. Neither do you."

"I know it's not a game to you. Any more than it is to me. I didn't care that it was a pretense for you in the beginning, and I don't care now, either. Because I knew in the end, it would end up exactly the way it was supposed to." He came closer. Closer. "Don't say it isn't real, what we have. We found each other after all this time, years—"

"Don't," she snapped. "I'm all right with petting and kissing if that's what will make you happy. But I'm not going to listen to whatever stories you have about—mates and destiny. I don't want to hear about how we met before or any of that."

"You know what I'm saying is true. And you remember that you knew me before we ever met here. You already confessed it. And I'll tell you why if you let me, if you'll just let yourself remember. We were young, just children—"

"Stop." She held up a hand and pressed it against Kai's chest, fingertips pressing hard into the bottom of his collar with a warning strength. "That's enough."

"Anzi—"

"I'm not saying I don't believe you. I'm not saying you're making all of this up. But you have to understand me." She narrowed her eyes. "What I'm doing is bigger than both of us. Do you want to know if I feel something when I look at you? Yes. Yes, I do. There. But I don't have time to stop so we can serenade each other in the moonlight. I don't have time to learn anything about us that won't help me save hundreds of thousands of people who are out there right now, dying and waiting and fighting. This connection you keep saying we have, if I decide to believe in it, is it going to help them? Is it going to go and pluck those people out of danger, or is it going to make the Emperor stop chasing your dragons? Is it going to change anything at all in the world except for—" She lifted her hand and twitched it between them with a flutter. "Us? Tell me."

He grabbed her wrist, making her grimace. "I understand. I'm not asking you to give up everything else for this. But I'm here, Anzi. I'm already here."

"And what about it? Should I turn around and chase the next sunset with you?"

"It's the way it—*we're* supposed to be. *Meant* to be."

In an instant, her other hand was wrapped around his wrist, locking it in place as she glared up at him. "Let's say I believe it. Let's say I believe in *meant to be.* Then answer me something. Can you guarantee it won't hold me back when I go off to do what I have to do? You're smart, Kai. You know I'm doing something dangerous. And you know I'm doing something important. You know I'm taking risks I never would have imagined before. You even asked me if I'm willing to turn against the Emperor. Do I really have to answer that? Do I really have to spell it out for you how committed I am? Because if you know me the way you say you do, then you would have given up this conversation a long time ago, because you would know I'm giving up everything for it."

"Anzi—"

"Just answer the question. Can you promise that if we"—she nodded her head in a fierce jerk—"happen, then it won't endanger anyone else?

That it won't distract me, or you? Can you guarantee it won't make things harder and more dangerous than they already are? Can you guarantee it won't just give both of us something more to lose?"

She waited for his answer. If not an answer, then a reaction, any reaction. The bobbing of a throat, a nervous swallow. The quickening of his breath. But there was nothing. Just the half-crazed, desperate flashing in his golden eyes and the dark pupils in them, blown wide open as he stared down at her. No words. Because she already knew his answer, and so did he.

"I know you mean it," she said softly. "I know you're not lying to me. Whether it's true or not, you believe what you say. And for what it's worth, I used to think it was all just...magic trickery, enchantment, but what the hell, maybe not. Maybe I'm not crazy and what you believe is the truth. But..." She let his wrist go. "The world is bigger than us. What would that make us if we put ourselves before it?"

His grip tightened around the base of her hand, thumb pressing hard against her inner wrist as if he were trying to dig deep for a pulse. For the truth. But she was hiding nothing. Everything she said—she meant it.

"Kai. You're a chieftain. A leader? I saw your retinue of guards already, and there have to be others you're responsible for."

"...Yes."

"If they were in danger, and you were the only one who could do anything about it. If you had to make a choice, who would you choose? Me, or the ones you're responsible for?"

A sharp gleam shone in his eyes. "I don't have to choose."

"If you *had to*," she insisted. "No twisting in the wind, no excuses. One choice only. Who?" She paused. "You know there's only one right answer. And if you don't know that..." She shrugged and pulled on her hand, trying to tug it away. "Then that's proof enough we're not meant to be. If fate exists, it would never destine me to be with someone who doesn't know how to put the greater first before the lesser."

"You aren't lesser. You would never be the lesser."

"I should be, if we're measuring my life against so many others. What needs to be done is bigger than both of us. I told you that already. And if you're the kind of man I think you are, then you understand. Don't you?" She stepped forward now, slowly. "I'm not saying it's forever. Maybe... maybe there's going to be time for this later on, in the future. When the job is done. But that time isn't now, and I can't let you stand in my way.

And I can't stand in your way either, if it comes at the cost of others. I won't do it."

He looked haunted, as if she had died in front of him just beyond his grasp. "You're my mate," he said quietly. "You're the only one in the world for me."

"I can respect that."

"We have mates, my kind," he insisted, voice dropping to a more insistent pitch. "We're different. We know. I can prove it to you."

"Save it for later, then. Because if you want me to be honest, if you want the truth—I'm not ready. I'm sorry. If I could help it, I would, but I can't and that's reality." Her smile felt like anything but, a grimace of pain mixed with a growing anxiety that Kai would never let this go. "It must mean I'm weak because I can't accept what you're telling me, but if that's what it is, then I have to accept that, too. I don't know how to change the way I feel. I can't just close my eyes and convince myself I'm ready when I'm not, that I'm ready to commit to something that's never even crossed my mind before. I can't order myself to be one way when I'm the other. If we could all do that, we wouldn't be the people we are."

She didn't know how to name the shadow that filled his expression. Didn't know how to measure the pain she could see there, the pain her words had laid upon him. And that only made her even more afraid. She couldn't remember the last time she'd felt like this. Maybe when Tet had loomed over her broken body, rearing back to strike her again for the thousandth time. Except now she felt like she was the one with bloodied hands and feet, like she was the one doing the hurting, the cutting, the breaking. But that wasn't what she wanted. Wasn't she allowed to speak her truth, too? Did she really have to twist herself into something else, to make room for whatever he demanded?

She balled her idle hand into a fist and tapped his chest with her knuckles twice. "I think you're a good man," she said. "I think you're dependable. Strong. Intelligent. A leader your people can trust. I won't pretend to know why you won't let me help keep your dragons safe, but maybe it's because you have some plan in motion that's beyond the both of us, too. It's hard for me to accept it, but what choice do I have? So I'll stand by, and I'll do what I can from where I am. Maybe we can figure out how to work together properly, with a little more time."

"Anzi."

"It can't just be about you and me. You know that, right?"

His mouth opened a little wider, ready to say something—and closed.

"You're my mate," he said again, every word heavy with resigned finality. "There's no one else for me. Only you."

She smiled. "Then survive long enough to change my mind. Things are going to heat up in the Imperial City, Kai. There's going to be fire, and there's going to be blood. I don't know about you, but I've been fighting for as long as I can remember, and I know when there's a war coming. Do you know what the people here call my kind, the ones who come from desertside? Besides *fringer*."

A twitch at the corner of his mouth told her he was coming around. For now. "What do they call you?" he asked, his voice lifting ever so slightly with a lofty inflection. "Tell me."

Her smile grew. "They call us crows. Because of the way we look, dark crow's eyes, and dark hair, like their feathers. And because we're also very, very good at knowing when there's going to be blood. You can see flocks of them sometimes flying over to-be-battlefields because they recognize the signs. Swarms of them, all ready to scavenge."

"And you think you're a crow now? Is that it?"

She pushed the heel of her wrist against his chest, palm scraping against the edge of his shoulder collar. "Don't tease," she mock-warned. "Trust my instincts."

His grip loosened on her hand at long last, but before releasing it, he lifted it to his lips to brush her knuckles with a fleeting kiss. "Trust mine, too," he said quietly. "I would tell you everything if I could, but it isn't up to me. That's not my decision to make."

She narrowed her eyes, confused. "You're a chieftain. Everything's up to you."

"Not everything. That isn't my way." He finally let her hand fall from his own. "My tribe is my family, not slaves to whatever I say. I take too many decisions away from the ones I care about already."

Her heart lurched, and she couldn't even try to convince herself it had been in a bad way. Kai's eyebrows suddenly knit together, and he leaned down to get a closer look at her face. She tried to move away, but it was too late.

"Are you blushing?" he asked. "I didn't know you could do that."

"I'm not," she snapped. "Get away from me. I'm tired of looking at you, and we have nothing else to talk about. Go! Go. I have to feed Netra before she—"

"What do you mean? We haven't even scratched the surface. Tell me how you have two dragons with you, one of them newborn. How did that happen, and when—"

A furious screech from the corner drowned out the rest of Kai's words, and it was just as well. "Fine," she said. "Then stay with me if you want. But I'm not waiting until she decides to shred everything in my room again to feed her. Bring Serqet and follow me down to the kitchens."

She gave him no chance to refuse. If he wanted to stick around, he was going to pull his weight, and he was certainly not going to peer into her face that closely again no matter how curious he was about the shade of pink on her cheeks. His breath on her lips had almost made her part them, and she had gotten another headful of that intoxicating scent of desert spice he always wore. He had delivered all that nonsense about mates and destiny when all he probably had had to do was lean in and press her against the nearest hard surface to convince her she could afford to waver a bit. Damn him, and damn herself, too. She needed to steel her mind against the memory of his hypnotically muscular physique, the resonant tones of his voice, sometimes rough, sometimes gentle, the cut of his regal cheekbones and the sheen of the sun that gleamed against his bronzed skin-

"Wasn't that the way to the kitchen?"

Anzi stopped short and whipped around, ignoring Netra chewing viciously on her hair. "What?"

Kai was standing a meter back and peering down a corridor. "The kitchens. I could have sworn it was this way."

She looked around and realized he was very, very right. Lost in thought, she had completely forgotten where they were heading.

Shit.

"You really are blushing this time. Let me see you, Anzi—"

"Hands off! Turn and get going, then, since you're so clever." She disguised her mortified expression with an angry scowl and jerked her chin in the opposite direction. "Go!"

He gave her a lingering look, then turn around as ordered. Slowly.

"What are you grinning about," she demanded. "You think something's funny?"

"Of course not."

She swallowed an angry breath, ready to sling a hot retort at him as he made his slow retreat, but nothing came. Her ears burned as if someone were holding a torch to them. Why had Kai looked like he'd caught her doing something red-handed? It was none of his business what she pondered in her own thoughts. Not even when it got her lost. She stomped after him, glaring at the back of his head as Serqet peered over the man's shoulder and blinked back at her.

Damn him. And damn him again.

...But, all right:

This view of his back was certainly very interesting.

~

THEY WERE STANDING outside her room in a perfect row when she returned later that evening. Her...gift, the four male concubines Tet had given her. Luckily, Kai was long gone, off to a meeting with the Emperor's numerous advisors somewhere in the city to discuss business. It seemed Tet was impatient to get things going...Did she really stand a chance at foiling his plans without exposing herself? She couldn't sacrifice her position, her sole vantage point, to save even the wild dragons Kai had brought, not when there was so much more at stake. Somehow, she had to pull this off without costing herself everything.

And after getting these men out of her hair.

"What are you all doing here?"

The foremost man bowed to her at the waist. His loincloth looked suspiciously loose. "His Excellency instructed us to keep you company anytime we receive word Chieftain Kaizat-Amun leaves the grounds. We live to serve."

She cringed. She didn't like the way he said *serve.* Not one bit. "That makes no sense," she said. "He'll be here in a matter of hours. His Excellency was very specific when he said you should only be accompanying me when Chieftain Kaizat-Amun is no longer staying with us."

"With all due respect, the instructions have been altered. When we receive word he is on his way, we will take leave of you then."

Her eyes narrowed. He was speaking with the utmost humility, yet there was something iron-hard behind his voice—the security of the Emperor's direct order. But why? What was happening all of a sudden, and why did she feel almost like she was being...

"Please, allow us to escort you inside. Would you enjoy a massage?"

The door opened, and she was ushered in before she could protest with Serqet in her arms and Netra coiled around her shoulders, growling. She was about to snap that she was in no mood for company and kick them all out—when she noticed it. Her eyes darted around. "You straight-ened the room."

"Of course. For your convenience. Would you like us to disrobe you now?"

They'd *straightened the room.* Never mind that they had entered it without her permission—disrespectful no matter how they clothed it as a service—but they had then tidied everything. In other words, they had gone through her scant possessions, touched nearly every part of the room in the process. The bed sheets had been replaced, the covers. Her armor and spare uniform had been washed, folded, and placed atop the vanity table, which had also been shifted ever so slightly out of position.

Something was wrong. She sensed it from the way she suspected the drawers of the vanity table had been opened and closed in her absence, from the way the bed's headboard was a touch closer to the wall than it had been before, from the way Tet had apparently sent these men to tend to her when that had to be the worst impromptu idea ever.

What do you think our real purpose is?

Letti's words breezed through her memory, unbidden. Anzi blinked.

To be entertainment?

She had been talking about herself as well as the other harem girls, the other palace concubines.

Just another warm body?

The men were watching her. Carefully. Not because they were eager to please and jump to her beck and call, but because-

Our main job is to collect information and report it.

She lifted her chin and looked at each of them in turn, measuring them with a suddenly cool gaze.

Spies. No, not spies. Keepers.

Tet knew.

65

Netra didn't like crowds. She barely tolerated company. So with the presence of the four strange men in the room, it was a miracle she hadn't yet leaped out at them and left her claws in their bare chests. Anzi kept her eyes glued to the dragonet whose spines were already raised and bristling with undisguised hostility. And since when had her teeth become so jagged? There had been a few strewn about here and there over the past several weeks, but Anzi hadn't noticed the new ones growing in. They looked too big for her maw and certainly big enough to sink and crush bone, too. She gave her a baleful glare, a wordless warning to behave, and was answered with a rebellious, wider display of those fierce dragon teeth. Was this what it was like to take care of a child? Constant disobedience and attitude? She would never have any of her own, she swore it. Then again, it was too late. Netra was all but her child anyway.

"I really have to order you to leave," she resorted to saying at last when she exhausted all other polite options. "I want to rest. I'm very tired. And as helpful as you—all of you—are trying to be, it's not." She pointed at the door and cast her gaze over each man in turn down the straight row in which they stood.

"If we can't change your mind, then we will wait outside your room. Please don't hesitate to call for us if you have need of anything."

She narrowed her eyes at them when they all bowed to her in unison.

"You don't have to do that. Didn't I arrange comfortable quarters for you all on an upper floor? Go and rest. I'm sure you all have better things to do than stand around waiting for orders that won't come. I'll be sleeping."

"If Madam can't be convinced to let us offer a relaxing massage to assist with that—"

"You really can't."

"—then we would be happy to stand by while you rest at your leisure. It's our privilege to be at your disposal. We live to serve."

She wasn't drunk on her newly minted authority as the latest inductee into the Premier Guard. She really wasn't. It was simply a matter of common sense that if she gave her supposed 'gifted' servants a direct order, they should have jumped to obey her no matter how eagerly they wanted to *serve*. Supposedly. It wasn't a leap at all to conclude with certainty that they were, then, no mere servants at all. They were daring to disobey her even behind a facade of servility because they had been instructed to by someone they feared more than her.

So her suspicion was correct. Tet. How much did he know? Did he only suspect, or had he seen something, or had someone reported her to him? She should have been more careful. But what exactly had it been that tipped him off? What had made him decide to keep a closer eye on her when he had been so pleased with her following her sabotage of

Colonel Bisset? Or maybe this was only insurance. Maybe...

"All right. So how will you all know when to leave? I never get advance notice when the chieftain returns, and I'm sure he'll be unhappy if he finds you here. His Excellency did say none of you should be around when he is."

"Someone has been assigned to inform us of the chieftain's whereabouts. When he enters the palace grounds, we will act accordingly."

There was something too smooth about his replies every time. Smooth-skinned with a pretty face, he was as slippery as he was beautiful. And she detected something more insidious and spiked under the calm exterior, something she hadn't noticed before because of his—and all the men's—ridiculous appearance. But how apt, how fitting. Under the painted, gilded exterior lurked something too dangerous by half.

"I see," she said. "Then that'll be all. If you'd like to wait in the hallway, be my guest. I'll be sleeping."

"As you wish."

They filed out in a row, every step synchronized like soldiers marching to a disciplined rhythm. That wasn't out of the question. Maybe they *were* soldiers after all, taken from their former station to take up this job of spying on her at all times. Tet had said he'd picked them out himself, hadn't he? What deceit, stirred in shallow truth. Or maybe that had been his way of slyly taunting her.

She had been wrong. She had underestimated him, assuming that after Bisset's disgracing, she was safely harbored within his favor. It sickened her to realize it now, but at least she had stumbled upon the truth sooner rather than later. The door closed behind the concubines, and she dropped down onto the foot of the bed with her hands gripping the covers. Damn it.

After a long moment, she turned her head, searching for the dragons who had gone wandering around the room to find somewhere to rest. There, in the far corner. "Netra," she called. "Look at me."

The dragonet deigned to obey, but Anzi said nothing upon locking gazes. Instead, she narrowed her eyes and fixed the reptile with a sudden glare. This had better work...

I know you understand me, she thought. Loudly, clearly. As forcefully as she could. And I know you can speak. Not just to me, but to others. There was that piscin girl, and I bet you screamed at Kai this morning just like you did to me. Am I right?

Netra said nothing and lowered her head to the floor again. Her snout wrinkled slightly.

If you won't talk, then I won't either, Anzi threatened. And you can feed yourself from now on. You're big enough to fish on your own, you're a big girl now. She paused and lifted her chin when she felt something like a rush of smug skepticism run through her mind. It was a foreign sensation, clearly coming from the dragon rather than herself. But it was no less recognizable for it. Instantly, Anzi jumped to her feet and sharpened her glare. You think I don't mean it? Fine. I'm off, then. And if you think I'm going to come around before you get hungry again, go ahead, be my guest. We'll all head to the river for a nice meal. I'll find Serqet all the best fish and you can sit there and watch. You've been bullying her so much I think it's about time anyway.

She reached down to pick up the younger red hatchling, and when she straightened, she found Netra scrambling to her feet.

That's what I thought. Now, are you going to stop being a brat and help me? She waited, Serqet wriggling slightly in her arms and waving her stinger for balance. This was it. She had been patient because yes, fine, she spoiled Netra far more than she should, but now she was going to be firm. Treasured and rare or not, even a dragon needed to learn manners, especially when she had been babied for this long already. Netra was more than capable of caring for herself now that she had grown so much, but she still insisted on being coddled.

Anzi was terrible at coddling. And she wasn't interested in learning how to do so now.

I'm not going to ask you again, she said. *If I can't rely on you to help me when I need it most, then I won't ask you to help me, ever. You can do like you always do, eating and sleeping and whatever else pleases you if that's what you want, but I'm risking everything for reasons I'm starting to think you understand, more than I suspect. So make your choice. Help me or not, Netra. It's up to you. It has to start with both of us being more open to each other, like this.*

It was an agonizingly long silence, both within her thoughts and without. Sliver by sliver, her hopes for a response dwindled, flickered, disappeared—

I know. The dragonet moved around in a circle, idly chasing her tail. Her voice in Anzi's head was lyrical and sharp at the same time, as cold as it was graceful. It reminded her of the chirping of birds, of trilling from the treetops, mixed with the crackling of icicles falling from the eaves of a house. *I wait.*

"Wait for what?" Anzi demanded, so overwhelmed by inexpressible excitement that she forgot to ask silently.

Time. More time.

Why? Time for what? You've spoken already when it suited you. Just not to me. Except twice, when you're screaming to be fed.

Netra lay back down on the floor in an elegant circle, snout resting on top of her curled tail. *You. Thoughts. Shut, all the time.*

What?

'You. Mind. Shut. *Always.* Netra was staring hard at her, spines twitching as they rose and fell along her back. *Bad. Don't like.*

…What was she saying? That it was her own fault Netra hadn't spoken to her? *How long have you been able to talk and understand what I say?*

Don't know.

'How do you not know that?'

Do you remember? When you learn? To speak?

Anzi scowled. *That's not the same thing. You haven't been but hatched for a couple of months. That's different from humans like us, we go months and sometimes years without remembering what happened in between when we're born and we're grown.*

Still same. You cannot speak. Mind shut.

She snorted. But the piscin girl's mind wasn't? How about Kai's, then? You screamed at him too, didn't you? I'll have to explain that when I see him again, so thanks for that.

He knows. Netra sounded even more smug than before. *Mind good. Open. He is like me.*

Like you?

Dragon. Good. You can be. You do not.

This was difficult. The dragonet's words in her mind were sharp and vivid enough that she thought she could understand if she just tried a little harder, but at the same time, they were too jagged and splintered to make full sense of. It was like staring into a broken mirror and trying to make out her full reflection—impossible, only in pieces.

Well, you're not going to be telling anything to Kai, are you? You understand how dangerous things are? We have to be discreet. It's important—

Not stupid, Netra hissed. *I see. I know. You are the blind.*

*Maybe so. But if it's like this, then we either have to work together or you have to keep out from underfoot so you don't slow me down. I'm not saying that to scold you—*she grimaced when the dragon made a sour sound—*but because I can't let anything happen to you. You know that, don't you?* She gave her another long look. *I won't let them hurt you, but you have to help me keep you safe.*

From Un-man. In red.

Red? Red... The Emperor? What's an Un-man? And yes, I meant him. But you don't know what he's capable of because he does his worst when he and I are alone—

Not stupid, Netra said again. *I know. I see. His mind, open. Bad way.*

His, too? What, is everyone better at it than I am? How do I do it, too?

His wrong. Un-man. Don't be. Like him.

That again. What does that even mean? In response, a barrage of sensations flooded her mind, and Anzi gave her head a fierce shake. The sensations fled. *What was that! Don't do that.*

You see? I try to explain. Cannot. Your mind. Shut.

This was getting them nowhere. Not only was Anzi getting increasingly frustrated, she could see that Netra was, too. Her tail was whipping back and forth across the floor, lashing against it so sharply her spikes were leaving scratches on the wood.

I'm not doing anything, she insisted. *How do I change that? What do you need me to do?*

You. Fighting too much. Be open. See me. See you. More.

This was futile. She would try again later when Netra didn't look like she was about to chew through whatever came close enough for her to snap her jaws at. A part of her wanted nothing more than to go find Kai and demand that he explain how to obtain an *open mind* suitable for proper communication with a dragon, and why the hell Netra seemed to respect and like *him* more than she did her from day one, but that wasn't possible. She had to be more careful now that she had spies watching her every move.

Danger. She was on the precipice with Tet watching her teeter on the brink, and with one misstep, one wrong breath, he would shove her over the edge. She would lose everything. Her life was only a secondary concern. Her real concern was everyone else. What happened if she was exposed and executed? Everyone around her would be cut down. And if they didn't already have plans to kill Kai, he would surely be the first to go, if nothing else for the sole reason that they coveted his dragons. And Letti, without a doubt. They would suspect her of conspiring with her. And Oza, too, even though she had been so careful to keep him out of this.

She took a deep breath and closed her eyes. Against the wall, Netra stirred, rubbing her scales along the wall with a grating whisper. The little dragonet had always been able to sense her emotions well, and vice versa. Serqet's tail was waving about, too. She couldn't agitate herself and them like this. Calm.

At least Netra would be more cooperative than before. She was growing up, and it was time she learned how to protect herself in case Anzi ever…In case something happened and Netra had to escape. She had to be strong and clever enough to take care of herself and Serqet, attentive always. It wasn't fair to put such burdens on the little dragonet, so young, so fragile, and Anzi wished with all her heart for nothing more than the chance to whisk her away to someplace safe, someplace kinder, but there was no more time for that.

Anzi would have to put in work, too. A *shut* mind—she had always been stubborn, so she begrudgingly believed it. What did she have to do to fix that? She didn't know, but she would make it happen. Whatever she had to do, whatever it took. Anything to save the dragons. Her dragons.

Netra. A clicking sound answered her. When did you get so big?

When you. Did not look.

Anzi sighed.

She would have to look harder from now on.

~

"Your Excellency?"

Tet turned, one finger still in his mouth as he licked off whatever was on it. "Oh! Darling, very good, you're here. Strawberries?"

"No, thank you."

"Oh, just one. There's no point in letting these people have their stupid greenhouses if we can't enjoy the fruits of their labor cost-free. Come here."

No point? Besides the fact that without the greenhouses, the Imperial City would not only fail to produce winter exports but also starve? "Yes, sir."

"Say *ahhh*. Good, how does that taste?"

She wanted to gag. Inhumanly long, skinny fingers dipped between her lips to deliver the red berry...and they had been noticeably damp on the tips. Anzi had never been squeamish, but the realization that she had just touched the spit of a man who treated dragons and humans alike as insects wanted to make her vomit the scant contents of her stomach and take a scouring medicinal bath. "Delicious, Your Excellency."

"Fantastic. You're not wearing your leg brace today, I see. Impressive recovery. Did the chieftain ask about how you were injured, by the way? You've been spending a little time with him again lately, which is very good, but we don't want him knowing too much, yes?"

"I told him I injured myself while training, sir."

"Hm, good. Nothing else?"

"No, sir."

"I suppose he hasn't had the time. I have him running back and forth so much he can't come to neck you while asking nosy questions." He rubbed his chin and nodded thoughtfully. "Either way, good. For now, keep him distracted. I've decided to invite him to house his dragons here to train with ours. His seem very unruly, I think he'll appreciate our brand of discipline once he sees it. What do you think?"

She wanted to gag again. "I think he'll be impressed, sir."

"I think the same way. Desert barbarians are a bit dense and mistrustful sometimes, but he's very agreeable lately. Ever since he came back, actually, remarkable change. He wasn't so bad before he left, but I really do like him more now. He brought two adult dragons, darling. Both male, though, which is disappointing...but deliberate, of course."

"Deliberate?"

"Well, he must have realized I would want to take possession of whatever he brought, don't you know? But without female dragons to bear more eggs, it's not much of a gain if I kill him now and commandeer them."

Her heart stopped. It took everything she had not to betray her shock. Already? Already thinking of killing him. "I didn't think of that, sir. Would you like me to try to persuade him to bring female dragons next time?"

Tet reached down to tweak her nose. "I like that about you. Always a step ahead, every time. I was going to tell you to do exactly that, believe it or not—but for now, we entertain him. Treasure him. Make him think he's on top of the world and that if he continues to cooperate, he'll stay there. I just need..." He brought his forefinger and thumb together. "A little more from him. Ideally, half a dozen female dragons, maybe a couple of male ones for breeding variety. But emphasis on the females."

"Yes, sir."

"Now, here's the plan, darling. Listen carefully. We're going to have a festival. A real one this time, not a half-assed one put together at the last second. We're inviting all the little people from everywhere within a few weeks' travel on horseback—I've already had wagons sent out to provide free transportation. We're going to fill the streets with them, all screaming, all running around...It'll be like setting fire to an anthill, if ants liked fire and were twice as irritating. We'll put the word out that wild dragons have reappeared, and that we're looking for more candidates for the Premier. That should do the trick."

She didn't dare frown and make evident her confusion, but what was Tet trying to accomplish by doing all of this? It would make the Imperial City an absolute madhouse, on top of a dozen more madhouses. "...Yes, sir."

"Oh, fine. Just ask me, darling. Go on."

"...Please forgive me. I only mean to say that I'm concerned. I don't really trust the chieftain, nor his men. Do we know they mean no harm? Are they a threat to us with their wild dragons?"

"Worry not. In the event that Alexandre can't fend them off on his own, there's always me. It's been a long, long time since I've had to resort to violence—it's so crude, Anzi, and I'm really not the little rascal I used to be, killing here and there and everywhere I looked. But I am a god, Anzi. And I do have a dragon. The king of dragons."

Something in her chest twisted at the words, hard and fast. "Is the king here—"

"You'll learn soon enough. Not now, I like to make it a nice surprise. And as for the festival—necessary! We're preparing to move north. We have to pound into the little people's heads that we have more than enough dragons to lay waste to everyone in the countryside, with more on the way. Once they're here and see with their own eyes that we have a new source without having to wait to hatch any—ah! That's all we need to keep them nice and obedient while we take care of things on the new front."

"...I'll do my best to convince the chieftain to bring more."

"That would be good, yes. But whether the chieftain does agree to bring me more dragons in time for the invasion or not, word will spread far and wide. They'll speak of our new army of a hundred dragon riders, each one able to raze a city alone. And my, Anzi. You haven't seen them yet. I'm not prone to blubbering, but they are magnificent. There's something truly different about the wild ones Kaizat has brought, it's very nice, really."

"I'm glad, sir."

"So am I. Why don't you see them yourself? They're being flown over as we speak. Go and be a good host and take them down to the Cave where Bastien can tend to them. Kaizat will be there, too, so make sure you leave a good impression."

His broad wink made her feel dirty. "I understand. I'll go right away."

"One more thing, Anzi." She turned back only to find another strawberry resting on her lips. "Say *ahhh.*"

This time, she really did almost vomit. But with titanic effort, she swallowed the berry whole to spare herself the sickening effort of chewing on something fed to her by those strange, spindly fingers.

"Oh, you're so adorable. Honestly. This is why I have to keep you at my side at all times. Maybe I should give you a little collar and have you do tricks for me, how about that?"

"As you wish, Your Excellency."

"That's what I like to hear. Now shoo."

66

Oh, hell.

Anzi stood utterly still as the dragon drew close, ridged upper lip curling in the beginning of a snarl. It was dark with only the standing torches lining the stone walkway to lend their weak light, but the blood red hue of the massive dragon was no less intimidating for it. Wild dragon, indeed. She could sense savagery, strength, hardened brutality. A truly fearsome creature, born and raised according to its birthright, not like the ones of the Empire. She remained motionless even when the dragon lowered his head and came so close the small ridged horn curving up from the tip of its snout almost brushed her face. Hot breaths puffed out in clouds of steam that carried away on the stiff winter breeze. No frill to speak of, but even without it, the dragon's head was terrifically large as it glared down at her, orange eyes flashing.

"You're not afraid."

She didn't turn to look at Kai. "I can move before he gores me." She paused. "He? She?"

"Does it matter?"

"Maybe to him. Her."

"Rest assured, it doesn't. He doesn't care."

So, a male dragon. "His name? What do I call him?"

Kai came strolling around from the creature's flank to stand next to her, and he peered down into her face with a curious expression. "You're the first to ask that," he said. "No one else has bothered. You're very interested in him, did that Bastien ask you to convince me to stud him out?"

She shot him a hot, furious look. She hadn't meant to be so angry, but the lightning flash of disgust that rose up inside her was too fast to hide. "Who do you think I am?" she snapped, and it was on the tip of her tongue to ask—*Tet?* But she didn't. She held back and satisfied herself with a continuing glare until the chieftain smiled and stroked her cheek with his knuckle. Still offended, she knocked his hand away—and leaned back immediately when the dragon growled inches from her nose.

"Careful," said Kai, and for a second, she thought he was talking to her. "She's mine. Leave her be."

Another protracted growl, this one strong enough to send vibrations straight through her body. She suppressed the shudder that rose from her bones in visceral response. Dangerous, a voice whispered from within her. Strong. This was a kind of dragon different from the ones she knew.

"I'm not going to do anything to Kai," she said, voice rigid and almost daring to be impatient in its undertones. "You have nothing to worry about."

The growl continued, but she waited with a pointed stare until it faded. At that, Kai leaned forward again. "Don't mind him. He'll behave."

"And I told you not to bring the dragons here. But you've brought both, and now I can't do anything about it." She looked behind her at where the second one stood waiting. That one was smaller than this red one, though not by much since she had to guess that both of them were close to ten meters from snout to tail. Slender and blue-green-scaled, with a strange peacock-like webbed frill bearing beautiful false eyes, this second dragon was far stranger and more ethereal than she had ever imagined one could look.

"Don't be deceived," Kai said suddenly. "She's the more unpredictable one. You'd never know you were on her bad side until your head's between her teeth already."

As if on cue, the beautiful creature bared her teeth in what could only be a sinister, deliberate smile. Long, terrible teeth like perfect rows of deadly daggers gleamed in the flickering torch light.

"Her name is Qinglong. You'd do well to watch her carefully. Sa-Khente is far tamer if you look past first impressions."

Sa-Khente was the giant red one, then, who was still breathing hard on her as if he were preparing to swallow her whole. But the other— Qinglong? She looked back at Kai with a nonplussed frown. "Qing...?"

"Yes. She's not native to the desert. Comes from the northeast edge of the Feng territories.

"But all dragons come from the desert or the southern tundras," she said. "And the Adaraat is their birthing ground. They aren't native anywhere else." Or had that teaching been false too?

"The Purge changed things," said Kai, and the light smile that had been curving his mouth disappeared. "The survivors scattered, and some of them made it to the border of the Feng lands. I'd imagine some are still there. It's been a long time, Anzi."

"But that's basilisk and gryphon territory. Always has been. It's unlivable for dra—"

"Dragons will do what they must to survive, just like everyone else. What do territories and rivalries mean in the face of survival? It was either lose many or lose everyone. So they migrated. Mortal enemies be damned."

Anzi looked away. She still didn't understand how any dragon could have survived the Purge at all, but if she looked past it, she could reluctantly understand the urgency of the threat of extinction that would have driven the remaining ones into dangerous territory. But basilisks and gryphons, some of them even working together in a symbiotic relationship in certain stretches of land—it would have been a massacre. However few dragons had escaped Tet's reach, most of them must have perished while trying to flee northward.

"Anzi?"

Startled, she turned to look back at Kai—and at the same time, reached up to rest her hand on the still-threatening snout of the giant red dragon growling at her. She didn't know why she did it if there was a reason at all, but the electric sensation that shot through the light touch drove out every thought in her head in an instant. And suddenly she was drifting, swirling, floating like a leaf on a stream as vague impressions of blurred images wrapped around her. She could make no sense of them, only that there was a great deal of sand...now greenery. Water. A mountainside, rocks crumbling under the weight of her claws and dropping down the rocky slopes. Her wings spreading, mighty and heavy—

She threw herself back, hand burning. Or was it freezing? It was raw from fingertip to wrist as if she had held it in fire, and a wave of pins and needles traveled back and forth, back and forth as she stumbled away with her face contorting in blended shock and confusion. Maybe even fear, if she could figure out what exactly had frightened her just now.

Kai was by her side before she could say a word. He held her with one hand grasping her elbow and the other reaching for her waist to right her before she could trip and fall over her feet. "Anzi!" His voice was sharp, alarmed, and she found herself absurdly sensitive to the guttural hitch of it at the very end when he pulled her close. "What's wrong?"

Over his shoulder, the crimson dragon stared at her in abrupt silence, no longer growling. She avoided its eyes, heart pounding and pulse throbbing. "I'm fine. Let go."

"Sa-Khente, get back!" he snapped without looking away from her. "Anzi, what did he do to—"

"He didn't do anything. Leave him alone." She shook herself free from his grasp. Her knees were still wobbly, but she couldn't blame that on the dragon. "We need to get him and—Qinglong? Down into the Cave. It's warmer down there."

"They'll be fine. It's you I'm worried about. Anzi, what happened?"

She stilled, wondering the same thing. But her stomach churned when she tried to pry apart the memory, so much so that she barely noticed when Kai snatched up her hand and turned it this way and that, looking for wounds. She shook him loose again. "It's fine, I was...My leg. It's still bothering me, and..."

She was still in the middle of formulating the lie when he stopped tugging on her hand. He paused as if he were listening to something, and that was, approximately, when she knew pretense was futile. She looked over his shoulder and examined the hulking red dragon with narrowed eyes and her mouth set in a hard line. Well. At least now she knew Netra wasn't the only one who could speak to others in their minds. She had suspected, but this was almost proof. "He speaks to you?" she asked. She kept her voice low; the two guards standing by the entrance to the underground Cave were close by. "That's what he's doing, isn't it. Right now."

Kai's golden gaze flicked back up from her hand to her face, and in the darkness, they shone with a spectral sheen. He remained silent, and she tried desperately to guess whether he was still speaking with Sa-Khente or if he was thinking of something evasive to respond with. She hoped it was the former...knew it was the latter. Damn him.

"We should talk again soon," he said quietly. "If we can both find time when we aren't surrounded by others."

She pursed her lips. Easier said than done. Ever since he had returned, she had noticed there were always attendants checking on him, messengers delivering useless invitations and reports, even harem girls offering to entertain them with songs and dancing. They were being watched even when they tried to retreat to her own room, and twice, Netra's superior hearing had caught palace maids—if they really were palace maids—lingering outside the door or the wall a little too long to be accidental. And that was only when Kai managed to make time to see her at all: Tet and his advisors monopolized his time far more aggressively than when he had visited the palace last. That couldn't be a coincidence. Anzi wanted to think Tet was only extra vigilant out of paranoia, but she had to consider the possibility that he knew something was about to go wrong. Maybe even knew she would have something to do with it. But then why was he making such a show of favoring her? He had nothing to gain from her by doing so that he couldn't get out of her with just another beating. Was it a game to him? Was he playing with her?

"You're taking so long I've come out to see what's going on!" a familiar voice called to them suddenly, cutting Anzi off just as she opened her mouth to reply. She closed it again quickly and turned her head to see Bastien emerging from the Cave's shadowed entrance...Ah. So he, too, was unwilling to leave them alone for long. She had never seen him come out into the open even once, not until tonight. It was too obvious. "But I'm pleased you've brought gifts for me, Chieftain," the man said with a wide grin as he ambled over, skinny arms crossed over his narrow chest. Out here, he looked far smaller than he did underground, but it only made him look more sinister. Anzi glared.

"Take good care of them," said Kai. "These two are my most...valuable."

Valuable? She gave him a sidelong glance. Sounded like something Tet would say, not Kai, which raised her suspicions all the more. He was up to something.

"Oh, my. That just makes me even more excited. Please, Chieftain, this way. I'll show you my own premium stock, how does that sound?"

"Please. I couldn't resist."

She was going to vomit if they didn't stop. With a surreptitious twitch, she turned and eyed the green-blue dragon as it crept over the grass and closer into the range of the torch lights. Her breath caught. Murky shades cleared and brightened into smooth turquoise, and the dragon's body was long and snake-like, similar to Netra's. But she could swear the creature reminded her more of a wyrm with its slender legs instead of the bulking, muscular stature she was accustomed to seeing. Indeed, the claws looked more like bird's feet, and not only that, she saw graceful, catfish-like whiskers drooping down the sides of the dragon's snout. This was like no dragon she'd ever imagined, much less seen before. She watched with wide eyes as the creature glided past her on silent feet. Not even the rustling of the grass betrayed its progress, and when the dragon caught Anzi's stare out of the corner of its own eye as it passed, she took in an involuntary breath. The bright, keen awareness in its gaze was more than human, and the whiskers floated up as if touched by a gentle breeze…

And then it was over. Qinglong the turquoise dragon went on ahead, disappearing down into the Cave after the others. With a steadying breath, Anzi followed her in.

BASTIEN MADE HER LEAVE. Her presence wasn't necessary, he said, and she needed to be doing her *real job* as he had so succinctly put it. After that, she had no choice but to leave him continue lecturing Kai on feeding and breeding regimens for dragons, so maybe it was just as well that she left. Listening to Bastien babble on about so disgustingly degrading made her want to pick him up by the throat and smash him into the wall.

At least she knew Kai's interest was insincere, that this was all a part of some secretive master plan he couldn't confide in her about. Had to be, she was certain of it. But the way he egged Bastien on into rambling more about his genius ideas, even suggesting that they exchange dragons to introduce 'new blood' made her want to bash their heads together anyway. Good thing Pierro and the others weren't here. Her patience was razor-thin as it was and none of them liked her very much anymore, if they ever had. Snapping at them all night would have battered their fragile camaraderie more than it could take. With an angry exhale, Anzi sat and crouched against the back wall of the chamber instead of nosing about the eggs as Bastien had wanted her to. He was busy lodging the newcomers and talking Kai's ears off. He wouldn't know she was stalling again, and she could buy these unborn dragons precious time before she inevitably released them into the world.

Except that one. One day or a hundred or ten thousand, it wouldn't matter to it. She stared at her left where the massive, black-and-silver mottled egg as long as her arm lay resting against the wall beside her. It looked even more misshapen than when she'd first seen it all those weeks ago, if that was possible. With a sad smile, she turned and sat cross-legged in front of it before running her hands down the shell.

"I can't do anything for you," she murmured. "You're the only one I can't hatch. It's a good thing, though. I'm sorry you're trapped, but...it's probably better this way. At least you're safe from what's out here, and they can't hurt you when they can't get to you in the first place." She balled her fist and knocked on the curved surface with light taps. "No one can break through this. Bastien said so, and if he's willing to admit it, then it's got to be true. So you're the only dragon he's ever had to confess to being beaten by."

The thought made her grin. Prince Bastard, the unhatched, the unhatchable. She hated to think it might be in pain, but least it was safe from Tet and his minions. And if it died unhatched, maybe it was a mercy. But gods, she could feel the life flowing under the surface, dark and murky but alive nonetheless. It was right there—right there! Past the impenetrable wall that was this magic-imbued shell. Maybe one day, someone would find out how to get past it. But it wouldn't be her. She hoped not.

"Hey...Look at you. Slacking instead of working hard? Might have to tattle."

She glared. "What are you doing here? No training tonight."

Pierro leaned against the chamber entryway and crossed his bulky arms over his chest, looking entirely too smug. "No training from *Bastien* tonight," he corrected. "Never said we couldn't train on our own. The grounds are open late, no one to get in the way."

"Knock yourself out."

"It's not just me. Doufan and Aimee are already waiting there. I told them I'd stop by and get you myself."

She snorted. "You came for nothing, then. I won't be joining you."

"You don't even like being here. Come on, this is your excuse to leave."

"I need to stay."

"Why? Because you have to babysit the chieftain? Come on..." He grinned and jerked his chin at her. "To tell you the truth, I'm starting to think you're straddling the fence. If the fence is two different men, that is."

"What?"

"You've got Oscar on the side already tying himself up in a knot over you. Even had you over for dinner. And then here's the chieftain, already half-naked for convenience. Tell me the truth. Have you fucked him yet?"

She stood, and the look in her eyes must have been enough to warn him off. He straightened and dropped his arms at his side, hand just happening to dangle by the hilt of his sword.

"Kidding, kidding," he said. "But really. Come with me and I won't tell Bastien you were playing around instead of working hard."

"You think that scares me?"

"I don't think anything scares you. But you don't need more attention than you're already getting, do you?"

She stilled, and the air was suddenly heavy and threatening. She narrowed her eyes-

"Because sooner or later," he continued with a smirk, "you're going to get caught with your pants down and Oscar's hand down there instead. You really have to work on that discretion, Anzi."

"...What?" she asked. She had thought he was accusing her of something more malevolent...the truth. Seemed he was too dense for that, luckily.

"Did you know we've been ordered to watch you?" His smirk grew wider. "Looks like you've fucked up. You used to be the perfect soldier, married only to her duty to the Empire. Inviolate virgin off-limits to, you know, all mortal men. But look at you now. Sneaking around with other soldiers when no one's looking, huh? And sitting around being lazy when you think you can get away with it. What were you even doing when I got here? Mumbling to yourself and groping that egg, you've got me all curious now."

"Shut up," she said flatly. "Don't waste my time."

"I'm just saying...Don't rock the boat." He shrugged. "We're not supposed to be on your side, you know. But the nicer you are to us..."

She said nothing, and his smile grew into a wide, triumphant grin.

"That's what I thought. Come on, entertain us. Bastien never has to know. He'll be gone all night anyway, jacking off now that he's got two new dragons down here. He won't even think to look for you. And the chieftain can find his own way back."

She hesitated. "You said someone told you to watch me. Who did?"

"Follow me out. I'll let you be nosy on the way."

67

Sparring was agonizing thanks to her hobbling leg and the occasional ripping spasms that made her grit her teeth against the crippling pain that flooded her from thigh to foot, but she wasn't going to show weakness. Pierro's growing smirk as the minutes slipped past was already making her want to murder him, and he was probably one stumble away from taunting her again, his favorite pastime.

She had to stop caring so much, she told herself as she and Doufan circled each other in the dirt. Two of the standing torches had gone out by the training ground they had chosen, but it was still bright enough to see the man's narrowed eyes and the angular, serpent-like face they peered out of. Doufan, the most mysterious of them all. Pierro was loud and brash; there could be no comparison. Aimee was quieter, but only in the haughtiest and most transparent of ways, and Anzi—Anzi had never been mysterious at all. Standoffish, yes, she could admit it now, but never mysterious. The immigrant soldier was different. He never spoke even when spoken to, never reacted to murmured insults toward his heritage, never flaunted even his most impressive accomplishments. She had no idea what kind of person he was, only that he was all too quiet and impenetrable. And a hell of a good fighter.

"*Agh!*" She swallowed the half-cry back and delivered a slashing parry against his own sword, a skinny little blade that shouldn't have been able to jar her leg as badly as it had. Both of their weapons were blunted, but damn if that didn't make it even worse. It felt like someone had taken a sledgehammer to her bad leg, twice.

"Hey, now, Dou. You shouldn't do that to her, you know she's got a limp."

"Shut up," she snapped without taking her eyes off the Feng soldier. "Stay out of it, Pierro."

"Hey, I'm just trying to help."

"No, you're gloating. Now shut up."

She didn't need his false sympathy. He was enjoying watching her get walloped by the one person who could even get close. Doufan with his thrice-damned, black magic-like affinity for any weapon he could get his hands on was living Pierro's dream for him with every strike he landed on her. And there could be no doubt he was even stronger and faster than when she had seen him last—or was he? She recalled once more that Doufan had always held back, even if it meant he lost. He'd never showed anyone the upper limits of what he was capable of. She hated people like him, people who crept around, sneaky and lying and deceptive. But maybe that was why she was so bad at all of this espionage and intrigue. She should have watched him more closely and picked up some tips instead.

But still. In the end, she was the superior fighter.

"Enough." She waved her hand at him when he got back up onto his feet, a new smearing of dirt over his uniform from when she had just sent him crashing onto the ground with a brutal kick. "You'd be dead already, anyway. That's enough."

"You would be, too."

"What?"

He didn't repeat himself. He spun his sword in his barely-twitching hand and moved away, swift and smooth as a silent shadow. She stared after him, wondering if he'd really just spoken or if she had only imagined it. Doufan didn't talk. Not unless he had no choice. Hearing his voice was a new and foreign experience every time, and she could count the times she remembered he had spoken on one hand.

"Wow, Anzi," Pierro called. "You must be tired. Haven't seen you beg off like that before."

"I told you to shut *up*," she snarled, both because his incessant sneering was riding her last nerve and also because he was right. Her leg felt like she'd just rolled it around on a bed of hot irons. If she went on, she couldn't be sure her healed muscles wouldn't rupture and snap after everything she (Doufan) had put it through. Damn opportunist knew how to exploit a weakness, and she had nothing but begrudging respect for it.

"Well, what now?"

"Nothing," she said. "I'm going back to the palace."

"Ah. Then I guess we'll have to go, too. Since we're supposed to keep our eyes on you and all." He added the last remark under his breath as he came close, just loud enough for her to hear and no one else. She narrowed her eyes.

"The Emperor trusts me," she said. She hadn't rebutted with anything earlier when he had mentioned it because she hadn't known exactly how to parry the gloating claim, but now she cautiously tested the waters. "If he told you to watch me closely, it's only because he wants you to learn from me. So do as I do. That's what His Excellency would want."

"Oh?" He took her practice swords from her and began moving back to the open weapons rack. Hanging on his next words despite herself, she followed. "What if," he said in a low, drawling voice. "What if...I told you His Excellency has no idea about it?"

She had to use every ounce of her willpower to conceal her surprise. Calm. In stride. She couldn't let Pierro know he'd rattled her with that one simple question. "Then you're wasting both your time and mine." She scoffed and turned away, affecting an air of jeering indifference—and gambling on the certainty that he would hurriedly say something else to make her linger. He loved having someone to hang on his every word. He and Oscar shared more than a passing family resemblance in that regard.

"Wait."

Perfect. "What. I'm not in the mood for games. Whatever political thing you've mired yourself in, it has nothing to do with me. Spy on me all you want for your grandfather and the other noble families, but—"

"It's not them who've put us up to this, you dunce. Hey!" He pulled up next to her, jostling her with his shoulder so she couldn't continue walking away. She rolled her eyes, maintaining her pretense of irritated impatience. "Listen to me, Anzi. I said it was all of us who were told to watch you, not just me. Why would my family ask Doufan to do anything? Aimee, maybe, since her family's always been close with mine, but you really think anyone in the upper districts would lower themselves to conspiring with an immigrant? Come on, now."

True. The attitudes toward outsiders among the upper crust were all generally the same. "Can you stop wasting my time, then. I'm not interested in gossip. Do whatever you want—"

"It's the colonel. Did you hear me? It's Colonel Bisset. He's even having us tail you wherever you go, if we can manage it. Told us to just this morning."

She paused. "And have you?"

"Have we what? Been following you around? Not yet. But you can believe we'll be doing it. We're not stupid enough to run up against him and defy direct orders. I don't know what his problem with you is and why he's giving us secret instructions, but either way, we've been told what to do. Simple as that. Even if he's not giving them on behalf of the Emperor, we have our orders."

"And you're warning me about it?"

"Sure." He shrugged. "Truth is, we don't want you doing stupid shit yet. I sure don't. Maybe when I'm sure that they'll pick me to replace you, but this early in the game? If you end up getting caught doing something you're not supposed to be doing, and you get"—he made a slicing gesture across his throat with his hand—"then we might be shit out of luck,too."

"So you're just helping yourself, in the end. You want me to stay out of trouble so your transition goes smoothly."

"What? Did you think I was tipping you off about the colonel out of the goodness of my heart?"

She turned to look at their fellow soldiers standing by the far bench. They were staring now. "Let's go," she said. "You're going to look suspicious talking to me like this. Do they know you're telling me everything?"

"Never said I was telling you everything. But no. I didn't bring it up to them. Then again, they're not stupid, and they probably would have done the same thing I just did if they're smart. We're not all dumber than you are, Anzi. You should keep that in mind. We got where we are because we're that good."

She didn't spare him even a glance. Anything she said in response would only encourage him to launch into another bitter rant about how she thought she was better than everyone and had no friends. The usual.

"Hey, I'm still talking—"

"Anything useful?" She stopped walking and looked over her shoulder at him. "If there's nothing else you want to tell me that I'll find relevant, then..."

Ordinarily, she would never brush off a willing blabbermouth like this. She would leech them for all the information she could get, resorting even to thinly veiled threats if it came to that, but she knew Pierro well enough to understand that wasn't the way to get him to spill his guts.

What got to him was being dismissed, being underestimated. *Ignored.* He would fold in half a second-

"When the festival comes around, we're to keep you and the chieftain separated at all times. He's up to something. We don't know what, and I have no idea what you've done to get on his bad side all of a sudden, but he's out for blood. You watch. He's coming for you."

The festival, only a few weeks to go. Preparations were underway and the streets would be filled to the brim with Imperial City natives and visitors from all over the land…She didn't yet know how, but if Bisset was going to do something to try to expose or sabotage her, it would happen then. With all eyes on her and everyone reveling in the celebration of the wild dragons' supposed return, it could be a prime opportunity to disgrace her in Tet's eyes. But how? What was the colonel planning? The man was loyal to Tet, she was certain of it. Surely he wouldn't be plotting to have her killed when she was still so valuable to the Emperor he served with such unswerving loyalty. Not over a single spat, even if he'd been roughed up for it, admittedly. He was decades and decades old, a battle-hardened man far older than anyone knew for certain. Would he let himself get bent out of shape by some soldier still wet behind the ears?

Or maybe he had always been that way. No longer blinded by the respect she used to lug around for him, perhaps he was far pettier and more bitter than she had ever realized. And Tet had humiliated him in front of her, no less. Maybe that was what had made Bisset snap, being disgraced in front of someone who used to serve under him. And maybe that was exactly along the vein of whatever he had planned for her now. If that were true, he was truly pathetic. But it also meant he was more dangerous than she'd been prepared for, an angry man with an axe to grind rather than a subdued former threat. This changed things.

"Thanks," she said, pitching her voice with just the right intonation to make herself sound like she was forcing her gratitude. "I appreciate the heads up."

"You still don't get it. You're not—"

"Maybe we should just head in, Pierro. Think we're all very tired…All of us." And with a long, pointed look, she headed off.

It was an entire week and a half before she could come face to face with Kai again. She had no idea where he'd been during that time, but she couldn't put the blame solely on him. She had been gone too, forced to tend to the dragon eggs with Bastien late into the night—even sleeping down there in the Cave in temporary quarters. Her punishment, it seemed, judging by the way the weasely little man breathed down her neck the entire time and watched her every move. He was still angry about when she had left that night to train with her auxiliaries instead of doing as he instructed, and now he no longer let her leave his sight. A damned unfortunate mistake, and yet if she hadn't gone and followed Pierro then, she might never have known about Bisset's machinations.

Or could it be that Pierro had been the one lying? Had he given her bad information in a devious move to mislead her? Damn him. Damn them. Damn everyone—Anzi had never been skillful at reading others motives' and understanding how their minds worked. Why couldn't everyone be plain and transparent, all their motives laid out on the table like detailed references for her to peruse? She could use one of those for Kai, too.

"Want to tell me why you brought a female dragon that night when it was supposed to be two male dragons?"

A hint of a smile curved his mouth. "Hello to you, too, Anzi. I've missed you."

She narrowed her eyes, delivering the most scorching glare possible to the man currently perched on her balcony. It was just like that first night he had made himself welcome, and it brought back memories that both annoyed her and made every part of her flush with a strange heat. But no, enough of that. There was no telling when he had to slip away again, no telling when someone would come slinking by and expose them. They finally had a chance to speak again.

"Answer the question," she demanded, keeping her voice low but sharp. "Before I went to go meet you and help you bring the wild dragons in, the Emperor specifically told me you would be bringing two male dragons. He even mentioned it was deliberate. That you didn't want to give him a chance to try to breed them." Her mouth twisted into an ugly scowl at the words. How degrading. She hated repeating them. "Qinglong wasn't supposed to be there, was she?"

His smile grew. "You didn't ask me anything about it that night. Why all of a sudden?"

"I was..." The truth was that she had been distracted. The realization hadn't even occurred to her until after it was too late, when she had been in the middle of sparring with the auxiliaries far away. "Just tell me. Why?

You know that Bastien is...like that. You know why he wants females. Even if you didn't realize it until after you'd brought her, you must have known you couldn't keep her there. Bastien was badgering you the entire time about taking her permanently. He's deranged, Kai. You don't know what he's like, how desperate he is. He thinks all dragons are his personal toys. He's sick. You don't know what he'll have done to her if you keep her there."

"I thought you've been keeping Bastien busy so as to avoid that."

"Excuse me?"

"Isn't that why you've been down there all this time? The few times I managed to sneak out to find you, you were always gone."

"Who's been telling you where I am?" She glared when he only continued to smile. "Tet? Someone else? Or are you spying on me? I'm going to figure things out on my own eventually. It's up to you whether it's in time for me to help you, too."

"Things are going the way they should. You don't need to worry."

"I'm sorry I can't believe that."

"Don't be." He slid off the carved balcony railing and moved toward the threshold where she stood. "I missed you."

"I..." She caught herself. She was obviously more exhausted than she realized; she had been about to parrot back the sentiment without thinking. "Good for you."

She faltered when the heat of his body radiated across the suddenly too-small space between them. Had his shoulders always been so broad? And how could he not be freezing cold in this weather? She was of hardy constitution and still balked at the idea of walking outside in this wintry cold without a warm layer to protect her. But here he was, torso bared for all the world to see except for his signature collar. Outrageous. Studded gemstones and gold jewelry—didn't the cold make the metal even more frigid against his skin? Her eyes darted down to his chest in what was supposed to be an idly critical once-over, and froze on the dusky nipples just under the edge of the drooping collar. They were pebbled against the cold, evidence that her suspicions had been correct...

"Is there something on my chest?"

She tore her eyes away immediately and fixed them back on his face with doubled intensity. Triple. Heat flooded her face, and she was glad the nighttime darkness would cover whatever shade had just attacked her cheeks. "If I let you in, are you going to explain why you're bending over backward to please them? I thought you hated the Empire. I thought you hated what they did to the dragons."

"Let's go inside first," he murmured, and he slid his hands around her waist. His palms were large and warm as they settled on her hips, and both of her legs chose that moment to wobble. Only because of her injury, of course. Never mind that her good leg was about to collapse, too. Half-dazed by the abrupt sensations filling her up from the inside, she let him walk her backward several paces until they were inside her room. He closed the door behind them with his foot, and from the corner, Netra raised her head to look at them, spines half-raised even as she remained curled up in her rag nest. Kai turned toward her as if listening to something, and after a wordless silence, returned his attention to Anzi once more. They must have just spoken to each other. She wished she knew what they had said.

"You don't need to worry so much," he said quietly. "Everything is fine. Do as you normally would, otherwise you'll only look more suspicious. They don't know anything for now."

"I'm not choosing to stay down there day in and day out, Kai. We're being kept apart, haven't you noticed?"

"Your Emperor—"

"Stop calling him *my* Emperor. And it's not him. There's someone else pulling the strings, I think. The colonel, you remember him? And he might have gotten Bastien in on it, too, but I can't tell for certain if he's just being the typical ass he always is or if he's making an extra effort. I don't know. I don't know anything yet. A lot of things happened that I don't have time to explain. They might have figured something out somehow."

His fingers ghosted down the side of her face, and she flinched in surprise. She hadn't even noticed him moving his hand. "You're doing too much," he murmured. "Be careful. I need you safe."

"Safe doesn't get things done."

It was hard to see in the weak moonlight filtering through the thick paper windows, but she thought she saw his expression harden even as he smiled, a curious combination of determination and satisfaction. "You're right," he said. "It doesn't."

"Kai, just let me help—"

He kissed her hard, stealing away the rest of what she meant to say right out of her head. When he finally pulled away—the second time, because he had ended up coming back for another kiss the first time he tried—she couldn't remember exactly why she had been angry moments ago.

"You should take your own advice before you give it," he said before she could pull her lost words back out of the ether. "Netra says she can hear someone coming. I have to go."

"Wait—"

He was gone again, disappeared into the night.

ANZI FELT his lips on hers again three days later when she awoke before dawn, a phantom memory of the heated kiss he'd last left her with. She wondered if she had been dreaming about it, and for a paralyzing moment of terror, considered the possibility that she had gone prancing over into Kai's mind again in the middle of the night like a gamboling horse looking for a choice, juicy patch of sweet grass. But she could remember nothing of it, only fragmented dreams and nothing else. Good. With a relieved sigh, she rolled out of bed and prepared for the day.

"You can go where you want today," Bastien told her with a grin when she trudged into the Cave. He was lying on his back on the table, head lolling off the foot of it as he stared at her upside down. "Finally, I can get you out of my hair."

She glared. "What was that?"

"You heard me. Leave me alone today. Been waiting to get rid of you for too long, now."

…Clearly, she wasn't hearing him correctly. But he only grinned wider as if he had just won the most marvelous prize in all the world.

"Alexandre apparently had some hassle to handle this morning outside the city, so he can't make me babysit you today. And I deserve a break. So get out of here. The eggs can wait, I'm sick of seeing your face."

She left, simmering. So it really had been Bisset. He had made Bastien hold her down here for the last two weeks while he—what? What was he trying to accomplish? Or was he simply trying to make sure she was under watch moment to moment? She ground her teeth together as she plotted several different ways to break the colonel's neck and end it all. It was nice to fantasize. And maybe one day, she really would be strong enough to knock him on his ass.

She took Netra and Serqet to the hidden river bend and spent her day there. Twice, she stood up and nearly made her way to the mages' Tower, determined to see Oza no matter the risk, but sat back down both times. She couldn't. He was even more vulnerable than she was, trapped in a prison home. He was just a boy, a child. She should never have left him there alone. It nauseated her, remembering how she had abandoned him for so long—and for what? Useless ambitions. And look at her now, unable to go to him now that she wanted to. What cruel irony, what stupid shortsightedness...

She drifted off under the sun, giving up on keeping an eye out for anyone who might have tailed her out here. It was quiet, other than Netra's continual bullying of the younger dragon. The bitter cold sliced in under her leathers, sapping her strength and lowering her guard, but she was exhausted and spared no wistful thoughts of warmth and soft bedding. She wouldn't spend a moment of freedom cooped up in the palace where the maids and other spies pressed their ears to her door and rummaged about her things while she was gone. If remaining there meant she might be able to casually run into Letti for the first time in days, but someone had been keeping them apart, too. It was no use.

She slept better here than she had in days, dozing off against a boulder with her arms wrapped around herself to stave off the cold. She didn't even dream. Just the bliss of dark sleep, undisturbed, calm and peaceful-

"Ah!"

She jerked awake and rolled over onto her side, gasping at the searing agony that ripped apart her chest and belly. She convulsed around it, squeezing herself with her arms as she struggled to make sense of what was happening while simultaneously trying to stop the pain, the pain, from ripping her open.

But it wasn't hers. The terrible burning—it came from something deeper than her own flesh, from somewhere in the recesses of her soul. It was coming from—

"Kai!"

68

If Anzi were in her right mind, she would have known better than to charge blindly in whatever direction was pulling her, especially when it brought her into the lower market district where she careened into angry citizens, none of whom recognized her or her mind-shattering urgency. Not that she cared. She shoved them all aside with more strength than she should have, sending people tumbling into vendor stalls and against building walls and occasionally, to the ground. None of it mattered. She ignored the furious shouting and cursing following her every hurried step, driving herself ever onward first this way, then that, then backward every time she became too terrified she had gone in the wrong direction to go any farther.

Somewhere, she was sure he was dying. She had no idea how she knew or why it was she could feel him—or maybe she would if only her mind weren't reeling and tearing apart, splintering under the weight of the pain that carved so much deeper because she knew it was Kai who suffered instead of her. But that was all she could think of. Him, it was him. Something had happened and she had no idea where he was or what had happened, and every second that passed as she wheeled wildly to and fro in search of him drove her steadily insane.

Someone knocked into her one too many times, and with an enraged, half-crazed shout, she turned and bent to pick up the unhitched wagon full of horse feed next to her from the bottom. She didn't even register the weight. In the next instant, the entirety of it, load and all, was flipping through the air to crash into the stone fountain five meters away. It landed with an almighty crash, bursting apart at the wheels, axle, and along the boards, pieces splashing into the water and showering the screaming market-goers with frigid sprays. The bags of feed were strewn all about, and there were several people shouting at her, around her, everywhere, begging her to go. But blinded by the terrible burning that coursed through her, filling every inch of her skin and bloating her like a leather skin about to tear open, Anzi could only turn and crash into the nearest stall and knock it over. The impact should have hurt. It should have brought her to her senses. But instead, she picked up what remained intact of the large wooden stand and flung it across the way, failing to notice the screaming retreat of the panicked merchant who waddled away with his hands over his head.

She couldn't find him. He was somewhere dangerous and inescapable and he was dying and she was here, useless, senseless, too far away to do anything about it. Someone was doing something to him and if only she could reach them, she would rend them limb from limb and tear their throat out with her teeth, but she didn't know where to go, how to get to Kai, whether it was too late too late too late—

Netra's heavy weight pouncing on her shoulders and the digging of claws into her skin brought her back out of insanity. The dragon had run along after her when she fled the river bend, half-hopping, half-running the entire time. Serqet must have been able to keep up too, somehow, as the hatchling cowered nearby. But here was Netra, now hovering before her a scant handspan away from Anzi's face as her gossamer white wings beat the air. She screeched again, louder and higher this time, and Anzi was finally able to push back the suffocating mass of terror that had clogged her awareness like fleece soaked in water.

"It's Kai," she croaked, voice half-gone. Her hand flew to her throat. "It's Kai—"

Netra screeched again, a harsh, scolding sound.

"I..." And it was then that understanding finally dawned on her. She looked around with wide, horrified eyes at the carnage she had wrought in her mindlessness. The heavy brazier that had been lit with a large flame was upside down, the kindling that had been stored inside only glowing with the smallest embers now. Every stall was overturned, too, with vegetables and fruits spilled out over the dirt as well as countless baubles and fabrics. She swallowed hard and grabbed her right wrist that still shook as if it were eager to go on and continue in the unbridled destruction.

No. She couldn't do this. She was being stupid, tapping into the panicked animal instincts inside her instead of using her wits. Kai—if Kai was in danger, then she only needed to find out where he was. All this destruction had accomplished nothing and never would. No, she needed to find the advisors, they would know. They would put a search out. She hurried forward, stumbling every other step until she eventually righted herself and headed for the palace. The upside of her outburst was that the street was now deserted, and she rushed unhindered.

If all was well, she would come back and sort this all out. Now that she was lucid again, she remembered all too clearly the terrified expressions on the people's faces, and guilt pulsed in her chest, hot and sickening. But as awful as she felt about what she had done, she knew she had to get to Kai first. She had to. If she couldn't find him, couldn't reach him— another wave of horrific pain stabbed and tore down her belly, and she gasped and wheezed as she ran on, never stopping.

She had to find him. No matter what.

When she reached the palace walls with Netra hopping behind her and Serqet clinging to one arm, she didn't bother waiting for the gate guard and the golem to open up the way. There—a rope ladder was being pulled back up, and she didn't stop to question who must have just used it. No time. It was already close to four meters up the wall, and she could see the soldiers up at the very top chatting as they proceeded to reel it up, but she didn't care about shouting at them to stop. She crouched, digging in as every muscle tensed, every sinew strained, then let fly in a running leap. She hit the wall so hard the impact rattled her teeth, but she had what she wanted, her free hand secured on the bottom rope rung. She kicked the stone wall hard, scrabbling for purchase when the ladder suddenly plummeted a meter, and surprised, indignant shouts came from the wall guards above. They could be angry about whatever they wanted to be later. Later!

"Pull me up!" she shouted. "Pull me up now!"

She had half-expected them to ignore her, the crazy fringer soldier scrabbling up the wal, but perhaps they had pieced together who she was from how she had leaped nearly three times her height up the wall.

"Drop me down!" she demanded as soon as she clambered over the top of the wall and leaped for the other side with the rope ladder still in hand. "Right now!"

They obeyed. From this close, they would have recognized her for sure, if not for her First Guard designation then at least as someone on the verge of rabid retaliation. They lowered her toward the palace grounds with all haste, but she leaped down the rest of the way when they were too slow. The impact jarred both knees, and if she were anyone else, they would be shattered into pieces, but with a stubborn crawl and a determined gnashing of her teeth, she was gone again. Panic pushed back the pain enough for her to sprint into the palace proper and head straight for the throne room without stumbling. She threw open the doors with no regard for the guards outside or for proper routine—and found no one. No one? Tet? Where was the Emperor? Where were his advisors? Where-

"If you're looking for His Excellency, he has been resting all day elsewhere. Express orders to not disturb him for anything, sir."

She whirled around, eyes narrowed in a furious scowl at the guard who dared to tell her exactly what she didn't want to hear. The man stiffened, drawing himself up and staring at Serqet in her arms and Netra hovering in the air behind her head.

"But his advisors were here!" he added quickly. "And there was a messenger who wanted to report that there'd been an attack on the visiting desert chieftain. He was brought here for treatment."

"He's—he's alive, then? The chieftain?"

"Yes, but he was in dire condition from what I understood. The healers will already be with him. It happened less than a half-hour ago."

She was sprinting past him and his fellow guard before the last words had left his mouth, and she shot down hallways and up winding stairs one after the other. There were several infirmaries Kai could have been taken to, but this was the closest one in the palace to where she was. And it didn't matter. If he wasn't here, then she would check every single-

"Kai!"

She was at his side in an instant. She had shoved aside the two soldiers standing in her way as well as a dark-skinned man in a striped desert robe and headcloth, barely seeing them. Just the man lying supine on the bed in front of her, two long, ugly gashes marring his abdomen. One stretched down from his chest, shallow at the top but sliced deep diagonally to his right hip, while the other was shorter but no less serious, a direct stab to the gut.

"He's unconscious," she choked out as she reached for his face, aching to touch, to feel, to know there was still life coursing under the bronzed skin splashed with blood. He was breathing, but it was so shallow and wet. No, no—"Who did this?"

"Please," the healer next to her wheezed, sweat pouring down the sides of his face. "He's been poisoned, and the wounds aren't closing properly. We need to focus."

She couldn't bear to step back, but she had to be silent so the physicians could keep Kai alive. Do something, she begged. Say something. Anything. But he was gone, walking the line of life and death, only his body fighting for survival. At least wherever he was, he couldn't feel the pain, a small mercy. She didn't know how she knew it, but when she reached to brush his hair from his forehead, she just did—somehow.

Fear. Terror. She didn't try to dissect and explain it away to herself the way she would if she were in her right mind. She didn't question why she thought she was dying inside, and outside, every part of her that existed and would ever exist. Didn't question why she could hardly take her eyes off his face as if he would disappear if she so much as blinked. Because it didn't matter. Not right now, if ever. Everything was wrong and it all hinged on this moment, these moments, this lifetime infinitely longer than eternity. What if he...

She hardly knew him. But it didn't matter. She couldn't lose him. Couldn't.. Something powerful swelled inside her, growing like a terrible shadow and rearing back to lash out, to kill, to hurt whoever had done this—

"Sir?"

She didn't realize she was the one being addressed at first. It was so foreign a thing to be addressed with respect that she reflexively looked around the room to see who the commanding officer in the room was, only to realize it was herself.

"Yes?" she managed to say despite her tongue feeling simultaneously withered yet too full in her mouth, dry and dying. "What is it."

The guards looked at each other before moving apart to reveal something on the floor a ways behind them, close to the door. "Something fell off...your leg, sir," the other said as he stood at awkward attention, trying to indicate the fallen splint while avoiding looking directly at it. "Would you like us to retrieve it?"

She stared at it as she fought the urge to throw something heavy at them for interrupting her, especially with something so inconsequential. What the dark hells did she care about broken wooden splints? She didn't even remember when it had begun falling apart. There were only three or four narrow slats left attached to each together on the floor, still connected. Had she lost the rest of the splint securing her bad leg while she had been going over the palace walls? Now that she thought about it, she had struck the stone hard, and then the landing…

A fresh twinge of pain sharp enough to make her stumble lanced through the back of her calf with no warning, and a grip on her arm pulled her up before she could grasp at the bed's headboard for balance. Serqet leaped out of her arms and skittered over to the corner to join Netra, and Anzi looked back, bleary-eyed. It was the man in the desert garb who had grabbed her, and his headcloth wrapped completely around his head revealed only dark eyes staring out at her. With a frown, she pulled away.

"Do not disturb him," the man said in a thick accent she couldn't place. "He is in a dangerous condition."

"I know that." Who was this man? One of Kai's bodyguards? He had no armor, no weapons. He couldn't possibly be. If Kai had been with someone who could protect him, someone to hurl away the attacker, someone to take the blow for him—this would never have happened. This mad had *better* not be a bodyguard.

"At ease," she snapped at the two soldiers who were still surreptitiously eyeing the broken remains of her splint on the floor. "You two stand guard at the door."

"Yes, sir." They filed out of the infirmary without another word. Anzi didn't usually care for exercising such unquestionable authority, but it was the perfect opportunity to interrogate this man

"Who are you?" she demanded. "Where were you when this happened?"

He ignored her and resumed watching the sleeping Kai, and the next few seconds passed in silence. It was only when her hand twitched at her side that he answered. She couldn't be sure whether he replied only because of the imminent threat of violence. "I am Neb Minnakhet," he said, deep voice half-muffled as he tightened the headcloth wrapping over his mouth. "I am his closest companion. He is in my care."

"He's in *our* care," she snapped. "His companion? What, where are his guards, then?"

"He chose not to have them accompany him today."

"Why would he do that! There are thousands of people streaming into the Imperial City every day now, and there'll be thousands more. Why would he—"

"He is not afraid," the man interrupted, and his tone was both disdainful and offended, almost angry. "And the young lord Kaizat-Amun would never have been lain low this way if not for…"

"For what?"

He turned away, ignoring her in earnest this time as he focused his attention on the chieftain. "You, healers. When will he rise?"

One of the elderly men on the other side wiped his brow with his sleeve. "We don't know," he panted as he moved his hands over Kai's chest and abdomen, fingers glowing with a green hue. "There's, there's poison. It's making this more difficult than we hoped it would be."

"Poison?"

"It's very potent, but we should have been able to neutralize it already. We're not sure why it's damaging him so much more than it should, but then again, these wounds are deep. Even without the poison…"

"Continue your work," Neb Minnakhet commanded as if they were his to order, his to jerk around on a lordly chain. Anzi nearly growled at him, an animal response that rose to her lips as if it had a life of its own. He glanced up, eyeing her sideways. "You should concern yourself with your own matters," he said, voice suddenly frosty and hard. "I'm sure you have many to tend to."

She almost reached over and punched him in the mouth. He'd said nothing directly insulting, but there was something ugly and roiling in his tone that betrayed the nature of his true thoughts. He didn't like her, and he was doing less and less to hide it the longer they spoke. But what did she care? He had been the one with Kai. This was as much his fault as it was the attacker's, although she knew once she found the latter, she would be unleashing her wrath with far less restraint on them.

An unhappy screech had her removing her glare from the man who stared back with such lofty scorn. Netra! She looked down at Kai, torn…

"You should go," Neb Minnakhet told her. "You have responsibilities you should be more attentive to. The lord is under my care, not yours."

She almost struck out at him again. They didn't even know each other, and he was speaking to her with such veiled insults. "He's my responsibility too," she said, her every syllable icy and ugly. "The Emperor has assigned me to him."

"And yet you weren't at his side today. I wonder."

"And you were, but failed to act when he needed it."

They turned toward each other in unison on either side of the seated healer, both tensing-

"Please," the physician panted. "We are focusing...very hard. If you could both leave the room to settle whatever disagreements you have, that would help us greatly." From the other side of the bed, the other two physicians made assenting noises, and Anzi ground her teeth as she stared down at Kai. He looked even worse than he had moments ago. These were the best physicians in the whole city, the whole Empire—why wasn't he waking up yet?

"I'll be back," she promised, letting her eyes fix on Kai's companion again. The last thing she wanted was to leave the chieftain's side, but she didn't dare interrupt the healers' work as they labored to mend the gushing wounds with their magic. They'd mentioned poison, too. Her heart hammered away, throbbing so painfully she thought it might fall apart with each pulse. "But I won't be going far. I'll be outside...right here."

"You won't be needed."

"We'll see about that. While I'm here, no one would be stupid enough to stab him...Twice." She whirled away just as she saw the man's eyes widen in fury and headed for the infirmary's exit. Good. She was only too happy to put him in his place if he dared to gloat despite his incompetence. And in the meantime, she would keep her distance—a short distance—and keep careful watch. Outside in the hallway, she stared as Netra glided up and down the wide corridor, occasionally picking a wriggling Serqet up in her claws and herding her back to Anzi whenever the hatching strayed too far.

Now that the keenest edge of her panic had fallen away and she stood here in dull silence, her body remembered the abuse she had subjected it to. Phantom pains streaked up and down her belly, piercing her insides, while her bad leg shook and wobbled under her weight. She needed to rest; she had hurt herself while sprinting here all the way from the lower districts. But she would be damned if she left Kai by himself again.

She settled back against the wall, eyes narrowed.

69

O nly Netra's terrible hunger was capable of moving Anzi from her post by the infirmary door where she could keep an unblinking eye on both Kai and his suspicious 'companion' Neb Minnakhet. Just a couple of hours after exiling herself to the hallway, she was forced to go in search of something for the dragon to eat.

The kitchens were only too happy to supply the imperious white drag-onet with all the meat she could possibly stuff into her gullet—how was she growing so quickly?—while Serqet wandered elsewhere, bumping into corners and exploring the tiny dust bunnies along the walls. The younger hatchling wasn't nearly as demanding and seemed to be able to go days without nourishment. And even when she *was* hungry, she seemed content to search for it on her own in the form of lizards, insects, and whatever else she could find rather than begging (screaming) for a meal.

Such polar opposites. It made her wonder even more about dragon nature than she already did. It was a welcome reprieve from the anguish of thinking only of Kai, of feeling nothing but the horrific pain still burning inside her. Nonetheless, she hurried back to the infirmary as soon as she was able with instructions for the kitchen to bring meals up later. She would be damned before she left Kai alone again.

Bisset. She ground her teeth. It was his fault, had to be. All these games as of late were his machinations, and everything must have led up to this.

Even the stupid male harem 'gift'—had putting spies on her been Tet's idea or a slippery suggestion from the colonel in the ear of the Emperor? They could have easily reported to Bisset that Kai was alone and left unguarded. And Bisset had made Bastien all but imprison her in the Cave for the last two weeks to monopolize her time. He had been the one to make it so that she wasn't there to stop this. What portion of the blame Tet shared, she didn't know, but Bisset would bear the brunt of it. When he returned, when she saw him next—she would make clear what that meant. No more crawling around in humble modesty to prevent any more clashes, no more creeping on tip-toe to keep the peace. To hell with peace.

She leaned back against the wall and crossed her arms, glaring hard at the floor. If anyone dared to move her now while Kai fought for life on the other side of the wall, let them try. They could join the chieftain in the infirmary on the next bed over and share in his hardships, personally.

IT WAS another few hours later when Anzi heard the slap-slap of sandals up the hallway, and the two palace maids that had been cleaning the stone friezes near the ceiling from atop wooden ladders suddenly scurried back down and turned to face the wall. The footsteps grew lounder until a familiar shape whirled around the corner and nearly ran her over.

"Idiots!" he shouted. "No one woke me! Doesn't this qualify as an emergency, I swear all of you have the intelligence of pill bugs! And now my one lifeline is as good as dead and I'll have to start all over, do none of you understand how important this is? All wasted!"

"Sir," cut in when he stopped to take a breath. "I'm told he still has a fighting chance. So long as the physicians can continue their work, we'll know in a little while whether Chieftain Kaizat-Amun will make it through the night."

"He'd better!" the Emperor snarled as he pushed back his billowing red sleeves to his elbows. "If they fail, I'll know they're incompetent, and they'll have no place here in my palace."

She was wise enough to understand he meant they'd have no place in life, either. Was that the hair-thin line the elderly men walked every day for the privilege of serving here? Succeed always—or die. Harrowing, but she couldn't sympathize. It was Kai's life at stake. She needed him back. Needed him alive.

"Well?" Tet demanded. "Where are the ones who did this? Why aren't they here in front of me?"

She started. He was right. She had been so consumed by raging frustration and penetrating fear that she hadn't even considered what had happened to Kai's attacker. Whoever it was that had dared, he must be dead now as any guards posted nearby would have retaliated in full fore, but no one had outright said so. No one had even made mention of it-

"Are you serious!" Tet exclaimed. "You didn't think of it either! I can't believe this. Go! Find out! Now!"

Yes. It gave her an excuse to slip back into the infirmary, too. With a swift half-bow, she obeyed and slipped back inside the room. There, the three healers, the two guards, and Neb Minnakhet remained at various locations close to the bed where Kai still lay motionless. She glided closer, barely feeling her boots strike the floor. Her vision narrowed to pinpoint tunnels as it focused on the barest rise and fall of the chieftain's chest.

"How is he now?" she asked. She could stall a moment longer before asking what Tet had sent her to inquire after. "Is he better? There's color in his face again. And the wounds, they look like they're bleeding less."

"Because we just cleaned the blood off of him again, with all due respect," the lead healer wheezed. "The wounds are still grave, and it's all we can do to keep them from worsening for now."

"The poison? It's counteracting your healing that much?"

"Yes. We don't understand why it's having an even more pronounced effect than normal, but we know it's a form of basilisk poison. It's already absorbed entirely into the chieftain's body, and it's so potent that if we stop for even a moment, we think it might kill him outright. We can't stop, madam. We need to focus."

Basilisk poison. Not home-concocted elixirs or viper poison or even wyrm poison. Basilisk poison. Those weren't even native to this side of the continent, and there were any number of deadlier poisons easier to acquire. It was pure symbolism, the motive. What greater enemy of the fabled dragons than the basilisks? And what greater irony than to kill a chieftain who promised a resurrection of the dragons with basilisk poison?

"Call for help when you need to rotate out," she said crisply. "Do whatever it takes to make sure you stay in top form. The chieftain's life isn't the only one that hangs in the balance." She paused, half-cursing herself for being the bearer of bad news, but they deserved to know. And secretly, a not-so-guilty part of her wanted them to work all the harder for it, as terrible as that was. "The Emperor is outside, and he is very determined to see his guest safe again."

All three healers glanced up at her in unison, and she knew they understood what she was saying. She turned away before she could see the fear blossom in their eyes. "You," she snapped at the guard standing behind her. She whirled around to face him. "He didn't bring his own guards, but you were escorting him when this happened. What happened to the attacker? Is he dead? Is he captured? Was there more than one?"

The guard paled. "Please forgive my incompetence. I wasn't able to keep the chieftain safe, but we were able to have the culprit hauled off to the dungeons for interrogation. He acted alone at the time, but he couldn't have done this without help. In the middle of a crowd and with such expensive poison—"

"One of you go and ask how much progress they've made with inter-rogation," she ordered. "Now." She didn't wait to see which of the guards went. She turned back around and caught Neb Minnakhet's stare as he watched her with the same guarded, disdainful gaze as he had earlier. What she wouldn't give to slam her fist in his haughty face right now. "You must have seen it happen, too. What did he look like? What did you see?"

He allowed himself a long silence before finally answering. "Someone from the coastal lands, and closer to the north. An outsider. I could see nothing more than that."

She wanted to make a sneering statement about how it must also have been such a powerful adversary that even the chieftain's close companion had been useless in stopping him, but that was pointless now. It wouldn't help Kai. Very little could.

She gave a stiff nod and left the room.

70

Tet paced back and forth. He hadn't stopped once in the past hour. The palace maids had dismissed themselves long ago, making sure to remain bowing deep at the waist as they walked backward so as not to look upon the Emperor's countenance. They had taken the ladders with them as well, and the friezes remained half-polished for now. They would come back only after the monarch had taken his leave.

The guard who had scurried off to the dungeons was another story. He had no choice but to drag back the prisoner and stand in the presence of the Emperor upon his return, sweating buckets. He wasn't merely starstruck, Anzi knew. If the Emperor realized he was the same man who had been guarding Kaizat when it all happened, he was as good as dead.

She didn't intend to betray him. She would never have trusted anyone but herself to do the job right anyway. As far as she was concerned, Bisset was the only one who needed to bleed for this, and the prisoner. She had taken the ends of the securing ropes herself when the guard arrived, both because the prisoner had no chance of escaping her and because she wanted a closer look. Minnakhet had been right. Coastal looks. He had the sea-beaten look of a deep seafarer, and although he was aging with a weathered face, there was a bitter, snarling vitality to him.

"You!" Tet snapped, and the slicing, inhuman tinge of furious voice sent an unsettling sensation scuttling down Anzi's back. "You little pissant. I'd snap your neck for all the work you've cost me, but I can't be bothered. The poison, how did you get a hold of it?"

It was odd to see the Emperor taking the initiative with such insistence. She watched as he pushed his sleeves up to his elbows and stepped forward to loom over both prisoner and guard, the latter of whom shrank back even more under his towering height. Gone was the lackadaisical demeanor of the Emperor who could barely be bothered to pay attention to anything other than himself. In its place was dark rage boiling up to the surface, ready to roast alive everything it touched.

"You'll nev-never get me to talk," the prisoner wheezed, and Anzi narrowed her eyes when she saw that he was half-laughing as he jeered his response. The glee wasn't a pretense, and neither was the pronounced difficulty of his breathing. She looked at Tet and inclined her head, drawing his attention.

"What! What is it."

"Sir, with respect, he'll be dead before you get the information we want out of him." She pinned her gaze on aging man again with a grimace. "He's too old for an assassin. If they sent someone so fragile, it was on purpose, someone who would be more likely to die under heavy interrogation. In other words, someone too weak to last long enough to talk, sir. I think I can hear the choking sickness in him." Like Oza.

"What kind of dishonest trickery...? Fine. Then tell me what I should do. I can't think right now, hurry up and come up with something."

Couldn't think? Of course. He didn't have his merry band of advisors here to fawn at his feet and spin elaborate schemes to get him whatever he wanted. But this was what she wanted, too. She needed to root out the source of the problem herself and find everyone who had had a hand in nearly killing Kai.

"He probably didn't work alone," she said. "I would put the prisoner on display and threaten to execute him if no one steps forward to save him. They wouldn't fall for it if they're typical assassins, but all of this feels too disorganized. Someone personally assaulting the chieftain in plain view should have made sure to kill himself before he could be caught, and in sending someone so weak, they sabotaged themselves. No organization or skill event. Possibly a small rebel cell. Those tend to be ruled by bonds of sentiment and camaraderie, so this prisoner may have offered himself up as the sacrifice as he has less years in him than a younger man." She paused. "But just a guess, sir. And even if no one steps forward, we can keep a close eye out for anyone who lingers too closely, someone who might be watching him to make sure he doesn't reveal what he knows under duress."

"You're cleverer and cleverer every time you open your mouth. I like it. String him up and let the birds peck out his eyes for a while, and let's see who folds."

"I'll never," the prisoner wheezed, and a trickle of blood dripped down the corner of his mouth. Two of his teeth were gone, probably knocked out over the course of his interrogation, and yet he spoke fearlessly. "I don't care if you kill me now or kill me later. I've done my part. Soon…" Blood mixed with saliva oozed down his chin again. "We'll have no more dragons. No more!"

"Oh, shut up. This really is about dragons again? As I thought. You, dimples, go and do the thing. Make sure he's chained up tight." Tet made an angry, dismissing gesture at the guard who immediately dragged the cackling man away. "What a headache. Anzi, stick to the chieftain and make sure no one gets in or out. Looks like the anti-dragon sentiment's reached our gates now with the festival bringing in all the wretches from around the land."

"Yes, sir."

"And you remember what I told you about Alexandre, yes?"

"I'll send him to you if he comes here. Yes, sir."

"Good. And where are your dragons?"

"Inside the infirmary. They're sleeping, sir."

"Good. Keep close watch over them. If we lose the chieftain and our best shot at getting new fertile females, the last thing we need is losing our second best options for breeding stock to this chaos. I'd bet the whole treasury someone's already after them. Now, I'm away, this has done me a bad turn and I need to sleep it off. Don't disappoint me, Anzi. I expect good news when I wake.."

She bowed her head. There was absolutely nothing she could do to guarantee that, but she couldn't bring herself to care. She was numb to everything but one thought, one desire, one need. She stood at the door after the Emperor left, hands pressed against the wood. Just beyond it, Kai was fighting for his life, and there was nothing she could do to help him. Nothing she could do to save him…

Or was there?

She looked up for a heart-stopping instant before barging into the infirmary with newfound determination, bordering on panic. Everyone whirled around, but she wasn't the slightest bit sorry for the crashing disturbance as she bore down on Kai's bed with all urgency. "Is he stable yet?" she demanded. "When can you let up?"

"We think he'll pull through at least for a night, madam. There's no telling tomorrow, but..."

She clamped her hand over the physician's shoulder, ignoring the glare Neb Minnahket sent her from her other side. "If you stop your healing here right now, he'll survive? Or not?"

"In truth, we would go a little longer since his condition is so delicate, but he's vulnerable to overflow, too. His body needs time to expel excess magic, or else..."

They didn't have to explain. She knew well enough what happened to those suffering from magic overflow, the internal rupturing and ruination that came from excessive healing. Besides possessing a soldier's familiarity with it, she had been injured grievously twice not too long ago. She had been warned. "I understand. Then can you leave him now? How much longer?"

The healers all glanced between each other, no doubt confused by her haste in dismissing them. But there was relief on their exhausted faces, too, and she knew they wouldn't put up a fight. Good. She nodded and took their unspoken responses for what they were, a plea for respite.

"You're all dismissed. Go and rest. You've done very well, and I'll be here when you return in the..." Morning? Evening? She hardly knew what time it was anymore. "...Go on. I'll be here."

They picked up their tools, herbs, and talismans before shuffling off, all but sagging with each step. She watched them until they disappeared through the far door, then cast a scrutinizing look around the infirmary to make sure she was alone with Kai.

And Neb Minnahkhet.

"You would do better to stay away," the man said, and although the corners of his eyes crinkled in an unseen smile behind his head wrap, she knew it was the most sardonic of expressions that was aimed at her. His bitter voice was tired and ragged, rewards wrought by his ceaseless vigil at the chieftain's side. Well, who cared? She had been standing outside just as long, even when feeding Netra and Serqet who lay sleeping outside. Exhausted? Never. And she felt more alive now than ever because she had a wild, senseless idea, ludicrous and reckless, but it was something. Hope.

"You," she said. "How well do you know Kai?" His eyes narrowed, and she saw the jut of his brow move under the cloth covering his forehead in an aggressive furrow. "I'm not trying to insult you," she snapped. "I'm asking to make sure. If you really want to help Kai, then tell me."

"You can't help him."

"Watch me."

They glared at each other.

"...Why are you asking? What are your intentions?"

If he would just stop fucking wasting her time—"Because," she said, "I need to know if I can trust you. This is the first time I've seen you, ever, and it just so happens to be right after he's nearly killed and can't confirm it? You could be a spy. Just because you're a desert native doesn't mean you're with him. You might not even be a desert native at all. Judging you by your color and your clothes is as stupid and shallow as trusting that you're on Kai's side just because you said so."

"I've been at his side since he was a child," the man hissed. "You are nothing to me, and he should never have come for you."

"Maybe I'm nothing to you, but that isn't the case with him, is it? You would know that if you're as close as you say." He took a menacing step forward, and she leaned in to match his stare just as ferociously. If he wanted to turn this into a fight for Kai's fate because he was too stubborn to see sense, she would at least make sure she came out on the winning end. Her fingers twitched at her sides. It would be easy. Barrel into him and send him to the ground, thrash him until she was satisfied.

"You," he growled. "He calls you his destined. He always said he would find a way to bring you to your senses, but I know better. You've been mired in this corruption for so long that this is all you are. We'll never trust you. And I'll lay down my life before I ever let you get to him."

Anger. Who did he think he was? But also relief, because if he knew that, then he was who he said he was.

"Well, I'm standing here," she said. "And you're doing nothing about it."

He scoffed. "The mate bond is strong. Corrupted or not, he is bewitched by you. I tolerate you now only because the love of you gives him the strength to fight."

"That's what I want to ask about." She planted her hands on her hips in a show of bravado and secretly, to hide the sudden shaking of her hands. "If you know what you do, then Kai trusts you, so I have to trust you too. And maybe you can help." She narrowed her eyes. "He had a way with dreams. He could heal me when I...went to him. In his head. How did he do that? Is it because—is it because of the..."

"Look at you," he sneered. "Your mate on the brink of death, and you still refuse the call. One of the purest forces in all life, all existence, and it fails to cut through the ugliness that has marred your soul down to the roots. What is it like living like that?"

"Shut up. Tell me how he healed me."

"Yes, it was because you are his mate. But you cannot."

"Why! I have magic. It's not strong, but if you tell me how—"

"I will not tell you more than I have to," he said coldly. "Do not think we are on the same side because I tolerate your presence here…for now. I allow you to stay only for his sake."

She wanted to slam her fist in his face to show him exactly what she thought of his *allowances*, but she needed answers. She needed to save Kai. And this man was the only one within reach who could help her do that.

"What do I need to do?" she asked. "Why can he do that for me and I can't for him? Is it because I don't *accept* him? Fine. I accept it. I answer the call. I don't care anymore. He needs my help."

"The gift of healing through a mate bond is only for our kind. Not you."

"And what, I can't learn?"

"As much as a worm can learn to fly. Impossible. Your mate bond is wasted on you. Kaizat-Amun deserves so much more than some mongrel blood with no right to his soul."

"Well, I'm what he's got. And you'll just stand there since you refuse to help me help him."

"You know nothing. How you could possibly be his destined is beyond me. A filthy collaborator of a corrupt empire built on blood and bones."

"Exactly how much has Kai confided in you? I guess it isn't much." She glared harder. "If you knew him well, then you would know I'm not the enemy, either."

"With your show of secretive treason? You have not fooled the rest of us despite how you have blinded Kaizat. If you were sincere, you would have died before helping your twisted abomination of a leader."

"I won't become a martyr with nothing to show for it."

"There are lines one does not cross, but you help your mad king more than you will ever harm him. You stand next to him and never think to slit his throat. You have already been corrupted. And to see you with stolen dragons, too. Look at them." He pointed suddenly at the corner where Netra and Serqet lay sleeping. "They will die young, broken. Dragons taken from eggs shattered before their time always do. How was it, reveling in the black magics he uses to break their shells?"

"You don't know anything. There was no black magic. I hatched them myself, so before you accuse me of something else, let me warn you that I have no patience to argue whether I'm allowed to help you save the man you allowed to get hurt in the first place."

He tensed, and so did she. If he was going to make a scene and insist on a fight, she was only too happy to oblige. She could manage it without disturbing Kai. Her fingers twitched again. But it wasn't to be. With another snort, he turned so he was looking down on Kai's face once more. "You are useless," he said flatly. "From here, it will depend on his endurance. The mate bond will not help him with that."

Damn it, and damn him. He could be wrong, didn't he see that? Why wasn't he trying harder? Why wasn't he as desperate as she was? "Then what about his own healing?" she demanded. "I've seen it before. It was when we met. Someone wounded him in a spar, and I saw his skin harden. It was black. It looked like scales." He stilled, and she knew she had stumbled upon something important. But what? "Can't he use that magic to close his wounds? Or does he have to be conscious to cast it? Or if it's desert magic, can't you or any of his guards do it instead?"

"Don't babble about things you have no understanding of."

"Then make me understand! Why are you so stubborn!"

"Says the one whose stubbornness drove him to risk himself this way. If you had any compassion for the man who would move heaven and earth to satisfy you, then you would never have let this happen."

"Me! I let this happen!" She drew herself up again, but he continued to ignore her while he straightened the covers over Kai's motionless body. And in the end...she had nothing else to say. She blamed Minnakhet for his failure, but she had abandoned Kai too. She should have tried to stay with him, tried to hold onto him...She should have fought harder.

It was too much. She was miserably young and ignorant suddenly, a baby left to crawl the streets alone. And she used to think she was so in control, so sure of herself. Now she knew better.

"Fine," she said. "It's my fault. But what's done is done, and it's too late to be wishful. Are you going to stand there and refuse to let me help because you have a grudge?"

He said nothing for a long moment, and she wondered if he was going to remain silent after all. But finally he sent her a half-look over his shoulder. "There is nothing you can do. And there is nothing I can do. Yes, he can heal. But no, it is not magic. Not the kind you think of. The basilisk poison stops him from healing, so he will have to endure with his own strength. If the poison weakens, his wounds will close."

"Why is the basilisk poison doing this to him? The healers should have been able to extract it the same as any other."

"He is weak to it."

She stirred, an unhappy, wry smile curving her mouth as she turned to look upon Kai's sleeping, stress-lined face. "Ironic."

"And why would that be ironic."

"Because dragons. I heard a basilisk is a dragon's weakness. And it turns out it's his, too." A flicker of something passed through her thoughts like a quick sputter of a flame, and she stopped mid-sentence to glance at Neb Minnakhet again. He was watching her straight-on now with a waiting expression, and something about it unsettled her deeply. Her stomach churned. "Why are you looking at me like that?"

"Do you know what your shortcoming is, woman?"

"Excuse me?"

"You refuse to accept what is in front of you if it does not suit you. Not until it is too late. Kaizat laughed about it to me, but I knew. I knew it would end like this."

"It's not ending at all," she snapped, ignoring his insinuation that he and Kai had gossiped about her. "He'll pull through. He will."

"We will see. If he does not open his eyes soon, he never will."

She turned away. If he wanted to deliver ominous predictions and fear the worst, that was his choice. Not hers. With a swift yank, she grabbed the chair the physician had been sitting in and sat down hard upon it. And damn it—before she could lose her nerve, she gripped Kai's limp hand on the bed and held fast, not caring if Neb Minnakhet commented on it.

He didn't. Not once. And some time later, he even excused himself with a bitter sigh and left them alone in the infirmary, perhaps to find sustenance at last. Good. Despite their unspoken truce, she still didn't like him.

But what coincidence. It was only when they were left alone, just her and Kai and no one else, that his eyes finally cracked open to reveal the gleaming golden irises she had missed so shamelessly.

"You're awake," she choked. She stumbled out of her chair to lean over him. "You're alive!"

"Yes," he said, sounding exhausted and equally surprised. "I guess I am."

71

Anzi didn't know how to describe the terrible swell of emotion that rose up inside her, if she could even call it something so mundane as emotion. Relief, anger, frustration, helplessness in the face of everything that had happened, all of it coalesced into a crippling weight that filled her up like molten metal poured into a cast. And underneath it all, she could feel the haunting shadows of pain in her belly and chest and knew without question they belonged to Kai. The bond he'd said they shared, the bond she hadn't had time for, the bond she couldn't afford to accept because it only made everything so much harder than it was already—it was here now. Looming larger than life and taking up the whole of her vision, her senses, planting itself in her path and forcing her to acknowledge it.

So what choice did she have? What could she say anymore? Do?

"You almost died," she said dumbly. "You might still."

"No." His voice was weak from disuse, fatigue, and no little amount of pain. She almost wished she felt more of it in the vain hopes that it would share and ease his burden. But no such thing existed. She had to stand here and watch him suffer, useless. "I'll be fine," he said. "Come here."

She let him pull on her hand, and he rested it over his bare chest away from his wound. His skin was feverish hot, burning so intensely she wondered how he hadn't melted yet. "What happened?" she asked. "How did someone..."

"Get close enough to attack me? My fault. He must have been following me for hours waiting for his chance. I saw him, but he looked harmless. Let down my guard."

"You can't catch your breath. Don't talk so much."

He tugged her hand up to his lips, and afraid of letting him strain himself, she offered no resistance when he laid a long kiss on her knuckles. "You're really attentive today."

"You almost died."

"If it's given me this much, it'll have been worth it." He laid another kiss on her hand, long and lingering. "But has it?" he asked, and he looked up at her with eyes that were still bloodshot and half-swollen.

"Has it what?"

"Gained me you."

"Stop. I don't know where you're getting the energy to try to woo me, but you should redirect it to getting back on your feet. It's been days." She pulled her hand free, but unable to help herself, pushed his hair back from his forehead and tugged on a corner of the pillow under his head. This. This was why she hadn't wanted...It was too much. Even now, she wanted to touch his lips, his cheek, his chest, his hands...He could slip away at any moment, and she was powerless. "Who's your bodyguard? I only know his name's Neb Minnakhet. He was with you but he couldn't protect you?"

"No need to be suspicious," he said with a tired smile. He reached for her hand again, and this time she let him hold onto it. "Like I said, it was my fault."

"He should have been close enough to—"

"He's not a warrior," he interrupted. "He's my guide."

"Guide?"

"Spiritual guide."

She narrowed her eyes at his serene expression. There was too much she didn't know, and here was yet another thing he had concealed from her. She had secrets too, but they weren't half so confusing as his. "There's more to it than you're telling me," she accused. "You say spiritual guide, but I'm starting to be able to read you. He's no priest."

"Something of a father to me."

"Your fath—"

"He's known me since before I became what I am."

Became what he was? What kind of riddling... "He hates me. I also hate him back."

"I know, but he'll come around. I won't let you go now that I have you. I'm not stupid enough to waste good luck when it finally finds me."

"You call this good luck! Look at you, laid open and almost dead—" She lifted the covers from his waist just then in an impulsive desire to prove her point—and the rest of her words died on her tongue. His grievous injuries were bare, left unbandaged because the fabric only seemed to exacerbate the wounds, which meant there was nothing concealing the rime of black that lined them. Shimmering…scaled. They were faded into the skin still, lighter than when she had last seen such a thing, but it was unmistakable. The day on the training grounds when Oscar had injured him, the scales that had covered it over…

"The poison's still in me," he murmured. "My body will do what it can to mend itself, but not much more than this."

She continued to stare. "What is that? That's not healing magic."

"No, it's not. Healing magic is rare among my kind."

The scales were slowly extending across the rest of the gashes, knitting together bit by bit with agonizing slowness. She watched them at work, open-mouthed and utterly lost for words. It took her far too long to find something appropriate to say. "You better not let the healers see that when they come back."

"I'll be too exhausted long before that to keep this up."

She swallowed, still staring. "What am I looking at, Kai?"

He tightened his grip on her hand. Warm. So warm. "You're cleverer than I am. You have to have some idea. Even if it sounds too unbelievable to be true."

She wished she didn't. But as she stared and stared, a memory drifted up and bobbed across the surface of her thoughts. Dark scales blacker than the night, gleaming…Golden eyes, peering up at her. Alert, intelligent. She opened her mouth, inhaled. Held it. "You said we met before, haven't you? A long time ago."

"We did."

His eyes were probing. Bright. Her pulse slammed against her throat at breakneck speed; her toes curled. "And you're weak to basilisk poison."

"I am."

"And…that wagon full of dragon remains." Her head was pounding, but she had to ask. It was impossible, but she had to hear the answer. She had to ask. "Where did you get those from, again?"

"Passed down," he answered. "Through family."

"You…"

"Yes? Anzi?"

He was still holding her hand tight as she watched more scales materialize over the gashes. Some were fading back into flesh, but she could see the wounds shrinking ever so slightly....so slowly. "Kai," she mumbled, her tongue feeling too large and dry in her mouth by far. "Are you a—"

The door to the infirmary opened then, and Neb Minnakhet strode in, already glaring. "What are you doing!" he demanded, and his gait tripled in speed as he bore down on her with sudden, burning suspicion flooding his expression. "What were you just doing to him!"

"Minnakh, I'm all right."

"Lord! You're awake. Move, woman!"

She would have backhanded the man to the floor if she weren't feeling so boneless. Move? As if the entire world weren't shifting under her feet and sending her toppling already? What did he know? "Are you like him?" she demanded. "Are you two the same?"

"Enough! Quiet!" Minnakhet snapped as he rushed around the bed to Kai's other side, but then his head shot up, face freezing. "The same? Lord, you didn't tell her—"

"I didn't say anything. I remember what I promised."

"I'm standing right here!" Anzi exploded. "And I'm not blind. I see what I see."

At her pointed words, the man looked down again and noted the lifted covers revealing Kai's scales. In the next instant, he yanked them back over the chieftain's body. "Get out!" he shouted. "We don't need your meddling. Get out—"

"Minnakh, stop. You know I respect your instincts, but trust mine, too. She's with me now."

"Lord, you know why she's not to to be trusted—"

"Anzi." He reached for her again, hand shaking with fatigued tremors. She grabbed it without a second thought. "I'm right, aren't I? You're with me now."

She heard the smile in his voice as he drifted off, exhaustion finally overtaking him...

"You're with me now."

≈

Neb Minnakhet banished her from the infirmary. Not that she was afraid of him, but after having seen the proof of his close relationship with Kai, she doubted slamming him into the wall was a good idea. She would have to tolerate him for no other reason than that. And, admittedly, because he was the only person in the palace whose loyalty to Kai she could be certain of. He would set his face against anyone who dared come close, even her—and that was exactly what she wanted.

Especially now that Bisset had returned.

"Where is he?"

"Heard he's been meeting with the advisors outside the palace." Letti glanced around again, searching the shadows around the hot springs for eavesdroppers. "But he'll be here soon. Julien says there's a guard change happening in the next hour and that the next rotation has been told to be ready for the colonel's arrival."

"Julien?"

"He doesn't know more than he has to, don't worry. He's just doing a favor for me by keeping an eye out."

Favors. Letti's good looks were a lethal a weapon as any. "You should go before they notice you're gone."

"It's fine. I'm more worried about you. They're really going to believe you wanted to take a bath here all of a sudden? Anyone would be suspicious. You never come this way."

Anzi leaned back against the rocks. "The Emperor himself told me to. He heard about Kai waking up, wants me to be in perfect form in case he needs some physical consolation after everything he's been through."

"Oh.."

"Mhm."

Letti scowled. "I still don't trust him. You shouldn't either. I don't care if you say this is part of your duties, you're getting too close."

"Hm."

"Don't *hm* me! Respect my experience. I know what I'm looking at, and I'm looking at someone who's smart, capable, and a badass warrior falling for some suspicious lout with nothing but nice muscles and a pretty face. He's not even rich! All that gold and jewelry is a sham, he can't spend that anywhere."

"All right, I'm leaving—"

"Wait. There's one more thing."

She rolled her eyes. "What is it."

"Something's going on at the Tower. The mages are training more. A lot more. Word is there's going to be a march soon, and they're sending everyone they can spare to the north."

Anzi said nothing. The mages were already being prepared for war. She had expected something like this, but she hadn't thought it would be so soon. What did this mean for Oza? She had been careful not to send him any messages or make mention of him to anyone ever since the incident with Tet, but now it wasn't safe for him to blend in and become inconspicuous, either. That would only mean he would be sent off to the northern front along with everyone else...

"Thanks, Letti. And...be careful."

"You know I am."

She was. She was more careful than Anzi, smarter and more shrewd with ears skilled at picking up the smallest nuggets of vital information and the sense to know which were valuable and which were useless. Anzi was lucky to have her on her side when the harem girl didn't even know what was going on...

She would have to tell her, eventually. Letti was risking so much for her. Just—not yet, not when things were still so unpredictable. For now, they parted ways again with hushed goodbyes before Anzi's unwelcome male concubines could come investigate why she was taking so long.

These were strange times. Dangerous times. And with war on the horizon, growing ever closer...

～

"You had Bastien keep me occupied on purpose."

"Strange tone you're taking with me."

Anzi let the double doors to the throne room latch closed behind her. Calmly. She could already feel her hands closing around Bisset's neck, but she could hold on a little longer. With the Emperor not yet arrived, she had the colonel all to herself—and she was going to make good use of it. Throttling him could come later.

"There's no one tone I have to take with you." With long, slow strides, she crossed the large room toward him. "I'm not your subordinate anymore."

"And how is that limp, soldier? It's a shame it's still so severe after this long. It might turn out to be a lifelong handicap."

"Wasn't so much of a handicap that I couldn't disgrace you."

He turned to face her just as she came to a stop behind him, and he stared down at her over his nose. He was colder, his expression more imperious and disdainful than she remembered. "You'll find that Tet's favor comes and goes. What you call a disgracing is just a momentary disfavor. And in the end, Tet understands that the ones who've survived the longest are the ones most capable. You're young. And you won't last long."

"Not if he has anything to say about it. As far as I can tell, I'm more valuable than you are by far. You must not like that. Which is why you're twisting things to disadvantage me even if it comes at the cost of everything else. I understand you've been whispering in his ear a lot lately."

"Careful what you accuse me of, soldier. Tet makes all final decisions. He might mistake your concern for my influence as disrespect for his authority."

"Oh, shut up," she said, and she felt cold satisfaction chill her from the inside out at the flash of rage that crossed his face. "Don't try to use him against me. All I have to do is let him know that you've been deliberately keeping me away from the chieftain, which left him vulnerable. We almost lost him. All our work, wasted."

A sneer curled up the corners of his mouth. "You were assigned to a more important job, I assure you. The Emperor agreed wholeheartedly."

"So you admit it was your idea, not his?"

"All for his glory. You should be more careful. Being valuable for the moment doesn't exempt you from being put down like a dog if you become too rowdy to control, soldier."

"I could say the same to you. Alexandre."

There was a full second's delay between her drawling his name and his reaction to the scorn in her voice. And in truth, the fury that exploded from him took her off guard. He held her up in the air with both hands around her throat, leaving her boots to dangle off the floor. The memory of Tet strangling the colonel against the wall flashed through her mind, and she wondered as she choked around his grip if that was exactly why he was choosing to do this in the first place, like passing off his humiliation to her the only way he knew how.

He was strong. Incredibly strong. There was no way she was going to be able to loosen his stranglehold. She released her struggling grip on Bisset's hands, forced to make the second's sacrifice of a crushed throat so she could hold onto his arms for leverage, and swung her legs up. They slid over his shoulders up to her knees to choke him in return, both of them locked in a furious grapple. She had picked an unwise fight, the rational part of her warned, but the rest of her wanted blood for the role he had played in Kai's near-assasstination. She held on tight, her grasp only loosening when Bisset her bodily onto the floor, knocking the wind out of her.

"Alexandre! You mad dog, what the hell are you doing!"

The timing of Tet's arrival could have been better. She might have been able to turn the fight, but now she would never know. At least it had looked at that instant as if she weren't fighting back, as that had been the moment her legs loosened from around Bisset's neck.

She made sure not to sneak in any more hits no matter how tempting, and when Tet tore them apart, she couldn't help but note with cold smugness how he handled Bisset far more roughly. Her neck felt like it was half-snapped, but it was worth it to see the blood trickling from the colonel's bottom lip. She'd knocked her boot in his face while moving to strangle him with her knees—accidental, of course.

"I'm sorry, Your Excellency," she hurried to say, voice hoarse and broken. "I think it was my disagreement with how he wants to handle the issue with the dragons, sir."

"Tet, ignore her. She's—"

"Shut the hell up, you stupid idiot. I'll tell you when I want to hear what you have to say. Anzi, explain."

Relief flooded her from head to toe. She'd half-expected him to thrash both of them at once after what he'd seen, but then again, that might be coming later anyway. She had to get this under control in a hurry while she still had the chance. And who knew what Bisset would say or do to manipulate things again? "The colonel was under the impression that I should prioritize hatching more eggs, even if it means leaving the chieftain undefended. But I think it's more efficient to use him to obtain more adult dragons of breeding age straightaway. It'll take too long to mature our own, and with the invasion so close, we'll hardly be ready in time."

"Tet, let me explain."

"Fine, you talk now. Because I have a half-dead chieftain in the palace and we almost lost our best source of war-ready dragons because you swore up and down Anzi was better put to use working with Bastien."

"The chieftain's unreliable, Tet. You know that. He wouldn't be doing this without ulterior motives. Whatever it is that he's planning, it's advantageous enough to him that he's willing to turn over his dragons. Live, adult dragons, Tet. Don't tell me you don't think that's suspicious."

"What the hell do I care about suspicious! We don't have time. How much longer do you think Ra is going to last? We need more—"

"Tet. We shouldn't talk about that now."

Ra? Anzi watched them both closely, eager to hear more. That was the name of Tet's dragon, wasn't it? What did they mean, what were they hiding? Because they were certainly hiding it now, falling silent as they looked at her.

Nothing? They weren't going to say anything more? So this was a secret she wasn't allowed in on. Then she would at least take care of the one thing she had come here to resolve.

"If I may speak, Your Excellency."

"Sure, sure. What is it."

She ignored Bisset's scornful glare and inclined her head at Tet. "I still sincerely think our best route to victory is through the chieftain. With one attempt already made on his life, I'm sure there are going to be more. Allow me to resume guarding him. I don't think we can trust the chieftain's own men to protect him, and despite Bisset's optimism, our men clearly aren't up to the task, either." Another dirty look. She ignored that one too. She was getting far too much pleasure out of subtly blaming him in every way possible. It was his choices that had nearly gotten Kai killed; she was going to make him regret it.

"Fine. Good." Tet nodded. "Do that—ah-ah-ah, shut up, Alexandre. You're getting too full of yourself and you're getting rusty at the same time. No. I'm not risking anything. Anzi, go stick to the chieftain and don't let him out of your sight. And I don't care how you manage it, get him on his feet again for the festival. You have until the end of the week. All the healers in the palace are at your disposal, understand?"

Oh, hell. She'd forgotten all about that. And from the rabid light in the Emperor's eyes, she knew there was no dissuading him. This was for the war effort, after all; he wouldn't fold.

"Yes, sir. I'll make sure of it."

"Good. Those harem boys, have they been around?"

"...Not since I've been with the chieftain in the infirmary, Your Excellency."

"Well—surprise. This is as good a time as any to let you know they're actually a bit more useful than I might have led you to believe. Keep them with you at all times, they'll be secondary protection."

"Sir?"

"They're assassins, dear. Just insurance, don't be so shocked. But when the festival's underway, keep them close at hand. I don't want a single fly slipping through to land on that man's head. Understand?"

Her stomach churned. Assassins. There could be no mistaking who they'd been meant to take out, should the need arise. Kai, her, either. "Yes, sir."

"Good. I don't want a damn thing messing this up for me. Now go."

Bisset sent her one final dirty look before she turned to take her leave. But it was his hushed words—pitched at just the right volume that she knew he must have meant for her to hear them—that made her nearly lurch forward and fall.

"Tet," she heard him say as she left through the doors. "We should discuss the mages now. There's one in particular I'm interested in using…"

The doors closed behind her before she could hear any more.

72

"Don't push yourself. You'll split your wounds open again."

Kai looked up with a smile, perched on the edge of the bed. "I was waiting for you."

"You were supposed to be resting."

"But you came knowing I wouldn't." He stretched out his hand toward her. "Do you want to help me leave this place? I'm sick of it. And so are the little ones."

She followed his gaze to the corner where Netra and Serqet were currently fighting over something—oh, no. "Get that out of your mouths!"

"Leave them. They should enjoy the time they have."

"That's yours," she said hotly as she whirled back around to shoot him a dirty look. "Why are you letting them play with it? You're teaching them bad habits."

"They'll never outgrow it. They say dragons love gold."

She ignored him and stomped toward them, but instead of displaying any hasty remorse over chewing on Kai's bejeweled collar, the dragons only redoubled their efforts to take it for themselves. Netra was on the verge of ripping it away when Anzi's hand clamped down over it and yanked it out of her maw. "Don't you hiss at me," she growled. "Go somewhere else and stop making trouble! Why are you always like this?"

You shame me but not her?

She was so incensed by the sheer rebelliousness in the dragonet's voice that it took her a second to realize her voice was—clear. Much clearer than before. No longer did it fade in and out of her mind with a frustrating scratchiness. There was still a chirping quality to it like birds trilling, but it was vivid. Bright. She hesitated, so shocked she forgot what she had been about to say. Netra had no such hesitations. She raised her spines and let out another angry hiss before reaching out to flip Serqet over on her armored back. And before Anzi could shout at her, she turned and scurried away toward the infirmary exit where the door remained open.

"Get back here!"

"Anzi."

She glared at Kai over her shoulder. "Let me go, I need to go get her."

But his hand remained clamped on her arm, and he pulled her back with a firm tug. She didn't know why she relented so easily and let him spin her around to face him, their knees touching. Could be because she didn't want him to strain himself and his wounds. Or maybe it was because now that she'd had a taste of what it was like to accept this, to accept him, she couldn't help but sneak another taste again and again. Just once more, every time.

"We need to talk." He stared up at her, golden eyes fixed on her face with an intensity that didn't match his soft murmur. "There's a lot we don't know that we should."

"Seems like your friend didn't want me to know anything at all."

"Neb Minnakhet means well." He paused, then amended his statement. "Means well for me."

"Hm."

"But aside from the things he wants me to keep to myself...there are other things, Anzi. Things that you need to know so you don't have to find out the hard way." He reached up, and it took all her willpower not to close her eyes in pure bliss under his warm touch. So good. So warm. The compelling power of it was so much stronger than it used to be, so much more demanding. It was as if the terror of almost losing him had broken open the dam that had held everything back, and now it was too late to put it all back together. It felt too right, too overdue. A single slow exhale found its way out between her parted lips as he ran his fingers over them, and the corners of his mouth turned up in a lazy smile.

"It could have been like this," he said. "But you're so stubborn."

"Don't know what you mean. Anyway, what were you saying?"

He dropped his hands down to her hips and rose from the bed without another gibe, but she could take no satisfaction in winning the argument. Not with the way his smile dropped away like a leaden weight. A shadow passed over his face as he drew her close. "It's about the little ones," he said softly. "Netra-hau and Was-Serqet."

"They told you their names?"

"Netra did. Serqet doesn't seem to be much of a talker." He furrowed his brow at her silence. "Sometimes it's like this," he said. "We all find it hard to reach out to those closest to us sometimes. Don't let it bother you."

"She talks to you easily enough. And to others. Not me."

"She loves you. You're her whole world. You know that."

"She has a peculiar way of showing it." She wrapped her hands around his forearms with the intent to remove his hands from her waist, but found herself slightly too preoccupied with the muscular tautness there. Against her better judgment, she let her fingers rest there. "Tell me what you were going to say about them."

"Anzi—"

"Just tell me. You're making me worried."

A quiet sigh told her she'd won the argument for now. "It's about their hatching. If there's even the slightest chance Minnakhet was right and they forced you to use—" He stopped suddenly and looked at the door. "She says someone's coming. Several."

In a flash, she extracted herself from his hold and faced the infirmary entrance, expecting the worst. Guards come to take Kai away on a whim? Had Tet finally cracked? Or maybe Bisset was sending assassins. He could have felt inspired by the recent turn of events and become spiteful enough to try it himself. She reached for the hilt of her swords, wrapping her hands around them and prepared to protect what was hers.

"My lord. My lady."

Oh, no.

Two bald heads, one behind them with long, lustrous dark hair, and another with radiant blond hair to his shoulders. Too familiar. It felt like it had been an eternity since she had seen them last—the male concubines she'd been gifted that had turned out to not be concubines after all. Assassins, Tet had said. Wonderful.

"What are you doing here?" she barked, the edges of her voice curling up like a bitter leaf. "We're speaking in private right now."

"Our apologies. We've been instructed to stay with you both at all times until the danger is past. I assure you we won't leave your sides before then. Two of us will be with you, and two with your honorable self, Chieftain Kaizat-Amun."

That sounded like a threat, not a reassurance. Tet might have admitted their true purpose to her, but that didn't mean she had run clear of all suspicion yet. And even if it did, her hackles rose at the idea of four trained assassins lurking anywhere near Kai. If they were good enough that they'd been trusted with the responsibility of watching over her, then they had to be fearsome fighters despite the pretty faces and hair. At least they had abandoned the loincloths and changed into loose civilian clothes, tunics and wool pants. She didn't know what would have happened if they'd shown up in their less shameless attire. Kai would have had something to say about that, she was sure of it.

"Fine," she said. "What's your name." The man who stood at the head of them was clearly their leader. She only needed to know his; the rest were incidental.

"Alain, my lady."

"All right, Alain. Stay in the hall. You don't have to close the door."

Alain's eyes moved from her to Kai and back again as if he were considering whether to defy her order, but to her relief, he bowed his bare head and backed away. The other three did the same until they were filed back out into the corridor outside…still watching through the doorway. And that was as good as she was going to get.

She turned around. "You should rest," she said quietly. "I'll stay here and keep watch."

"Who are those."

"Think of them as bodyguards. Troublesome ones."

"They smell of sex."

She nearly choked, only just managing to catch herself with a timely knitting of her brow and a fierce, annoyed glare. "You can't possibly—smell that. Stop it. Get back in bed and relax."

But he was staring around her arm at them with an increasingly dark expression. "I can. What kind of bodyguards are these that they release rutting scents?"

Rutting scents? She had no idea what that meant and she was sure she had no interest in finding out. "Don't worry about it. But you won't be able to get rid of them, and neither can I. Not even if we leave the palace."

"You've met them before. You recognized them. From where?"

There was something guttural and aggressive rumbling in his voice, and she wondered how it was that Kai's intuition could be so sharp. He always seemed to know too much no matter how much she concealed. "They were assigned to me by the Emperor some time ago. It's not important. Come on, get back under the—"

"No. I'm up." He surged to his feet, suddenly far more full of vigor than he had been a moment ago. "Let's take a walk."

"A walk? Where?"

"Out."

"They have to come with us," she reminded him, dropping her voice to a near whisper. "If you're trying to get rid of them, it's useless. And suspicious. Don't do anything that'll attract more attention. We don't want that."

She didn't know what exactly about her bodyguards-assassins had made Kai so hostile, but she feared for a tense moment that he would start a fight. There was something different about him suddenly, something primal, bordering on uncontrolled. She reached for his wrist and wrapped her hand around it. "It's fine. Ignore them. You're being too obvious."

Another long silence passed before he relented. For now. She could feel the thrumming of his aggression under his skin, was still worried he would act on it...ignoring how strangely thrilling it felt. What? No. Shut up, she scolded herself.

"Now's a good time to tell you," she added. "Soldiers have the man who tried to kill you in custody. They're displaying him right now to the public."

"I know. Minnakh told me."

She waved a hand in front of his face. "Stop looking at them. Look at me."

His golden eyes finally left the doorway to rest on her face. "Don't ever be alone with them," he said, his voice dipping into an abrupt growl. "Stay with me from now on."

"I have things to do tonight. I can't stay with you all day. And you need to rest."

"After. I want to go see the man."

"It's outside the palace grounds, Kai."

"I know."

Right. Minnakh the talker. The nosy, talkative tattler who would rather waste everyone's time suspecting her rather than the real enemy, and the reason Kai couldn't simply tell her everything he knew so they could work together. Yes, she had secrets of her own. But she had been on the brink of revealing to him, and she knew the reverse had been true just moments ago, too. Until the damn false concubine men made their entrance and ruined everything.

"If you're sure you're feeling up to it…"

"I am. Let's go."

But just before she could lead the way out of the infirmary, he grabbed her arm and pulled her close into a sudden kiss, fierce and possessive. She was about to chalk it up to his exasperating habit of touching her whenever he felt like it when she noticed he was staring past her at the men in the hallway even as he nibbled on her bottom lip, his hand cupping the back of her head and tilting it so he could he could see them. Whatever was bothering him about them, he hadn't managed to shake it off. With an annoyed sound, she pushed him away.

"Come on," she said. "I'll take you to him."

"WOULD you like us to wake him up, sir?"

Anzi frowned. "Leave him. I can do that myself."

The guards posted at either side of the raised wooden scaffold nodded, and she glanced back around at the harem-men-turned-bodyguards lined up a short distance away on the ground. Next to her, Kai remained motionless as he looked down at the kneeling man tied to the posts on the left and right.

"He's an older man," Anzi remarked. "I figured it was because they were hoping his body would give out under interrogation before they got the truth out of him. Or maybe he got sentimental and decided to sacrifice himself for the cause to save a younger man."

Kai continued in his silence, and when she shifted her weight onto her left foot, the wooden board under it creaked with a loud groan. The prisoner awakened then, gasping for breath as if he'd been underwater, and the fog in his eyes cleared as he stared up at them with unveiled hatred.

"You," he snarled as he glared up at the chieftain. "The one they say will bring the dragons back."

"Yes. I'm alive."

"You don't deserve to be." And through cracked, dry lips, the prisoner spat at his feet. There wasn't enough saliva to make it more than a speck of spittle, but he'd tried. "You and whatever cursed beasts you bring, may you all face swift judgment."

"The dragons are innocent. Don't curse them."

"Innocent! Burning our children alive, destroying our homes, our minds. Men will do terrible things to each other in the name of war, but dragons are what gave men the power the power to delight in it." He spat again. "May the gods do to you and your cursed demon creatures what they deserve. Filth. Evil. There will be a reckoning."

Kai stared, and Anzi saw a flicker of something wounded in his eyes.

"Yes," he said. "There will be."

73

They didn't have a moment alone, ever. Anzi couldn't so much as look at Kai without Alain and his fellow damned *spies* pinning her with the most intent of stares. And it was deliberate. Maybe Tet trusted her more now than before, but he must have told them to make it clear she was every bit the pressed prisoner she'd always been. Kai knew it too, although his restlessness appeared to come from a different direction than mere frustration at being watched.

"They reek," he snarled on the morning of the festival as she turned him around and wrapped fresh linen bandages around his waist. "How long is he going to keep them around you?"

"They're watching you, too. And they smell fine. Stop saying they smell like—*sex*, you don't just go around saying that in front of people. It's crass. This isn't the lower districts, we use our nicer words here."

That was enough to make him peel his fierce glare away from the men outside the infirmary. She even thought she saw the corners of his mouth twitch upward. "Nicer words?" he repeated. "Since when does my Anzi pretend she's anything but the thorniest woman to walk the earth?"

"I'm not—" She broke off, but only to tug the last strip of bandaging tight around him with what might have been spiteful force. She was rewarded with an audible grunt, but to her chagrin, found him still smiling when she looked up. "Don't ride my nerves today," she warned. "I'm stressed and you're not helping."

"I'm not?"

"No."

"Then maybe this"—he snaked his arms around her waist and yanked her close, driving the breath from her lungs when she realized how close their lips were—"will help."

"We are way too late, don't even think about—"

She didn't know why she even bothered. It was like trying to reason with a wall, teaching him to keep his hands to himself so she didn't look like a hussy to the other soldiers. And he should be worrying about his own image, too. After the assassination attempt that had happened in full view of the public and in broad daylight, no less, his reputation as a fierce, desert-dwelling warrior chieftain had suffered. That wasn't only an issue of pride. Showing such vulnerability invited more danger, more hostility. Many in the Imperial City were already hostile to foreigners no matter how rich and handsome, even if they brought magnificent dragons with them. If Chieftain Kaizat-Amun lost the popular favor of the people too soon...

"You taste like summer," he whispered against her mouth when he finally broke the kiss. "You're more than I ever imagined you'd be. And I already had such high hopes in the first place..."

"You're ridiculous and embarrassing."

"I am?"

"Yes. Now let me go before I run out of patience with you."

"I can't help but notice you're holding onto me. You must be confused."

She looked down.

Damn it.

"Anzi, come back—"

"Netra!" she snapped, face burning. "Stop chewing on his collar and bring it over."

A blessed lull gave her some peace. Yes, she was glad Kai was back on his feet and gradually recovering from the effects of the basilisk poison, and yes, she could no longer deny how right it felt to be with him, to hear and see and taste, to touch him and be touched by him anymore, but there was too much on her mind for her to truly embrace the relief. Things weren't good. She kept her hands steady and her face steadier because she had no choice, but it was nothing more than false bravado. It was as if the attempted assassination had triggered a slew of brewing disasters, and now everything was spiraling, crumbling. Bastien had sent word earlier that two more dragons were on the verge of hatching with or without her. Letti had failed to show up for their planned rendezvous at the baths as well, which meant something had gone wrong and that Anzi should expect trouble. She had even tried to reach out to Oscar, tentatively asking Pierro about him even though she knew it would only make her look even more besotted (the thought made her want to vomit). But there, too, she had found no success. Oscar was gone on a short march along with a great deal many of the other garrisoned soldiers, and he wouldn't be returning until the festival began when all the troops filed back into the Imperial City in unified parade.

And worst of all, Oza must be in trouble, too. She had no proof, but she knew she was being far from paranoid about what Bisset had said to Tet the last time she'd been with them. He had made deliberate mention of the mages, knowing full well her brother was among them. Trapped. Imprisoned in the Tower where he had nowhere to run. How could she have ever thought this was good for Oza? How could she have ever believed this was the best their world had to offer? Penned in like swine and turned into weapons for the Empire, instruments of conquest and warfare. How could she ever have thought any of this was right? But she could do nothing. Showing any reaction was weakness and would only egg Bisset on all the more. She had to wait…to be patient.

"What's wrong?"

She moved Kai's hand away from her face and motioned for him to step aside so they could leave. She crooked the fingers of her other hand at Netra and Serqet with a stern look as well. "Nothing's wrong if you'll just get a move on. We're supposed to be in the courtyard already. Bastien's probably lost his mind by now."

"He can wait."

"No, he can't." She gave him a swift but significant look out of sight of their unwanted retinue of 'protectors' outside, a warning for him to mind the prying eyes and ears nearby. "We have a lot to do before we start parading you down the streets to the adoring public. Come on."

He held her arm tight for a long moment as if he were about to cast aside all common sense and demand she stay and tell him everything. But finally, he loosened his grip, letting his fingers slide down her arm and brush against her hand. "Stay with me today," he said quietly. "Don't leave my side."

She rolled her eyes. "You don't have to remind me. Apparently, I can't trust anyone to be competent enough to keep one old man from stabbing you, so—" She stopped when he tilted her head up with firm fingers under her chin.

"Stay close."

She narrowed her eyes. There was something strange gleaming in his eyes, a hidden darkness in his expression that made her suspicious. Stay close? He would never be this insistent with her for his own sake. "What's going on? You asked me what's wrong a minute ago, but you're the one who's acting off."

He caressed her cheek, a fleeting touch only, before leaning away again. "It's dangerous times. Don't wander off."

"Of course not."

Bastien was furious when they finally arrived, but once he was done fuming and tossing out passive aggressive remarks, he led them to where he had stabled the dragons in a vast inner chamber in the Cave. To Anzi's surprise, a familiar, massive blue dragon waited there alongside the crimson Sa-Khente and the turquoise Qinglong. Bisset's dragon partner. She stared at the enormous creature that dwarfed the other two at least two-fold. Was it her imagination or was she even larger than Anzi remembered?

Bastien dragged Kai away so they could do final inspections with the condition of his wild dragons before the parade, leaving Anzi behind. For a long, protracted moment, she resisted the urge to move closer to Bisset's dragoness, to reach out and touch. She had always been in awe of the enormous creature ever since she'd first seen her from a distance, soaring into the clouds with a wingspan that looked like it could cast an entire village into shadow. A lord of beasts and man, great and elegant and terrible all at once...

Her feet moved without her knowledge, without her consent. Closer. Closer. And Bisset's dragon watched all the while with its massive head resting upon the stone, blue, blue eyes staring, staring...

And then they touched. Or rather, Anzi touched her. A creature of such proportions should be warm to the touch, heated by limitless inner fire, surely. But no. Cool, like lake water in late autumn against bare skin. And the scales that had looked smooth and glossy were rough to the touch instead. But most disturbing, most disconcerting was the thick surges of energy she felt pumping inside the dragoness, under her thick scaled hide. She could feel every labored breath, every contraction of the two massive hearts that passed the creature's blood. Slow and heavy...exhausted.

Against her palm, she could feel the dragon—dying.

In an instant, her mouth ran dry and her tongue became leaden, weighed down by the horror of witnessing such an unnatural thing with not just her sight, but every single one of her senses. It was worse than sickness, disease. It was wrong. Something was terribly, terribly wrong, and yet Anzi could do nothing about it except stroke the dragon's snout and run her fingertips down the chipped scales of her face in a pathetic attempt to give comfort. She could hear Bastien and Kai still murmuring between themselves on the other side of the cavern, their voices echoing and rebounding between the domed walls and ceiling endlessly, and yet her mind blotted them out as easily as if they were nothing more than the dripping of water somewhere in the distance. She lowered herself to a kneel, still staring at the creature's blank blue eye, and placed both of her hands along its upper lip.

"Damn you, Bisset," she whispered. "You piece of shit."

It took longer than it should have for Bastien to let Kai go, but when he launched into another rambling rant concerning his ideas about dragon breeding and pedigrees, Anzi knew it was time to separate them. Kai looked relieved. "Can you go first?" She nodded in the vague direction of the Cave's exit. "I need to talk to Bastien about something. Don't need Alain coming down here."

"How long will you be?"

"I'll be quick. Don't let them take you anywhere. Wait for me."

When he left, Anzi gestured at Bastien to follow her. She caught Sa-Khente's eyes—had they always been so orange and angry?—before leading the way back to the other side of the chamber. Gods above and below, wild dragons were something else. There was something truly intimidating about Sa-Khente that had nothing to do with his size or his blood-red hue. Qinglong exuded a similarly dangerous aura for that matter even with her serene appearance, no doubt a deceptive one...But she wasn't pulling Bastien aside to talk about either of them.

"You never said Bisset's dragon is dying." She pointed. "Look at her. What's he doing to her? Is he crazy or stupid or both? She needs rest."

But despite her harsh words and tone, the man grinned at her as if she'd said something hilarious. "Rest? Rest, really?"

"Don't waste my time with this routine. Just say whatever it is you want to say instead of trying to make me feel stupid."

He sighed and shook his head, looking decidedly put-out as if she had taken away his favorite toy. "Fine. But only because I'm exhausted and need to sleep while you all take my precious cargo and flaunt them to the common people who don't deserve it. Yes, Alexandre's dragon is dying, why are you acting so surprised? I told you we outlive our dragons."

"Stolen immortality."

"Don't get uppity with me." He wagged a finger at her. "All that does is rile you up, and you haven't forgotten what happened the last time you got too overexcited with me?" When her face tightened, he was quick to wink and laugh once more. "Just kidding, relax. You're too tense. But really, what do you think Tet's having you rush so many hatchings for? It's not just to get your auxiliaries saddled up. They're expendable. We need suitable dragons for those of us who need a refresher before we head north."

"...A refresher?"

"Half of us have been hard at work. You don't think our dragons are about used up? Some of them still have some strength left in them, but it's best to go with a fresh batch when we leave the Imperial City. We won't be able to come all the way back here one at a time whenever our dragons wither, it's too far. You've got to think ahead."

She had to force herself not to wrap her hands around his throat. He sounded so smug, so matter-of-fact. How could he say these things? Wasn't he even the slightest bit ashamed? "They should be hatching their own. You told me when I first came down here that I needed to find the one that responded best to my—"

"Yes, I remember that, don't you worry. But there's no point anymore. Getting them to hatch is the hardest part since there's almost no force on earth that can get through something as well-protected as a healthy dragon egg. Otherwise? They can pick and choose whichever dragon they like. It's easier this way. And fear not, you're doing marvelous. I found a third egg this morning about to hatch. It's clear you don't even have to do anything. You just being around them is giving us great results.

That was the last thing she wanted to hear. Truly.

"And then the more experienced ones of us will enchant the dragons to grow fast enough to be useful in time. Alexandre's the best we have. Look what he's done with her. She's enormous. And she'd be growing even more if he hadn't worked and flown her to death. She's only a handful of decades old, don't remember. Alexandre may be a pompous tit, but he's the best we've got at quickening dragons. At least this one lasted long enough to leave quite the impression on this generation. Really helped with recruiting."

She barely understood anything he said. All she had to go off of was her limited knowledge born of a few months spent with her own hatchlings and terrible guesses that were probably ludicrously inaccurate. More than ever, she wished she had asked Kai every question she ever had about dragons while she'd had the chance. Now it was too late. They were never out of earshot of at least one of Tet's loyal cronies, whether that was Bastien or Bisset or the harem men or, hell, probably even the guards posted down every corridor and outside every room she happened to pass by in the palace.

Hemmed in. Trapped. Just like Oza in the mages' Tower. Everyone was trapped.

"Well," he said after slapping his hand on the snout of Bisset's dragon with such supreme disrespect that she almost reached out and ripped his arm away. "You'd best get going. Tet's been ranting and raving about all the...whatever's the big deal today."

She glared. "Don't even think about trying to pull a fast one with the chieftain's dragons," she said. "I know you, but I know him, too. If you mess this up..."

"Oh, shush. The only thing I would have been interested in is studding the red one out to one of our females, but in case you haven't noticed, all of our riders with fertile female dragons haven't made it back to the city yet. Maybe in a few days. The festival will still be going on then. Too bad Alexandre's is too worn out to be any use."

She glared harder. "I heard you begging him to give you Qinglong."

"Ugh. You use their names too much." He pretended to shudder. "Your affection for dragons was cute at first, but now it's a little..."

This was going nowhere. She shot him a final murderous look before turning on her heel to leave.

"Don't do that," she muttered out of the corner of her mouth. "They're watching."

"All the more reason."

"I'm serious. We don't need more attention on us than we have already." Anzi tried to discreetly peel Kai's fingers off of her waist as they stood outside the blacksmith's shop with the harem men watching their every move. Gods help her. Something about their presence drove him mad, and she didn't understand why. It wasn't mere jealousy. It sparked a

primal reaction in him that made his golden eyes glow hard and bright—
and with violence. Thankfully, the door opened before he had a chance to
do something even more obnoxious like kiss her for no reason in full
view of the growing crowd milling about on the street.

She turned to see a blacksmith apprentice shuffle out with a pair of
the most beautiful swords she'd ever seen. Anzi had never gawked over
weapons before. She preferred bare hands to blades, plain grappling to
fancy maneuvers. But as the apprentice launched into an obviously practiced spiel concerning the many glorious qualities of the slender, elegant
twin swords, she was already reaching for them, hands itching to wrap
around the twin hilts trimmed in beautiful gold. The yellow sheen
reminded her of glowing sunlight, of heated honey…of Kai's eyes. Bright,
and hot enough to melt through even the most resilient, stubborn barriers. But the blade's hue. Black? The color of obsidian. She had never seen
that before.

"…We're not quite sure what happened," the apprentice stammered.
"But my master thought you'd like it anyhow. He said something must
have happened when he had you imbue the ore with your magic when we
were first commissioned for this. It made the process take far longer than
it should have, but he says they're the most beautiful blades he's ever been
privileged to labor over. He wanted to thank you himself, but he was
called away right away to work on other urgent jobs for the Imperial
Army."

She felt Kai draw up close behind her, and warm breath from his
murmur of approval hummed against the back of her neck. She hoped he
didn't notice her shiver. "They're beautiful," he remarked. "Your magic is
one of a kind if it could do this."

Black and white steel. She licked her lips. "My magic's actually terrible.
I don't know if this is a good or a bad thing."

He pressed a soft kiss to her shoulder while the apprentice stared,
goggle-eyed. "We'll find out soon enough."

"What was that?"

"Nothing. Come. We're due to meet the Emperor now, aren't we?
Should we get a move on, or are we going to sneak away elsewhere?"

She sheathed the swords in their slender scabbards and secured them
to her hips. To the apprentice, she handed over her old military-issue
ones; he would know what to do with them. "Thank you. Tell your master
I'm grateful for his hard work."

"Our privilege. We hove to serve for many a First Guard."

Her stomach lurched. "Of course. We'll be going, then."

Kai wisely opted not to disturb her with more talk. He did wrap his hand around hers and grasp it tight, though whether it was out of possessiveness or comfort, she wasn't sure. Both, maybe? There was a part of her that still couldn't believe anyone could possibly desire her so much—more than one part; most parts of her, actually—but she was beginning to accept it. She felt the same way after all, didn't she? No matter how much she tried to control and rein it in.

The Emperor's massive retinue of guards and concubines had almost fully assembled by the time she and Kai reached the stone bridge outside the palace walls. The ground was still rumbling with the last quakes of the stone golem's efforts, and the clear waters that ran along the branched Annat River under the bridge rippled with rhythmic waves. So scenic. So beautiful. Despite everything that had happened, Anzi might have still appreciated it if she didn't lock eyes with Letti in that very moment. Damn it. She had hoped the woman would escape selection for the Emperor's personal entourage, but that had been a fool's hope. How could one of the most beautiful, if not the most beautiful women in the Imperial Harem go unnoticed? They would simply have to avoid looking at or talking to each other, avoid attention.

At the very center of the assembled entourage was a beautiful white palanquin, balanced on the shoulders of four scantily clad, muscular men. Gorgeous flowers, slender vines, and various talismans for luck, prosperity, and virtue draped and hung all over the vehicle, and the silk curtains at the front billowed in the breeze with dreamlike grace. The Emperor was inside, of course. He wouldn't be showing his face to the people, but they would fall all over themselves in fainting fits anyway. Before they could begin the procession, a familiar, twiggy, too-spindly hand snaked out between the gauzy white curtains and beckoned at Anzi with a crook of the pointer finger. She hesitated at first, uncertain, but there was no one else Tet would be gesturing at.

She made her way between the other members of the entourage, squeezing between the palanquin bearers. Good thing Kai had already gotten into his own vehicle behind Tet's posse. He would have bristled at her rubbing shoulders with half-naked men. She peeked in through the curtains, training the grimace on her face into something more subservient and yielding—and froze. She stared, unblinking and unthinking, every inch of her body frozen in place.

"Isn't this perfect!" Tet exclaimed, sitting cross-legged inside. His favored golden veil was thrown over the top of his head, revealing his excited expression as he pointed at the much smaller figure sitting next to him. "Anzi! My present to you. Today, we'll all be spending time together like a real family."

She opened her mouth. No sound came out.

"Well? Anzi? Do you like your present or not!"

She bowed her head, the best pretense of gratitude she could offer while rendered mute. Her heart was tangled in her ribcage, her pulse throbbing so hard she thought Tet would surely see it. But she had to stay calm. "Thank you. I'm very grateful."

"Wonderful! Well? Go on, say hello!"

She forced a smile and turned her head to look at his guest.

"Hey, Oza," she said. "It's good to see you."

74

When Anzi withdrew from the gauzy curtains, Bisset was watching her from where he stood flanking the palanquin. He wore no expression, stone-cold and emotionless as always, but behind the marble indifference lay an insidious spite directed at none other than her. She knew. So did he. He wouldn't be looking at her otherwise. He was sending a clear message he knew she would decipher behind his inscrutable face. And she would have gone for his head for that if not for one thing: she had to stay alive to protect Oza. And Letti, too, if Bisset knew about her. And why wouldn't he? It seemed all he did now was seek out her weaknesses and threaten them. She should have known he would act quickly. She had thought she could stall until she was no longer under close watch and move then. This was her fault.

A flurry of suspicion slipped through her. She still believed he had a greater hand in plotting Kai's attempted assassination than through mere neglect and the unwise decision to convince Tet to separate her from the chieftain. It would be in line with the rest of his malicious moves against her. Either way, she would make sure never to leave Kai alone with him. Tet might think Bisset was loyal, but in him was the need to press others down, greater than the need to serve his Emperor. She couldn't even trust the man to act according to Tet's benefit. He was out for himself and himself only.

"Forward!" The colonel's voice rang out, cutting through the early morning air, and the procession advanced. She fell into step on the other side of the palanquin, hands close to her swords and her eyes glued in his direction to watch for the slightest disturbance. If he did anything to Oza, if anything happened to Oza because of his whispered machinations, she would make him pay.

...But at least Oza looked well, and more significantly, seemed to understand not all was as it seemed. His safety was more important than anything else, but she couldn't deny she had felt a heavy weight sinking deep down in her gut at the thought that he would think he had been avoiding him all over again. She hadn't wanted to disappoint him, hadn't wanted to see it in his eyes. But it wasn't disappointment she had found there. It had been wariness, furtiveness, maybe a flash of relief. On the one hand, it was good he knew things were awry, but on the other hand, his awareness of it meant he had encountered trouble of his own in their time apart.

Her fingers twitched. One leap, one swipe. She could jump on top of the palanquin and leap down on Bisset's head, sword cleaving down toward his skull to reave it in two. One strike, and it could all be over. But she wasn't stupid. Even if she had continued to grow stronger and more skillful in the past several months as she seemed to have done the last few years, she was still weaker than Bisset. He had decades of experience and a body hardened and strengthened by innate magic...black magic, too. Not to mention her damned leg yet hobbled and shuddered if she moved it the wrong way. If she went head to head with the son of a bitch now, she knew she would lose. It was as simple as arithmetic. And yet she couldn't help but thirst for it anyway.

Patience. Time. She needed to hold fast and wait for the chance to strike, clean and swift. She would only have the one...

As they turned onto the main street where thousands gathered on the sides and screamed and cheered, Anzi glanced around, pretending to observe their surroundings for threats. In truth, she looked for Letti and Kai, making sure they were still where they were supposed to be. The harem girls were at the very front, leading the way with their beautiful, gauzy veils and dresses, and she saw a flash of Letti's light pink dress somewhere between the dozen women. She hoped that was her, at least. And Kai? She eyed the second palanquin that came behind Tet's, this one black and golden. It had no curtain and she could see him staring at her with undisguised intensity. But that was unsafe. There were almost certainly more assassins lying in wait, and they could fire arrows from a distance instead of having to fight through an unruly crowd. The guards, magisters, they were probably all too useless to interept a single arrow. It was up to her. It was up to her to protect Oza and Letti and Kai. And Netra and Serqet, too. Her pulse raced. They would be with Bastien, waiting to make their appearance as had been planned in the next few minutes. In fact, all the dragons present in the Imperial City would be there, those that could fly wheeling in the sky in magnificent flight to awe the massive throng of people lining every street, every road. The ones that couldn't fly would remain in Bastien's hands…allegedly safe and sound. Yeah, right. Anzi couldn't wait for the first day of this stupid, damned festival to be over so she could take them back and get them away from the man. Her breathing quickened; her heart pounded. They marched on.

Soon, she heard the screaming and the roaring of the crowd swell to a crashing crescendo behind her, and she thought she could hear Netra's triumphant cries from the sky. She shouldn't be doing that. She should be trying to stay inconspicuous, unnoticed. Whatever insanity was brewing in the Imperial City thanks to the impromptu mass festival, whoever made the loudest sounds, whoever stuck out the most haphazardly would be the first to taste fire. And Netra was not ready for fire. Anzi clenched her fists and tried to send a mental scolding to the dragonet, but it went unanswered. Were they too far to communicate? Or was Netra ignoring her? Dark hells, she didn't know. The rushing of her blood was so loud in her ears that it drowned out even the deafening noise of the crowd, and she squeezed her eyes shut with a furrowed brow to try to recall her composure.

Calm. Patience. Easy…

When they finally reached the end of the planned route and stopped where they had begun on the main street, Anzi breathed a sigh of relief. Despite the chaos of tens of thousands, even hundreds of thousands of souls screaming and shrieking and stomping in mad celebration, no one had tried to disrupt the event yet. Didn't mean it wouldn't happen, especially now that the most dangerous part of the festival's commencement was upon them, namely, the opening of the palace grounds to the public. This was the second time in less than half a year such a thing was happening—unheard of, and not even for the New Year's celebration!— and it promised to be a far greater revelry than the gala before. The Imperial City natives thronging together in suffocating numbers were bad enough, but the horde coming in from the other cities as well promised record pandemonium. Not to mention the great number of foreigners streaming into the city even now and more due to arrive in the coming days as the festival ramped up to its climax. Between them all, assassins could be hiding anywhere, ready to strike, and after the mistake with the old man no one really knew what to do anything about, Anzi was certain the next crop of killers would be more careful.

Where was he, anyway? And what had happened to him? Kai had insisted that day she had let him out of the palace that the man be taken off the scaffold, but shortly after, the old man had managed to get a hold of a sharp object in the dungeons and tried to kill himself with it. He'd been stopped and saved—doomed, in other words—but now languished in a feverish coma last she'd heard. She wondered how it was he had managed to find something to hurt himself with in the first place when the dungeons were so well guarded, but now wasn't the time to dwell on it. She had to keep an eye on everyone. Had to keep them safe. Somehow.

From the stone bridge where the procession had paused, she watched along with everyone else as the dragons soared over the city. There were Kai's dragons, both of them; she noticed them first. It was hard not to with how gracefully they rode the thermals and banked with tight turns even at their prodigious size. Their scales gleamed under the winter sun, red as running blood and the other a captivating turquoise. A primal energy hummed through her as she watched them, and she wished for a wistful moment she was up there with them. Wild dragons, indeed. And there, Netra. How had she grown so much? She used to be so small, so fragile, but now she was so big that from snout tip to tail, she would probably be longer than Anzi was tall soon. This last week especially, she had grown by leaps and bounds, and her wingspan was growing even faster than the rest of her body.

But Anzi felt no pride. How could she? The faster Netra grew, the more valuable she became to Tet and the rest of the Premier Guard, and the more peril she was in. War was looming, and Anzi was beginning to fear that Netra would be towed off alone to the northern front without her while she was forced to stay behind and hatch more eggs.

Things were happening too fast now. She couldn't keep up. And no matter how fast she ran, no matter how high she leaped, no matter how hard and savagely she fought, the odds continued to stack against her. Would Bisset use the *quickening* power Bastien had so cryptically mentioned on Netra? It made the dragons grow, he had said. However that happened, it was unnatural and wrong, and she would sooner snap

Bisset's neck than let her near Netra. She'd seen more than enough destructive evidence of how that would end.

On cue, her jaw tightened when she glimpsed Bisset's dragoness next. But it neither soared nor hovered in the air as the others did, nor did it ride the wind with effortless grace. Instead, the blue behemoth brought up the rear from far, far behind, and now that Anzi paid attention, now that she knew what she was looking for, she could see the dragoness's fatigue in every labored beat of her massive wings and in the exhausted up-down rhythm of her body as the creature struggled to stay in the air. She hadn't always been that way. Anzi had flown on her back so many times and had never sensed it. Or had she simply never noticed because her ignorance had blinded her? Now that she thought back, she could remember how the dragoness would always choose to lie down and rest whenever she wasn't made to fly. She could remember how her head always drooped, how she never stirred until she had no choice.

She was dying. She was dying, and there was nothing Anzi could do about it. Meanwhile, the crowd had no idea—all they saw was a massive dragon far larger than the others with wings enormous enough to cast a shadow long and deep over their heads. They screamed, cheered, waved their hats and pointed up at Bisset's dragon as if she weren't crumbling to pieces before their very eyes.

Anzi looked away. She couldn't watch anymore. She glanced at Tet's palanquin and at Letti, busying herself with making sure all was right, then looked back at Kai's carriage. To her surprise, he was leaning forward past his curtains and staring directly at her, golden eyes flashing like blades in the dark. She jumped when she felt a foreign sensation churn and roil in her chest, heat and power and—helplessness.

Helplessness?

She stared back, and for the first time, she noticed something different within herself—something changed, turned. She didn't know how else to describe it. But whatever it was, it rose up and flared inside her like wings as she held Kai's stare, and she thought she could feel the touch of his hand breezing along her skin across the distance. She whirled back around, breathing hard. She didn't know what that had been—she felt it even now—but she wasn't interested in deciphering whatever mysterious magic afflicted her this time. She would blame it on the bond he claimed they shared (the bond she believed in more and more with every passing day, damn it) and set it aside for later examination. Maybe yell at him for it, too.

But gods above, had she been feeling his emotions just now? Had that been him inside her, echoing and swirling deep down underneath even her own awareness?

"Open the gate!" Bisset's gravelly order had everyone straightening their postures in a haste. Not her. This had been the most critical time, the easiest opportunity for any assassin to try his hand while the procession was stopped for nearly half an hour while the crowd admired the flying dragons and filtered in closer and closer toward the palace walls to try to get a head start in. But in just a minute, the window would be past and she could breathe a little easier.

…So long as nothing happened in that next minute. Her stomach twisted, and she sucked in her next breath between her teeth, eyes roving the rooftops, the crowd, the waterway, even the very ground. But nothing. The guards were doing well keeping the people away from the Emperor's retinue, and with the stone golem on the other side of the wall already opening the massive gate, Anzi felt the tension in her body beginning to loosen.

Yes, finally! The procession filed back into the palace grounds through the stone tunnel, the footsteps of the soldiers guarding the palanquins marching in comforting unison. She sighed. For all her secret ideas of rebellion and treason—the stomping of the boots, the flash of blue and white uniforms, the arms and legs swinging in perfect synchrony—she felt so at home in the middle of it all.

Even if, she thought bitterly as they went up the steps and entered the palace proper, that was only because she had forgotten what home really felt like.

"Don't," she murmured when Letti sidled up to her after the Emperor's posse dissolved in a hurry, once inside. "Low profile. Don't even look at me."

But Letti shook her head, and Anzi thought she saw a flicker of nervousness in her bright blue eyes past the charming smile she wore. "You haven't been keeping up!" the harem girl chirped. "Haven't you heard? I'll be with you this whole week!"

She stared, uncomprehending.

"Anzi, say something." Letti waved a hand in front of her face, and the faint smell of lilac wafted into her nose. She leaned back.

"I don't know what you're talking about. I'll be with His Excellency the Emperor and our guest, the chieftain." The other guards and concubines —the Imperial Harem's as well as her own, damn them all—were too close for her to speak with familiarity, so she carved her voice with a cold demeanor as she replied. She didn't know what the hell Letti was doing talking to her in the open like this especially with Bisset just outside the doors, but she wasn't going to seal their fate by playing into it.

"I'll be with you all," the woman insisted with a bright smile. Too bright. And again, a nervous light glimmered in her eyes, lingering long enough this time that Anzi recognized it for what it was. Her heart lurched. "Because the very nice man over there told me that the most industrious woman in the Imperial Harem should get to enjoy special privileges too, in a time like this."

'In a time like this?' 'Special privileges?' Her throat tightened. "And which very nice man told you that?"

She shouldn't have bothered asking. As if he'd heard, she saw the colonel turn his head and look at her over the heads of everyone else rushing in and out of the palace, and for an instant, time hiccupped, stopped. It froze them in a bubble, and she stared at him as he stared back —until his mouth twisted up in a familiar faint shadow of a cruel smirk.

The bubble popped; time unfroze and rolled on. Bisset disappeared to inspect the guard lining up along the main hallway while Anzi considered the benefits and consequences of lunging between the soldiers and attendants to drive straight through his spine.

"Anzi, stop." Letti's whisper barely reached her ears over the noise, but that was intentional, of course. "He knows. I was so stupid. Anzi. It's my fault. I'm sorry."

"He knows what?"

"That you and I are friends. That we've been talking. He might know."

"He might not. He might just be using you to frighten me."

"Yes, I know."

"How did he find out about us?"

Letti shook her head again. "I was so stupid. It was Noemi."

A violent shiver vibrated through Anzi's entire body at the mere mention of the name. "The bitch," she said flatly. "I remember her. I remember her well." She swiveled her head this way and that as she took two swift steps forward, searching—

"Stop, Anzi. You can't. Don't, please." Letti clamped her hands around her arms. "It's done. She's been spying on you, and on me. She doesn't know anything either other than that we're friends, but she thinks I'm using you to get special favors. Like getting permission to leave the palace when no one else can, things like that. So she's been reporting about us."

"Shit."

"I know, I'm sorry. She's been so quiet that I thought she'd decided to just…" She pulled in her bottom lip and gnawed on it. "I was wrong. I underestimated her."

"Not your fault."

"It is."

"No. I shouldn't have put you in that position in the first place. But we have nothing to lose now, so stay close to me, got it?"

"But I—"

"It's too late. The best we can do is make sure I'm close by in case something happens to you. And if Bisset has his way, that's exactly what's going to happen."

"Well, you won't have to worry about where I am. I can't leave His Excellency's side at all once they take us up to there." The harem girl pointed up at the sweeping balcony level above the great hall. "I'll be there all night."

"I'll stay with you. Don't worry."

With a sad smile, Letti reached up to cup her face in both hands before Anzi could object. "If I weren't so scared," she said, "I'd be really touched. I missed you."

"You're right to be scared. Don't do anything rash, Letti. I'm going to make sure things go right."

"I'm not the one you should be worried about." The harem girl glanced around, eyes darting furtively from face to passing face. "Is it true? Do you think someone's going to try to kill your chieftain again?"

Her chieftain, again. But it wasn't worth it to correct her. "Yes. The festival was a reckless idea, but it's too late now. And it's to build war fever, which is already working, so there's no chance it'll be cut early."

"Things are happening so fast, Anzi. I've never seen things so chaotic before."

"I know. Keep your head down, let's get up to the balcony before the colonel gets any more creative ideas."

"Is he the one behind everything that's happened to you? All of it?"

There was no easy way to answer that question. She wanted to say no, that in the end, it was Tet who bore the blame for everything—and yet the more she waited, the more she saw, the more she believed the colonel had more than just the ear of the Emperor. He wasn't the loyal, unswerving soldier she had always thought he was. He was devious. Scheming. He dug in and forced everything to move around him instead, even the Emperor himself.

"Let's just go," said Anzi. "We'll be late."

IN THE END, it was Tet who would be last to arrive.

Kai, one of his tribal brothers, and the harem men were the only ones waiting at the center of the balcony, the highest point. From here, they could see the milling people inside the great hall as well as see clear through to the outside through the transparent dragon fire glass that made up the top half of the forward facing wall. It was a sight to behold, truly, and Anzi might have enjoyed it if she weren't in a towering mood. She elbowed past Kai's companion with a dark look and stood next to the chieftain by his grand chair.

"Where's Neb Minnakhet?" she muttered. "Thought he was supposed to protect you."

"Not today." He reached up to run his hand up her elbow before wrapping it around her arm. "Don't forget what I told you. Stay close."

"I'm going to try, but you're not the only one I have to be worried about." She glanced to the other side, where Letti waited for one of the guards standing by to bring her a chair as well. "There's her."

"And your brother," he added. "I know. But I'm not telling you to stay close for my sake. Just stay close, Anzi."

"Did you have any idea he was going to bring Oza from the Tower?" she demanded, still in a murmur. She had to swallow down a rush of fresh agitation and rage before continuing. "Never mind," she ground out between clenched teeth before Kai could answer. "You couldn't have known if I didn't, and there's nothing we could have done about it anyway. It was Bisset, that son of a bitch. He keeps pushing and pushing, but he doesn't know I have my limits. I'll crack soon. Right on top of him."

The grip on her arm tightened, and she looked down to see Kai watching her with an inscrutable expression.

"What?" she asked. "What is it?"

"Bringing Oza wasn't his idea," he said quietly. "It was mine."

75

B efore Anzi could demand an explanation, the clanking of metal from behind made both of them turn. Two soldiers outfitted in the signature armor of the Emperor's personal guard appeared at the top of the winding steps with the monarch right behind them.

He was wearing something different than usual, robes of soft gold and white thread rather than Imperial red. It made him look even more unearthly, if that was even possible, or maybe it was how he stood more than half a meter taller than his guards as he grinned and plumped his garment around himself. "Greetings!" he exclaimed. "Things are going fantastic. We're doing wonderfully, everyone." He clapped his hands once, and his two guards as well as the harem men standing nearby bowed and backed away out of sight behind the crimson curtains. "Great, we don't need to stuff this place with so many bodies. Ah, Oza, come out here."

Anzi's breath caught in her chest like an ugly clot of tangled roots when she saw the young boy sidle out from behind Tet. He was taller than when she'd seen him last—but skinnier, too, and she narrowed her eyes when she saw telltale red markings on the back of his hands. Needle-thin and long, she knew exactly what had caused those: a rapping of something sharp and thin, much like the ones the magisters liked to use to discipline their students when they weren't performing to their desired standards. Oza was the most gifted young mage in a generation. In several generations. What would he have done to deserve being disciplined, especially when the Magisien body treasured him so much? He was not a spoiled boy, but as far as she knew, he was pampered and given greatly preferential treatment.

Did it have to do with her? Was he being punished to get to her? If Bisset had gone so far as to instigate physical violence against Oza, she wasn't sure she wouldn't leap down from the balcony right on top of his head the moment she spotted him in the aristocratic crowd milling around below. Older he might, and stronger than she was—but not wiser, if he thought she was going to helplessly accept this. Even a worm squirmed underfoot when the heel dug in, and she was no worm. She was no *fucking* worm.

…Except it hadn't been Bisset to bring Oza here. She couldn't understand why Kai would ever do that. Why? What had he meant to accomplish! Had he done it in innocent ignorance, a careless suggestion because he hadn't realized the full import of it? Was it her fault for not telling him everything, for waiting to see if she could trust him before she gave away everything she had learned in her time here at the palace? She should have told him. She should have told him she was surrounded by enemies, made it clear that Bisset was among the worst of them. She should have—

"I don't understand. Is this just what you're like when you're happy? Why do you always look so angry? You're harder to please than a cat, I swear." Tet jabbed a finger at her and down at Oza. "You, too! Both of you. I have to say, I make special concessions for you and I get no appreciation at all. None!"

Anzi's eyes flickered back up to the Emperor and his scowling face. His anger at her stoic reaction seemed genuine, and she had the small comfort that whatever the circumstances that had led to Oza being here, it wasn't because Tet was trying to punish her and drag her back into line. In fact, the greater danger now was if she didn't fake her gratitude quickly enough. His grimace was deepening even now as he glared at her, and she hurried to bow her head to him.

"I'm sorry, Your Excellency," she said. "Oza is unable to speak. And I'll do my best to be more open. It's a challenge for me."

She listened for his response, and when she heard a familiar huff of mixed resignation and frustration, she knew it was safe to look up again. And indeed, Tet was ruffling Oza's hair—ignoring the boy's furious expression, thankfully—and rolling his eyes. "Right," he said. "I forgot this one's a mute. So many of you interesting types with all sorts of impediments. It's actually a bit cute, isn't it?" He ruffled Oza's hair a second time, and Anzi had to hold herself back from warning him that the boy didn't like to be touched that way, or in any way, really. That would be stupid of her and likely deadly, too—for both her and Oza. His patience and her restraint were the only things keeping Tet from having one of his quiet, smiling meltdowns, and she was in no mood to receive a second beating from the man. Her entire body tingled with the mere memory of it even months later. And Oza? He wasn't a fighter. One glancing blow in the wrong place, and...

"Well, let's sit and have a nice break. That stroll out there was so tiring. All those people screaming and being idiots, don't you hate it?" Tet made a show of wiping sweat from his brow, a gesture that was meaningless to Anzi because the man hadn't so much as twitched a finger outside his palanquin the entire time. "All of us here together, very good! And you, come here." He settled into the grand throne-like chair next to Kai's and crooked a finger at Letti, who had been standing quietly by. "Alexandre was telling me all about you. Your hair really is the color of spun gold, so very beautiful. I remember when I used to have a taste for that. And your eyes! Why, you're prettier than I am. Ha-ha!"

When Letti glided close enough for Tet to take her hand and place it on the raised armrest of his chair, Anzi felt a queasy churning rise inside her. The harem girl was hiding it well, but she knew her expressions well enough to know—Letti was terrified. The calm smile she wore was nothing but a front. Still, it remained steady as ever even when Tet reached up to dig his forefinger and thumb at various points around her face, even pulling the corners of her mouth back to inspect her teeth as if she were a dog to be sold at auction.

"Pristine condition! My friend, Kaizat—do you want this one, too?"

Anzi's eyes darted back over to the chieftain, and she ignored the other kind of rumbling that spread across her chest like a wave of cold fire. She would have closed her eyes if she could to beat back the confused hostility fast growing inside her, but she found herself unable to look away as she stared, waiting, watching. Damn it, she was being stupid about something so petty when Letti's very life could be in danger at this rate, but even so—

"She's beautiful, but I'll have to decline. I'm already claimed."

Her stomach lurched, pleased. Too pleased. The next thing she knew, Tet was throwing his head back in laughter so hard that his gold-veiled head knocked against the top of his chair. "I see," he said, nearly choking, and it was the closest Anzi had ever seen the man come to being graceless.

"But I assure you, if you're talking about my dear Anzi over on your other side, she's more than happy to share. She's a darling. You don't mind, do you, Anzi?"

A darling? She was a breath away from grabbing hold of a piece of the balcony's stone railing and tearing it apart in her hands. She didn't have the time or patience to discuss *sharing* Kai with anyone. Did she give a damn? She did not. Not one. Who cared if she could see him watching her out of the corner of her eye, golden eyes gleaming with a metallic sheen? She was too preoccupied with making sure nothing went wrong and that neither Letti nor Oza accidentally stirred up trouble. She was worried about important things, significant things, and she had no time to be—

"See? She's not jealous. That's a childish thing. Look at her, fine warrior. So do you want this one or not?" Tet picked up Letti's hand and wagged it at the chieftain. "Don't forget, I did warn you that I can't let you keep Anzi. I hate to keep anything from a dear, supportive friend such as you, but this is different. Violetta—that's your name, right? Good— Violetta's unattached, and I'm more than happy to give her to you as a souvenir to remember me by. She's also got, what do they call it? Classical training. And I hear from time to time that the skills of anyone in my harem border on magical. Hands, mouth, all."

Anzi's skin crawled. She was still busy trying to split her vigil between everyone, especially Oza who had just taken up Letti's recently vacated seat, but listening to Tet speak of Letti as if she were no more than a toy to be enjoyed made her want to lash out once again. It was getting harder and harder to stay quiet.

"I'm satisfied," said Kai. "No need."

"Hm. Well, if you change your mind…" Tet waved the harem girl away. "Let's watch the show, then. Those crazy acrobats come up with something more deadly every year. I swear they're the only things left in the world that make me feel excited anymore. Look, there's that one about to swing on the rope with only his teeth holding on. I wonder if they'll fall out."

Oza had always been better at sitting still than Anzi, and she was thankful for his quiet ways more than ever as he remained planted in his chair, barely moving. Next to him, Letti sat just as quietly, and there was even a convincing, serene smile on her face. How had things come to this? What had been the fatal misstep? If she had endangered only herself, she would have forgiven it, but for her mistakes to cost everyone she cared about…

"Tet, my friend."

Anzi's gaze fell on Kai once more, and she narrowed her eyes at the tone he took. Smooth and disarming, it didn't suit him. Not when he was addressing the Emperor. But she said nothing and only listened, absorbing every word.

"Hm? What is it?"

"You have a dragon, too, don't you? I haven't seen him."

"Sure, you have. I have my other riders flying in soon over the course of the week, they're coming from way out in the sticks or something."

"I mean yours. You have one of your own, don't you?"

Anzi stilled. That was right. Bastien had even named him—Ra, the Emperor's dragon. How could she have forgotten? But instead of answering, Tet burst into a peal of laughter that sent a cold shiver running down her spine.

"Not to worry, my friend. My dragon isn't one for crowds, so he'll stay where he is. You don't mind, do you?"

Kai returned his attention to the performance going on below. "It would be an honor to see him soon. I was under the impression he would show himself today along with the other dragons."

"Oh, no, not him." The Emperor's face split in a grin so wide it looked thoroughly sinister, and the hair on Anzi's arms stood up straight even though she only saw it in her periphery. "He's under the weather, so let's not disturb him."

She waited for them to say anything more, itching to learn more about the mysterious Ra, though she dreaded to hear it at the same time considering all the atrocities committed against dragons that she knew of already. But surely it would be different with the Emperor's dragon. Selfish and greedy as he was, wouldn't he at least prize his own companion enough to treat it well by sheer virtue of his possessiveness, the way a greedy merchant might polish his most valuable jewels with loving care? But she heard nothing more. Neither man said anything after that, and the performance below wound down to its conclusion several hours later. It had been a grueling affair with over two dozen different performers all engaging in death-defying acts to make the spectators scream and cover their faces again and again. But it was nearly over now, as morning had turned to evening already. Through the translucent dragon glass looking out over the Imperial City, Anzi could see darkness falling. Winter days were so short, but she couldn't bemoan them. The faster end of day came, the sooner she could get Oza and Letti out of here. And the sooner she could ask Kai what he had been thinking, having her brother brought to the enemy's doorstep.

Please be a misunderstanding, she thought. Please-

An intense rumbling rocked the palace, hurtling Anzi to full attention. A wave of screams pierced the massive hall when the final pair of performers lost their balance and tumbled to the ground, and Anzi steadied herself with arms flung outward as she looked back to make sure the others were unharmed. Then again, another rumbling, even louder and more intense this time, one powerful enough to send Anzi out of her chair.

"Earthquake!" someone screamed, and then it was chaos. The people below clambered over each other in a mad dash for safety, all shrieking and crying. Anzi thought she saw several people disappear into the crowd under trampling feet, but she couldn't get to them from here. She would trust the soldiers posted below to do what they must. In the meantime, she had her own duties.

"Everyone, follow me," she said sharply. "Out to the—"

"The Tower's under attack!" one of the guards behind her shouted, and when she looked out the glass portion of the far wall, she found it to be true: though darkness was fast falling, an unmistakable plume of roiling, thick smoke poured out of the top of the dark spire in the distance.

Her eyes widened. She had no idea what was happening, but she did know one thing. She needed to get Oza, Letti, and Kai out of here. "Follow me down!" she insisted in a second attempt to bring order to the group, but she never had the chance to finish what she meant to say. Half her words were still tumbling off her tongue when she whirled around and saw something that choked her to stunned silence:

Kai, standing in front of Tet.

With his black-scaled hand buried in the Emperor's chest.

76

I t happened before Anzi had even the slightest chance to react. Not only Kai's sudden, brutal assault on Tet, but what happened next, too—the explosion of the translucent, swirled dragon glass that made up the top half of the far wall looking out over the city. And as countless shards showered over the entirety of the great domed hall with a piercing, shattered cacophony, the dim sky darkened, far more quickly than any sunset could cause.

Shadows! The shadows of wings as two large shapes crashed in, then unfurled, revealing winged dragon-like figures, half reptile and half-man. They deflected a hail of arrows before flaring their wings again. And although they were on the distant end of the great hall, Anzi felt it the instant they raised their heads and stared at her. No, not her, at them—everyone on the balcony. Their wings beat twice, gaining air as they prepared to fly straight toward them.

"This is it, then!" Tet shouted over the growing cries and horrified shouts rising from the packed crowd below the balcony. "Magnificent, wonderful!"

There was something wet and blubbering in his voice, and Anzi knew it could be nothing other than blood. But something was wrong. Something was terribly wrong, because as everyone stared in paralyzed shock, even the guards who'd initially rushed forward, Tet rose from his grand chair. Kai's hand slipped out of the terrible wound in his chest, and the chieftain stumbled back, grimacing as he gripped his hand that was smeared crimson with silvery splotches. No, not hand. Claws. Anzi threw out her arm and pushed Letti back, who had hurried forward as well. Was she reckless or merely foolish, she raged, but trying to drown her horror with forced anger was futile. Her leg twinged with renewed pain as she shoved the harem girl back toward Oza who, being the smart boy he was, had begun inching away already.

"Oh, yes," Tet shouted, his voice rising even more, and the exhilaration flaring in his growing shouts of glee made Anzi shudder as she stared up at him. He towered over everyone even more than he normally did, and she had to crane her neck back to continue to look upon his wide-eyed, grinning face even though he was standing several meters away from her now. And Kai, oh, no, *Kai*—

He lunged forward again, his other hand changing form into elongated claws as well, but Tet caught him by the wrists as easily as if he were stopping a mere child. It was as if he weren't bleeding copious amounts over his robe at all, even though thick rivulets streamed down to the marble floor and everywhere from the balcony's white stone railing to the chairs to the curtains on the side were splattered red with metallic threads. And dark hells, were they—was the blood steaming? It was, and smoking, and if Anzi wasn't imagining everything in this impossible fever dream, she thought she could see Tet's blood eating through the fabric of the curtains with a hungry hiss.

The winged reptile-men were more than halfway here. It was clear they were with Tet, inhuman allies of the chieftain. But they wouldn't make it here in time to save Kai. None of them would.

Anzi knew what she had to do. This was stupid, suicidal, and if she were wise, she would have known to throw her lot in with the monstrous, overwhelming thing that was Tet the Emperor. That way, she could gain his trust and exploit it in the future...because there was no chance she could defeat him. Not before when he had all but torn her apart with the brutal beating months earlier, and not now when she had a half-crippled leg. But if it was stupid and suicidal to save Kai, if it was stupid and suicidal to forget everything else for just one pivotal, crushing, mind-rending moment and throw herself into the abyss, then stupid she was. Because this couldn't be it. She would not pay the price with Kai's life—

But when she lunged forward toward them, swords drawn in both hands and arcing forward from the side to slash at the arms holding Kai captive, an invisible blast of power crashed into her and hurled her backward. She slammed into the balcony railing on the opposite side, thrown clear across the distance and nearly sent hurtling over the edge.

"Stay back, dear!" Tet shouted, voice drowned in maniacal, cackling glee. "I don't need you! Let me enjoy myself before I cut his hide off and wave it around like a banner."

He thought she'd been leaping in to protect him. A jarring, terrifying mercy, because as Anzi choked out a wheezing breath and slid off the railing to the floor, she couldn't imagine what Tet might have done to her if he'd been meaning to hurt her. Just that, the single expulsion of magic that had flung her like a rag doll, must have cracked her ribs where they had smashed into the stone behind her. Her entire body vibrated from the impact even now, and when she moved her trembling arms, she realized belatedly how reckless she had been. But what choice did she have! Kai was still there, still struggling as black scales enveloped his arm and chest to no avail. He had yet to free himself, and worse, now he reached for her as if he should be worried about anyone but himself. Was he stupid! She was fine, he was the one in danger! Anzi doubled over and crawled forward, ignoring the searing pain in her back and her sides—only for an incoming rush of wind to nearly bowl her over. She caught herself, collapsed on her forearm, and looked up when two shadows loomed over the entire balcony. The groaning of the stone made everyone else scramble backward, arms and legs tangling as the balcony began to come away from the wall—

"Anzi!"

She made a sharp, panicked gesture when Letti tried to run toward her, but smart Oza, clever boy, grabbed the harem girl by the arm and pulled her back. Anzi shot him an approving glance before struggling to her feet as well, but nearly fell over again when the entire balcony tilted with a ferocious, grinding noise under the weight of the two dragons that landed upon it right in front of her. She stared, breathless, as she grabbed for the wall to pull herself back up to her feet. Dragons—right in front of her, even if they were turned away. The screaming from below was even more deafening now as men, women, and children tried to escape the chaos, but the noise all died away in her ears as she watched the two crea-tures advanced upon Tet with savage growls rumbling from their scaled throats. They were small, she thought vaguely, as her mind worked furi-ously to keep track of the insanity according to her methodical soldier's habits. They were scarcely more than perhaps six meters long, but that was still plenty big enough to be dangerous. The tip of one of their swishing tails smashed against her, crushing her to the wall and sending searing pain screaming down her injured back and her bad leg.

And they were big enough to alarm Tet, who proceeded to drop Kai's hands and begin backing away. But he was still smiling, still laughing.

"So that's why you wanted to know where my dragon is, ah? Ah?" he cackled. "You'll never find him without me. Go on, try to kill me—even if you could, it won't help you!"

Kai tried to lunge at him again, but another invisible wave of magic burst outward and sent everyone reeling back. Even the dragons, who had to take to the air and beat their wings against the force to steady themselves. But at least they were alive. Anzi looked back, suddenly fearful, but she saw no one there except the guards who were pointing their shaking swords at the scene. They were only men, after all, even if they were the Emperor's personal guard. Soldiers who had never thought they would encounter anything fiercer than mortal, two legged enemies who looked just like them...

There was blood dripping into Anzi's eye from a cut that had opened over her brow, and she wiped it away in a hurry with the back of her hand as she dived for her fallen swords on the ground. She didn't know what was happening anymore, but there wasn't a chance in all the dark hells that she was going to continue disarmed. And if this was her chance to rush in and end Tet with the help of two dragons, however unexpected the aid, then she was certainly going to—

"Wh—hey, where's the boy! *Where's the boy!*"

She froze. The boy? His head swiveled, eyes wide open and crazed. His grin was gone, and if she didn't know any better, she would have said the Emperor looked panicked.

"The BOY!" he screamed once more, then pointed at the guards. "I need him! Get him! Don't let these idiots get anywhere near the kid, go! Go!"

The boy? Did he mean—Oza? But why! He was only here because he was being used against her, anyway, what was he—

THE GUARDS TURNED tail and fled, armor clanking, and a horrific, dark fear filled Anzi's heart. But there was no time to think, no time to try to puzzle out what was happening anymore. The dragons crashed down upon the balcony again, this time landing directly upon the Emperor, and the balcony finally met its limits: with a final groan, it tore away from the walls, and everyone plummeted toward the ground in a hail of giant stone chunks and a thick cloud of white dust. Anzi reached for something to hold onto, anything, but a blur of black flashed in her vision. Without thinking, she let go of the metal sconce—

—and found herself in Kai's arms as he bounded off the last piece of the balcony's edge to fall away. And then they were airborne, the wind knocked out of her as he crashed into the wall shoulder first, shielding her from the impact. There were more screams as people dodged out of the way below, and she somehow managed to angle her swords away from both Kai and herself just in time to avoid beheading either of them. They rolled horizontally once across the wall with the momentum, sliding roughly, and she goggled at the black, reptilian wings that exploded out of Kai's back. One of them caught the tip of her sword as it ripped outward and expanded, just on the edge, and although she angled it away yet again, it was too slow. He let out a pained grunt and flinched as he crushed her to his chest. But even more worrying was what happened next. They hovered in the air high above the ground, but an abrupt shudder raced through his body so violently that it rattled her to the bone as well. And then—one of his wings shrank, sinking back into his body as if something were yanking it back inside his flesh. Her eyes widened, and she let out a choking shout when they plummeted several meters at a terrifying slant.

"Hold on!"

She would have even if he hadn't said to, but never had she felt so helpless before. A familiar queasiness struck her at the worst of times, swirling in her gut as Kai's shrunken wing burst outward again to catch them mid-fall. But it wasn't to last. This time, the other wing withered and faltered, and then it happened a third time just before they crashed into the ground at a punishing angle. They landed in a heap, rolling over and over with Kai's arms wrapped around her, and every part of her body felt bruised and jarred when they finally slid and slammed to a stop against the base of a pillar. The people had deserted this area already, and there were no trampling feet to dodge as Anzi loosened herself from his grasp and sat up. She sheathed her swords, clumsily, before reaching down to pull Kai up against the pillar. She was too numb to stand up herself, so she kneeled in front of him, panting, wide-eyed.

"You," she said. "You're not human."

"I'm a dragon, Anzi."

"But you're a man."

"I'm both." He grasped her wrists and pulled her closer. "There are only a few of us. Not enough to fight for long. I thought I could kill him, but there's something wrong. He has black magic strong enough to keep him alive even when I crush his heart."

"I know. You should have told me! I could have warned you that—"

"That what? Did you know he would be powerful enough to defy death like that?" He stroked her cheek, and despite the crashing chaos and violence swirling all around them in the crumbling palace, she felt something settle inside herself like a key sliding into place. "I wouldn't have believed you, even if you'd tried to tell me. I want to kill him. I know he hurt you. I feel it still, the mark he left on you, how you fear him. I know it."

"…I thought you killed him," she confessed, swiftly dragging the subject back to the present. She glanced back, saw the two dragon from earlier slashing, biting, writhing as they battled something unseen. They were on the ground again, wings folded against their sides, and she knew what was happening in an instant. No matter how unbelievable, Tet was forcing them to retreat, beating them back even as they thrashed and gnashed their teeth at him. "He's even stronger than I thought," she breathed, and she turned to look at Kai again. "You have to leave. Leave with—whoever those two are. Leave before he kills all of you. This has gone sideways."

"You have to come with me."

"I can't. I can't—Oza's here. So's Letti."

"I won't leave without you."

She ripped his hands off her wrists with a furious, desperate sound. "Don't try that with me! I know there's something wrong with you, isn't there. You were changing. You were changing—I saw your wings come out and your face was changing, your hands, the scales—but you couldn't keep the form. That's why we fell. Tell me!"

He grimaced, and she noticed then the rattling of his breath, how hard he had to fight to stay sitting up. "It's the basilisk poison," he rasped. "I thought I'd healed enough that it wouldn't interfere with today, but there must have been enough left inside me to do this. I didn't realize until I tried to shift. I've made a mistake."

"You idiot," she cursed, and she wiped away a trickle of blood that dribbled out from his mouth. She hoped it hadn't come from within him, that he had simply bitten his tongue, but something told her such hope was in vain. "I'm going to get you out of here. Your friends behind us—I'll try to help them, but I need to get you out of here first."

"Don't. Just come with me. They'll hold him off long enough, and then I'll call them back. I won't let them die for this."

"Call them back?"

"We speak to each other. In our minds. They'll hear me."

She shook her head. "I'm—"

"Anzi, please. Come with me. I would never do anything to hurt you." His fingers trailed down her jaw. "Come with me."

"That's not why I can't go. Oza's somewhere out there and Tet—Tet wants him. I have to get him out." She shoved herself back up to her feet. "And Netra and Serqet are still in the Cave. The dragons you let Bastien take, are they like you?"

"Yes. They're our generals. They'll bring your hatchlings. That was the plan, they were supposed to infiltrate and rescue any captured—"

A particularly deafening crash behind them made Anzi whirl around. "We don't have time for this," she hissed. "Swear to me. Are Netra and Serqet safe?"

"They already are. They're being taken out of the city as we speak."

He knew that because of his mental communication with his allies, no doubt, but her fists clenched at her sides. How could she trust strangers with the safety of her dragons? And yet Kai's expression was earnest. He meant what he said, and she had to believe. She had to trust him, if no one else.

"Then I'm going to go find Oza and Letti. You need to escape with your men before Tet kills them, or the mages come and..." She paused. "The Tower. You attacked the Tower, too. That's what it was, why we saw the smoke there...why you had Oza brought out." But there was no more time. She grabbed his wrists and pulled him to his feet just as a furious roar filled the air. "Go!"

"Anzi—!"

She didn't wait for him to speak. She took him by the arm and ran toward the crumbling exit of the great hall, and just before the great archway could collapse over them, hurled herself forward as she dragged Kai along behind her. Something struck her on the head and the arm, and a stone chunk clipped the back of her heel, but she couldn't stop. Couldn't slow down.

"Go!" she screamed as she let go of Kai's arm, and she used the thick dust that rose up all around them to slip away before he could catch her.

He was wounded. He would never make it out alive if he had to take her, too. And she had never been good at being saved, anyway. Who was she? Even with a twisted limp and cracked ribs, even with a bleeding head and full of fear, she was Anzi. She was still a warrior. A fighter. And this time, she was fighting for what she wanted, now.

There were people screaming all over the palace grounds, but it was hard to see through the smoke and dust rising everywhere around her. She saw flashes of white and blue somewhere over the towering walls like strikes of lightning, but something was different about them—explosive, unnatural. Still, she couldn't stop to stare. The ground shook as all the wall gates opened at once, no doubt the work of the guards who must have panicked and commanded the golems to lift the stones so that the people could escape through the tunnels out onto the streets. But she cursed them for it, fiercely. If Oza and Letti made it out into the city, they were as good as lost to her. And those unnatural lightning strikes outside colored blue and green and all sorts of dangerous hues she didn't trust— the outside was dangerous. They could die before she ever had a chance to find them again.

"Oza!" she screamed. "Letti!"

She shoved aside the men and women streaming out, parting the crowd that crammed toward the closest open tunnel in a writhing mass. But this was futile. She couldn't see anyone in this sea of faces, this screaming mob. She needed to get higher, somehow, some way—

She surged through the people, barely noticing them. Her leg twinged again and again, but she didn't stop until she reached the edge of the crowd that stayed well away from the enormous stone golem that towered next to the tunnel entrance, its arms raised up and stationary as it held the gate open with its magic. Stable enough for her. She shoul- dered her way into the cleared patch of grass, breathing hard now that she was free of all the panicking, frenzied bodies crashing into her. And once she reached the golem's foot, she clutched at the crags and crevices all over its body and began climbing her way up. When she reached its bulky shoulder, she ignored the shouts of the soldier manning the golem from below and scanned the grounds. But it was dark enough now that it was so hard to see anything in clear detail, too dim to tell anyone apart from the crowd. Gods above and below, she prayed to them all that she could find them.

A terrible, explosive sound from beyond the palace wall had her swiveling her head to look out in the distance. There, a flash of spectral green lit up the sky, a lightning strike-like column of power crackling down toward the ground. The illumination cast a fierce glow all around it, revealing for an instant the shape of a dragon even further out, framed against the light. Broad wings, a yellowish shade she'd never seen before. She had no idea who it was and in this moment, didn't care at all. She had to find Oza and Letti even if the world fell apart around her. She grabbed onto the side of the golem's head, hand planted against the rough surface as she looked down again and frantically searched the crowd.

There! A flash of pink, darkened by the coming night. She didn't know how she spotted it in the chaos, but there could be no mistaking it. With a furious, determined shout, she launched herself off the golem's shoulder and dropped to the ground below like a rock.

The walls of the Imperial Palace continued to crumble…

77

Anzi hit the ground so hard it made her teeth rattle, but she managed to land on her feet and tuck into a roll to protect her knees from the impact. In truth, it was easier than it should have been—just a half-year ago, she would never have considered leaping down from such a towering height, but she was desperate and determined as she shoved through the crowd to find that flash of pink she had seen a moment ago. If she had wasted even a single second longer for fear of her own safety, she would surely lose Letti.

But desperate or no, the aching pain that throbbed in her calf and foot was a bitch. She bit down hard on the inside of her cheek, cursing Bisset for crippling her, but there was no time to be bitter about it for long. There—!

She wrenched Letti back by the shoulder and found bright blue eyes staring back at her, wide and panicked. They were filled with no small amount of fear and hostility, but as soon as she recognized Anzi, relief flooded her face as she slumped toward her. Anzi caught her in a tight embrace, her heart feeling like it was going to pound right through her ribcage. "Are you all right!" she shouted over the crowd that slammed into her over and over again as it tried to swim past her. "Where's Oza! The boy who was with you, my brother!"

"I'm trying to find him!" the harem girl sobbed back, not bothering to comment on her own dirty, dust-covered state. "I don't know what happened. The guards knocked me aside and grabbed him from me, then they said something about how they had to get him to the safest place they could. But they went out there! How can it be safer outside the walls than inside them! Anzi, I don't know what's happening anymore!"

"Calm down! I know where they took him. You get to embassy in the upper district. You know where that is, right? Where they take the lesser diplomats and the merchants to stay?"

"Yes, but I can't leave you! I'll help you find him. I can come with you!"

"You'll only slow me down." Anzi shook her roughly by the shoulders to bring her back to her senses and make her look into her eyes again instead of looking around wildly. "Listen to me! I can't focus on finding Oza if I think you're in danger. Understand? I need you to get to the embassy and take cover."

"But why would it be safer there! The whole city's in shambles by now!"

"No. Not there." They were on the ground so it was impossible to see over the towering palace walls, but she pointed at them anyhow to indicate what was on the other side. "The dragons have attacked the mages' Tower, and they're concentrating their attacks there now. Can't you hear it? The noise on the opposite side of the city's lessened. And the dragons aren't attacking civilians—they're attacking our most fortified points. The palace, the Tower, the North and the South barracks, all of our garrisoned forces. You'll be safest if you go to the embassy."

"But—!"

Anzi didn't have time to convince her any further. She had to hope the woman was smart enough not to try to follow her and do anything reckless, to go straightaway to the building and take cover there. In truth, she wasn't sure at all if the dragons would overlook the building and its inhabitants at all, but she had to rely on her familiarity with Kai's ways if nothing else. His grievances were with the Empire and its corruptions, with especial resentment against those who had had a personal hand in its atrocities against dragonkind as well as other innocents. So the embassy was the safest place from his wrath and that of his allies, wasn't it? It would be inhabited by only foreigners, poorer foreigners who weren't favored enough by the Empire to earn lodgings inside the Imperial Palace.

She had to hope. She wasn't even certain that Kai knew of the embassy as well as she hoped he did, but she had to hope. She rushed on, all but flinging people aside as she surged out of the crowd to head for the place she suspected the guards had taken Oza. There was only one place such simple-minded idiots would consider 'safe' in a time like this if even the palace was falling, only one place they would mistake for being immune to the terrible attacks exploding all over the city. They would be wrong since anyone with the remotest intelligence would know the only safe places were away from the Imperial City, but this was all part of the Service training they were conditioned to. If the Palace fell and the escape tunnel underneath was inaccessible, then the next place to flee would be the dungeons.

Letti had been wrong. She had thought the guards were taking Oza outside the palace, but they would have cut through the crowd and run along the inner edge of the wall until they reached the northernmost gate. The dungeon entrance was closest to there, and the dimwitted guards would have foolishly taken Oza inside without a single intelligent thought as to how reckless it was to hunker down in a stone pit when the world was falling apart all around them.

When she reached the dungeon entrance, it was as she had expected. The doors were no doubt barred closed from the inside, even if she had a battering ram to crash through the thick wooden portcullis that had been dropped down in front of that. She inserted her fingers into the mesh pattern of the gate, looking frantically from left to right in an attempt to find any weakness in the barrier. But there was none at all, and the lever and pulley to open the portcullis back up was all the way on the other side —close to the inner door. She cursed, nearly sobbing in rage and frustration, and flung herself forward in a frenzied attempt to bash through with her own body. The thing shuddered and rattled so loudly that if she had the chance, the time, she would have stopped dead in her tracks to wonder how she had struck it so hard. But she couldn't stop. Couldn't slow down.

The explosions all over the city, the lightning crack of magic from the sky lightning up the night, the green and blue and white flashes that made the distant screams of the crowds refresh anew—this was no mere skirmish, no short-lived ambush that would leave its mark before fleeing. This was war. Whether Kai knew yet the full meaning of what he had done, whether he and his tribe of impossible, dragon-shifting men were ready for the storm that would descend upon them in the form of the Emperor's blood thirsty dragon riders flying in from all over the continent—it would happen, and Anzi would have to helplessly watch the bloodletting.

She was afraid. She didn't know if she had ever felt this afraid before on the battlefield. Why was it so much more terrifying here when she knew this place better than she did any foreign land, any occupied and annexed territory? But the fear didn't matter. All she knew was that she needed to save Oza, and then she would gather up everyone else one by one. With another bash of her shoulder, she rammed into the portcullis, knowing that her swords would chip and shatter before they ever cut through the enchanted wood.

Wait—enchanted. Stupid! She cursed herself for her blind panic and backed away, making sure to stay well away from the arrows that were now occasionally peppering the grass around her. The soldiers on the wall must be trying to shoot up at the sky to bring down the circling dragons, stupid idiots, and she had to make a clumsy, hasty prayer that no stray projectiles would find their way into Letti's neck as she fled the grounds.

But she couldn't focus on more than one thing at a time, not like this. She had to save Oza first, and then she would find Letti after that. Right now, she needed to get this gate down no matter what, and there was only one way she was going to be able to manage it in time. After backing up to a safe distance, she dropped to one knee for leverage, planting herself in the grass and leaning forward over her thigh. Her arms were outstretched, palms cupped and facing forward.

She hadn't done this in earnest in a while, only expelling her arcane power in short, controlled bursts as she trained herself to use it more artfully, but this was no time for artfulness. This was no time for precision, for careful accuracy, for efficiency. She needed only power, to hit hard and mercilessly and destroy all obstacles in her path. Like this gods-damned gate—!

With a strangled shout, she released a ferocious blast from her palms. The magic burned her skin as it left her body, streaming out of her palms and leaving them as raw as if she had held them over a fire to roast, then slammed into the wood with a terrible splintering sound that made her heart leap. A shimmering energy surged over the entirety of the gate and she recognized it in an instant as the protective charm laid over it, but she wouldn't let that stop her. She steadied herself and tried again, and again, and again, shouting each time in deranged fury as the portcullis began to give way against the concussive, furious strength of her magic.

Maybe she would never be like the mages of the Tower, but she didn't need to be. She only needed rage. She scrambled up to her feet and rushed forward, heedless as she charged through the splintered hole torn through the middle of the wooden gate. She barreled down the short passage that led to the inner doors a few meters ahead, knew it was barred closed, knew exactly what they would be holding the doors closed with, an iron piece fitted between the handles inside. But she didn't care. And even though explosive pain tore through her body the instant she bashed her shoulder into the doors, it was all worth it for the triumphant instant that she crashed right on through, destroying both the wood of the double doors and twisting the iron bar on impact as easily as if they were no more than toothpicks.

She clambered through the splintered entrance she had just made, ignoring the scratching of the broken pieces against her exposed skin. Who cared about her tattered uniform and that one of her leather shoulder guards had disappeared along with a forearm greave? She didn't need those to get to Oza, and judging by the panicked shouts and barked orders coming from inside, that was exactly where the guards had gone.

The cells were half-filled with various prisoners, but she didn't have time to free them even if she could be sure they didn't deserve to be trapped down here. She rushed past them, ignoring their echoing calls, and headed all the way to the back where three guards brandished their weapons at her.

She didn't care about them. Didn't care about them at all except how fast she could drop them to the floor with swift strikes that knocked them unconscious, didn't care about anything except this one thing:

"Oza!" She stuck out her hand for him to take, ever present of his repulsion to touch. She couldn't afford to trigger an episode right now; she had to let this happen on his own terms. "Oza, I need you to grab onto my sleeve. We need to get out of here. Please, Oza! Wake up!"

He was staring at her, stunned and shaken. The guards must have manhandled him fiercely and set him off in that time, she thought with a curse—but she didn't have time to figure that out and get him to cooperate. He stared past her over her shoulder, and in a flash of intuition, looked back as well. Someone stood there in the dimness, a familiar sight —confusing, but familiar nonetheless.

"Doufan," she snapped. "What are you doing here? I don't need any help, get yourself out off the palace grounds and head for—"

"I'm not here to help." He hefted the glaive in his hand and let it lazily point in her direction as she stared. "I'm here to get rid of you."

78

"**D**on't do this," said Anzi. She shifted, making certain she was concealing every part of Oza from Doufan's view. "You're not going to like how this ends."

His glaive twisted in his grasp, a small rolling of the handle that made the keen edge of the curved blade on the end gleam under the torch light. "I'm obligated to make you an offer since that's our way," he said just as blithely. "Give me the boy, and I'll make it painless for you."

"It? And what's 'it' supposed to be? You're getting ahead of yourself." She grasped the hilts of her swords and unsheathed them an inch. The other soldier's glaive tip edged upward as well. "This is a bad time for you to play Bisset's lapdog. The whole city's falling apart. Get out of here, and I won't bring this up to His Excellency when we see him next. Consider it a favor repaid if you don't say a word about the guards."

But he said nothing, and something about his cold composure and sharp, deliberate regard of her felt different than usual. She didn't know what exactly, just that it made him appear far more sinister in the dim light than he ever had before. But she was going to have to get over it. Everyone was suddenly wanting Oza, but they would have to walk over her corpse to get him. She was getting her brother out of here in intact even if it meant she had to cut Doufan to ribbons. The only problem was that she was already battered and tired, and in pain too. Half her leathers were missing on top of that, whereas he looked untouched and in top form. Indeed, not a hair out of place.

"I don't have to keep him alive," he said suddenly.

"What?"

The man pointed at her chest, but she knew what he was really indicating. "I don't have to keep him alive," he repeated. "It's up to you whether he has it easy or not. If it comes down to it, I can eliminate either one of you, then both. Make your choice."

She didn't have to. She already had.

They leaped at the same time and clashed in the center in a shower of sparks as the magic running through her black blades screamed against his glaive. His weapon was stronger, and by all accounts should be able to shatter her blades if she so much as nicked his in the wrong direction, but the magic would hold out. The bigger problem was her raw hands— expelling so much uncontrolled power earlier through her palms had torn the skin and exhausted the sinews there. With every swing, her grip weakened around the hilts, and soon, she could feel a layer of blood beginning to slicken her grasp.

What was worse was that the rear of the dungeons here was so cramped. She could hardly swing her sword except in short slashes and cuts without nicking one of the bars or the low ceiling or the ground, whereas Doufan's glaive could jab and strike freely. His reach was far longer, too, and she couldn't hope to get enough momentum in her strikes to try to break his guard. Meanwhile, he was breaking hers more and more with every blow, and if she didn't figure out a way to shove him back, he was going to back her right into Oza, and there was nowhere the boy could run.

He always had been better than her where weapons were involved. But when she shot off a wave of magic at him that he neatly dodged with his eyes still fixed on her, she knew she had underestimated him far more than she had ever expected. Of course she had known he was always holding back in their spars, but this much? How had he kept this hidden for so long?

"Yield," he said when she leaped back closer to Oza with her guard up and swords crossed in front of her. "Your stubbornness will get all of us killed. I don't mind death, but I think you'd rather keep your brother alive."

She glanced up at the ceiling for a fraction of a second, noting the ominous crumbling of stone pieces. Her second magic bolt had gone astray and hit something that was already weak; that combined with the continuous shaking from aboveground had made the underground dungeon more unstable. Shit. But she couldn't show her fear. "Since when do you taunt and talk trash in the middle of a fight?" she jeered. "Picked that up from Pierro, have you? Spending too much time with him."

The look he gave her was cool, inscrutable. He shifted his glaive tip up so that it was pointing toward her instead of at the floor once more. "He's dead."

"What's that?"

"He's dead. I killed him. Just before I came here."

She stilled. There was nothing but stony earnestness on his face, absolute uncaring indifference. He didn't care if she knew, didn't care that he'd just told her. It was as if he'd commented on her bad footing or on the changed weather, nothing more. "Is Bisset out of his mind? The auxiliaries were already attuning to the eggs. His Excellency is going to be angry as all hell—and you're just as crazy for going along with it. It's the Emperor you should be most afraid of, not the colonel."

The impatient, irritated look that crossed his face was the first hint of emotion she had seen him wear. Something flickered on the edge of her understanding, but not enough that she could grasp it.

"You kill Aimee, too?" she asked. "Got rid of everyone in your way so that you can get to the top after all of this?"

"She wasn't in my way. She's still alive."

Again, that cold dispassion that sent goosebumps crawling up and down her arms. In his way? Pierro had interfered with this insanity? Her stomach lurched. Pierro had been the only one on her side, or the one who had been least hostile to her, if nothing else. He was the one who had alerted her to Bisset's insidious treachery, he was the one who had helped her even if he thought it was because she and his cousin had some dirty tryst going on. In the end, Pierro had been one of the few people in all the city, in all her life, that she had asked for help from.

And now he was dead. She knew better than to doubt Doufan, who would never say such a thing lightly. Not even this new side of him that was infinitely more dangerous than before.

"Are you yielding, then?" he asked in the silence, and she gritted her teeth.

"In your dreams."

They clashed again, this time so hard that another shower of rubble came down over their heads. But she couldn't let that stop her. She parried a terrible chain of strikes with her swords, the impact so jarring that it had her hands and arms ringing like gongs. And again and again, the tips of her blades scraped against the walls as she tried to angle her slashes and swings to break past his guard. If only she could get close enough to deliver one kick, just one, or catch his weapon mid-swing, but Doufan was too good for that. She swallowed back a curse when his blade tore through the front of her uniform and slashed down her chest; how was he getting faster instead of slowing down?

Damn him. Damn him and all his secrets. If she had a chance, she would shake the answers out of him upside down and bury him alive afterward. But right now, her only worry was getting Oza away from him—

A small hand grabbed at her arm, nearly making her jump out of her skin. Before she could warn him to step back, what was he doing! he stuck out one trembling hand past her—and shout out a stream of white fire so ferocious and hot that it singed the skin of her face even though she turned away. It jetted toward Doufan, roaring as if it had life, and blossomed around him to swallow him up whole.

Except it didn't. Anzi gaped when he pulled back his glaive and spun it in front of himself without retreating a single step, and the silver glint of the blade fanned in a rapid circle as it channeled away every lick of the flames. No, not away—it absorbed it all as if it were eating up the fire magic. And when every flickering flame disappeared, the man hefted his weapon once as if testing its weight anew before pointing it directly at them.

"That's all I needed," he said flatly. "You know what this is. Give up now, or both of you will burn."

Shit! Shit! She felt Oza draw back behind her with a shaky, strangled sound, but she grabbed onto his shoulder from behind to keep him steady. It wasn't his fault. He had been clever to think of fire, something that should have roasted Doufan alive without compromising the stability of the crumbling dungeon ceiling. And he had been so, so brave to try to help her. How could he have known that the soldier would be carrying an anti-hex enchantment in his glaive? Anzi had felt nothing on the weapon to suggest such a thing when they had crossed blades again and again just a moment ago, but then again, she had only been looking for the telltale sign of enchantment against the physical, not the spectral. And his glaive was empowered not against chipping and shattering—but against magic and spells. Against not soldiers, but mages.

And now, he had a glowing, fire-imbued glaive in his hand, the same one he directed squarely at them now.

"Your brother has no defensive ability," he said calmly. "We've been watching him closely. Neither do you. If I release this, you burn. Understand?"

She understood. She understood very well. But what she also understood was that she would never, ever, *ever* lay herself down and roll over, just like she would never let him take Oza. Fuck him, and fuck whoever else was a part of this, too. With a furious shout, she discarded all the rest of her common sense and decided to do the purely idiotic, the purely desperate—and released a final wave of arcane power from her body. She didn't care that it wasn't accurate, and neither did she care that Doufan spun away the blunt of the blast from himself with another rapid twirling of his glowing red glaive.

Because she wasn't aiming for him. No. She was going to bring the entire dungeon down over his head.

Her magic crashed into the walls and the ceiling, and scarcely before she even had time to blink, the cracks in the stone ground and opened up with terrible groans. She thought she saw Doufan leap back and run toward the dungeon's exit, but it was too late for her to do the same. Even if Oza could keep up, she wasn't certain they would have made it out, anyway. Unlike Doufan, they were on the inside, farther away from freedom. So that left only one thing for her to do.

Just as the dungeon's ceiling crumbled overhead and brought down fearsome stone chunks all around them, she whirled around, grabbed Oza to herself, and bore him down to the ground under her body...

79

The falling stones should have crushed her. She had never visited the dungeons often enough to know exactly how far underground this lower level was, but the weight of the upper cells alone should have flattened her. And Oza, too, no matter how much she wanted to believe otherwise. Sheer determination and panic wouldn't have been enough for her to save him.

Or shouldn't have been. But as she groaned under the weight of the solid slabs threatening to drive her into the ground and take Oza as well, she realized dimly that she wasn't dead. That wasn't possible, and yet here she was, breathing, however laborious and painful each rattling, shallow inhale. Her arms and legs trembled madly, struggling to support the weight of every piece of debris fallen on top of her so she didn't suffocate Oza underneath, and she felt no give as she shifted left and right—but she was alive. She was conscious. And although they were buried in darkness under the rubble and she couldn't see whether his eyes were open, she thought she could hear him breathing too.

She could have sobbed. She had thought for sure she had let him die the instant she felt the impossible weight crash down upon her, had believed and dreaded feeling his body break and shatter under hers. But she was holding on. She was holding on somehow, and no matter what it took, she was going to get them out of this. She could feel the bruises already mottling every inch of her body and the gashes opened up all over her by sharp pieces that had torn through her uniform and remaining leather guards. But none of that mattered. Bones, flesh, they were resources she could expend if she could only keep Oza safe.

She opened her mouth to say his name and see if he was conscious, but the dust swirling in the cramped space between them made it impossible to make a sound without choking. It was only on the third strangled try that she managed to croak his name.

A loud, answering exhale made her wilt in relief, only for her to tense and lean back again when she felt the rubble groaning on top of her. Shit. But she couldn't stay still, either. The adrenaline was making her think she could hold out, but the realistic soldier's mind that spoke over the panicked relief told her she had only moments before she buckled and caved. She had to get out. She had to get Oza out.

"Move your hands," she wheezed in cracked syllables, "protect your face. Now."

She felt him try to move, but to no avail. She cursed again and made up her mind—there wasn't enough time to be indecisive. "I'm going to try to stand up. I might lose my footing. So keep pulling on your hands until they're loose again, and as soon as you can, cover your face. Nose and mouth. Got it?"

He huffed again in answer, and she took a deep breath to ready herself. Her muscles were burning, aching, and soon, she knew they would be screaming in pain once her body had a moment to process everything that had happened to it, but for now, she was going to drag it past its limits. Whatever it took. Whatever the cost. An arm, a leg, broken ribs and limbs and spine, she would gladly pay the price if it meant Oza could walk away safe. But she couldn't give those up either, because she was the only one in all the world who could protect him. And if she sacrificed herself, who would take care of him?

She closed her eyes—and heaved.

The rubble groaned; the stones creaked. Her voice tore out of her dust-smothered throat in a cracked, dragging shout as she strained upward against a weight unimaginable, every tendon and sinew feeling like they were going to tear out of place if she went on. But she had to. She couldn't stop. If she let up for an instant, a half an instant, if she paused for a single breath or to steady her grip, all was lost. One slip, and...

More, she begged herself, just a little more. But as her elbows weakened and the toes of her boots began to slip, as more dust filtered down from the shattered, grinding slabs on her back and head, she knew begging was futile. No more. Anzi had never been kind to herself. She had never been soft and begged herself to work harder, to give a little more. She was hard, sharp, merciless, always the most ruthless to herself while sparing what kindness she could afford only for a precious few.

"Get *up!*" she screamed at herself, and even to her ears, she sounded bloody, violent, full of fury. And she was, she *was*—as she tore herself up out of the earth, arms straining and blood racing through her body, heart pumping so fiercely she thought it might burst into pieces inside her. Frantic, frenzied power raged through her veins, and every vessel swelled inside her as the rubble fell apart to either side of her body. She lifted back and forced chunks larger than she was wide to fall away, more, more...Until, at last, she tasted air. She felt wetness on her cheeks as her body creaked and screamed, and her chest rose and fell with heavy gasps as she fought harder, harder, to taste the precious, cool wind seeping through the cracks.

She must have fallen unconscious the last few seconds, her body moving mechanically on its own. When she came to again from the blackness, she was lying sideways out of the depression she had carved a way out of, and Oza was crawling up to lean next to her. He reached for her face, skinny fingers prodding at her cheeks. She moved away, hardly able to breathe past the terrible, wrenching pain in every part of her, but slumped over with a shudder before she could shift but a finger's width.

It was dark now, she thought dimly, complete night. Far in the distant sky, she could still see the same flashes of fierce light that flooded the sky, beams of crackling energy that surged earthward. It was beautiful. Terrible and beautiful at the same time, fearsome and inviting. She tried to reach out to touch it. It looked so close, and she thought she could feel her body lifting up on wings to fly closer. Strange, she didn't feel as if she were in her own body anymore...No, it was more like—it was as if she were there already, right in front of all that glorious, blinding light, expelling it from her open maw and-

The crack of a hard slap to her face brought her back to her senses. Not the pain, but the sound, and her head was still lollingas she turned to look at Oza who stared at her with narrowed eyes. He took her by the shoulders and shook her as hard as he could with his meager strength, and only then did her mind begin to clear. But with renewed awareness and full consciousness came also the pain again, and she almost crumbled as her legs wobbled under her.

But she had to stay strong just for a little longer. Oza was not yet safe. No matter how much she wanted to lie down and curl up like a cat, no matter how exhausted and spent, she had to keep going.

She wasn't surprised when he began coughing after she pushed him up over the side. He kneeled on the grass, shoulders rising and falling with hacks as he fought for breath, and she dragged herself up so she could straighten his back with a hand flat against his spine. She helped him breathe, to soothe the tightening in his throat and his chest, and she gave genuine thanks to the gods when he began to calm. It hadn't been a bad one this time, a lucky thing since she had none of the herbs on her that would have helped him had the choking become more severe. Did he have some on him, she wondered, her thoughts still half-blurred. She patted down his now-filthy mage robes and searched his inner pocket, only to find crushed leaves and roots remaining.

"I'll carry you," she said, and when he protested with a thump to her chest, she grabbed his wrists and shook her head. "I'll be fine. It'll be worse if I make you walk and you have an episode. If that happens, there's nothing we can do."

He thumped her chest again, his skinny face the palest she had ever seen it as he stared up at her, terrified.

"I'm fine," she said again, and this time, she made sure to make her voice stronger. It was almost more than she could bear, but she had to make him believe she was all right. "You know me. Don't be afraid. I can do whatever I have to do. Got it?"

Her voice was hoarse and her body numb from head to toe, but she said it anyway. Because she knew it was true. Because she had no choice.

He balled his fist in his wide sleeve and reached up to wipe her face. It was still wet, she realized, and she made a clumsy attempt to use her sleeve to wipe at her eyes, nose, and mouth. But when she pulled her arm away, she saw dark blotches on her sleeve. Too dark. It was nighttime with no illumination to see their color with, but she knew better than to think tears and sweat could ever blacken the white of her uniform so.

No wonder Oza was scared. But that was all right. She could do this. She turned around and got down on one knee, the scabbards of her swords scraping along the dirt and grass. Miraculously, they hadn't shattered after she had sheathed her swords just in time, but that was what top tier enchantments did for someone. Not that she expected to be able to wield them again if trouble found her once more…She could carry Oza to the ends of the earth if she had to, but lunging and slashing were beyond her. It took everything she had to stay upright as she began to jog out toward the closest gate tunnel with the boy on her back, his arms wrapped around her neck and her hands behind his crooked knees.

He was so skinny, so small for his age. He couldn't make it out here all alone, not with everyone wanting him for their own ends. She had left him like that all this time, all these years—now she was going to make things right. She would stay with him. She would make it through for him. He had no one but her, so she couldn't crumble here. If she fell, who would protect him? Who would take care of him?

Kai, she thought distantly. Kai—and Letti, who had tried to run away with him before the guards had taken him away from her. If she could just make it to them, if her broken body could last just long enough for her to stumble her way to them...

She was delirious. Must have been, because otherwise, she would have known better than to lower her guard that way. But how could she not be delirious, how could she not be lost in the sea of raucous, deafening noises echoing and booming all over the Imperial City, some so close she could feel the whole earth shaking under her feet? It was light, then dark, then light again, and it was only silent when she sank into her thoughts and ignored everything else, focusing solely on the next step, then the next, then the next...

Of course it would cost her. It had to. Oza's panicked thumping on her shoulder nearly made her collapse to her feet, but it was the only reason she managed to avoid being skewered through the back and out the stomach. The singular stumble, the happenstance evasion—that was the only thing that saved her from death at the end of Doufan's glaive.

He was alive. Not only was he alive, but he was in far better condition than she was. He was bleeding, sure, but there was nothing to suggest he was too hurt to stab at her again, which he did three more times as she scrambled back. She was too disoriented to think of letting Oza down so she could maneuver better, but even if the thought had occurred to her in time, she wasn't sure she would have. The way Doufan stood at the ready, eyes eagle-fierce, she knew he was looking to kill them both now. Some part of her wanted to laugh at how ridiculous he looked, dusted gray and white from head to toe with stone grit and debris still in his rock-powdered dark hair, especially since she knew she looked the same way. But this was no time to laugh. He lunged forward again, and she leaped back only to teeter on numb feet, nearly falling.

Her hands were useless, and her vision blurred in and out. Every part of her throbbed with buried pain, and each desperate twist and jump threatened to unleash it all in a flood. She had to do something. Please, just one more, she whispered to listening forces, wherever they might be, and then she prepared to lower Oza and steel herself for one more fight—

THWACK!

Doufan stumbled, shielding the side of his head with one hand and clutching his glaive tight in the other. It was no longer pointed at her. Instead, he angled his body so that he was half-turned toward the source of whatever object ha struck him so hard that Anzi had heard it over the continuous explosions in the distance. If she had been smart, if she had been vigilant, she would have taken the chance to turn tail and run, but all she did was stare at the young woman suddenly standing there.

"Don't," said Doufan, although his voice was so low and quiet that she shouldn't have been able to hear him. "Go back, Aimee."

It was dark, but the glow of the moon and the occasional flashes of magic lightning in the sky lit up the woman's face. Wet? Tears. She had been crying. But she said nothing as she levitated another sizable rock from the ground and sent it whizzing at him a second time. He dodged this one, but still made no move to retaliate. Her hands were clenched into fists at her sides, and Anzi watched as a glimmering teardrop fell from her chin and disappeared. There was blood on her hands, she thought, or at least something dark enough to pass for it. Maybe. And her white-blonde hair was mussed to hell and back as if she had been in some kind of fierce tussle. But that blood—maybe it wasn't hers. She looked fine, unhurt. Then whose...?

"You should have stayed where I left you," he said. "Someone would have cut you loose after all of this is over."

"You killed him. You killed him like it was nothing."

"And I let you live. Don't waste that."

Anzi breathed in carefully, slowly. She had always thought there was something between those two—but apparently not, in Doufan's case. Had he killed Pierro in front of her? Had she perhaps tried to intervene? Obviously, she'd been restrained afterward—maybe that was where the blood on her hands was from. Anzi began to back away with cautious steps...

"Was any of it even real?"

Another crack of thunder nearly drowned her out, but Aimee's question fell like a heavy anchor on the seabed, anyway. Anzi felt every word cut into her heart as if she were the one who'd been betrayed. She backed away again, eyes darting between the two. This wasn't her fight. She had never trusted either of them anyway—what did it matter that they were tangled up in a lover's quarrel on top of everything else? It seemed more and more that Doufan had been an infiltrator all along, no matter how outrageous it was that someone who had lived in the Capital ever since he was a boy could possibly be allegiant to anyone but the Empire.

It wasn't Anzi's business. She turned and ran before she could hear another word of it, thankful for the distraction. But it wouldn't last long. Doufan had always been stronger, more dangerous. She guessed Aimee would last all of a minute or two before she ended up the same way Pierro had, or worse.

She didn't look back to see. The time the other woman was giving her, this chance to get away—she wouldn't waste it. And so what if a creeping horror crept over her conscience at the thought of leaving Aimee to die at the hands of someone she thought she had known—intimately? She had to make a trade. Aimee, or Oza...and the decision couldn't be easier.

Aimee had made her bed and intended to roost. Anzi wouldn't stop her. She fled as fast as she could, strength miraculously renewed by the shocking scene she had just witnessed and all the implications that came with it. How much had she now known? How much had she been blind to all this time? She had assumed she was the Emperor's most prized possession all this time because she could hatch dragon eggs for him, but he wanted Oza for some reason as well that had nothing to do with her. He was a gifted boy, a child prodigy in the arcane arts, but he was no warrior. His talents lay in other fields, but what of them could make him so valuable to not only the Emperor, but to Doufan and whoever he was loyal to? And how, how could she not have known Doufan was a traitor all this time? Not that she held it against him since she was a traitor, too —but how?

Her head swirled and thumped with every thought at the same time, but she had to put them all away. She headed straight through the now-deserted tunnel gate, sparing only a second to wonder where the stone golem guarding it had gone. After that, the thought vanished, and she ran with limping strides on and on and on until she thought she could go no farther. But she had to. She had to, both for the trembling boy on her back and also for—

"Letti!"

"Oh, gods, Anzi, what's happened to you!" The harem girl sprinted out of the remains of the embassy house and held her face in her hands. Her pink dress was a mess, all the sheer organza fabric in shreds while the hem carried enough dirt and dust that it looked nearly black against the night.

"Get in," she croaked. "There's a basement, hide down there with Oza."

"The colonel was here!" Letti cried, and another thundering boom echoed from across the city. But strangely, or rather thankfully, the explosive thunderclaps were far fewer between and seemed more distant—out toward the edges of the Imperial City now. And yet the other woman's words made Anzi's skin crawl in renewed fear.

"What? He found you? What did he want!"

"No—he was riding his dragon, the giant blue one, and he was chasing some other dragon all the way here. B-but something happened. The colonel's dragon just fell out of the sky with no warning! That's why the embassy house is all fallen apart. It fell on top of the building then rolled down the hill! I was watching out the window, he didn't see me—but, but the colonel just jumped off before it could take him with it, and then he ran off to keep chasing the other dragon. He just—he just left the poor thing, but I'm too scared to go and see."

This was all too confusing. Anzi shook her swimming head, and finally, she let Oza down when he thumped her shoulder. "Get inside, it's not safe yet."

But a tug on her wrist said that wasn't an option. Numb and bewildered, she followed the boy as he towed her around the embassy house that lay in shambles, and when he crooked a finger at Letti, she seemed to understand what he wanted and hurried forward to lead the way.

80

It really was Bisset's dragon. Massive and sprawling, she lay in a heap at the bottom of the hill, her enormous head half buried in the stream that ran across what used to be the embassy house's garden. Anzi's heart dropped, and despite the battered state of her body, a surge of panicked strength helped her stumble down on shaky legs. She rushed past Oza and Letti and nearly fell to the ground on top of the creature's snout, only managing to catch herself by bracing one hand right above the scaly upper lip. But the groaning, rumbling sound of pain that echoed from deep within the dragon's belly made Anzi recoil in instant regret and yank her hand away.

"What has he done to you?" she whispered. Her throat was raw and her lips cracked; her voice was too quiet for anyone but herself to hear. But she asked anyway—never expecting an answer. It came in brief flashes instead of words, glimpses into something that touched her with darkness, heaviness—with the end. Anzi struggled to breathe, her chest suddenly full and thick with something that wouldn't give way. No, not just her chest, but all of her, every inch. She was suddenly too big, too swollen, too heavy to do anything but double over and fall on her hands. She clutched at the grass, disoriented in the midst of the stream of terrible, suffocating sensations that filled her from head to toe—and realized this was her. The dragon. She was feeling her, being her. Somehow, the creature had entered her mind and melded them together as one. She could see both from her own eyes and from that of the dragon's, could see both the magnificent, dying behemoth in front of her as well as the image of herself, how she looked in the creature's eyes.

And gods, she was so small. Small and pathetic and torn apart, bleeding from every orifice and her hair matted in stone dust and dirt. Was this really what she looked like to others right now? She lifted her hand to run her fingers down her face. It was strange how her mind could —see her, see herself, how she felt both inside and outside her body at the same time...

And how it felt to be a dragon, too.

Because she could feel her wings crumpled against her sides, leaden and stiffening. She could feel her heavy forelimbs that had buckled under her weight, the rear legs that stuck out at awkward ankles further up the hill, too heavy to move. She could feel the water that lapped against her snout, some of it entering her nostrils with every breath. She could feel pain, deathly pain, the end that called and tugged at her too-tired body, the magic that ran so thin and weak in a body that used to be able to soar over the air currents and taste the sun, the clouds, the wind...

He did this to you, she murmured. She couldn't bring herself to even say his name. Such a grotesque, twisted, filthy man didn't deserve to have his name spoken aloud. Ever. *He's drained you of all your magic. Your life.*

But she knew she would receive no answer. Not in words, at least. Because the colonel had taken more than just the dragon's strength and immortality—he had rotted her mind, too, and stolen her ability to think and speak anymore. The dragon hardly ever even knew when she was hungry, when she was cold, only pain...

He drained the last of you while fighting Kai's allies. She reached out with a shaky hand to touch the creature again, but this time only to stroke her scales with a gentle touch. With her Other sight, she could see Oza and Letti standing behind her with frightened expressions, but her mind was so full of—of two presences, both the dragon's and her own—that she couldn't spare them more than a passing thought. This was more important. This was... *He can't get away with this.*

But even as she spoke the words in her mind, she knew there was nothing she could do. Even at her best, she knew Bisset would have strung her up easily, powered by the spirit and strength of all the dragons he must have corrupted and drained in his lifetime, but now she was— this. Useless. Weak. She hung her head, furious at her pathetic shortcomings. How could she be so fragile? She was a warrior. She was a fighter. She...

She was only human. Despite all the wild blood that was supposed to be surging in her veins, in the end, she was nothing. A hollow, burning rage filled Anzi's skin like shadows swimming inside her, rage at how she had failed at every single thing she set out to do. She couldn't protect her own brother, or one single harem girl. She couldn't protect her hatchlings, whom she'd entrusted to Kai's men, strangers. And she couldn't protect this beautiful, magnificent, battered queen of the skies, either. It was only when the dragoness let out a long, loud exhale of steam from her nostrils that Anzi awoke from the wordless fury that filled every corner of her being. She looked up again and stared at the one giant blue eye that stared back—and saw a vision.

Something back in the Cave, she thought, as a flickering memory brushed against her mind. The dragoness was trying to tell her something, unable to communicate through any other method. What was it? An—an egg? No, not just any egg. Another flash of memory, closer this time, to something mottled gray and black and various other earthy colors...She knew what this was. It was the misshapen egg that Bastien always made fun of, Prince Bastard. But it was unhatchable. In this memory, why was it moving so much? Struggling...and breaking? Anzi had closed her eyes to try to concentrate on the faltering memory the dragoness was passing onto her, but they flew open as she realized what she was seeing. Something had happened down below after the dragons had been taken back, right after their flight during the festival parade. The wild dragons, the red and the blue-green one, had done something while Bastien wasn't looking, and many of the eggs had begun shaking and rattling around in their nests.

"We have to get—get to the..." Anzi could hardly get the words out as she fought her way back to her feet "Have to get to the Cave!"

Oza and Letti ran up to catch her, but it wasn't because of the pain that she nearly keeled over again. It was the sudden disappearance of the dragon from her mind, and for a terrifying moment, she thought the creature had faded away and died. But she found the dragon staring at her still, her eye blinking once, slowly, at her from above the stream's surface.

I'll be back for you, Anzi promised. *Thank you for showing me. I'll find a way to—to—*

Find a way to what? Save them all? In her heart of hearts, she knew it was too late for the great creature before her who had been laid low by black magic and a blacker soul, the filthy, rotted thing that was Bisset. His greed had already killed her. But it wasn't too late for the little ones, the helpless, vulnerable hatchlings inside the Cave who had yet to take a single breath outside their eggs. They hadn't tasted life yet, still had a chance to escape this hell, to be free…

That was what she was telling her. That was what she was telling Anzi even if she could no longer speak. Through the linking of their souls, she had asked her for the one thing that would make her death a worthwhile one—only if Anzi could save the one she could.

"I'll be back," she promised again. And she felt another rippling wave of new strength enter her. It surged upward from the earth and entered her body through the bottom of her feet, and it filled her legs, her belly, her arms. Even the pain lessened. "I'll be back. Oza, Letti, you stay here and wait for me, and then we'll escape. Kai's forces are withdrawing by now, and after the fighting's over, the Imperial Army will give out the order to lock the gates permanently."

"What—you sound like you're going somewhere! You can't leave!" Letti cried.

"You'll be safe. Oza, you're Tower-trained. And you have fire magic. Burn alive anyone who comes close, but stay hidden until I come back. I'll be back soon, the wall isn't but a few minutes' run from here if I move fast."

"I'm not worried about us! I'm worried about you! Look at you, you're bleeding everywhere."

"I *was*," she corrected. "Not anymore." Because it was true. At some point, although her face was still caked in it, she had stopped bleeding. Strange. She had thought it was only a surge of frantic adrenaline crashing through her veins that had reenergized her, but she felt stronger. Strong enough to fight, run. "Stay here with the dragoness. The last person I need finding you is Bisset, and I also know this is the last place he'll come looking."

"How do you know that?" Letti asked. "How could you possib—"

"Because he doesn't care about her. She's nothing to him now, useless. Look at her." Anzi turned and ran her hand gently along the dragon's head again. "This is what I meant. The riders aren't heroes. They're not champions. They do this, they kill dragons and drain them. And she won't last long, now. Which means he won't come looking for her for a long while, and you'll be safe until then."

"Please," the harem girl begged as she tugged on Anzi's uniform.

"Please don't go. Let's escape together, you don't have to do this. Your brother needs you. I need you! Why are you always putting yourself in danger!"

But even when the woman burst into terrified tears, she had to harden her heart. She had to do this. She could feel the pull, the power. It wasn't only guilt and sorrow and pity that made her do this—she could feel the pure need swallowing her up and urging her to come away, come away quickly.

"Don't be scared," she said and squeezed Letti's arm before pulling away. "Oza, take good care of her. Be waiting, I won't be long."

Her main worry was that she would find Doufan waiting for her, glaive at the ready and hunched over Aimee's corpse, but she stayed well away, heading straight for the palace. She hoped with all fierceness that he was gone by now, and if he was as determined to catch her as he seemed, he would have already left to try to track her down. And it wouldn't have taken him but a minute, perhaps less, to dispatch Aimee and leave in search again. Either way, Anzi kept her head down and stayed low to the ground as she sprinted on. Please be gone, she begged. She didn't think she could last another fight.

There was still no one guarding the tunnel gates, and again, Anzi wondered where the golems had gone. They were too slow to be used to fight dragons, and more importantly, earthbound. Where could they have been sent? What, had the orders been to get the golems to pick up boulders and try to fling them skyward to bring down at least one clumsy and unlucky dragon? That would only lead to senseless death when it fell down again, crushing civilians and allies indiscriminately.

No matter. So driven was she that she was nearly flying over the ground through the deserted, crumbling palace as she headed straight for the courtyard, everything blurring past her in a streak. Maybe the dragon had lent her the power of her wings, too, while they shared their spirits. The thought made it all the more painful, reminding her how little time the creature had to live. She had barely had a spark anymore. No more than a handful of days left…What Bisset had done was unforgivable. It was the first time Anzi had seen the final result of such twisted magic, even though Bastien had told her about it long before.

Her fists clenched at her sides as she skidded down the Cave's passageway entrance. Most of the torches had fallen out of their sconces, but even bathed in darkness, she knew where to go. She ran faster than ever, legs pumping as if they hadn't been shaking so hard she couldn't stand just minutes before, until she grabbed the wall and dragged herself to a stop just as she turned the last corner. It struck her as odd that she had been moving so fast that it took all her strength to stop her own momentum, and even odder that it hurt far less than it should have to do that in the first place, but right now, she had to worry about *that* egg, not herself. The others, she could do nothing for. It tore at her to know she was abandoning them, but gods willing, when the day came that she could return and save them all...

She hurried to the rear of the darkened egg chamber. Bastien would never have cared enough to move the egg, and she groped in the darkness for it—only to open her mouth in a silent gasp when she felt a rigid line and shards under her fingertips. Then, before she could fully understand what she was touching, what she was feeling, a damp nose nudged at her hand.

The egg. It hadn't broken completely, but the hatchling inside was coming out. His entire frilled and horned head was poking out of the hole he had made on his own somehow, and an exhilarated sob tore itself out of Anzi's throat before she got to work. The unhatchable, unbreakable egg, the one thing in the entire Imperial City that neither the elements nor any curse nor the sharpest weapons could even nick—this little thing had humbled them all. Except it wasn't so little. She felt its head, far larger than even Netra's, and she had hatched months ago. How big, she couldn't tell yet. With grunts of effort, she ignored the cuts that opened on her palms as well as the throbbing pain that renewed themselves in her muscles as she ripped off the rest of the front of the egg shard by shard. It was thick and sharp and impossibly strong, but the protective magic was gone. The hatchling was free.

It was too big to gather up in her arms, she realized when she helped the dragon out of the egg. Indeed, when it uncoiled itself with a cracking of bones falling into place and flared its wings, she thought it was too big to be called a hatchling at all. The massive size of the egg aside, it must also have been because he was trapped in there for so long. Despite being contained within it, he had grown, and grown well.

She ushered it out of the darkened chamber, but it was already following her without the encouragement. Its large claws clicked against the stone floor so loudly and heavily that she was afraid for a moment it would alert whoever was close by, but the Cave was deserted. No guards at all. How could the dragon eggs be left unprotected like this? At least Bastien should have remained behind, what had happened—

Oh, shit.

Now that her eyes were adjusted to the darkness, she saw something hanging high up on the wall in the main hall just before she headed back toward the Cave's exit. It was left impaled on one of the torch scones high up, the curved metal protruding through the chest. Legs hung limply below it, still twitching, and she let her eyes trail up slightly until she found the outline of a head.

She quieted her heavy breathing, and in the silence, she could hear the wheezing, struggling breaths of someone in their death throes. Bastien. Bastien was meeting the end he deserved. What had Kai said earlier? That the wild dragons were no wild dragons at all, but his generals, Sa-Khente and Qinglong. They must have attacked Bastien and left him to die this way, left hanging on the wall like decoration, a war victory fixture.

…It was no less than he deserved. No, that wasn't right. For everything Bastien had done to dragonkind since he began this two hundred years ago, the countless dragon hatchlings whose deaths he must have been a part of, the countless more that he must have helped enslave…he deserved so much worse. If Anzi weren't in a hurry to get back to Oza and Letti, she would have finished the job. But maybe the torment before death was fitting, too, no matter how much it would have satisfied her disgusted rage to slice his throat and end it for good. With a final glare, she turned and sprinted out, the hatchling following behind her at a half-hopping pace.

⤳

"Let's go."

"A-Anzi? What is th…?"

"A hatchling," she said shortly. "He can fly, a little. He's fast enough to keep up with me, so he won't slow us down. And he's dark enough to blend in. Anyone come by here while I was gone?"

"No," Letti stammered, and she looked back at Oza who was standing over and staring at the massive dragoness still lying in a battered, broken heap with her head over the stream. "But the noises have stopped. I think the fighting is over."

"We need to move before the gates close. Don't stop for anything."

"But you're hurt, how can you—!"

"I'll be fine," she said, and strangely, felt as if she were only half-lying. Again, she was aware of a strange rejuvenation in her body, a winding thing that was both simultaneously cool and warm as it threaded along her body. It was slow and steady, but she was sure it was refreshing her, and although she still felt as if a house had fallen down on top of her— which, really, one had—she thought she could keep running and running and never stop.

But it wasn't to be. Anzi spared only a second to give the dying drag-oness one last goodbye, a quick one so that she wouldn't crumble under the guilt of leaving her to her demise with such indignity, such injustice. But when she turned and gestured for the others to follow her to the other hilltop looking over the stream, there was someone already there, waiting for her.

"Doufan," she growled, her hackles rising as she stared up at the man framed in hazy moonlight. She glanced around quickly while motioning for Oza and Letti to retreat. It seemed at the time he had been working alone, but who knew? There could be plenty of other infiltrators in the city, not just him. They could be lying in wait to ambush her.

"You can't escape me," he said. "I have a way to find you anywhere you go."

At Doufan's side, someone suddenly appeared like an apparition, sliding out of the darkness to stand next to him. She recognized him... that long, flowing braid draped over the front of the shoulder. All he needed was a loin cloth instead of leather armor. Damn it, that was one of the harem men. She was so tired of being surrounded by enemies and stopped in her tracks no matter where she tried to go. But sshe was even more tired of running. Maybe this was a sign. Maybe this meant she had to fight her way out the way she always did, by blood and bone, even if it cost her her life. She wrapped her hands around her sword hilts and felt the magic of their enchantment thrumming along her grip. Doufan would have to work for what he wanted, and she wouldn't let him have it except over her corpse.

So come, she thought. Come and get it.

"For what it's worth," he said, "I don't want to have to kill you and your brother. But it has to be done. I have to protect them all, and for as long as you two are alive, I can't do that."

She had no idea what he was talking about, and she didn't care. She tensed, and as soon as his glaive twitched up and he descended the hill at breakneck speed, she unsheathed her blades and began running to meet him halfway—

But it wasn't to be.Because in that instant, a fierce, overwhelming wind buffeted them both. It knocked Doufan to the ground, pinning him almost flat and forcing him to brace himself with the glaive stabbed into the grass, while Anzi stumbled backward down the slope where the wind wasn't so powerful. And despite the dangerousness of taking her eyes off the weapons master, she looked back when a bone-rattling, air-rending, terrible, all-consuming roar began to build behind her. It grew and grew…as the great blue dragon rose, hovering over the ground. Her wings beat again with an enormous leathery flap, sending another hurricane-like gale to knock aside loose stones and flatten grass and force Anzi to back up even more if she didn't want to end up with her nose planted in the ground.

Oh, gods. The dragon—she was flying. Not only that, but she could see Oza and Letti on the base of her neck, looking as tiny as ants as they clung to the saddle. The Prince was there too, clinging to the great dragon's side with what must be hooks at the joints of his wings, like a bat's. And again and again, the great dragon slowly beat her wings as she descended upon them. Anzi glanced back with bleary, wind-blinded eyes to see Doufan now bowled away along with his harem assassin comrade, and that was all she managed to do before enormous talons wrapped around her and lifted her into the sky.

81

The dragon's talons threatened to crush her ribs with their perilous strength, but she clutched at them with a determined fire and grit her teeth against the pain. She had just been given a second lease on life, and Oza and Letti, too. If Doufan had run her through, he would have gone after them next without a doubt, and they wouldn't have stood a chance. It chilled her to think how close they had all been to meeting their end just moments before, but as they rose higher and higher over the Imperial City, exhilaration and relief filled her instead, swallowing up all the fear that had weighed her down like the night clouds blanketing the moon.

They were leaving. They were leaving, and she had managed to keep everyone alive. Her heart pounded harder when she thought of Kai and how she had had to leave him, but surely he would have done the smart thing and left the Imperial City as she had told him to do before parting ways. And he would be safe, she told herself. He—he was a dragon, after all, not just some ordinary man.

All at once, the terrible burdens of everything she had experienced in the last hour crashed down upon her, and she shuddered in the dragon's talons while holding tight to it with all her strength so that she didn't fall unconscious. She was exhausted down to the bone, so tired that she couldn't even see straight anymore. It was worse even than the pain that wracked her entire body, every joint, every inch of her skin, even. But she couldn't fall asleep now. She—she had so much to think about. So much to absorb, to understand.

Kai, a dragon. She had seen the wings burst out of his back. But that wasn't all. She had heard of winged men before, the half-breeds like Rania who had inhuman traits like that. But Kai's men, the ones he had said could shift—she had seen with her own eyes how their entire bodies had morphed from human to dragon within seconds. Their arms had become scaled and thick and muscular, and their heads had elongated and grown either frills or horns or both. Tails, claws, everything. That had to mean Kai could do the same, if it weren't for the basilisk poison that had stopped his transformation.

She wondered what he would have looked like. Would he have grown as big as Sa-Khente and Qinglong? Or would he have been smaller and more agile like the two leaner dragons who had come crashing into the palace to attack the Emperor? She knew what color he would have been, at least, that pitch-black shade so dark it seemed to swallow up all light and let them gleam from his scales with a beautiful, staggering grace. But she knew so little else. Nothing.

…Which only proved to her how stupid and blind she had been all along. She should have known. She should have guessed. Hadn't she seen the signs? The first day they had met, she had seen the gleam of hard scales on his arm where Oscar had injured him, even if he had covered it quickly. She had seen them and then—ignored them, because it didn't fit within her understanding. And the other signs, the strength that was more than human, and the speed. If nothing else, that should have made it plain his gifts weren't the products of mere desert magic.

Neb-Minnakhet had been right. The man had told her this was her shortcoming. He had said it with a cold, condescending sternness that made her wish she could punch him even now, but he was right. And—he had been afraid this same stubbornness would hurt Kai, too.

And she had.

If she had been more open, if she had trusted him, if she had let herself lean on him, then maybe…Maybe he wouldn't have been poisoned, maybe he wouldn't have nearly died. She pressed her lips together to hold back the nauseated groan churning in her chest and throat. She felt sick to her stomach. It was the queasiness that she felt whenever she flew, except it was so much worse now. The fatigue and pain was causing it, no doubt, but that was no reassurance when she nearly puked in mid-air. Lucky that she had nothing in her stomach to vomit, and lucky that the dragon was clutching her so tightly. The next wave of sickening vertigo had her eyes rolling up into her head and her body convulsing in its grasp.

Thoughts of Kai, as well as Doufan, Aimee, and even Bisset were still swirling around in her head as her consciousness wavered. No, she thought helplessly, distantly, as her body began to shut down. What was causing this? This was no mere airsickness, even compounded by exhaustion and pain. It was something else, something terrible—

She couldn't crane her neck all the way around to see, but suddenly, a deep, resonant rumbling grew and grew...from the Imperial City far below. But the dragon never stopped climbing the currents and soaring higher, never once hesitating or angling her serpentine neck to look back. If anything, she picked up speed and rose almost vertically toward the cloud cover, as if she were running away from whatever was the cause of the growing noise.

Before Anzi shuddered and lost all consciousness, she managed to twist and around sneak one glimpse, just one—and her mouth hung open in a paralyzed gape as something truly titanic rise from within the bowels of the Imperial City. The—whatever it was came from underground, knocking down buildings as the earth caved in on it then slid away, and the whole of the city trembled before falling apart. The worst of it was near the center, under the palace. And as the earth there fell away and revealed something golden and mottled white, something enormous— truly, inconceivably, heart-stoppingly enormous, dwarfing even the blue dragoness—rose from the ground. And with a slow, ascending roar at the heavens, the titanic dragon bellowed its discontent for all to hear. It was so loud it made her ears pop, especially as it grew and grew and grew until it felt as if the entire sky were filled with that one roar, and still it grew—

Anzi shuddered again one final time, then slumped over in the blue dragon's talons.

~

She awoke with a start. How long had it been? They were still in the air, and wriggling free of whatever was holding her captive could end only in death. But the memories came flooding back all at once, and she breathed a sigh of relief. That was right. They had all escaped the Imperial City thanks to...

She looked up, and at the sight of the heaving underbody of their dragon rescuer, she felt her heart clench with dread. They needed to land soon, or else she would fall right out of the sky and bring everyone else down with her, too. She had to be exhausted. And as Anzi let her senses roam and expand, she could indeed feel the terrible tiredness that the dragon radiated, rough and suffering and so, so drained. She was dying. Dying faster than before because she was using up the precious little strength she had left. But no matter how much Anzi tried to connect their minds again and beg her to please, please land so that she could rest, the dragoness ignored her pleas and continued on. There was a manic energy to how she ignored Anzi—or as manic as the creature's sluggish mind could be. Why? It was almost as if she were afraid, fleeing from something. Could it be the massive thing that had risen from below the Imperial City? The impossible thing, and yet unmistakable: a true titan of a dragon, easily as big as a hundred of the blue behemoth here with her. Anzi's mind still failed to truly understand what she had seen, and maybe it was the exhaustion too, but all of her thoughts simply went blank whenever she tried to revisit the memory and make sense of it.

Either way, the dragoness was not going to stop.

Go back to sleep. We can't stop.

She started, and her chest heaved with shocked, almost-panicky breaths. "Kai?" she cried out, and she whirled around in the dragoness's talons to find him. And find him she did, clinging to the other talon. He was back to his ordinary form, the one she knew so well, and thankfully missing no limbs. There were gashes on his body, but they didn't seem deep enough to be life threatening. And yet there was a shadowed cast to his face that told her he was far from fine. Her heart throbbed as she stared back at him. The wind was too loud for them to hear each other even if she shouted. She would have to follow his lead and cautiously use this—this strange mental speech as he was if she wanted to hear him, to speak to him.

Kai?

Go to sleep, he repeated as he stared back at her. *You're hurt. Badly.*

What about you?

She thought she saw him smile, but it was too dark to know for sure. His golden eyes gleamed as if he were, though. *I'm fine now that I see you,* he said. *It took me a while to catch up.*

Oh, hell—that was right. He hadn't been able to transform when they were together. *How did you? I thought the basilisk poison was stopping you from flying. How did you find us? Did you wait until we passed over you? Why would you not run as far as you could when you got away?*

I never left, he interrupted. *How can you think I would leave that place without you?*

She didn't know what to do. If she could, she would have fought herself free, leaped over to his side, and shaken him like a cat would a rat for being so reckless.

I can't shift anymore, he added gently. *I gave it my all to do it one time, all the way, and catch you before you disappeared. I need to rest now. She won't mind the extra weight, she's so heavy that she hasn't even noticed I'm coming along.*

He looked up, and she followed his gaze. He was right. The dragoness had to weigh ten thousand of Kai, at least. He would be little more than a fly to her. But his words suggested that he, too, understood the dire straights she was in, and in the moonlight, she could see a stony sadness in his glowing eyes that made her own burn with a hint of hot, frustrated tears.

They were watching her die right in front of them. And they could do nothing about it.

Go to sleep, he said for the third time. *We have to fly through the next several days. We'll stop only for an hour or so at a time.*

She can't! She's ready to collapse any second.

Believe in her. She's doing this for you.

She tried to think of something to say back. Tried to juggle both the relief, gratitude, and immense guilt all at once. Not only that, but the confusion too—she and Kai were speaking through their minds, their thoughts, as if they were using their voices. It had shocked her when she and Netra had done that, but this was different. They were both—humans, or at least shaped like humans. This felt wrong and strange and nonsensical.

Except it didn't. His voice in her head, in her heart, in her soul…it felt right. It felt good, and warm, and strong and everything else that made her want to keep doing exactly this.

Never mind that she would never have let him in so easily before. So much had changed, both outside her and within. It made her want to bury her face in her hands and ignore the world until she could set things aright in her head, neat and orderly.

Where are we going? she asked instead. *How does she know where to go?*

She doesn't. But we're guiding her. It's a straight line from here.

How will she know when to land?

Don't worry, I'll take care of it.

But she didn't want him to 'take care of it'—she wanted to help, to be useful, since she had done nothing at all except get hurt and be saved all night. Had she even accomplished one single thing tonight herself? Getting Oza and herself out of the collapsed dungeon didn't count; it was her fault he had been there in the first place. Besides that—nothing. It made her feel sick, even sicker than she already was. The queasiness was still raging inside her at full strength, but her eyes fluttered shut anyway. Sleep beckoned again...

~

SHE WOKE up to Kai's voice in her mind again, and by then, it was daylight. Something about being in the Adaraat desert made the sun shine hot and bright, or maybe it was because springtime was closer than she'd realized. That was right. She'd met Kai back in the late autumn, and it had been an entire season already. The world had changed so much. When they landed, the dragoness released her above the ground first as she hovered a meter high in the air. She landed easily on her feet, far more gracefully than she had expected she would be able to, and flexed the stiff muscles of her body that felt better already. She loved the freedom of flight, and yet she couldn't deny how rejuvenating the sensation of solid earth was—

"You!"

Anzi looked up at Letti's enraged, terrified cry only to see her sliding off the dragon's back and wing in a hurry. It said something for her training that the woman could manage to do something like that for the first time with such grace and poise, but what was concerning was how she dashed over to stand in front of Anzi and turn her back to her. What was she...?

Oh. Now she saw. Letti hadn't been shouting at her, but rather at Kai who had been walking over to join her. And now the woman was standing between them and barring the chieftain's path in a clearly defensive posture—along with a short, needle-thin knife in her hands that looked barely dangerous enough to pose a threat to a small animal. And Kai was no small animal. He continued walking toward them, his strides slow but fearless.

"Stay back!" Letti cried, but there was a telling warble in her throat as she jabbed the knife toward him with both hands from a distance. "Don't come any closer to her! Not one step!"

Anzi moved up and placed a reassuring hand on her shoulder. Her dress was in tatters, and there were grass blades stuck all over the fabric. Most of her hairpins had disappeared as well. But despite her unkempt appearance—she was the most charming and beautiful Anzi had seen her yet. She smiled when Letti jabbed the knife toward Kai again with shaking hands. "Letti," she said. "It's fine. Relax."

"No! It's him! He's followed you here—"

"He's been with us the whole time. You didn't see him because he was underneath the dragon, with me."

But even that wasn't enough to convince her. Kai advanced another step, and Anzi sent him a glare over the woman's shoulder. "Give us a minute," she snapped. "Stop doing that. I know you're doing it on purpose to scare her."

And indeed, there was a gleam in his eyes that the dawn light reflected, something sharp and dangerous. Maybe even jealous, as if he had a genuine problem with Letti standing between them. But that would be ridiculous. He couldn't possibly feel threatened by a slip of a woman in a frilly dress and a tiny toothpick dagger in her hands that she clearly had very little training with.

Maybe.

"It's not his fault," Anzi said sternly, resorting to being firm with her since using her most coddling, gentle voice hadn't done anything. Figured. She had always been bad at that. "Leave him alone. Oza, come down here with us and bring the Prince with you—"

"Stay BACK!"

"LETTI! Calm down!"

But the squabbling argument ended as abruptly as it began when shadows fell upon them. Not just those, but the sound of footsteps moving in the sands of the desert where they had landed, too, and Anzi looked around to see them suddenly surrounded on all sides by a dozen men in various forms of desert garb. And above, several dragons whirled around in a circle, pinning them down below. One of them, she recognized instantly. The turquoise dragon, Qinglong, one of Kai's so-called generals. She had been down in the Cave when the attack began, or at least, was supposed to be.

She glanced around for Sa-Khente and failed to find him, but who knew? Maybe he was in his...man form, one of these people currently surrounding them.

Why did they look so aggressive? She narrowed her eyes and let her hands fall to her sword hilts. She wasn't about to let them hurt those with her. Not in the slightest, not a single one—

"Enough," Kai growled, and his strong voice carrying over the sands, even above the loud heaving of the great dragon curled up close by. "They're not the enemy. They're with me."

She continued to glare between them all, but he turned to her with a lingering look, one decidedly softer than before.

"This is Anzi, my mate," he announced, and the word sent a shiver down her back despite everything. "And Anzi—this is my Hunt."

He paused.

"The dragon shifters."

82

Oza was still perched atop the dragon's back, motionless, and Anzi refrained from telling him a second time to come down from there. The hostile expressions on the faces of everyone present told her he was in the safest place he could be, high above, and she briefly wished Letti hadn't come down yet either. But it was too late. They were surrounded, and despite Kai's sharp command, no one was lowering their guard. Only a few of them were carrying weapons, but she knew well enough they had no need of manmade blades. Not if they really were *dragon shifters.*

Out of the corner of her eye, something gray and black flitted down the great dragon's side, and she let herself glance there for a precious half-second to see the Prince crawling upside down off the elder dragon's neck. His wings were outstretched as he climbed down with his thumb-like claw hooks, and now she saw something else peculiar. He had four wings now, two smaller ones that the main ones overlapped halfway. And the gnarled horns protruding from his head that looked more like ram's horns than a dragon's, those hadn't been there before. At the movement, many of the warriors standing around them shifted to face both dragons with bared teeth and aggressive stances. Anzi bristled.

"Leave them alone!" she demanded in the voice she usually reserved for cowing younger rowdy recruits. "He's no threat to you. Neither is she."

But some of them pressed in anyway with slow steps—

"That's enough."

It was a growling command, a simmering threat, and it sent a shiver down Anzi's spine even though the words hadn't been directed at her at all. She stared at Kai, wondering what kind of magic he had just used to make his voice penetrate her to the soul. And judging from the way every one of his allies fell back, she guessed she wasn't the only one who'd felt the spectral—no, elemental reverberation down to her very bones. But they seemed far more affected, all in their various ways: some of them took several steps back, and others dropped down to a crouch in instant submission. The sand under their feet whispered and rolled down the wavy dunes, and then there was silence.

Letti was immune. To be sure, Kai's guttural command had made the woman flinch, but she still looked like she wanted to kick him in the groin.

"Take the others to the camp and see to them," said Kai. His voice was still harsh, but the resonant, arcane force in it that had shaken the air was gone now. "My mate stays here. With me."

Letti seemed about to snap back with an unkind retort, but Anzi's hand shot up to squeeze her behind her elbow. The harem girl choked in surprise, jumping like a startled rabbit before looking back over her shoulder. Her bright blue eyes were wide open in fright and confusion, and Anzi could feel her shaking in her grip. But she was trying to be brave —so brave.

"It's okay," said Anzi. "I'll be fine, and so will you. Oza, can you come here and help Letti?"

For a second, she thought he wasn't going to come, but one brief shared look between them later, he was sliding from his high perch and picking his way down from the resting dragon's great wing. And when his sandals touched down on the sand, he looked left and right, hands flexing under the wide sleeves of his robe as if he were ready to cast a spell, but the curiosity in his eyes assured Anzi he would do nothing rash. Of course he wouldn't. He was a smart boy, cleverer than she was by half.

"Anzi—"

"Everything is fine. Take care of Oza for me. I'll find out everything we need to know, and I'll come find you. Besides, you're all torn up. Go find something decent to wear unless you want to keep showing off your bum like that to everyone."

With a small squawk, the woman twisted around and pulled on her dress to see for herself. And indeed, a sizable tear in the fabric was perilously close to the top of the swell of her rear. Fast as lightning, she slapped her hand over the rip and glared at Anzi with wide, shining eyes as if to demand an explanation for why she had said nothing until now. But all she had for her was a small smile in return, because for the first time, despite Letti's obvious misgivings and even her own about Kai's so-called Hunt who all seemed to hate her, things seemed...better.

And if she chased this feeling, maybe things might even feel right again.

Oza was the one who moved first. He tapped the harem girl's foot with his own to get her attention before turning to lead the way. Before Anzi could warn her, Letti reached for his shoulder—perhaps to get him to slow down or maybe to dust off the dirt on his robe—and he recoiled with an angry, tight expression.

"He doesn't like being touched," Anzi murmured. "Don't worry, just go and I'll be there soon."

It was sheer trust and nothing else; she could see the warring emotions in Letti's eyes before it finally won out. With a defeated, tremulous sigh, the harem girl relented, and soon she disappeared over the dune with Oza and all the men who retreated to escort them off. One by one, they all crept away until only Anzi and Kai were left alone with the dragons.

She had so much to say but didn't know where to start. All she knew was that Kai owed her answers first, not the other way around, and also that what they had done was irreversible in so many ways. She had abandoned the Imperial City long before she had been ready, leaving behind all the dragon eggs she had promised herself she would rescue. But that was her fault, too. If she had been honest and told Kai everything, he would have had the chance to help. Maybe they wouldn't have had to abandon everything to the wind and run away with nothing in the end.

She turned to face the dragon who had saved her, saved everyone, and stared into her glassy blue eyes. She was the one who had salvaged everything, in the end. One dragon, dying, suffering. And there was nothing to be done about it...

"Anzi."

Strong arms slid under her arms and wrapped around her waist from behind. Their warmth was a different kind altogether from that of the sun beating down on her skin, and after a hesitant pause, she rested her hands on his forearms. "Are you trying to heal me?" she asked. "Because I'd rather leave it to an actual physician. You're exhausted."

He buried his nose against her neck, and when she rolled her shoulder in a half-hearted attempt to dislodge him, he only tightened his hold. "I don't have the strength," he admitted. "But I would if I could."

"Are you their healer on top of being their leader?"

He chuckled against her hair. "No. I can only do this with you. That's the nature of the mate bond. You have a lot to learn."

"Not here, though." She tugged on his arms, although she couldn't deny the temptation to let him drape himself over her forever. It must have been the fatigue that making her waver so much. She would never be such a slave to her whimsies otherwise. "Look. She needs help." She wriggled out of his arms as soon as she felt them slacken, knowing she needed to take advantage before he snatched her back to him. She was kneeling in the sand by the dragon's fallen head a few seconds later, running her fingers along the rough scales of her snout. At her elbow, the Prince lingered, all four of his wings pressed against his body in a noticeably lopsided way.

"Netra and Serqet are with your men, right?" she asked. "You said they would take care of them."

"Yes. They're receiving a kingly treatment right now." Kai hovered over her as he, too, observed the great creature before them. "I can't say they'll treat this hatchling the same way. He's swollen with corruption. They'll want to cast him out."

"What about her?"

"This one's been forcibly bonded for decades with black magic. They won't want to have anything to do with her, either."

Anger flared through her, hot and hard. "It wasn't her fault. Not his, either. They're going to abandon them both because of something they couldn't control?"

"They're afraid. The kind of magic Tet and his thralls use can infect us all, from dragon to dragon. It's why Qinglong couldn't bring any of the eggs. All tainted."

She shook her head. She was still trying to understand the chaos that had upended her life; there was no room in her head for talk of thralls and tainted eggs. "She's dying. And he hatched last night. She guided me to him. I would never have known, I would never have gone back for him. But she showed me."

"...She spoke to you?"

"Her memories."

"You always surprise me, Anzi. She hasn't been able to communicate in a long, long time. That she did with you is unbelievable."

"Isn't that how you told her where to land?"

"No. I can speak to her, and I can compel her as a Prime. But she could never answer back, because she's empty. A husk."

"What's a Prime—?" No. Never mind. She didn't want to know. She turned back to the dragon and stroked her scales, slowly. "There has to be something we can do. She's still fighting, Kai. She's trying so hard. You didn't see what she did back in the City."

"There's nothing we can do now. She'll be gone by nightfall."

How could he say it so easily? She was alive. She was here. She was right here—

"There's an oasis nearby, or should be soon. You should rest for now, and I'll wake you when it's time."

Fat chance. She wasn't leaving. "What do you mean, the oasis 'should be' near soon? Are we still on the move?"

"We're staying here; Nebt-Ash is coming to us. She brings the oasis waters with her."

She didn't know what that meant, either. What was more frustrating than her continued ignorance was that Kai was being open and honest. It was just that she could understand nothing he was saying. What a small, cramped world she had been born into, and what miserable darkness she had lived in all her life. It was as if she were opening her eyes for the first time, but the light was too blinding. Too unknowable. She clenched her fists atop the dragon's snout and bowed her head.

"I have to stay with her," she said. "There's something…"

"It's over, Anzi. Let her pass in peace. It's probably the first time in her life she's ever been free. And if she gave up the last of her strength to bring you here, then I think she would want you to take care of yourself so it isn't in vain. You can come back to see her and rest here if you want, but you need food, water. Rest."

She raised her head again to look directly at the massive blue eye staring back at her. Was Kai right? She couldn't know. When she tried to reach the dragon's mind, a tentative prod, there was no answer. It was like shouting into a cave, except one where even the echoes remained silent.

"All right," she said. "You have clothes for me?"

He didn't answer. Instead, he pulled her up with a hand under her elbow, and when she didn't resist, slowly spun her and pulled her into a deep embrace. His arms slid around her, and when she allowed herself at long last to fall against him without reserve, she noticed something. "Your collar," she mumbled. "It's gone."

"I was in a hurry to catch up. It broke when my wings came out. It doesn't matter."

She frowned and tried to pull back, but he held her tight and pressed her to his chest, his head resting on top of hers. "Your magic doesn't preserve your…belongings?"

His chuckle vibrated against her, deep and low. "No. I'm not very good at that."

"…Then what happens to your clothes if you change all the way? Into a dragon, I mean?"

"They'd be in tatters."

"And when you shift back…?"

She felt him smile against her hair. "I'm not a shy man. I could show you later."

She sighed. She was covered in dust, blood, and so wind-chafed that every inch of exposed skin felt like she had run it over rough stone for a fortnight. And yet here Kai was, suggesting she was anything but repulsive in her unkempt, grime-covered state. "Clothes," she said again. "I need to change into something that has more intact thread than holes."

"The ones who stayed behind in the camp are holding onto our supplies. We have spare clothes for all of you, and something to eat."

"The Prince needs to eat, too." She shifted against him to try to move away again. She failed a second time. "The hatchling, I mean."

"…We'll bring him something to eat when we come back here. It's not far."

"Kai!"

"I would if I didn't want to frighten them, believe me. But he's brimming with black magic. I don't even know if it's safe for you to touch him either. I can't allow him to come with us into the camp with everyone else. I'm sorry."

There was no persuading him, and she was too tired to fight him for long. Instead, she resolved to come back here straightaway. She wasn't leaving them here alone. Both dragons.

"I'll be back," she promised aloud as Kai guided her away. "Wait for me."

∼

THE TENT WASN'T LARGE, and between the three women—Letti, Anzi, and a pretty Feng woman who said nothing—there was little room to move around. It had been a hassle for the latter two to change into their new clothes, but neither could complain after all the trouble their host had gone to. She was some kind of water mage, and behind the tent, away from everyone else's eyes, she had set out a single basin and filled it so they could bathe. She did it twice, once for each, before handing over the beautiful, flowing, Feng-style wrapped-front garments that Letti had positively cried over. Apparently, all someone needed to placate and win over the harem girl was provide gifts of priceless silk. She had taken the red one, leaving Anzi with the green, and they now stood in the tent (stooped over slightly to avoid bumping their heads) as they stared at each other.

"I knew it," Letti announced. "Green goes perfectly with your eyes."

Anzi fixed her with with an unimpressed, dead-eyed stare. "Right. Because green matches black so much better than red does, and not because you really like your pinks and reds."

"Hey! I mean it! Look, don't you remember when I said the same thing about this?" With that, Letti reached down and picked up her pile of remaining hairpins and fished out a familiar emerald hair brooch. "Come here and turn around."

She was too exhausted to argue after their grueling days-long journey and offered no resistance as Letti fussed with her hair and eventually put it up in a plain, loose knot.

"There! Oh, look at you. You're even more beautiful than the night you wore my dress! I'm going to cry."

"Please don't," Anzi said tiredly, but it was too late. A few minutes later, she was patting the harem girl on the back as she sobbed into her hands, and she didn't blame her. It wasn't silly emotions getting the better of her; it was the chaos and shock of her world ending. She had held it in for so long. And Anzi hadn't even asked—had she left behind loved ones? Family, friends? She had to have, but she hadn't hesitated to follow Anzi wherever she went, straight into the barren Adaraat Desert with nothing but the clothes on her back. She was just a slip of a thing, but she was so much stronger than Anzi ever had been. Not in body, perhaps, but certainly in spirit. Devoting herself to the people she cared about and to the things she thought were right, not blindly throwing herself into the allegiance of corrupt nations and kings only to be so disappointed in the end...

The tent flap opened, and both of them looked up to see their host reentering their company. She was wearing a dress like theirs, too, though hers was blue and white and patterned with embroidered flowers, and it settled around her knees gracefully when she kneeled on the leather hide set out across the tent bottom.

"You're Qinglong, aren't you?" asked Anzi. "One of Kai's generals. You and Sa-Khente infiltrated the Cave."

She had to be. And she was a gorgeous woman, with dangerous features but calm, like peaceful water. But still waters ran deepest, and Anzi knew dark things lurked within. Behind those hazel eyes and the small, prim smile was the blood lust of someone who had had a part in hanging Bastien up on a metal sconce right through his chest.

"I'm the current Qinglong," she said. "So yes, you can call me that."

That suggested she had another name, a real one, and that 'Qinglong' was only a title, but Anzi had no interest in prying further if the woman volunteered nothing first. "Well," she said. "Thank you for all your help. Can Letti rest here while I see to my brother? She needs it."

The harem girl looked about to argue, but it was no use because it was true. There was no hiding the flicker of relief on her face, and she sat back down with a faint nod when Anzi sent her a stern look.

"She can."

"Thank you. I'll excuse myself." But before she could pass through the tent flaps, an iron vise of a grip wrapped around her wrist. She wrenched it away reflexively and whirled around. "Yes? Did you need something?"

Despite Anzi's testiness, Qinglong's serene expression never flickered. "Find Khente first," she said simply. "There's someone you need to see."

"I will. Letti, call for me if you need me."

Anzi disappeared from the tent.

83

I t was easy to find Sa-Khente. He was with Kai on the other side of the small camp, just over the large dune. She hadn't asked where either of them were and had simply followed the niggling feeling inside her that told her to go *that way, that way,* and she had. At its end, she had found the chieftain with a new ceremonial golden collar around his shoulders, and an exceedingly tall man standing beside him.

She gave up trying to explain to herself how she had known Kai would be here, and there was a knowing, satisfied gleam in his golden eyes as he watched her approach over his shoulder. It was as if he was reeling her in despite standing still, and it was only when she came within arm's reach that he turned and pulled her close with his arms around her waist, ignoring the man standing next to him.

"Kai—"

"Sa. Look at my mate, standing here with me. You had so little faith."

The large man grunted, and past his shoulder, Anzi caught a glimpse of something wriggling on the sand. With narrowed eyes, she tried to push Kai away so she could get a better look, but ended up gasping with a half-choke when he suddenly captured her mouth in a fast, fierce kiss. He let her go in seconds, far more quickly than he usually did, and she stood mesmerized for a moment trying to decide whether to be irritated or disappointed.

"What's that there?" she asked, opting to pretend it never happened.

He was too disorienting. The less she thought about being pressed to his bronze-kissed skin and the ripple of his muscles as he moved, the better, and that included feeling things like anger and annoyance toward him which always, always led to her thoughts then wandering in directions she disapproved of.

"One of our prisoners," he said. "But she's just a child, so we'll take her someplace safe and leave her there. But she and Netra-hau know each other, and we're mystified."

Knew…? No. It couldn't be—

It was.

"Rania! What the hell are you doing here!"

The girl was trussed up on the sand with fabric binds wrapped around her from shoulders to feet, and a gag in her mouth prevented her from screaming the insults she no doubt had stored in that terribly rude mouth of hers. But she looked exhausted, and despite rolling over and meeting Anzi's eyes, she made not a single muffled sound to protest what was happening to her. Wait, had she been tied up like this the entire flight here? And then perhaps clutched in someone's talons until this morning? Anzi was still horribly stiff from her own experience, and that was after a soothing bath in magically summoned water. She couldn't imagine Rania would be feeling much better.

"She's part piscin," Anzi said suddenly. "She needs water."

"We know. We gave her everything from our water skins. And Qing can help her if she needs it, but she should be fine."

Upon closer examination, she acknowledged the truth of what Kai said. She looked healthy, with no hint of the leathery tightness that would have colored her face if she were drying out. With a sigh of relief, she dropped to a crouch next to her and shook her head. "What are you *doing* here," she hissed even though she knew she wouldn't get a reply. In all honesty, she was of the opinion that it would be better to leave Rania tied up, too. At least for now. She was sure to be a headache as soon as the binds and gag came off. But there was one other thing. "You said she was 'one' of your prisoners? Who else?"

"The one who tried to kill me," Kai said dryly. "He was being smuggled out by the girl, but then she tried to intercept us before we could leave the city. Netra-hau broke away and tried to go to her, so we had no choice but to bring all of them if we didn't want to waste time. How do you know her?"

Anzi stood back up. "Lumenera. She's part of the resistance."

"That's a coastal city. Explains both of them. Using the festival to plan an assassination was clever. The one time almost anyone can enter the Imperial City, and I must have looked like an easy enough target in a crowd." He fixed his own stare on Rania. "But this is your only warning. I'm not your enemy unless you force my hand. We're all fighting against the same thing."

"It's useless. She and the others in Lumenera all hate dragons. It's ingrained in them, how they associate dragons with the Empire. Been like that for too long to change their minds now."

"Then why is she so attached to Netra-hau?"

"...I don't know. They just suited each other, I guess." Anzi sighed and rubbed her eyes. "I can't believe you two tried to kill Kai. Who is he to you? One of Isvan's men?" She reached down to tug the gag away from Rania's mouth so she could answer only for a large hand block her way.

"She's our prisoner, not yours," the large man said. The indigo turban veil wrapped around his head concealed most of his face, but she could see easily the mistrust in his orange-red eyes. "Leave it."

"Sa, Anzi is—"

"Your mate. Which blinds you."

There was something familiar about the way he spoke. The mistrust, the aggression...Calmer, but definitely bore a resemblance both in voice and in garb—"You remind me of Minnakhet," she said shortly. "He and I don't have a good understanding, either."

"That's *Neb*-Minnakhet to someone like you," the man growled, but before Anzi could ask what the significance of a single syllable could be in such a long name, Kai pulled him back with a firm hand on the larger man's shoulder.

"She doesn't know our ways," he said calmly. "And as I said, that's my mate. I'll be responsible for her, so if you've ever trusted me, then I'm asking you to show me that now."

"She's not one of us. And she's already practiced the black magic, how else would she have hatched those dragons?"

"And yet they're not tainted."

"Too early for them to show the signs," Khente insisted, "and we should thank the gods we were in time to save them from her before she corrupted them." He turned his glare on her again. "Your plotting is plain to see. To everyone."

She glared back. "Nothing I say will convince you or make you think any better of me. Let's end this before it gets out of hand."

Luckily for everyone, Rania chose that moment to struggle and growl something behind her gag. This time, Anzi ripped her gag away before anyone could stop her, and was surprised by the first thing that came out of her mouth: "Where's Netra!" Rania demanded in a cracked voice. "Where are you keeping her, and what do you want with her!"

Anzi clapped her hand over Rania's mouth. "Shush," she snapped. "You're in the camp of the man your friend stabbed with a poisoned blade. You're in no position to make demands." The girl looked outraged as if Anzi had just betrayed her, but she had more to say. "You were all supposed to wait to make your move until I sent a signal. You almost took out your greatest ally. The man your friend attacked, the one standing behind me right now? He got close to killing the Emperor, closer than anyone else has ever managed before. His hand was inside the Emperor's chest, do you understand me? Inside. His. Chest." She prodded Rania's chest hard with each final syllable, and the girl's face crumpled in joint confusion, fear, and skepticism. But she knew. She knew Anzi wouldn't lie about this because what did Anzi care about her opinion? Not enough to lie, that was for sure.

"But..."

"Yes, the Emperor's still alive. He's got some kind of magic sustaining him past death, or something. But that's not what we need to talk about now." She narrowed her eyes. "Who's your friend? Isvan sent him, didn't he?"

The girl looked uncertain suddenly. Her angular little head twitched left and right as she looked past Anzi and at the two men looming over them both with stone-cold expressions. "There were a lot of us there. Six. I think...I think two of them are dead..."

"Well, they came to make war, and war kills." Unbelievable. Kai and his men had planned to assassinate Tet during the festival, while simultaneously, the Lumeneran rebels had been plotting to kill Kai, or perhaps both leaders. What terrible, terrible timing. "This is why I told you all to *wait,*" she said again, her voice colder and angrier than before. "This could have all been so different. All you had to do was stay where you were and I would have—"

"We thought you were dead!" shouted Rania. "What were we supposed to think!"

"Something sensible, that's what." She stood up. "We don't need to do this now. Your friend, I'm not going to vouch for him because he's the one who tried to kill Kai, and it's not my place to forgive and forget even if I wanted to. I'm vouching for *you* because you're half the size of the next smallest person in camp, and you can't run anywhere anyway. No water for miles around except what these people give you. Got it?"

She looked like she wanted to stab Anzi. Let her try. Even in her battered state, she would have no trouble squashing a child's face into the sand, and her conscience would more than allow for it, too. To hell with everything. How could all of it have gone so wrong. How could she have let this happen?

"I'll keep an eye on her," she said. "She'll never be out of our sight, if you even had to worry about it in the first place. She'd last all of one league before she collapses in the desert somewhere. And don't get any stupid ideas"—she grasped Rania's chin with rough fingers—"because this is nothing like your nice, easy, coastal lands. We're leagues deep into the Adaraat Desert. Your kind isn't even supposed to be able to survive here. You need to be careful."

The girl wriggled away with a sneer. "There you go again. All you're looking at when you see me is that, huh? Just the nasty fish girl, nothing else."

"Be quiet. I'm helping you."

Miraculously, Sa-Khente said nothing else, and Kai gave her a nod to let her know he had no objections. She didn't want to linger, knowing now that she had at least a partial hand in what had happened to him, and before the guilt could make her sick, she ripped the binds off Rania, pulled her to her feet, and steered her back to the other side of the small camp. Meanwhile, she cast her eyes about for Oza, but saw no sign of him.

"Stay here," she ordered when she reached Qing's tent. "If you do anything, and I mean anything, Rania, I can't protect you anymore. And leave Letti alone. She's sleeping, so be quiet."

The instant the girl crawled inside, sand and dirt and all, she grabbed for the water skin that Qing wordlessly held out for her. Anzi didn't stick around to watch. Her head was full of woolly confusion. She needed a break from at least one problem. "Have you seen my brother?" she asked when she passed by one of Kai's men by another tent. He scowled and looked as if he were going to tell her to find him herself, but he must have figured the sooner he told her the answer, the sooner he could be rid of her.

"With the tainted," he said. "The boy went down to go see them."

It was on the tip of Anzi's tongue to say that being 'tainted' was a mark of honor, proof they had survived a system corrupt and terrible. But she knew better than to start a fight.

She didn't see Kai anywhere nearby, but that was to be expected. He had still been discussing things with Sa-Khente when she hauled Rania away, and in truth, it was as if he could sense that she needed space. Space from him, space to think about her accidental part in what had happened to him and nearly claimed his life. The memory of him in that bed, laid wide open and bleeding everywhere and so, so close to death—it was so stark and vivid in her mind that she had to stop for a moment and pause as she climbed the next dune. Her neglect had almost caused that. It was sheer luck that Kai had survived...

Later, she would have to ask Rania why they had chosen to use basilisk poison. She suspected it only held a symbolic meaning, that they couldn't have known it would be especially deadly to Kai as a dragon shifter, but she had to be certain.

"Oza? How are you feeling?"

He was lying up against the fallen dragon's snout, and the difference in size made him look even smaller than usual. Or maybe that was also the clothes he wore, a loose desert robe far too big for him with vertical stripes of dark red and brown. The hood was pulled over his head, shielding him from both the sun beating down as well as the shower of sand that pelted him from a stiff desert wind just as Anzi reached him.

He shrugged and jabbed a thumb over his shoulder.

"Yeah. I know. She saved our lives. And the other one sleeping by her nose—did I tell you? They call him the Prince. Prince Bastard. I guess I should find out his real name soon, huh?"

He pulled his knees up to his chest, and she took that as an invitation to sit next to him against the dragon. She was sleeping too, breathing rattled. She was near the end.

"I wish I could do more," she whispered. "It doesn't feel real."

He said nothing, but she was used to that. What surprised her was the hesitant, reluctant finger on her knee, and she smiled at him, slow and tired and sagging, nearly broken. But she couldn't fold here no matter how weighed down. She raised her hand with her palm turned skyward and fingers relaxed in a gentle half curl. And as they used to do, the way things used to be so long ago—he touched her fingertips to his, gentle, light. But he tolerated it only for a moment and pulled away again. That was enough, though. More than she deserved.

"Sorry for everything," she whispered. "I know you have lots of questions. Do you want to stay here with me? I'll tell you all about what's happened."

He nodded, and she hung her head in mixed relief and dread. She was glad she didn't have to stay here alone as she felt the dragon dying against them, her breaths growing fractionally shorter and shallower with every inhale, every exhale. But she dreaded explaining all of her mistakes, all of her shortcomings, everything she had done wrong. Still, Oza deserved the truth. She would give it to him.

He was silent, of course, while she spoke on and on. There was so much to say. And even when the sun began setting and Kai appeared with a question in his eyes, she wasn't done telling Oza everything.

"Are you all right?" he asked. He kept what he must have thought was a respectful distance; now she knew for certain he was trying to be gentle with her. But she didn't need him to be gentle. She needed someone to tell her she had been so stupid, so selfish, so hopelessly pathetic.

"Could you come here?" she asked softly. The fading sunset made the light gleam brighter in his golden eyes. They looked so warm. She wanted to feel that. To feel reassuring heat and solid strength. And she was done denying she needed Kai. Yes, she needed him—his touch on her arm, his kiss on her brow, the look in his eyes when he caught hers. "Oza. You remember him, right? Kaizat-Amun. He was the one who came to the Tower. He's…helped me a lot."

The boy shrugged. A good sign. If he didn't like Kai, she would have known, very quickly. And possibly unpleasantly. It was lucky that they could get along. When Kai settled down on her left and his arm came around to drape over her shoulders, she leaned into his side with a sigh. If he was surprised by her receptiveness, he didn't show it, and he pressed his lips to her temple in a long, soft kiss.

"I consulted with Minnakh and Khente," he confessed. "I asked them if there's any way at all to save her. They said there isn't."

Her heart was already so low it couldn't possibly sink any further. A small mercy. "I know," she said. "It's too late."

"You did your best."

"No. I didn't. But from now on, I will."

She rambled a little to Oza, continuing the long saga of all the happenings he had missed, but fell silent soon after. The sun was so low. The horizon's red glow was nearly faded. "I don't even know her name," she said at last. "I want to wake her and ask, but I don't think she remembers it, either." Kai's arm tightened around her, and out of the corner of her eye, she saw Oza's chin drop to his chest. Shame filled every part of her in an instant, hot and terrible.

"You're with her to the end," Kai murmured into her hair. "That's more than she probably ever thought possible."

"He left her there. Just threw her away. After everything, he just…"

She couldn't even bring herself to say the bastard's name. The son of a bitch. The trash, the filth, the walking cesspool.

"I think it's good she can free of him in her final moments, at least. Let her find some peace in that."

Peace? Peace, where? Against her back, she could feel the dragon barely moving anymore. She was dying before her time, all her vitality stolen, the life she was meant to live. From the egg onward, she had been nothing but a slave for a man who deserved nothing less than a terrible, agonizing, slow death for everything he had done. For everyone he had hurt.

"She deserves a name," she whispered. "Anything. I can't let him take that from her."

"Anzi…"

"But I don't know what to—" Her breath caught. Her eyes burned. A slow tear leaked out of the corner of her eye, singeing her skin as it trailed down to her lip. "I've always known what it is if I look closely enough. And listen. But—"

"Anzi, it's okay."

"She deserves a name," she said again. "We can't let her die nameless."

A long silence stretched on. Oza touched her knee again, this time with his little finger, but she could take no comfort in even that.

"I can give her a name, if you want." Kai's voice was softer than ever as he whispered into her ear. "We'll make a strong name. One she can take with her into the next life."

"Do it." Her voice was desperate, even as it was quiet and broken. "She doesn't have long. Hurry—"

"Shu," he said. "The name of one of the old gods. He was light, and air. Weightlessness, perfect flight. I think she might want to take the spirit of that with her."

Shu. Good, that was good. She could leave behind the massive body that had failed her in the end, and maybe…maybe she would fly high soon. Higher, higher, without ever becoming tired.

"And I'll give her my own name," he added. "Shu-Amunet."

Anzi shot to her feet before Kai could stop her, and Oza's hand fell away from her knee. She spun and planted her hands on the dragon's snout, hard enough that she awoke: one large, glassy eye fluttered open, the scales clicking against each other as the creature struggled to awaken. She would be gone in a moment, no more. But she had time enough for one thing.

"Your name is Shu-Amunet," Anzi croaked. Her throat was dry, painful, tongue too large for her mouth. She scraped her fingernails along the gigantic scales she had always admired, always looked at with wonder. But it wasn't the scales she looked at now. She held the great dragon's stare, willing herself to reach out and touch her mind, even for a fleeting instant, a single breath.

"Good night," she said as the last of the sun's rays finally dipped below the horizon. "Good night, Shu-Amunet—"

A final sigh, one last exhale that blew up a cloud of sand and dust—

And then she was gone.

84

Amunet's body was too massive to bury in good time, but more importantly, tradition held that a dragon's body not be buried underneath the earth, anyway. Anzi accepted this when Kai told her, and she watched carefully as he plucked several scales below her eye before turning back to face her. "They're typically passed down in families. You're the closest she has, so it should go to you."

That wasn't true. There was one other. She turned to look at the mottled gray-black hatchling who sat quietly by Amunet's snout, utterly motionless. He looked even bigger today than he had yesterday, but perhaps that was simply his body now uncompressing after all those decades trapped inside his egg. It horrified Anzi to know that he hadn't been dormant as all other hatchlings were before they came out into the world; he had been active and aware for a long, long time. He had moved around and tried to free himself so many times, and she had seen it with her own eyes whenever the egg rocked back and forth with his efforts.

But he was free now, and it was because Shu-Amunet had guided Anzi to him that night. And unlike so many of his trapped, captive brethren, he had escaped the grasp of Tet and his Premier Guard. Like Netra and Serqet, he was his own self, uncorrupted, unbroken.

But no one else believed that, at least not among Kai's allies.

"What did they say?" she asked the next morning when he returned from his brief foray back into the main body of the camp. "You can't tell me they're suspicious of a hatchling. He was literally—he literally hatched yesterday, Kai!"

"I know. I know that." He took her face in his hands and kissed the rest of her argument away. "But they're afraid anyway. Give them time. They'll come around."

"I don't care if they hate me and think they can't trust me. But he's done nothing wrong. And neither has Oza, but I see the way they look at him. They kept him locked up in a tower, Kai! He was a prisoner!"

"I know. And they know that, too. But they're afraid you're not sincere, that you have doubts. They think the Empire's teachings are too ingrained in you. But they'll see soon enough and understand they're wrong."

She couldn't say anything after that, even on Oza's behalf. After all, she had done terrible things she could never atone for…fought for the Imperial Army against enemies and spilled their blood solely because she trusted the leadership that told her to. She had fought to expand the Empire's borders for years and on dozens of battlefields, helped clear the way so the Empire could conquer, annex, and terrorize the cities and their peoples that came under their control. Everything she had done for years had only been in service of that and nothing else.

But at least she was free now. It hadn't happened the way she had planned and she couldn't help but dread finding out what consequences she would have to pay in the end, but for now, she was free. Just like the Prince. And just like Amunet.

"Letti's still sleeping," she told Kai later, when they were standing on the edge of the camp. "Oza stayed up with us all night so he'll be sleeping for a while yet, too."

"Hm. My tent is over there."

She gave him a look. "I thought you were telling me your friend is coming soon. And that she wanted to see me."

"Hm?"

She punched him in the shoulder this time, but lightly: he kept saying he was fine, but she could tell with every wince and hitched breath that he was still suffering from the aftereffects of the basilisk poison, even weeks later. Damn that….that old man. Him and Isvan and Rania, too. But despite how she wanted to rail at them for letting their stupid emotions and knee-jerk reactions guide them into such foolishness, such rashness, she was in no position to say anything. She had let emotions guide her too, hadn't she, for far too long.

For now, Rania lurked in the tent with Qing, who kept a close eye on her. Her friend the old man, the would-be-assassin, remained under Sa-Khente's supervision.

"So, my tent…"

Unbelievable. For a man who could be so serious sometimes, Kai joked around too much. When she looked up into his eyes, however, she realized suddenly he wasn't joking at all. There was a starved light in his golden eyes as he watched her, his gaze hawk-like and intense enough to make the hairs on the back of her neck stand on end. She realized in that moment how the dress Qing had given her slipped a little too easily off her shoulders, and she quickly hitched the wraps of the garment tighter around herself.

"Anzi—"

"If you're about to say what I think you're about to say….you'd better not." She glared. "All of your men are here. My brother and my friend are here. You have two prisoners in tow who almost got you killed. This is not the time to…"

"To what?" He stepped closer and slid his hands over her hips. His fingertips dug into the flesh there, grinding against bone. It would have hurt anyone else, but something about the barely-restrained strength, primal, so animal, made her heart lurch and skip several beats in a way that wasn't….wasn't all bad. Maybe. "When will it be the right time? Tell me."

"To talk, you mean."

"Anzi." He yanked her close, and she let out a surprised yell when he pulled her flush against him. "You know exactly what I mean."

"This is the worst possible time you could—Kai! Stop that!"

There were people far too close, and he had had the gall to almost grind her against him as he kissed her neck. This was unacceptable. And no, she was not going to talk about how her whole body lit up with a strange fire as he had touched her like that, and especially when he had crushed her against him and moved like—like that. Gods, no. Not one word. She squeezed her arm between them, ready to push him away with a firm shove, but somehow between that second and the next, her body forgot to follow through, and soon after, her head was lolling back and her eyelashes fluttering as his tongue trailed down her neck to her collar-bone, then to—

"Chief-tain-Kai-zat-A-mun."

The clipped, hard syllables that came from behind her sent a shiver down her back for very, very different reasons. That was the kind of voice she associated with barracks officers, who stalked from bed to bed with their hands clasped behind their backs and hunted down even the slightest signs of untidiness. Kai resisted, but after she yanked on his arm and gave him a stern look, regretfully pulled away so they could face the man who had come to interrupt them.

"...Long time no see, Neb Minnakhet," she said as she brushed unseen dust off her dress. "I'm glad to see you're in one piece."

The cold look she got in return assured her he didn't feel the same way about her. "Nebt Ash arrives. Our scout has said she will be here in less than an hour. Can I trust you'll be ready to enter her audience once she's here?"

The sarcasm in his voice grated on her nerves so much she nearly forgot her embarrassment at having been caught red-handed necking with the tribe's chieftain. What she wouldn't give to kick this man right in the throat and let him know exactly what she really thought of him behind the necessary courtesy she extended.

But, in truth, she had to be thankful this one time. Whether he had intended to or not, he had just saved both Kai and her from doing something hasty and thoughtless. Not that she didn't want to be close to Kai, and not that she regretted letting him into her full trust at long last, but... this wasn't the time. She clung to him for comfort as much as awkward desire, drew on his strength to get past the grief that still rang hard and cold from the night before. In the wake of Amunet's death, Anzi knew she was unintentionally throwing herself wildly into her other emotions to distract herself.

That wasn't fair to Kai—and not to herself, either. Now wasn't the time...

"I'm already prepared," she said just as stiffly, pretending complete obliviousness as to Minnakhet's real meaning and criticisms. "But no one's told me who she is, other than that she's a woman. And has something to do with an oasis."

"You'll know when she decides you'll know." He nodded at Kai behind her, clearly done with the conversation. "We're making preparations to take Duat's body to its final resting place. We need you to come bless him before we close the final rites."

Anzi's blood ran cold. Body? Duat? Was that one of Kai's men...? But of course there had been casualties from the attack, she realized far too late. How could there not be? She didn't know exactly how many of the men in this camp had gone to invade and how many had stayed behind, but it unlikely that all of them would have gotten out intact. She swallowed past the lump in her throat and looked up at Kai, only to see a darkly shuttered look of pain on his face that she hadn't seen before.

He had hidden it so well. Or maybe it was because she had been so absorbed in her own troubles, her own grief, that she hadn't spotted his. Guilt washed through her, leaving her cold and bare.

"I'll be there soon. Go on ahead of me."

"Lord..."

"I will. It'll take a while so I may miss Ash when she comes, but we can't put off the last rites. So I want to be sure Anzi knows what to expect."

The solemnity in his voice seemed enough to mollify the older man, and after a few seconds of suspicious glancing between their faces, he relented with a reluctant, sharp nod. "We're waiting for you in the tent, Lord."

"It won't be but a minute."

When the man departed, Anzi and Kai were alone again. She pressed her lips together and took a moment to put together the words she wanted to say. "I didn't know you lost one of your men."

"It may be more. The other two are being cared for the best they can. Once Ash comes, she may be able to help, but none of us are exceptional healers. They'll likely carry these wounds the rest of their lives."

"I'm sorry. I know what that's like."

He pulled her to himself again with his hands around her waist, but instead of giving into desire, he seemed to do it only for comfort. He held on tight, nearly crushing her in his embrace, and buried his face between her neck and shoulder. "I want to kill them every time I see you limping," he admitted in a muffled voice. "I wish I'd at least finished off Bisset if not Tet."

"It's better now. And I know the feeling."

"We'll go from city to city until we find a healer gifted enough to heal you. The Imperial City can't have a monopoly on all of them."

"I appreciate that, but your men would need it more." She stroked his bare back in soothing circles. How guilty he must be feeling. She wouldn't know it since she had always distanced herself from others, never assuming responsibility for their lives...but he was different. He wasn't stubborn and cold and standoffish; he was a leader to his people, however small the nation. "Anything I should know before this Ash person gets here?" she added. "I thought you'd be with me when she came."

She felt him smile against her neck. "Do you want me to be?"

"I'll be fine," she answered, expertly evading the question. Damn him. Even in the depths of the most somber conversation..."I'm sorry for your loss. I didn't even stop to think about..."

"You had your own loss to bear. Don't worry." He pulled back, but didn't let her go until he kissed her on the brow, then once more on the lips. He lingered there as if he couldn't quite manage to make up his mind and release her, so she did the hard part for him and pushed him away.

"Then you better take care of that while I'm handling this, this Nebt-Ash business." She jerked her chin in the direction of the camp. "Go before your lovely friend decides he wants to gut me."

And with a chuckle, he left her. She looked out past the dunes after he did so, and spotted something moving not too far away: a mirage?

She squinted and shielded her eyes from the sun with a hand over her brow. No, she thought. Not a mirage—it was definitely real, and it was coming closer.

The shape of palm trees. An oasis.

85

It was so hard to trust unknown magic, still. She was such a hypocrite. Hadn't she resorted to using her own not too long ago to save Oza? And yet she couldn't scold away the uneasiness lurching and twisting in her gut as the oasis sailed over the sands, like the desert was but water on the sea. This wasn't the cold, pruned Empire anymore. This was the wild Adaraat where the desert nomads wandered, and strange foreign magic came from here. Not rigorously trained and schooled magic with rules and pinpoint regulations in the ranks, but free magic, unconstrained, unpredictable. Like the kind that could move vibrant palm trees over sand - or a spring, because there was no mistaking that sound, however distant: water. But it stopped moving suddenly, and after a moment, she understood it was waiting for her. She glanced behind her at the camp's edge, wondering if anyone was watching her, and indeed, met the gazes of a few of Kai's men as they watched on eagerly. Time to go. Best not to disappoint.

It wasn't far, a brisk walk of a few minutes brought her close enough to count the individual fronds in the palm trees that surrounded the oasis. The burbling of a spring was now clearer than ever, and her mouth watered at the thought of touching cool, fresh water to her tongue. Qinglong and her magic was crucial enough, but Anzi had fast learned any water produced that way, materialized out of the desert air, was always lukewarm and carried a stale, almost baked quality into the mouth.

She missed vibrant, verdant earth. She missed cool, flowing water that flowed from cascades and between boulders. She walked on, almost hypnotized...

It was only when her feet touched exactly that that she realized she was standing within the oasis. She had meant to stop at the very edge of it and observe her surroundings, to take in all the potential dangers that lurked behind every damp, gleaming leaf and the bobbing fronds that seemed to bow to her, but somehow she was already here. Not only that, but she couldn't seem to stop walking. Was she under enchantment, she wondered, but it wasn't that. It was herself, it had to be. She knew her own mind. It was more like—there was something waiting for her, and she had been waiting for it in return for so long.

Grass rustled beneath her boots, so stiff and vibrant that as soon as she lifted one foot, the blades sprang up again, unbent. There was a stream now, too, flowing outward, and if she followed it, she was certain she would find what it was she had been secretly expecting all this time. With every step, her heart swelled, and she gawked at every sight, no matter how small. Butterflies fluttered by her of every scintillating hue, their large, glossy wings shimmering in the faint, gentle light that shared absolutely no resemblance with the blinding desert sun she had been walking under only moments ago. There were bluebells on the ground mixed with violets, shades of stunning blue and purple with flared white lilies among them. Oh, gods above and below, were those moonflowers climbing up the palm tree trunks? She had only ever seen those drawn on prints, nowhere else.

"Oh, my...she's just the way I thought she would be."

Anzi was too well-trained to ever simply startle at an unexpected voice. She drew her swords in a flash, crossing the black blades in front of her with a spark flying from the enchanted steel. Her heart pounded, her pulse throbbed—and she felt more alive than ever. Her body thrummed with a strange, rapid flow as if she were riding along rapids straight for a crashing waterfall, or perhaps as if she were the rapids and waterfall herself. She could barely contain it, and her arms shook so hard that her blades scraped against each other with tremors. And it was all because of the old, wizened woman standing in front of her, graceful and ancient and yet full of youthful, devious energy. Her dark skin gleamed with a hint of an arcane obsidian glow, and could it be? A faint aura swirled around her with the scent of fire and wet woods. She didn't know how that was possible out here in the middle of a barren desert no matter a spectral oasis or not.

"It's you," said Anzi, her voice climbing to a higher pitch in sheer amazement. "I—I know you."

"Oh, yes," the old woman said, and she slid one bent forearm under the flap of flowing white fabric in front of her elegant wrap dress. One corner of it went over a shoulder, the other side draped under the opposite arm. Gold trim, but when she looked closer, it was threaded into a pattern of ancient letterings Anzi couldn't decipher. And there were beads, wooden beads of all colors strung about her neck and draping low over her chest, necklaces upon necklaces upon necklaces. A strange headdress over her hair as well, which was tied and fashioned into braids both trailing down in front of her shoulders and styled up in a swirl on the back of her head. Ornamental earrings and binds in her hair, too, all of it—everything about the woman was fearsome and full of life.

"Welcome to my paradise," she said, then threw her head back in a hearty laugh. "I knew I'd see you again, I just expected it to be sooner. But everything comes in good time. It always does. Now, how long has it been since we met, hm? Have you grown any, or are you still the same hard-headed little cricket of girl who turned her nose up at the old, old ways?"

The voice of the old crone in her head from back when Bisset had brought her to the desert outpost—after the wyrms had attacked her. There could be no mistake. It was her, the very same.

"You're not a demon," said Anzi, still stunned. "I thought—"

"You think everyone outside your understanding is a demon, hm? Is that what it is? Or was, maybe. You seem different, little girl—not quite a little green thing anymore, are you?" The old woman wandered closer, taking deliberate, weighty steps toward her. Her beads rattled against each other, and Anzi was reminded almost of marbles rolling across the floor in a rhythmic cascade...

"I hope not," she said. Her voice was stronger than she'd dared to hope. Good. She didn't know why she felt such instinctive reverential awe in this woman's presence when she knew nothing about her, but she wouldn't be taken it by it so easily. She wouldn't let herself. She raised her chin. "Who are you? And what are you? A wild blooded mage? A sage of the free magic from the other side of the Adaraat?"

"Do you know what's there, girl? There on the other side, like you say?"

"Unconquered land."

"Oh, look how quickly you said that. It's been nailed right into you, that way of talking. You stink of the ways of the abomination and his lovely little Empire, or whatever he calls his dominion."

Anzi pressed her lips together. The old woman was right: the words had come out of her mouth without foresight. *Unconquered land.* What a dismissive way to refer to peoples and nations, even if she hadn't meant it that way. "That was my mistake."

"Hm...and a girl quick to admit when she had placed her foot on the wrong stone. You're stubborn, but humble. Gracious in your faults."

...What was happening? Praise? Compliments? Why? And now the old woman was walking around her in a slow circle as if inspecting her for cracks or secret compartments. Anzi turned her head and watched her out of the corner of her eye. "I'm slow to wisdom," she said. "I've decided I'm going to be more careful about the way I perceive others, that's all."

"Good...But don't expect too much from yourself, sweet child. We've never been the type to be overly careful. It's not in our bones, you know. There's too much of the wind and fire in us, and there are all those people who say the earth is steady when it's the least steadfast thing of all. And that's what we're made of, aren't we? Oh, little girl..." She stopped in front of Anzi and tipped her head back. The tall white headdress seemed almost to ripple, and a breeze ruffled the grass so loudly under their feet that the sound drowned out the rush of blood in Anzi's ears for a moment. "You'll do just fine. A little work, and a lot of time, and you'll be ready."

Goosebumps flooded her skin at the note of finality in the woman's voice. What was she talking about? "Who are you? And what are you?" she asked again, louder this time to try to assert what dominance she could despite knowing full well she was trying to punch above her weight. How she knew, she couldn't explain, but there was something about her way— "What did you want with me?"

"Who am I? I'm the Woman Lord of the Last Green, the one known to the old ones as She Who Refreshes. The dragons you're with call me Nebt-Ash, Lady Ash, of the one Oasis. I'm the spirit of the waning, meant to preserve. And one day, maybe even restore."

That answered none of her questions. She opened her mouth to argue and accuse her of being deliberately cryptic and vague—

"We're the avatars of the disappearing, the embers that cling to the wood. We protect. And preserve. And we build back up what has been pulled down. Some called us gods and goddesses in the long-ago, but that was never right. That's not what we are."

Ash circled her again, veined and wrinkled hands clasped behind her back as she prowled. She stopped in front of her once more.

"I'm old, little girl. I don't remember a time I wasn't. I'm the Druid of all the land that used to be here before it became eaten up by the sand and sun and wind. And you…"

Her teeth flashed white against her dark skin.

"…You are the Druid of the dragons."

oosebumps raced up Anzi's arms as if a wintry chill had suddenly replaced the ever-present heat of the Adaraat. "Druid? Of the dragons?" She scowled at Ash, wondering if the woman was crazy or if she was simply trying to get under her skin with such strange talk. "I thought you were going to answer my questions, not raise more."

"Who said I would answer anything?" The old woman threw her head back with such ferocity it was a wonder her headdress didn't fall off, and laughed and laughed. "The old way would have been to leave you to find those answers yourself. All I would have had to do was open your eyes so you could see."

"Open my eyes to what, old woman. Get on with it."

"So angry! And so hasty." She laughed again, and her wooden beads rattled around her neck. "You wouldn't be so impatient to leave if you were wiser. Go on, then. Ask me. What is it you want to know first?"

"Tell me what a Druid is, in simple terms. Let's start with that."

Instead of answering right away, Ash turned in a slow circle and clasped her wrinkled hands behind her back. With an indulgent sigh, she strolled off, and Anzi had no choice but to follow.

They arrived at the edge of the water and stood under the shadow of the wet rock face from whence a spring of water fountained forth—strange, that hadn't been visible at all between the palm trees from outside the oasis—and only then did the elder speak. "The Druids were once many. But that was in the long-ago days, back before we became so few and the gods were still what they were. Oh, my, I still remember the stories that say we used to stream in by the hundreds to serve the gods on platters of gold and silver. The only ones blessed to look upon their faces and live."

Anzi nearly choked on her spit, but Ash was already gone, no longer admiring the spring but strolling around the edges of the burbling water. "Serve the what? The gods? They're..."

"They're what? What do you think the gods were, little girl?"

"Not real, for one! I'm not a newborn to tell stories to."

"Not real? What makes you say that? Don't you call on the names of the gods yourself when you need them? Hm?"

If this woman would stop ambling forward and just turn to look her in the eye, maybe this conversation would actually go somewhere useful. "If the gods did exist, they've never protected us. They've never helped us. Everything we do is the work of our own hands."

"Is it? Then let's not think of rewards and blessings. What about divine punishment and scourging, little one? When the gods are angry, they strike down the unworthy and make known their wrath, don't they?"

"Please. I don't need stories, I need answers. And I'll either get them or I'll leave you be. It's your choice...Lady Ash."

"Oho, your cutting mockery isn't lost on me. Then let me ask you: if there is a man you know who cannot be killed, a true monster who possesses powers greater than any mortal, a man who strikes fear into the hearts of even the greatest warriors because he can never be struck down —who is this? And what would he be to you? What do you call that one who is greater than a man?"

She stopped in her tracks and stared at the back of Ash's head in sudden, hesitant silence. "Are you talking about Tet?"

"And see how all the daring courage vanishes. Just like that!" The woman snapped her fingers in the air and held them there, then turned around with a knowing smile. "The man you call Tet has outlived all the people of his kingdom and more besides, and he'll live on for centuries yet if he has his way. A mortal blow would never kill him anymore, either, and he could sweep away dozens of lesser men with a flick of a finger. And dragons too, but you know that already. Do you agree? Would this man not be a god to the people? An angry god, a scourging god."

"He uses dark magics. That's how he does it."

"To them, does it matter the reason, the how? Isn't it enough that he's more powerful than they could ever imagine or ever be in their wildest dreams? True, he wasn't born special. He was neither strong nor quick, not even born into a heritage among the gods or the Druids, but he became the way he was because of one thing." She tapped the side of her head with a crooked finger. "He was clever, and he was greedy. For more than thousand years, he's searched for the secrets to make himself what he's always wanted to be and finally, he's on the cusp of achieving it."

"A thousand years?"

"You already know he's long-lived, don't you?"

Of course she did. "Because he steals it from the dragons. That immortality doesn't belong to him." She turned and scowled at the water. "Bastien didn't trust me enough yet to let me in on the rituals, but I was getting there. I could have found a way to stop them, or to reverse it. I should have been faster."

"To even touch the knowledge of dark rituals would taint you irrevocably, sweet thing. He would have had you truly in his thrall, like the others, no matter your intentions. That's what happened to the others too, I'm sure."

Thrall, thrall…it wasn't the first time she was hearing that exact word. "What do you mean, thrall?" she asked, even more suspicious than she'd been before. She turned her head and fixed narrowed eyes on the old woman. "It means something specific, doesn't it? What is it?"

"Thralls are how we gain power beyond ourselves. Our vassals, loyal ones—not mere servants who live to serve, but those who would even in death."

"What! You're talking about undead arts, necromancy!"

"Necromancy's a lost art, and it's better that way. No, no. Thralls hover in the space between life and death, neither in one realm nor the other. They are bridges between so their master can walk the path made from their own souls…And no ordinary man can withstand it. Tet chooses only the strongest, ablest slaves to serve as his handmaids and manservants. He chains them to himself using those black rites, and they feed him power, life. In return, he lets them keep the scraps."

"The…scraps?"

"Haven't you noticed the ones closest to him are particularly strong and dangerous? Gifted beyond what men should be able to bear. Never mightier than him, but still fearsome things."

Of course. The dragon riders were all supposed to be powerful, but

Bisset was famed throughout the Imperial Army for his incredible skill in battle, nigh undefeatable. Except by the Emperor, anyway. "So Tet does something to bond them to him, and they drain the dragons of their immortality to pass it onto him through the rites. And he gives his most loyal followers more power? To make it attractive to serve him."

"That *is* the result, but not his true purpose." The woman gave her a searching look. "He was young, once upon a time. He was there before the Adaraat was cursed to become a barren wasteland, before the great cities here fell. He was already corrupted before I ever came to be—that's how old he is."

"There used to be *cities* here?"

"Have you never wondered why even when it should be bitter winter, it remains the same out here in the desert? Always just as scorching?" Ash flicked her hand in a vague gesture. "The Adaraat was turned into this because of Tet. And that's how I was born—the killing of the great land that used to be here, when it cried out to me."

"Tet…cursed the desert? You're losing me."

"He wasn't the one who cursed it. This is the wasteland meant to be impossible to conquer, the land forbidden to him. The great kings and warlords who used to reign here sacrificed everything they had to build a bulwark against him, a stretch of empty land so vast he couldn't send his men to cross it, not without losing far more than he would gain. So they did it, and to this day, it protects the lands far to the east where they remain safe from him. For now."

That explained a few of the longstanding questions she had always wondered and some she had never even thought of. But it did nothing nothing to help her now. "I don't understand. What does this all have to do with gods and Druids? I don't care what you say, he's not a god—and there is definitely a way to stop him. I need help, not riddles."

"Your preconceptions about the gods precedes you. All right. Let's say he isn't a god—yet. But he does have one in his thrall."

"What?"

"There is a great dragon, a lord among dragons, king of kings. It chose Tet when he was young, and it loved and cherished him so much it gave him long life and health to let him stay by its side for all time. Tet kept this god company for centuries—and then realized he wanted more, because he discovered that the great dragon who had taken him under his wing started out in life as just a tiny little thing too, just like him. And he became greedy. He thought, why not me? Why should I be only in the service of a god when I can become a god myself, too?"

"Can we stop saying *god*."

"Get used to it." Ash wagged a finger at her. "Tet's already enslaved the one who used to be master over him, the Dragon King, and bent him to his will. No one knows truly how he did it, but it happened. And now he uses the Dragon King to search out the other gods so he can—"

"The Dragon King, is it possible that that's supposed to be Ra—ow!" Anzi stepped back and sent the woman a furious look. Out of nowhere, the latter had pulled up a handful of thick reeds from the edge of the water and slapped the back of her hand with the stiff cattails.

"Don't interrupt! You say you want answers but all you do is ask, ask, ask. Now...where was I?"

"...At the end of whatever you wanted to say, I hope."

"Impudent girl. Fine. This is what you need to know. Tet controls the Dragon King, which means all dragonkind is ultimately obedient to him if he wishes it, should they be overtaken by that power. But he wants more. Needs more. He's going to capture the other gods, and when he does, he'll be sure to perform his dark rites on them to take their power. If he does that, if all that power exists in one form, under one man—"

"That's enough," Anzi said sharply. "I get it. I get it..." She trailed off, heart pounding. She still didn't believe in this god-talk nonsense, but there had to be some truth to what she was saying. Maybe the real story was that Tet was after powerful relics that would make him even more dangerous than he was already, something like that. If she took out all the fairy tale ridiculousness, things even started to make sense. The existence of the fabled Dragon King certainly did, considering she had seen what had been the unmistakable shape of a titanic white-and-gold reptilian head crashing up from the ground back in the Imperial City.

"So you know about Tet." She began to pace back and forth. "And you know about me, too."

"Hm...a little. You're a hard one to crack."

"But you told me I was a Druid. Obviously, you know more about me than you should. Is there more?"

"Oh, yes. I knew it the moment little Kaizat-Amun told me about you and that he had met his mate. I felt your power and your essence through the bond, faint but true. Something I never forgot how to do, but something I can no longer teach, either. Been so long..."

And now the old woman was rambling. Great. Anzi needed to get this conversation back on track. "We'll talk about Kai too, in a second," she said forcefully. "But I need to know something. When I was still back there in the Imperial City, I noticed Tet was more interested in my brother Oza than he was in me. I don't even know why he was interested in either of us in the first place, while we're at it—is it because he thinks I'm a Druid, too? Does he think Oza is the same?"

"The stubbornness of youth. *Think* you're a Druid? The sooner you accept what I say as truth, the better it will be for you. For everyone."

"...Anyway..."

"He couldn't know for certain you're a Druid, only guess. Even if he was raised by the ones who came before me, he himself was only ever a boy who captured a god too benevolent to him. He didn't have the gift, which is why he had to steal his power from elsewhere."

"Then why did he want me so badly? It couldn't have been by chance. And why did he want Oza? Is my brother a Druid or not?"

"There are no others here, just us. Your brother is no Druid or else I would have sensed it by now."

"So why in the dark hells is Oza so important to him!"

"I'm not all-knowing, little one. Seers only see what they can. But it's long been said someone who births a Druid carries a little of that power for the rest of their lives, and all the progeny that come after are meant for great things, too. It's simply that the mother of a Druid only ever rarely gives birth again, and only with great difficulty. Tell me, is there something special about him? What do you know?"

"...He's definitely gifted. He's so young but his understanding of magic is phenomenal. The only thing stopping him is a fragile body that can't contain his power."

"Mm, yes, fragile bodies. That's to be expected of any child born to a woman who's already birthed a Druid. How old is he?"

"Eleven years."

"Ha. He's already defied fate if he's lived that long. I will see him tonight, then, and we shall see if I can find some answers—"

"Ah, let's slow down there for a minute. He's fine."

"Still suspicious of me? Hee-hee, then who will you go to for the answers? Oh, that's right, there's one other who can give those to you. But I don't think you want to go and ask Tet himself, do you?"

Damn it. "You've been no help. I have more questions than you've given me answers now. All I've gotten from you is that Druids served the gods, and Tet wants to capture the gods to...I guess become one. And something about the Dragon King. Which I'm not going to ask you about because I'm going to ask Kai instead. I used to think he was frustrating, but you're even worse. I ask questions and you dodge with fairy tales and nonsense talk."

Ash cackled. "I'm as plain as war paint. Maybe you should listen to me more closely and open that stubborn mind. Go on, then. Ask me something else...something about little Kaizat-Amun, perhaps...?"

"As a matter of fact, yes."

"Oho, and something you don't dare ask him yourself! Endearing. Come on then, what is it."

She bristled. She hated speaking to condescending elderly types, damn it. "How is it that we're connected? He calls me his mate. Humans don't have mates, and I'm not a dragon, so explain that to me. Or are you going to tell me it's because I'm a *Druid* again?"

"That's an easy one. Yes. You have a soul scraped and pressed and molded together from the suffering of dragonkind. Your soul is the soul of all dragons, now and then and forever. Of course you can have a mate. What, don't tell me you still think you're too human for that? After everything you've done."

She grimaced, lips pressing tighter and tighter as she struggled to find an argument. But other than the eye-rolling ridiculousness of the *Druid* talk, she had to admit she had known for while now that she was different. Too different, she might have said not too long ago, but that was when she used to think inhuman blood was something dirty and dishonest. Now...how could she think that, knowing what she did now?

"I still don't understand this mate business. There's no free will. No freedom. How can someone decide that for me?" She wrapped her arms around herself in an uneasy huddle, then quickly disguised the anxious movement by crossing her arms over her chest instead. "I'm not an animal to be paired off against my will. It's not right."

"Hm? Then would you rather choose someone else? Who?"

She raised her chin in a defiant gesture. "It's not about that. I should still get to choose for myself."

"You have a point." The old woman nodded, then turned on her heel and began marching away. "I'll go find him, little girl. You have nothing to worry about, I'll fix this."

"What?" Anzi followed after her. "Fix what?"

"Break the mate bond. It's about time he finds some other nice woman to settle down with and get over you. Both of you can stop wasting your time, and he'll even have little children running about soon enough—"

"What! Stop it! What are you do—" Anzi's feet picked up speed all on their own, and she nearly collided with Ash when the woman abruptly spun back around with a wide grin.

"Got you! Heh. Look at that, all in a lather just because of a little joke."

"This isn't the time for jokes!"

"Oh, don't worry. The only ones who can break the mate bond are just two. You and Kaizat-Amun, no one else. Have no fear."

Her heart dropped. "You—what did you just say? He can break the mate bond? I thought mate bonds were forever?"

Ash cackled, holding her belly with her wrinkled hands. "Look how frightened you are. See that? You talk about free will and choices when you've already made yours. Hm? What do you say to that? If you could *choose* anyone else, then, who would you go to? And who would he go to? Or would you perhaps wring the neck of any other woman who might vie for his touch?"

"It's…enough! Anyway, you answered my question about that, so—"

"Changing the subject? When we've only just begun? Let's see. Maybe I should tell you about how to make the mate bond final. How about that? He'll be yours, and you'll be his, just like any other bonded pair."

Anzi swallowed. Hard. "…I'm not interested in talking about that with you. That's between me and Kai. No one else."

"Hee-hee, you hesitated."

"Well, I see this conversation is over." She stomped past Ash, face awash with a horrific heat, but a strong grip on her arm stopped her before she could go but three paces. "What!"

"All right, all right, don't be angry." The old woman sighed and released her grip so she could adjust her headdress with both hands. "Enough teasing from me for now. I called you here is to untangle the power inside you that you keep buried. It wouldn't be good to do it in front of the others. To show them how young your power is and how little you know of it—they have too little faith in you as it is."

"Faith?" Anzi snorted. "They think I'm the enemy."

"Even so. But come. Your magic is strong, only young. Too young to even dream of fighting the abomination Tet with, but you also have a strong body—especially so long as you stay connected to the earth from whence we came. It's ironic that a Druid could be mated to a dragon that spends half its life in the wind, but stranger things have happened."

"Connected to the earth? You mean I—"

"Come. Into the water. That's where my power is strongest, and that's where I'll show you yours."

Anzi wasn't about to trust her on virtue of her word alone. Maybe Kai and his tribe knew her well enough to do that, but something about the reverent way everyone addressed the so-called Nebt-Ash felt wrong, which was why Anzi went out of her way to be so brusque with her. It reminded her too closely of Tet, how all who looked upon him did so with worshipful eyes. As she kneeled on her good leg and wafted air from the water's surface toward her nose, she kept her eyes fixed on Ash, noting everything from the way the old woman's skin tightened and shone to the way her white dress floated and swayed on the water's surface contrary to the direction the ripples were moving in.

"It's not poisoned, little one." Ash grinned and pointed at her. "Though you won't know for sure until you step in, would you?"

"If Kai didn't trust you, I wouldn't be so hasty."

"Heh...smart. Let's see, then."

Let's see, indeed. Anzi dipped her fingers into the water, briefly at first, then sank them until her knuckles were immersed. Clean water. With a grimace, she held back a wince when her calf throbbed, then carefully unfastened the wrap of her dress so she could place it on the grass. Now only in her undergarments, she slid into the oasis's waters at last. It was colder than she thought it would be, but the true alarm came when she descended waist-deep and the water began climbing up her body. When she attempted to scramble back up the bank, Ash grabbed her arm with a splash and held her steady.

"Be calm," she crooned, and Anzi looked up to see the woman's face was no longer wizened and creased but smooth, youthful. What in the world? Anzi wasn't schooled in wild magic enough to know whether it was illusion or true rejuvenation, but it was clear this was what Ash had meant when she said her power was strongest here. Something in the water. "The Druid who mentored me had mastery of a dormant volcano. Consider yourself lucky!"

The water continued to climb her body, sloshing up her chest now far higher than it should, and Anzi had to fight every instinct in her body that told her to flee before she was trapped and drowning. But she wouldn't have made it in time anyway. In two blinks, the water streaked up her arms, back, and chest in a dozen streaming tendrils before enveloping her entire head, nose and mouth and all. She flailed, hands slapping at her face to try to clear it away so she could breathe, but the water swarmed her arms and pulled her down, down, down.

Sunlight gleamed and cut down from the surface, the rays shattering into a thousand streaks and scintillating with the current. To her right, a thick cloud of bubbles, and to her left, Ash's legs as the woman waded her way over to help her up. No, not help her—she was pushing her down further! Anzi tried to strike out at her, fear and regret blossoming as she cursed herself for foolishly trusting a stranger. And yet she had no choice but to succumb as the water pulled her down, down, down into a darkening abyss, as the last of her breath ran out and she gulped mouthfuls of the cold void. Ash disappeared as did the sunlight, and soon it was as if she were miles below the earth, descending into another realm entirely.

Whatever happened now, she would have to make her peace with it.

THE FIRST THING she noticed was how close to the ground she was. Was she kneeling? No. She was simply—short. Very short. A child's height. She looked down at herself to solve the mystery of her missing stature, only to find she was now running. But she felt like a ghost in her own body, swimming against a woolen force rather than feeling the impact of each footfall on the packed desert dirt and sand, the tame heat of the warm night, or the scratch of her desert garb against her skin. Ah, this was so familiar that her heart ached.

The body that was both hers and not-hers stopped, and a ghostly sensation of movement flowed through her when her child-self looked down at the ground, weapon held at the ready at her side.

…A wyrm. A medium sized one, dark as night. There was something strange about it, familiar and thrilling. Oh! She remembered this now. It was back when she was not yet in the Service. No, wait, it was when she had been Selected but not yet fully inducted into the Imperial Army. Eight years ago, it had to be, long, long before her world began falling apart and the truth showed itself through the cracks.

She choked at the flash of golden eyes below, a molten yellow she knew so well now. But back then, she hadn't known, hadn't had a clue. Not only that, but the wyrm rose to its feet, revealing slender legs and that it was not a wyrm after all, but a dragon—

She was still fighting the heady rush of emotion that threatened to drown her when the vision disappeared without warning, and suddenly she was being pulled through the earth, far and fast and without end. She tried to shout and struggle, but she had no form. She was energy following a compulsion, nothing more. Under rocks, through dirt and sand, past serpents and lizards and desert mice burrowing under the desert, she was dragged past them all faster and faster until everything was simply a red-brown blur.

When it stopped, she was ripped out of the earth with a shower of sand, but the power controlling her body didn't stop. She was yanked upward toward the sky, tumbling and rolling and careening higher and higher until she was sure she would punch right through the clouds, but just before she could, the compulsion released her. Her eyes widened, but what could she do—except plummet? And earthward she came, stomach lurching hard and twisting into knots. Limbs flailed as she sought in vain for purchase. But nothing, nothing was going to stop her from splattering on the ground from such a terrifying height, and her eyes watered from the fierce wind until tears blinded her and streamed down her face. Oh, gods, what was happening, she would make sure she picked Ash up and hurled her into the sun from the afterlife, she swore it—

She hit the ground hard, spread-eagle and feeling like she would rather be dead than alive. Whatever this magic was, she hated it and it hated her right back. She groaned and tried to turn over on her side to vomit, but the most she could do was fight to sit up and wheeze. At least she could move, but her arms were heavy and slow as if she were pushing against water.

…Water, damn it. That was it. This was all a hallucination. An illusion in her mind. In reality, she was still in the water, drowning, dying. How long would this magic last? How long had it lasted already? She cursed her lack of knowledge of deep magics. Oza would have known what to do. But this wasn't Oza's fight; this was hers. And besides, she felt as alive as ever. If she wasn't dead yet, she still had a chance.

Or so she thought, until a massive shadow fell over her, enveloping all the land from east to west and north to south, blocking out the sun entirely. It was as dark as night, no rays of the sun penetrating the gloom, and her jaw dropped in a soundless gape as a massive dragon descended upon her, golden wings outstretched as far as the eye could see. An enormous head crowned with a heavy frill and a dozen horns craned down toward her as the dragon's descent slowed.

It landed before her with a prodigious cloud of dust, and then there was an eye in front of her face as big as her entire body. She could see nothing past the dragon's head in her entire field of vision, and her feet remained planted where she stood in numb shock as the great, glassy golden eye with its vertically slit pupil observed her for a paralyzing eternity.

Oh, she thought in a small voice. She knew who this was. She had seen him once before. The one who had risen from the depths of the Imperial City's underground as she fled with the others, the reptilian head and wings crashing through the buildings and streets like a true nightmare come to life and swollen with true, awe-inspiring magnificence—

Here, she thought, was the Dragon King.

87

Could she even call this creature a dragon? Could she even call it a creature indeed—so massive, so titanic, so enormous that it seemed to take up the whole world from end to end that it couldn't be a product of creation at all. He was so all-encompassing that mountains could come out of him, the highest ones, and the deepest trenches, and sprawling valleys in between.

And just as disturbing, the glassy golden eye that dwarfed her entirely was still staring at her, unblinking. What was it waiting for? It was clearly seeing her. It had come to her. And now it said...nothing.

But this wasn't real, after all—this was all in her mind. If she concentrated hard enough, she could still feel the waters of Ash's oasis weighing cold and heavy on her skin, although the sensation was ghostly and faint as if she were only feeling its echoes from another life. But it wasn't. That was her real life, that was the real world. This other one, this hallucination was the false one.

And yet the presence of this nameless, ageless, leviathan of a dragon felt the farthest thing from illusory. If this was only in her mind, then her mind must be a fearsome thing to summon this feeling of standing before something so present, so staggeringly existent that it demolished all inferior beings, this wall of living wisdom in front of her that she could never dream of understanding.

A huffing breath far to the left of her where the dragon's snout was turned made her twitch and pause. His head was so large the sound felt distant although still loud as anything, like listening to a volcanic eruption rumbling far off. But it was an unmistakable sign that he was alive, which she was beginning to doubt in favor of thinking he was simply a malevolent, massive spirit come to haunt her.

And still he waited. She girded herself, preparing for the worst but calm. She had been truly afraid so rarely in her life, and every one of those less than handful instances had all been in the last several months of her life upon entering the cruel, twisted inner world of the Empire, of Tet's secrets and horrors. This? She would not be afraid. She would not be cowed. If he waited, then she would speak first.

"What am I doing here?" she demanded, raising her voice to a near-shout. She didn't know to what extent normal rules of the world applied in this made-up one, but common sense told her the dragon's ears must be so far back on his enormous head that he couldn't hear her if she spoke normally. A human couldn't hear the cries of the ant, the squirming of a worm, the footsteps of a caterpillar creeping tremulously along a leaf. She would have to speak loudly, without fear, and prove herself so much more. "Who are you? Are you the Dragon King? The one Ash spoke of? I saw you when you were rising up from underneath the Imperial City, at least your head. I know it's you."

Or was it?

She blinked. The once-hazy memory flickered into clarity, and she now remembered white streaks and patches covering more than half the titan's scaly body from head to wings to tail. The discolorations had not lessened the majesty of the Dragon King—if that was what he was—but they had certainly dulled his luster. On the other hand, as she looked on now and peered left to right as far as she could while leaning back to fit more of the dragon in her vision, she could see no break in the pure golden sheen of his scales, not a single fluctuation of color that wasn't just a more beautiful shade of metallic yellow than the last.

"No," she murmured. "Not the same."

Or—

"Is this how you were before?" She straightened again and looked head on at the staring eye. "I can't imagine there are two of you in the world. I don't think there's enough space in all the land for more than one of you. That has to have been you back then in the Imperial City...but you look different. Healthier." Healthier? Was that the word she meant? "Younger," she amended, half-rambling, and she paused again when she realized that felt far more accurate. Was the illusion somehow giving her the intuitive knowledge she needed to comprehend what was happening to her?

Maybe. But one would think she wouldn't have to be screaming by herself at a mute dragon, her pitiful voice bouncing uselessly off into the void.

"Say something!" she snapped, her impatience and uneasiness swelling to dwarf even the intimidation of being the size of a gnat compared to the one before her. "Or do something, anything! I'm here and can't get out, and the longer I do nothing, the sooner I drown out there in the real world because that damned woman is holding me down! Clearly I'm here for a reason. So I'm ready! Show me!"

What had she been expecting, she wondered as the earth began to rumble and her heart dropped. She staggered, falling to the side as the world warped around her, twisting one way and the other like someone disturbing the formerly calm surface of a pond by stirring it fast and hard with a reed. Or the surface of tar, more like, thick and terrible and sickening…

And then it stopped. She squinted, uncertain of what had happened until she realized she could see her reflection in the dragon's eye that was still lowered and staring down at her, angled. Despite the deep shadows clinging to everything below the looming head, just enough sunlight reflected off the ground and glimmered above that she could see an unfamiliar outline shimmering in the glassy eye. That wasn't her. She looked different, like…a man. A young man with soft, fair curls, slender. She could see nothing more exact than that thanks to the dimness.

Shit, she thought in paralyzed horror when suddenly, she realized she could no longer move, either. This body—it wasn't hers. It was almost like when she had walked in her dreams to join Kai from hundreds of leagues away, their spirits binding to each other so they could speak through their spirits. She was trapped in the confines of this body like water sloshing around helplessly in a jug, and worse, the jug was indifferent. It couldn't feel her at all. And it felt displaced in time as if she were slipping her foot into a sandal that lay on the floor across the room.

Get out of here, she hissed to herself, but it was no use. The rumbling began again under her feet, and the dragon's eye loomed even closer, making her reflection all the clearer for it. It took one more look, just one, and she grimaced, knowing for a certainty now whose reflection exactly that was.

Tet's.

88

"Hello," he says. "I guess this is where I die, then."

The Dragon King doesn't move a single muscle, and Tet watches with a deceptively serene smile as the monster among monsters stares him down, his giant golden eye shining as if it's spinning and spinning and spinning in the silence. Or maybe that's just the vertigo threatening to topple Tet to the side as he contemplates how short his life was, and how unfortunate and wretched it is to die from sliding down a dragon's gullet or, if he's unlucky, from being crunched between savage teeth three times as long as his entire body.

Yes, he's small. So maybe the Dragon King will spare him, consider him unworthy of the trouble to swallow him up.

"Please don't keep me in suspense. I'm not dead yet, but it really does feel like I'm dying here."

The swell of dark, deep sounds that rumbles up from the ground into his feet is a mystery at first. He thinks maybe the earth is opening up to drop him into the depths of a never-ending abyss, an appropriately mythic and dramatic demise for someone who's literally staring into the eye of a dragon so large it alone could crush entire villages. Several at once, actually. And despite always having been told that it's an honor to die a splendid death, far better than meeting an undignified one of neither glory nor remembrance, he can't imagine this will be any more satisfying to him.

Oh, please, he thinks as the rumbling grows and grows and the earth's trembling increases to a speedy vibration. Please, let me live, let the Dragon King drop dead so I can live my pathetic life that I've wasted until now.

It's an entire handful of seconds before Tet realizes the earth is not, in fact, splitting apart in dramatic fashion. It's...the King, growling. Which also isn't good by any means since growling implies anger which in turn suggests death by crunch, but at least he has one last chance to appease the god.

"I'm boring dead, you know. I'm great fun so long as I'm still breathing to make ill-timed jokes and make light of deadly peril. If it pleases you, Your Divinity."

So he's never been good at appeasing anyone or anything. He has no friends, and the entire village hates him. Even his parents like to pretend he's dead sometimes because it's easier than dealing with all the people he's pissed off while wandering around in places he shouldn't. Like in neighboring villages where he can't keep his mouth shut whenever he comes across a huddled group of brawny, burly men twice his size and he picks a fight anyway. Things like that. And this one...Well, this one's the worst he's ever gotten himself into. Sure, the people warned him not to wander out toward the valley since there have been sightings of gods and demons in the distance, but that only made Tet even more curious. So yes, he packed some supplies (his mother would say he stole them from the family pantry, silly woman) and promptly set off on a seven-day journey toward that very same valley where the old gods are rumored to walk— and found one.

"Please stop growling at me. I can't feel my bones anymore."

Well. Surprise. It doesn't stop. What does change, however, is that the Dragon King angles its massive head even closer toward him, the length of its snout buried in the grass with the enormous eye looming down from several feet above him...And then it enters Tet's mind.

He has no idea what happens between the time it starts and the time it ends. All he knows is that when the dragon finally withdraws the mental probe, he's lying flat on his back on the grass with drool dripping out of the side of his mouth and his head lolling in the grass. He feels like someone's stuck a hundred hollow reeds in his flesh and blown into them all simultaneously until he's puffed up like a pig bladder about to burst at the seams. He knows he isn't dead, though. Death wouldn't be nearly this catastrophic. But there's one good thing that results from the terrible experience: he's seen into the mind of a god, and now he knows what it's like in there.

It's lonely.

"That's a shame," he says some time later when he remembers how to speak again (it took a while). "It's rough being alone. I just never thought a god would have any shortage of friends. But it makes sense. You're too different from the rest of the dragons, too large, too powerful. I have the opposite problem, funny enough, but I do get it. It's like you're standing on one side of the rope bridge hanging over a chasm, and whenever you try to take a step to cross, the people on the other side start sawing away at it. Yeah, I get it."

And it's a miracle. He's babbling, but somehow, the god deigns to understand him, to understand human speech and even respond. The growl that comes from the Dragon King is smaller than the one that came before, even if it still reverberates through the whole valley. And it's a humming growl of assent, not the menacing kind...Tet thinks.

Yeah. That's right. He's starting to understand the god, and he won't try to modestly deny it to himself like the other kowtowing villagers would. He's always known he's different from the rest. It's not that far of a leap to say he's even *special*. Who could deny it now? He's stroking the snout of a god, the fearsome Dragon King, the king of kings and lord of lords who carries entire worlds on his wings. If that doesn't make Tet special, then what would? And the dragon agrees. Not in words, but the sensations that flow through Tet's mind are approving ones. And dare he say it, once he gets used to the sheer massive breadth of the mental presence that belongs to the Dragon King, he thinks the god is...excited. Excited to be speaking to him, to a mere human, like stumbling upon a discovery of gold and gems.

And he knows why.

"Hey," he says as he continues to stroke small circles into the single golden scale that's as large as his body is long. "I'll be different from the rest. Those other dragons, they're scared of you, they run away from you, they only follow you when you command them into doing it then scatter again after—but I'll follow you forever. You won't be lonely anymore."

He never goes back home after that. Why would he? He's like—like a prince now, the Dragon King's most trusted companion. Its *only* companion. And he learns about all the things a god can do. For instance, when the King calls to his kind with a deafening, bellowing roar across the land, when the King uses the power of his primordial voice that holds dominance over all other dragons, they come at his call no matter how they fear being in his terrifying presence. It's like lighting a torch to attract the moths; they can't resist it. They scatter after he releases the compulsion, but they do come…and that's when Tet thinks of an idea one day.

Why not just make them stay? he asks in his mind—for by now, he's mastered the art of speaking silently to the Dragon King thanks to their bond. Next time, have them gather around and make them stay with you. And we'll all just hang out together. What's so wrong with that? It's not hurting them any.

When it happens, Tet almost can't believe it even though he's the one who suggested it in the first place. He has some crazy good ideas, doesn't he? And it swells his pride to know the Dragon King treats him as an equal, albeit a fragile one. No, not an equal—it's almost like Tet's the one leading the dragon. His ideas, his words, all of them are taken seriously, and when he babbles on about his life and all his wandering thoughts about every little thing, the King never dismisses him the way the villagers did. The way even his own family did. And best of all, he never has to swallow down anyone's scorn again. No one can ever scold him, ridicule him, beat him, ever. Ha! He wishes they would all try. How incredible would it be to see the expressions on their faces when he tells them—*you'll regret that!* and an old god himself rises up to take vengeance on his behalf? He shivers, wondering if there will ever come a day when he can flaunt his newfound position in life as the companion of a divine. He wishes they would all regret, but they don't know anything. They probably all think he's dead and muttering 'good riddance' to themselves.

So yes, he does wish he can go and show off, it's true. But he's also afraid that if he goes back to human civilization with the Dragon King, the god will find someone more interesting than he is and change his mind. No. He can't let the dragon meet anyone else. Not ever. He likes being special. He likes being the only one. If he ever loses this, he thinks he might die.

And then it happens: he finds out he's not quite as special as he thought he was. Ever. Because that's when he meets his first Druid, someone who should only exist in fables and fancy tales. Servants of the gods, gifted with fragments of their power, meant to preserve the old and carry on the flames that flickered. They have magic, Tet marvels. They're not just humans who keep the gods company. They have power. They have strength. And when they roam the land in service to their respective god-masters, the people don't fawn over them because of who they serve. They fawn over them—because of *them*, and no one else.

How come he doesn't have that? He's envious. And it's because the Dragon King doesn't have human subjects. Worshipers. There's no one who can come close enough to admire him, no one who can resent him the way he resents the Druids. It makes him angry.

But he's still too afraid to ask for what he thinks he deserves. So he waits and waits, hoping it's just a matter of time. That's all, he tells himself. If he's patient, surely the Dragon King will gift him real power just like the other gods do their own loyal servants, and those damned Druids will never be able to look down on him. He's special, he reminds himself. He's the only one of his kind, the only companion of the Dragon King. Those other gods? They have multitudes of servants to do their bidding, legions of them, but he's a one and only. Of course he'll have his just rewards in the end, and it'll be so much better than the rest. He ought to start thinking of a title. The Dragon Prince. No, wait, something stronger, more fearsome, because when he gets his powers, he's sure to be strong enough to topple mountains and sunder storms. He won't be like all the other Druids, common servants who have to share power between themselves. Because he's special, he's always been special. Just him.

Too special to wait, he realizes before long. And why should he? It belongs to him, truly. And the fact that he's a humble human for now doesn't matter. He was always better than everyone else, meant for great things. The Dragon King wasn't born a god either. He knows that since he's seen all its secrets now, into its mind. And it's colossal and ancient and powerful, but deep inside, the King still a lost child in need of a guiding hand. Tet's that guiding hand. He can be, always. And in exchange, it's only fair he benefits, too. And with interest added since he's had to wait so long for equal exchange.

It's a long road to attain what he desires, but what he lacks in courage, he makes up for in patience, in doggedness. He'll do whatever it takes to get the Dragon King to do for him what no other god has ever dared: to give Tet not only a piece of itself, a mere fragment, but the whole of its power, shared between them. Because Tet's special. He knows it. Believes in it with all his heart.

Oh, yes.

It's everything he deserves.

89

The memory passed over, through, and around her like a surge of stormy water sloshing through a ditch. It tossed Anzi around and spun her like a top, and an invisible force ripped her out of Tet's body and consciousness like a slab of meat pulled off a hook. She came free with a gasping scream, every part of her utterly raw and freezing and vulnerable as if someone had taken a blade and flayed the skin off her bones before tossing her out into a wintry blizzard.

But the sensation of soul-deep coldness faded fast, and it wasn't long before she stopped shivering as her body soaked up the rays of the hot Adaraat sun. So she was back here again. Whatever kind of magic Ash was using on her, it had pulled her across the land from place to place. She'd recognized the first one, her home village on the fringes of the desert when she had been but a child. The second was far from here, to the south where the flatlands began to roll up and down to meet the mountainous region. And now she was back to the desert again, but not on its edges like before. This was the very heart of it, the center, the singular point of the Adaraat from which its strange magic and ever-lasting curse of barrenness radiated, strong and deep and terrible. She had never been here before, but the knowledge came from outside of her, from—that.

She looked around, eyes narrowed. It was all sand here, rippling dunes in every direction as far as the eye could see, except for the strange piles of large, monolithic stones arranged in a perfect circle just ahead. Clearly, she was supposed to go there. It annoyed her that this magic insisted on such ritualistic minutiae when it could just show her what she needed to know—or rather, what Ash wanted her to learn. But she was trapped in this world now, and she had to play by its rules. So she strode forward, every step kicking up sand as she stomped up the way.

There, in the middle of the circle of stacked stones, something that looked like an altar. Maybe. A sacrificial table, a raised platform underneath it upon which to gather around and pray. There was even a semi-hollow shaped stone bowl on top of the wavy, smooth surface. Not only that, but when she drew close enough to peer into it, she saw water inside. Clear water, pure and cool. She leaned back, knowing instinctively it was not for her, nor anyone at all.

"What am I doing here?" she asked loudly. "What's going on? Am I supposed to do something?" She looked around again, counting each stone monolith and peering at each from a distance in case any of them held clues. Magic seals, symbols to guide her next step, anything. But there was nothing, nothing except…wait, were those faint handprints all over them?

Before she could investigate, a familiar voice had her whirling around, lips curled in a ready snarl and her hands reaching for her swords—that were no longer there. As she glared at the smiling Tet who stood on the other side of the sacrificial altar, her hands groped twice more at her hips before giving up and dropping uselessly at her sides.

"Hello, there," he said cheerily. He swayed from side to side like some slender sapling caught in a stiff wind. "Looks like you're even more special than I thought you'd be. This was not something I foresaw."

She glared harder still. This thing, this mirage, spoke just like him. It was as if someone had plucked him from her mind and given him identical shape, something even closer than a twin. It sickened her to think Ash's visions would inflict her with this when she was so furious, so murderous, when she wanted so badly to grab Tet by the throat and hurl him into the ground over and over again. Him and Bisset both.

"Oh, my. With that kind of face, I'd think you're unhappy to see me. But fear not! I know you're only afraid and confused. No need, though. It is truly I, your beloved Ra-Tet. I have to admit, I didn't know you could do this, but with the desperate straits you're in, your spirit is reaching out for whatever help it can get. I dread to think what condition your physical body is in."

The Tet-thing sighed, and Anzi's furious grimace faltered. It couldn't be...

"Well, at least your efforts in seducing the chieftain won't come to naught," he continued. "Alexandre is almost at the Territory Five outpost, but you have to stay alive long enough for the rescue. So keep our former friend Kaizat happy. I'm assuming he's availed himself of your body in the meantime since, well, you know all men are the same, and war spoils are war spoils. My condolences for your suffering, but as a woman on the battlefield risking capture at any time, I'm sure you knew something like that was inevitable." He coughed delicately behind his long, spindly hand. "I heard if you just let it happen, it hurts less, so may I suggest simply lying there whenever he does what he does. You poor thing."

His sympathy was sickeningly syrupy and patronizing, as if he were watching someone set fire to an anthill he couldn't quite bring himself to feel genuine sorrow for. And his words—the filthy, disgusting words he said about both her and Kai, accusing him of something she would never disrespect him by putting into words even in the privacy of her own thoughts. But worst of all was the realization that this was no mere hallucination, no made-up vision in her head imagined by Ash's magic. The man standing there on the other side of the altar, staring at her with those slender furrowed eyebrows and slow, pitying blinks—that was Tet. The real Tet.

How was he here in front of her? Had Ash known this could happen? Why would she do this? Anzi retreated one step, then another, and another. She needed to get out of here. She had to get out.

"Anzi? Wait, where are you going? Ah, no, you're fading...But have no fear, my darling plum flower. I can feel where you are now, and as soon as I wake up, I'll have the mages send a message to the outpost to tell Alexandre which direction to take up pursuit."

And then he was gone. Anzi blinked, thoroughly confused and unsettled by what had just happened. She hadn't imagined it, and yet what now? As suddenly as he had appeared, Tet's visage was now gone. Completely. It was as if he had never been standing there, and she even carefully walked around the altar in case he had dropped to a crouch and was hiding behind the stone. It seemed like something he might do.

But he wasn't there. He was gone.

She spun around, staring up at the sky, around the stones, glaring all the while. "Ash!" she shouted. "What was that! I don't know how you did that, but you just gave away our position—did you hear him? He's sending someone here!"

But no one answered, and with a gnashing of her teeth, she turned back to stare down at the stone table. What was she supposed to be waiting for? Could Ash even hear her? Had she not seen what just happened? That had definitely been Tet's presence before her, like when she had walked in her dreams to Kai before. She could only be grateful that she hadn't given away her true feelings and motives, and that Tet thought she needed rescuing. It made possible a counterattack, an ambush, preparation, anything that wasn't sitting like ducks in the middle of nowhere. Or maybe she should allow herself to be taken back to Tet without a fight, where she could spy on him. All she had to do was stage an escape since he believed she was an unwilling captive, even if it would mean she couldn't stab Bisset in the back when he got here and properly *thank* him for his timely rescue. Gods knew he deserved it, but...

No. All of that could come later. First, she needed to figure out how escape this damned dream world. Magic, she swore. Damn it! Boiling with impotent rage, she slammed her fists down on the stone altar—and found it cool to the touch. Too cool, under the heat of this desert sun, invitingly so.

Her fury dissipated, leaving her in a bare daze. Hello, she wanted to call. Who was that? Because there was something calling to her, urging her to succumb, to fall into the current and follow instead of fighting. She had already fought all her life, now she needed to surrender. And it felt so right to listen to it, like a thread sliding into the eye of a needle, a guiding whisper.

Damn, she hated magic. It was everything she wasn't. Mysterious, elusive, never straightforward. But even she could take a hint like that. With a reluctant sigh and one final suspicious, lingering look, she turned and lifted herself up onto the surface. She swung her legs up and scooted back so she could lie perfectly along the length of it, and it was only when she breathed out and folded her hands over her chest, peacefully, that it occurred to her...she was lying on a sacrificial altar.

Her eyes shot open, but it was too late. Whatever was supposed to happen was already here.

The first tidal wave of energy that surged from the stone surface and into her back made her scream, and her voice pierced the desert silence like the shattering of glass. If she could listen to herself, she might have even sworn her voice echoed unnaturally between the circular array of monoliths. But she didn't, because the heat that seared her made it impossible for her to feel, see, hear anything anymore. And the light that beamed up all around her widened until it came from not only the table she lay upon but also the raised stone dais around it, and it was blinding and melting and all things, all things at once.

And then in an instant, it all disappeared, shrinking into a single beam of needle-thin white light that pierced straight through her back and out her chest. It went all the way up into the sky, so bright its brilliance stood out even in the glare of the midday Adaraat sun overhead. Anzi didn't have the strength to even wilt in relief at the sudden change, but that wasn't the last of it anyway. Another savage lurch of energy raced through her, lighting her up from head to toe then back again and back again and back again as if every drop of the blood rushing through her veins had turned into lightning, into molten lava, into star-bright fire that swelled and bubbled up inside every part of her, down to the seed of her soul.

And then it exploded from her, but not upward. Instead, branching lines of energy streaked out of her flesh and raced down the stone altar, then down the dais, then under the sand and out in every direction across the desert, burrowing fast and hard. Millions of jagged lines like lightning strikes painted across the sand, reaching, reaching, reaching—

Anzi stared up at the sky, but she saw nothing of it. Her mind was gone, entirely elsewhere, racing through the desert along every branching path of white light that shone through the sand. If she were coherent, if she had her wits about her, she would have wondered how it was possible to be in so many places at once, but all she could do was wait in numb silence as her fragmented mind followed each searching lance of light and power, on and on, until one of them dived deep into the earth, surging below the surface sand toward something that lay hidden underneath.

And it was...a wyrm. A wyrm, Anzi thought in wandering, swimming confusion, and not just one but many. This one was only the first, and every time another burrowing branch of white light cut down deep into the desert's gullet and connected with another wriggling reptile, that fragment of Anzi's mind stayed with it, anchored tight. She had no idea what was happening—hadn't for a while now, and was helpless against the current that carried her forward. All she knew was that somehow, she had broken out of the vision, or at least her mind had, and she was sensing the wyrms that hid in the far reaches of the Adaraat. Her presence lingered with them, slivers of her awareness clinging to their scales and feeling their every breath, their every heartbeat, fast and low and humming, as some of them dug after prey while others slept, some above ground, many below...

When her mind split off one too many times, she felt a terrible twinge like a vicious cramp along her entire body, and every branch of traveling light stopped short before sputtering in place. They all held steady for a moment as she struggled and sucked in a long, deep breath, her back arching off the stone altar upon which she lay. Until all at once, every single wyrm linked to her mind turned in her direction. From the ones that had been mid-feast to the ones that had been asleep underground, every single one stopped what they were doing and turned to face her with their sharp, diamond-shaped heads motionless and their eyes trained on her from every direction, from every distance. And then, in unison, they opened their maws and let out a terrible screech as if to tell her that yes, they could see her, she could never hide from them like this, ever.

It wasn't the sound, but the reverberations of their very lives all together that shattered her into countless pieces, like rupturing glass. Every trailing light tore away and raced back toward her as if she were yanking upon them all hand over hand, as if her body were a spinning wheel spooling up thread in the wrong direction until at last, they exploded into her all at once, making her shine and burst into spindles of light exploding from her flesh from head to toe—

With a strangled, gurgling shout, Anzi surged up from the water, showering everything in sight with a ferocious fountain of droplets. It took a moment for her to realize she was no longer in the dream world but back in her own body again, and as she panted hard and fast while coughing out the water in her lungs, she threw a glare in the direction of the old woman standing before her.

"Welcome back," said Ash with a wide, white smile. "Now, you can be strong."

90

"So who goes first," Anzi said flatly as she wiped the water off her face with an angry hand. More coughs tickled at the back of her throat as she spoke, but she was too incensed to stop and get them out. "I already know you have a lecture prepared for me, probably a riddling one, but this time I have one for you, too."

"Aha, then maybe I should keep it to myself just to be contrary..."

"That would mean it's not important enough to impress me. I'll go first, then. Did you know that damned Tet could enter my mind like that or not, before you used your magic on me? And did you know he could not only talk to me, but also track me down? Did you have any idea of that or not?"

"Calm, little one. You're agitated."

"I have every reason."

"No." Ash shook her head with a knowing smile. "Put aside your emotions for a moment. Think. How could he possibly be in your mind? Truly?"

"*You've* been in my mind," she fired back. "And Kai. And all sorts of people including dragons, because apparently my head is open to anyone and anything who wants to take up space there. I've already gotten used to the idea that my mind is no longer my own. I'm more concerned about the fact that your magic exposed me to—"

"Anzi, I know it seemed real, whatever you saw, but understand:

whatever it is that was shown to you in your vision is only a stepping stone to the truth. Your truth. Only you can understand your power, and everything you saw is only meant to aid you in that. If you saw the abomination in your vision, then pry deeper. Question why it is that when you looked deep within yourself, he was the face you saw, the voice you heard. Look past what seemed real and find the meaning underneath it."

"I'm telling you I saw Tet! He was real! I spoke to him, and he said he was sending the colonel here to get me."

"Let me ask you this. Are there reasons they would be buried so deeply in your heart?"

Something about her tone, knowing and lilting and rich with other-worldly wisdom Anzi couldn't help but mistrust—because what had she learned about trusting solely in the capacity of others?—made her narrow her eyes. "What's that supposed to mean?" she asked, her voice lower, darker. "Buried deeply in my heart? If you're asking if I have any lingering loyalty to them after everything that's happened, you're wrong. Or if you're saying I'm so terrified of them that Tet's likeness appeared to me in the vision, then you're also wrong. I'm not afraid."

"Are you not? Hm. Maybe not now, but what if you were standing before them? What would you do if they came against you, right here?"

"They're—" Anzi struggled to shove aside her rising anger, impatience, and panic. She knew what she had seen! It had been Tet's face, Tet's voice, Tet's smug, repulsive mannerisms, all of it. She couldn't have possibly imagined anything so real. Like hell there was a 'true meaning' behind it. Tet was sending Bisset, and everyone needed to get out of here before they were converged on by the colonel and his forces. They had to get away, and all Ash was doing was preaching to her as if she were some ignorant child. "My history with them has no bearing on this. Ash! Listen to me." She lifted her hands out of the water with a fountaining spray and planted them on the other woman's shoulders. "Bisset is going to outnumber us. There were other riders coming. And what condition are we in! Kai's still unwell, I know it even if he hides it. And everyone is exhausted. We can't fight like this!"

All the mischief was gone from Ash's eyes as she watched her with a pensive expression. there was no sparkle, no excitable gleam. Instead, despite the newfound youth that tightened and smoothed what used to be Ash's wizened, wrinkled skin, there was an ancient knowingness in her gaze that made Anzi feel foolish and clumsy. The rest of her frenzied, sharp words died in her throat, and in the silence, the spring burbled out of the stone above their heads as they stared at each other.

"Druid magic is a strange thing," Ash said at last. "It's never the same from one to the next. And the fewer of us live, the more powerful. We were already almost gone by the time I came around. But you and I are here, and we may never find another. That means you will surpass me, born into a generation I can never hope to match, but that also means you're the only one who can bring back the balance we used to have. Whatever you saw, whatever your mind showed you, you were meant to see so you could understand yourself and the power that resides inside you. What you have to do is understand it."

Every part of Anzi rebelled. Why wasn't she paying attention! She knew what she had seen, and if only she would listen!

"I see you won't believe me," said Ash. "Good. I would be disappointed if you were so gullible and ready to trust. But if you can believe anyone, it's me. What should I do to earn your faith?"

"Nothing," Anzi snapped. "I'm done acting on faith. I know what I saw, Ash! Can't you go into my mind and see it too?"

"You should know by now it doesn't work that way. Only you know what you saw, and you'll never truly be able to explain it to anyone else." Ash's eyes crinkled up at the corners. "That's the nature of your Druid magic, the heritage we share. You're young, so it'll take time to come into your power, but you must know more now than you did before. Tell me. What have you learned?"

It killed her to shove aside the urgency of Tet and Bisset's imminent attack. How could this feeling of sheer dread mixed with equal parts fury and—yes, she would admit it—fear, how could any of it have been false? A mere vision to be interpreted? An illusion? No. It couldn't be. It had been too real. Terrifying.

But she would get nowhere with her insistence. For now, they had time, so she would extract what knowledge she could from Ash then return to Kai to warn him. Even if this old woman was useless, surely Kai would trust her instincts.

"It has something to do with the wyrms," Anzi said stiffly once she made her decision. "They could see me, and I could see them."

"The wyrms, ha? That makes sense. It was before my time, but I know the Druids of old who inherited the spirits of dragons had bonds with their lesser cousins, too. You know, the people of Feng believe a wyrm will even transform into a dragon if they survive a thousand years…"

"No stories, thanks. So you said I'm the Druid of the dragons, but all it lets me do is—that." She grimaced, so disappointed it was almost crushing. "There was nothing else. The second part of the vision was…" The memory flowed back into her, rising and flaring like a suddenly remembered dream. "It was Tet! I was in Tet's mind. I saw the Dragon King, it looked like the creature I saw in the Imperial City."

"Calm down," Ash urged. "Yes. Little Kaizat and I guessed long ago that the abomination has been hiding the Dragon King somewhere. It was a mystery for a long time simply because the King should be too large to be concealed at all. If you saw him, then you understand."

"I don't know if they're the same. The one in the vision was enormous. The one in the City was massive too, but I mean—this one, he was so big I couldn't even…I can't explain it. He was just bigger." And the scales she had seen of the one crashing up from underground had been white and gold, nowhere near the brilliance of the Dragon King in her vision. Or maybe it was age? Disease? Bisset had stolen nearly all the life and power out of his dragon, who could say Tet hadn't done the same? Though it was hard to imagine he could do such a thing to one powerful enough to be called one of the old gods.

"Hm. A mystery I can shed no light on. I've never seen the King, either then or now. And you say you were in whose mind? Tet's?"

"It was him. Without a doubt. But it was when he was younger, and…I don't know. Maybe I wasn't in his mind. It felt like I was looking from the outside in, except I had a foot in the door. Like I was hearing echoes, not the real thing."

Her words sounded hollow even to her own ears; there was no way she was going to be able to explain it to Ash in a way she would understand. Besides, she was more worried about—

"Wait. I was in Tet's mind, and you won't argue that. But you think the Tet I saw in the second vision was fake? How do you know that wasn't just as real?"

But Ash shook her head. "You saw the afterimage of him. As the Druid meant to protect the dragons, of course you would have a connection to the Dragon King, or at least what he used to be. And once upon a time, the man you know as Tet was indeed his loyal servant. But for your minds to be truly connected—well. That would require something special I doubt you have." Suddenly, the woman's eyes found their mischievous twinkle again. "For instance, Kaizat and you share a bond, so you can speak to each other that way. He's told me you've done this several times.

So you are lovers in spirit...even if that's yet to be in body. Can you say the same for you and Tet? Are you a troublesome woman of many loves? Hm?"

Anzi didn't know whether to be furious that Ash was poking her nose into private business between her and Kai, or to be utterly nauseated at the horrifying attempt at a tease. "Please don't make me sick. You have no idea..."

"Ha-ha. Then it's settled. Rest easy, Anzi. If nothing else, trust that your bond with Kai is special, and you won't find it with anyone else in the entire world."

"I've had dragons in my mind, too. And you."

"Was it the same? I think not. You traveled leagues to be with your fated mate in your dreams, don't flatter the false king by thinking him capable of the same privilege. And dragons speaking to you—that's to be expected since all dragons can speak to those around them that way, and especially to you since you are who you are."

"And you? You spoke to me from a distance, too. That time when I scouted the desert trying to find out why the wyrms were starting to swarm into human territory, you found me then."

"We're sisters in spirit, little one. True Druids will always find each other, and I wasn't so far away." She grinned. "You just couldn't see me. And speaking to you that way is a far cry from how you can bond with little Kaizat. It brings a tear to my eye to see how he's all grown up and wooing a woman now."

She was not going to talk about wooing and being wooed with this... this crone. Despite the cool water lapping against her chest and odd breeze that kept flitting around the oasis, Anzi's face had never felt hotter. "Enough! I'm not here to talk about that. I want to know how I'm going to get stronger. What should I do? This Druid thing and whatever else, how do I train it? I have magic, but it's never worked well for me."

"Of course not. You're no mere magician or sorceress. You're a true heir to the first magics, the ones that shaped our whole world from the beginning of time. Ah...but the Druids fell before I was old enough to learn the rituals and carry them out for our younger brethren. You will have to come into them the hard way, I'm afraid."

Great. Exactly what she wanted to hear. "So there's nothing I can do?" she demanded. "I've come all the way here and I'm useless?"

"Don't say that, little one. You're powerful, and you're shrewd, and you've a gift no one else has that was meant for you from the beginning. You've been chosen by fate for this, Anzi. Have faith in yourself."

Faith again. And in herself? That was even more laughable than believing blindly in someone else. There were only two people on earth she was more disgusted with—after Tet and Bisset, it was herself that she was most disappointed in for all the years of blindness, of stupidly following her heart when she should have paid attention, opened her eyes, and seen the truth. She clenched her fists below the water, too frustrated to speak. Why was it that she was always the ignorant one now, the burden, the one who was always behind when she used to be the one who ran at the fore of the pack?

"There is one thing you can do, if you want answers." Ash's words made her look up, eyes narrowed. "Another link to the primal magics, one that I sadly can't guide you along."

Cryptic advice again. Please, would she just get on with it. "Tell me!"

"Ah. Well." A sly smile curved Ash's mouth. "One of the oldest forces in the world is the mate bond, isn't it?"

Was it? "I don't know."

"Then I suppose you should get some answers, shouldn't you?" The woman's smile split into a toothy grin. "I've done my duty here and awakened you to the first seeds of your power. Now you have to seek out the rest of the trail yourself. Go. Find him. Get your answers."

"You're just trying to foist me onto him."

"If only I could be so lucky. Hee-hee! No, little one. I'll be staying with the tribe for a while since I can be of some help. Not to you, but to Kaizat's wounded brothers. I'll be at hand if you need me, but I think you will want to speak with him—privately."

She didn't like how Ash kept waggling her eyebrows. Not one bit. She sent the woman a dirty look.

...But maybe she had a point. She was grasping at straws trying to figure this out, and besides, she still needed to warn Kai about the possibility of an imminent attack. Maybe Ash was convinced it was all some elusive thing with a hidden meaning, but as far as Anzi knew, the vision had been a simple stroke of luck and a timely warning. Right, then. She turned and marched out of the water, her clothes and hair sopping wet.

"Have fun!" Ash called out from behind her. "I'll be around~ Though you probably won't need me."

Damn right. Face burning and fists clenched, Anzi hurried out of the oasis and back toward the campsite.

91

No matter how skeptical Anzi was of strange magic unconstrained by regulation and study and training, she couldn't deny that Ash's power was a wonder. This place, the Oasis, was no mere natural formation she was simply transporting. It was the culmination of her power, the Druid power she spoke of, something that had been given life by the woman's very magical essence. And now that Anzi had been plunged into the depths of the water at its heart, the same water Ash had said was where her power was greatest, Anzi could now sense the echoes of that same aged, layered presence everywhere around her as she made her retreat. The leaves of the bushes she brushed against, the breeze as it whipped her hair over her shoulder, even the crunching of stiff grass blades under her feet—all of it felt like Ash, as if the woman were gliding behind her and breathing, speaking into her ear.

It was the eeriest thing she had ever felt. It reminded her of when she had first stepped into the Cave, that sensation of being surrounded by something far greater than she was. And it reminded her of when she had stepped into the egg chamber for the first time, the realization that she had found something great and terrible after an eternity.

Myths. Gods. *Druids.* Old stories passed down by barbarian tribes and the primitive people predating the Empire. But this was the new age; everyone knew such things didn't exist. There were rules and reasons for everything, rational explanations. The greatest mages used calculations, runes of power, carefully constructed arrays to manipulate arcane energy, and whoever still believed that magic was some wondrous, unknowable thing from the gods were even more backwards than the fringers everyone else looked down on.

And yet, here it was. Wonderment. Anzi stopped at the edge of the Oasis where grass faded into sand. Here, the breeze stopped, and if she took one step farther, she would be leaving the inexplicably vibrant palm trees, the burbling waters, the butterflies. It was like hovering on the brink of waking up, still half-dreaming…and she didn't want to wake.

She dropped into a squat, feeling a queasiness inside that wasn't too unlike the sickness that overtook her whenever she was in the air. This world she had slipped into after abandoning the one she had known all her life—even after plunging herself into it, it was so hard to accept, to walk backward and follow primal footprints instead of walking in the understanding she'd been born into.

But the rules she had always abided by, she now had to set aside. Druids, gods, unlettered magic, these would have to be her weapons out here against the Empire. Maybe now that she had reconnected with Oza, he could help her learn to understand this world. He had always been gifted with magic. Speaking of him, she needed to check on everyone from him to Letti to the piscin girl, and all the dragons. Somehow, she had gone from being a determined loner to toting around a whole tribe just like Kai.

With a sigh, she stood—and fell like a rock, planting face-first in the sand with all the grace of a sack of rocks. She lay there, stunned, breathing in loose, warm sand but too stunned to do anything about it for a full moment. It happened so fast she didn't know why she was on the ground at all until she blinked and her thoughts fell back into order. It wasn't her limp that had betrayed her, but rather a newfound pressure wrapped around her mind, so heavy and sudden it had momentarily disconnected her from all feeling in her body.

She recognized this sensation. She recognized the way her mind spread and radiated in all directions like water rippling outward. It rolled and tumbled on, all of her senses, and then she could feel them: hints of life, flickering lights. Warmth. All of them inside the camp just ahead, she could feel them moving over the sand, stopping, moving again. The thrum of energy that passed through their bodies and into her, the echo of their every breath and every beat of their heart, their pulse.

It was them. Her eyes widened, eyelashes brushing against the warm grains of sand. Every single one of them, Kai's tribesmen, and she could feel too the dragons who lay curled up behind her tent. There was Netra, her energy pulsing through her slender body like fracturing icebergs and a frigid current rushing below a frozen surface. There was Serqet, slow and steady, life force creeping like a scorpion crawling over sand dunes, click-clicking. There was the Prince, the one with no name, too muddled and dark and dense for her to see into—and was that Kai? Brimming with heat, a bright corona of energy flashing around him, pulsing with life. The ones he was with and all the rest of the others couldn't even compare.

It took her several more steadying breaths before she could crawl back onto her hands and knees. By now, she was a mess again. The sand clung all over her damp skin and sword scabbards, and more annoyingly, her dress and hair as well. Qinglong wasn't getting her dress back in mint condition.

She sighed. Her mind was still partly scattered, and even now she could sense the life pulsing all over the campsite ahead, but her awareness was slowly funneling back into her body once more. She wasn't even alarmed. What else should she have expected after being subjected to Ash's strange magic? She should have known it would change her to the core. In her vision, she had sensed the wyrms all over the Adaraat. This was too similar to be a coincidence even if the range of her newfound ability wasn't nearly so impressive. And it also couldn't be a coincidence that she could sense the dragons as well as the dragon shifters, but no one else. Oza, Letti, and Rania all remained invisible to her even though she knew for a fact they were also there.

Anzi glanced over her shoulder when she got to her feet, wondering if she should swallow her pride and go back in, ask for Ash's insight… but that could come later when she wasn't so frustrated at the woman. Right now, she needed to see Kai.

Kai. Mates. Fated mates. The surface of her mind rebelled at the thought that she was a slave to someone's destiny. She never wanted to give her soul unconditionally to anything ever again, not after she had tasted the bitterness of it with such pain, such darkness. But Kai was different. He had to be. He made her feel wonderful, terrible, undone and pulled together all at once. His every touch gentle or firm made her want more. Hearing his voice made her blood hum in her veins in answer. Mates. She had thought it was a thing only for inhumans and animals, for wild things with primitive magic. A sign of inferiority, captive to a will not their own. But this desire to be near him that only continued to grow with every passing second, this thing that was simultaneously strong yet tremulous, steady yet restless, like a river contained by a dam but crashing against it over and over and over again, it was richer and fuller than anything she'd ever...

She shook her head. First, she needed to get cleaned up. She could sense he was still with his tribesmen anyway—this strange ability was coming in handy already—and hardly in a position to entertain the barrage of questions she had for him. A quick bath and a moment to check on everyone she was responsible for, and then she would wait for him.

~

LETTI FOUGHT Anzi's hair with a comb she had managed to keep intact during their violent escape from the Imperial City. Leave it to her to secure the greatest necessities...When Anzi muttered so, the harem girl slapped her on the shoulder with the jade comb before resuming her grooming.

"Making snide comments when you're so eager to look pretty. Stones, glass houses."

"I don't care about looking pretty."

"Oh, so you're staying still and letting me do you up fancy like this for no reason? It's not for your new man who can't ever seem to find a shirt?"

"He's used to desert heat, Letti."

"Aaaand you're not denying he's your man. I'll always support you because I love and cherish you, but you could do better."

"He's not my man," Anzi snapped, far too late. "We're just..."

"Complicated? Please. I've heard that too many times. Oza, what do you think? Is she full of it?"

From the corner of the tent where he pored over Qinglong's various scrolls with the Feng woman quietly passing him more and more to examine, the boy said nothing. Aside from greeting Anzi upon her return with a brief nod, he had ignored everything and everyone except one water magic-wielding dragon shifter general...She didn't know whether it amused her or made her uneasy. That he had felt an immediate draw to a strange woman he'd never met before when he normally reserved but the coolest of opinions for all—was even Oza vulnerable to boyhood puppy love?

"All right, you're done. Your dress is probably dry now. But please,

please don't do whatever it was that you did to it again." Letti stood up and moved toward the tent's exit in a crouch, pausing only to throw her a scolding look. "The thread is good, strong Feng silk, but it's not steel. Right, Madam Qing? Qinglong?"

The woman looked up with a faint smile and a bound codex in her hands. Anzi had never been a scholar, but her eyes widened at the sight. A book? A whole book, out here past the advanced technology of the Empire? Feng civilization was still dozens, perhaps hundreds of broken up territories ruled by constantly fighting warlords. How could they have enough peace and stability to encourage scholarly arts? Or was that another lie, she wondered, meant to make the Feng look primitive. Past the veneer of the Empire's teachings, she knew so little of the world...

"I would advise you to take care of your attire," the woman said, and although the words were reproachful, her voice was nonchalant with a gentle flow, a calm stream. There was even a half-smile curving her lips just so, like a raindrop dangling from the tip of a curling leaf. "Not so much for your modesty since the women here aren't so shy, but because you will be a distraction. To Kai."

It was the first time she had heard anyone else address him that way. Kai? Hearing it sent a jolt through her, and she had no idea whether she was jealous or simply surprised...And she wasn't going to wonder about it, either. It was just aname. She lifted her chin. "If he can be distracted by some skin, then he's not half the man I think he is."

"You shouldn't set your expectations so high." Qing's smile remained faint and gentle, but there was a cutting amusement in her voice, crisp and elegant. "Men are men, sometimes."

From the side, Letti made a hm-*hm* noise of absolute affirmation. But interesting. There was a glint in the Feng woman's eyes that betrayed a hidden motive behind her lackadaisical words. A test, Anzi guessed, to see how she would respond. Too bad. She wasn't here to play word games and be probed, especially not when it came to Kai.

"Aren't you his general?" She held Qing's stare. "Seems strange that one of his most trusted companions would disparage him to a stranger from an enemy nation."

"Is that what you think you are?"

"It's what you think I am. Otherwise, you wouldn't be trying to test me like this." Anzi didn't wait for a response and turned so she could rise and leave the tent. Her senses were running amok again; she couldn't stop herself from feeling the quickening of Qinglong's pulse, the flare of her watery aura. "I need to speak to Kai. If anyone needs me, you know where I'll be."

Letti sounded like she was about to say something, but Anzi was outside before she could hear it. She grabbed her now-dry dress from where it hung on a planted stave and rounded the tent to see Rania lurking behind it, hiding in the tent's shade while leaning back against the empty wash basin. There, curled up beside her folded legs was Netra, sleeping with her serpentine head resting across the piscin girl's thigh.

She didn't belong here. This girl, Rania, with a growing mess of dark curly hair where there used to be only a fuzzy layer the first time they met. It was long enough for the ends to cover the tips of her ears. Had so much time passed already since that night in Lumenera? That night she had imagined she could raise up a secret army of dragon riders in some distant coastal city, lead them into battle not gloriously, but cleverly, against a tyrant emperor who had broken her whole world. This girl, small and skinny with slitted gills under her jaw on either side, this girl glaring up at her like any other ordinary street urchin with an attitude—how could things have changed so much that she could end up here in the middle of the Adaraat with a band of dragon shifting renegades and runaways from the Empire? She must feel even more place out of place than Anzi did. It was almost enough to make her feel sorry for the girl, except for one thing. The strength in her eyes. Determination. And the way her slender, webbed hand curled over Netra's snout? She must have figured herself out, gotten over her hatred of dragons. Was that infant bond she had with Netra-hau so strong, that it had pushed away everything else so she could be here now? With the dragon who had chosen her as a companion? It wasn't even a mate bond. It was something else Anzi didn't understand, probably some mystical thing that only dragons could. And yet it had been powerful enough to make Rania change her mind and come here, the middle of nowhere, a place that should be death to her water-dwelling blood.

Well, if Rania could adapt to this dangerous, unpredictable, insane new world, then so could Anzi.

"I thought you were going to be a burden," said Anzi. "But you've been watching and learning while staying out of everyone's way. You're smart."

"I know."

"Your friend who attacked the chieftain. Is he going to cooperate, too?"

Rania snorted. "You're behind. He died last night."

What! "They executed him?"

"No. He killed himself. Bit his tongue and rolled on his back in the middle of the night, let himself drown in the blood. He was half-crazy to begin with anyway. The only reason he even took on the mission in the first place. Right before, when he saw Netra come in with me when I asked to see him, he spat on me and told me I was a disgrace for betraying the cause. Said if I was so desperate that even I'd become a snake-loving traitor, then he'd rather die than meet the same fate." She grimaced and shifted further into the shade that the tent casted over her body. "I just didn't think he'd meant it."

"And what about you? Made your peace with dragons?"

"...I just know I'm ready to follow my heart. And I'm not stupid. I can tell these people, these...dragons, they're not like..."

"The dragon riders you know," Anzi finished. "You're right. The ones that are enslaved to the Empire, Tet controls them all. He told me one time he could even kill them with a thought. I don't know how much is true, but I can tell you they're not the evil creatures you grew up thinking they are."

Rania said nothing to that. A moment of silence passed, and then Anzi nodded at her hand that was still absently stroking Netra's head. "Your hands are different," she remarked. "Webbing. You didn't have those before."

The piscin girl glanced down. "Yeah. I've been changing."

Changing. Anzi pulled in her bottom lip and bit on it, thinking hard. Was it so easy? To change... "I'll come back later. Take care of Netra."

"What about them?" Rania noddedover her shoulder, indicating the other side of the large basin. Behind it, Anzi could sense them: Serqet burrowing into the sand, quietly, looking for prey, while the Prince coiled into himself in motionless sleep. The heat was doing it to them, making them drowsy...They too adapted, through their own means.

"They're fine. Netra's the one who's hating the heat the most. Like I said, take care of her."

It was that simple. Not easy—just simple. Seeing the beautiful, immaculate white-blue dragonet lying there upon Rania's leg like a beloved sister, to see her making her own way—her own dragon way, instead of sticking to Anzi's side. Growing up, growing away...How could it ever be easy? But things had come to this. They were in the middle of no man's land. And here, things were changing...changing...had changed so much.

Over the far dunes and past the campsite, past anyone's eyes, was the carcass of Shu-Amunet, the dragon who had lived so long shackled to the will of wicked, disgusting men. She lay baking under the sun. Dead. Free. Before she had gone on, she'd made a decision too. How tired she must have been. How resigned. How strong, so impossibly strong. To see death coming but not only meet it stolidly, but to fly toward it, sacrificing the last of her strength to save others. She had burned so bright, the last hair's breadth of the candle wick flaming with unmatched fury...then gone.

Anzi readjusted her scabbards over her hips and waited outside Kai's tent. She couldn't hear what they were saying inside, but she let her senses expand once more. Cautiously, with resignation but also with strength, and the knowledge that if everything else around her was changing, she had to do the same. She had never been a coward. Never would be. And within the tent, she sensed Kai and three others, kneeling and gathered around a weakened brother. She knew without a doubt he would die. His life was already flickering with its last sputters. But there was something else in him, something...

She made up her mind and moved toward the tent's entrance. There wasn't enough time to stop to ask for permission. She simply pushed her way inside in a crouch and let the heavy hide flap close behind her. Everyone looked up.

"What are you doing here—" one of them hissed, but she pointed at the sweating, wheezing man lying on the bedroll before them all.

"There's something inside him," she said. "I don't know what it is, but I know it's killing him." She did. The spectral vision she had been granted was telling her so, guiding her, and she could follow. She knew she could.

Kai reached for her, and she ignored the shocked expressions of the other men in the tent as she moved toward him. She took his hand, sure and unhesitating, and joined him to kneel at his side where he made room for her. "What are you talking about?" he asked in a murmur, voice urgent. "Do you know what's happening to him? Are you seeing something?"

She nodded, eyes roving up and down the dying man's body that lay upon the sweat-drenched bedroll.

"Yes," she said. "I am now."

92

"A nzi—"

"I'll explain after," she said between gritted teeth. "Just give me room."

Easier demanded than given. She doubted anything Kai said to his men would make them back off as she roved her hands over their fallen comrade's form. He was young, perhaps only a little older than she was, and now naked as she had thrown off the animal skin covering so she could inspect the wounds on his flesh. But it wasn't his modesty the tribesmen worried for. Out of the corner of her eye, she could see one of them with his hand hovering by his thigh where he must be carrying a unfriendly blade. Kai's vouching for her didn't mean much, it seemed, and even if he used that strange voice from before that he'd subdued his men with, she knew it would do nothing to change their minds.

But she wasn't here to beg for their approval. They could mistrust her all they wanted. She was still the only one who could do anything about this dying man. Without her, all they could do was watch him die, and that was all they *had* been doing before she barged into the tent and upended their suspicious sensibilities. If they wanted her to save him, they were going to have to learn quick to trust her....even if she wasn't sure she could save him at all.

"What is she doing," one of the other men growled as if she couldn't hear him, and she threw him a glancing glare, all she could afford.

"If you think you can do something to save his life, then feel free," she retorted. "If not, just leave me to it."

"All you're doing is waving your hands around."

Kai shifted beside her, but before he could order his man to hush, she threw him a glower as well until he settled, reluctantly mollified. Good. She didn't need him defending her honor. She could fight her own battles. "At least I'm trying," she said, voice low and hard. "I'm no healer, so I don't know what I'm looking at, but damn you, I'm still trying. So if you all want to keep complaining, do it outside the tent where you won't be distracting me and getting your friend killed."

Kai's hand slid onto her thigh, hiding under her billowing sleeve. She didn't know if it was magic or simply the reassurance of his touch, but immediately the blood pounding in her ears softened ever so slightly, and her pulse slowed, slowed...

"Is there anything I can do to help?" he murmured in her ear. "Just say the word."

"Nothing. I barely know what I'm looking at." Her own words were soft, just quiet enough for him to hear and no one else. Despite her convincing performance of gritty bravado a second ago, a spiraling helplessness whirled inside her now. The trails of murky poison flowing under her hands, the ones under this young man's skin and eating away at the life inside him, she had no idea how to get them out. Whatever they were, they were tearing him apart from the inside, and his wounds were bleeding, so much blood, too much—and they were growing. With every second that passed, what little hope there was for him withered all the more. She clenched her teeth, vision blurring from how hard she was glaring down at the shivering body. It wasn't her physical sight granting her this otherworldly vision. Even with her eyes closed, she would be able to sense the silvery trails rushing through the weakening veins. But what else was she to do? She wished she could simply tear out of this man's body like stubborn vines from the ground. How weak was she that she couldn't fight back against even this? She poured herself into it, giving up all she was—

She started, breath catching, and sat back on her heels to steady herself. That sensation, like a stinging across her skin from head to toe. It had hurt. Badly. But...

"Did his eyes just open?" One of the men whispered from the other end before someone else shushed him, but he was right. He hadn't imagined it, and neither had she. This man was still alive, still fighting, and whatever she had done just now had given him a fighting chance. She leaned forward once more, determination renewed now that she'd finally seen some reward for her efforts, no matter how clumsy. She still had not a sliver of an idea what she was doing, but she closed her eyes, breathed in. She had to find that moment again, that instant in which she'd been both here and there...within herself and without. Like in the vision, when her spirit had been ripped out of her and pulled in every direction like frayed strands of a rope unraveling, falling apart. It had happened just now, again, for a single eyeblink without her even knowing it. Once more, she thought furiously, again, *again.* The world around her shrank until all she could see, hear, feel was the rush of blood in her ears...and in the man's veins. Gurgling. Pounding. The whisper of something opening and closing and opening again, and the thump-thump of a heartbeat. But his was so quiet, so weak. She could hardly hear it. She had to get closer.

Something wrapped around her forearm when she leaned forward even more, her hands pressed flat upon the man's bare chest. Kai? Yes, it was him, trying to hold her steady; he must have thought she was keeling over. But that wasn't it. She had to get closer, closer, closer to that gleaming, dark shadow she could see mingling inside the man as her consciousness chased after it through arteries and veins that were slowly crumbling all around her.

"What is she doing! Stop her!" she heard someone else shout in a panic, but it was too late. Warmth coated her fingertips, slid up to her knuckles, hot and burning and all things awful at once.

"She's killing him, stop her, stop her!"

She didn't know if Kai truly believed the frantic accusations and thought she meant harm, or if he thought she was the one who needed saving. But in the next instant, she felt him yank her back by the shoulder, and her fingers slid out of the dying man's open gash on his abdomen. Coated red with dark streaks, she'd plunged them into his wound in search of the thing just out of reach, just beyond the darkened curve past her senses, because what choice had she had?

"Gods, what is that!"

Someone else's voice this time, but Anzi didn't care to play guessing games as to who was shouting in horror and who was letting out a string of garbled curses. Everyone except Kai was scrambling away from her, and for good reason: in her hands, a slender, worm-like tendril of shimmering silver and black squirmed and twisted, and she nearly lost her grip on it before realizing what was happening. She squeezed, intent on crushing it in her palms, then stopped. Whatever it was, its form was soft, squishy, nauseatingly yielding. If she crushed it, would it splatter everywhere and infect the others? For unknowable reasons, it wasn't able to hurt her other than sting and burn, but if it made contact with someone else—no, she couldn't let that happen. This thing had nearly killed the gasping man before her. She had no doubt it could do the same to the others. It was already hungering for them, reaching.

"Anzi, let go of it!"

"Kai, don't touch it, get away!"

He reached for her, ignoring how she struggled to keep the writhing tendril away from him. He was afraid for her, but he didn't know, didn't understand. She was the only one who could do this. In his fear for her, he would damn himself. If only she could shove him away and get out of this tent, she could do something about this poisonous thing in her hands. Ash, she thought wildly. That old woman would know what to do, she knew everything, right? Wise and old and she knew so much, so she had to have an answer for this. But Ash wasn't here. It was only her, and she was the only one who could keep Kai away from danger. She wriggled back when he bore her down to the ground and tried to wrestle the silvery-black worm from her grip, and if she didn't get up on her feet, he would restrain her and grab the poison because of his damned superior reach.

She exploded to her feet in one desperate leap, sending the entire tent toppling and sprawling off to the side when her head hit the heavy cloth. She heard the tent pins tear out of the sand and land with heavy thumps somewhere else, but she was already gone.

"Anzi, stop!"

She did, but only when she was sure she was out of range. He might be stronger, but she was quicker. Far quicker. She whirled around, holding up the still-squirming tendril, and he stopped short at the look in her eyes. "Don't come near me," she warned. "This isn't for you to handle."

"Let go of it!"

"And let it infect someone else? I don't think so. Stay back!" No matter how he stared at her, no matter how hot his golden eyes flashed and begged, demanded, commanded her to come toward him, she felt no urge to bend. Instinct told her she needed to keep this silvery tenril away from him, and that was what she was going to do.

"Anzi. Come here."

That voice. It was the one he'd used on his tribesmen just yesterday when they had all gathered around her with threatening glares and weapons at the ready. He'd subdued them with it, that voice laced with magic, power, nature, heat, and they had all subjected themselves to the aura of sheer dominance he'd exuded. It raised the hair on the back of her neck even now. But she shook her head, slowly, dark eyes fixed on his face. In her peripheral vision, she could see his men keeping their distance while others gathered around. Some of them must be thinking she had finally revealed her true colors and was turning on them. Admittedly, things weren't looking good.

"Don't," she said flatly. "Whatever you're trying to do, it doesn't work on me. And in case you haven't noticed, I'm fine." She raised her hand, presenting the writhing worm. It was as long as her forearm, as thick around as two of her fingers. The top of it was more bulbous as if it were a head, but there were no eyes, no mouth, no identifying marks along any part of it. Hell, she didn't even know if it was truly alive. "This isn't all of it. There's more of this in your man. I don't know what it is, but it's killing him, and if you don't let me do what I have to do, he is going to *die*. And if any of you touch this? You'll also die. Look!" She waved the thing around, and everyone but Kai drew back as if struck by some deep primordial dread as they stared at the thing in her hand. "But I can touch it, and I'm not dying. That means something. Kai, you need to let me do what I have to do if you want me to save his life. Make your choice."

No one moved. No one made a sound. He stared and stared, but she held his gaze as steady as ever.

"...Someone go find Nebt-Ash," he said in a low, harsh voice. When no one moved, he barked again in a half-snarl this time. *"Go!"*

Several scrambled away. The rest began to inch backward, and Anzi knew why: the radiant power thickening the air, the savage, animal presence emanating from Kai—oppressive, dominating, compelling.

But not to her. She tilted her head back, challenging him. She could still see him thinking, scheming, but tere was no need for him to be afraid for her. This was the most powerful she had ever felt. She was in control. She had no idea what she was doing but just as firmly knew what she had done was right.

"You can't help him while still holding onto that," said Kai, and he pointed at the wriggling tendril in her grasp. His voice was deceptively smooth now, disarming, as if to try to put her at ease. But didn't he know? Wasn't it he who'd insisted they had an intimate bond? Of course she could read him. She took a step back and gave him a warning look. "Let me help," he insisted, and she heard the first threads of frustration break through and enter his words. "You don't even know what that is."

"Neither do you," she shot back. "You would have said what it is by now if you did."

"All the more reason to stop *touching* it, Anzi!"

"Not until I know how to kill it. Safely. Without spreading more of it around. It's fighting me right now, trying to get to you. I'm not going to let it." But he had a point. The job was unfinished, but she couldn't go back toward that dying man still panting on his bedroll like this. Even now, she could sense there were more poisonous worms inside him, two of them. But what could she do about them when this one was still struggling to possess flesh again?

A hulking movement out of the corner of her eye made her glance around at it. Quick, darting. Taking her eyes off of Kai might give him ideas, and no one wanted that. But when she realized who it was that had joined her, she blinked and turned toward it completely, too surprised.

"…What are you doing here?" she asked aloud as if the dragon could answer. For a dragon it was. The Prince, with his muddy brown, black, and gray hide and drooping, leathery wings dragging along in the sand. He was coming toward her, looking straight at her.

No. Wait. He wasn't looking at her. He was looking at her hand, at the worm. And with each dragging claw that scraped across the sand, she noticed the tendril writhing less and less in her grip, weakening…softening, until it felt like but a dead, soggy stretch of seaweed. And when she looked down at it, that was almost exactly what it resembled. A limp, black-tinged translucent thing, no longer shimmering silver, no longer alive.

The Prince came to a stop a meter away and watched her expectantly. In the silence, Anzi's mind whirled, working furiously to deduce what was happening. But it was clear as day even if she didn't understand the reason behind it. This dragon, this mute, mutant, misshapen dragon with no name, was able to deaden the poison tendril with his mere presence.

"I think we have a solution," she said crisply as she turned back to Kai. "Now I just need you to get out of the way."

93

She could sense the mistrustful glares fixed upon her as she hurried back to the bedroll where the young man had begun gasping for breath, a good sign no matter his pain because any breathing was better than none. That was fine with her. They could question her all they liked from a distance. She expected nothing from them anyway, just the space to do what she needed to do.

The Prince lumbered to her side and sat on his haunches like some kind of frilled, giant mastiff, ready to do whatever it was he'd done before to kill that poison tendril. But this was no good. The sun glared off the sand, rays baking the man's wounds, and his nakedness was going to kill him in this direct heat. She kneeled by his side and looked frantically around, rolling up her billowing sleeves once more. "Kai! He needs shade. The hotter he is, the harder it is for me to find the poison in him."

She had thought he would bark out an order for someone to help him erect the fallen tent again, but instead he stalked toward her, barefooted and radiating an animal determination that made her tense. Was he still going to try to stop her? Even after what he'd seen? Forget her, they could save a dying man right now if he would just let her take this one chance—

"Everyone else stay back," he snapped, and before the last word left his lips, something large and dark erupted out from behind him. It unfurled like a sail, wide and massive and utterly opaque, even the thinner unscaled membranes that made up the bulk of the single wing.

Wing, Anzi marveled. She swallowed hard when Kai crossed the last stride of the distance between them with his left wing outstretched. Enormous. From behind his shoulder to the very tip of the wing, it was easily two meters, and she suspected it would span even wider if he were wholly transformed. She had yet to see him in his dragon form. What would he look like?

"Are you sure you should be doing that?" she asked in a low voice when he kneeled next to her, his unfurled, curved wing providing a wide shadow for both her and his fallen comrade. "What about the basilisk poison. It's still in you, isn't it?"

"I can do this much. But whatever you're doing, do it quickly." He leaned in, and for an instant, she thought he was going to kiss her. But he only hovered there, breathing warmly against her face. "I shouldn't be letting you do this," he said quietly. "This is too risky."

"If we have a chance to save him, we have to take it. He's your comrade. He fought by your side."

"I know." Something hard and painful came over his golden eyes, flashing bright. "His older brothers were the ones who held Tet off while I escaped. When I failed. Now he's the only one, and I promised them I'd protect him."

The two dragons who had crashed in and attacked the balcony. Them? They had both died? Anzi bit the inside of her cheek, fighting to keep the questions down. This just made it all the more dire, the feverish need to save Kai's subordinate. He hadn't been able to save his fallen tribesmen. She couldn't make him mourn yet another one.

"Move farther back," she warned him. "You're just as vulnerable as everyone else."

"I'm staying here. You need my shade."

"Kai, please. As far back as you can."

But he refused to move from her side, and time was running out. The few minutes she'd bought for the dying young man were going to go waste if she didn't act now. With a frustrated growl, she gave up and let Kai be. She would just have to be careful enough for the both of them. But it was different doing this in the daylight, even shaded under Kai's wing, because this time, she could feel everyone's eyes on her. Exposed, vulnerable. She didn't like letting everyone see her struggle, didn't want them to see her in her incompetence and breaking out in a cold sweat in the middle of steaming desert heat. She wished more than ever that she hadn't sent the tent flying, that she could do this alone, hidden. Because if she failed—

"So you can't kill those things while they're still inside him," she murmured, speaking to the Prince who had put his blunt snout by her elbow. She flexed her fingers and willed her other-vision to return, squinting. "Kai, what's his name? And how exactly did he get hurt? These wounds don't look like they're from a fight."

"Masal. He was with the wing attacking the Tower that night, but he had no injuries except for a few flesh wounds when he shifted back to human form. It was when we were carrying out the final rites yesterday and this morning for his eldest brother, then for his other brother. Sometime between then, he started acting strange. I thought it was grief…"

"It's not your fault. You couldn't have known. Tet might have done this to his brothers, then it infected Masal when he was with them after everyone got here. I'm assuming he spent time with their bodies alone, or might have even been with them when they passed?" He nodded at that, and she nodded back. With one last quick look at her other side where the Prince continued to sit motionless, she got to work.

Whatever it was that the dragon had done to kill the living poison a moment ago, he wasn't doing it now. Or couldn't, she guessed, until she did her part first. Intuition urged her on, and she found the open gash once more with steady fingers. It was an unpleasant sensation and no doubt even worse for others to watch, but with a sharp huff, she planted her fingertips into the wound, deep, and savagely called forth the poison coursing through Masal's body.

It made no sense. Even if she could explain away how she was able to sense it at all, she shouldn't be able to make it respond. That was what rational sense told her, anyway. But it was happening, and she was grateful. This strange new ability she had unearthed was the only reason Masal would live to see tomorrow. And she had to make that happen, no matter what. Had to. His brothers had died in the assault and given their lives for a cause butchered and botched while Kai had to bear the weight of the failure on his shoulders alone. That was the burden of a leader, wasn't it? Comrades lost, lives torn away, and he had shown so little weakness that it was easy for Anzi to forget he must be in such pain. He shouldn't have to bear that alone. She could have done things differently. There had to have been some other way, she just hadn't looked hard enough, hadn't been smart enough, hadn't been diligent enough…

"I have them," she muttered through clenched teeth. She could feel them squirming out of the wound, the ropes of living poison that tried to fight her every inch of the way. But she wouldn't lose to this. With a growl, she yanked the thread-thin trails of silver and black out of Masal's chest and watched as they thickened and lengthened as soon as they touched air. But they faded to black just as quickly before falling limp in her grasp.

The Prince. Again, he had done the same thing, killed the malevolent...whatever they were as easily as if he'd born to do it. She stared at him, ignoring Kai's repeated tugs on her wrist. "How are you doing that?" she asked aloud. She had to, because she couldn't communicate through her mind with this dragon the way she could with Netra. And until now, she had assumed it was because this one was still a hatchling, far too young, but that wasn't it, was it? Because it wasn't an infant's mind she sensed past the dark fog inside the Prince's head, but a walled mind, murky and unresponsive, caked in centuries' worth of dust and grime. No name, just like Shu-Amunet before they had named her themselves, no emotions, nothing.

She didn't fear him, this hatchling born too late, but she did fear what it meant. For him. For her. Maybe—for everyone.

"It's done." Her knees scraped against the sand as she turned toward Kai with narrowed eyes and fists still clenched around the lifeless tendrils. "Masal's going to make it if your people can take care of those wounds. But I need you to gather everyone else here so I can check if the poison's infected anyone else. And there's one more thing."

Kai's larger hand enveloped hers, warmer than the desert heat. "What is it?"

"Bisset's on his way here. I'm sure of it now."

94

F ive. There were five others who had been infected out of the roughly dozen and a half who made up Kai's warrior troupe, and of them, only one had begun to show signs of the living poison that had burrowed into their veins. It was a grueling three hours of inspection and labor, far more difficult than it had been with Masal because these slivers were so much smaller and that much harder to see. Anzi had checked and rechecked every man, woman, and beast in the camp and Oza, too, fueled by growing paranoia and fear whenever she found the damnable silver threads hiding in their bodies. But what made it truly difficult was the exhaustion that set in. Not only when she extracted the poison through fresh, deep incisions she had been forced to make because there was no other way to draw it out, but even the expansion of her very senses to search for it in the first place.

This unknown, unfamiliar power she had discovered had come with a price. It came from within her, an instinctive ability, but it was clumsy and heavy and cost her throbbing headaches while dulling her other senses. Twice, Kai tried to order her to stop, the first when she had to kneel and bow her head when the vertigo threatened to topple her, and the second when she staggered out of Kai's tent to retch empty sounds for several minutes. A good thing she hadn't eaten. Besides, it was a good teaching moment for Kai, she thought to herself with a mixture of fatigue and satisfaction. He had been a leader too long, surrounded only by those who answered to him. But Anzi wasn't one of them. She knew what she had to do, and whether he liked it or not, she was going to do it.

"You're exhausted. You should have listened to me." He kneeled in front of her now, wielding a wet cloth he had just dipped into the large bowl by their side. Qinglong had dropped by after the last man was helped out by his comrades a few minutes ago, carrying the bowl full of water in her hands. She had said nothing and simply left after placing it on the sand next to Anzi.

"You don't understand," she mumbled, eyes closed and hand pressed against her forehead. This headache was blinding. She had never been prone to pains and discomforts in her life so she had little to compare it to, but she was certain this had to be the lord of all headaches ever to exist. Even the muffled light that shone through the tent fabric made her eyes throb behind their lids, and every little sound clawed the inside of her head like talons scraping tree bark. "We can't stop and dawdle. There's no time, Kai. And I'm not just talking about how fast that poison spreads and grows. Our problems are only starting."

She cracked open one eye against her better judgment, but only to make sure the Prince was still huddling where he had retreated to the corner of the tent. He betrayed no exhaution, no emotion, ever. Even Serqet could display stubborn aggression whenever Netra bullied her too much, but from him, nothing. Only his gentle dragon presence.

"You said Bisset was on his way here earlier." Kai wiped her brow again, leaving a damp trail over her forehead. She didn't have the heart to tell him it did no good; the water Qinglong summoned was lukewarm at best and did nothing to cool her. "Anzi?"

"Sorry. Head hurts." She squeezed her eyes shut and tried to will away the ache behind them with nothing but fierce determination. She failed. "Yes, Bisset's coming. I know I can't prove it, and Ash thinks I'm wrong, but it was real. You have to know—I talked to Tet. He was there. He was right in front of me."

"What? What do you mean?" His voice roughened, and a strong hand clamped down on her shoulder, forcing her to turn to face him squarely. "Explain."

She did. She knew she sounded crazy as she talked about visions and other-sight and how she had been inside what Ash had called the after-image of Tet, and she knew the grand and harrowing way she tried to describe it all was falling flat on both their ears. Damn it, she had never been an orator, a speech-giver. All she had were plain words and passion, rushed and tumbling words.

"Listen," she insisted. "I know she's wiser than I am and knows so much more than I do, but she wasn't there. She wasn't there, Kai. I won't believe in protection from the gods and ignore the signs. That's her way, not mine. I have to do something."

"You said you can sense dragons now. And wyrms."

"I think so. Including your tribesmen. Or—maybe not the wyrms, I haven't sensed any since I left the Oasis. Could be I imagined it."

"I thought you—?"

"In the vision, I could. But we're in deep desert, and I can't sense anything except the dragons and your warriors. I find it hard to believe there's not a single wyrm hiding somewhere in range. I might not be able to sense them for some reason in the real world, only in the vision. I won't assume anything until I know for certain."

"All right, not wyrms, then. Just the dragons and us, the shifters." He cradled the side of her jaw in his palm with a contemplative frown. "Would you be able to sense them crossing the desert? If Tet sends his slavers here."

Slavers. The word was jarring to hear, but it was true even if she'd spent her whole life thinking of the Premier as dragon riders. The name was too noble for them, for what they really did. Slavers, she repeated silently. "I don't think I could sense them from that far off. Not until it's too late to get away. I don't know since I have no idea how far it reaches, only that I can't feel anything beyond the edge of it all…"

"That's all right. You're doing unbelievable things I never could have imagined." He curled his fingertips along the side of her face and traced his thumb over her cheek. "I never knew things would be like this."

"I always try to prepare for the worst," she began to mutter, but he shook his head.

"No. I meant I have you now. Right here. I always dreamed of taking you away from it all even though I knew you'd never come willingly, but here you are."

"It took me too long to figure out the truth."

"It's not just that." He leaned in and hovered close, barely a finger's width away, and despite all her lifelong training in self-restraint and iron control, she found her gaze sliding down to rest on his mouth. It was very close. Very. "You wanted to stay there when you still had faith in them, so you could protect your king. And then when you learned the truth, you wanted to stay to protect the ones who couldn't protect themselves. I thought it was futile. I even started to think you were sure to die, that it might happen right in front of me. One mistake, one wrong word...It could have been over."

"I know," she mumbled, still staring at his mouth. "I was careful."

"I would have stayed with you if you hadn't left. After the assault. I was looking for you, I couldn't leave."

Her anger flared briefly, just strong enough that it distracted her from the sight of his moving lips for a second. "And you could have died for it!" she snapped. "You don't even know how long it'll take for you to recover. Basilisk poison, Kai! That's what traders kill the most dangerous wyrms with, if they can even get their hands on some in the first place. Even the low-grade stock could have hurt you—and I don't know anything about dragon shifters and how you all survived the Purge and dark hells, how you can even exist, but I know I had to sit there by your bed while you were *dying* because some old man stuck you with a dagger a couple of times. Dying, Kai! If it had been someone more skilled, if that poison had been in the hands of someone who'd actually known what they were doing and went for your heart or your neck and head, you wouldn't be here."

She had had a lot more stored up. All the buried fear, anger, and frustration from months and months of burdensome weight, she had only barely begun to tap into it, but when Kai pulled her forward in a kiss and dragged her into his lap, the rest of her words were very suddenly out of reach...

"You're not supposed to...'s important...need to talk while we can..." she mumbled against his mouth when they parted at long last. But he was still breathing hotly over her lips, and a wisp of steam curled out from between his before he captured her mouth again. She moaned against him, angry, surprised, and all too thrilled when his hand dragged off of her hip and began working apart the wrap of her dress. It had the misfortune (good fortune?) of being in the Feng-style of attire, which meant there were no pesky accessories to deal with. Just his hand bunching up the green fabric, and here was the other one, pulling on the side of the dress's collar that lay atop the other and formed the deep valley cut...

"I wanted to have you the instant I saw you," he growled as he attacked her jaw next. "But we were in Tet's territory and there was nothing I could do. And now that I have you here, I still do nothing."

This? Clearly, their ideas of *nothing* were completely irreconcilable.

His hand was still trying to slide up from the bottom of the flowing garment, and she was very much still in his lap. And yes, for a moment, for one terrible half of a half-moment, she wondered if maybe—what if they were quick and...?

But no. No! People were dying. Here. They were dying!

"Your men," she gasped out, finally forcing herself to gather up her wits and push him away. "How many are wounded? How many can fight?"

And just like that, her question deadened the terrible, melting ferocity that he had been radiating so fiercely all of a sudden. He dragged his mouth away from her jaw, let his hands drift back down and rest on her thighs, over her rumpled dress. And most sobering of all, his forehead dropped to rest on her shoulder.

"...Kai?"

"Stay like this," he mumbled. "I know this is all I can have, for now...so stay like this. I won't ask for anything more."

He had been so indomitable a second ago as his hands roved around her body, searching for bare skin and curves and only a heartbeat away from finding them. Hard, hot strength and fire, he had felt larger than life, larger than the reality bearing down on them like a wild storm. But now, so abruptly... With hesitant motions, she reached up bit by bit until her fingers were in his dark hair, and before she could lose her nerve, she tangled them there, watching the black strands curve over her hand as she stroked them, soft and light. At her touch, a low growl rumbled from Kai's throat, and she paused, wondering if she had done something wrong. But it was the opposite: when she stopped, he moved his head against her palm, urging her to continue.

Ah...such vulnerability she had never seen from him. Not like this. She could feel it, through—what was it? The mate bond, perhaps. Echoes of terrible guilt, resignation, helpless fury.

"If there's any chance my family's in danger," he said quietly, "I'll act. So tell me, and don't worry about Ash. We venerate her as our guide and speaker for the gods, but...you're right. I didn't grow up with faith in the gods the way the others did. So I'm listening."

"I..." She reached for the words, but reluctantly now. Before, she had been so eager to convince him of the danger, so determined to make him understand how much peril they were all in, but now...Now, she wished she didn't have to. "It wasn't your fault," she said softly, still running her fingers through his hair over and over. He shifted, and his forehead moved from her shoulder to rest closer against the curve of her neck. "You did the best you could. You're leading your men, and they're following you."

"The attack was a failure. I lost good men, Anzi. I failed. He was right there in front of me, and I failed…I got them killed. And Masal's brothers, I was so certain they could get away, that they could cover my weakness and…"

"Your hand was in his chest. No one could have known Tet would live through that. And if you failed, then so did I." She moved her hand to the back of his neck and let it rest there. "You did the best you could."

"Tell me about Bisset. You said you saw Tet in the vision, that he's sending the colonel here. How many dragons?"

"Your guess is as good as mine. I never met any of the other riders, I only know that every single one in the region was on the way to the Imperial City, and they were supposed to fly in over the course of the week's festivities. But Kai, there's something else."

"Hm?"

"I won't know ahead of time if they're drawing close. Not until they land or otherwise touch earth." She paused, frowning. "Earlier, you sent someone to find Ash. I felt it when he shifted, Kai. I could feel it, his footsteps, when he changed—but when he lifted up into the air, I lost him. So if Bisset and the others are flying straight to this location, then…"

"You won't be able to detect them," he finished.

"I wish I could be more useful. I'm sorry."

"Shh…Don't say that." He stroked her thigh without looking up. "You've been through so much."

"So have you. More than me." She licked her lips, preparing for her next words. She could already guess what he would say, but she had to try anyway. "I'm going to go intercept them. Tet wants me, so I'll go and say I escaped. We'll figure out how to make it look convincing. Once they pick me up, they're sure to return to the Imperial City, which means they won't find you or your men."

"Anzi!" He lifted his head, brow furrowing, mouth twisting into an angry grimace—

"Can half of your men even fight?" she interrupted. "And the ones that can are exhausted. They fought and then had to fly here without rest. It's been a day since they could settle down. Meanwhile, the First Guards who come here will be fresh. It won't be a fight, it'll be a slaughter. This is the only way to—"

"No."

His answer was so flat, so final, so stubborn that she wanted to tear her hair out. Was this what it was like for others when they tried to argue with her? Only Kai's adamant belief she couldn't take care of herself could possibly rival her stubbornness. "There's no other way," she insisted. "No other way that won't end in bloodshed."

"I won't let them have you. Not again."

"I'll find a way to get out of there again. And besides, we need a spy in the city. Someone who can get close. That way, we can try again—"

"No."

Gods. Time was so short, but he was going to sit there and hold her in his lap and refuse to budge. How long would it take to convince him to see reason? No matter how much he cared about her, no matter how much he valued this thing, this mate bond that drew them together across leagues and leagues and even time—she really did have to ask him about that, their very first meeting back when she was but a child—no matter what, she couldn't let him sacrifice his people for her. And he wouldn't. Because if he did, if he was capable of that, he wasn't the man she thought she knew. Wasn't the man she could feel herself falling for faster and faster, inexorably, undeniably, as she stared into his eyes flashing with menacing anger.

"Your man just got back," she said in the silence. "He's on the ground....shifting back to human form now. He must have brought Ash with him from the Oasis."

"Anzi," he growled. "I'm not letting you play decoy to save everyone else. I'm not giving you away again."

She sighed. "Let's just talk to Ash first. We'll figure it out."

er leg ached, badly, even though Anzi had done nothing at all to strain it. Her only labor since morning after leaving Ash's dominion was to perform the crudest half-surgeries known to man on a handful of Kai's warriors, and she had been kneeling for most of that. Her body couldn't be so weak, could it? Or was she imagining it all because of the fatigue and the haunting sensations of feeling warm flesh pull apart under her fingers as she searched for poison no one else could touch? What was this strange new world she had plummeted into with no preparation, no wisdom, nothing at all?

No—she had Kai, who pulled her close and kissed her on the brow before letting her go so she could walk to meet Ash. She had Letti and Oza here in the camp on the other end of it, safe and sound. Netra and Serqet were here too, thank to Kai's tribesmen who had brought them here instead of abandoning them. Had Anzi remembered to thank anyone for that? Maybe she didn't have to since they had made that decision on their own—how could they leave behind their brethren, after all—but she regretted it all the same.

They were all afraid. Not only of her, but of the traces of the Empire she had dragged along behind her, the same Empire that had wiped out their people. And now that she had had some time to think about it, she knew now how the ancestors of these wandering men and woman had survived the Purge: they must have disguised themselves as humans, escaped in the guise of their two-legged forms and disowned their dragon heritage to escape death. How bitter they must be, but more than that, how terrified. They had launched an attack on the Empire in full faith that they could strike at the heart of it and kill the Emperor, kill the man who'd spelled so much death and destruction upon them while enslaving their captive cousins at the same time. And then...they had failed.

Kai hid his weakness from them, his despair. Because he was their leader and had to be strong even when he fell. The rest of them hid theirs, too, because what was a king without his people? They had to hold their heads up just as he did. So how could she blame them mistrusting her? She had served their enemy all her life, and the things she had done were irreversible. She had killed in the name of her king, her Emperor, had worshipped him the same way these people worshipped their own gods. She had been ready to commit herself to a man who had savaged whole peoples to stake his claim on a land that had never belonged to him. Of course they didn't want her here. She was a reminder of everything they had tried to fight against—and lost.

But it wasn't over yet. Because now, she was going to fight, too.

"Ash," she said, and her voice was steady and hard as she fixed her gaze on the old woman's face. She was back to her wizened appearance now, no longer the youthful thing she'd transformed into upon entering the spring at the heart of her oasis, and her clothes were still damp. It gave her a curiously mundane air.

"I needed to rest, little one. But Kaizat sent one of his men to come fetch me. I can only guess that was your fault." She reached up to press her fingertip against Anzi's nose, mouth curved in a wide smile.

This was no time for playfulness. Anzi steeled herself. "I need help putting together a plan to divert Bisset when he gets here. And because I know you'll say it was all in my head and I'm being ridiculous, I've already told Kai. And he's not willing to take the same chances you are."

"...Anzi, you're so very young."

"Young. Stupid. Stubborn. I don't care what you call me. And I see you. You feel sorry for me because you think I'm chasing my tail like a dog, too blinded by what I think I know."

"If you see that, then you should take my advice and—"

"You might think you know, but how can you be sure? I saw him, Ash. He spoke to me. It was him, I felt it."

The old woman sighed. "So now you abandon the people you've found because you can't help but be drawn back to the life you left behind."

"That's not it. At all."

"My magic doesn't transport the spirit, Anzi." She squinted and stood with her arms akimbo, mouth turned down in a frown. "It never has. It grows what is dormant, brings life to what's barren. The things you saw are signs and portents about you, and your destiny. If you saw Tet in your vision, he meant something deeper than you know."

"Spare me. If I'm wrong about this, I'll come back with my tail tucked between my legs. What harm is it for me to be careful. And maybe I'll come back after finding it was all in my imagination. But do you think I want this? Do you think I want to abandon everyone, including my brother and the only friend I ever made in the Imperial City?"

Ash smiled with her eyes. "Only friend you ever made? Hm."

She bristled. "This is not the time. Your teasing about Kai and me isn't welcome right now."

"Or ever. An old crone like me gets so bored sometimes."

This was why she couldn't stand the woman. And fine, Anzi knew there was a possibility Ash was right, because who could know her magic better than she did? But something told her it wasn't so. She had to act. She had to.

"There's something else you should know," Ash said suddenly, and her smile was gone, replaced by a somber expression. "You could never have made contact with Tet's spirit because he can't touch your mind that way. I can, because Druids have always been near one another in the spirit. So can little Kaizat because, my dear one, he is your mate. And the dragons have always been able to speak this way."

"And Tet learned how, too, then. He's had plenty of time to learn."

"Foolish girl. It's not possible for him. You can do this because you are the Druid of all dragons. Those ones back there despise you, but they can't deny you're special. They can feel it. It's why they're so afraid of you, because they can feel the power you wield…over them. Haven't you seen the signs?"

Yes. The way she could hatch dragon eggs so effortlessly where hundreds of others must have tried and failed. The way she had been able to know Netra's and Serqet's true names scarcely before they were even self-aware enough to do anything but screech and cry. And there were other fleeting things, like the time she had touched Sa-Khente back in the Imperial Palace's courtyard and, just for a moment, melded minds with him. She had forgotten about that until now, but Ash's gentle reminder brought so many scattered pieces of selectively forgotten memories back.

Memories that had been too confusing to confront at the time, so Anzi had shoved them all away and chosen to keep her life neat, simple. But she couldn't do that anymore.

"The abomination was never a Druid, dear one," Ash continued. "It was why he became so greedy. He was already old when I was young, and he was full of bitterness and envy. That's why he is the way he is. Because he will never be like us, touched by the gods in the truest of ways, even though he had the favor of the Dragon King for a time. He simply wasn't worthy."

Gods, worthiness, Druids—all this superstitious magic talk boiled down to one thing for Anzi: Ash could provide no proof that everyone would be safe if she did nothing. And she wouldn't take that chance.

"You can make fun of me for being paranoid if I was wrong all along," she said crisply. "But I'm leaving. I'm going to go in a straight line toward the direction of the Imperial City and intercept Bisset before he can get here, because if he reaches us, it'll be a massacre. Everyone here's either wounded, exhausted, or both, and the few who can fight will get trampled because there's no way in darkest hell that the colonel will come without a horde. A fast moving one. Likely an entire band of First Guards because he wouldn't leave this to chance."

"Hm…Kaizat will die before he lets you go."

"…That's why I need your help. I need you to convince him since he won't listen to me. It's obvious he respects your wisdom, so if you say—"

"The mate bond doesn't bow to wisdom, Anzi. Except yours, it seems. I've never seen someone so cold to the draw. You're a true Druid, through and through, able to withstand even such temptation."

"…Thank you?"

"Ha. Kaizat curses the gods every day for your clear mind."

"Good to know. So will you help me or not?"

"Ah…but how could I convince him? What is it I can tell him to change his mind when you could not?" Ash leaned over to peek around Anzi's shoulder at Kai who stood far back, though he continued to stare at them as if he wanted nothing more than to stalk up and pull Anzi away to keep for himself. "Look at him. Truly a wretch. It's fortunate you were never born a tease, too, on top of everything else. He would go mad."

"Enough of that. Please. Ash."

"So boring, you are. Go on, tell me your grand plan, then."

Her heart pounded. "I can't let Kai or any of his people fall into Tet's hands. The poison…it would have killed them. The only reason I was able to do anything now was because you happened to get here in time this morning to…do whatever it was you did to me. But it took everything I had, and if it happens again, I don't know if I can save them all."

"What are you talking about? What poison? Speak, Anzi."

She did. In a rush and in an undertone, she explained what had happened in the half-day that had passed since they parted ways, and when she finished, Ash's face was contorted in an ugly grimace.

"That abomination," she said between her teeth. "An insult to all things natural and good. I don't know what curse it was that birthed whatever you found in their bodies, but it must be some forbidden magic he's unearthed. Old rites, ones that are lost to us."

"So you don't know a countermeasure."

"No. No, I do not."

"And I'm the only one who can do anything about it. You see? Ash, I can't let Kai come with me. Or any of his men. I have to return to the Imperial City…"

"Aha. So you do want to go back."

"Stop it, Ash. There's no one else who can do what I can. The tribe failed and got away, but next time, it'll be a true massacre. They only got as far as they did because the Empire never expected the ambush, but Tet will be ready now. Kai knows it too."

"Hmph. So, what do you think it is that I can do? Because there's nothing I can say to him that will make him change his mind. He'll want to stay with you no matter what."

"I know. So I need you to lie to him."

Ash's eyebrows went up. "What's that?"

Her stomach twisted, and she hesitated before continuing. "Tell him you're taking me somewhere. Pretend this conversation we're having now is about you convincing me I was wrong. But I won't listen, and you want to—I don't know. What is it that people do? Take pilgrimages? Tell him you're taking me on some spiritual journey or whatever it takes to convince him to let us go alone."

"Ah, you sly thing. Kaizat would never forgive me. You want me to go with you as a guarantee of your return so he won't follow you, but you'll send me off while you go ahead."

"It's the only way. He won't trust anyone else. And you're the only one who might be willing to do this for me."

"He'll never forgive me," Ash repeated. "That trust will be gone. And I already know it'll be for nothing."

"It's not nothing. What I saw was real, not some mystical vision."

"The older Druids, back when we were many, told me about him. When he came to them to seek wisdom after failing to obtain what he wanted so badly, the favor of the gods, they took pity on him. But he was a hopeless case. He may have used dark magics to gain power, but he will never be one of us. The connection we Druids have to one another, he will never have it."

Enough. She wasn't going to do this again. She'd said her share and that was that. "A day's travel in one direction," she said forcefully, although she kept her voice low so Kai couldn't hear her. "That's all I ask. If it's a false alarm, I'll come find you again and we'll go back together, and he'll be none the wiser for it."

"And if you're right? You'll be leaving him here. You'll hurt him more than he can bear."

"He'll have to bear it." She swallowed. "He's stronger than I am. I'm weak, Ash. I can't let him come with me. I've already had to sit at his side and be afraid of losing him once. I can't do it again. I have to do this alone."

"Poor girl. You'll admit the truth to me, but not him?"

She set her mouth in a hard grimace. "Will you do it or not?"

"You are so stubborn, girl. All right. We will leave before dawn. But only because I know we'll be returning together anyhow. You'll understand soon enough that I speak the truth, and that you fear for nothing."

"Then all the better. I'll celebrate if you were right all along."

The old woman rolled her eyes and waved her away. "I'll speak to him now. Don't forget—you ask me to deceive someone who has only the utmost faith in me. You ask me to use it against him, and cut him deeper than any blade."

"Only if I'm right about everything, otherwise he'll never even find out. But you're not worried, are you? You think I'm wrong anyway."

"It's your heart and mind I worry for. But go. I will speak to him."

nzi didn't want to know how Ash had managed to convince him. All she knew was that Kai was in a towering mood, terrible and brooding, and she could feel it from across the camp. It was fainter here in Qinglong's tent that had somehow become extremely crowded within the last day—Oza and Letti as well as all three of her dragons along with Rania, too—but she could sense Kai's anger nonetheless. Something had changed between them without her even noticing, something beyond simple attraction and other mundane feelings. Maybe it had been back when he first kissed her on the bridge, or maybe it had been that day when she had sat by him, watching the healers labor to save his life before the basilisk poison could kill him. Or maybe it had been during the flight here, when she had first tasted real freedom away from the shadow of the Empire.

But things were different now, and the part of her that used to be afraid of defining those very changes—wasn't so afraid anymore. Whatever the strange magic behind it all, whatever freak incident had caused her to become this way, she couldn't deny the truth that had waited so patiently for her to realize it. Kai was hers. And she was his. They were mates, as surely as she could feel his presence tickling at the edge of her mind, and this awareness, this connection they had came from something other than her newfound ability to sense dragonkind. It was a shame she had realized it so late, just hours before she needed to leave, but there had been so few chances to truly understand it. Yes, she wanted to be with him, wanted to stay—but she was the only one who could do what had to be done. How bitter it was to lose him like this, and for who knew how long? When would she see him again after she vanished tonight?

What a powerful thing the mate bond was that it could make her miss his presence, his warmth, the rumble of his voice in her ear before she had even left. What a compelling, all-powerful, terrifying force to make her feel so unlike herself, so out of control, so irrational. And worse, it made her regretful—all she could think about now was how there was no more time. She hardly knew Kai, nothing more than his name, and she had only just learned he was a dragon shifter. Hell, she had only just learned such a thing even existed. And they were supposed to be mates...

"Oza, what's that?" She kneeled next to him as he pored over half a dozen scrolls laid out in a confusing array around him. And an open book, too, the same one Anzi had marveled at before. Qing was watching him with a small smile from the corner, looking pleased with herself and with him, too, as she nodded at something Anzi didn't understand. "Are you trying to teach him things from your country?" she asked, then quickly added, "That's good. He likes learning. I'm glad you're getting along." Truly, she had no issue with her brother learning Feng philosophies and whatever else they were bonding over. He had always been a gifted scholar mage through and through. She hadn't known he knew how to read Feng script, though...That was new.

"Teach him?" Qing repeated, and she chuckled, sending a soft and pleasant sound trickling around the tent. "No. I'm the one learning from him."

Anzi blinked, then stared down at Oza until he looked up at her, but all he did was shrug and turn his attention back to the scrolls again. "What do you mean, learning from him?"

"He's memorizing everything. And translating. I only had the two clean sheets with me that he already interpreted the old words on, but I intend to find more shortly when we return to civilization. What's written on there is ancient script, copied meticulously by scribes far more skilled than I. But I go nowhere without them. Family treasures. It just so happened that young Oza was able to read and understand them, which I can't fathom because knowledge of this script is impossible."

It was the most the Feng woman had ever said at once. Whatever all these writings and various drawings meant, it was important to her. Anzi narrowed her eyes and tried to make sense of them again, but she was only passably literate even in her native tongue...Imperial Army training had never encouraged education beyond what was necessary on the battlefield, especially for someone like her. She was most useful with a blade in her hands, not quills.

"Oza? They taught you Feng script at the Tower?"

"You misunderstand," Qing interrupted, and the woman leaned back with her legs crossed under her, looking supremely contented and smug. "That isn't Feng script, even if it was transcribed by my people. It's older than all of us."

Older than the Feng nations? But they were the oldest civilization in all the known land, fractured though they might be. "So whose nation, then?"

"None. When I called them the old words, I meant it. There's no name for this language, so we only call it the old tongue when spoken, and the old words when written. It can't be learned, only known, innately. Your brother is a very special young man."

Anzi blinked again, utterly confused. A language that couldn't be learned? And one he hadn't learned at the Tower, either, as part of his mage education. So how? Well, either way, it was the happiest she'd seen him in...ever. He wasn't smiling, but the way he worked furiously as he went from scroll to scroll, reading the vertical script so quickly she couldn't understand how he could possibly be processing anything he looked at—he was enjoying himself, truly. Oza had always been a genius, the brightest among generations. He had always been special.

But a niggling sense tickled at her. This. All of this. Did it have something to do with why Tet had wanted to hold onto him so badly? It was just the kind of mysterious and eerie thing she could imagine he knew about. After all, even though it gave her goosebumps and she had been avoiding thinking about it, Tet had known, too, about the wyrms. How? How did Tet know these things? Just like Ash—what was it about Anzi that made it so these people understood more about her than she did herself? She clenched her fists in her lap as Oza's eyes darted from scroll to open scroll spread out over the thin woolen blanket protecting them from the sand underneath. Whatever the reason for his knowledge of things that should be beyond him, she wouldn't let him fall into the hands of the Empire again. He was only a little older than when she had gone into Service, and he had already been in servitude for eight years now. She wouldn't let them have a single one more. He would not end up like she did.

"I have to go," she said, making sure to keep her voice casual and light. She was supposed to only be gone for a few days at most, and the only one who could know the truth was Ash. Maybe Oza would hate her for abandoning him again like she'd already done, like she'd already regretted, but he didn't have to forgive her. If it meant she could spare him, she would accept his anger forever, again and again and again.

He looked at her again, but she could see that more than half his mind was still working furiously on this new work he had found. The look in his dark eyes was exasperated, not worried, and she nodded at him with a half-smile.

"I'm not just annoying you," she told him. "I'm telling you to be careful and take care of yourself since I'll have to be gone for a little while. Longer this time. You shouldn't expect me to come back for at least a few days." He frowned this time, and his irritated expression quickly changed to a questioning one. "It's all right. But you need to keep an eye on Letti—"

"What? Huh? What's happened?"

"Go back to sleep, Letti."

"Ohh…this heat is terrible for me, I can barely keep my eyes open."

"You don't have to. I'm not leaving until a little before sunrise since I need to rest before I go—"

"You're going somewhere again? Where?"

She sighed. "Just sleep. We can talk when you're awake."

Even though she didn't know if that was going to happen at all. She almost hoped the former harem girl would sleep straight through the evening, night, and the morning. It was even harder to deceive her than Oza after knowing everything Letti had been through, and especially for her sake. But Anzi would punish herself in due time. Right now, she had to ensure everyone else's safety even if it meant they would be angry with her. Even if it meant Kai's tribesmen would think she was truly a traitor or whatever else they might think when they discovered she wasn't coming back.

She hoped she was wrong. She hoped it really was all in her head and that the vision of Tet had been the result of paranoia and fear and nothing else. But that wasn't a chance she could take, ignoring the danger no one else could see. Kai most of all. He had already courted death and was still recovering, but if she gave in to her most secret, wistful wishes and confessed the truth to him, he would choose to come with her to intercept Tet's men. And if they found Kai again, he was dead. He couldn't fight in his condition. He could hardly even shift. So it had to be her. It had to be Anzi, and Anzi alone.

"I'll be back later," she said softly as she watched Oza hard at work. Letti's soft, sleeping breaths filtered through the tent again as Anzi got to her feet, and Qing sent her a half-smile just as she turned to leave. She hoped this wasn't goodbye. She hoped she could slip back into the tent before sunrise and find her brother and her closest friend waiting for her. She almost wished they had suspected something, wished she could have one last farewell. Greedy. Selfish, for wishing for a second that someone would realize the truth and stop her. She should be relieved they knew nothing, not feeling slowly crushed under the weight of it...

"Anzi."

She sucked in a sharp breath when she realized where she was. Kai's tent? When had she gotten here? And how long had she been sitting here in silence while waiting for him to return? She stared up at him as he hovered under the raised tent flap, his golden eyes gleaming in the darkness that had settled over the desert and around them both.

She opened her mouth, but there were no words in her throat, on her tongue, or even in her mind. She could only hold his gaze, frozen in the realization that if she was right, this was the last time she would see him in who knew how long? How many days apart would they be, how many months? Years? Surely Tet wouldn't let her slip out of his grasp again so easily. It would be so hard to get away long enough to find Kai again no matter how hot this mate bond burned inside her, flaring like a starburst in the night sky. But they could speak through dreams. That would be all right and no one would know, no one would stop her. And he would be angry at first that she had lied to him and left him behind, but he would forgive her...

She was a warrior. Things like this that left no mark, hurts that couldn't bruise the flesh, she should be strong enough to withstand them. But it couldn't be wrong to regret how little time she had left, how much time had slipped by, and to miss his touch before she'd even left.

The heavy flap closed behind him as he slipped inside, just a silhouette now with gleaming eyes she couldn't look away from. She still had yet to say anything, and even when he lowered himself to lean over her and press her down upon the woolen blanket spread out inside the tent, the words wouldn't come. But he was warm and strong and heavy against her as he kissed her neck and slipped his hand inside the open wrap of her dress, so maybe they didn't need words after all. She moaned when his hand found her breast, and she pressed the side of her head against his as he continued to attack her shoulder, her jaw, all warm tongue and lips against her bare skin. She didn't spare a thought for anyone else whose tent might be too close to hear, and it seemed Kai didn't care either. He didn't have his golden collar, the new one he'd begun wearing after losing the first one, and she was suddenly glad for it since it meant he didn't have to stop to throw it off. Her hands slid up his chest and wandered over his shoulders until they laced together behind his neck, and by then his mouth was on her breasts, then her belly, then below—

She could have cried. She wanted to, felt like she should. What a deception she was leading, giving in to the mate bond she hadn't even truly been certain about until now only because she couldn't bear to hesitate any longer. Because she couldn't bear to lose him, and only be able to see him again after tonight in her dreams from far, far away. There was no more time. The sun would rise in a few hours, and she was supposed to be resting, but as Kai's teeth scraped their way up her chest and to the side of her neck, she was shaking and wanting, needing, panting aloud as he moved up between her bare legs and held steady—

"I'll be with you to the end of my days," he rasped in her ear. "You're all I need."

And for now, she could believe it. She could forget about his people who waited out there for him to lead them now and forever, for everyone else who had known him and loved him far longer than she had. She barely even knew her own feelings, these stunted holdovers from a repressed adolescence where she had never been permitted to feel anything like this before. But what she did know was that this felt so right even if it had been out of desperation, rushed and heady and panicked, and she cried out when he entered her at long last in one savage, wild thrust. All animal, all need, no words or rational thought—

He held on, fanged teeth breaking the skin as she felt his primal energy take over and thrum under his skin like melted lightning coursing through his veins. She could feel parts of his body twitching, shifting between dragon and man, like the half-wing that shot out of his shoulder blade when he groaned over her, or the scales that rose under her palms when she hung on, crying out every time their bodies collided. His teeth grew ever sharper, dragging all over her in a way she knew would leave marks for a long, long time, until—

"Ah!" She thrashed under him, eyes rolling back and her entire body shaking under his weight. She knew nothing else other than this intoxicating heat, the feel of his large, strong hands on her, the ripple of muscle and sinew under hers, the way he completed her so thoroughly as he snarled over her mouth in a groaning kiss.

"You're mine," she thought she heard him say somewhere beyond the haze, and then his teeth found some tender spot between her neck and shoulder as his movements became even more ferocious, utterly untamed. "You're mine—"

She came again, and this time, so did he. And maybe she had done something terrible to him tonight by snatching this one last gift, this one final moment before slipping away again, but she needed so much strength that she didn't have. And maybe, maybe that needed strength would come from the searing tidal wave of power that rushed through her entire body as they climaxed together, the way she could now feel his presence under every inch of her skin the same way she knew he could feel her, and maybe she could hold this feeling close to her chest even after she took one last look at his sleeping form and crept away in the night...

97

"You're running away. I never thought you could be so timid."

"It's not about being timid. I knew he would try to stop me. Doesn't matter what you told him, he would have changed his mind in the end and gotten in my way."

"Oho, what a chill I feel in the middle of all this heat. Tell me, how do you think he will feel when he wakes up to see you gone?"

"Don't try to guilt me." Anzi straightened her uniform. It was in tatters, missing a forearm bracer, a shoulder guard, waist split, half of one pant leg missing. That night in the Imperial City had torn a hole or burst seams in just about everything, especially after the fight with Doufan and the collapse of the dungeon. Even the flight in Shu-Amunet's massive claws had done their share of damage. But all the better. It would make her story of forced kidnapping more plausible.

"No guilt, then," Ash snickered. "But some regret? You must be wishing you could stay a little longer now that you've had a taste."

"Excuse you?"

"My, you seemed to be having great fun with little Kaizat, weren't you? Shameless. I brought him up like my own child and can't help but disapprove. For his people, to fulfill the mate bond must be preceded by ceremony, ritual. But there you went and tempted him to misbehave! He must be planning already for a true marriage once you return. You should be prepared, he won't be satisfied with less."

"Assuming we make it back." The words slipped out with a wistful tone she hadn't meant to betray. Damn it. She gestured across the sands in the direction of the Imperial City—she had checked earlier in the day and compare their course to the sun's path. That way. "And now's not the time for talk of marriage. Are you crazy? I barely even know him."

"Ho-ha, you hesitated."

"Would you stop."

"Should have stopped yourself if you're so uncertain." Ash wagged a finger at her. "You've begun fulfilling the bond. It's too late to stop now."

"Great. Then I'll figure it out if we get back, how about that?"

She didn't know if she could stand this. As soon as she had traveled half a day's worth in the right direction, she would send Ash off. It would have been better to wait an entire day so she could keep an eye on the troublemaking old woman and make sure she didn't go back on her word to warn Kai what was really happening, but at this rate, she was going to end up fighting Ash herself if she didn't stop poking her about her personal affairs. They had nothing to do with anyone else insofar as the mate bond was concerned...Her face burned as she recalled the Druid's gleeful teasing. Who else knew about last night? She had been trying to be quiet, but she had no recollection of how loud she might have been. And certainly Kai hadn't cared about quieting himself either.

Her chest tightened, and she clenched her fists at her sides. Just remembering his touch made her crave him even more, and a bleak, dark desolation opened up inside her at the thought that every step only took her farther away from him. And despite what everyone else thought—Anzi was certain of it: she wouldn't be seeing him again for a long time. She knew what she had seen, knew what was coming. But at least he would be safe. And as for hesrelf, if for no other reason but to see them all again, everyone she loved, everyone she couldn't bear to lose, she would survive, and she would find them once more. She swore it.

"This is getting to be too much. Come, Anzi. No more walking."

"It hasn't even been an hour." She stopped and turned to see that Ash had planted herself in place with her hands on her hips. There was a scowl on her wrinkled face, and even her headdress was tilted at what seemed like an angry angle if that was possible. "Ash, if you want to leave me now, go ahead. I just want you to swear on...all Druid-kind and the gods that you won't go and have Kaizat chase after me."

"This girl has her mate on the brain!" the old woman crowed, and a mischievous twinkling appeared in her eyes. "Hu-hu, if only to torment you, I certainly won't. You clearly want me to go and fetch him which is why you keep bringing it up. Well, it'll teach you a lesson about leaving him again, won't it?"

Anzi rolled her eyes. "If that's what you think."

"I think you're great fun, little one. No, I'll come with you if only to see the look on your face when you realize you should have been listening to me. But we should go in luxury. My old bones have such a difficult time in the heat…"

"You live in the desert, Ash."

"In my little paradise! I abhor the heat. Come. It will be so comfortable. I love being comfortable."

"Are you—are you about to summon your Oasis here and move us from inside it? Is that what this is about?" Anzi narrowed her eyes. "It'll attract the attention of everything within miles. They'll sense the water flowing, and I don't want to run into whatever desert monsters we've been lucky to avoid until now. I know the stories."

"Don't be silly. We're not nearly deep enough into the desert to run into the sand monsters."

"Then, I don't want Bisset and his scouts to spot your Oasis from the skies. That thing has got to be visible for entire leagues, and they'll investigate whether they think it's a mirage or not. I can't risk that."

Ash clucked her tongue several times, shaking her head. "A half-day. When evening approaches again and the heat fades a little, I'll leave you and go. Until then, come. Join me."

"…Ash, I want you to conserve your strength and your magic in case things go wrong. Don't waste it for my sake when I don't even need it, I'm used to traveling harsh terrain. Just go. I might even have to return in a few days anyway if things aren't as I think."

"And I've already said I won't leave you. You're a stubborn little sprout, I will have to keep my eye on you. Infant Druids are known to be troublesome." She wagged her finger at me again. "And that means I'm coming with you, lounging at my leisure whether you join me or not."

Anzi was about to object again, but the desert was already rumbling under her feet. And that smug grin on the old woman's face was enough to drain her of at least half her resolve already… "Ash, I mean it. If you're exhausted and Bisset appears—"

"Ha-ha! Then I won't fight. I'll run away and leave you to get your hands dirty, as the youthful should."

"I didn't want you to get tangled up in this anyway. But you'll need your strength to escape."

"Say what you like, I'm already—" Ash's teasing was drowned out by a sudden and loud shower of sand as a palm tree erupted from underground. "See?"

Anzi pinched the bridge of her nose to stave off an irritated headache. She didn't know how much she believed in this primitive and superstitious Druid nonsense, but what the old woman had said about Druids being stubborn was obviously true. This was like trying to make an ox walk backwards. "This is reckless. You're only making trouble for me."

"And if you try to leave me—" Ash peeked around yet another palm tree that erupted out of the sand, and by now, Anzi could feel tufts of grass sprouting under her feet, too. "I'll just follow you anyway! Be more like me, little one. Learn to take your pleasures where you can, even in hardship. Though perhaps you already know something of that. Ho-ho."

It was almost enough to make her smile. Not because she was happy, but because this old woman who should be so wise and composed was acting like a fool, and somehow, it softened the ragged edges of Anzi's fears. Maybe things weren't so bad after all. Maybe Ash was right, and she only needed to trust, to be calm, to have faith...

"A half-day's travel," she relented, though in truth, she didn't have a choice. An unruly hedge had popped up out of the materializing oasis to hem her inside its bounds. "And then we have to part ways. I won't get you mixed up in this."

"Whatever you say, little one." Ash winked and plucked a berry from a freshly sprouted bush by her elbow. "Things will be all right. You'll see."

Would she?

She hoped.

THIS WAS FASTER than simply walking, Anzi had to admit, but that only made her dread the passing seconds all the more. The swifter they moved, the closer they came to the Imperial City, and although it was no dragon's flight, she could feel the distance shortening and twining around her neck like a choking noose. If only she could lift it. If only she could toss it down and demand Ash turn back because now she knew she'd been wrong all along. If only she could take back her fears and pretend everything was all right.

"So gloomy! Come here and share your worries."

She turned to glare at Ash, who sat atop a protruding crag over the spring with her skinny legs crossed and her dress hiked up over knobby knees. Share her worries? She knew exactly what they were. "We need to part ways here. You go elsewhere while I move forward."

"Oh? But you said a half-day's travel. You change your mind now?"

"This isn't a game. Stop this thing." She waved her hand around, struggling for the right word to call this arcane 'transport' by. It wasn't as if it were some simple carriage. "Turn in a different direction while I walk from here."

"Ho-ho, and what would you do if I tagged along? You're bound to faint in the heat. You flew on the back of a dragon to come to the Adaraat. You'll be a dry husk before you find the edges of it alone." Ash waggled a finger at her, something that was fast becoming a most infuriating gesture. Anzi had to hold back from baring her teeth, a strangely animal-istic response she hadn't been expecting from herself but ignored anyway.

"I don't need to get out. Bisset is moving in a straight line here."

"If he's coming."

"Have it your way, believe he isn't. It won't change my mind."

"Calm, little one. You'll curdle your insides looking so angry."

"You're the one curdling—" Anzi sucked in a deep breath, struggling to calm herself and speak past the tangled storm of mixed anger and fear growing in her belly. "Just stop. I'll jump out of your Oasis if I have to. You can go rushing on ahead if you like to your death."

"So prickly. You've spent too long in the desert, you're turning from girl to cactus—aht! Patience! Fine, we will walk in heat and without cool water since you are so adamant that suffering needlessly is glorious."

She wasn't going to let Ash bait her with such teasing and needling. She was already dissolving the Oasis again anyway, which was all she wanted, and despite herself, she marveled still at the way the Oasis collapsed in on itself with mystic grace. The palm trees sank down under the sands while the spring drained and dried up like a puddle disappearing a hundred times faster than it should with a final sparkle and gleam. The bushes rustled and whispered to nothing, the fruits shrank back into overhanging branches, and the butterflies that had floated from bloom to blossom blinked out of existence as if they'd never been there. And they never had, she knew now. Those glowing, winged insects were nothing but magical manifestations, not true animals. That was why there were no fish in the water, no birds singing in the trees. She frowned. This

Oasis, it was definitely capable of life. The plants weren't false conjurations, she'd felt them under her feet herself.

"How do you do this?" she asked just as the last bits of greenery vanished into the desert sand. "How are you creating life out of nothing? But only plants, no beasts…"

"Such miracles you expect of me," Ash teased as she ambled across the way to stand in front of her. "I told you before. We Druids have a task from the gods to preserve what is dying. I don't summon life, I only let it flow. The Adaraat was cursed long ago to stop the abomination's invasion to the east, but they preserved something at the very heart of it because it was in the nature of the magic to do so…You cannot curse the ground upon which you stand, after all."

"So your Oasis is the last bit of healthy land that never died?"

"Once upon a time, I wouldn't have been able to move it so. But the Druids were already rare when I was young thanks to the abomination's betrayal and bloodshed…and I've told you. After we became few, we also became stronger. The gods are still on our side, little one. Don't be fearful. We'll be victorious in the end. We can't lose with them on our side."

The simultaneously casual and exhilarated note in the old woman's voice made Anzi grimace. She hated this most of all: blind belief that went far beyond optimism. This was what lost battles, wars. This was what blinded little soldier girls into thinking her leader and nation were infallible…

The squinting of Ash's eyes made her narrow her own. She was looking over Anzi's shoulder and up at the sky with her head inclined, and there was a disbelieving shadow on her face that flickered and grew. "I don't believe it," the old woman murmured. "It can't be."

Gods on high and darkest of hells. Anzi felt the breath leave her lungs as she turned, terror growing in her gut. No, she thought. Not like this. It was too soon, too soon! How could they already be here, it was impossible! She groped backward for the old woman's arm and found it. "Go," she snapped, her eyes still glued to the sky. "Get out of here!"

There, flocked in a swarm of beating wings, came the shape of dragons in all their fury, all their glory. There had to be almost a dozen of them, and oh, they were large, large enough to send thrills of dread through her entire body—

"I said get out of here!"

98

"It's impossible."

"Obviously, it's not," Anzi snarled, and she shoved Ash's shoulder in a vain attempt to send her away. But the old woman only stumbled to the side and continued staring into the distance at the unmistakable shape of dragons in flight. "Go! Do you realize what they'll do if they catch you with me? They'll drag you along no matter what I say!"

"This makes no sense. There's not a Druid among them. They can't sense you. Can't sense us."

"If you had listened to me—" No. This wasn't the time to argue. It would solve nothing. Ash was here and they would take her prisoner if she didn't get away in time, assuming they hadn't seen her yet from the sky, but worse, they were too close. Too close! It hadn't been but a few hours since they had left Kai's camp, and a dragon in flight could cross the distance they'd traveled in a tenth of that time. She knew better than to hope Bisset wasn't among them, too, and she had served under him long enough to know he would leave no stone unturned. Even if he didn't suspect she had turned traitor to the Empire, he would send out scouts from this position in all directions in search of the chieftain and his men who had 'kidnapped' her the way Tet thought they had. And gods, they were so close that no more than an hour—no, a half-hour's flight was sure to expose Kai and his men.

"This wasn't a coincidence," she said once she'd fought her voice back down to a calm monotone. "They could have gone in any direction into the Adaraat, but they came this way. If they'd deviated but a few degrees, they would have missed us completely. But they didn't."

"I don't understand…"

"There's nothing to understand. They had a way to find me. I told you Tet was in my head, that it wasn't just a vision. He has power beyond what anyone expected, and we knew this. We knew this! We were in no position to underestimate him, Ash. This was never the time to have faith in stories and myths."

"He was never powerful in magic. And one can't scry for anyone through the Adaraat in the first place. The curse of the desert makes blind all who try to look into it."

"Stop relying on whatever old magic laws and superstition you were taught," Anzi said fiercely. "Look! They're coming! Why are you denying anything when you can see it in front of you!"

To this, Ash said nothing and only stared in dumb confusion.

"You have to leave, Ash. I'm going to go as far as I can to meet them and try to stop them from coming any closer. I'm hoping we can see them a lot better than they can see us thanks to their size, which means there's a chance they haven't seen you. So you need to leave."

But the old woman shook her head. "No, I'm not leaving."

"Ash!"

"Look at you. Ready to throw yourself into the lion's den, not believing in your power even now. But if this is happening, this is how it was meant to be. Anzi, you need to understand. Tthings greater than us are already moving. They shape things as we speak. Don't lose faith, little one."

"Just go!"

"You had to fight sometime." The woman's eyes slid over to meet hers, wide and unafraid. The sheer calmness in them was so unnerving that Anzi felt a frigid chill race down her back despite the sweltering heat of the desert. "Don't you think they'll ask questions about how you escaped? And they're too close now even if they believe. They'll find Kaizat."

"I know! I'll figure it out. Just go before they see me!" Her uniform was in shreds but the blue and white of it would stick out from all this sand like a damned fire in a forest. It could be a matter of seconds before they saw her, and then soon after, Ash.

"Stop, Anzi."

"What! What is it now!"

Ash's hands rose and wrapped around her upper arms. Though her strength was no greater than a typical human's and lesser than Anzi's by far, she let the old woman pin her arms to her sides and stare at her. Damn this. Damn all of it. She had wanted so badly to be wrong, but her instincts had told her rightly that the mystical things Ash said were nothing. And now...

"Don't let this shake you," said Ash. "You had to know this was coming. This is when you need to make your stand. And Anzi...you will win. You know that."

"Are you insane. You were wrong once already. Don't you dare."

"So, you'll go back? Continue to play the part of that Tet boy's puppet, slink around in the shadows forever? You made it out once. How can you go back and crawl at his feet?"

"Because it's the only way! What am I supposed to do, fight here? And lose? I'm not here to be a martyr for a lost cause. I'm here to win, Ash. That means I'll do whatever it takes to protect everyone—even you. Do I care about my pride? Not anymore. So don't ask me to fight against odds I can't overcome. I told you I won't believe in things without the proof in my hands, before my eyes, right in front of me—and that means I won't start a fight I can't possibly win. Yes, I'm going back. Yes! I'm leaving everyone. But I'm doing this so we can survive. So *they* can survive."

Ash's face hardened in stern disgust. "Druids were never meant to be cowards."

"If you want to call it cowardice, that must mean I'm no Druid, then. I don't care what you call me. I see only one path ahead that won't annihilate everyone I care about in the next hour, and that means I take that road until I find another way off of it. So go! Get out of here. And you won't tell Kai about this...he can't know. Promise me, Ash. I know what I'm asking of you, but you know you're the only thing standing between Kai and death. He's still hurt. Still weak. But he'll come after me and throw himself on every blade if he thinks it'll make a difference—and it won't."

"You can't run and hide forever. Believe in yourself. Fight back."

"It's only for now. I promise I'll make things right in the future, I'm just not ready yet. Believe me, I know it—but I'll find everyone again, and you know what? After that, I'll do what you say. I'll follow your Druid philosophy and religion and everything else. Today, I just need this one thing. Ash, please."

There was no time left...Please, Anzi begged silently. Please.

"I'm leaving you, then. You will have to come to terms with what happens here this day, you know."

Relief and gratitude flooded her entire being. "I know. I promise I know. But I'll make things right, I will."

And just like that, the old woman turned and shuffled away over the sands.

ANZI SPRINTED in a straight line toward the oncoming dragon swarm. It was a shame she wouldn't be able to give it back to Qinglong, but doing so would have raised suspicion. There was no sensible explanation for wanting to leave the dress behind, after all. Qing would have then gone to Kai, who would have deduced in an instant what Anzi intended to do, and all her hasty plans would have turned to dust.

But he was safe now, and so were the others. She just had to do her part.

Giving herself several convincing wounds had been easy. A few shallow nicks to refresh her old wounds from that night in the Imperial City, a slap with the flat of her blade against bared flesh to leave proper bruises. It was incredible how quickly her body had healed in the handful of days since then, though, and she spared a faltering moment to wonder if maybe she had become stronger than she thought, if maybe she stood a chance after all...But no. Better to be two parts sure than half-uncertain.

It wasn't long before the dragons descended. They were so close she could tell each of their scintillating colors, shades of green, red, yellow, and more. There were six of them large enough to take her breath away, and although none came close to the size of Shu-Amunet, they were still easily the size of Sa-Khente's and Qinglong's dragon forms if Anzi's squinting guess was accurate. The rest were smaller, but at this distance, she couldn't hazard a more precise guess as to their sizes. And they were still dangerous. One slip up, one wrong word...

Her mouth dried up when they tilted into a nosedive, and she resisted the urge to hurry out of the way. She had to play the part of exhausted runaway captive eternally grateful to see them, and that meant she stayed right here, unmoving. Their shadows blocked out the sun, and if her heart weren't in her throat, she would have been thankful for the cool shade. But her tongue was swollen in her mouth and her hands grew cold as she tried to pick out Bisset from among the Guard. No auxiliary riders, them, but true ones, Tet's loyal Premier. But now she wondered, whatever had happened to Doufan? And Aimee? He had killed her, hadn't he, just like he'd killed Pierro. But did Bisset know he had been an infiltrator all along, and the harem men too? He had to have found out by now and handled it—or had he? She had been the only one to see the proof of it. Doufan could have killed everyone else who knew, and then after the battle was over, taken up his position again just like before. Could she exploit that? When she returned, she could expose him, gain credibility.

There, at last. They were so close she could see the dragon's gleaming eyes above her, and it was far too late to change her mind now. Something inside her burned and spread like poisonous fire as the shadows darkened and grew around her until finally, the winged creatures in the sky lifted up from their dive to circle her like ominous tempest winds. They landed one at a time upon the sand, some of them so heavily they sent vibrations through the grains to tremble under her bare feet. She had decided to chuck her tattered boots long ago so her worse-for-wear condition would be all the more persuasive, and she was glad for it when several of the uniformed riders leaned around their dragons to peer down at her with mixed consternation and fascination at the mess they saw. Good. The more pitiful and pathetic she looked, the more distracting.

"You fought your way free then?" someone called down from one of the towering dragons, and she tore her eyes away from one particular reptile titan who had six horns curving out from its massive head to meet the stranger's vaguely amused stare. "Alexandre, you must be disappointed. She's more alive than you'd hoped."

She betrayed nothing, not a fleck of emotion as someone else began sliding off the blueish-purple dragon looming to her right. A large wing unfurled and slapped down on the sand, sending up a faint cloud of red and yellow dust with it. So many dragons, she thought, throat tightening as she counted them all once more with a swift once-over. But fewer than she'd thought. She had counted a dozen at first, but there were ten—two of them had strange double-wing appendages which explained the extra wings she'd glimpsed high in the sky while they were all grouped together. It reminded her of the Prince with his extra wings as well, and she narrowed her eyes as she pondered the possible connection. Was it a natural formation on some dragons, or was it some kind of mutation spawned by black magic?

Here he was. Bisset, landing on the sand with a muffled thump and proceeding to lay his cold, unfeeling glare upon her. He kept his distance, however, and there was a new stiffness to his posture that she wasn't accustomed to. It was only then that she noticed the dark shadows tracing over his face and down his neck into his stiff collar. Bruises? Good. So his healing was no stronger than hers, at least. She would note that for the future.

"Alexandre, come on. She's one of us, you'll get over it." It was the same man as before, and there was an amused lightness in his voice. "You should saddle her up. Make up and be friends, you know how Tet feels about grudges."

"And better keep her close this time," said a different voice from behind her, and this one had a touch of a jeering note. "Tet's going to actually kill you this time if you let her get snatched up again."

She had to control herself to keep the flood of icy relief from making her crumple to the ground. Yes! She had already known Tet assumed she'd been captured, but this was confirmation of her greatest hopes, that the Emperor blamed his former right hand man for it. After all, it had been Bisset's own dragon that had picked her up from the ground in her claw. Oh, her only regret was that she never got to see what kind of punishment Bisset had gotten for his negligence. She fought to keep the sneer from rising to her lips. So those were where the bruises were from, all the faded markings shadowing his skin like wraiths. What she would give to know what he'd looked like after Tet was done.

But one additional pleasure outweighed the regret: now she knew for a certainty the man had truly fallen out of his liege's favor. Could she take it up instead? This was her chance, the thing they needed to begin carving a new path to victory after such a brutal loss. It even made leaving Kai worth it. She felt a twitching in her chest at the thought of him, and for a second, she thought she could feel his presence drawing nearer to her across the sands, warm, strong, and bright. She could carry this sensation with her all the way back to the Imperium and imagine it was all real.

Maybe he wouldn't forgive her for this, but she would rather be unforgiven and save his life than appease a dead man. She couldn't let that happen. Not ever.

"I have information," she rasped, and she didn't have to fake the terrible hoarseness of her voice. She had been so anxious that her throat had gone dry seconds after they all landed. "At least a dozen of them survived the battle in the City, but after they captured and brought me to the Adaraat, there was something spreading through the camp like a sickness and killing them all. It happened quickly, and most of them were so weak they succumbed within hours."

"Tet's blood. Damn it, we needed to take them all alive if we could." It was the first man again. Was he in a position of seniority like Bisset? He was doing an awful lot of talking, and it made sense that these men would have their personal hierarchy even if Tet insisted everyone was equal. But where was she in that heirarchy, then? "How many do you think survived, Anzi?"

"Not but a handful," she answered. "It was how I fought free. They retreated and left me behind when they realized I was too much trouble."

"We should be able to find corpses then. You'll need to retrace your steps and show us."

And that was Bisset. The first words he'd spoken in her presence, and they were as cold as winter ice. She wondered if he might possibly suspect her...Maybe. But even if that were the case, as long as she had the ear of the Emperor and kept the colonel in disfavor, she would be all right. She'd prepared for this, and Ash's decision to use her magic to transport them via the moving Oasis solved this perfectly: no footprints. There were only the wavy, untouched dunes that had reformed in their wake as they slid across the sands, and once Ash was distant enough, she would have summoned the Oasis once more to make her escape. No traces. Nothing to follow.

"That way," she croaked, and pointed in the wrong direction—the direction Ash had veered off toward. The footsteps she would have left behind before summoning the Oasis would be disturbed enough by now by the desert wind, if they even remained at all. No one would be able to tell they weren't Anzi's and traveling in the wrong direction. And at the trail's end, they would simply vanish. "I'm at the end of my strength," she added, affecting exhausted modesty. "If you need to leave me behind while sending someone to scout, I understand."

"Nah, little lady. Some of us will stay behind and recuperate, isn't that right, Alexandre? And you can stay with us and rest. You need it." The first man again. He slid off his six-horned dragon with practiced grace, and she observed the rider's strange black tattoos that decorated his face. Curling, mystical—magic arrays? "I'm Benhad. It's good to see competent new blood. We've been inundated with too many failures the last few decades. I heard you're the one who's set all the dragon eggs alight back in the Imperial City. All due to hatch before another year's turn."

Her stomach lurched. But she knew this already, and this was one of the reasons she had to go back, too. She had to take responsibility for what she'd done unwittingly, stirring up life within all the long-dormant eggs with her magic. But less than a year's turn?

The group split in half: Bisset said nothing to her as he handpicked four others to accompany him in case he found resistance while scouting. The other four remained behind with her, evidently a guarding body meant to ensure her safety until she returned to the Imperium. They introduced themselves while the dragons lay down in the sand, quiet and obedient. Two of them were towering, including Benhad's, between ten and fifteen meters long from head to tail, while the other three ranged roughly a few meters shorter. They were smaller than she'd expected, or maybe she was only less impressed because she was used to the sight of dragons by now.

How life had changed, and so quickly. But she had adapted. She would win.

An hour passed as she gave Benhad a false briefing on her 'captivity', being specific enough to make them nod along but remaining vague enough that they could find nothing to contradict or find holes in. They expressed great interest in Kai time and time again in particular, and despite the danger, every mention of him made her chest loosen and the warmth that filled her in secret soothed the ache in her bones. She would be so far away soon. She was leaving him behind. But she would let this phantom sensation deceive her. Every time she spoke of him, he felt a little closer, a burst of flaring heat in her spirit that made her imagine she would turn around and see him cresting the far dune as he walked toward her. She would cradle that fantasy with her when she left.

Another hour passed, and she forced herself to settle down as the sun set. She had sent Bisset off on a wild goose chase in a random direction; he wouldn't find Kai and the others. None of them would. She had nothing to worry about, and she needed to keep spinning her plan for the future in the meantime.

"A damn shame you didn't see if the man kicked it," one of the other men grunted from where he leaned up against his dragon's folded fore-limb. Rowan, Anzi remembered. Skinny, gangling thing with flaming red hair and freckles dusting his cheeks, he looked so innocent and friendly. "If they lose their chieftain, they're as good as gone."

"Don't be daft," another of the riders muttered. "We'd still have to track down the rest."

"Eh. Just hope he did get infected and die. Anzi said he looked sick, and how many people do you know who can withstand Tet's blood? He's as good as dead."

Something to think about, if Anzi could possibly concentrate instead of fighting to keep from smiling every time she so much as thought of Kai. Tet's blood—it seemed they were talking about the living poison she'd extracted from the infected dragon shifters. Was that really the source of it? But Kai hadn't been sick; she'd checked him thoroughly for any sign of it. And he'd been the one to plunge his hand into Tet's very chest. If the Emperor's blood was truly the source, then surely Kai would have been the first to show the signs. There was too much she didn't know.

Ho-ho...There you are.

She froze. Looked up. The other men were bickering amongst themselves and didn't notice her horrified reaction to the familiar voice echoing in her mind. *'Ash! What are you—"*

I told you, Anzi, didn't I? That there would be a reckoning for the choices you make. Well, I made my own long before you did. You're not the only crafty one among us.

She couldn't breathe, couldn't even see in front of herself anymore. Panic bloomed through her entire being, and she realized all at once that she hadn't been imagining Kai's approaching presence at all. It had been real all along, had been there, coming closer and closer and she had thought it was only the delusions of a yearning mind. *You brought him here. You—!*

I've brought them all, little one. I told you, it's time to fight.

Anzi's heart skipped a beat.

Ash...what have you done.

99

Please, *take him back,* she begged as she struggled to keep her face stone-solemn and unaffected. *It's not too late. Ash, you know what the plan was. Take him back! All of them!*

This was the plan all along, and it's time you learn to put your faith in fate. This is your destiny. Not just yours, but everyone's, and you have to rise to meet it. This is what you were born into the world to do, to be. If you believe nothing else, then believe in that.

What do you mean, this was the plan? Ash!

Last night when you begged me to lie to Kaizat, did you think I'd done it? I didn't. What I told him was to trust me just as I'm telling you to trust me now, and he did. Do you know it? I've guided the half-dragons since before he was born, for the last two hundred years since they dispersed and wandered and gathered together at last, one by one. I was there when their grandfathers' grandfathers came to find me in the desert, drawn by destiny, and it was I who raised them like babes in the nest. That was me, Anzi. We two might be the last Druids in all existence, and you think we were meant for small, petty things only? We are here. We live. We do what we must!

She was raving. Her words were nonsense, all of it. Was she saying she had told Kai everything Anzi had been planning, that she was leaving in secret to infiltrate Tet's confidence once more? That couldn't be. No matter how sound the logic, how sensible the reasoning, Kai would never have agreed. So Ash must have withheld that from him—but what had she meant by telling him to 'trust' her? Anzi blanched, and someone across the way saw how her face contorted. He sent her a look mixed with rough sympathy and amusement, no doubt thinking she was suffering some small aneurysm from the pain of her battered condition. Idiot—how could he possibly know the terror ripping out the seams of her composure, the throbbing of her heart so panicked and fierce it felt as if it would burst out of her chest?

Because now she could guess, approximately. Anzi had left earlier than she'd planned to, earlier than Ash had expected, but she must have agreed upon some signal with Kai the night before while they spoke privately. Not a predetermined signal, just an assurance that he would know what to do when the time came. And when he woke up, he must have panicked, searched for Anzi the way she would for him if their positions had been reversed. But he'd guessed already that she was up to something, and he had trusted the old Druid: that must have been why Ash had summoned her Oasis in the first place, so Kai could spot them in the distance through the desert haze and follow them without revealing himself. But surely she would have sensed him and the rest of his dragon warriors when they took up pursuit. Surely—unless they had shifted and pursued by air. They wouldn't have even had to climb to any height. Simply removing themselves from the ground cut them off from her vision in the blink of an eye, just like how she could never have sensed Bisset's or his men's approach through the air either.

She'd been followed all this time with Ash betraying her, leading Kai and his men after them all along. She had promised to help. She had promised to help keep him safe, Kai and everyone else. And now she was going to get them all killed.

Anzi.

Not Ash this time, but a different voice, strong and masculine and familiar. She wanted to pound her fist into the sand, overwhelmed by both fury, fear, and though she hated to admit it when she knew how damned he was for coming here, no little happiness. Feeling Kai's presence in her mind was more quenching than any drink of cold water in punishing heat, more soothing than a breeze from over a salt sea.

Go back, she begged even though she knew it was futile. *You have to let me go.*

How? Look at us. We're one now. I'm here, Anzi.

His voice had never been more crushing and exhilarating all at once. Her heart soared, her heart sank. She could feel all of her spirit rejoicing as he drew closer and closer over unseen dunes, and at the same time dread filled every dark crevice of her being as she struggled to hold herself together.

I left Oza and Letti to you...

They're safe back at camp. And your piscin girl, and your children.

Her children? Her hatchlings, the dragons she'd left behind. Her heart twisted. *Kai, please...It's not too late. Ash won't listen, but—*

Everyone will be exactly where we left them when you come back. They're waiting for you, and I'm not going back alone, not without you.

You're still hurt! You should never have come here. How many of your men can even fight with you? How long will they last? And Bisset could come back any minute now, I have no idea where he is.

I'm coming to get you, Anzi. And this time, I won't let you go. Not again. I've done it too many times already.

He wouldn't listen. His voice in her mind was fevered, not with fear or desperation but with hunger, hunger for the coming fight and hunger for her. She had always sensed the beast in him but never like this, never so primal and wild. Her breath caught in her chest and tangled inside like vines, and she didn't know what to think, not when she knew Kai was still so weak he hadn't even been able to shift more than a wing at most yesterday, not when she knew half his men wouldn't last another fight. She had been ready! She swore it, even if she couldn't deny how she'd secretly hoped she wouldn't have to be because no matter this was the only way she could have savd him. The only way she could have saved them all...

But it was too late now. She had to do something because if she didn't, she would be letting these men collapse on Kai and his warriors. She had to find out a way to cripple and disable at least one or more of these men, not only skew the odds but ensure they were in her favor. This was everything she'd trained for, she realized as her hand slid discreetly to the hilts of her swords, to be the vanguard force that opened up the way. Because she was stronger, faster, could leap higher and hit harder than anyone else she knew. Oh, forget about Bisset, forget about Tet—she was here, and they weren't. Only these men and their dragons.

She didn't hate being a fighter. She'd only ever begun to hate being a soldier, Tet's soldier, a fist of the Empire used to batter the weak and helpless. But to rise up like this? It was what she knew best. And although every instinct told her this was futile because she would hardly be able to take down one man much less all five of the ones lounging and ambling around her, she had no choice but to defy them all.

The vanguard force, she reminded herself. She had always been the one to take the hardest missions, to drop first into the battlefield and draw the savagery of the enemy so her allies could sweep in from behind. Because who was she?

She was Anzi. Always had been. Always would be.

How far are you, Kai. At least tell me that.

You still can't feel me even after we've already started to complete our bond. His voice was still battle-fevered, but there was a teasing, thrilled, thrumming note in it that made her skin tingle. I've been inside you and you're still so slow to let me in.

Kai!

Things are going to be different soon, love. I'm going to teach you all about it, everything. When this is over...

Just tell me how close you are.

Close enough. I can feel you. You can feel me too, can't you? Wait for me.

Despair welled up in her chest once more like a heavy storm, but it was past time for weakness. If they were already there, she had scarcely more than a minute at most. Five men. Five dragons, two of them large enough to rival Sa-Khente and Qinglong's size in their dragon forms and all five of them large enough to worry her.

Her hands tightened around her hilts. Squeezed. No one noticed. How could they? And why would they? What she was about to do was madness. But if this was what it meant to be mad, then so be it, and filled by the strength of the earth and fear, fury, love—

She attacked.

100

A nzi had no time for a poetic entry into battle. She had no time for battle either while she was at it and hoped desperately she could be more assassin instead, striking at vulnerable heart and tearing apart the enemy before they could fight back and resist. But that was impossible. She was faster than any ordinary man, stronger and more agile even in this battered state she'd earned from the night of the great battle, but these men were riders too. First Guards, men of the Premier just like her. Of course she never made it to a killing stroke on the first try and in the first moments of what could only end in the bloodiest ways.

"Get her down!" Benhad shouted from her right, so she went to the left with deadly slices of her sword, aiming for whatever part of the closest man she could reach. When she found only air, she didn't stop: she pressed on, dashing after her target who backed up into his motionless dragon as he drew his own weapon. She had to bring down at least one of these men. More if she could, but at least one—it was her job to tilt the odds just so. The hardest missions with the greatest reward, those had always been her lot from the moment she graduated from Service training, and this was no different. Bring down the threats, soften the wave, if she failed here then she deserved to fall anyway.

"Alive, not dead!" Benhad shouted again just as something sliced through the air less than a finger's width away from her throat. "Watch it, Olivier!"

No wonder she'd sensed weakness in Olivier and known to go after him first. A name like that, he was native Empire, living the cushiest life and the least threatening of everyone here. She bore down on him with three times more savagery than before, and when he tried to retreat up the body of his dragon and take flight or whatever other genius solution he was trying to enact, she followed him up, scurrying up to the back and launching herself at the soldier with no caution, no care. Because now she understood as she let her senses stretch into the Other vision how the dragon under her feet—no, all five dragons here—were no threat to her until their riders demanded they act. They were simply dead sentinels now, staring mindlessly at the fray with slow-blinking eyes and nothng more.

"Burn her!" someone else shouted, and she grimaced. End it, just one of them, she thought furiously and threw herself at Olivier to slash at anything vital she could reach. If not the heart or the head, then a leg, an arm, something to cripple him and render him at least half-useless in the coming fight. Because this wasn't a fight yet, not even close; this was just the butchering before the bleeding and she had to be of use before they could rally to fight Kai head to head, before they could hurt him, hurt everyone—

"She got me!" The man's garbled scream came after a spray of blood from his bicep and right before Anzi choked out a gasp at the sensation of steel sinking between her ribs. But she'd never thought she would get away unscathed; she'd been ready. Before the blade could skewer her from behind, she threw herself forward once more and crashed into Olivier where he had scrambled back all the way against the base of his dragon's neck to escape her reach. The cold steel slid back out the scant knuckle's length it had entered, and although she could feel blood wetting the back of her tattered uniform in the next instant, she set her mouth in a hard triumphant line in mid-air just before she and Olivier crashed to the sand.

They were all coming for her now, no longer sitting stunned or hesitating in case they were mistaking the situation. Benhad and the three others were upon her now while this one writhed under her, his upper arm nearly severed with how deeply she had cut him. But she couldn't turn her back on this one, couldn't have mercy. Besides how he deserved death for being complicit in this, for having enslaved a dragon for his own, the same one who stared down at him now with empty reptilian eyes, Anzi couldn't afford to let him heal up and rejoin the fray while she fought the others. She raised her swords, one aiming to stab down at his chest while the other angled behind her to parry the blow that came hammering toward her from someone else—

"Fuck!"

Fuck, she agreed, and her teeth set in a frustrated grind when she was sent stumbling forward with no one pinned under her blade. He had rolled out of the way just in time and even managed to hurl a fistful of sand into her eyes to boot with his good hand, and now she had no choice but to spin around and begin backing away before the four men advancing on her in a semicircle. The dragons had yet to move, though, which meant the soldiers were still hoping to take her in in one piece. Otherwise, they would have had their thralls roast her until she was but a smoking hunk of charred meat.

Her mind expanded, reaching, scratching, at those of each of the dragons lounging nearby. But it was like trying to fight her way through solid stone, no give and all impassivity. It was like how Shu-Amunet's mind had been but worse. At least she had retained a sliver of self-awareness, a spark of conscious desire that had escaped the cruel control of Bisset's conditioning, but these? She despaired even as she hefted her swords again, seeing ever more clearly the truth she had been afraid of for a while now. These dragons were gone. Long gone. Their bodies remained, enslaved to the will of their corrupt riders, but all that made them truly living had long since vanished. Like knocking upon hollow wood, somehow their stone-filled and stone-encased mind echoed, echoed, echoed in their barrenness. There was nothing left to appeal to.

"Drop your weapons and think about what you're doing," Benhad rumbled as he advanced one step for each one she retreated. "Whatever they've done to you, use your training and fight back."

Exactly the luck she needed. They thought she was bespelled under the magic of the enemy, forced to act against her own comrades. Of course. Why would they doubt her loyalty to the Empire? She was famous for being one of its greatest soldiers, and a First. The longer she let them think so, the better. She trained her face to show no emotion as if she were a dead thing too, just like those dragons watching on blankly who were but only shells of themselve, and dashed across the sand straight toward the row of outstretched weapons pointing at her. She had no time to hesitate, no time to strategize other than with the swiftest of knee-jerk reactions and primal instincts as she hacked downward, swung sideways, spun and delivered bone-breaking kicks at whatever limbs were unlucky enough to test her reach. Because just beyond that dune right behind them all, she could feel them approaching: Kai and his warriors.

Two of them had alighted upon the ground, and her heart throbbed when her Other-sense detected their weakness, the likely reason they hurried across the last leg of the distance on their clawed feet rather than stay in flight. The others must still be in the air, she hoped, but how many? How many had made it here and were strong enough to fight? There were only the five men here and their five dragons—four and a half if she counted Olivier's crippled dominant arm. If there were enough of them and she fought and fought hard, fought harder than she ever had in her entire life, maybe they could end this with no casualties to mourn.

She'd never dreamed of it before, winning a battle with no losses. But now she had no choice but to stretch for it no matter how unlikely, because those were all Kai's men. Kai's comrades. His brothers in arms who had been with him from the desert to the Imperial City, had lain down their lives and would do it again and again no matter how many times they fell and rose up. Those were Kai's men, and he would grieve every one just like how he'd crumbled under the weight of those who he'd lost already.

Anzi's swords glowed bright somehow despite the magicked blackness of the blades, and they threw strange sparks now every time she ground them against the soldiers' weapons again and again and again in light-ning-fast flurries. Metal screamed, piercing the men's grunts as they fought against her superhuman strength and speed. Any second now, they would realize they couldn't take it easy on her anymore, but all she needed was one more in, one more vulnerability, one more opening so she could clear the way—

"Benhad! Behind us!"

Shit! One of them had turned around and glimpsed the shapes that rose up over the dune's crest. They were so close that had she been able to keep them distracted for three, no, two seconds longer, it would have been the perfect ambush. But it was too late now. She could see Kai hanging on to the side of Sa-Khente's dragon form, already disembarking even though the blood-red titan reptile was still in flight. Oh, gods, she thought as she lunged and stabbed her sword into the closest rider's gut, please, be safe—

She gasped when something pierced her ribs from the side, and she thought she heard Kai bellow with impossibly animal—no, demonic rage as he dropped down to land on the sand in a cloud of dust. But he needn't have worried. Who was she?

Anzi called on every sliver of experience, knowledge, and instinct she had ever touched now as she flung herself away from the blade that tried to carve out the flesh between her lower ribs. Olivier was fumbling with something behind two of his comrades who shielded him, holding a hand to his gushing arm and grunting as he struggled to take something out of the bag saddled over his dragon's back. Damn it, he probably had an emergency healing cantrip tucked away in there, much like how she used to carry one when she was still on typical patrol.

What about these men? Did they have healing spells hidden away too? She'd accounted for it, though, even if they did: all she had to do was disable them so they couldn't use the cantrips in time or force them to exhaust it as quickly as possible. The Empire's magic was orderly and efficient, but without a healer, such spells still took time to cast. And that was when she had to strike, hard and fast. Disable, stall, whittle them down one by one. She came in again with a terrible sideways cleave powerful enough to hurl Benhad backward when he parried her blow, then in the next instant sliced up with the other sword to sever the arm of the next man unlucky enough to think he saw an opening then. Her every movement was tight, brutal, ferocious. She had been born to fight, always, throwing away sophistication for primal efficiency and chasing the kill, chasing the kill, end it, end them, end everything. She spared no strength, no furor as she whirled upon them like a hurricane, both Benhad and his cursing one-armed comrade who were now spitting guttural commands at their respective dragons as they tried to pincer her from either side. The other two had already taken flight to meet Kai's warriors, no, three— Olivier had either given up on trying to heal his arm first or he had cast the cantrip halfway and hoped it was enough to get him by.

She hoped it wouldn't be. She hoped he bled out, hoped he would fall off his enslaved dragon and plummeted to the sands below to shatter like glass. She had already failed, screamed every voice that bubbled up inside, because she had let even a single one of them go so they could attack Kai. She should have wiped them all out long before he ever got here, should have broken every bone in their bodies and torn them apart in her hands so they couldn't get to him. But it was too late, and now the bellowing of dragons filled the desert like terrible storms growing, growing, growing until they tore themselves from the sky and wrapped around them all with a squeezing, suffocating grasp. Not war cries, not the shouting of concerted determination the way humans shouted at their enemies as they ran across a battlefield to each other, but killing cries, destroying cries, the purest expressions of survival. They ripped through the desert sunset like promises of death, and the first clash of titanic body against titanic body sent a cascade of broken scales showering down upon the sand and everyone's heads.

And that was only the beginning. In the next heartbeat, streaks of every color whirled and wheeled through the air, dragons tangling with dragons, teeth bared and sinking into scaled flesh, gnashing and crushing. Fearsome claws lacerated whatever soft flesh they could find unprotected, and Anzi had no idea who was who as the giant reptiles rolled and somersaulted above while locked into lethal embrace with the enemy.

But she couldn't afford to stand still. She had her own fight to win, and she had to do it before Bisset and his men returned to reinforce their ranks. She didn't know when they would be back and could only guess they would be here before true evening fell, but sunset was already dying. They had to end this quickly, end this *now* while they still outnumbered the soldiers escape.

Silver drops splattered all along the sands like metallic rain, and when she lunged again for Benhad and his second with her swords moving so fast they were but a shimmering blur, dragon blood blinded her in one eye as it landed on her forehead and dripped down to her cheek. Still, she raged on, ignoring the strain that made her left leg tremble more and more with each pounding stomp, vicious kick, or even fleeting footwork to dodge the soldier's desperate attacks. She needed to kill them now or else Bisset would return, and she saw no path to victory if he reached them in time to mop up. But no matter how hard she fought, she couldn't break into their defense, only chip, and time was running out. If she could afford to whittle them down, she knew she would outlast them even with a bum leg, but how many minutes did she have? No, not minutes, seconds —the roaring of the dragons overhead would echo for leagues around, and Bisset would have spurred his men on even faster by now.

But where was Kai? He needed to get out of here, needed to be ready to call for a retreat because between him and his little over half a dozen warriors who had made it here, there was no chance of survival unless they finished this in the next moment. But that wasn't happening, so he needed to be ready to run, fly, escape. She reached out with her Sight to find him since she couldn't take her eyes off these damned two—

Her stomach lurched when her senses rushed through the sand in search of him in all directions. The dragon blood that continued to shower the desert even now littered the sands and sank between the grains, trickling ever downward into the dryness that swallowed it all up. She could tell which traces of blood belonged to whom—that one Sa-Khente, that one Qinglong, and gods, they were indeed locked tooth and claw and wing with their enemies when Anzi dared to glance skyward for half an instant; would they survive?

But most terrifying of all was when she felt Kai's blood there sinking into the sands. Her heart swelled, her pulse throbbed, and in the next breath she found him at the surface. She couldn't see his wounds, couldn't tell how badly he was hurt, but oh, there was so much blood buried below his feet and she didn't know who had done it. How had his men let the enemy reach him at all! There were more of them than there were of Bisset's men; these were only half his force. If they could only barely hold their own against a fewer number…!

But that was unfair. She couldn't curse them for their incompetence when she, too, was failing to protect him. And all his men, every single one who had managed to come here, were still battle-weary from the terrible fight back at the Capital. This had been a fool's attempt, a suicidal charge—Ash! she cursed, heart shattering as she felt Kai tumble to the ground. A wave of residual pain echoed into her mind, something like a fierce burning, and she realized that the soldiers attacking him were magic-proficient. Gods—she had to get to him, had to get to him before they killed him, and he should never have been here when everyone knew full well that the basilisk poison yet weakened his body.

She despaired. Ash, Ash had promised. Ash had promised she wouldn't let this happen, that she would help her keep everyone safe. And now…

Fight on, Anzi! I'm here. I'm protecting him.

Get him away from here! She rained ferocious strikes at Benhad's sword, letting black and white sparks fly as a sharp scent suddenly filled the air. The smell of magic? But why? Neither she nor they were casting anything. But she had no time to wonder such things. She aimed for his hands, for the hilt of his weapon so she could disable him since she couldn't break his guard quickly enough. His second leaped to his rescue, countering her twin swords as they both panted and sweated. Fall! she demanded. Fall, fall, fall—! *I said get him out of here, Ash! Or by the gods you believe in, I'll spill the weight of his blood out of you.*

And I said to fight on! Here it is, your fate and your destiny. No matter what happens here, no matter the cost, know you'll be victorious.

And the old woman sounded so sure, so exhilarated that Anzi had no choice but to falter. Not in the fight but in her mind, the rational part of her that knew there was no hope. Could it be? Could it be that Ash had seen something of the beyond, had looked in from the outside somehow and seen the path ahead? Could it be that Ash was right? Hope hurt worse than her wounds that bled and gushed, but in a moment of weakness—she grabbed on. She grabbed on and determined to see it through, determined to take every one of these men with her into the darkest hells no matter what it took.

That's it, little one. Fight on! Win! This is the way!

Blind, deaf, unfeeling. Anzi had to shut out every part of her that begged her to run back to Kai and drag him away herself to save him. She had to sell herself to the blood, to the violence, to the earth-shattering, air-rending screams and roars of the dragons in the sky and the smell of acrid sweat from the men she fought. Her senses heightened, her feet quickened, she hurled herself at them until finally, Benhad's second collapsed with a gurgling cry. A fountain of blood gushed from his neck, and with the only good hand he had left since she had left his other as a mere stump, he tried to stifle the flow with wheezing, choking gasps.

She launched herself forward to finish him for good because who the hell knew with those of the First Guard, they could be even hardier than she was, and finally earned her first taste of final blood this battle. She sank her black blade into his chest with her eyes still glued on Benhad who had retreated, knowing he stood no chance of defending his fallen comrade any longer, and now he, too, was ripe for the felling. Anzi had never fallen prey to blood lust before and never would—it was one of her greatest strengths, clear-headed intent uncolored by greed for carnage, but somehow the drumbeat adrenaline pounding through her veins and sending fire through every part of her both physical and spiritual made her wild, burning, reckless, open—

—no, not adrenaline. Desperation. Desperation because despite this small victory and how she could sense Kai was still alive, still fighting back, this fight was not in their favor. Not for long. And yes, even as the fearful through pressed against her mind, the bleeding, battered body of an enemy dragon crashed to the sand and made the desert rumble, but that changed nothing. Because they were winning but had not yet won, because they had not stolen victory quickly enough—

—because just over the next dune, she saw him:

Bisset and the rest of his men.

101

W as there nothing else she could do? Nothing at all? Anzi took a deep and angled slash to her midriff that tore the tattered remains of her uniform almost completely in two while at the same time, beheading Benhad at last in exchange, and yet it wasn't triumph she felt but stunned disbelief. She had thrown her faith into Ash's words because she had no choice but to fight on anyway, but here that faith proved futile as ever. Five newcomer dragons in the fight, some of them rivaling Kai's generals in size, and the five First Guards riding atop them as well. Outnumbered, outpowered, fighting like this would mean everyone died. No path to victory, no opening, no vulnerability to exploit. And for every one she might find if she looked hard enough, the shifter tribe had a dozen more.

Please, she begged the gods, the spirits, even herself. The fate and destiny Ash insisted would meet her here, where were they? Please, let there be something I can do, she screamed into the windstorm swallowing up her mind. If she were truly the Druid of dragons as Ash had said, then surely there was something she could do, some stone she had left unturned. In desperation, she sank her consciousness into the desert once more and reached out, straining in vain for the wyrms as she had done in her vision back in Ash's Oasis spring. They were but the cousins of dragons, the old woman had said, so if she could connect with the one then this should be possible, too. And if it wasn't—there was no one else, nothing else she could petition or command aid from, no way to even the numbers, the odds.

And oh, the odds—

She sent her mind surging forward, blood and heart burning within her, but uncomprehending, purely animal, the serpents slithered off into the desert to flee from her presence the instant she made contact. They had never been susceptible, she realized, heart sinking. The second she had touched them, she realized. They had no higher reasoning or capacity to obey her demands, whether they were fierce commands or begging pleas. They weren't war dogs who could learn to listen to their masters' whistles and clicks. They were serpents, with serpents' minds. But she should have known that.

Still, she had to try, so she tried and tried and tried until her eyes watered and she nearly collapsed mid-run. But the wyrms fled until they disappeared past the range of her Sight entirely. This couldn't be it. This couldn't be the end. *Ash!* she bellowed in her mind, praying the old woman was listening. This mental communication was still so foreign to her that she never knew if she was ranting to herself or making contact. *They have reinforcements! Tell me I can communicate with the enslaved dragons and make them stop, there has to be something I can do to make them fight back against the control. Ash!*

Spare your nobility for the ones you can save, little one. You can do nothing for the ones eaten up by Tet's black magic, it's too late for them. Only death can free those dragons.

Then how do we fight them at all! They outnumber us!

With faith! Fight on, Anzi, and win! The gods are with us!

At the old woman's exuberant words, Anzi wanted to vomit as she ran across the sand to join Kai and protect him from the three remaining soldiers. Her earlier guess had been right. Olivier was back in the fight with his arm done up in a hasty tourniquet. That could only mean the healing cantrip hadn't done enough work yet to let him loosen the cloth binds. And against him and his two comrades, Kai fought alone—no, not alone. Ash was keeping her distance but with him nonetheless, casting strange magic that glowed from her eyes and mouth while she mumbled under her breath. It was only then that Anzi noticed the soldiers hacking at something around their feet in between trying to land blows on the winged chieftain.

The closer she came, the more she saw: green and brown curls of wood and leaves sprouting from within the sand to wrap around ankles and tug downward, to ruin footing and send them tripping and tumbling. More than once, they tried to get to her, but Kai intercepted with black claws drenched in blood. He had more than held his own, and yet he hadn't managed to land a killing blow on any of them yet. That would change once Anzi got there, and she gnashed her teeth as she powered up the dune, ignoring the screaming of the sinews in her faltering leg. She couldn't fall now. Bisset was seconds away with his men, and she could see dark shapes against the setting sun as they dived to join the bloody fray.

Two of the enemy's dragons were dead now, having plummeted earthward to land on the sand with almighty crashes, but Kai's warriors were no longer the greater number now with Bisset's reinforcements. And the ground fight had just become even more perilous. It didn't matter that Olivier screamed in agony as Anzi plunged one sword clean through his spine and out his chest, didn't matter that Kai leaped in to take advantage of the distraction by killing yet another soldier, because several more men landed on the sand with their weapons at the ready.

Wait. Something was wrong. In the heat of the fighting, she hadn't noticed, but as she shoved Olivier off her blade with a bare foot to his chest, she looked up to take a swift headcount of everyone in the air. Kai's generals were still fighting, thrashing their tails and digging into whatever enemy flesh they could find with their claws, and there were six others besides them, a few worryingly small but viciously struggling for survival and victory all the same. And on the ground, it was only Kai, Ash, and herself against the fresh handful of reinforcements who had come rushing into the battle just now.

But something was wrong, either her eyes or her count—because of the enemy, including the two unmoving dragons lying motionless on the sand, Anzi counted one fewer than she should. There should have been ten enemy dragons and ten riders paired with them, two of the former disabled and five of the latter dead, she thought as she leaped backward to dodge a whirling spear tip that had already taken a slicing chunk out of her thigh a few seconds ago. But the count was *wrong*. She dared to glance skyward and count again, paying the grim price of a slash to her face that simultaneously rattled every bone in her skull and neck as she crashed to the ground.

"Anzi!"

"Watch out!" she howled, instantly furious and terrified at Kai who attempted to dash in to protect her. She didn't need his help—he needed hers! Already she could see him bleeding from countless wounds all over his torso and his tattered pants, from his nose and mouth. He didn't even have the strength to keep his wings; all he could summon were his black claws that were noticeably smaller than before, too.

Keep them away from Ash! she screamed across their bond, and when she saw his eyes narrow as she scrambled back to her feet, she knew she had somehow forced open the mental connection as she'd intended. Good, at least this way they could strategize in secret, but then there was no time to plot or plan anyway. These three men who were advancing on her and Kai with their weapons at the ready were far more skilled than the ones before. It made sense; Bisset would have taken his best with him when he took his scouting party ahead. Olivier, Benhad, and the rest of the men who'd stayed behind had been formidable, but these men...

She had assumed Bisset and their fifth man were still in the sky riding their dragons. She could see magic being cast in the air, war magic, and so hadn't questioned it. Had been thankful, even, because she knew that if Bisset were in the ground fight, she might have lost already. But now she wondered, because a third count made it unmistakably clear: one enemy dragon was missing. Did that mean a rider was missing from the fight, too? Her gut twisted with a savage dread, but she had to finish this before she could even dream of pausing long enough to figure out this newest conundrum. These three men, the two riders up in the sky, and the one, two, seven dragons locked in a ferocious fight to the death with Kai's shifter warriors. Silver blood peppered and splattered all over the sand in puddles, the sand now so saturated it couldn't suck up the moisture quickly enough. And her heart flew into her throat when she saw two smaller dragons, Kai's men, scream in mortal agony as they spiraled to the ground.

The sound that erupted from her throat was inhuman. There was no other word to describe it even though she was the very source. Layered with explosive, corrosive venom and every part of it drowned in rage-blind fury, she felt it rip from her throat like a living thing tearing itself out into the world. And it was, it must have been, because the magic that thundered out of the deepest parts of her and shot into the sky to form a white fog looked like a living thing indeed.

Yes! That's it, Anzi! Go on!

Ash's exhilarated voice rang inside her head as if they had won already, but she didn't know. She didn't know that as the fog-thing shifted and twisted into shape, Anzi's body weakened and withered like a dying husk, and she fell to the ground, torn through by this foreign pain far greater than any she had ever endured before. Not ready, she thought dully. It was an instinctive notion, an awareness that came from her Other sense rather than any logical knowledge. *Not ready.* This power she was about to use, it was still too young. If she used it now, there was no telling what what happen. She had to wait, had to let it grow first, it was too soon, said the voice.

Butwhat choice did she have? Another dragon fell to the ground with a terrible cry, and she knew even blinded that it was one of Kai's men. Her senses roiled and curled under the sands, searching desperately for any way to turn the tide of the battle before it became a complete massacre. And now Kai leaped in front of her fallen body to take blows meant for her, his teeth silver with blood but running in mixed rivulets of red, too, like an ordinary human's. Half-shifted, half-blooded, and he was going to die in this neither-state if she didn't figure out a way to save him.

No, too soon, too soon, the voice whispered again, but one of the men was now sprinting toward Ash while the other two continued to bear down on Kai with furious, vicious strikes. He couldn't hold on for much longer, a few seconds at most as the veins in his neck stood out and pumped that gods-damned basilisk poison through his body. But he would never retreat either because she was here, and he would die if she did nothing.

She would pay the price later, but she had to save Kai now. She had to save Ash. She had to save the dragons, both Kai's tribesmen and the ones held captive in their black magic thrall, even if it meant that their freedom could only come with their death. Because she knew intimately that given the choice, if she could choose death over the captivity of her soul, then she, too, would surely choose the latter.

She was the Druid of the dragons. She didn't care that it was nonsense, the product of superstitious divining and whatever other authority Ash begged. In this moment, all she cared about was saving the dragons, the dragons she had vowed to find a way to protect when she at last accepted the truth. Her mate, her mate's people, all of them.

So—she let go.

Her spirit divided, and half of it left her body in a violent storm and entered the fog. Her mind split too, and went on to expand in a flash until it took up the entirety of the mass of fluid, raw, unshaped magic hovering above. Time slowed; the world moved at a snail's pace as her spirit reshaped itself again and again and again until it somehow fit. It wasn't perfect, far from it, and again the terrible knowledge that neither her body nor her spirit were prepared for this struck her like a bolt of lightning. It was a final warning to stop before it became irreversible, before she committed to the consequences she didn't know but should be terrified of, but...Her eyes opened, both those of her physical body and those of her Other-form, her Other-body in the sky, and she knew this was the only choice she could make. Her mind wobbled one final time along with her legs, and then her physical half picked up her fallen swords. In the air, she spread her wings, her half-incorporeal, ghostly wings, because somehow the mass of white-fog magic had taken on the shape of a misshapen dragon. She could see herself, she thought dumbly, below on the ground as she yanked Kai away from an oncoming blow and went on the offensive. She could see herself, tattered and torn, and when she looked up and looked down at the same time, the world fell into place.

A few others had paused to witness the sight, but the battle had raged on uninterrupted everywhere else. Five of Kai's warriors were dead or dying now, each of them falling faster than the last as their numbers dwindled, then toppled. Only Qinglong, Sa-Khente, and one other dragon remained with scarcely any casualties in kind on the other side. It was past time to act, to unleash. She had to trust this division of her very soul and let it save her, save all of them. On the ground, Kai tackled the soldier chasing after Ash while Anzi stabbed the point of one sword straight through the chest of one of her own quarries. The grind of bone and armor would have stopped anyone weaker, but she was far from weak and power coursed through her body like fire at night, windstorm through a canyon, crashing rapids swollen after heavy rains. She drove her sword deep into him until her hilt met his chest, and she turned and shoved him into his comrade, using the gurgling body as a shield. Victory. She could taste it. Not just here, but above, too, because simultaneously in the sky, her other self sent out surging flames of white that made Bisset's dragons bellow and roar in agony as they wheeled away to escape. Her fog-like, shifting, draconic body took up the pursuit, soaring upward, diving down, claws shattering scales and rending flesh. The silvery streaks of blood that should have littered her spirit-sending were absent, however, simply floating right through the incorporeal form to rain down on the sand below.

That wasn't right. The urgent thought made her scramble for answers, and she turned her mind to Ash once more. *I need more strength!* she cried. *This isn't enough!*

Then find it where you must! the old woman screamed back, and for the first time, Anzi thought she detected uncertainty in the voice that echoed in her mind. But she couldn't doubt now. She had to keep going, keep going and never stop—

There! Gathered between the sands were the crystallized remains of Ash's Druid magic, and even though they were but residue, power was power and she needed every ounce before her own crumbled. She dived toward the ground, her dragon self, and crashed into the desert. But she didn't crash at all. Still incorporeal—even more so than she had been in the beginning now that her strength was already beginning to fade, her spectral body simply sank into the sands like a ghost.

Power. Finally. She breathed it in and drank it down like blessed water, and that was exactly what it tasted like. Ash's Druid magic—it was of the earth, she realized distantly. It was nothing mysterious, had nothing to do with a sacred Oasis—it was simply earth magic distilled into this potent, particular form. But now wasn't the time to examine the answer to the mystery. Now was the time to fight on, and win. Khente and Qing were yet fighting off the remainder of the Thralled dragons when Anzi's spirit-born form burst out of the sand. It was no longer white but green now with streaks of brown, all the translucent and faint parts of it filled with the earthy hues of Ash's magic. And it was with that joined power that she could now rise, rise and crash into the enemy dragons and deliver the generals from the mass of tangled wings and claws that would have killed them had Anzi been but a moment slower.

On the ground and in her physical body, she exulted. She could feel her body tearing apart as her mind collapsed upon itself under the strain, too soft and too young to withstand such a thing, but she was saving them all, she marveled, even as she grieved at the same time for each dead and dying thrall that slammed down onto the ground below.

Kai had finished off his man even injured and battered as he was, and he reappeared behind the last remaining soldier before impaling him from behind with one pitch-black clawed hand. In the same instant, Anzi's own swords plunged into the man, one in the throat, one in the gut, and she met Kai's golden eyes above the soldier's lolling head. Without a word, she ripped her blades out of the gurgling body and stepped back.

The fight in the sky ended with a bellowing roar from Sa-Khente as he bit through the serpentine neck of the last remaining enemy—and then it was over. Anzi breathed in, breathed out, and at long last allowed her spirit to rejoin again. The spectral dragon in the sky that carried half her mind dissipated into the wind, and she was whole once more.

"Anzi," Kai rasped when she turned her eyes upon him. His voice was hoarse with exertion and emotion, pain and muffled grief. "You're hurt."

You're hurt worse, she tried to say, but blood filled her mouth and dribbled down her chin when she opened it to speak. He caught her as she stumbled, but she pushed him away with a choking gasp. She was no soft spring foot soldier. She had trained all her life to overcome pain, to welcome it with open arms. And after Tet—well, almost nothing could come close to that kind of suffering...almost nothing. The shadow of agony clawing at the edges of her mind and creeping closer and closer promised to change her mind, but that would come later. The price of her power invoked prematurely, she wouldn't be able to avoid that.

Later.

"There was one soldier in the sky," she panted after spitting out a mouthful of tangy blood. "He was casting binding magic while still riding his dragon. It...it was enough to get your men killed. He would paralyze them and set up the kill..."

"I know. I never thought it was going to be like this."

"I did." She hung her head and closed her eyes. "I knew..."

This was why she hadn't wanted them to come after her, she had been about to say. This was why she had begged Ash not to drag Kai and his men here. And she had done it anyway. And now? Dead. Dead. More bodies, more fallen brothers and sisters for them to grieve...How many did that reduce his tribe to? How many dragon shifters remained to carry on their legacy and fight?

"Some of them are still alive," she whispered. "Your men. Three... maybe four, but I don't know if it's too late for the last one. Is there anyone who can heal them?"

"I can make them shift back to human form even if they're unconscious. It'll help them heal faster with a smaller body, if they survive long enough."

Grief. She could hear it threatening to break through with every syllable, and she knew he didn't want to lose himself to his despair and rage here. With a nod, she let it go and struggled to her feet when she saw Ash approach. And behind her, with her Sight, she sensed Qinglong approaching too. She was badly hurt. The general, not the Druid, who had come away nearly unscathed after all of this carnage.

"Stay down," Kai ordered, but she shook her head and picked up her swords. She spared herself only a second to examine them. One was still black from tip to hilt, the same night-dark hue it had been when first crafted for her, but the other had changed. The blade was a shimmering silver-white, and so was the hilt. It had happened right after she had figured out how to divide her spirit and summon a dragon-sending to carry part of it into the sky, and she wondered once more exactly what kind of enchantments were buried into these swords.

"Kai," Qing murmured when she came to a limping stop next to Anzi. "Khente—it's not good. Come see."

The two left to tend to their fallen comrades, and Anzi stared uselessly at the ground. She could tell which ones were already dead and which ones stood a chance of surviving, but her tongue stiffened and her lips pressed together in silence. It was only when Ash came to stand before her that she finally looked up.

"You shouldn't have done this," she said softly. There was no anger in her voice. No despair. She was too exhausted for either. "I asked you to trust me. Now look."

"What happened was supposed to happen. The gods were with us. How could we have won otherwise? This is the path fate intended."

Fate. Gods. She was still prattling on about that when they were surrounded by the corpses of Kai's dead kinsmen. "I have to go," she said. "Bisset is still out there. He either never showed up to the battle or disappeared in the middle of it, but he's not here."

"Bisset?"

"Tet's colonel. I have to find him before he has a chance to report to Tet what happened. But I don't know how. We'll never catch up to him without wings...And everyone's too hurt."

"It's too late if he's gone flying off," said Ash. "Forget about that. We'll help Kaizat here and take care of his men. And you need to treat your wounds."

Anzi looked down at herself and wiped away the dried blood crusting over her lashes. "I'll heal fine." Her response was curt, acidic. "I just need clothes. My uniform's torn and sticking to the wounds, they'll get infected at this rate. I'll find something to wear once we return to camp."

"No need. Kaizat wanted me to hold onto this, your dress. You should change out of those rags now while you can."

She was right. Not just because the frayed and torn threads were making her wounds burn, but also because the fact that she was wearing them in the wake of the battle made her want to vomit. She wanted to be rid of all traces of her former life, disown every part of it that had led her here. She would go down cursing Tet and his gods-damned Empire to the grave no matter whether she went on to win the war or not...

But Ash was right. It would be impossible to catch up to Bisset now anyway, so she needed to come up with plans anew. Could she still infiltrate the Imperial City and enter Tet's confidence even after all of this? She couldn't be certain Bisset had never been here. He could have retreated midway, meaning he would have seen sure proof of her betrayal. But if he had never been here, if he had seen nothing, maybe there was still a chance to make it work. Or that could be too risky, and she was better off training up a rebellion in annexed cities the way she'd been planning to, starting with Lumenera...

Muddled in her thoughts as she went from dragon to dragon, checking again with her own hands whether they were truly dead or not, it was only then that she realized she could hear something in the back of her mind. A faint voice, twinkling, like snow crystals and ice chimes...She froze, gripping the edges of her dress.

Netra? Is that you? What's wrong?

But it wasn't in words that the response came. Distant, so distant she could barely hear anything at all, it was nothing but shards of fear and panic. The wailing of a child for a missing mother, of chicks left too long in the nest alone...

"Ah—ah—!" Words wouldn't come. Blinded by fevered terror, Anzi whirled around and stumbled in the direction the voice had come radiating from. She hadn't gone but a dozen steps when a large, blood-smeared hand wrapped around her arm.

"Anzi! What's wrong?" Kai took her by the shoulders, voice urgent. "Qing, help me take a look—"

She clutched at him, struggling to unearth whatever strength she had left as she dug her fingers into his forearms. She was so tired and the pain was already creeping in to overtake her, but—

"Bisset!" she choked out. "He's at the camp!"

102

S he was exhausted but unable to sleep as Ash transported her and Kai back to camp. Qing had implored him not to go, but there was no dissuading him now that his men were stable and those who could be saved had been saved. After all, those were his men back at camp, too, the ones who had had to remain behind.

No one said a thing as the Oasis slithered through the sands. Kai, despite how exhausted he must be and fearing for his defenseless men on top of that, took Anzi to the spring and bathed her gently. Her wounds refused to close, and even when he slid his hands over them to try to impart healing power through their mate bond, they remained angry and red and gushed blood anew anytime she shifted too much.

"It'll be all right," he murmured as he kissed her wounds while she sat numbly in the water. "We'll be there soon."

Soon wasn't enough. Night was already falling, and it had been that long since she heard Netra's fading cry for help in her mind. How long had she been calling for her while Anzi went on oblivious, deafened by adrenaline in pitched battle? The thought was anguish, pure agony. Bisset could have been hurting Netra in that very moment, and Oza, and Letti, and the other dragons. Her brother, her friend, her *children*. Her heart sank lower and lower as she waited to hear Netra again...But silence. Only silence. Was Rania was still alive, or had she given her life in vain?

And Kai's tribesmen, how many had Bisset killed by now? All of them, probably, of the ones remaining in camp.

Anzi doubled over more than once in the water, stomach heaving, but there was nothing to vomit. Kai soothed her time and again and despite how she knew he must be suffering also, she could find no words to comfort him. Nothing from the void that opened up inside her and sucked in every emotion until it was heavy and dark with every terrible fear trapped inside it.

And then they were there. Anzi was already dressed again with her swords in her hands as she rushed out of the Oasis and charged into the camp, throwing all caution to the wind. There, she could sense Bisset's new dragon moving around in the rear, and a terrible, horrific weight caved inside her chest. They were by Qing's tent. Oza. He had him. She could sense Netra, Serqet, and the Prince huddled by the much larger dragon holding them all hostage, too, and since it was Bisset, they were probably muzzled and tied together like how wyrm traders captured their quarry. They were gathered too close together for it to be anything willing.

She was nearly there now. Almost—

"I can finally be rid of you, Anzi. My patience has been rewarded."

Bisset. Bisset was standing there. She came to a stop, hands clamped so tightly around the hilts of her swords that she could feel the gash over her knuckles widen and bleed. The tent behind the colonel was no longer standing, slashed to shreds. And on the ground, tangled in the fabric that should have been covering the bottom of the tent, Letti's motionless body lay at a strange angle. Crouched next to her was Oza, who had his small, skinny hands hovering over her body. When he turned to look at Anzi, there was a dead look in his eyes she couldn't decipher. More than ever, she regretted all the years she had abandoned him to the darkness of the Tower and the Magisters. Now she couldn't even read him anymore. Was Letti dead? No, because then Oza wouldn't be hovering over her that way. But he was casting no magic, either, or it could be he was trying and failing. It could be anything. What she did know was that Rania was still alive, because the piscin girl was curled into the fetal position a few meters away from Bisset and gasping, bleeding.

"She tried to attack me. I think she knows now how unintelligent that is. As you do." The colonel's soulless blue gaze slid from Anzi's face to Kai, who stood next to her with his shoulders tensed and hands already shifted back to draconic claws. "I wouldn't," he added coolly. "Anzi can inform you in no uncertain terms how that would end. Or maybe I'll let the dragon speak for me, in fire."

She didn't have to look to know he spoke of the enormous, burly creature he'd taken on as his new thrall. Blueish purple, nowhere near the titanic proportions of Shu-Amunet but large enough to more than rival Sa-Khente in size. Ten meters? Eleven? A rumbling growl echoed within its slightly open maw as it answered to Bisset's imperious gesture.

"One breath, and I win. Or will you put me to the test?"

She couldn't. She didn't dare, and she would never give him the pleasure of it. He would only enjoy it too much. "What do you want, Bisset. You left them alive for a reason, and you waited here. For me."

The colonel sent a lazy glance to his right. "Entertainment. One kick and her ribs broke. I think a few of them might have gone into her lungs. I could put her out of her misery if you want. I'm training this dragon to eat humans so we can cut down on the quantity of butchered meat we spend in the Imperial City."

His words were so emotionless, so deadpan that she didn't know if he was taunting her or if he spoke the truth. Both, more likely. "What do you want," she repeated. "Tell me what you *want*."

"Sir." A faint smile curved his mouth. "Tell me what you want, *sir*."

She narrowed her eyes and stopped Kai from advancing with one arm thrown sideways to bar him. She didn't care about her pride. Bisset's dragon was so close it could roast them, and while she didn't much care about herself, she didn't know if Kai would leap out of the way in time. And Ash was here, too. She was furious at the woman, but she couldn't let her die, either.

"Tell me what you want," she said slowly. "...Sir."

"Should be obvious. I'm holding your beloved brother hostage as well as your prostitute friend, which should be enough to keep you in line. And as for you, Chieftain Kaizat, the Emperor would love to invite you back to the city, so you'll both be returning with me. I imagine he won't be pleased." His smile faded, and his typical icy, solemn expression replaced it once more. "He's not a forgiving man even in his best moments. I look forward to seeing what he does to you."

Anzi's mind raced, searching for a way to pierce through the hopelessness, to wrest victory from the colonel's hands though she could see nothing but defeat. She prayed Kai would continue to stay motionless, and she didn't dare to even speak to him through their minds lest Bisset detect the slightest change in the air and condemn them for it. And Ash, too—this time, she needed the old woman to stay still and hold her tongue.

"How did you find the camp?" she asked casually, stalling for time. Bisset would see through it in an instant. But she had to do something. "I pointed you in the other direction. Away from here."

"I saw dragons taking flight in the distance. It was so far away I nearly missed it, but I've spent too many years with dragons in my service to not recognize them even as specks against the desert. I imagine they're all wiped out now along with your men, Chieftain. I sent my soldiers ahead and came here alone, found only the infirm and the weak remaining."

So Bisset didn't know yet about the dragon shifters. She had thought for sure he would have pieced it together somehow, but even with the additional subtle clue of Kai's transformed hands, he hadn't realized the truth. When he returned to Tet, his report would be incomplete. Anzi let that console her to balance the horror of knowing Oza, Letti, and Kai were all going to be taken captive again. And Rania, too, since she had been left alive for some reason.

The man must have seen her eyes flit to the gasping, collapsed piscin girl. "I recognize her," he said simply. "From Lumenera. You protected her, said she had some bond with your dragon. I've decided she might be of use or at least worthy of study, so she'll be coming along as well. All the more to ensure your cooperation, Anzi. The only one who won't be necessary is the elderly one beside you. Otherwise, I'm pleased. Excellent resources."

She was still listening, but her gaze fixed on his dragon now. That was her greatest obstacle, but surely it could prove her greatest chance, too. There must be some way to spark life inside the dead mind, to open it up and make it hear her pleas and wake up or be reborn or whatever it took to free itself from Bisset's control.

"It's no use trying to communicate with it. I held onto the dragon before this one because she was particularly receptive to my quickening magic, but she always had a spark of resistance I didn't like. I made sure not to overvalue size this time. This one's mind is gone completely, more effective than the last."

Her desperate attempts to speak into the mind of his dragon thrall met with nothing. Bisset was right—it was futile.

But there was more. "You're only the latest in a long line of your kind," he said almost gently. "You have a new trick or two that your predecessors never displayed, but that's the case with each one we collect. The newer ones are always more powerful and promising than the last, and we know how to identify the potentials by their interactions with the wyrms—the wyrms always know. Those of the old days would have referred to you as a Druid. Much like the one next to you."

Her breathing stopped. He knew? Tet must have told him.

"But your name was written in history when you were still young, at your Selection—few children can lift twice their weight. You were exceptional, and you would have lived a good life before Tet used your life to lengthen his. But your end was always decided, even before you rebelled."

Every word he said only increased her confusion—and yet answered her questions, too, at the same time. Cold dread coiled in her belly and weighed her down like an anchor.

"Tet will take his chances with your successor. Once you die, the next Druid will be stronger since there will be fewer of you. Narrower distribution of the hereditary power." His gaze moved to Ash. "This one, for example. I'll be killing you so we can prune the stock and concentrate the quality of the next one who'll be born with a remnant of pure magic. You can try to escape, but it'll only be more painful for you."

Next to Anzi, the old woman sneered. "Run?" she demanded. "You think I'm going to run from a minion of the abomination. How can a servant of the gods flee before a pretender?"

"You talk the way I always imagined a primitive would. Tet tells me it was common, this idealistic, logic-defying mentality. He admired the devotion of the zealot hierarchy your magical order built so much that he modeled the entire foundation of his new Empire on that. Blind faith, undying loyalty, and the worship of a rarely-seen godly figurehead who remains distant always so he can remain perfect in the faith forever. We pass on thanks to your so-called Druid order for his massive success. We have zealots of our own. In fact, Anzi used to be one of our most unconditionally loyal. I'm disappointed she failed to uphold it."

She could barely breathe. Every part of her ached with the horrifying realization that everything he said—rang true.

"The fewer of you exist, the more concentrated the ancestral magic," he said. "So unfortunately, it does mean I need to kill you now."

"We are secure. Fate brought you here, and fate will see you defeat—"

It happened so fast Anzi had no time to react, nor Kai next to her. One second, Bisset was standing a full two meters away, sword tucked in its sheath. In the next, he was in front of Ash, the sword piercing her through from chest to back in a gruesome impaling. The old woman gurgled and convulsed around the blade, wizened hands clutching at it uselessly.

Anzi braced to rush him, obeying instinctive reaction and ignoring the cool logic that told her to stay away—but before she could move a single muscle, she gasped around the cold steel that tore through her next. She staggered back into Kai's arms when it pulled out of her in the next second, blood gushing from the wound even harder with each frantic beat of her heart.

"Anzi! *No!*" But Kai's *no* meant nothing...Nothing. He had no choice but to abandon her side and lunge forward to stop Bisset from finishing the job, and she watched through bleary eyes as they did battle. She turned her head over the sand, feeling the grains fill her hair and dig into her skin, and searched through blurring vision for Oza. Brave boy, he was getting up, or trying, and now she saw he had not come away unhurt after all even though she'd seen no blood on him. Bisset had done something to both his legs, possibly broken them, and injured an arm too—that was why he couldn't cast magic earlier. A wave of fresh agony washed through her again, and she vomited blood with a gurgling cry as it forced her severed muscles to ripple around her gaping wound.

Kai...She had to stop Bisset from killing him. There he was again trying to protect her, shield her, but he was already exhausted and still poison-weakened. He was but an ordinary man like this, and against Bisset, ordinary wasn't enough. Ah...She couldn't lose here. She had made it this far, and if she could only be strong for a moment longer, a few seconds, if only she could find that strength she had discovered earlier... but her body was exhausted, her spirit spent. She couldn't even lift a single finger anymore; the power was gone and not coming back. There was no wind to blow the ember back to life, and it would fade away forever...

Kai was somehow holding Bisset back, snarling like a true dragon as he lunged and slashed and even tackled the colonel head on whenever the former two failed. But time was running out. Silver-red blood splattered down upon her crumpled body, and she knew then there was no more time for hesitation. A moment longer and Kai would find himself dying on the sand just like her. She rolled over and dragged herself over to Ash. The old woman was dying. There was fear in her eyes as well as despair for the first time. Anzi was too numb to offer her comfort.

"We have to stop him," she rasped, blood dribbling from the corners of her mouth. "I have to do something—"

But the old woman offered no sagely advice, no secret to victory in this final, desperate moment. "It wasn't supposed to be like this," Ash whispered. "Why...why did this happen...How could it..."

Finally she had seen and understood. But it was too late now. There was no point in Anzi telling her that blind faith had been naïve, stupid, selfish. That this was no fairy tale endeavor protected by the favor of kind gods looking down upon them, ready to bestow favors to soothe their pains like handmaidens to masters. Fate? Destiny? If they existed, they were cold mistresses only. This was war, this was death, this was punishment for being so ready to believe in infallible higher powers and never questioning the truth, the lesson she had had to learn herself, too, the hard way.

It was too late for Ash to learn. She would have only regret. Anzi watched as the old woman's eyes glassed over, teeth gnashing as yet another frayed strand of hope burned away. Or had it? She stared as wisps of green energy floated up from the old woman's body, and then—she saw it. The thread-narrow path to life, one more flickering chance.

She sucked in a noisy breath, ignoring the tearing, ripping pain of the wound between her chest and gut, and the spectral wisps curled toward her. More, she thought. More. Because some of it was beginning to make sense now, things that Anzi had said compared to Bisset's revelations. Both had mentioned the fewer Druids existed, the more powerful they were, and he had said something else too, that it had to do with the distribution of power. If that was the case, then since Ash was long gone and no longer needed it—Anzi would take her share, too.

Deep down, she knew this would break her. That last ember she was blowing upon now, once she did this, it would die once and for all. It would shatter into a thousand pieces never to come together again, and she would never be the same. But she was already broken anyway. Bum leg, a hole in her chest, and burdened by despair—she looked forward to the end.

Bisset had noticed her stirring, and he tried to charge past Kai to get to her. But Kai, beloved Kai, her mate and her partner and her other half, held him off as she wrapped cold, shaking fingers around Ash's temples and drained the last of the remaining magic in her body. It came to her so easily that she could imagine it had belonged to her all along, and then it filled her body like warm water and soft music, the swaying of leaves and the shifting of dirt under her bare feet...

When she rose up, she was both strong and weak, outside of her body and within it. Her senses were far removed from her physical body, fading into some other awareness far, far away...With her last remaining strength, she would finish this. She would protect everyone even if it meant her end. She wasn't brave enough to go on by herself. If that made her a coward, then so be it. Kai hadn't noticed yet how she stood behind him, renewed with the life of another, and he continued to rail against Bisset even as she raised her swords above her head, breathed in the moonlight now shining down in full over the Adaraat—and unleashed.

She spun, slicing her swords in a fierce circle around herself, and the power that rushed out of her in a deluge blew the sand away under everyone with the force of a savage twister. Tents toppled and hurtled off in random directions along with the belongings that had been in them, even limp bodies. Everything, everything—and if she were in her right mind, she would have tried to hold back for fear of hurting Oza, Letti, and Rania in the middle of it all. But she was gone, gone, gone and all she could do was let her magic speak. It exploded out of her in waves and gales, and Kai scrambled against the force of it to dodge around Bisset's collapsed form. Distantly, Anzi noted how he picked up Letti with one arm and reached for Oza next, but he too was driven off by the pressure of her magic swirling in a violent storm around them all.

When the wind lessened, the landscape had changed: gone was the campsite, and now this patch of desert was sunk several meters below the rest. This must have been the site of an ancient city, Anzi thought when she saw the broken and crumbling ruins now unearthed from beneath thick layers of sand. She felt strangely like she had discovered a great and wondrous gift, a surpassingly joyous secret. Nothing could dampen it, not even when Bisset picked himself back up and leaped at her with sword drawn.

She should have been afraid, but with calm-numb awareness, mind breaking, she read Bisset's incoming assault like a series of unraveled secrets. There, his sword was coming for her throat. And there, his booted foot was planted into the packed sand for traction so he could put all of his strength behind the blow. And there...an opening. With one fluid movement, she severed his arm at the shoulder. He drew back, stunned and staring and bleeding profusely from the stump while she stared back, dead-eyed and gone.

They clashed again, but not before he did something else, something that made the last speck of her consciousness scream and writhe from a place deep inside herself that she could no longer reach. She could do nothing as he barked a command to his dragon, and the great creature rose up into the air to obey. No, she thought. Please, no. But there was nothing she could do but fight back as Bisset set upon her again, and far behind him, his dragon knocked Kai aside with its massive bulk before grabbing Oza in its talons and flying away.

By the time she cleaved through Bisset's skull then beheaded him, by the time his body fell to the sand with a thump and left her standing there half-dead, she could no longer remember anything at all. All she knew was that she had had one objective, to remove this man, this threat, this danger—and now it was done. Everything was done.

Her little dragon had called, and here had been her answer.

With a whispering breath, Anzi fell to the sand, eyes open.

"I can't feel her anymore," Kai murmured as he rocked the unresponsive body back and forth in his arms. "Qing, I can't feel her. She's gone."

"She's alive, Kai. That's better than I expected. I don't know how she survived or how she's surviving still, but she has. So be patient—we'll find a healer to wake her."

"You don't understand. I should be able to feel her whether she's awake or asleep. But I can't. The mate bond, it's gone."

Qinglong sighed. Last night had been disastrous. They had taken a fight they shouldn't have gambled on, and they had paid for it many times over. Nearly a third of their troupe dead, and Sa-Khente had yet to heal enough to even speak.

"Kai, you have to let her go. She'll heal faster if you leave her be."

It hurt to see her old friend like this, bent and twisted so far she could hardly recognize him. But she had no words of sympathy to offer, nothing that could soften the blow. She had yet to tell him what she had divined while examining Anzi's body: that she could sense no power in her anymore. No magic, no spirit. She had never seen this before. It was as if she were extinguished entirely. Would she ever wake up? And if she did—would she ever regain her power? That very thing was likely the reason Kai no longer felt the mate bond...because the other end of it simply didn't exist anymore.

But not all was lost. Even thought they had lost the boy and their only remaining Druid lay nearly dead in an unwaking sleep, the woman had at least dispatched the one known as Bisset. That one had been dangerous.

Nearly as dangerous as the abomination himself, and somehow he was dead in the sand at Anzi's hands along with a considerable force of almost a dozen corrupted dragons and the same number of elite Empire soldiers. This little warrior was more powerful than anyone in the tribe had ever thought, and Qing hoped they all regretted now how coldly they had treated her.

She had nearly died for them. Might still. It was an undeniable sacrifice that could not be surpassed, sure evidence where her true loyalties lay.

Qing sighed again. "She'll be all right, Kai. Be at peace."

He held Anzi close, his entire body shaking with a cruel mixture of rage, fear, and grief. She had to peel him away from her at long last, but even then she knew his mind and heart were still with her. Until Anzi awoke, he would never be in one piece again…

Weeks later, far from the desert, she was still tending to Anzi's sleeping form. She sat at her bedside, examining her eyes, mouth, anything that might offer a flickering hope of recovery. And that was when she heard the first sound sighing from the girl's throat, a tiny, slow leak of air that she almost missed. Qing sat back and took a deep breath.

"Welcome back," she murmured, but it was too late. Anzi was asleep once more, and Qing leaned forward to push her hair back from her forehead. Ah, well. Progress. Any was better than none, and she and everyone else would wait as long as they had to. She would need to let Kai know once he returned.

"Come back to us soon," she murmured as she tapped the woman's slack cheek. "You're needed more than ever."

Outside, the moon shone brightly…